From

Ever After

By #1 *New York Times*
Bestselling Author
Nora Roberts

Under him she lifted and moved as if they'd danced this dance together for a lifetime. Flowed with and against him, now fluid, now strong. And the quickening pulse that rose in her was like his own.

Her scent was soap, her taste fresh as rain.

He watched her glide up, the faerie again, soaring on one long spread of wings. As she crested, her eyes opened, met his. And she smiled.

No one had brought her so much, or shown her how much she had to offer. Her body quivered from the thrill of it, and in her heart was the boundless joy of finding home.

She arched up, opened so he would fill her. As he slid inside her, the beauty dazzled, and the power hummed.

While they took each other, neither noticed the star carved in silver, glowing blue as flame.

Titles in the Once Upon series

Once Upon A Star

★

NORA ROBERTS
JILL GREGORY
RUTH RYAN LANGAN
MARIANNE WILLMAN

JOVE BOOKS, NEW YORK

This is a work of fiction. Names, characters, places, and incidents either are the product of the author's imagination or are used fictitiously, and any resemblance to actual persons, living or dead, business establishments, events or locales is entirely coincidental.

ONCE UPON A STAR

A Jove Book / published by arrangement with
the authors

PRINTING HISTORY
Jove edition / December 1999

10 9 8

CONTENTS

Once Upon A Star

EVER AFTER

★

Nora Roberts

To my sisters in magic—
Ruth, Marianne, and Jill

1

"This," the old woman said, "is for you."

Allena studied the pendant that swung gently from the thickly braided links of a silver chain. Really, she'd only come in to browse. Her budget didn't allow for impulse buys—which were, of course, the most fun and the most satisfying. And her affection for all things impulsive was the very reason she couldn't afford to indulge herself.

She shouldn't have entered the shop at all. But who could resist a tiny little place tucked into the waterfront of a charming Irish village? Especially a place called Charms and Cures.

Certainly not Allena Kennedy.

"It's beautiful, but I—"

"There's only one." The woman's eyes were faded and blue, like the sea that slapped and spewed against the stone wall barely a stone's throw from the door. Her hair was steel gray and bundled into a bun that lay heavy on her thin neck.

She wore a fascinating rattle of chains and pins, but there was nothing, Allena thought, like the pendant she held in her bony fingers. "Only one?"

"The silver was cured in Dagda's Cauldron over the Midsummer's fire and carved by the finger of Merlin. He that was Arthur's."

"Merlin?"

Allena was a sucker for tales of magic and heroics. Her stepsister Margaret would have sniffed and said no, she was simply a sucker.

"The high king's sorcerer wandered through Ireland in his time. It was here he found the Giant's Dance, and coveting it for Arthur, floated it away over the Irish Sea to Britain. But while he took magic from this land, some he also left." Watching Allena, she set the pendant swaying. "Here is some, and it belongs to you."

"Well, I really can't . . ." But Allena trailed off, her gaze locked on the pendant. It was a long oval, dulled and tarnished a bit, and centered in it was a carving in the shape of a bursting star.

It seemed to catch the murky, cloud-filtered light coming through the small shop window, hold it, expand it, so that it glittered hypnotically in Allena's eyes. It seemed the star shimmered.

"I just came in to look around."

"Sure and if you don't look, you can't find, can you? You came looking, all the way from America."

She'd come, Allena tried to remember, to assist Margaret with the tour group. Margaret's business, A Civilized Adventure, was very successful—and very regimented. Everyone said that Allena needed some regimentation. And Margaret had been clear, brutally clear, that this opportunity was her last chance.

"Be organized, be prepared, and be on time," Margaret had told her as she'd sat behind her polished desk in her perfectly terrifying and perfectly ordered office in New York. "If you can manage that, there might be a chance for you. If you can't, I wash my hands of you, Lena."

It wouldn't be the first time someone had washed their

hands of her. In the past three years she'd lost three jobs. Well, four, but it didn't seem necessary to count those hideous two days she'd spent as assistant to her uncle's mother-in-law's sister.

It wasn't as if she'd spilled ink on the white Valentino gown on purpose. And if the Social Dragon hadn't insisted that she use a fountain pen—I mean, really—for all correspondence, there wouldn't have been ink to spill.

But that wasn't the point, she reminded herself as she stared at the pendant. She'd lost that job and all the others, and now Margaret was giving her a chance to prove she wasn't a complete moron.

Which, Allena feared, she probably was.

"You need to find your place."

Blinking, Allena managed to tear her gaze away from the pendant and look back into the old woman's eyes. They seemed so kind and wise. "Maybe I don't have one."

"Oh, there now, each of us has one, but there are those who don't fit so easily into the world the way others see it. And us. You've only been looking in the wrong places. Till now. This," she said again, "belongs to you."

"I really can't afford it." There was apology in her voice, even as she reached out. Just to touch. And touching, she felt heat from the silver, and terrible longing inside her. A thrill raced up her spine even as something heavy seemed to settle over her heart.

It couldn't hurt to try it on. Surely there was no harm in just seeing how it looked on her, how it felt.

As if in a dream, she took the chain from the old woman, slipped it around her neck. The heaviness in her heart shifted. For a moment, the light through the window strengthened, beamed brilliantly over the trinkets and pots of herbs and odd little stones crammed on the shelves and counters.

An image swam into her mind, an image of knights and dragons, of wild wind and water, of a circle of stones standing alone under a black and raging sky.

Then a shadow that was a man, standing still as the stones, as if waiting.

In her heart she knew he waited for her, as no one had before and no one would after. And would wait, eternally.

Allena closed her hand over the pendant, ran her thumb over the star. Joy burst through her, clear as the sunlight. Ah, she thought. Of course. It's mine. Just as I'm his, and he's mine.

"How much is it?" she heard herself say, and knew no price would be too dear.

"Ten pounds, as a token."

"Ten?" She was already reaching for her purse. "It has to be worth more." A king's ransom, a sorcerer's spell, a lover's dream.

"It is, of course." But the woman merely held out her hand for the single note. "And so are you. Go on your journey, *a chuid,* and see."

"Thank you."

"You're a good lass," the woman said as Allena walked to the door. And when it shut, her smile turned bright and crafty. "He won't be pleased, but you'll bring him 'round by Midsummer's Eve. And if you need a bit of help, well, that will be my pleasure."

Outside, Allena stared at the sea wall, the dock, the line of cottages as if coming out of a dream. Odd, she thought, hadn't that all been wonderfully odd? She traced a finger over the pendant again. Only one, cast in Dagda's Cauldron, carved by Merlin.

Of course, Margaret would sneer and tell her that the old woman had a dozen more in the stockroom ready to pass them off to birdbrained tourists. And Margaret, as always, was probably right. But it didn't matter.

She had the pendant and a wonderful story to go with it. And all for ten pounds. Quite a bargain.

She glanced up now, wincing. The sky was heavy with clouds, and all of them were thick and gray. Margaret would not be pleased that the weather wasn't falling in line with today's plans. The ferry ride to the island had been meticulously arranged.

Tea and scones would be served on the trip over, while Margaret lectured her twenty-person group on the history of the place they were about to visit. It had been Allena's job to type up Margaret's notes and print the handouts.

First stop would be the visitors' center for orientation. There would be a tour of a ruined abbey and graveyard, which Allena looked forward to, then lunch, picnic style, which the hotel had provided in hampers. Lunch was to last precisely sixty minutes.

They would then visit the beehive cottages, and Margaret would deliver a lecture on their history and purpose. The group would be allotted an hour to wander on their own, into the village, the shops, down to the beach, before gathering at four-thirty on the dot for high tea at the restored castle, with, naturally, another lecture on that particular spot.

It was Allena's job to keep all of Margaret's lecture notes in order, to help herd the group, to watch valuables, to haul parcels should there be any, and to generally make herself available for any and all menial chores.

For this she would be paid a reasonable salary by Margaret's definition. But, more important, it was explained, she would receive training and experience that, her family hoped, would teach her responsibility and maturity. Which, by the age of twenty-five, she should have learned already.

There was no point in explaining that she didn't want to be responsible and mature if it turned her into another Margaret. Here she was, four days into her first tour and already something inside her was screaming to run away.

Dutifully, she quashed the rebellion, glanced at her watch. Stared at it, dumbfounded.

That couldn't be. It was impossible. She'd only meant to slip into the shop for a few minutes. She couldn't possibly have spent an hour in there. She couldn't—oh, God, she *couldn't* have missed the ferry.

Margaret would murder her.

Gripping the strap of her bag, she began to run.

She had long, dancer's legs and a slim build. The sturdy walking shoes Margaret had ordered her to buy slapped pavement on her race to the ferry dock. Her bag bounced heavily against her hip. Inside was everything ordered from the Civilized Adventure directive and a great deal more.

The wind kicked in from the sea and sent her short blond hair into alarmed spikes around her sharp-boned face. The alarm was in her eyes, gray as the clouds, as well. It turned quickly to despair and self-disgust when she reached the dock and saw the ferry chugging away.

"Damn it!" Allena grabbed her own hair and pulled viciously. "That's it and that's all. I might as well jump in and drown myself." Which would be more pleasant, she had no doubt, than the icy lecture Margaret would deliver.

She'd be fired, of course, there was no doubt of it. But she was used to that little by-product of her professional endeavors. The method of termination would be torture.

Unless . . . There had to be another way to get to the island. If she could get there, throw herself on Margaret's stingy supply of mercy, work like a dog, forfeit her salary. Make an excuse. Surely she'd be able to come up with some reason for missing the damn ferry.

She looked around frantically. There were boats, and if there were boats, there were people who drove boats. She'd hire a boat, pay whatever it cost.

"Are you lost, then?"

Startled, she lifted a hand, closed it tight over her pendant. There was a young man—hardly more than a boy, really, she noted—standing beside a small white boat. He wore a cap over his straw-colored hair and watched her out of laughing green eyes.

"No, not lost, late. I was supposed to be on the ferry." She gestured, then let her arms fall. "I lost track of time."

"Well, time's not such a matter in the scheme of things."

"It is to my sister. I work for her." Quickly now, she headed down toward him where the sea lapped the shore. "Is this your boat, or your father's?"

"Aye, it happens it's mine."

It was small, but to her inexperienced eye looked cheerful. She had to hope that made it seaworthy. "Could you take me over? I need to catch up. I'll pay whatever you need."

It was just that sort of statement, Allena thought the minute the words left her mouth, that would make Margaret cringe. But then bargaining wasn't a priority at the moment. Survival was.

"I'll take you where you need to be." His eyes sparkled as he held out a hand. "For ten pounds."

"Today everything's ten pounds." She reached for her purse, but he shook his head.

"It was your hand I was reaching for, lady, not payment. Payment comes when you get where you're going."

"Oh, thanks." She put her hand in his and let him help her into the boat.

She sat starboard on a little bench while he cast off. Closing her eyes with relief, she listened to the boy whistle as he went about settling to stern and starting the motor. "I'm very grateful," she began. "My sister's going to be furious with me. I don't know what I was thinking of."

He turned the boat, a slow and smooth motion. "And couldn't she have waited just a bit?"

"Margaret?" The thought made Allena smile. "It wouldn't have occurred to her."

The bow lifted, and the little boat picked up speed. "It would have occurred to you," he said, and then they were skimming over the water.

Thrilled, she turned her face to the wind. Oh, this was better, much better, than any tame ferry ride, lecture included. It was almost worth the price she would pay at the end, and she didn't mean the pounds.

"Do you fish?" she called out to him.

"When they're biting."

"It must be wonderful to do what you want, when you want. And to live so near the water. Do you love it?"

"I've a fondness for it, yes. Men put restrictions on men. That's an odd thing to my way of thinking."

"I have a terrible time with restrictions. I can never remember them." The boat leaped, bounced hard and made her laugh. "At this rate, we'll beat the ferry."

The idea of that, the image of her standing on shore and giving Margaret a smug look when the ferry docked, entertained Allena so much she didn't give a thought to the shiver of lightning overhead or the sudden, ominous roar of the sea.

When the rain began to pelt her, she looked around again, shocked that she could see nothing but water, the rise and fall of it, the curtain that closed off light.

"Oh, she won't like this a bit. Are we nearly there?"

"Nearly, aye, nearly." His voice was a kind of crooning that smoothed nerves before they could fray. "Do you see there, through the storm? There, just ahead, is where you need to be."

She turned. Through the rain and wind, she saw the darker shadow of land, a rise of hills, the dip of valley in shapes only. But she knew, she already knew.

"It's beautiful," she murmured.

Like smoke, it drifted closer. She could see the crash of surf now and the cliffs that hulked high above. Then in the flash of lightning, she thought, just for an instant, she saw a man.

Before she could speak, the boat was rocking in the surf, and the boy leaping out into the thrashing water to pull them to shore.

"I can't thank you enough, really." Drenched, euphoric, she climbed out onto the wet sand. "You'll wait for the storm to pass, won't you?" she asked as she dug for her wallet.

"I'll wait until it's time to go. You'll find your way, lady. Through the rain. The path's there."

"Thanks." She passed the note into his hand. She'd go to the visitors' center, take shelter, find Margaret and do penance. "If you come up with me, I'll buy you some tea. You can dry off."

"Oh, I'm used to the wet. Someone's waiting for you," he said, then climbed back into his boat.

"Yes, of course." She started to run, then stopped. She hadn't even asked his name. "I'm sorry, but—" When she rushed back, there was nothing there but the crash of water against the shore.

Alarmed that he'd sailed back into that rising storm, she

called out, began to hurry along what she could see of the shore to try to find him. Lightning flashed overhead, more vicious than exciting now, and the wind slapped at her like a furious hand.

Hunching against it, she jogged up the rise, onto a path. She'd get to shelter, tell someone about the boy. What had she been thinking of, not insisting that he come with her and wait until the weather cleared?

She stumbled, fell, jarring her bones with the impact, panting to catch her breath as the world went suddenly mad around her. Everything was howling wind, blasting lights, booming thunder. She struggled to her feet and pushed on.

It wasn't fear she felt, and that baffled her. She should be terrified. Why instead was she exhilarated? Where did this wicked thrill of anticipation, of *knowledge*, come from?

She had to keep going. There was something, someone, waiting. If she could just keep going.

The way was steep, the rain blinding. Somewhere along the way she lost her bag, but didn't notice.

In the next flash of light, she saw it. The circle of stones, rising out of the rough ground like dancers trapped in time. In her head, or perhaps her heart, she heard the song buried inside them.

With something like joy, she rushed forward, her hand around the pendant.

The song rose, like a crescendo, filling her, washing over her like a wave.

And as she reached the circle, took her first step inside, lightning struck the center, the bolt as clear and well-defined as a flaming arrow. She watched the blue fire rise in a tower, higher, higher still, until it seemed to pierce the low-hanging clouds. She felt the iced heat of it on her skin, in her bones. The power of it hammered her heart.

And she fainted.

2

THE STORM MADE him restless. Part of the tempest seemed to be inside him, churning, crashing, waiting to strike out. He couldn't work. His concentration was fractured. He had no desire to read, to putter, to simply be. And all of those things were why he had come back to the island.

Or so he told himself.

His family had held the land, worked it, guarded it, for generations. The O'Neils of Dolman had planted their seed here, spilled their blood and the blood of their enemies for as far back as time was marked. And further still, back into the murky time that was told only in songs.

Leaving here, going to Dublin to study, and to work, had been Conal's rebellion, his escape from what others so blithely accepted as his fate. He would not, as he'd told his father, be the passive pawn in the chess game of his own destiny.

He would make his destiny.

And yet, here he was, in the cottage where the O'Neils had lived and died, where his own father had passed the last day of his life only months before. Telling himself it had been his choice didn't seem quite so certain on a day where the wind lashed and screamed and the same violence of nature seemed to thrash inside him.

The dog, Hugh, which had been his father's companion for the last year of his life, paced from window to window, ears pricked up and a low sound rumbling in his throat, more whimper than growl.

Whatever was brewing, the dog sensed it as well, so that his big gray bulk streamed through the cottage like blown smoke. Conal gave a soft command in Gaelic, and Hugh came over, bumping his big head under Conal's big hand.

There they stood, watching the storm together, the large gray dog and the tall, broad-shouldered man, each with a wary expression. Conal felt the dog shudder. Nerves or anticipation? Something, all Conal could think, was out there in the storm.

Waiting.

"The hell with it. Let's see what it is."

Even as he spoke, the dog leaped toward the door, prancing with impatience as Conal tugged a long black slicker off the peg. He swirled it on over rough boots and rougher jeans and a black sweater that had seen too many washings.

When he opened the door, the dog shot out, straight into the jaws of the gale. "Hugh! *Cuir uait!*"

And though the dog did stop, skidding in the wet, he didn't bound back to Conal's side. Instead he stood, ears still pricked, despite the pounding rain, as if to say *hurry!*

Cursing under his breath, Conal picked up his own pace, and let the dog take the lead.

His black hair, nearly shoulder-length and heavy now with rain, streamed back in the wind from a sharply-honed face. He had the high, long cheekbones of the Celts, a narrow, almost aristocratic nose, and a well-defined mouth that could look, as it did now, hard as granite. His eyes were a deep and passionate blue.

His mother had said they were eyes that saw too much, and still looked for more.

Now they peered through the rain, and down, as Hugh climbed, at the turbulent toss of the sea. With the storm, the day was almost black as night, and he cursed again at his own foolishness in being out in it.

He lost sight of Hugh around a turn on the cliff path. More irritated than alarmed, he called the dog again, but all that answered was the low-throated, urgent bark. Perfect, was all Conal could think. Now the both of us will likely slip off the edge and bash our brains on the rocks.

He almost turned away, at that point very nearly retreated, for the dog was surefooted and knew his way home. But he wanted to go on—too much wanted to go on. As if something was tugging him forward, luring him on, higher and higher still, to where the shadow of the stone dance stood, singing through the wind.

Because part of him believed it, part of him he had never been able to fully quiet, he deliberately turned away. He would go home, build up the fire, and have a glass of whiskey in front of it until the storm blew itself out.

Then the howl came, a wild and primitive call that spoke of wolves and eerie moonlight. The shudder that ran down Conal's spine was as primal as the call. Grimly now, he continued up the path to see what caused young Hugh to bay.

The stones rose, gleaming with wet, haloed by the lightning strikes so that they almost seemed to glow. A scent came to him, ozone and perfume. Hot, sweet, and seductive.

The dog sat, his handsome head thrown back, his great throat rippling with his feral call. There was something in it, Conal thought, that was somehow triumphant.

"The stones don't need guarding," Conal muttered. He strode forward, intending to grab the dog by the collar and drag them both back to the warmth of the cottage.

And saw that it wasn't the stones Hugh guarded, but the woman who lay between them.

Half in and half out of the circle, with one arm stretched

toward the center, she lay on her side almost as if sleeping. For a moment he thought he imagined her, and wanted to believe he did. But when he reached her side, his fingers instinctively going to her throat to check her pulse, he felt the warm beat of life.

At his touch her lashes fluttered. Her eyes opened. They were gray as the stones and met his with a sudden and impossible awareness. A smile curved her lips, parted them as she lifted a hand to his cheek.

"There you are," she said, and with a sigh closed her eyes again. Her hand slid away from his cheek to fall onto the rain-trampled grass.

Delirious, he told himself, and most likely a lunatic. Who else would climb the cliffs in a storm? Ignoring the fact that he'd done so himself, he turned her over, seeing no choice but to cart her back to the cottage.

And when he started to gather her into his arms, he saw the pendant, saw the carving on it in another spit of lightning.

His belly pitched. His heart gave one violent knock against his chest, like an angry fist.

"Damn it."

He stayed crouched as he was, closing his eyes while the rain battered both of them.

She woke slowly, as if floating lazily through layers of thin, white clouds. A feeling of well-being cushioned her, like satin pillows edged with the softest of lace. Savoring it, she lay still while sunlight played on her eyelids, cruised warm over her face. She could smell smoke, a pleasant, earthy scent, and another fragrance, a bit darker, that was man.

She enjoyed that mix, and when she opened her eyes, her first thought was she'd never been happier in her life.

It lasted seconds only, that sensation of joy and safety, of contentment and place. Then she shot up in bed, confused, alarmed, lost.

Margaret! She'd missed the ferry. The boat. The boy in the boat. And the storm. She'd gotten caught in it and had lost her way. She couldn't quite remember, couldn't quite separate the blurry images.

Stones, higher than a man and ringed in a circle. The blue fire that burned in the center without scorching the grass. The wild scream of the wind. The low hum of the stones.

A wolf howling. Then a man. Tall, dark, fierce, with eyes as blue as that impossible fire. Such anger in his face. But it hadn't frightened her. It had amused her. How strange.

Dreams, of course. Just dreams. She'd been in some sort of accident.

Now she was in someone's house, someone's bed. A simple room, she thought, looking around to orient herself. No, not simple, she corrected, spartan. Plain white walls, bare wood floor, no curtains at the window. There was a dresser, a table and lamp and the bed. As far as she could tell, there was nothing else in the room but herself.

Gingerly now, she touched her head to see if there were bumps or cuts, but found nothing to worry her. Using the same caution, she turned back the sheet, let out a little sigh of relief. Whatever sort of accident there'd been, it didn't appear to have hurt her.

Then she gaped, realizing she wore nothing but a shirt, and it wasn't her own. A man's shirt, faded blue cotton, frayed at the cuffs. And huge.

Okay, that was okay. She'd been caught in the storm. Obviously she had gotten soaked. She had to be grateful that someone had taken care of her.

When she climbed out of bed, the shirt hung halfway to her knees. Modest enough. At her first step, the dog came to the door. Her heart gave a little hitch, then settled.

"So at least you're real. Aren't you handsome?" She held out a hand and had the pleasure of him coming to her to rub his body against her legs. "And friendly. Good to know. Where's everyone else?"

With one hand on the dog's head, she walked to the bedroom door and discovered a living area that was every bit as spartan. A couch and chair, a low burning fire, a couple of tables. With some relief she saw her clothes laid over a screen in front of the fire.

A check found them still damp. So, she hadn't been asleep—unconscious—for long. The practical thing to do, now that she'd apparently done everything impractical, was to find her rescuer, thank him, wait for her clothes to dry, then track down Margaret and beg for mercy.

The last part would be unpleasant, and probably fruitless, but it had to be done.

Bolstering herself for the task, Allena went to the door, opened it. And let out a soft cry of sheer delight.

The watery sunlight shimmered over the hills, and the hills rolled up green in one direction, tumbled down in the other toward the rock-strewn shore. The sea reared and crashed, the walls of waves high and wonderful. She had an urge to rush out, to the edge of the slope, and watch the water rage.

Just outside the cottage was a garden gone wild so that flowers tangled with weeds and tumbled over themselves. The smell of them, of the air, of the sea had her gulping in air, holding her breath as if to keep that single sharp taste inside her forever.

Unable to resist, she stepped out, the dog beside her, and lifted her face to the sky.

Oh, this place! Was there ever a more perfect spot? If it were hers, she would stand here every morning and thank God for it.

Beside her, the dog let out one quiet woof, at which she rested her hand on his head again and glanced over at the little building, with its rough stone, thatched roof, wide-open windows.

She started to smile, then the door of it opened. The man who came out stopped as she did, stared as she did. Then with his mouth hard set, he started forward.

His face swam in front of her. The crash of the sea filled her head with roaring. Dizzy, she held out a hand to him, much as she had to the dog.

She saw his mouth move, thought she heard him swear, but she was already pitching forward into the dark.

3

SHE LOOKED LIKE a faerie, standing there in a wavery
sunbeam. Tall and slender, her bright hair cropped short,
her eyes long-lidded, tilted at the tips, and enormous.

Not a beauty. Her face was too sharp for true beauty,
and her mouth a bit top-heavy. But it was an intriguing
face, even in rest.

He'd thought about it even after he'd dumped her in bed
after carrying her in from the storm. Undressing her had
been an annoying necessity, which he'd handled with the
aloof detachment of a doctor. Then, once she was dry and
settled, he'd left her, without a backward glance, to burn
off some of the anger in work.

He worked very well in a temper.

He didn't want her here. He didn't want her. And, he
told himself, he wouldn't have her, no matter what the fates
decreed.

He was his own man.

But now when he came out, saw her standing in the

18

doorway, in the sunlight, he felt the shock of it sweep through him—longing, possession, recognition, delight, and despair. All of those in one hard wave rose inside him, swamped him.

Before he could gain his feet, she was swaying.

He didn't manage to catch her. Oh, in the storybooks, he imagined, his feet would have grown wings and he'd have flown across the yard to pluck her nimbly into his arms before she swooned. But as it was, she slid to the ground, melted wax pooling into the cup and taking all the candle as well, before he'd closed half the distance.

By the time he reached her, those long gray eyes were already opening again, cloudy and dazed. She stared at him, the corners of her mouth trembling up.

"I guess I'm not steady yet," she said in that pretty American voice. "I know it's a cliché and predictable, but I have to say it—where am I?"

She looked ridiculously appealing, lying there between the flowers, and made him all too aware she wore nothing but one of his shirts. "You're on O'Neil land."

"I got lost—a bad habit of mine. The storm came up so fast."

"Why are you here?"

"Oh, I got separated from the group. Well, I was late— another bad habit—and missed the ferry. But the boy brought me in his boat." She sat up then. "I hope he's all right. He must be, as he seemed to know what he was doing and it was such a quick trip anyway. Is the visitors' center far?"

"The visitors' center?"

"I should be able to catch up with them, though it won't do me a lot of good. Margaret'll fire me, and I deserve it."

"And who is Margaret?"

"My stepsister. She owns A Civilized Adventure. I'm working for her—or I did work for her for the last twenty-three days." She let out a breath, tried the smile again. "I'm sorry. I'm Allena Kennedy, the moron. Thank you for helping me."

He glanced down at the hand she held out, then with

some reluctance took it. Instead of shaking it, he pulled her to her feet. "I've a feeling you're more lost than you know, Miss Kennedy, as there's no visitors' center here on Dolman Island."

"Dolman? But that's not right." The hand in his flexed, balled into a little fist of nerves. "I'm not supposed to be on Dolman Island. Oh, damn it. Damn it! It's my fault. I wasn't specific with the boy. He seemed to know where I was going, was supposed to be going. Or maybe he got turned around in the storm, too. I hope he's all right."

She paused, looked around, sighed. "Not just fired," she murmured. "Disinherited, banished, and mortified all in one morning. I guess all I can do is go back to the hotel and wait to face the music."

"Well, it won't be today."

"Excuse me?"

Conal looked out to sea, studying the crashing wall of waves. "You won't find your way back today, and likely not tomorrow, as there's more coming our way."

"But—" She was talking to his back as he walked inside as though he hadn't just sealed her doom. "I have to get back. She'll be worried."

"There'll be no ferry service in these seas, and no boatman with a brain in his head would chance the trip back to the mainland."

She sat on the arm of a chair, closed her eyes. "Well, that caps it. Is there a phone? Could I use your phone to call the hotel and leave a message?"

"The phones are out."

"Of course they are." She watched him go to the fire to add some bricks of turf. Her clothes hung on the screen like a recrimination. "Mr. O'Neil?"

"Conal." He straightened, turned to her. "All the women I undress and put into bed call me Conal."

It was a test, deliberately provocative. But she didn't flush or fire. Instead her eyes lit with humor. "All the men who undress me and put me into bed call me Lena."

"I prefer Allena."

"Really? So do I, but it seems to be too many syllables

for most people. Anyway, Conal, is there a hotel or a bed-and-breakfast where I can stay until the ferry's running again?''

''There's no hotel on Dolman. It's a rare tourist who comes this far. And the nearest village, of which there are but three, is more than eight kilometers away.''

She gave him a level look. ''Am I staying here?''

''Apparently.''

She nodded, rubbing her hand absently over Hugh's broad back as she took stock of her surroundings. ''I appreciate it, and I'll try not to be a nuisance.''

''It's a bit late for that, but we'll deal with it.'' When her only response was to lift her eyebrows and stare steadily, he felt a tug of shame. ''Can you make a proper pot of tea?''

''Yes.''

He gestured toward the kitchen that was separated from the living area by a short counter. ''The makings are in there. I've a few things to see to, then we'll talk this out over a cup.''

''Fine.'' The word was rigidly and properly polite. Only the single gunshot bang of a cupboard door as he started out again told him she was miffed.

She'd make the damn tea, she thought, jerking the faucet on to fill the kettle, which was no easy matter since the cast-iron sink was loaded with dishes. And she'd be grateful for Conal O'Neil's hospitality, however reluctantly, however *rudely* given.

Was it her fault she'd ended up on the wrong island? Was it her fault she'd gotten turned around in a storm and passed out and had to be carted back to his house? Was it her fault she had nowhere else to go?

Well, yes. She rolled her eyes and began to empty the dishes out of the sink so that she could fill it with soapy water and wash them. Yes, technically it *was* her fault. Which just made it all the more annoying.

When she got back to New York she would be jobless. Again. And once more she'd be the object of pity, puzzlement, and pursed lips. And that was her fault, too. Her family expected her to fail now—flighty, scatterbrained Lena.

Worse, she realized, was that she expected it, too.

The problem was she wasn't particularly good at anything. She had no real skill, no craft, and no driving ambitions.

She wasn't lazy, though she knew Margaret would disagree. Work didn't frighten her. Business did.

But that was tomorrow's problem, she reminded herself as she dealt with the dishes and waited for the kettle to boil. Today's problem was Conal O'Neil and how to handle the situation she'd put them both into.

A situation, she thought, as she went about stacking dishes, wiping counters, heating the teapot, that should have been thrilling. A storm-swept island; a handsome, brooding man; a cozy, if rustic, cottage isolated from the world.

This, she decided, perking up, was an adventure. She was going to find a way to enjoy it before the axe fell.

When Conal came back in, the old teapot was sitting snugly in a frayed and faded cozy. Cups and saucers were set on the table, and the table scrubbed clean. The sink was empty, the counters sparkling, and the chocolate biscuits he'd had in a tin were arranged prettily on a plate.

"I was hungry." She was already nibbling on one. "I hope you don't mind."

"No." He'd nearly forgotten what it was like to sit down and have tea in tidiness. Her little temper snap appeared to be over as well, he noted. She looked quietly at home in his kitchen, in his shirt.

"So." She sat down to pour. The one thing she was good at was conversation. She'd often been told she was too good at it. "You live here alone?"

"I do."

"With your dog."

"Hugh. He was my father's. My father died some months back."

She didn't say she was sorry, as so many—too many— would have. But her eyes said it, and that made it matter more. "It's a beautiful spot. A perfect spot. That's what I was thinking before I fell into your garden. You grew up here?''

''I did.''

''I grew up in New York, in the city. It never fit, some-how.'' She studied him over her teacup. ''This fits you. It's wonderful to find the right fit. Everyone in my family fits except me. My parents and Margaret and James—my brother and sister. Their mother died when Margaret was twelve and James ten. Their father met my mother a couple of years later, then they married and had me.''

''And you're Cinderella?''

''No, nothing as romantic as that.'' But she sighed and thought how lovely it would be. ''Just the misfit. They're all brilliant, you see. Every one of them. My father's a doctor, a surgeon. My mother's a lawyer. James is a wildly successful cosmetic surgeon, and Margaret has her own business with A Civilized Adventure.''

''Who would want an adventure civilized?''

''Yes.'' Delighted, Allena slapped a palm on the table. ''That's exactly what I thought. I mean, wouldn't regi-menting it mean it wasn't an adventure at all? But saying that to Margaret earned me a twenty-minute lecture, and since her business is thriving, there you go.''

The light was already shifting, he noted, as a new sea of clouds washed in. But there was enough of the sun yet to sprinkle over her hair, into her eyes. And make his fingers itch for a pencil.

He knew just what he would do with her, exactly how it would be. Planning it, he let his gaze wander over her. And nearly jolted when he saw the pendant. He'd all but forgotten it.

''Where did you get that?''

She'd seen those vivid blue eyes travel down, had felt a shiver of response, and now another of relief that—she hoped—it was the pendant that interested him.

''This? It's the heart of my problem.''

She'd meant it as a joke, but his gaze returned to her face, all but seared the flesh with the heat of it. ''Where did you get it?''

Though the edge to his voice puzzled her, she shrugged. "There was a little shop near the waterfront. The display window was just crammed with things. Wonderful things. Magic."

"Magic."

"Elves and dragons, books and jewelry in lovely, fascinating shapes. A hodgepodge, but a crafty one. Irresistible. I only meant to go in for a minute. I had time before we were to meet at the ferry. But the old woman showed me this, and somehow while we were talking, time just went away. I didn't mean to buy it, either. But I do a lot of things I don't mean to do."

"You don't know what it is?"

"No." She closed her hand over it, felt that low vibration that couldn't be there, blinked as something tried to slide in on the edge of her vision. "It feels old, but it can't be old, not valuably old, because it only cost ten pounds."

"Value's different for one than for another." He reached out. It was irresistible. With his eyes steady and level he closed his hand over hers that held the pendant.

The jolt snapped into her, sharp as an electric current. The air seemed to turn the blue of lightning. She was on her feet, her head tipping back to keep her eyes locked with his as he shoved back from the table with enough violence to send his chair crashing.

That same violence was in him when his mouth crushed hers. The need, so bright, so strong, so right, whipped through her even as the wind rushed sudden and sharp through the window at her back. Her hand fisted in his hair, her body lifted itself to his.

And fit.

The pounding of her heart was like a song, each note a thrill. Here, with him, it was enough, even if the world crumbled to dust around them.

He couldn't stop. The taste of her was like water, cool and clean, after a lifetime of thirst. Empty pockets he hadn't known he carried inside him filled, bulged, overflowed. His blood was a rage of heat, his body weak with wanting. He gathered the back of the shirt in his bunched fingers, prepared to rip.

Then they dropped the pendant they held between them to reach for each other. And he snapped back as if from a blow.

"This is not what I want." He took her shoulders, intending to shake her, but only held her. She looked dazed. Faerie-struck. "This is not what I'll accept."

"Would you let me go?" Her voice was low, but it didn't quaver. When he did, and stepped back, she let out a short, quiet breath. There was no point in being a coward, she told herself.

"I have a couple of choices here," she began. "One is I hit my head when I fell and I have a concussion. The other is that I just fell in love with you. I think I prefer the concussion theory, and I imagine you do, too."

"You didn't hit your head." He jammed his hands in his pockets and strode away from her. The room was suddenly too small. "And people don't fall in love in an instant, over one kiss."

"Sensible ones don't. I'm not sensible. Ask anyone." But if there was ever a time to try to be, it was now.

"I think I should get dressed, take a walk, clear my head or whatever."

"Another's storm's brewing."

Allena tugged her clothes off the screen. "You're telling me," she muttered and marched into the bedroom.

4

CONAL WASN'T IN the cottage when she came out again, but Hugh sat by the fire as if waiting for her. He got up as she came through and pranced to the door, turning his big head so that his eyes met hers.

"Want a walk? Me, too."

It was a pity about the gardens, Allena thought as she paused between them. She'd have enjoyed getting down into them, yanking out those choking weeds, pinching off deadheads. An hour's pleasant work, she thought, maybe two, and instead of looking wild and neglected, those tumbling blossoms would just look wild. Which is what was needed here.

Not her job, she told herself, not her home, not her place. She cast an eye at the little outbuilding. He was probably in there doing . . . whatever the hell he did. And doing it, she imagined, angrily.

Why was there so much anger in him?

Not her problem, she thought, not her business, not her man.

Though for a moment, when their hands and mouths were joined, he had seemed to be.

I don't want this. I don't want you.

He'd made himself very clear. And she was tired of finding herself plopped down where she wasn't wanted.

The wind raced in off the sea, driving thick black-edged clouds toward the island. As she began to walk, she could see the pale and hopeful blue being gradually, inevitably consumed.

Conal was right. A storm was coming.

Walking along the shoreline couldn't do any harm. She wouldn't climb the hills, though she longed to. She would just stick to the long curve of surf and sand and enjoy the jittery thrill of watching the fierce waves crash.

Hugh seemed content to walk at her side. Almost, she thought, like a guard.

Eight kilometers to the nearest village, she remembered. That wasn't so very far. She could wait for the weather to clear, then walk it if Conal wouldn't drive her. There'd been a truck parked between the cottage and the outbuilding, a sleek and modern thing, anachronistic but surely serviceable.

Why had he kissed her like that?

No, that wasn't right. It hadn't been his doing. It had simply happened, to both of them. For both of them. There'd been a roar in her head, in her blood, that she'd never experienced before. More than passion, she thought now, more than lust. It was a kind of desperate recognition.

There you are. Finally. At last.

That, of course, was ridiculous, but she had no other way to explain what had spurted to life inside her. And what had spread from that first hot gush felt like love.

You couldn't love what you didn't know. You couldn't love where there was no understanding, no foundation, no history. Her head told her all these sensible, rational things. And her heart laughed at them.

It didn't matter. She could be conflicted, puzzled, annoyed, even willing to accept. But it didn't matter when he didn't want her or what had flamed to life between them.

She stopped, let the wind beat its frantic wings over her, let the spray from the waves fly on her. Overhead a gull, white as the moon, let out its triumphant scream and streamed off in the current of electric air.

Oh, she envied that freedom, for the heart of flight was inside her. To simply fly away, wherever the wind took her. And to know that when she landed, it would be her place, her time, her triumph.

But you have to live in the present, don't you, Lena? Her mother's patient and puzzled voice murmured in her ear. *You have to apply yourself, to pay attention. You can't keep drifting this way and make something of yourself. It's time you focused on a career, put your considerable energy into making your mark.*

And under that voice, unsaid, was *You disappoint me.*

"I know it. I'm sorry. It's awful. I wish I could tell you how awful it is to know I'm your only failure."

She would do better, Allena promised herself. She'd talk Margaret into giving her a second chance. Somehow. Then she'd work harder, pay more attention, be responsible, be practical.

Be miserable.

The dog bumped his head against her leg, rubbed his warm fur against her. The small gesture comforted her and turning away from the water, she continued to walk along its verge.

She'd come out to clear her head, she reminded herself, not to fill it with more problems. Surely there couldn't be a more perfect spot for easing heart and mind. Under those threatening skies, the rough hills shone, the wicked cliffs gleamed. Wildflowers, dots and splashes of color, tangled in the green and gray, and she saw a shadowy spread of purple that was heather.

She wanted to gather it, fill her arms with it, bury her face in the scent. Delighted with the idea, she turned to scramble over rocks where sprigs of it thrived in the thin soil, then higher to mounds bumpy and thick until the fragrance of it overpowered even the primitive perfume of the sea.

When her arms were full, she wanted more. Laughing, she hurried along a narrow path. Then stopped dead. Startled, she shook her head. She heard the oddest hum. She started to step forward again, and couldn't. Simply couldn't. It was as if a wall of glass stood between her and the next slope of rock and flowers.

"My God, what is this?"

She lifted a trembling hand, sending sprigs of heather falling, then flying free in the wind. She felt no barrier, but only a kind of heat when her hand pressed the air. And try as she might, she couldn't push through it.

Lightning burst. Thunder rolled. Through it, she heard the sound of her name. She looked down to the beach, half expecting to see dragons or sorcerers. But it was only Conal, standing with his legs spread, his hair flying, and his eyes annoyed.

"Come down from there. You've no business clambering up the rocks when a storm's breaking."

What a picture she made. He'd come after her out of responsibility, he liked to think. But he'd been dumbstruck when he'd seen her walking the cliff path in the eerie light, her hair fluttering, her arms overflowing with flowers. It made him want to climb after her, to whirl her and her flowers into his arms, to press his mouth to hers again while the wind whipped savagely over them.

Because he wanted it, could all but taste her, his tone was blade-sharp when she met him on the beach. "Have you no more sense than to pick flowers in such weather?"

"Apparently not. Would you walk down there?"

"What?"

"Just humor me, and walk down the beach five more feet."

"Maybe you did rattle your brains." He started to grab her hand, pull her away, but she took a nimble step aside.

"Please. It'll only take you a minute."

He hissed out an oath, then strode off, one foot, two, three. His abrupt halt had Allena closing her eyes, shivering once. "You can't do it, can you? You can't go any farther than that. Neither could I." She opened her eyes again, met his furious ones when he turned. "What does it mean?"

"It means we deal with it. We'll go back. I've no desire to find myself drenched to the skin a second time in one day."

He said nothing on the way back, and she let him have his silence. The first fat drops of rain splattered as they reached the cottage door.

"Do you have anything to put these in?" she asked him. "They'll need water, and I'd like to keep my hands busy while you explain things to me."

He shrugged, made a vague gesture toward the kitchen, then went to add more turf to the fire.

It was a downpour. The wind rose to a howl, and she began to gather vases and bottles and bowls. When he remained silent, scowling into the fire, she heated up the tea.

He glanced over when she poured the cups, then went into the kitchen himself to take out a bottle of whiskey. A healthy dollop went into his own tea, then he lifted a brow, holding the bottle over hers.

"Well, why not?"

But when it was laced, she picked up the flowers instead of the cup and began to tuck them into vases. "What is this place? Who are you?"

"I've told you that already."

"You gave me names." The homey task calmed her, as she'd known it would. When her gaze lifted to his again, it was direct and patient. "That's not what I meant."

He studied her, then nodded. Whether she could handle it or not, she deserved to know. "Do you know how far out in the sea you are?"

"A mile, two?"

"More than ten."

"Ten? But it couldn't have taken more than twenty minutes to get here—and in rough weather."

"More than ten miles out is Dolman Island from the southwest coast of Ireland. Here we straddle the Atlantic and Celtic Seas. Some say the silkies come here, to shed their hides and sun on the rocks in human form. And the faeries come out of their rafts under the hills to dance in the moonlight.''

Allena slipped the stems of shorter blossoms into a squat bottle. "Do you say it?"

"Some say," he continued without answering, "that my great-grandmother left her raft, her palace under the hill, and pledged herself to my great-grandfather on the night of the summer solstice while they stood by the king stone of the dance on the cliffs. One hundred years ago. As a hundred years before, another with my blood stood with his woman in that same place to pledge. And a century before that as well, and always on that same night in that same place when the star shows itself."

She touched her pendant. "This star?"

"They say."

"And in two days it's the solstice, and your turn?"

"If I believed my great-grandmother was other than a simple woman, that I have elfin blood in my veins and could be directed to pledge to a woman because of the way a star shines through the stones, I wouldn't be in this place."

"I see." She nodded and carried one of the vases into the living room to set it on a table. "So you're here to prove that everything you've just told me is nonsense."

"Can you believe otherwise?"

She had no idea what she believed, but had a feeling there was a great deal, a very great deal, that she *could* believe. "Why couldn't I walk away from here, Conal? Why couldn't you?"

She left the question hanging, walked back into the kitchen. She took a sip of her tea, felt the hot flow of whiskey slide into her, then began to select her other arrangements and put them where she liked. "It would be hard for you, being told this story since you were a child, being expected to accept it."

"Can you accept it?" he demanded. "Can you just shrug off education and reason and accept that you're to belong to me because a legend says so?"

"I would've said no." Pleasing herself, she set bottles

of heather on the narrow stone mantel over the simmering fire. "I would have been intrigued, amused, maybe a little thrilled at the idea of it all. Then I would have laughed it off. I would have," she said as she turned to face him. "Until I kissed you and felt what I felt inside me, and inside you."

"Desire's an easy thing."

"That's right, and if that had been it, if that had been all, we'd both have acted on it. If that had been all, you wouldn't be angry now, with yourself and with me."

"You're awfully bloody calm about it."

"I know." She smiled then, couldn't help herself. "Isn't that odd? But then, I'm odd. Everyone says so. Lena, the duck out of water, the square peg, the fumbler always just off center. But I don't feel odd or out of place here. So it's easier for me to be calm."

Nor did she look out of place, he thought, wandering through the cottage placing her flowers. "I don't believe in magic."

"And I've looked for it all my life." She took a sprig of heather, held it out to him. "So, I'll make you a promise."

"You don't owe me promises. You don't owe me anything."

"It's free. I won't hold you with legends or magic. When I can leave, if that's what you want, I'll go."

"Why?"

"I'm in love with you, and love doesn't cling."

Humbled, he took the heather, slipped it into her hair. "Allena, it takes clear eyes to recognize what's in the heart so easily. I don't have them. I'll hurt you." He skimmed his fingers down her cheek. "And I find I'd rather not."

"I'm fairly sturdy. I've never been in love before, Conal, and I might be terrible at it. But right now it suits me, and that's enough."

He refused to believe anything could be so simple. "I'm drawn to you. I want my hands on you. I want you under me. If that's all, it might not be enough for you, or for me in the end. So it's best to stand back."

He walked to the peg, tugged down his slicker. "I need to work," he said, and went out into the rain.

It would be more than she'd had, she realized, and knew that if necessary, she could make it enough.

The storm was only a grumble when he came back. Evening was falling, soft and misty. The first thing he noticed when he stepped inside, was the scent. Something hot and rich that reminded his stomach it was empty.

Then he noticed the little changes in the living room. Just a few subtle touches: a table shifted, cushions smoothed. He wouldn't have noticed the dust, but he noticed the absence of it, and the faint tang of polish.

She'd kept the fire going, and the light, mixed with that of the candles she'd found and set about, was welcoming. She'd put music on as well and was humming along to it as she worked in the kitchen.

Even as he hung up his slicker, the tension he'd carried through his work simply slid off his shoulders.

"I made some soup," she called out. "I hunted up some herbs from the kitchen bed, foraged around in here. You didn't have a lot to work with, so it's pretty basic."

"It smells fine. I'm grateful."

"Well, we have to eat, don't we?"

"You wouldn't say that so easy if I'd been the one doing the cooking." She'd already set the table, making the mismatched plates and bowls look cheerful and clever instead of careless. There were candles there, too, and one of the bottles of wine he'd brought from Dublin stood breathing on the counter.

She was making biscuits.

"Allena, you needn't have gone to such trouble."

"Oh, I like puttering around. Cooking's kind of a hobby." She poured him wine. "Actually, I took lessons. I took a lot of lessons. This time I thought maybe I'd be a chef or open my own restaurant."

"And?"

"There's a lot more to running a restaurant than cooking. I'm horrible at business. As for the chef idea, I realized you had to cook pretty much the same things night after night, and on demand, to suit the menu, you know? So, it turned into one of my many hobbies.'' She slipped the biscuits into the oven. ''But at least this one has a practical purpose. So.'' She dusted her hands on the dishcloth she'd tucked into her waistband. ''I hope you're hungry.''

He flashed a grin that made her heart leap. ''I'm next to starving.''

''Good.'' She set out the dish of cheese and olives she'd put together. ''Then you won't be critical.''

Where he would have ladled the soup straight from the kettle, she poured it into a thick white bowl. Already she'd hunted out the glass dish his mother had used for butter and that he hadn't seen for years. The biscuits went in a basket lined with a cloth of blue and white checks. When she started to serve the soup, he laid a hand over hers.

''I'll do it. Sit.''

The scents alone were enough to make him weep in gratitude. The first taste of herbed broth thick with hunks of vegetables made him close his eyes in pleasure.

When he opened them again, she was watching him with amused delight. ''I like your hobby,'' he told her. ''I hope you'll feel free to indulge yourself with it as long as you're here.''

She selected a biscuit, studied it. It was so gratifying to see him smile. ''That's very generous of you.''

''I've been living on my own poor skills for some months now.'' His eyes met hers, held. ''You make me realize what I've missed. I'm a moody man, Allena.''

''Really?'' Her voice was so mild the insult nearly slipped by him. But he was quick.

He laughed, shook his head, and spooned up more soup. ''It won't be a quiet couple of days, I'm thinking.''

5

HE SLEPT IN his studio. It seemed the wisest course.

He wanted her, and that was a problem. He had no doubt she would have shared the bed with him, shared herself with him. As much as he would have preferred that to the chilly and narrow cot crammed into his work space, it didn't seem fair to take advantage of her romantic notions.

She fancied herself in love with him.

It was baffling, really, to think that a woman could make such a decision, state it right out, in a fingersnap of time. But then, Allena Kennedy wasn't like any of the other women who'd passed in and out of his life. A complicated package, she was, he thought. It would have been easy to dismiss her as a simple, almost foolish sort. At a first and casual glance.

But Conal wasn't one for casual glances. There were layers to her—thoughtful, bubbling, passionate, and compassionate layers. Odd, wasn't it? he mused, that she didn't seem to recognize them in herself.

That lack of awareness added one more layer, and that was sweetness.

Absently, with his eyes still gritty from a restless night, he began to sketch. Allena Kennedy from New York City, the square peg in what appeared to be a family of conformists. The woman who had yet to find herself, yet seemed perfectly content to deal with where she'd landed. A modern woman, certainly, but one who still accepted tales of magic.

No, more than accepted, he thought now. She embraced them. As if she'd just been waiting to be told where it was she'd been going all along.

That he wouldn't do, refused to do. All his life he'd been told this day would come. He wouldn't passively fall in, give up his own will. He had come back to this place at this time to prove it.

And he could almost hear the fates giggling.

Scowling, he studied what he'd drawn. It was Allena with her long eyes and sharp bones, the short and shaggy hair that suited that angular face and slender neck. And at her back, he'd sketched in the hint of faerie wings.

They suited her as well.

It annoyed the hell out of him.

Conal tossed the pad aside. He had work to do, and he'd get to it as soon as he'd had some tea.

The wind was still up. The morning sun was slipping through the stacked clouds to dance over the water. The only thunder now was the crash and boom of waves on the shore. He loved the look of it, that changing and capricious sea. His years in Dublin hadn't been able to feed this single need in him, for the water and the sky and the rough and simple land that was his.

However often he left, wherever he went, he would always be drawn back. For here was heart and soul.

Turning away from the sea, he saw her.

She knelt in the garden, flowers rioting around her and the quiet morning sun shimmering over her hair. Her face was turned away from him, but he could see it in his mind. She would have that half-dreaming, contented look in her eyes as she tugged away the weeds he'd ignored.

Already the flowers looked cheerful, as if pleased with the attention after weeks of neglect.

There was smoke pluming from the chimney, a broom propped against the front wall. She'd dug a basket out of God knew where, and in this she tossed the weeds. Her feet were bare.

Warmth slid into him before he could stop it and murmured *welcome* in his ear.

"You don't have to do that."

She looked up at his voice, and she was indeed happy. "They needed it. Besides, I love flowers. I have pots of them all over my apartment, but this is so much better. I've never seen snapdragons so big." She traced a finger on a spike of butter-yellow blooms. "They always make me think of Alice."

"Alice?"

"In Wonderland. I've already made tea." She got to her feet, then winced at the dirt on the knees of her trousers. "I guess I should've been more careful. It's not like I have a vast wardrobe to choose from at the moment. So. How do you like your eggs?"

He started to tell her she wasn't obliged to cook his breakfast. But he remembered just how fine the soup had been the night before. "Scrambled would be nice, if it's no trouble."

"None, and it's the least I can do for kicking you out of your own bed." She stepped up to the door, then turned. Her eyes were eloquent, and patient. "You could have stayed."

"I know it."

She held his gaze another moment, then nodded. "You had some bacon in your freezer. I took it out last night to thaw. Oh, and your shower dripped. It just needed a new washer."

He paused at the doorway, remembered, as he hadn't in years, to wipe his feet. "You fixed the shower?"

"Well, it dripped." She was already walking into the

kitchen. "You probably want to clean up. I'll get breakfast started."

He scratched the back of his neck. "I'm grateful."

She slanted him a look. "So am I."

When he went into the bedroom, she did a quick dance, hugged herself. Oh, she loved this place. It was a storybook, and she was right in the middle of it. She'd awakened that morning half believing it had all been a dream. But then she'd opened her eyes to that misty early light, had smelled the faint drift of smoke from the dying fire, the tang of heather she'd put beside the bed.

It was a dream. The most wonderful, the most real dream she'd ever had. And she was going to keep it.

He didn't want it, didn't want her. But that could change. There were two days yet to open his heart. How could his stay closed when hers was so full? Love was nothing like she'd expected it to be.

It was so much more brilliant.

She needed the hope, the faith, that on one of the days left to her he would wake up and feel what she did.

Love, she discovered, was so huge it filled every space inside with brightness. There was no room for shadows, for doubts.

She was in love, with the man, with the place, with the promise. It wasn't just in the rush of an instant, though there was that thrill as well. But twined with it was a lovely, settled comfort, an ease of being, of knowing. And that was something she wanted for him.

For once in her life, she vowed, she wouldn't fail. She would not lose.

Closing her eyes, she touched the star that hung between her breasts. "I'll make it happen," she whispered, then with a happy sigh, she started breakfast.

He didn't know what to make of it. He couldn't have said just what state the bathroom had been in before, but he was dead certain it hadn't sparkled. There may or may not have been fresh towels out the last time he'd seen it. But he thought not. There hadn't been a bottle of flowers on the windowsill.

The shower had dripped, that he remembered. He'd meant to get to that.

He could be certain that it was a great deal more pleasant to shower and shave in a room where the porcelain gleamed and the air smelled faintly of lemon and flowers.

Because of it, he guiltily wiped up after himself and hung the towel to dry instead of tossing it on the floor.

The bedroom showed her touch as well. The bed was tidily made, the pillows fluffed up. She'd opened the windows wide to bring in the sun and the breeze. It made him realize he'd lived entirely too long with dust and dark.

Then he stepped out. She was singing in the kitchen. A pretty voice. And the scents that wafted to him were those of childhood. Bread toasting, bacon frying.

There was a rumble he recognized as the washer spinning a load. He could only shake his head.

"How long have you been up and about?" he asked her.

"I woke up at dawn." She turned to pass him a mug of tea over the counter. "It was so gorgeous I couldn't get back to sleep. I've been piddling."

"You've a rare knack for piddling."

"My father calls it nervous energy. Oh, I let Hugh out. He bolted to the door the minute my feet hit the floor, so I figured that was the routine."

"He likes to run around in the mornings. Dog piddling, I suppose."

It made her laugh as she scooped his eggs from skillet to plate. "He's terrific company. I felt very safe and snug with him curled up at the foot of the bed last night."

"He's deserted me for a pretty face." He sat, then caught her hand. "Where's yours?"

"I had something earlier. I'll let you eat in peace. My father hates to be chattered at over breakfast. I'll just hang out the wash."

"I'm not your father. Would you sit? Please." He waited until she took a seat and for the first time noticed nerves in the way she linked her fingers together. Now what was that about? ''Allena, do you think I expect you to cater to me this way? Cook and serve and tidy?''

''No, of course not.'' The lift had gone out of her voice, out of her eyes. ''I've overstepped. I'm always doing that. I didn't think.''

''That's not what I meant. Not at all.'' His eyes were keen, part of his gift, and they saw how her shoulders had braced, her body tensed. ''What are you doing? Waiting for the lecture?'' With a shake of his head, he began to eat. ''They've done what they could, haven't they, to stifle you? Why is it people are always so desperate to mold another into their vision, their way? I'm saying only that you're not obliged to cook my meals and scrub my bath. While you're here you should do what pleases you.''

''I guess I have been.''

''Fine. You won't hear any complaints from me. I don't know what you've done with these humble eggs unless it's magic.''

She relaxed again. ''Thyme and dill, from your very neglected herb bed. If I had a house, I'd plant herbs, and gardens.'' Imagining it, she propped her chin on her fist. ''I'd have stepping-stones wandering through it, with a little bench so you could just stop and sit and look. It would be best if it was near the water so I could hear the beat of it the way I did last night. Pounding, like a quickened heart.''

She blinked out of the image, found him staring at her. ''What? Oh, I was running on again.'' She started to get up, but he took her hand a second time.

''Come with me.''

He got to his feet, pulled her to hers. ''The dishes—''

''Can wait. This can't.''

He'd already started it that morning with the sketch. In his head, it was all but finished, and the energy of it was driving him, so he strode quickly out of the house, toward his studio. She had to run to keep up.

''Conal, slow down. I'm not going anywhere.''

Ignoring her, he shoved open the door, pulled her in after him. ''Stand by the window.''

But she was already moving in, eyes wide and delighted. "You're an artist. This is wonderful. You sculpt."

The single room was nearly as big as the main area of the cottage. And much more cramped. A worktable stood in the center, crowded with tools and hunks of stone, pots of clay. A half dozen sketch pads were tossed around. Shelves and smaller tables were jammed with examples of his work. Mystical, magical creatures that danced and flew.

A blue mermaid combed her hair on a rock. A white dragon breathed fire. Faeries no bigger than her thumb ringed in a circle with faces sly. A sorcerer nearly as tall as she, held his arms high and wept.

"They're all so alive, so vivid." She couldn't help herself, she had to touch, and so she ran her finger down the rippling hair of the mermaid. "I've seen this before," she murmured. "Not quite this, but the same feeling of it, but in bronze. At a gallery in New York."

She looked over then where he was impatiently flipping through a sketch pad. "I've seen your work in New York. You must be famous."

His answer was a grunt.

"I wanted to buy it—the mermaid. I was with my mother, and I couldn't because she'd have reminded me I couldn't afford the price. I went back the next day, because I couldn't stop thinking about it, but it was already sold."

"In front of the window, turn to me."

"That was two years ago, and I've thought about her a dozen times since. Isn't it amazing that she was yours?"

Muttering an oath, he strode to her, pulled her to the window. "Lift your head, like that. Hold it there. And be quiet."

"Are you going to draw me?"

"No, I'm after building a boat here. Of course I'm drawing you. Now be quiet for one bloody minute."

She shut her mouth, but couldn't do anything about the grin that trembled on her lips. And that, he thought, was precisely what he wanted. Just that trace of humor, of energy, of personal delight.

He would do a clay model, he thought, and cast her in

bronze. Something that gleamed gold and warmed to the touch. She wasn't for stone or wood. He did three quick studies of her face, moving around her for a change of angle. Then he lowered his pad.

"I need the line of your body. Your shape. Take off your clothes."

"Excuse me?"

"I have to see how you're made. The clothes are in the way of you."

"You want me to pose nude?"

With an effort, he brought himself back from his plans, met her eyes. "If this was a matter of sex, I wouldn't have slept on that rock in the corner last night. You've my word I won't touch you. But I have to see you."

"If this was a matter of sex, I wouldn't be so nervous. Okay." She shut her eyes a minute, bolstered her courage. "I'm like a bowl of fruit," she told herself and unbuttoned her shirt.

When she slipped it off, folded it, set it aside, Conal lifted a brow. "No, you're like a woman. If I wanted a bowl of fruit, I'd get one."

6

SHE WAS SLIM, leaning toward angular, and exactly right. Eyes narrowed, mind focused, he flipped up a fresh page and began.

"No, keep your head up," he ordered, faintly irritated that she should be so exactly right. "Hold your arms back. Just a bit more. Palms down and flat. No, you're not a flaming penguin, spread your fingers a little. Ah."

It was then he noticed the faint flush spreading over her skin, the stiffness in her movements. Moron, he told himself and bit back a sigh. Of course she was nervous and embarrassed. And he'd done nothing to put her at ease.

He'd grown too used, he supposed, to professional models who undraped without a thought. She liked to talk, so he would let her talk.

"Tell me about these lessons of yours."

"What?"

"The lessons. You said you'd taken a number of lessons on this and that. What was it you studied?"

She pressed her lips together, fought back the foolish urge to cross her arms over her breasts. "I thought you said I wasn't supposed to talk."

"Now I'm saying you can."

She heard the exasperation, rolled her eyes. What was she, a mind reader? "I, ah, took art lessons."

"Did you now? Turn to the right just a bit. And what did you learn from them?"

"That I'm not an artist." She smiled a little. "I'm told I have a good eye for color and shapes and aesthetics, but no great skill with the execution."

Yes, it was better when she talked. Her face became mobile again. Alive again. "That discouraged you?"

"Not really. I draw now and then when I'm in the mood."

"Another hobby?"

"Oh, I'm loaded with them. Like music. I took music lessons."

Ah, she was relaxing. The doe-in-the-crosshairs look was fading from her eyes. "What's your instrument?"

"The flute. I'm reasonably adept, but I'm never going to have a chair with the Philharmonic."

She shrugged, and he bit back a sharp order for her not to change the line.

"I took a course in computer programming, and that was a complete wash. As most of my business courses were, which scuttled the idea I had of opening a little craft shop. I could handle the craft part, but not the shop part."

Her gaze was drawn back to the mermaid. She coveted that, not just the piece itself, but the talent and vision that had created it.

"Stand on your toes. That's it, that's lovely. Hold a minute. Why don't you take on a partner?"

"For what?"

"The shop, if it's what you want. Someone business-minded."

"Mostly because I have enough business sense to know I could never afford the rent in New York, the start-up costs." She moved a shoulder. "Overhead, equipment, stock. I guess running a business is a study in stress. Margaret always says so."

Ah, he thought, the inestimable Margaret, whom he'd already decided to detest. "What do you care what she says? No, that's not right. It's not quite right. Turn around. You have a beautiful back."

"I do?" Surprise had her turning her head to look at him.

"There! Hold that. Lower your chin a little more to your shoulder, keep your eyes on me."

That was what he wanted. No shyness here. Coyness was something different altogether. There was a hint of that in the upward angle of her gaze, the tilt of her head. And just a bit of smugness as well, in the slight curve of her lips.

Allena of the Faeries, he thought, already eager to begin in clay. He ripped the sheets off the pad, began tacking them to the wall.

"I'll do better with you as well as the sketches. Relax a minute while I prep the clay." As he passed, he touched a hand absently to her shoulder. He stopped. "Christ, you're cold. Why didn't you say something?"

She was turning toward him, a slow shift of her body. "I didn't notice."

"I didn't think to keep the fire going." His hand skimmed over her shoulder, fingers tracing the blade where he imagined wings. "I'll build one now." Even as he spoke he was leaning toward her, his eyes locked on hers. Her lips parted, and he could feel the flutter of her breath.

He jerked back, like a man snapping out of a dream. Lifted his hand, then held them both up, away from her. "I said I wouldn't touch you. I'm sorry."

The rising wave of anticipation in her broke, then vanished as he walked away to yank a blanket from the cot. "I wish you weren't. Sorry, I mean."

He stood with the table between them, the blanket in his hands, and felt like a man drowning. There was no shyness in her now, nor coyness. But the patience was there, and the promise.

"I don't want this need for you. Do you understand?"

"You want me to say yes." She was laid bare now, she realized. Much more than her body laid bare. "It would make it easier if I said that I understand. But I can't, I don't. I want that need, Conal. And you."

"Another place, another time," he murmured. "There'd be no need to understand. Another place, another time, I'd want it as well."

"This is here," she said quietly. "And this is now. It's still your choice."

He wanted to be sure of it, wanted to know there was nothing but her. "Will you take that off?"

She lifted a hand to the pendant, her last shield. Saying nothing, she slipped the chain over her head, then walked to the table, set it down. "Do you think I'll feel differently without it?"

"There's no magic between us now. We're only who and what we are." He stepped to her, swept the blanket around her shoulders. "It's as much your choice as mine, Allena. You've a right to say no."

"Then . . ." She laid her hands on his shoulders, brought her lips to within a breath of his. "I've also a right to say yes."

It was she who closed that tenuous distance so mouths and bodies met. And she who let the blanket drop when her arms went around him.

She gave, completely, utterly. All the love, so newly discovered in her heart, poured out for him. Her lips seduced, her hands soothed, her body yielded.

There was a choice. She had made hers, but he still had his own. To draw back, step away and refuse. Or to gather close and take. Before his blood could take over, before it was all need and heat, he took her face in his hands until their eyes met again.

"With no promises, Allena."

He suffered. She could see the clouds and worry in his eyes, and said what she hoped would comfort. And be the truth as well. "And no regrets."

His thumbs skimmed over her cheeks, tracing the shape

of her face as skillfully as he'd drawn it on paper. ''Be with me, then.''

The cot was hard and narrow, but might have been a bed of rose petals as they lay on it. The air was chill, still damp from the storm, but she felt only warmth when his body covered hers.

Here. At last.

He knew his hands were big, the palms rough and calloused from his work, and very often careless. He would not be careless with her, would not rush through the moment they offered each other. So he touched her, gently, giving himself the pleasure of the body he'd sketched. Long limbs, long bones, and soft white skin. Her sigh was like music, the song his name.

She tugged off his sweater, sighing again when flesh met flesh, and again murmuring his name against the pulse of his own throat. With only that, she gave him the sweetness he'd denied himself. Whatever he had of that simple gift inside him, he offered back.

Under him she lifted and moved as if they'd danced this dance together for a lifetime. Flowed with and against him, now fluid, now strong. And the quickening pulse that rose in her was like his own.

Her scent was soap, her taste fresh as rain.

He watched her glide up, the faerie again, soaring on one long spread of wings. As she crested, her eyes opened, met his. And she smiled.

No one had brought her so much, or shown her how much she had to offer. Her body quivered from the thrill of it, and in her heart was the boundless joy of finding home.

She arched up, opened so he would fill her. As he slid inside her, the beauty dazzled, and the power hummed.

While they took each other, neither noticed the star carved in silver, glowing blue as flame.

She lay over him now, snug under his arm with her cheek upon his chest. It was lovely to hear how his heart still pounded. A kind of rage, she thought, though he'd been the most tender of lovers.

No one could have shown her that kind of caring if there wasn't caring inside. And that, she thought, closing her eyes, was enough.

"You're cold," he murmured.

"Am not." She snuggled against him and would have frozen to the bone before she let him move. But she lifted her head so she could grin at him.

"Allena Kennedy." His fingers trailed lightly down the back of her neck. "You look smug."

"I feel smug. Do you mind?"

"I would be a foolish man to mind."

She bent down to kiss his chin, a sweet and casual gesture that moved him. "And Conal O'Neil is not a foolish man. Or is he?" She angled her head. "If we can't go beyond a certain point and walk to the village, wouldn't it follow that no one from the village can come here?"

"I suppose it would."

"Then let's do something foolish. Let's go swim naked in the sea."

"You want to swim naked in the sea?"

"I've always wanted to. I just realized it this minute." She rolled off the cot and tugged at his hand. "Come be foolish with me, Conal."

"*Leannan,* the first wave'll flatten you."

"Will not." *Leannan.* She had no idea what it meant, but it sounded tender, and made her want to dance. She raked both hands through her hair, then the light of challenge lighted her eyes. "Race you."

She darted off like a rabbit and had him scrambling up. "Wait. Damn it, the seas are too rough for you."

Bird bones, he thought, snatching up the blanket on his way. She would crack half a dozen of them in minutes.

No, she didn't run like a rabbit, he realized. She ran like a bloody gazelle, with long, loping strides that had her nearly at the foaming surf. He called out her name, rushing after her. His heart simply stopped when she raced into the water and dived under its towering wall.

"Sweet Jesus."

He'd gotten no farther than the beach when she surfaced, laughing. "Oh, it's cold!" She struggled to the shallows, slicking her hair back, lifted her face, her arms. For the second time his heart stopped, but now it had nothing to do with alarm.

"You're a vision, Allena."

"No one's ever said that to me before." She held out a hand. "No one's ever looked at me the way you do. Ride the sea with me."

It had been, he decided, much too long since he'd been foolish. "Hold on, then."

It tossed them up, a rush of power. It sucked them down into a blind, thundering world. The tumult of it was freedom, a cocky dare to fate. Wrapped around each other, they spun as the waves rolled over them.

Breathless, they surfaced, only to plunge in again. Her scream wasn't one of fear, but a cry of victory as, latched around him, she was swept into the air again.

"You'll drown us both!" he shouted, but his eyes were lit with wicked humor.

"I won't. I can't. Nothing but wonders today. Once more." She locked her arms around his neck. "Let's go under just once more."

To her shrieking delight, he snatched her off her feet and dived into the cresting wave with her.

When they stumbled out, panting, their hands were linked.

"Your teeth are chattering."

"I know. I loved it." But she snuggled into the blanket he wrapped around them both. "I've never done anything like that. I guess you've done it dozens of times."

"Not with the likes of you."

It was, she thought, the perfect thing to say. She held the words to her for a moment even as she held him. Hard against her heart.

"What does *leannan* mean?"

"Hmm?" Her head was on his shoulder, her arms linked

around his waist. Everything inside him was completely at peace.

"*Leannan.* You said that to me, I wondered what it means."

His hand paused in midstroke on her hair. "It's a casual term," he said carefully. "A bit of an endearment, is all. 'Sweetheart' would be the closest."

"I like it."

He closed his eyes. "Allena, you ask for too little."

And hope for everything, she thought. "You shouldn't worry, Conal. I'm not. Now, before we both turn blue out here, I'll make fresh tea, and you'll build up the fire." She kissed him. "Right after I pick up some of these shells."

She wiggled away, leaving him holding the blanket and shaking his head. Most of the shells that littered the beach had been broken by the waves, but that didn't appear to bother her. He left her to it and went into the studio to tug on his jeans.

She had a pile of shells when he came back, offering her his sweater and her pendant.

"I won't wear it if it bothers you."

"It's yours." Deliberately, as if challenging the fates, he slipped it around her neck. "Here, put this on before you freeze."

She bundled into it, then crouched to put the shells into the blanket. "I love you, Conal, whether I'm wearing it or not. And since loving you makes me happy, it shouldn't worry you."

She rose. "Don't spoil it," she murmured. "Let's just take today, then see about tomorrow."

"All right." He took her hand, brought it to his lips. "I'll give you a promise after all."

"I'll take it."

"Today will always be precious to me, and so will you."

7

SHE DUG OUT an ancient pair of Conal's jeans, found a
hunk of frayed rope, and went to work with scissors. As a
fashion statement the chopped jeans, rough belt, and baggy
sweater said Island Shipwreck, but they did the job.

As he insisted on making the tea this time around, she
busied herself hanging the wash. And dreaming.

It could be just this way, she thought. Long, wonderful
days together. Conal would work in his studio, and she'd
tend the house, the gardens . . . and, oh, the children when
they came along.

She would paint the shutters and the little back porch.
She'd put an arbor in front, plant roses—the only roses she
would have—so that they'd climb up and twine and ramble
and it would be like walking through a fairy tale every time
she went into the house.

And it would be her fairy tale, ever after.

They would need to add rooms, of course, for those children. A second floor, she imagined, with dormer windows.

Another bath, a bigger kitchen, but nothing that would take away from the lovely cottage-by-the-sea feeling.

She'd make wonderful meals, keep the windows sparkling, sew curtains that would flutter in the breeze.

She stopped, pegging a sheet that flapped wetly. Her mother would be appalled. Household chores were something you hired other people to do because you had a career. You were a professional . . . something.

Of course, it was all just fantasy, she told herself as she moved down the clothesline. She had to make a living somehow. But she'd worry about that later. For now, she was going to enjoy the moment, the thrilling rush of being in love, the jittery ache of waiting to be loved in return.

They would have today, and their tomorrow. Whatever happened after, she'd have no regrets.

With the last of the laundry hung, she stepped back, lifted the basket to rest it on her hip. She saw Hugh prancing down the hill.

"Well, so you decided to come home. What have you got there?" Her eyes widened as she recognized the brown bulk he carried in his mouth. "My bag!"

She dropped the basket and rushed to him. And Hugh, sensing a game, began to race in circles around her.

Conal watched from the doorway. The tea was steeping in the pot, and he'd been about to call to her. Now he simply stood.

Sheets billowed like sails in the wind. He caught the clean, wet scent of them, and the drift of rosemary and lemon balm from the herb bed she'd weeded that morning. Her laughter lifted up, bright and delighted, as she raced with the dog.

His tattered old jeans hung on her, though she'd hacked them off to above her ankles. She'd rolled up the cuffs, pushed up the sleeves on his sweater, but now as she ran around with Hugh, they'd come down again and fell over her hands. She hadn't put on her shoes.

She was a joy to watch. And when, he wondered, had he stopped letting joy into his life? The shadow of his fate had grown longer with each passing year. He'd huddled under it, he thought now, telling himself he was standing clear.

He had let no one touch him, let nothing be important to him but his work. He had estranged himself from his father and his home. Those had been his choices, and his right. Now, watching Allena play tug-of-war with the big dog in a yard filled with sun and sailing white sheets, he wondered for the first time what he'd missed along the way.

And still, whatever he'd missed, she was here.

The pendant was here.

The solstice was closing in.

He could refuse it. He could deny it. However much this woman called to his blood, he would, at the end of that longest day, determine his own fate.

It would not be magic that forced his destiny, but his own will.

He saw Allena yank, Hugh release. She stumbled back, clutching something to her chest, then landed hard on her back. Conal was out the door and across the yard in a single skipping heartbeat.

"Are you hurt?" He issued one sharp order to the dog in Gaelic that had Hugh hanging his head.

"Of course not." She started to sit up, but Conal was already gathering her, stroking, murmuring something in Gaelic that sounded lovely. Loving. Her heart did one long, slow cartwheel. "Conal."

"The damn dog probably outweighs you, and you've bones like a bird."

"We were just playing. There, now, you've hurt Hugh's feelings. Come here, baby, it's okay."

While Conal sat back on his heels and scowled, she hugged and cuddled the dog. "It's all right. He didn't mean it, whatever it was. Did you, Conal?"

Conal caught the sidelong glance the dog sent him, and had to call it smug. "I did."

She only laughed and kissed Hugh's nose. "Such a smart dog, such a good dog," she crooned. "He found my bag and brought it home. I, on the other hand, am a moron. I forgot all about it."

Conal studied the oversized purse. It was wet, filthy, and now riddled with teeth marks. That didn't seem to bother her a bit. "It's taken a beating."

"I must've dropped it in the storm. Everything's in here. My passport, my credit cards, my ticket. My makeup." She hugged the bag, thrilled to have her lipstick back. "Oh, and dozens of things. Including my copy of Margaret's itinerary. Do you think the phone's working now?"

Without waiting for him to answer, she leaped up. "I can call her hotel, let her know I'm all right. She must be frantic."

She dashed into the house, clutching the bag, and Conal stayed as he was.

He didn't want the phones to be working. He didn't want that to break their bubble. Realizing it left him shaken. Here, he thought, at the first chance to reach out of their world, she'd run to do it.

Of course she had. He pressed his fingers to his eyes. Wouldn't he have done the same? She had a life beyond this, beyond him. The romance of it had swept her away for a while, just as it had nearly swept him. She would get her feet back under her and move on. That was as it should be. And what he wanted.

But when he rose to go after her, there was an ache inside him that hadn't been there before.

"I got through." Allena sent him a brilliant smile. She stood by the counter, the phone in her hand and what appeared to be half her worldly goods dumped on the table. "She's checked in, and they're going to ring her room. I only hope she didn't call my parents. I'd hate to think they'd—Margaret! Oh, I'm so glad you're—"

She broke off again, and Conal watched the light in her eyes go dim. "Yes, I know. I'm so sorry. I missed the ferry and . . ."

Saying nothing, he moved past her and got down mugs for tea. He had no intention of leaving her to her privacy.

"Yes, you're right, it was irresponsible. Inexcusable, yes, that, too, to leave you shorthanded this way. I tried to . . ."

He saw the moment she gave up, when her shoulders

slumped and her face went carefully blank. "I understand. No, of course, you can't be expected to keep me on after this. Oh, yes, I know it was against your better judgment in the first place. You were very clear about that. I'm sorry I let you down. Yes, again."

Shame, fatigue, resignation closed in on her, a dingy fog of failure. She shut her eyes. "No, Margaret, excuses don't matter when people are depending on you. Did you call Mom and Dad? No, you're right. What would have been the point?"

"Bloody bitch," Conal muttered. They'd just see how Margaret liked being on the other end of a tongue-lashing, he decided, and grabbed the phone out of Allena's hand. The buzz of the dial tone left him no victim for his outrage.

"She had to go," Allena managed. "Schedule. I should—Excuse me."

"No, damned if I will." He took her shoulders in a firm grip before she could escape. There were tears on her lashes. He wanted Margaret's neck in his hands. "You'll not go off to lick your wounds. Why did you take that from her?"

"She was right. I was irresponsible. She has every reason to fire me. She'd never have taken me on in the first place without family pressure."

"Family pressure? Bugger it. Where was her family concern? Did she ask if you were all right? What had happened? Where you were? Did she once ask you why?"

"No."

A tear spilled over, slid down her cheek and inflamed him. "Where is your anger?" he demanded.

"What good does it do to be angry?" Wearily, she brushed the tear away. "I brought it on myself. I don't care about the job. That's the problem, really. I don't care about it. I wouldn't have taken it if I'd had a choice. Margaret's probably right. I bungle this way on purpose."

"Margaret is a jackass."

"No, really, she's not." She managed a wobbly grin. "She's just very disciplined and goal-oriented. Well, there's no use whining about it." She patted his hand, then moved away to pour the tea. "I'll call my parents after I've settled down a little, explain . . . oh, God."

Pressing her palms to the counter, she squeezed her eyes shut. "I *hate* disappointing them this way. Over and over, like a cycle I can't break. If I could just do something, if I could just be good at something."

Shaking her head, she went to the refrigerator to take out last night's soup to heat for lunch. "You don't know how much I envy you your talent and your confidence in it. My mother always said if I'd just focus my energies instead of scattering them a dozen different ways, I'd move beyond mediocre."

"It should have shamed her to say such a thing to you."

Surprised by the violence in his tone, she turned back. "She didn't mean it the way I made it sound. You have to understand, they're all so smart and clever and, well, dedicated to what they do. My father's chief of surgery, my mother's a partner in one of the most prestigious law firms on the East Coast. And I can't do *anything*."

There was the anger. It whipped through her as she slammed the pot on the stove. Pleased to see it, Conal folded his arms, leaned back, and watched it build.

"There's James with his glossy practice and his gorgeous trophy wife and certified genius child, who's a complete brat, by the way, but everyone says she's simply precocious. As if precocious and rude are synonymous. And Margaret with her perfect office and her perfect wardrobe and her perfect home and her perfectly detestable husband, who won't see anything but art films and collects coins."

She dumped soup into the pot. "And every Thanksgiving they all sit around patting each other on the back over how successful and brilliant they are. Then they look at me as if I'm some sort of alien who got dumped on the doorstep and had to be taken in for humanitarian purposes. And I can't be a doctor or a lawyer or a goddamn Indian chief no matter how hard I try because I just can't *do* anything."

"Now *you* should be ashamed."

"What?" She pressed her fingers to her temples. Temper

made her dizzy, and fuzzy-headed, which is why she usually tried to avoid it. "What?"

"Come here." He grabbed her hand, pulled her into the living room. "What did you do here?"

"About what?"

"What are the things you did in here?"

"I . . . dusted?"

"To hell and back again with the dust, Allena. Look here at your flowers and candles and your bowl of broken shells. And out here."

He dragged her to the door, shoved it open. "Here's a garden that was suffering from neglect until the morning. Where's the sand that was all over the walk that I didn't even notice until it was gone? There are sheets drying in the wind out back and soup heating in the kitchen. The bloody shower doesn't drip now. Who did those things?"

"Anyone can sweep a walk, Conal."

"Not everyone thinks to. Not everyone cares to. And not everyone finds pleasure in the doing of it. In one day you made a home out of this place, and it hasn't been one in too long, so that I'd all but forgotten the feel of a home around me. Do you think that's nothing? Do you think there's no value in that?"

"It's just . . . ordinary," she said for lack of a better word. "I can't make a career out of picking wildflowers."

"A living can be made where you find it, if a living must be made. You've a need to pick wildflowers and seashells, Allena. And there are those who are grateful for it, and notice the difference you make."

If she hadn't loved him already, she would have fallen at that moment with his words still echoing and his eyes dark with impatience. "That's the kindest thing anyone's ever said to me." She laid her hands on his cheeks. "The very kindest." Softly, she touched her lips to his. "Thank you."

Before he could speak, she shook her head, then rested it on his shoulder.

8

THEY SHUT OUT the world. Turned off time. Conal would have bristled at the idea that they were making a kind of magic, but for Allena there was no other word for it.

She posed for him again, in the studio where the afternoon sun slanted through the windows. And she watched herself be born in clay.

Because she asked, he told her of his years in Dublin. His studies and his work. The lean student years when he'd lived on tinned food and art. Then the recognition that had come, like a miracle, in a dingy gallery.

The first sale had given him the luxury of time, room to work without the constant worry of paying the rent. And the sales that followed had given him the luxury of choice, so that he'd been able to afford a studio of his own.

Still, though he spoke of it easily, she noticed that when he talked of Dublin, he didn't refer to it as home. But she said nothing.

Later, when he'd covered the clay with a damp cloth and

washed in the little sink, they went for a walk along the shore. They spoke of a hundred things, but never once of the star she wore against her heart, or the stone circle that threw its shadows from the cliff.

They made love while the sun was still bright, and the warmth of it glowed on her skin when she rose over him.

As the day moved to evening, the light remained, shimmering as though it would never give way to night. She entertained herself mending the old lace curtains she'd found on a shelf in the closet while Conal sketched and the dog curled into a nap on the floor between them.

She had the most expressive face, he thought. Dreamy now as she sat and sewed. Everything she felt moved into her eyes of soft, clear gray. The witch behind those eyes had yet to wake. And when she did, he imagined that any man she cast them on would be spellbound.

How easily she had settled in—to him, his home, his life. Without a break of rhythm, he thought, and with such contentment. And how easy it would be to settle in to her. Even with these edgy flashes of need and desire, there was a comfort beneath.

What was he to do about her? Where was he to put these feelings she'd brought to life inside him? And how was he to know if they were real?

"Conal?" She spoke quietly. His troubled thoughts were like a humming in the air, a warning. "Can't you put it aside for now? Can't you be content to wait and see?"

"No." It irritated him that she'd read his mood in his silence. "Letting others shape your life is your way, not mine."

Her hand jerked, as if it had been slapped, then continued to move smoothly. "Yes, you're right. I've spent my life trying to please people I love, and it hasn't gotten me anywhere. They don't love me enough to accept me."

He felt a hitch in his gut, as if he'd shoved her away when he should have taken hold. "Allena."

"No, it's all right. They do love me, under it all, just not as much, or in the same way, or . . . however I love them. They want things for me that I'm not capable of—

or that I just don't want for myself enough to make a real effort. I can't put restrictions on my feelings. I'm not made that way.''

"And I can." He rose, paced. "It's not a matter of feelings, but of being. I can't and won't be led. I care for you more than should be possible in this short a time."

"And because of that you don't trust what's happened, what's happening between us." She nodded and, clipping the thread, set her needle aside. "That's reasonable."

"What do you know of reason?" he demanded. "You're the damnedest, most irrational woman I've ever met."

She smiled at that, quick and bright. "It's so much easier to recognize reason when you have so little yourself."

His lips twitched, but he sat down. "How can you be so calm in the middle of all this?"

"I've had the most amazing two days of my life, the most exciting, the most beautiful." She spread her hands. "Nothing can ever take that away from me now that I've had it. And I'll have one more. One more long and wonderful day. So . . ." She got to her feet, stretched. "I think I'll get a glass of wine and go outside and watch the stars come out."

"No." He took her hand, rose. "I'll get the wine."

It was a perfect night, the sky as clear as glass. The sea swept in, drew back, then burst again in a shower of water that caught those last shimmers of day and sparkled like jewels.

"You should have benches," Allena began. "Here and here, with curved seats and high backs, in cedar that would go silver in the weather."

He wondered why he hadn't thought of it himself, for he loved to sit and watch the sea. "What else would you have, were you me?"

"Well, I'd put big pots near the benches and fill them with flowers that spilled out and spiked up. Dark blue crocks," she decided, then slanted him a look. "You could make them."

"I suppose I could. Flowerpots." The idea was amusing.

No one had ever expected flowerpots from him before. He skimmed a hand over her hair as he sipped his wine and realized he would enjoy making them for her, would like to see her pleasure in them.

"Dark blue," she repeated, "to match the shutters when they're fixed up with the paint I found in the laundry room."

"Now I'm painting shutters?"

"No, no, no, your talents are much too lofty for such mundane chores. You make the pots, sturdy ones, and I'll paint the shutters."

"I know when someone's laughing at me."

She merely sent him a sly wink and walked down toward the water. "Do you know what I'm supposed to be doing tonight?"

"What would that be?"

"I should be manning the slide projector for Margaret's after-dinner lecture on megalithic sites."

"Well, then, you've had a narrow escape, haven't you?"

"You're telling me. Do you know what I'm going to do instead?"

"Ah, come back inside and make wild love with me?"

She laughed and spun in a circle. "I'm definitely putting that on the schedule. But first, I'm going to build a sand castle."

"A sand castle, is it?"

"A grand one," she claimed and plopped down on the beach to begin. "The construction of sand castles is one of my many talents. Of course, I'd do better work if I had a spade and a bucket. Both of which," she added, looking up at him from under her lashes, "can be found in the laundry room."

"And I suppose, as my talent for this particular art is in doubt, I'm delegated to fetch."

"Your legs are longer, so you'll get there and back faster."

"Can't argue with that."

He brought back the garden spade and the mop bucket, along with the bottle of wine.

As the first bold stars came to life, he sat and watched her build her castle of sand.

"You need a tower on that end," he told her. "You've left it undefended."

"It's a castle, not a fortress, and my little world here is at peace. However, I'd think a famous artist could manage to build a tower if he saw the need for one."

He finished off his glass of wine, screwed the stem in the sand, and picked up the challenge.

She added more turrets, carefully shaping, then smoothing them with the edge of her spade. And driven by his obviously superior talent with his hands, began to add to the structure, elaborately.

"And what, I'd like to know, is that lump you've got there?"

"It's the stables, or will be when I'm finished."

"It's out of proportion." He started to reach over to show her, but she slapped his hand away. "As you like, but your horses would have to be the size of Hugh to fit in there."

She sniffed, rocked back on her heels. Damn it, he was right. "I'm not finished," she said coolly. She scooped up more sand and worked it in. "And what is that supposed to be?"

"It will be the drawbridge."

"A drawbridge?" Delighted, she leaned over to study the platform he fashioned with his quick, clever hands. "Oh, that's wonderful. You're definitely sand castle–skilled. I know just what it needs."

She scrambled up and raced to the house. She came back with some wooden kitchen matches and a bit of red ribbon that she'd cut in a triangle.

"Chain would be better, but we'll be innovative." She poked the tip of the long match into the side of the drawbridge, slid the other end into the castle wall. "Fortunately, the royal family here is having a ball, so the drawbridge stays down." She set a second match in the other side.

She broke a third match, looped her ribbon around it,

then hoisted her makeshift flag on the topmost tower. "Now that's a sand castle."

She plucked up the bottle of wine and poured for both of them. "To Dolman Castle." A dream, she thought, they'd made together.

After clinking her glass to his, she drew up her knees and looked out to sea. "It's a beautiful night. So many stars. You can't see sky like this in New York, just slices of it, pieces between buildings, so you forget how big it is."

"When I was a boy, I used to come out at night and sit here."

She turned her head, rested her cheek on her knee. "What else did you do when you were a boy?"

"Climbed the cliffs, played with my friends in the village, worked very hard to get out of chores that would have taken less time and less effort than the eluding of them took. Fished with my father."

He fell into silence, and the depth of it had Allena reaching out to take his hand. "You miss him."

"I left him, alone. I didn't know he was ill that last year. He never told me, never once asked me to come back and tend to him. He died by himself rather than ask me for that."

"He knew you'd come back."

"He should have told me. I could've brought him to Dublin, gotten him to hospital, for treatments, specialists."

"It's always so much harder on the ones who're left behind," she murmured. "He wanted to be here, Conal. To die here."

"Oh, aye, to die here, that was his choice. And knowing he was ill, and frail, he climbed the cliffs. And there at the stone dance is where his heart gave out. That was his choice."

"It makes you angry."

"It makes me helpless, which is the same thing to me. So I miss him, and I regret the time and distance that was between us—the time and distance I put between us. I sent him money instead of myself. And he left me all he had. The cottage, and Hugh.''

He turned to her then and pulled the chain at her neck until the pendant slid clear. ''And this. He left this for me in that small wood box you see on the dresser in the bedroom.''

The shiver raced over her skin, chill and damp. ''I don't understand.''

''His mother had given it to him on his eighteenth birthday, as it had been given to her. And he gave it to my mother on the day he asked her to marry him, at the stone circle, as is the O'Neil tradition. She wore it always. And gave it back to him, to hold for me, on the night she died.''

Cured in Dagda's Cauldron. Carved by the finger of Merlin. ''It's yours,'' she murmured.

''No. No longer mine, never mine as I refused it. The day I buried my father, I came here and I threw this into the sea. That, I told myself, was the end of things.''

There's only one, the old woman had told her. It belonged to her. She had found it, or it had found her. And led her, Allena thought, to him. How could she feel anything but joy at knowing it? And how, being who he was, could Conal feel anything but anger?

For her it was a key. For him a lock.

Allena touched his cheek. ''I don't know how to comfort you.''

''Neither do I.'' He rose, pulled her to her feet. ''No more of this tonight. No more castles and stars. I want what's real. My need is real enough.'' He swept her up. ''And so are you.''

9

SHE COULDN'T SLEEP. No matter how short the night, she couldn't bear to waste it in dreams. So she lay quiet, and wakeful, reliving every moment of the day that had passed.

They'd ended it, she thought now, with love. Not the slow and tender sort they'd brought each other the first time. There'd been a desperation in Conal when he carried her into bed from the beach. A kind of fierce urgency that had streaked from him and into her so that her hands had been as impatient as his, her mouth as hungry.

And her body, she thought, oh, her body had been so very alive.

That kind of craving was another sort of beauty, wasn't it? A need that deep, that strong, that *willful* could dig deep and lasting roots.

Why wouldn't he let himself love her?

She turned to him, and in sleep he drew her against him. *I'm here*, she wanted to say. *I belong here. I know it.*

But she kept the words inside her, and simply took his

mouth with hers. Soft, seductive, drawing what she needed and giving back. Slow and silky, a mating of lips and tongues. The heat from bodies wrapped close weighing heavy on the limbs.

He drifted into desire as a man drifts through mists. The air was thick, and sweet, and she was there for him. Warm and willing. And real.

He heard her breath catch and sigh out, felt her heart beat to match the rhythm of his own. And she moved against him, under him, bewitching in the dark.

When he slid into her, she took him in with a welcome that was home. Together they lifted and fell, steady and smooth. Mouths met again as he felt her rise up to peak, as he lost himself, gave himself. And emptied.

"Allena." He said her name, only her name as he once more gathered her against him. Comforted, settled, he slipped back into sleep never knowing that she wept.

Before dawn she rose, afraid that if she stayed beside him any longer in the dark she would ask—more afraid that if he offered some pale substitute for love and lifetimes, she would snatch at it, pitifully.

She dressed in silence and went out to wait for the dawn of the longest day.

There was no moon now, and no stars, nothing to break that endless, spreading dark. She could see the fall of land, the rise of sea, and to the west the powerful shadows of the jagged cliffs where the stone circle stood, and waited.

The pendant weighed heavy on her neck.

Only hours left, she thought. She wouldn't lose hope, though it was hard in this dark and lonely hour to cling to it. She'd been sent here, brought here, it didn't matter. What mattered was that she was here, and here she had found all the answers she needed.

She had to believe that Conal would find his in the day that was left to them.

She watched dawn break, a slow, almost sly shifting of light that gave the sky a polish. Mists slipped and slid over the ground, rose into the air like a damp curtain. And there, in the east, it flamed, gold, then spread to red over sky and water, brighter, and brighter still, until the world woke.

The air went from gray to the shimmer of a pearl.

On the beach, the castle had been swamped by the tide. And seeing what could be so easily washed away broke her heart a little.

She turned away from it and went back inside.

She needed to keep her hands busy, her mind busy. She could do nothing about the state of her heart, but she wouldn't mope, today of all days.

When Hugh came padding out, she opened the door so he could race through. She put on the kettle for tea. She already knew how Conal liked his, almost viciously strong with no sugar or cream to dilute the punch.

While it steeped, she got a small pot from a cupboard. Conal had mentioned there were berries ripening this time of year. If she could find them, and there were enough, they'd have fresh fruit for breakfast.

She went out the back, past the herb garden and a huge shrub covered with dozens of conical purple blossoms that smelled like potpourri. She wondered how they would look dried and spearing out of a big copper urn.

Ground fog played around her ankles as she walked and made her think it was something like wading in a shallow river. The wind didn't reach it, but fluttered at her hair as she climbed the gentle rise behind the cottage. Far off was the sound of Hugh's deep-throated bark, and somewhere nearer, the liquid trill of a bird. Over it all was the forever sound of the sea.

On impulse, she slipped off her shoes to walk barefoot over the cool, wet grass.

The hill dipped, then rose again. Steeper now, with the mist thickening like layers of filmy curtain. She glanced back once, saw the cottage was merely a silhouette behind the fog. A prickle over her skin had her pausing, nearly turning back. Then she heard the dog bark again, just up ahead.

She called out to him, turned in the direction of his bark, and kept climbing. On the top of the next rise was a scattering of trees sculpted by wind, and with them the bushes, brambles, and berries she hunted.

Pleased with her find, she set down her shoes and began to pick. And taste. And climb still higher to where the ripest grew. She would make pancakes, she thought, and mix the berries in the batter.

Her pot was half full when she scrambled up on a rock to reach a solitary bush pregnant with fat fruit of rich and deep purple.

"The most tempting are always the ones just out of reach."

Allena's breath caught, and she nearly overturned her pot when she saw the woman standing on the rough track on the other side of the bush.

Her hair was dark and hung past her waist. Her eyes were the moody green of the ocean at dawn. She smiled and rested her hand on Hugh's head as he sat patiently beside her.

"I didn't know anyone was here." Could be here, she thought. "I—" She looked back now, with some alarm, and couldn't see the cottage. "I walked farther than I realized."

"It's a good morning for a walk, and for berry picking. Those you have there'd make a fine mixed jam."

"I've picked too many. I wasn't paying attention."

The woman's face softened. "Sure, you can never pick too many as long as someone eats them. Don't fret," she said quietly. "He's sleeping still. His mind's quiet when he sleeps."

Allena let out a long breath. "Who are you?"

"Whoever you need me to be. An old woman in a shop, a young boy in a boat."

"Oh." Surrendering to shaky legs, she sat on the rock. "God."

"It shouldn't worry you. There's no harm meant. Not to you, or to him. He's part of me."

"His great-grandmother. He said—they say—"

The woman's smile widened. "They do indeed."

Struggling for composure, Allena reached under her

sweater, drew out the pendant. "This is yours."

"It belongs to whom it belongs to . . . until it belongs to another."

"Conal said he threw it into the sea."

"Such a temper that boy has." Her laugh was light and rich as cream over whiskey. "It does me proud. He could throw it to the moon, and still it would come to whom it belongs to when it was time. This time is yours."

"He doesn't want to love me."

"Oh, child." She touched Allena's cheek, and it was like the brush of wings. "Love can't be wanted away. It simply is, and you already know that. You have a patient heart."

"Sometimes patience is just cowardice."

"That's wise." The woman nodded, obviously pleased, and helped herself to one of the berries in the pot. "And true as well. But already you understand him, and are coming to understand yourself, which is always a more difficult matter. That's considerable for such a short time. And you love him."

"Yes, I love him. But he won't accept love through magic."

"Tonight, when the longest day meets the shortest night, when the star cuts through with power and light, the choice you make, both you and he, will be what was always meant to be."

Then she took Allena's face in her hands, kissed both her cheeks. "Your heart will know," she said and slipped into the mist like a ghost.

"How?" Allena closed her eyes. "You didn't give us enough time."

When Hugh bumped his head against her legs, she bent down to bury her face in his neck. "Not enough time," she murmured. "Not enough to mope about it, either. I don't know what to do, except the next thing. I guess that's breakfast."

She wandered back the way she had come, with Hugh for company on this trip. The fog was already burning off at the edges and drawing into itself. It seemed that fate had decreed one more clear day for her.

When the cottage came into view, she saw Conal on the little back porch, waiting for her.

"You worried me." He walked out to meet her, knowing his sense of relief was out of proportion. "What are you doing, roaming away in the mist?"

"Berries." She held up the pot. "You'll never guess what I . . ." She trailed off as his gaze tracked down to the pendant.

"I'll never guess what?"

No, she thought, she couldn't tell him what had happened, whom she had seen. Not when the shadows were in his eyes, and her heart was sinking because of them. "What I'm going to make for breakfast."

He dipped a hand into the pot. "Berries?"

"Watch," she told him and took her gatherings into the house. "And learn."

He did watch, and it soothed him. He'd wakened reaching for her, and that had disturbed him. How could a man spend one night with a woman, then find his bed so cold, so empty when she wasn't in it? Then that panic, that drawing down in the gut, when he hadn't been able to find her. Now she was here, mixing her batter in a bowl, and the world was right again.

Was there a name for this other than love?

"You really need a griddle." She set the bowl aside to heat a skillet. "But we'll make do."

"Allena."

"Hmm?" She glanced back. Something in his eyes made her dizzy. "Yes?" When she turned, the pendant swung, and caught at the sunlight.

The star seemed to flash straight into his eyes, taunting him. Without moving, Conal took a deliberate step back. No, he would not speak of love.

"Where are your shoes?"

"My shoes?" He'd spoken with such gentle affection that her eyes stung as she looked down at her own bare feet. "I must have left them behind. Silly of me."

"So you wander barefoot through the dew, pretty Allena?"

Words strangled in her throat. She threw her arms around him, burying her face at his shoulder as emotions whirled inside her.

"Allena." He pressed his lips to her hair and wished, for both of them, he could break this last chain that held his heart. "What am I to do about you?"

Love me. Just love me. I can handle all of the rest. "I can make you happy. If only you'd let me, I can make you happy."

"And what of you? There are two of us here. How can you believe, and accept, all I've told you and be willing to change your life for it?" He drew her back, touched a fingertip to the pendant. "How can you, Allena, so easily accept this?"

"Because it belongs to me." She let out a shaky breath, then took one in, and her voice was stronger. "Until it belongs to another."

Steadier, she took a ladle from a drawer and spooned batter into the skillet. "You think I'm naive, and gullible, and so needy for love that I'll believe anything that offers the possibility of it?"

"I think you have a soft heart."

"And a malleable one?" The cool gaze she sent him was a surprise, as was her nod. "You may be right. Trying to fit yourself into forms so that the people you love will love you back the way you want keeps the heart malleable. And while I hope to be done with that, while I'm going to try to be done with that, I prefer having a heart that accepts imprints from others."

A patient heart, she thought, but by God if it was a cowardly one.

Deftly, she flipped the pancakes. "What hardened yours, Conal?"

"You've good aim when you decide to notch the arrow."

"Maybe I haven't reached into the quiver often enough." But she would now. Movements smooth and unhurried, she turned the pancakes onto a platter, spooned more batter into the pan. "Why don't you ever speak of your mother?"

Bull's-eye, he thought, and said nothing as she set him a place at the table.

"I have a right to know."

"You do, yes."

She got out honey, cinnamon, poured the tea. "Sit down. Your breakfast will get cold."

With a half laugh, he did as she asked. She was a puzzle, and why had he believed he'd already solved her? He waited until she'd emptied the skillet, turned it off, and come to the table to join him.

"My mother was from the near village," he began. "Her father was a fisherman, and her mother died in childbirth when my own mother was a girl. The baby died as well, so my mother was the youngest and the only daughter and pampered, she told me, by her father and brothers."

"You have uncles in the village?"

"I do. Three, and their families. Though some of the younger have gone to the mainland or beyond. My father was an only child."

She drizzled honey on her pancakes, passed the bottle to Conal. He had family, she thought, and still kept so much alone. "So you have cousins here, too?"

"Some number of them. We played together when I was a boy. It was from them that I first heard of what runs in me. I thought it a story, like others you hear, like silkies and mermaids and faerie forts."

He ate because it was there and she'd gone to the trouble to make it. "My mother liked to draw, to sketch, and she taught me how to see things. How to make what you see come out in pencil and chalk. My father, he loved the sea, and thought I would follow him there. But she gave me clay for my eighth birthday. And I . . ."

He paused, lifted his hands, stared at them through narrowed eyes. They were very like his father's. Big, blunt, and with strength in them. But they had never been made for casting nets.

"The shaping of it, the finding what was inside it . . . I

was compelled to see. And wood, carving away at it until you could show others what you'd seen in it. She understood that. She knew that.''

''Your father was disappointed?''

''Puzzled more, I think.'' Conal moved his shoulders, picked up his fork again. ''How could a man make a living, after all, whittling at wood or chipping at hunks of rock? But it pleased my mother, so he let it be. For her, and I learned later, because in his mind my fate was already set. So whether I sculpted or fished wouldn't matter in the end.''

When he fell silent, looked back at the pendant, Allena slipped it under her sweater. And feeling the quiet heat of it against her heart, waited for him to continue.

10

"AFTER ME, MY parents tried for more children. Twice my mother miscarried, and the second, late in her term . . . damaged her. I was young, but I remember her having to stay in bed a long time and how pale she was even when she could get up. My father set a chair out for her, so she could be outside and watch the sea. She was never well after that, but I didn't know."

"You were just a boy." When she touched a hand to his, he looked down, smiled a little.

"Soft heart, Allena." He turned his hand over, squeezed hers once, then released. "She was ill the summer I was twelve. Three times that spring, my father took her on the ferry, and I stayed with my cousins. She was dying, and no one could find a way to save her. Part of me knew that, but I pushed it out of my mind. Every time she came home again, I was certain it was all right."

"Poor little boy," Allena murmured.

"He doesn't deserve as much sympathy as you think. That summer, when I was twelve, she walked down to the sea with me. She should've been in bed, but she wouldn't go. She told me of the stone dance and the star and my place in it. She showed me the pendant you're wearing now, though I'd seen it countless times before. She closed my hand around it with her own, and I felt it breathe.

"I was so angry. I wasn't different from the other lads I knew, no different from my cousins and playmates. Why would she say so? She told me I was young to have it passed on to me, but she and my father had discussed it. He'd agreed to let her do it, in her time and her own way. She wanted to give me the pendant before she left us."

"You didn't want it."

"No, by God, I didn't. I wanted her. I wanted things to be as they were. When she was well and I was nothing more than a lad running over the hills. I wanted her singing in the kitchen again, the way she did before she was ill."

Everything inside her ached for him, but when she reached out, Conal waved her off. "I shouted at her, and I ran from her. She called after me, and tried to come after me, but I was strong and healthy and she wasn't. Even when I heard her weeping, I didn't look back. I went and hid in my uncle's boat shed. It wasn't till the next morning that my father found me.

"He didn't take a strap to me as I might have expected, or drag me home by the ear as I deserved. He just sat down beside me, pulled me against him, and told me my mother had died in the night."

His eyes were vivid as they met Allena's. She wondered that the force of them didn't burn away the tears that swam in her own. "I loved her. And my last words to her were the bitter jabs of an angry child."

"Do you think—oh, Conal, can you possibly believe those words are what she took with her?"

"I left her alone."

"And you still blame a frightened and confused twelve-year-old boy for that? Shame on you for your lack of compassion."

Her words jolted him. He rose as she did. "Years later, when I was a man, I did the same with my father."

"That's self-indulgent and untrue." Briskly, she stacked plates, carried them to the sink. It wasn't sympathy he needed, she realized. But plain, hard truth. "You told me yourself you didn't know he was ill. He didn't tell you."

She ran the water hot, poured detergent into it, stared hard at the rising foam. "You curse the idea you have— what did you call it—elfin blood—but you sure as hell appear to enjoy the notion of playing God."

If she'd thrown the skillet at his head he'd have been less shocked. "That's easy for you to say, when you can walk away from all of this tomorrow."

"That's right, I can." She turned the faucet off and turned to him. "I can, finally, do whatever I want to do. I can thank you for that, for helping me see what I was letting happen, for showing me that I have something of value to give. And I want to give it, Conal. I want to make a home and a family and a life for someone who values me, who understands me and who loves me. I won't take less ever again. But you will. You're still hiding in the boat shed, only now you call it a studio."

Vile and hateful words rose up in his throat. But he was no longer a young boy, and he rejected them for the sharper blade of ice. "I've told you what you asked to know. I understand what you want, but you have no understanding of what I need."

He walked out, letting the door slap shut behind him.

"You're wrong," she said quietly. "I do understand."

She kept herself busy through the morning. If she did indeed go away the next day, she would leave something of herself behind. He wouldn't be allowed to forget her.

She hung the curtains she'd mended, pleased when the sunlight filtered through the lace into patterns on the floor. In the laundry room she found tools and brushes and everything she needed. With a kind of defiance she hauled it all outside. She was going to scrape and paint the damn shutters.

The work calmed her, and that malleable heart she'd spoken of began to ache. Now and then she glanced over at the studio. He was in there, she knew. Where else would he be? Though part of her wanted to give up, to go to him, she did understand his needs.

He needed time.

"But it's running out," she murmured. Stepping back, she studied the results of her labors. The paint gleamed wet and blue, and behind the windows the lace fluttered in the breeze.

Now that it was done and there was nothing else, her body seemed to cave in on itself with fatigue. Nearly stumbling with it, she went into the house. She would lie down for a little while, catch up on the sleep she'd lost the night before.

Just an hour, she told herself and, stretching out on the bed, went under fast and deep.

Conal stepped back from his own work. His hands were smeared with clay to the wrists, and his eyes half blind with concentration.

Allena of the Faeries. She stood tall, slim, her head cocked slyly over one shoulder, her eyes long and her mouth bowed with secrets. She wasn't beautiful, nor was she meant to be. But how could anyone look away?

How could he?

Her wings were spread as if she would fly off at any moment. Or fold them again and stay, if you asked her.

He wouldn't ask her. Not when she was bound by something that was beyond both of them.

God, she'd infuriated him. He went to the sink, began to scrub his hands and arms. Snipping and sniping at him that way, telling him what he thought and felt. He had a mind of his own and he'd made it up. He'd done nothing but tell her the truth of that, of everything, from the beginning.

He wanted peace and quiet and his work. And his pride, he thought, as his hands dripped water. The pride that refused to accept that his path was already cut. In the end, would he be left with only that?

The emptiness stretched out before him, staggeringly

deep. Were these, then, after all, his choices? All or nothing? Acceptance or loneliness?

Hands unsteady, he picked up a towel, drying off as he turned and studied the clay figure. "You already know, don't you? You knew from the first."

He tossed the towel aside, strode to the door. The light shifted, dimmed even as he yanked it open. Storm clouds crept in, already shadowing the sea.

He turned for the cottage, and what he saw stopped him in his tracks. She'd painted the shutters, was all he could think. The curtains she'd hung danced gaily in the rising wind. She'd hung a basket beside the door and filled it with flowers.

How was a man to resist such a woman?

How could it be a trap when she'd left everything, even herself, unlocked and unguarded?

All or nothing? Why should he live with nothing?

He strode toward the cottage and three steps from the door found the way barred to him. "No." Denial, and a lick of fear, roughened his voice as he shoved uselessly at the air. "Damn you! You'd keep me from her now?"

He called out to her, but her name was whisked away by the rising wind, and the first drops of rain pelted down.

"All right, then. So be it." Panting, he stepped back. "We'll see what comes at the end of the day."

So he went through the storm to the place that called to his blood.

She woke with a start, the sound of her own name in her ears. And woke in the dark.

"Conal?" Disoriented, she climbed out of bed, reached for the lamp. But no light beamed when she turned the switch. A storm, she thought blearily. It was storming. She needed to close the windows.

She fumbled for the candle, then her hand jerked and knocked it off the little table.

Dark? How could it be dark?

Time. What time was it? Frantically she searched for the candle, found a match. Before she could light it, lightning flashed and she saw the dial of the little wind-up clock.

Eleven o'clock.

No! It was impossible. She'd slept away all but the last hour of the longest day.

"Conal?" She rushed out of the room, out of the house, into the wind. Rain drenched her as she ran to his studio, fought to open the door.

Gone. He was gone. Struggling against despair, she felt along the wall for the shelves, and on the shelves for the flashlight she'd seen there.

The thin beam made her sigh with relief, then her breath caught again at what stood in the line of that light.

Her own face, her own body, made fanciful with wings. Did he see her that way? Clever and confident and lovely?

"I feel that way. For the first time in my life, I feel that way."

Slowly, she shut the light off, set it aside. She knew where he'd gone, and understood, somehow, that she was meant to find her own way there, as he had, in the dark.

The world went wild as she walked, as wild as the day she had come to this place. The ground shook, and the sky split, and the sea roared like a dragon.

Instead of fear, all she felt was the thrill of being part of it. This day wouldn't pass into night without her. Closing her hand over the star between her breasts, she followed the route that was clear as a map in her head.

Steep and rough was the path that cut through rock, and slippery with wet. But she never hesitated, never faltered. The stones loomed above, giants dancing in the tempest. In its heart, the midsummer fire burned, bright and gold, despite the driving rain.

And facing it, the shadow that was a man.

Her heart, as she'd been told, knew.

"Conal."

He turned to her. His eyes were fierce as if whatever wild was in the night pranced in him as well. "Allena."

"No, I've something to say." She walked forward, unhurried though the air trembled. "There's always a choice, Conal, always another direction. Do you think I'd want you without your heart? Do you think I'd hold you with this?"

In a violent move she pulled the pendant from around her neck and threw it.

"No!" He grabbed for it, but the star only brushed his fingertips before it landed inside the circle. "Can you cast it off so easily? And me with it?"

"If I have to. I can go, make a life without you, and part of me will always grieve. Or I can stay, make a home with you, bear your children, and love you for everything you are. Those are my choices. You have yours."

She held out her arms. "There's nothing but me here to hold you. There never was."

Emotions tumbled through him, end over end. "Twice I've let the people I loved go without telling them. Even when I came here tonight I thought I might do so again."

He pushed dripping hair away from his face. "I'm a moody man, Allena."

"So you told me once before. I never would have known it otherwise."

His breath came out in a half laugh. "You'd slap at me at such a time?" He took a step toward her. "You painted the shutters."

"So what?"

"I'll make you pots in dark blue, to fill with your flowers."

"Why?"

"Because I love you."

She opened her mouth, closed it again, took a careful breath. "Because I painted the shutters?"

"Yes. Because you would think to. Because you mended my mother's curtains. Because you pick berries. Because you swim naked in the sea. Because you look at me and see who I am. Whatever brought you here, brought us here, doesn't matter. What I feel for you is all there is. Please, God, don't leave me."

"Conal." The storm, inside her and around her, quieted. "You only have to ask."

"They say there's magic here, but it's you who brought it. Would you take me, Allena?" He reached for her hand, clasped it. "And give yourself to me. Make that home and that life and those children with me. I pledge to you I'll love you, and I'll treasure you, ever hour of every day." He lifted her hand, pressed his lips to it. "I'd lost something, and you brought it back to me. You've brought me my heart."

So, she thought, he'd found the key after all. "I'll take you, Conal, and give myself to you." Her eyes were dry and clear and steady. "And everything we make, we'll make together. I promise to love you now and ever after."

As she wrapped her arms around him, the mists cleared. In the dark sea of the sky a star began to pulse. The fire shimmered down to a pool of gold flame, tipped red as ruby. The air went sharp and cool so the stones stood out like a carving in glass.

And they sang in whispers.

"Do you hear it?" Allena murmured.

"Yes. There." He turned her, held her close to his side as the shimmering beam from the midsummer star shot through the stones and like an arrow pinned its light to its mate on the ground.

The pendant burst blue, a clean fire, star-shaped and brilliant. While star joined star, the circle was the world, full of light and sound and power.

Then the longest day passed, slipping into the shortest night. The light rippled, softened, faded. The stones sighed to silence.

Conal drew her farther into the circle. The fire rose up again, and shot sparks into her eyes, stroked warmth over his skin. He bent to pick up the pendant, and slipping the chain around her neck, sealed the promise.

"This belongs to you, and so do I."

"It belongs to me." She pressed their joined hands against it. "Until it belongs to another. I'll always be yours."

She kissed him there, inside the echo of magic, then stepped back. "Come home," she said.

● ● ●

Some say that the faeries came out of their raft to celebrate and danced round the midsummer fire while the star showered the last of its light. But those who had magic in their hearts and had pledged it left the circle, walked from the cliffs and along the quiet beach to the cottage with dark blue shutters that waited by the sea.

CATCH A FALLING STAR

★

Jill Gregory

1

"Come to the window, my lady, I beg you. Perhaps you will see a falling star and can make a wish, and all of this will vanish like a bad dream."

Else, the youngest of Princess Lianna's ladies-in-waiting, spoke through tears. She turned from the castle window and gazed imploringly at the slender, sable-haired princess, who sat with legs curled beneath her on the gilded bed before the fire. The princess's chamber was filled with women, all weeping, with reddened cheeks and eyes and faces damp with tears. Only Lianna herself, lovely and regal in her sapphire silk gown trimmed in gold thread, remained dry-eyed and composed, her heart-shaped face as calm as a new day.

"A falling star? A wish?" Despite the churning of her stomach, Lianna gave her head a shake, sending her dark locks flying about her pale face. She even smiled grimly at Else as she sprang catlike off the bed, her gown billowing about her. "If I only had the chance, I would wish Ambrose the Barbarian a bloody death and an eternity in hellfire!''

She paced to the window, peering out at the silent black sky aglitter with a thousand stars. Not one fell from its destined place. There would be no help there. "Wishes and stars and magic will not avail me now,'' she said softly, half to herself. "Nothing will.''

A half-remembered spell of her grandmother's floated through her mind, tinkling like a fairy song. *Comes the night of a falling star . . .*

The rest danced away into the recesses of her memory, a chant from long-ago days of childhood. But she was no longer a child, Lianna reminded herself, her fingers tightening upon her skirt. She was a woman, full-grown, pledged to wed.

Old spells and rhymes could not save her from that.

She turned from the window, her shoulders straight and determined. "Falling star or no, I am going to marry the Barbarian come morn, and that is that.''

Her old nurse, Meeg, sunk in a chair in the corner, let out a wail, the sound echoing through the firelit chamber where velvet bed hangings and rich tapestries and fragrant rushes softened the chill coming off the old stone walls of the castle. Lianna's mouth trembled as she turned to gaze at the old woman. Meeg had been lady-in-waiting to her grandmother, a great lady renowned for her goodness and her magic, whom Lianna only dimly remembered, with fondness and awe. But Meeg had told her stories about her grandmother and helped her to see that she, Lianna, had inherited the knack for magic that blessed the women of her family, skipping every other generation, then returning afresh. It was Meeg who had raised her like a mother since she was twelve years old when her own mother had died giving birth to a stillborn son. Meeg, who had crooned to her when she had nightmares, encouraged her interest in the healing arts and simple spells, taught her to listen to the whispers of her own heart and follow the sigh of the wind. Now, weak as a baby bird and nearly blind, the old woman refused all of the fine gifts Lianna sought to give her, would not even wear the ermine robe Lianna had ordered made for her—save on state occasions—and still made up her own bed, swept her floor, spent hours at embroidery all done by touch and instinct—refusing to rest and lie about as Lianna kept insisting she had earned the right to do.

"Oh, Meeg," the girl said softly, kneeling beside the woman and wrapping her arms around her. "Do not weep for me—I am not afraid of Ambrose." She repressed a shudder, thinking of the bridegroom she had not yet met, the fearsome warlord known as the Barbarian. "He cannot be as bad as they say." She bit her lip, praying her words would prove true. "And even if he is, I still must do what I can for Penmarren, and for my father. Another battle, waged either against Ambrose or Loth, will kill him. This way, there will be peace with Ambrose, and he will protect Penmarren from Prince Loth. It is the only way to save my father—and our kingdom."

"We must delay, child. There is always the chance that Prince Constantine might return."

Lianna shook her head. Her cousin Constantine, Prince of Wyborn, had been trying to raise an army in the east, an army that could match the strength of Loth or Ambrose, and to bring that army to Penmarren's aid. But all the spring and summer and autumn had passed, and he had not returned, nor sent word. "We do not know what has become of him. Now we cannot wait any longer. If I do not wed Ambrose on the morrow, he will tear Penmarren apart like a wild dog. Or leave us to Loth, which will be just as bad." Her lips tightened. "This is the only way."

"But you . . . you, my beautiful little one, will be shackled to a barbarian." Her voice cracking, Meeg tore her fingers from her wet dumpling of a face and stared into the princess's wide-set violet eyes, her own eyes filled with pain. "A man whose castle is cursed, who they say eats the hearts of his enemies for breakfast—who takes no prisoners on the battlefield, a man who they say . . . who they say . . ."

She straggled off, choking on the rest.

"A man who they say killed his first wife," Lianna completed for her quietly. She saw Else press her white lips together and Kira and Gwenlyn wring their hands. Her own blood pounded in her ears as she spoke the words, yet she struggled to keep her face composed and her voice steady. "Rumors."

She was pleased that she managed to sound brisk and unconcerned. "He cannot be as brutal as they say. If everything that is said about him were true, he would be the devil himself. No, I am not afraid. Let Ambrose be afraid of *me*," she added with a toss of her head. "Didn't I tame and ride the wildest steed in our kingdom? Didn't I once spear a boar that had felled three men? Haven't I broken hearts of knights and princes from lands as far away as Galeron? Let Ambrose the Barbarian fear *me!*"

The women exchanged hopeful glances despite their misgivings, taking heart from her bravery. Though they knew what she said was true, they couldn't help but fear for her. She was slender, delicate, yet as fiery as a candle's flame. Lianna had grown up wild and free, racing through the trees and meadows of the gentle land like a fairy child, eluding those set to guard her, making friends with every creature she encountered, playing at sword fighting with sticks and branches, stealing destriers from the stables to test their speed, returning home to the castle at nightfall with muddy gown and dirt-streaked face, leaves in her hair and scrapes upon knees, toes, and bare feet.

Her mother, Queen Felice, had disapproved of her antics and made no attempt to hide her displeasure, but the king delighted in her bravery and curiosity and warm, impulsive nature, and she was allowed to roam at will—until she began to grow into womanhood.

When her mother died shortly after Lianna's twelfth summer, the king had become more protective, and Lianna, sensing his heavy heart and heightened concern, had allowed herself to wander less and less. She had applied herself to mastering her royal duties and threw herself into becoming her father's friend and confidante as well as his daughter, hoping to lessen his loneliness.

She had grown into a beautiful, independent young

woman, beloved by her people, respected by even her father's most somber advisers.

But a man like Ambrose the Barbarian—he would see nothing but a trophy to be displayed in his castle, a vessel to bear his heir, a princess of indisputably royal blood who would buy a bastard duke respectability and greater power. The woman who had served Lianna all her life shuddered to think what would become of her when she was locked away in Crow's Keep, in the cold and distant kingdom of Blackenstar, as Ambrose's wife—and his prisoner.

A knock at the door made every woman turn in dread.

''Your Highness, your father the king requests your presence in his chambers.'' Her father's servant, Ulf, bowed low, his seamed old face as grim as those of all the others in the castle.

Lianna was only too glad to escape. It was a strain to keep up her spirits in front of those who cared for her. How she wished she could be alone—alone to try to master her fear and her own crawling dread. She had been raised every inch a princess and knew her duty. She was not the first royal daughter to be given over to an enemy as a trophy of war—or in this case, as a prize that would bring peace. If it would save her father and her people, she would gladly suffer the fate of being Ambrose's bride. What choice did she have?

Yet she was only human and she couldn't help but be afraid. The stories told about Ambrose were fearsome. He was a warrior, first and foremost, a man born a bastard youngest son of a fierce nobleman, a man who had wrested his kingdom from a series of half brothers and brutish warlords who had quarreled over pieces of it, all of them slabbering to have it all. His reputation on the battlefield was legendary, his ruthlessness the stuff of stories told to frighten children into obedient behavior, his cruelty, lust for women, and crude disregard of civilized behavior were all part and parcel of his dark legend.

And, a small scared voice inside reminded her, *he killed his first wife when she'd been unable to give him a child.*

A shudder rippled through her as she made her way

through the long, torchlit hall, across the solar, to the king's chambers. Ambrose might be a crude barbarian, but she was a princess. She would not cower before him, nor weep, nor seek to escape her fate. She would do her duty with her head held high, and she would not let anyone—least of all the beast she was to marry—see her quail or quiver.

"Lianna, child. My dear child." Her father stroked her head as she bent over his bed and kissed his cheek. The sight of him so weak and frail flooded her with pain. As a little girl she had known her father to be tall and strong, with his shock of white hair and ruddy face, his merry smile. But a battle wound had left him lame in one leg, with a creeping sickness that kept him confined to his bed. In the last skirmish, when Penmarren had been forced to drive Loth's men from their southern border, he had been carried onto the field in a litter.

Only his captain-of-arms, the brave soldier Rufus, had saved him from a death blow.

"Don't fear for me, Father." Lianna spoke soothingly. "As I told my ladies, I am not afraid. Well, not very afraid," she added with a trembling smile. "It will be all right."

"I hope and pray that is so, child." The king waved his hand, dismissing the servants hovering nearby in the gilded chamber. "Leave us," he commanded.

When they were alone and Lianna had seated herself comfortably upon the edge of his bed, he struggled to a sitting position and huffed as she propped tasseled pillows behind him.

"Listen to me, Lianna. Don't fuss with me, child. I have news—hopeful news."

For the first time she noted that his cheeks were flushed and his eyes bright. Her heart jolted in her chest. "Constantine?" she whispered, scarcely daring to hope.

He nodded and grasped her hand. "He is coming. By all that is holy, he is coming. Not in time to stop the wedding, I fear, but if all goes well, my dear, you will be Ambrose's bride for no more than a fortnight—at most!" He spoke in a whisper, as if fearful that even the walls might have ears.

Lianna's heart began to thud. Constantine and his army were coming to save her from a lifetime wed to Ambrose. She had only to wait, to endure—to stay alive for the brief time she was married to the Barbarian, and then she could return home in honor to Penmarren.

"Such wonderful news, Father!" Her eyes glowed. "Tell me all of what he said," she urged eagerly.

"Your cousin has gathered an army—a mighty army, Lianna—one that is nearly twice the strength of Loth's and very near in size and ferocity to that of Ambrose! He has been beyond the Crystal Sea and has found fighting men as fearsome as any Ambrose might boast, and they have sworn allegiance to him. They have to cross the sea and make their way through Dunhelm, amass horses and weapons and supplies, but they are coming. No one is to know," the king added quickly. "If Ambrose were to suspect what is afoot, it would be disastrous for us all—and very dangerous for you, my child."

Lianna's eyes sparked violet fire, and she nodded. "We won't speak of it again, Father. But what am I to do? How can I help? Surely while I am in the Barbarian's keep there is some way that I can be of use to Constantine."

"No. That's too dangerous. It is bad enough that you must go off with that monster." His voice trembled, and fury and helplessness shone from his sunken blue eyes, still sharp despite his sickness. "If I were a younger man, and stronger, I would never allow him within a mile of these castle walls, much less to dare demand your hand in marriage. He's nothing but a bastard, a blackguard, a murd—" He broke off, his face purple, his breath coming heavily in his chest.

He'd been about to say "murderer," Lianna knew. Her hand shook a little as she touched his arm. "Hush, Father. Don't upset yourself. It does no good to think what could have been or should be. My marriage to this man will buy time to keep our kingdom safe."

"But Constantine will come for you, I swear it." His white brows drew together. "So be ready, girl. We'll get word to you somehow and you must be ready to flee, or to hide—whatever is called for when the hour draws near.''

''I will be ready.'' Lianna's mind was already leaping ahead to the day when the gates of the Barbarian's keep would be flung down, when Constantine and his army would crash through and storm the castle, when perhaps even the bastard Ambrose himself would be slain.

''If only we could delay the wedding.'' Her father's tone was heavy. ''But at the least, we can try to keep the Barbarian here for several more days, drunk and entertained with wedding feasts and festivities.''

He fell silent. Lianna knew they were both thinking the same thing. Such things would delay her being taken from Penmarren, carried off to the dark, distant, and forbidding Blackenstar, but it would not delay the wedding night itself. The moment when she would be alone with Ambrose in their marriage bed, when he would claim her in the most elemental way as his bride.

''I am not afraid,'' she whispered as steadily as she could. ''I know what must be done. And he won't dare harm me—not until I bear him a child, the heir he is rumored to want so badly. And long before then, Constantine will have rescued me and perhaps will even have run the Barbarian through like the wild pig that he is—''

She broke off as urgent knocking sounded at the door. Not the brisk polite rapping with which Ulf had summoned her to her father's side, but forceful and repeated *thwacks* that sounded as if they would smash the door to bits.

''Come in!'' the king bellowed, and Lianna looked up in astonishment as the door burst open and a broad, gold-haired soldier with a scar that slashed across the entire left side of his fleshy face strode into the king's lamplit chamber like a lion invading another's den. He was not one of her father's knights. He was clearly Ambrose's man. His river-green eyes, colder than the frost that clung to the winter trees outside the window, swept the room and fell upon Lianna, then shifted to the glaring king.

Two more soldiers followed him into the room, men equally as large, with expressions equally as grim.

''King Penmarren,'' the scar-faced soldier rasped in a

thick voice, "Duke Ambrose has received news. He must ride this very night to Blackenstar to protect his eastern border—we leave within the hour. Your daughter . . ." He riveted his sharp gaze upon Lianna, who had jumped up, her hands to her throat.

"Ah, this must be the dark beauty we've heard about." Lusty approval glistened in his eyes. "My lady, you will wed the duke at once and depart with us now. Come." He stepped toward her, stretching out an arm. "I will take you to Ambrose—"

Lianna jerked back out of reach and stared at him in wide-eyed astonishment. "I am not going anywhere with you."

"By all that's holy, how dare you try to lay your hands upon my daughter!" the king roared. He struggled upward in the bed, his voice rising in a harsh command. "Guards! Guards, restrain this man!"

Three soldiers of Penmarren rushed in. Two grabbed the gold-haired man, each by one arm, and the third planted himself between the intruder and the king and princess.

"Fools, do you think you can stop me? Stop any of us? Think hard, Penmarren. You don't want to fight Ambrose, do you? You've struck a bargain—now keep it!"

The soldier's voice was a barely disguised sneer. "Your pitiful troops are scattered, protecting your borders from Loth. What do you have here? Fifty men? One hundred at most? We have three hundred fighting men encamped in your fields and forests, all at alert, awaiting only the call to battle. We could take the castle and burn the village before the sun is near to rising. Ambrose's men are trained to fight in darkness, snow, and storm."

"What do you want?" the king croaked.

"We want what we came for, Your Highness. Your daughter as bride to Ambrose. Then we'll send one hundred of those men to fortify your borders against Loth. And we'll be gone."

"I agreed to the marriage, but it is to take place tomorrow. Not tonight. You can't expect me to turn my daughter over to Ambrose and let him ride off with her in the dead of night to a battle.''

''I've no time to waste with you!'' The gold-haired man shook off the king's guards and lunged forward, shoving aside the soldier who stood between him and the king. In a flash, he had a dagger in his hand, its glinting blade only inches from the king's chest.

''Ambrose gave me orders to fetch his betrothed. If you want them married before they ride for Blackenstar, you'd best rouse your cardinal from his bed and get him down to the courtyard quick-like, because as soon as Ambrose hits his saddle, we are off—*with* your daughter. With or without your permission—Your Highness!''

Trembling all over, Lianna stared at the dagger pointed at her father's chest. Leave Penmarren tonight? Be dragged off like a prisoner? Like a prize of war—without a proper wedding, or her ladies-in-waiting to accompany her, or even a chance to bid her father a solemn farewell, much less time to pack her belongings?

''This is outrageous!'' the king sputtered, but as another half dozen of Ambrose's soldiers charged in, unsheathing their swords to hold off the guards, Lianna realized that there was nothing any of them could do to stop the events that Ambrose the Barbarian had set in motion.

''Father, don't disturb yourself,'' she cried, knowing that resistance would only lead to full-scale bloodshed and battle. ''I . . . I will go. It is only a few hours sooner,'' she finished on a ragged breath and suddenly thrust herself forward, between her father and the man who held the dagger.

''Put your weapon away. Do you think I would let you hurt my father?'' she demanded. Her hand came up, and the soldier's eyes flickered down to the dagger she gripped, a gold-and-ruby-handled dagger with a blade that shone in the lantern light.

Ambrose's soldier grinned. ''They said you were feisty. Ambrose will have his hands full with you, my lady.'' His grin widening, he sheathed his own weapon.

''Come, then, Princess, I will take you to your husband.''

''He is not my husband yet,'' Lianna retorted. But at the

same moment she realized the uselessness of the situation. Ambrose had made up his mind, and he was obviously accustomed to having things his way. In this situation, neither she, nor her father, nor anyone else in Penmarren could stop him.

Until Constantine arrived.

Up to that point, all she could do was her duty—and avoid endangering her father and those in the castle any further.

"Tell the men to put down their swords, and I will go with you." Her tone was quiet but full of command.

The man gave a signal, and Ambrose's soldiers lowered their weapons. Penmarren's guards swarmed around the king's bedside.

"Father, I will see you in the courtyard," Lianna said softly. For a moment their eyes met and held. Lianna did her best to silently reassure him, though her own heart was pounding and her chest was so tight she could scarcely draw breath.

"I will . . . bring the cardinal," he whispered hoarsely and held out his thin, blue-veined hand.

She clutched it, her slender fingers clinging to his gnarled ones, and then as the gold-haired soldier growled impatiently, she turned with a rustle of her skirts and sailed out the door.

"This way, my lady." The man jerked a thick arm toward the great hall. He put a hand at her back and swept her along before him, his pace forcing her almost to run. "Hurry, now. There's a good girl. There's no time to waste."

"Then by all means," Lianna said breathlessly, her face every bit as grim and set as his as he propelled her along the narrow corridor, "let us find your cursed Barbarian. When I lay eyes on him, there is much I wish to say!"

2

"Just as you asked, Ambrose—I've brought her. I give you Princess Lianna."

With a laugh, the gold-haired soldier thrust her forward toward the man seated at a long trestle table in an anteroom off the great hall. The man had been scribbling swiftly upon a map, but at the soldier's words he halted his task, and lifted his head sharply.

Lianna was frozen to the spot. As she met his cold, hard gaze, both panic and surprise rose in her like drowning tides.

A great strapping giant gazed back at her, a giant with the broadest shoulders she'd ever seen and raven-black hair as startlingly dark as her own.

May the angels save me, she thought wildly. The man was pure warrior, more rugged than an oak. He couldn't be more than thirty, but he looked to be the toughest, strongest man she had ever seen—and the most handsome. His chest beneath its dark plum tunic was massive and thick with muscles, and beneath his cropped black hair, ice-gray eyes glinted like shards in the torchlight that threw dancing amber shafts across the table where he sat.

She caught her breath. She had not expected him to be handsome. But he was—brutally, swarthily handsome. There was something dangerous and alive and vibrant about him, something magnetic that came not so much from the harsh lines of his face, the keen, deep-set eyes, that aggressive nose and chin, but from the sheer power and raw forcefulness that seemed to emanate from him. It radiated from those gray eyes and that immense body like dark slashes of lightning.

She could find no trace of emotion, neither pity nor amiability—and certainly not even a flicker of gentleness—in the impassive way he studied her. Unlike other men she had met, who openly revealed their admiration of her charms, Ambrose the Barbarian showed nothing upon that handsome countenance but swift, ruthless appraisal.

Lianna's pulse raced. She wanted to stride forward and slap him as his gaze boldly swept up and down the curves of her body, as if he were seeing everything that was hidden beneath the elegant sapphire gown. He took in her slender waist, the swell of her breasts, and his expression remained unchanged—but his eyes darkened to the color of smoke.

His gaze missed nothing and at last came to rest upon her pale, defiant face and the sable hair that fell loose and tumbling past her shoulders.

"Satisfied?" Lianna asked between clenched teeth.

To her surprise, amusement flickered across his swarthy features as he stood, towering before her like an implacable mountain.

But he made no answer.

His silence unnerved her even more than the imposing sight of him.

She'd planned to be elaborately gowned and coiffed when she first met this man, protected by dazzling jewels and royal raiment and all her carefully cultivated dignity—wrapped in her power and position, using them as a shield against this bastard warrior who was so far beneath her. Never had she thought to meet him face-to-face like this—

breathless, her hair flying, her heart pounding as uncertainty and panic collided within her.

She struggled for composure, but it was difficult to feel composed when he was regarding her as if she were a chunk of ham brought forth on a platter for his inspection before he picked up his knife to dine.

"I demand to know the meaning of this, Duke Ambrose." She took a deep breath. "Why have I been literally dragged from my father's side, forced to meet you here, and informed that we are leaving Penmarren within the—"

"Bring the horses now, Beorn. I'll meet you in the court-yard shortly with my bride." Ambrose cut her off without preamble, shifting his intense glance to the soldier. "What of the cardinal?"

"They're fetching him."

Ambrose nodded. "Make haste, then," he said curtly, and the gold-haired soldier hurried out, leaving them alone in the antechamber.

Swiftly the barbarian duke strode around the table.

Lianna had to fight the urge to back away. In his rich purple tunic of heavy wool, fastened at the shoulder by a distinctive star-shaped brooch of gold, onyx, and rubies, with that powerful body and harsh, thoughtful face, he was formidable—he might have been a young dark prince, born to command. Not the ragged, coarse bastard she had envisioned but a leader of men, a warrior/ruler who looked every inch as royal as she—and a hundredfold more dangerous.

"Silence," Ambrose said softly. "Good. I don't like chatter in a woman."

"Do you really think I care what you like?" she asked haughtily as he paused less than a foot from her.

Surprise flickered momentarily in those intent gray eyes, and perhaps another shadow of amusement, but just as quickly vanished. Ambrose had no time or patience for spoiled princesses, however beautiful they might be. And this one was the most beautiful he'd ever beheld, with her gorgeous spill of velvety hair and those eyes like amethyst stars. But she was not a prize to be cherished and indulged, he thought harshly. She was a necessity—a weapon of sorts—and all that mattered was that they be wed and she be ensconced under guard in the keep as soon as possible. His holdings, all that he'd fought for his entire life, were being threatened by an old enemy, his clever cousin Sandar of Kenelm, who had planned a surprise attack meant to wrest Blackenstar away. He needed to reach his land's eastern border without delay to make sure that Sandar failed.

And that he paid.

Ambrose also needed to learn how Sandar had discovered he was to be away at this time fetching his royal bride, with a large portion of his army dispersed—and thus temporarily vulnerable.

It reeked of treachery. If there was indeed a traitor in his camp, he, too, must be found. And made to pay.

So he looked at the lovely black-haired girl glaring at him and spoke brusquely. "You are as beautiful as they say, I suppose, if one cares for such an elegant, icy type of female." He ignored her gasp and continued calmly. "And you are clearly royal. It shows in every inch of you. That is good, for it's the reason I chose you." A slight pause, and his eyes narrowed upon her. "But they tell me you also possess powers. Is this true?"

Lianna drew in her breath. How dare he! Her magic was a difficult subject. Her mother had hated her powers, perhaps because she herself didn't possess them, and from the time she was a child Lianna had learned to keep them quiet, nearly hidden, as a matter of course. Even after her mother's death, she rarely openly displayed the few small gifts she possessed. But everyone seemed to know of them all the same.

"There is some magic in me, my lord duke," she said stiffly. "Not enough to turn you into a toad, I'm afraid."

For one brief moment a grin tugged at those hard lips, then his expression turned cool once more. "Be advised, when you reach Blackenstar, you may do what you will with small, harmless charms and tricks, but I will not have you practicing spells or employing potions. That is forbidden. Do you understand?''

"And if I disobey? Punishment by death?'' she retorted, but then recoiled as the blood drained from his face and every muscle in his body went rigid.

She suddenly remembered the first wife, the one he was rumored to have killed, and her mocking remark rang through her head like an ominously tolling bell.

Ambrose spoke with dangerous quiet. "You have an undaunted spirit, Princess—as well as beauty, royal blood, and power. Use them wisely and do not anger me, and you will live a long and contented life.''

"They say you anger readily, my lord. That may not be an easy thing to avoid.''

"They say many things about me, Lianna. Some are even true.'' His voice was rough. "You'll have to make your own judgments.''

"I already have,'' she murmured sweetly, but there was contempt dripping from the words.

He gripped her arm and yanked her closer, so close she gasped. His touch sent a sizzling warmth through her. She would have jerked away, but she knew her strength was no match for his and so she went still, gazing up into his eyes, her lips parting.

He smelled of sweat and leather and horses. There was the dark shadow of beard on his lean jaw. She had never been quite this intimately close to a man before, even those who had dared to kiss her—chaste, temperate kisses, hesitant, almost meek. There was nothing meek about Ambrose the Barbarian. His eyes glinted like coals in the torchlight. They ignited something inside her: fear, perhaps—or was it fascination?

Lianna knew better than to struggle. She would not break free, not if he didn't want her to. She nearly whimpered because her skin burned hot where his strong fingers touched.

He was entirely too powerful. Too close. Too handsome.

She swallowed and kept silent, though it took all of her will to meet those hard, stern eyes.

"I learned long ago never to judge early, or in ignorance," he said softly. "Such blunders prove fatal. You'd be wise to remember that."

Waves of fear enveloped her, but Lianna lifted her chin and spoke with all the calm she could muster. "Are you threatening me, my lord?"

"Who would threaten such a fine royal lady?" he asked silkily, the clamp of his fingers tightening. His gray eyes raked her as her own eyes widened. "As brides go, you have all the attributes I seek. And yet I tend to prefer a woman who thinks before she speaks, who does not deliberately try to offend, but rather tries to please." He swept an arm around her waist, pressing her up against him, letting her feel his superior strength. Indeed, he could break her in two if he chose, and they both knew it. "Still, my spoiled, sharp-tongued princess, if you learn to mind your tongue and please me in our marriage bed, you'll do. Aye, my lady Lianna, you'll do."

She drew in her breath, her face flushed a vivid pink. "How dare you," she whispered, in a voice as cold and furious as midwinter snow.

He met those wide, flashing eyes, his own hard as granite. "If it's wooing and pretty words you want, you won't get them from me. I've neither the time nor the nature to indulge such things. This is a business arrangement, Princess, one you've been raised to understand. If you don't know what this marriage is about, don't blame me for it—and don't expect me to coddle you. I am first and foremost a warrior and I've got a battle to fight. A savage one, at that."

He pushed her away. But as he began to wheel toward the table, Lianna grabbed his arm.

"Coddle?" she flashed. Her fingers gripped hard, terrifying muscle, but she rushed on anyway, driven by an anger that was deep and scorching. "I'd never expect that, my lord duke—especially not from a man like you! Only a barbarian would treat his intended bride with such callousness as you have shown this night—"

"Exactly." His nod was weary. "I am what I am. You do understand. Now go."

"Go?"

"Go to your chambers and ready yourself for the journey. Take what belongings you can gather in the next few moments. There isn't much time, so seize that which is most precious to you, and the rest will be sent for later."

"But my ladies-in-waiting! They must pack for themselves as well as for me . . ."

"No ladies-in-waiting, Princess. They'll be sent for later, when Crow's Keep is once more secure. For now, you'll have to manage like a soldier."

Desperation surged through her. "Why don't you go and fight your battle and then come back to Penmarren, and we'll have a proper civilized wedding ceremony—oh!"

He seized her so suddenly that she gulped back the rest of her words, nearly choking on them. His strength seemed to pulse through her, dazzling her senses, weakening her knees. She who had been taught to use a sword by her father's own man-at-arms, who had killed a boar, who had met with equanimity kings and counts and rulers from lands near and far, found herself trembling as she stared into the lean, dark face of this barbarian from Blackenstar.

"There is *nothing* proper or civilized about me, Princess. The sooner you understand that, the better off you'll be. Now, I have no more time to waste chattering with you—either go and pack what you can and meet me in the courtyard in the blink of an eye, or you and your precious kingdom of Penmarren will know exactly what kind of barbarian I really am."

Her chest constricted with fear, Lianna read the furious determination in his face. "You're hurting me," she whispered.

He glanced down, as if unaware, at the spot where he gripped her wrists, his strong fingers digging into her flesh. With an oath muttered under his breath, he released her.

"Go!"

She went. She turned and swept toward the corridor, refusing to run, refusing to look desperate and afraid, though heaven knew that was how she felt. As she reached the outer hall, she heard his voice call sharply behind her.

"Don't make me come looking for you, Princess! I have urgent business, and if you cause me a moment's delay, it will not go well for you or for those you hold dear."

Lianna did run then. She fled through the great hall and the solar, up a short flight of stairs, and down the corridor that led to her own quarters. All the castle was aflurry about her—guards and servants running, shouting, colliding, as the news spread from the tower to the cellar that the Barbarian of Blackenstar was leaving at any moment and taking the Princess Lianna with him.

"Princess . . . is it true?" Else gasped, her face whiter than the snows that still clung to the winter trees beyond the window.

"Please, by the stars, no!" Meeg whispered, but one look at Lianna's taut, pale face, and she dropped her head into her hands.

"I must get to the courtyard. I am to be married at once and leave immediately after for Blackenstar." She managed to say it without bursting into tears, though they clogged her throat and burned behind her eyelids. It would not do to collapse in a quivering heap now—it would not serve her father, her kingdom, or herself. What was it her mother had always told her?

You do not have what it takes to be a true princess, Lianna. Running through the woods like a squirrel. You lack dignity. Grace. A princess never speaks without considering her words or acts without considering the effects of her deeds. You are impulsive, emotional, and unreliable. You disappoint me.

"I must take only some clothing and necessities. Else, Bronwen, help me, if you please. Fill my trunk—quickly. I am to meet Ambrose immediately, or he will . . . he will . . ." Her voice faded, but she summoned it back. "I must go down without delay," she finished desperately.

Else and Bronwen began frantically tossing clothing, boxes of jewels, colored hose, snoods, and other belongings into a silver-edged trunk.

"A marriage gown," Meeg gasped out. "Surely you must have time to don your marriage gown."

"No time," Lianna muttered, dragging her crimson velvet cloak from its peg and throwing it around her shoulders. "We will be riding for Blackenstar as soon as the wedding is done. I dare not make him come in search of me, or who knows what those I leave behind will suffer. The man is a beast. 'Barbarian' is too kind a word for him . . . He is . . ."

She stopped short. The horror and pain on her nurse's beloved face made her curse her own tongue. "He is not that bad, dearest," she whispered. "He is quite handsome, at least. I am sure we shall deal well together."

But it was a lie, and every woman in the room knew it, especially Meeg. She caught Princess Lianna's lovely face in her doughy hands and spoke to her so softly no one else could hear.

"Take care, Lianna. Watch your tongue, child, I beg you. Do not anger him. He is a dangerous man."

A dangerous man? Lianna bit back a hysterical laugh. That was true a hundredfold. She wanted to claim that she wouldn't be intimidated by any man—least of all a graceless bastard who didn't deserve the noble title of duke that he had snatched for himself, but she knew such rash words would only alarm Meeg further.

"I will take care, Meeg," she promised softly, a catch in her throat. "Do not fear for me. I promise you—all will be well."

All will be well—when Constantine comes for me, she finished silently, grimly. Then she was running down the hall again, the manservant Ludd following with her trunk and all her ladies trailing after, weeping.

The night whipped around her in a flurry of icy, bitter winds. Wrapped in her crimson cloak, a few wild strands of hair escaping from her hood to fly about her face, she shivered and prayed that she would survive the hours ahead.

They'd been riding nearly all the night, it seemed to her, and she wondered that dawn had not yet begun to glimmer on the horizon. But, no, darkness still shrouded the great dark forest through which they rode—she could not even see the stars—and the cold was unrelenting.

Behind her in the saddle, the Barbarian's large, well-muscled frame was warm and hard, but his arms around her were every bit as unrelenting as the cold.

Lianna knew that if she were riding alone or in a litter she might well have frozen to death by now. It grated on her to be grateful to him for anything—after all, she would be in her own soft, warm, and very safe featherbed right now if not for him—but she had to acknowledge that she was thankful for the very solid bulk of his body behind her, for his warmth and strength, which partly shielded her from the fierce night wind, and for his arms, which held her upright in the saddle—for she was so weary, her body aching and exhausted, that without his grip, she was certain she would slide right off the horse and simply die of cold and misery upon the forest floor.

As they rode, the wedding itself whirled through her mind, a blur that seemed more like a dream than a real event. She saw her father's face, ashen and furious as he gave her away to the Barbarian of Blackenstar, and the cardinal, his collar askew, his voice trembling at the unexpected late-night turn of events, concern for her glistening in his sad, ancient eyes as he guided Ambrose and her through the sacred vows.

With torchlight smoking in the courtyard, and incense burning, and women muttering prayers, Ambrose's men had chafed impatiently, horses had snorted and pranced, and the groom himself, cloaked, wearing hauberk and sword, had barked out his vows in a quick, rough tone that had made Lianna repeat hers with deliberate slowness. Then just as they'd finished and Ambrose had scooped her up in his arms and hoisted her into the saddle, Meeg had pushed forward, breaking free of the knot of women and going straight to the Barbarian himself.

"Duke Ambrose!"

He'd turned back, staring at the short, heavy woman with the seamed face and faded eyes.

"Lady, I have no time—-"

"Be good to her." It was an order—gruff, quick—yet oddly pleading. "My Lianna. If you dare to hurt her, I will hunt you down myself. She's a good child. Her heart is pure. If you hurt her—"

"Ease your mind, old woman. I will not harm her." Ambrose spoke so softly that Lianna was certain only she and Meeg had heard. "Go to your bed and rest easy. She will not suffer at my hands."

Meeg stared at him as the seconds beat on, precious seconds, while horses whinnied, men seethed to be off, the wind whipped at the nobles and servants gathered in the courtyard to see their princess wed.

Then Meeg nodded and stepped back. The king cried, "Have courage, my daughter!" and with one last glimpse of her father's anguished face, Lianna was swept away upon the Barbarian's black destrier, and she could only gaze back in longing at her beloved castle as the dark night closed around her.

Since then they'd been riding for hours. Or perhaps days . . .

Lianna didn't realize she'd fallen asleep until she felt herself being lifted down from the steed. Her eyes fluttered open and for a moment she stared in confusion at the swarthily handsome face so close to hers.

"She needs rest." The man's words came to her as if from a great distance. His voice was deep, not at all unpleasant. "Or else I'll have another dead bride on my hands."

A chill pierced her, and she came fully awake, her heart lurching.

"Ambrose."

"Yes, Princess." He was carrying her in his arms, she realized, and then she saw that the great forest had given way to a hamlet, and a churning black river flowed to her right. To her left was a cluster of ramshackle buildings that huddled like stooped monsters in the night.

"Where are we?"

"An inn in Kyrdwyk where it will be safe to spend what

remains of the night. No more than three or four hours—then we'll have to ride again."

She moaned and tried to struggle free of his arms. "Put me down. I can walk."

"I doubt it."

She realized he was right. Her body ached and weariness dragged at her so that she could scarcely see or think. But she detested her own weakness and vowed he should not know of it.

"You underestimate me. I am well able to—"

"If you're going to argue with me every time you speak, there is going to be real trouble between us." He strode into the inn, where a man in a greasy dark tunic and cap raced down the stairs, staring in stupefaction.

"A dozen of my men and I need quarters for the night. Others will be camped outside. They'll need food in the morning. See that you have enough for all."

"Aye, sir, my lord. As you wish. Let me show you to a room."

Goggle-eyed at the sight of the large, armed, and obviously dangerous soldiers who stomped into the tiny inn, the landlord stumbled over his own feet as he led the dark-haired duke to the best room of his house.

Entering the musty, low-ceilinged chamber, Ambrose gave it a swift glance. It had a hearth. That was something. But not much. The mattress was of straw, the planked floor sticky with spilled ale, the blankets moth-eaten and nearly threadbare.

But the fire would warm the woman in his arms and the bed would afford her some much-needed sleep, and those were his chief concerns at the moment.

He had to reach Blackenstar before the invaders from the east did, but he couldn't afford to kill his bride getting there.

"Sleep while you may." He tossed her down upon the bed, noting how swiftly she bounced up to glare at him.

"Build a fire and bring the lady some refreshment," he ordered the landlord over his shoulder and then left the dim chamber to find William and Beorn and set out orders for the men.

Lianna wanted no refreshment, only sleep. As the fire sprang to life in the hearth, and the landlord bowed and scraped his way out the door, she huddled in her gown and cloak upon the lumpy mattress, which smelled like a pig had been the last to lie upon it. She thought briefly, longingly, of her own bed made of softest feathers, her room delicately scented with rushes and sweet spices, of the hot spiced drink Else brought her each night in the winter before she retired. Then she pushed the thoughts away.

Those days were gone—for now. If she ever wanted to return to Castle Penmarren, to her life there as her father's daughter and a princess held in esteem by her people, she had first to get through the next fortnight wed to the Barbarian.

And that meant getting through her wedding night.

She had expected it would take place in Penmarren Castle, at least. Not here in some filthy inn on the road, in the middle of the night, with the smell of pig nearly choking her.

She must have drifted off into sleep again, because suddenly she was jerked awake by a heavy form dropping down beside her and the bed dipping low with a resounding creak.

Ambrose sprawled alongside her, fully clothed, the long, heavy length of him taking up nearly the entire bed.

In shock she recoiled and tried to shift herself away from any contact with him, but she mistook the width of the bed. With a strangled cry, she tumbled over the edge to land with a most unprincesslike thud upon the floor.

3

A DEEP RUMBLE of laughter shook the rafters of the chamber.

"Come back to bed, Princess. I've already swallowed three virgins whole for my supper—I won't eat you alive, at least not tonight."

Her cheeks burned. And her rump ached. Not to mention her elbow. She wanted to march out of the room and demand that the landlord give her another chamber—but she couldn't. Ambrose was her husband and there was no escaping him.

Not until Constantine came and, with any luck, lopped off his head.

So she rose with all the dignity she could muster, yanked her cloak tight about her shoulders, and tried to avoid her husband's eyes as she began to carefully settle herself upon the bed once more, but he reached out a giant arm and before she could move he tugged her unceremoniously down beside him, clamped an arm across her chest, and drew her close by his side.

"Next time you fall out of bed you might injure yourself," he growled. "Then the world would say I raised my hand to you on our bridal night."

Staring into his eyes, Lianna saw that they were tinged with amusement, but also a shadow of bitterness. "I'd best keep you close or my reputation will suffer," he said softly.

A strange dizziness assailed her at his nearness. Something about him made her senses reel. *Fear*, she told herself. *Dread*.

"I wouldn't worry, my lord," she said with honeyed sweetness, "your reputation could not sink much lower than it already has."

She felt him move beside her, the bunch of powerful muscles, the catlike spring as he came up in one smooth, powerful motion. He had removed his hauberk but wore tunic and cloak as he loomed over her, his face dark and harsh in the dancing glow of the fire.

"You're wrong, Princess." He spoke in a low tone. "It could."

Lianna didn't dare try to move. She couldn't escape him if she tried. He hadn't yet touched her, or tried to hold her there, but if she moved, he would, sure as a lion would pin down a lamb.

"D-do what you want with me, then." She took a deep breath. "I know what is expected of me as your w-wife. G-go ahead."

She squeezed her eyes tight shut and braced herself for the worst.

Nothing happened.

She waited, sensing him above her, hearing his soft breathing, aware of the sizzling air that seemed to tingle around her.

She braced herself to be roughly touched, grabbed, her cloak and gown ripped, flung to the floor, but . . . nothing happened.

She opened her eyes.

Ambrose was just as he had been before. Except for one thing. Now his gray eyes no longer glittered threateningly. In the waving firelight that sent golden-orange shadows through the dingy room, they shone with faint amusement.

Was he *laughing*—at *her*?

"What are you waiting for?" she bit out between clenched teeth. "Midsummer's Eve?"

A low rumble of laughter sounded deep in his chest. "I've a fierce battle to plan and win, Lianna. My castle is endangered. And our road is not without peril. I think—for now—for this one night, at least—I am able to withstand your many and considerable charms," he chuckled.

So he did not mean to . . . he would not . . . she didn't have to . . .

She carefully hid the relief that surged through her. Thank the heavens she would be spared having to couple with this monstrous creature—at least for tonight. If a tiny bit of disappointment nibbled at the corners of her heart she pushed it away. Why should she feel disappointment? Because Ambrose the Barbarian wasn't so tempted by her beauty and femininity that he would forget the very real troubles besetting him and wish only to kiss her, touch her, and bed her?

That was preposterous. She didn't want him even to look at her, much less place those large, rough hands upon her . . . much less . . .

She pushed that thought away, too, deciding that fatigue was turning her mind to mush and confusing her thoughts with nonsense.

She struggled up to a sitting position then, half fearing that he would try to push her down, but he leaned back and allowed her to rise. Her hood dangled down her back and her black hair tumbled in her face as she stared into those deep, disconcertingly intelligent eyes. "Very wise to set your priorities, my lord. My father taught me when I was young that if a man wants to hold on to his kingdom he should consider well his choices and his actions. If your land is being threatened, and your castle is at risk I agree that nothing else can possibly be as important as . . ."

He reached out and pushed her back down onto the straw mattress, and a hand clamped over her mouth.

"Ye gods, woman, do you always talk so much? I may have to kiss you just to keep you quiet!"

"That won't . . . be necessary."

Ambrose lifted one dark brow. "Frightened?"

"Of you, my lord?" Lianna forced a laugh, though she felt none too confident sprawled on the bed with him nearly atop her. "H-hardly!"

It was his turn to laugh. Suddenly his hands pinioned hers above her head and he leaned closer, his weight pressing down over her. "Prove it, my brave lady." Gray eyes gleamed down into hers. "Let me kiss you."

Lianna's blood pounded in her ears. "But you said . . ."

"One kiss—only one."

Her gaze dropped from those gleaming eyes to the hard, implacable mouth. Heat twisted through her. She squirmed in a futile effort to break free, then went still. "I cannot stop you," she whispered bitterly.

"Yes. You can, Princess." He released her hands, and his knuckle moved downward to gently brush her cheek. "If you are afraid, simply tell me no."

"I'm *not* afraid. I've never met the man to make me afraid . . ."

"Then your answer is yes."

Slowly, he leaned down. Close, closer. His eyes glinted silver, his breath whispered on her cheek. One big hand slid through her hair, stirring a strange feeling in the pit of her stomach. "Yes?" he persisted, his mouth an inch from hers.

Suddenly the room was no longer cold—it was hot, dizzyingly hot. Gazing into that darkly handsome face, she trembled, and felt the fire of his lips though they were still a breath away from hers. She tried to form her lips to speak the word "no."

"Yes," she heard herself whisper and knew that she was in terrible trouble now, drawn forward toward something she couldn't name—or resist.

Ambrose's head dipped lower and his lips swooped down upon hers. Firm, masculine lips—yet warm, yielding. Commanding. He laid claim to her mouth with a kiss that was hungry and intense, a warrior's kiss, giving no quarter. Without warning, his tongue darted inside her parted lips—searching, branding.

Conquering.

Lianna moaned at the shocking pleasure that invaded her senses. The dingy room vanished, the strange inn, even the straw bed. There was only Ambrose, only the kiss, only the flame of it eating her up, sparking a spiraling pleasure inside her. His hand moved through her hair, slid down to cup her nape. A delicious melting sensation rolled through her.

The kiss never ended, he merely deepened it and continued, plundering with sure, smooth strokes that demolished her defenses.

But when his hand slipped inside her cloak to close about her breast, shock struck her, and sense rushed back. "N-no!" She struggled free of the fierce pleasure. "Stop . . . Ambrose . . . stop."

She pressed hard against his chest and he drew back at last, his hand dropping, his mouth ceasing its relentless assault.

Why, his breath was coming as fast as hers, Lianna noted as she stared wild-eyed at him. And there was a flush to his swarthy skin.

"You . . . promised. Just one . . . kiss!"

"You *are* afraid," he taunted softly, a smile curling his lips. He reached for her again.

"No!"

"Then one more . . ."

"No!"

Ambrose sighed and released her. Reluctantly, he shifted in the bed, leaving a slight space between them. "As you wish." There was a tinge of mockery in his voice, and something else—regret. "We'll finish this game at Crow's Keep, then—when I have sent Sandar to a bloody grave." He grinned at her.

"You are very sure of yourself," Lianna said breathlessly, her heart still pounding from the soul-stirring heat of his kiss.

"I know my strong points." Again the swift grin that transformed his dark face and stunned her almost as much as the kiss had. One hand reached out and gently tugged on a gleaming black curl that framed her face.

"Sleep then, Princess. Gather your strength. The ride we've just completed from Penmarren is child's play compared with what lies ahead."

And before she could speak, the grin faded and he settled down on his side, facing her, and closed his eyes.

It took a few moments for Lianna's breath to calm, for her heartbeat to slow and steady. Soundlessly, she raised up on one elbow and studied the man beside her. Impossibly handsome, she thought helplessly, as the firelight gilded his strong features, glinted off the dark sheen of his cropped hair. Impossibly powerful, she thought in dismay, recalling the heady, dizzying effects of his kiss.

She studied his closed eyes, with their unexpectedly thick lashes. For some reason, every time those eyes flickered over her, she felt a jolt. Like lightning striking her. Strange. She'd never felt any such thing before, not when any of the noble or royal suitors who had come to court had looked at her. Not a one.

It is naught but fear, she told herself, and settled her head gingerly upon the pillow once more. *And loathing. Nothing more.*

But when he'd kissed her—such strange feelings had churned through her. Why, oh, why, had she accepted his dare? He'd stirred up emotions and sensations inside her she hadn't known were there. And what if . . . the next time he kissed her, touched her, claimed her fully as his wife, those sensations returned?

She tossed fitfully, but as the fire hissed and danced, and night crept toward morning, eventually fatigue stole over her. Now that she wasn't cold any longer, now that the warmth of the fire and of the kiss and of the man lying beside her had banished the ice in her blood, she felt sleep coming to claim her, dragging her down.

She must sleep while she could. Or she wouldn't be strong enough to endure a fortnight wed to this man, who shifted suddenly in his sleep and dropped his powerful arm across her. A man with no scruples, she reminded herself, a bastard with not a drop of royal blood in his veins, a man who made her flesh crawl every time he looked at her. Well, perhaps not crawl . . . more like *tingle.*

Morning came in a blink.

They rode for two more days and nights—with only brief intervals of rest, meals, and sleep. By the time they reached Blackenstar, Lianna could only stare blearily at the forbidding, mountainous country through which they traveled, at the dark forests whose trees loomed taller, denser, and more threateningly than any she had seen in Penmarren.

They left the mountains behind late in the day, and as dusk approached and thick, glistening snowflakes began to fall, they reached a frozen river and then rolling farmland frosted with ice. Not long after that, they came to a village and heard the sounds of the sea. Beyond the cottages and workshops and the local inn, with smoke curling from the chimneys to dissipate in the dark slate sky, Lianna had her first glimpse of Crow's Keep.

Her heart constricted at the sight of the great stone castle rising from the rocky cliffs at the very edge of the sea.

With its weathered gray stone, looming towers, and fortified battlements all flying the star-shaped black-and-crimson flags of Blackenstar, the huge keep looked chillingly impregnable. A fine silver mist clung to the tower and dwindled down over the bailey, and the iron gates appeared as forbidding as those leading to a dungeon. High above, black crows circled and squawked, swooping from treetop to battlements, their dark wings beating against wind and sky.

Ambrose spoke from behind her in the saddle, his arms snug around her waist, his deep voice carrying over the wind.

"I'll leave you at the gate. My seneschal, Randolph, will show you to your quarters and acquaint you with all you need to know."

"Do you mean that you are going into battle now—this

very night?'' Half turning in the saddle, she stared at him incredulously. Weariness tugged at every bone in her body. She marveled at his strength to proceed straight into battle after their grueling ride.

"I must catch Sandar unawares before he can cross the Crystal Sea. There is no way in hell I will let him reach within arrow's distance of Crow's Keep or the village.'' Then he spoke again, in her ear.

"Do I take it that you regret the postponement of our first real night together as husband and wife?''

"I am thankful for it!''

He laughed, which made Lianna immediately try to squirm forward, as far away from his muscled body as she could, but Ambrose's arms tightened around her waist and drew her back.

"When I return we'll make up for the time we've lost.''

"Not if your battle leaves you dead—or grievously wounded!''

"Ah, your concern touches me, Princess.''

She twisted around to look at him and saw that beneath his dark brows, Ambrose the Barbarian's gray eyes glinted silver as the mist.

"Does it indeed? I am surprised that anything could touch you, my lord,'' she retorted in her haughtiest tones.

"Those daggers from your eyes could kill me if they reached my heart. If I but *had* a heart,'' he mused.

"Daggers? Really, my lord.'' She spoke coldly, in the manner her mother would have employed when addressing a stableboy. "Indeed, I wish you safe journey.''

"You lie, Princess. You know you hope that Sandar runs me through.'' He caught her chin in his hand and raised it, forcing her to meet his eyes. "Why don't you just say it?''

"That would be unfitting speech for a princess of royal blood.''

To her chagrin, he threw back his head and laughed. "I am pleased to see that I have got my money's worth with this bargain. Go ahead. Be just as royal and haughty as you want. Especially when you're in my bed.'' His voice grew deeper, huskier. "I've conquered every petty king and noble who has sneered at me, and I'll conquer you, too."

"How dare you . . ."

"This is as far as I'll go."

He pulled the destrier to a sudden halt and swung off the steed with surprising litheness for such a large man. Without a word he swept Lianna down beside him.

All around her the company drew up. They were near the portcullis, where soldiers in armor guarded the gates, awaiting orders from their duke.

The wind blasted around Lianna, slicing right through the heavy velvet cloak, whipping her hood back like a banner.

"William—you stay behind." Ambrose addressed a stout, bearded man with hair and whiskers the color of summer wheat who spurred his horse forward at the duke's words. "Guard my lady and the keep well! Take her to Randolph and see that she is made comfortable and shown the respect due her."

Sir William saluted sharply and rode toward the gate to await the lady of the castle.

Lianna began to stride toward him, but Ambrose gripped her wrist and tugged her back.

She was conscious of the men on horseback all around them, watching, smiling, as their duke prepared to bid farewell to his bride.

"Not so fast, my lady. I have something for you before we part." To her surprise, he removed the gold-and-ruby star-brooch from the shoulder of his cloak and pinned it to hers.

"It is a bridal gift. I command you to wear it always. It is a symbol that you are under my protection."

"But who is to protect me from you?" She gazed defiantly up at him as the wind tore at her hair.

"No one can protect you from me." Ambrose pulled her closer. She shivered and his hands tightened at her waist. His voice dropped. "No doubt a chaste public kiss is appropriate even for royalty," he said slowly. "Am I correct?"

She was unnerved by his touch, by the way his eyes gleamed at her through the cold mist, but she nodded with outward calm. "You are correct. Most proper of all would be for you to kiss my hand—oh!"

Her startled cry was cut off as he swept her into his arms and his lips clamped down to claim hers. Heat and dazzling confusion suffused her as Ambrose the Barbarian roughly and thoroughly kissed her, holding her taut against him, his warm mouth waging a lusty battle against hers, his arms locking her entire body against his.

Struggling would be undignified and unbecoming a princess, Lianna thought dimly before she couldn't think at all. She felt as if she was drowning, drowning in a hot sea of sparkling pleasure as his hand fisted in her hair and his mouth set hers afire.

The dark keep, the men on horseback, the mist, and the sea—all blurred to nothingness as the man she had wed against her will held her in arms of iron and kissed her to the depths of her soul.

When he drew back, Lianna could only stare blankly up at him, her eyes wide and glazed, her lips swollen and parted.

She couldn't speak. Couldn't break the spell.

Heaven help her, what evil magic was this? She wanted him to kiss her again!

But he only smiled, his eyes dancing as snowflakes melted upon her upturned face. He spoke so that only she could hear his words.

"I'll be back before you can miss me, Lianna. And I'll teach you about all the things a proper, true-blood princess doesn't know."

As he vaulted back upon the destrier, the laughter and shouts of his men rang out. Then he was off, straight through the village again, toward the dark wood that bordered the sea, his soldiers thundering after him.

Still shaken, her face hot despite the numbing cold, Lianna walked with as much dignity as she could muster toward those massive gates. William and the soldiers manning them bowed their heads in deference as the portcullis lifted and the new lady of the castle passed through into the great courtyard of Crow's Keep.

4

Ambrose's kiss had chased all thoughts out of her mind—including her fears about this castle—but as the thunder of hoofbeats faded and the keep loomed before her, and servants and scullery maids peeped out at her in silent awe, and knights and pages and stableboys hurried forth to get a glimpse of her, she once more had to fight off a sense of dread.

The castle was much more stark than Penmarren. Everything was well ordered, large and spacious, with tapestries upon the walls, and tables and chests inlaid with gold and precious jewels, but there was a chill that seemed to mist from the stone walls, a sense of foreboding that clung to the recessed shadows of the great hall.

Surely the rumors that the place was cursed were as baseless as the one that claimed Ambrose had murdered his wife, Lianna told herself as she proceeded with the seneschal, Randolph, through the great hall.

At any rate, it would do her no good to appear afraid.

It was easy for Lianna to meet those who lived and worked in the castle, to greet the cook, Berta, and the scullery maids, the pages and the squires, and the men-at-arms who guarded the keep. She knew the role of lady of the castle well, and it took no effort for her to smile, nod, and murmur questions or instructions to those who bowed or curtsied as she passed.

But during all that time, and especially that evening as she prepared herself for bed, she could not forget the parting kiss that Ambrose had bestowed upon her.

She sat by the window in the lofty bedchamber she had been given, drawing her silver hairbrush through her hair and thinking about that moment when his lips had seared hers.

She'd had many suitors—tall, short, fair, dark- or russet-haired, young, old, kindly or stern—and one or two had even been bold enough to kiss her when no one was about and when, eager to discover what it was like, she had made it known that she was willing.

But none of them had kissed her like that. None of them had affected her like that. None of them had ever clouded her brain, assaulted her heart, made her blood pound like a tempestuous sea in her ears.

Only Ambrose.

A barbarian.

She was ashamed. He was not worthy of whatever feelings had begun to alight in her heart toward him. He was all that she had been raised to despise. He had in effect forced her at swordpoint to marry him!

And she would have her revenge when Constantine came to free her.

But for some reason she found little comfort in that notion tonight. She wondered where Ambrose was, how he fared against Sandar. If he was hurt.

The thought tore through her and she caught her breath, taken aback by the pain that sliced her heart.

Surely she would not care if Ambrose had been hurt, even if he were dead. She would celebrate. Wouldn't she?

She closed her eyes and remembered again the feel of

his steely arms around her, the deep roughness of his voice—and his mouth, bruising and hungry upon hers as he bade her farewell.

Her sleep that night was uneasy. She was in a strange bed, in a keep rumored to be cursed, with crows flapping at her window—and a husband far afield, fighting an enemy.

He had many enemies, this barbarian.

She wondered, just before sleep claimed her at last, if he had ever had a friend.

The next two days dragged by. Each hour Lianna found herself listening for the thunder of hoofbeats that would signal Ambrose's return. It did not come.

She took her meals alone in her room. They were served by a stoop-shouldered stern-faced woman named Marthe, who uttered not a word but only nodded or shook her head when Lianna spoke to her. She wondered if the servants were all so fearful of Ambrose that they dared not speak lest they offend him or someone who would report to him.

She thought of her own beloved nurse, of Else and Gwenlyn and Kira—and her heart ached with missing them.

On the second afternoon, she felt as if the walls of the castle were closing in upon her. She threw her cloak over her simple gown of cream-colored wool, tucked her braid inside the hood, and headed toward the bailey. The star-brooch winked at her shoulder as she hurried through the halls and all she passed bent their heads or bowed as she went by.

Their deference, born of fear, Lianna guessed, increased her desperation to be alone, to have time to think about what she could do in this time when Ambrose was gone that might help Constantine.

Perhaps there were maps, documents showing the placement of Ambrose's troops, how many men he commanded, where he might be vulnerable.

Surely there must be something she could do to help Penmarren defeat him. She needed to get away alone for a while to think and plan. And perhaps she could gather some herbs, even now, in the dead of winter. Even dead roots would serve for some of her healing draughts. She'd not had time to pack her herbs and healing medicines when she'd left Penmarren, and she didn't like being without them.

An idea came to her in a flash. Perhaps she would come across a plant that could be useful during Constantine's attack. Kittle plants or umsbar weed, which could be used to make a sleeping draught—something tasteless but powerful to slip into the ale drunk by Blackenstar's knights—and by the Barbarian Duke himself on the day Constantine stormed the castle.

Her stomach clenched at the thought, but she pushed the unease away. Whatever she could do to help Constantine and Penmarren—and to free herself from Ambrose—she must do. It was not wrong, she told herself, heading out toward the bailey with a brisk step. It was her duty.

But when she stepped out into the courtyard, making for the stable, she was dismayed to see William bearing down on her.

"Yes?" She stared at him questioningly, though she knew full well why he was there.

"Does my lady wish to leave the protection of the castle grounds? It is not advisable."

"Oh? Am I a prisoner?" It wasn't as if she could escape—she was much too far from Penmarren to try reaching it alone on horseback.

"Of course not, my lady." William smiled. "But you are our honored duchess, and if you wish to ride out, I must accompany you. The duke ordered me to guard you well, and I must obey those orders. Besides," he added with a slight bow, "it is a pleasure to protect so lovely a lady."

"I wonder what he would do to you should you fail in your duty." Lianna kept walking toward the stables, and the knight easily kept pace with her. "You are frightened of him, are you not?"

"Frightened, my lady?" William sounded amused. "No. But I respect him. I owe him. Why, he has made me his captain-of-arms when I have served him for fewer years than others—like Beorn. He has granted me an estate—farmland and a manor house—when the wars are finished and Blackenstar is secure. I will carry out whatever service he asks of me without hesitation.''

Lianna doubted that Ambrose could inspire loyalty. Fear, yes. That she could imagine. William was merely too wise to say so, however—and besides, no man liked to admit fear of another. She surveyed him closely, but could read only calm in his expression. ''The servant woman, Marthe. Do you know her? *She* is fearful even to speak! I can only imagine what she has suffered in the duke's employ.''

''Marthe.'' Sir William halted before the stable doors, and Lianna did, too, turning to face him. The knight shook his head, his face somber. ''No, my lady. You mistake the matter.''

''It is true. She does not speak.''

''Aye, that is true, but not because she is fearful of Duke Ambrose. She is devoted to him. Marthe was attacked—ravaged—when she was a young maid in his father's court. She worked in the old duke's household, and one day she was returning from the village with her parcels and was set upon by men traveling along the road. She was grievously hurt, but she recovered—except after that day, and the horrors she experienced, she never spoke again.''

''Oh.'' Lianna bit her lip, her heart going out to the silent stick of a woman who had served her meals since she'd arrived. ''I see.''

''If it were not for Duke Ambrose, no one knows what might have become of her. He was only a lad of sixteen summers at the time, but he set out to find the men and bring them to justice. Which he did, I might add. He killed them all.''

Lianna sucked in her breath. ''I see,'' she repeated shakily. Perhaps Ambrose was not such a complete brute as he had been painted. He had cared enough for a servant girl to punish the men who had harmed her. That didn't fit with the legends told of him from forest to sea.

''And if it weren't for Ambrose, who knows what would

have become of Marthe?'' William continued in his quiet way. "She was too ill and skittish to work for some time, and afterward, when she didn't speak, many might have sent her packing as useless. But Ambrose found a place for her in a manor house where she could serve a gentle and quiet lady. And when he himself became duke, he brought her back to his own household. He has always made certain she had a livelihood, food to eat, shelter, and no one is allowed to mistreat her. I know few men who would take such pains for a servant, but Ambrose is loyal to all those who are loyal to him.''

"Well, yes. It would seem so." Lianna was too stunned by all she'd heard to think of anything else to say. She needed time, time to mull over what William had told her.

They went into the stables together and he helped her to mount a splendid white mare, then he himself took a dun horse with the thickest mane she had ever seen. Lianna waited until they had ridden out past the gates before she gave a low cry.

"What is wrong, my lady?''

"I have forgotten my gloves, and the air is cold.'' She shivered. The air *was* cold, but her gloves were shoved deep inside the pockets of her velvet cloak. There was no need for William to know that, however.

"Would you kindly go back to the hall and ask Marthe to fetch them for me? If you please?''

The knight hesitated, eyeing her uneasily, but he could hardly tell the duke's bride to fetch her own gloves. "Perhaps you'd care to ride back within the gates while I do so?'' he said at last.

Lianna gave a laugh and flashed him her most brilliant smile. "The guards are right there watching,'' she pointed out. "Where do you think I might flee, Sir William, in the twinkling you will be gone? And with the guards to see my every move?''

He warmed under the power of that sunny smile.

"Very well, my lady. I will return, as you say, in a twinkling.''

And I will be gone in a twinkling, Lianna thought, but she kept the bright smile upon her face.

She waited only until he had dismounted in the yard and disappeared inside the castle before kicking the mare and galloping straight for the belt of trees that lined the road.

"My lady! Halt! Halt!" The guards ran after her, calling for her to stop, shouting for Sir William, but she was off like the wind, her hood blowing back, her braid bouncing free, her sights set on the glorious shadowy depths of the forest.

Moments later, she found a curving track that led along a rocky outcropping, and this she followed, knowing that the rocks would leave no telltale hoofprints for Sir William to follow. Many was the time she had escaped her nurse, her ladies-in-waiting, or one of the soldiers sent to guard her on her expeditions in search of berries or healing herbs. She had long ago mastered all the tricks involved in eluding those who would follow her.

And on this bright, cold day her tricks worked like a charm, just as they always had. In a short time she found herself deep within the shadows of the forest, surrounded by the bare winter trees, her mare picking its way along a rutted path glossy with patches of melting snow.

When she spotted the dull purple roots of umsbar weed straggling beside a rock, she dismounted and began to gather some, careful not to crush them. Looking around, she found kittle as well, peeking out from some dead leaves clustered at the base of a pine, and filled the deep pockets of her cloak. She had just spotted some dead lavender at the rim of a gully when she heard a woman's scream.

Her head flew up and she listened, her heart thudding. A man's shout followed, quickly joined by more, and above all, the continuous, bloodcurdling shrieks of the woman.

The fracas came from straight ahead, just beyond a thicket of pines. Leaving her mare, Lianna dashed through the trees at a run, her kid boots making little noise on the forest floor, but when she reached the clearing beyond the trees, she skidded to a halt and her hand groped for the dagger hidden in the folds of her gown.

Three men—outlaws by the look of their filthy, tattered clothes, scarred and cruel faces, and the knives and sticks they brandished—had attacked a peddler's wagon. The peddler and his gray-haired wife were frantically trying to beat them off as their terrified horse reared and whinnied. Even as she watched, one of the outlaws dashed in and swung a stick at the man, knocking him to the ground.

The woman screamed again as the outlaw arced his blade at her husband. At the last moment he rolled aside, nearly under the horse's hooves, but the knife slashed his arm and blood spilled into the earth as he howled in agony.

"Halt!" Lianna darted forward, her dagger clenched, her eyes blazing at the outlaws closing in upon the fallen man.

They paused, staring at her, as startled as if she had sprung down from the very sky.

Then the one who had slashed the peddler grinned toothlessly, and the others joined him.

"What's this, lads? A pretty maid joins the fun. Our luck is truly in, I say!"

The woman and her husband stared in shock as the outlaws turned their attention upon the lovely young woman whose elegant face was flushed with fury.

"Welcome, beauty," the tallest of the three muttered. They left the man lying on his side and fanned out as they approached her—two of them gripping knives, the shortest man clenching a long stick whose tip had been sharpened to an evil point. "Put down that shiny blade and come join us," the tall one barked. "There's no turning away now."

"Stand back." Fear clawed at Lianna, nearly overriding the outrage that had filled her when she saw the plight of the peddler and his wife. But she refused to step back even a pace as the men advanced.

"Come no closer," she warned. "I order you to leave this place at once—in the name of Ambrose, Duke of Blackenstar."

These words made the outlaws laugh. They did pause, though, and surveyed Lianna with uproarious amusement. The burly man brandished his knife overhead.

"I don't see no Duke of Blackenstar. Do you, Werric?"

"All I sees is a wisp of a woman who looks like she'll be as tasty a morsel as any I've known."

The tall one, obviously the leader, stepped forward, his black eyes glistening like chunks of coal. "You two see to the peddler," he ordered, his gaze riveted on Lianna. "Kill him and take whatever gold or silver you find. Do what you want with that screeching woman. This tasty morsel is mine."

Lianna's blood froze. She could hear the woman in the wagon weeping as if from a long way off. She saw the peddler struggling to gain his feet, but he swayed and fell into a pool of his own blood. "I am under the protection of the Duke of Blackenstar," she said desperately. "If you harm me, or these people traveling his roads, you'll have his wrath to deal with. See here?" She touched the star-brooch glittering at her shoulder. "I wear the brooch of Blackenstar. You'd best beware!"

A flicker of doubt crossed their faces.

"Go now—while you still may!" she commanded, and prayed through the frantic drumming of her heart that they would be cowed enough in that moment to obey.

But the leader began to curse, and his hands tightened on his knife. "I might be feared of a man, but not of a brooch. Or of any woman who thinks to trick me. I'll take you, my fine lady, *and* your star-brooch. It'll fetch a handsome price in the marketplace."

And with that, he leapt toward her. Lianna slashed out with the dagger and caught him in the stomach. With a strangled gurgle of surprise and pain, he stared at her, then down at the blood pouring from the wound. Then he fell to his knees, the knife slipping from his slack fingers.

"Kill . . . her!" he rasped as the other two rushed forward.

The old woman staggered down from the wagon and picked up a rock, shrieking as she headed into the battle. Lianna scarcely had time to notice. The outlaw with the stick struck her full across the shoulders, a whacking blow that sent her reeling sideways into a tree.

Before she could recover, the third outlaw seized her arm

and wrenched her jeweled dagger from her. Holding his knife in one hand and her dagger in the other, he grinned grotesquely and came at her.

Through the terror sweeping over her, she heard a great roar, felt a whooshing rush behind her, and before she knew what was happening, the clearing was filled with a great charging horse and Ambrose leaned low in the saddle, bearing down upon the outlaw like a dark bolt of fire.

The man shrieked and tried to parry the blow, but Ambrose drove the glittering sword through his heart with one swift thrust.

Screams. Blood. Death.

Through a fog of horror, Lianna watched as the outlaw tumbled into the dirt and Ambrose spun his horse toward the other two, for the leader, bloodied and hurt, had grabbed his knife and hurled himself to his feet, his face savage with fury as he returned to the fray.

Two against one.

There was nothing to do but watch, her heart in her throat, as the duke fought both of them—his face calm, determined, and utterly ruthless. Neither man stood a chance, Lianna realized after that first awful moment. Ambrose fought with single-minded purpose and sublime skill, and before the peddler's woman even had time to run to her husband and kneel at his side, it was over.

The outlaws lay dead beneath the clouded sky, and Ambrose himself turned his destrier and surveyed Lianna as though he would like to run her through as well.

For a long moment she met his harsh gaze, unable to look away, shaken by the way he had fought for her, killed for her, and fully aware of what would have happened if he had not come when he had. And then the sobs of the woman penetrated her shock.

With a choked cry, she ran to the wagon and knelt beside the fallen man.

"There, now, let me see." She spoke quietly to the weeping woman, who raised a grimy, pockmarked face to her.

The knife wound was deep. The man had lost much blood and lay in a faint.

She heard Ambrose approach behind her, but focused her attention on the peddler. The ancient spells came easily to her lips as she pulled a sprig of umsbar from her pocket, crushed it between her fingers, and sprinkled the coarse brown powder on the wound. She asked the woman for bandages and salve, if they carried any in the wagon, then returned her attention to the fallen man as his wife went in search of them.

The moments blurred as Lianna ministered to the man, and by the time the wound was bound up they had been joined in the clearing by Sir William and Beorn and half a dozen other knights, who stood silently behind Ambrose and watched.

Gently Lianna lay her hands upon the man's brow and closed her eyes. Her lips moved, the old spells of healing sprang forth sweet as song.

At last she felt the faint, hot pulsing beneath her fingertips, and at the same moment she heard him moan. She opened her eyes.

Another groan came from the man.

"Will he live, then, my lady?" The woman clasped her hands to her throat.

Lianna nodded wearily, her vision dazed. She was utterly drained.

"He can recover in the hall. My men will take him to the keep." Ambrose turned and quietly gave orders to Sir William, then lifted Lianna to her feet. She sagged against him, her knees buckling at the weakness that assailed her.

Without a word, Ambrose lifted her and set her upon his destrier.

"My mare," she murmured softly. "Back there."

"William will fetch her." Ambrose spoke curtly, tightly controlled anger in his voice.

He swung up behind her, and once again they rode together toward the castle.

They did not speak until they were nearly at the gates. Then Ambrose addressed her, his voice so cold it was like a bucket of icy spring water poured over her.

"Why did you run away? Did you really think you could travel back to Penmarren in safety on your own? You would never have reached the border. And if you had— and your father took you in, I would have made war on your people. Is that what you wanted?"

"No . . . I wasn't going to run away. I would never bring your anger down upon my people!" Lianna cried. Her head was swimming—the result of conjuring up the spells, of the deep concentration needed to ensure the man's healing. She fought to think and speak coherently.

"I only wanted some time alone. In the open air. I am used to going about freely out-of-doors . . . gathering herbs and medicines . . ."

"I told you the first night we met that I would have you brew no potions."

"Not potions—herbal draughts, healing medicines. You said I might do as I pleased . . ."

"Not that." They reached the portcullis and the guards opened the gate, saluting.

Lianna turned in the saddle and risked a glance at his face. It was thunderous.

"Go to your quarters and await me there. You will not be allowed out of your rooms without my leave. A guard will be posted."

"You can't keep me a prisoner!"

"Can't I?" His mocking smile made Lianna wish to strike him. "You will see what it means to cross me."

Lianna couldn't reach the castle soon enough. She refused even to look at him when he helped her down from the horse, his hands tight at her waist as he set her upon the ground. Though she was dizzy from the weariness besetting her, the same weariness that always drained her after the exertion of the healing spells, she held her head high and walked swiftly and with dignity straight into the hall, never once looking back.

She knew exactly what she was going to do.

5

DARKNESS CLOAKED HER chamber when she awoke.

Candles flickered, streaming pale ribbons of light upon the walls, the rush-strewn floor, the crimson bed hangings. Pushing herself up slowly in the bed, Lianna gazed about her, relieved to see that she was alone.

Her head was clearer than it had been, thank heavens. Sleep had cured her of the aftermath of the magic. But she felt fear and panic churning within her. She was a prisoner, not only of the keep but of her own chambers. She who loved to roam the woods and hills, to feel the breeze flying through her hair, was locked here within these dank old stone walls.

Until Ambrose granted permission for her to leave.

Cold sweat broke out upon her skin, and she had to force herself to remain calm.

Someone—Marthe, no doubt—had left a tray for her on the table near the window. She had no appetite, but to distract herself from her predicament she tiptoed barefoot across the room and found on the tray thick slabs of bread, a wedge of cheese, a dish of eggs in jelly, and a plate of sliced venison and turnips. She tasted a bite of bread, then a sip from the goblet of wine that stood beside the plate.

She turned to the window and stared out at the magnificent star-bright night.

Else's plea the night she was taken from her home flashed into her mind. *Come to the window, my lady, I beg you. Perhaps you will see a falling star and can make a wish, and all of this will vanish like a bad dream.*

Again the faint shiver of memory ran through her, and a distant song tinkled somewhere in her brain. Her grandmother's spells—something about a falling star and . . . a curse? Had there been something about a curse in that same spell? And dreams . . . coming true . . .

She closed her eyes and felt the gentle stroke of her grandmother's beautiful hands upon her hair, heard that low, witch-husky voice as if it whispered in her ear once again. *Comes the night of a falling star . . .*

No. This time it was different.

Catch yourself a falling star. . . . And love will . . .

The sound of the door opening banished the fragile wisp of memory and everything else except the hot tension that flooded the room as she whirled and saw Ambrose's large frame filling the doorway.

"You slept a long while, Princess."

"I fear not long enough."

Lianna moved from the window, holding her head high, eyeing him with the haughtiness her mother had reserved for the lowest of stableboys. She remembered now what she must do, what she had vowed silently to do when he had carried her back to this keep as his prisoner.

She would aid Constantine in every way possible. She would find a means of ensuring that Ambrose the Barbarian lost everything he craved in the world—and threatened no one ever again.

"You didn't touch your supper." Ambrose stalked into the room and kicked the door closed behind him.

"Supper? Too common a word, my lord," she chided

tightly. "Why, this repast is a veritable feast. I thought prisoners were served up stale bread and water."

"That can be arranged."

She nodded coolly. "Of that I have no doubt."

As his gaze raked her, she became suddenly aware that she wore only a sheer ivory sleeping gown, with pale lemon flowers embroidered upon it. Marthe must have helped her out of her day garments, just as she had helped her into bed. Vaguely Lianna remembered the woman's somber gray face swimming before her, but that was all.

But now it was Ambrose who stood there, studying her, a hard dark gleam in his eyes that Lianna didn't care for. A gleam that made her throat tighten and her own heartbeat race.

With fear, she told herself. *Nothing more.* But a heady excitement like that of too much wine seemed to burst inside her chest.

"I am not well, my lord. If you must lecture me, let it be on the morrow. I am in need of sleep."

"It is not a lecture I had in mind for you, bride." Ambrose came closer. One big hand reached out and captured her hair, twining through the loose, lustrous black curls.

"And you do not look sickly to me. You look quite lovely."

"The aftereffects of my magic—"

"Are gone," he finished for her, his tone taking on a firm note. "It is clear that sleep has refreshed you. Your eyes are as bright and clear as ever, your cheeks delectably flushed. You look as lovely as I have ever seen you."

Lianna caught her breath. "Well, I . . . I . . . have no wish to speak to you at the moment."

"We needn't speak." He took another step forward.

Lianna backed up. "Then good night."

"It will be a good night," Ambrose agreed and advanced again.

Lianna retreated two more steps to counter his forward ones, only to come sharply up against the window embrasure. She gasped as he closed in upon her and seized her by the arms.

"Wait, my lord—"

"Wait?" Ambrose pulled her closer, one muscular arm snaking around her waist. There was a tautness about his mouth, a tension in his powerful limbs, that filled Lianna with a kind of strange and wonderful panic. "For what should I wait, Princess? My battle is over. Sandar is defeated, his ships burned. The keep is safe—for now."

"Then . . . you should celebrate. There is wine . . ."

"I intend to celebrate. With my beautiful—and disobedient—bride." Suddenly he swung her toward the velvet-covered bed and sent her sprawling backward upon it.

Before she could spring up, he was upon her, pinning her beneath him. His eyes gleamed silver in the candlelight and anger stamped his face.

"You may be royal, Lianna, but you are also foolhardy. You might have been killed today if I hadn't returned in time, found you in time. You were told to stay in the keep, to let Sir William guard you, yet you ran off—straight into danger. You were told—no, *forbidden*—to mix potions, yet you were gathering plants and herbs for just that purpose. If it is taming you want and need, Princess, I'll damn well give it to you!"

"Let me go!" Lianna struggled futilely beneath him. He was far too powerful, and though she twisted and writhed and kicked, it was all to no avail. Her hair straggled across her face, her breath came in deep, gasping rasps, but Ambrose held her down easily, his weight pressing her relentlessly into the softness of the bed, his hard face showing no sign of pity for her helplessness.

"If you don't release me right this very moment, I will . . . I will . . ."

"Yes?" Ambrose asked, his lip curling.

She stared up at him, a red film of rage across her eyes. "I will turn you into a worm and mash you up and feed you to a falcon!" she gasped.

He laughed, the sound rumbling clear up to the rafters.

"You dare to laugh? You think I won't?" she fumed, frustrated by a strand of hair that fell and lingered across her eyes.

"You, Lianna, are a healer," he said at last, gazing into her eyes with a piercing intensity that nearly took her breath away. "Not a sorceress. I may be a bastard and not royal-born, but I am not stupid. I saw what you did with that man back there. I heard the spells."

He brushed the wayward lock of hair out of her eyes, smoothing it away from her creamy cheeks.

Lianna stared at him. "Then you know I never planned to use those plants and herbs to concoct any dark potions!"

Her words made sense. He admitted it. No doubt she only wanted to find healing plants, but Ambrose couldn't afford to take chances. Not after what had happened with Madeline.

He resolved to take the herbs and plants she'd gathered to the wise woman of the village, who knew such things, and make certain they could not be used for poisons or potions that addled the senses.

As he stared down at her, still frantically struggling beneath him, he couldn't help but feel a rush of admiration for her courage. She was hopelessly outmatched in this battle, yet she still fought with both her body and her mind.

He hadn't expected to get such a fiery beauty when he'd set his sights on the princess of Penmarren. He needed a royal bride, someone to bring respectability to his title so that his heir might rule in peace one day, without this incessant fighting. He needed someone who could help him to end this vicious curse of war and strife that seemed to shadow all who tried to lay claim to power in this land.

He'd had no personal hopes of a woman who would interest him beyond the usual reasons men were interested in women.

But this one not only interested him—she enticed him. Something his pale, secretive first bride in their very brief marriage never had done.

With her eyes bright as the flowers that grew in the mountains of Blackenstar, her creamy skin and ripe lips that were pinker than sunrise, she was the most sensuous female he'd ever seen. And her velvety hair—how did it happen that it always smelled like roses? Was that some magic, too?

"If you don't stop struggling you'll wear yourself out and be no use to me at all this evening," he told her gruffly and was intrigued to see her lovely eyes shoot sparks of even hotter blue fire.

"Barbarian! I will never stop struggling. If you're going to treat me like a hostage, a prisoner, like a serf here to serve your pleasure, then I will behave like one and fight you with my every breath!"

"I think you would," he growled, meeting her fierce glare with a thoughtful look. "Woman, if you show this much passion when we consummate our marriage vows, you just might tire me out."

But he laughed as he said it and suddenly released her arms. He shifted off her and Lianna shot upright, sweeping her hair back from her face. She sprang off the bed and across the room, her breasts rising and falling in such a way that Ambrose could not take his eyes off her.

He came slowly to his feet. She was magnificent. Slender and elegant in her chemise, which clung to her pretty white breasts and rounded hips. Beautiful, proud, elegant—and frightened. Though she fought to keep from showing it, he saw that behind the sparkle in her eyes there was a tinge of fear. Her lips trembled, though she stood straight and tall—a delicate yet formidable warrior woman.

She would never admit her fear. He could see that. She would rather die than beg him to be gentle.

He had bedded many women in his time, all of them willing—eager, even—for his touch. Yet this one, his bride, feared him, despised him. He knew she considered him beneath her. He wanted suddenly to command her senses, her mind, her body, to melt her ice with fire and have her come eagerly into his arms and his bed.

He went to her, moving slowly so as not to frighten her any more than she already was. He saw her back up apace, then stop herself, no doubt knowing that she couldn't escape him a step at a time.

"Lianna." He reached out and cupped that dainty chin in his fingers, forcing her head up. The candlelight spilled over her, setting her pale skin aglow.

"Be calm. I've no intention of hurting you."

"You already have!"

He raised his brows. "I have not."

She hated to admit it, but it was true. He had curbed his strength carefully and had done her no harm. Yet.

"Perhaps it is your pride that is hurt," he said and ran a finger along the sumptuous curve of her lip.

She trembled all over. And a new fear consumed her as she stared into Ambrose's eyes. He would see that she herself was torn—torn between a strange, heated attraction to him and a desire to flee. Something piercing and brilliant in those silver-gray eyes seemed able to read her soul, her heart.

She struggled for the frosty dignity that would be her only protection.

"I told you once—at the inn—that I know my duty, and I do," she said quickly. "But there is no need to rush into anything, my lord. Is there? You must be fatigued from your battle . . ."

"I am not."

"And perhaps injured . . ."

"Nary a scratch."

"And we scarcely know each other!" she rushed on.

"That can be easily remedied."

He was grinning at her! Lianna's heart flipped over, and she cursed it for a traitor.

She ought to be furious with him at the way he'd treated her tonight, and yet . . .

There was a weakness in her knees that made her actually long to lean into him, to feel his arms snug around her again. Surely, surely, he couldn't read that in her eyes.

"Wait . . . my lord." In desperation, she wrenched away and retreated to the window. Beyond, the darkness gleamed, a half-moon glistened in a pale curve of light, and the stars glittered pure as crystals. "Look at the night. It is so lovely. Perhaps if we gaze out for a while at the moon . . . and the . . . sky . . . we will see a falling star," Lianna chattered, scarcely knowing what she said.

Ambrose pulled her away from the window and into his

arms. "Now why would I care to see a falling star, Lianna, when I can gaze into your eyes?" he said softly.

Her skin burned where he touched her. This odd tingling sensation, the leaping in her heart, had never happened before—not when any of her suitors had touched her, looked at her, complimented her. Confusion warred with panic in her head, and Lianna found herself gazing up at him in desperate appeal.

"Kind w-words, my lord, but . . . they say if you make a wish upon a falling star, it will come true . . ."

"What would you wish for, Lianna? I would know."

"Wish for?"

He nodded, and his hand slid down through her curls, slowly, gently, and cupped her nape. His fingers were strong and warm against her skin, sending delicious shivers down her arms.

"I would wish. . . ." Suddenly the words burst from her. "That you would not stand so close to me . . . or hold me so . . ."

"But you are my lawful wife," he reminded her, his voice low, firm, and not the least bit reassuring. "And you are ready to do your duty. You married me of your own free will and in good faith, and I can do with you as I please. Whatever I please."

She sucked in her breath, every inch of her tensing. "Then I would wish that you were human and not a barbarous monster!"

She tried to pull away from him, but found herself inexorably caught, held, imprisoned by arms far stronger than any that had ever touched her. "I would wish that you would show patience, mercy, understanding, that I could somehow touch your heart . . . if you had a heart!"

"Touch my heart?" He stared down into her eyes, his own glinting with amusement. He leaned closer, his strong, handsome face only inches from hers. "You have a better chance to *catch* a falling star, Lianna, than you do to touch a warrior's heart."

"That, my lord, is obvious," she cried, and kicked at

him, but instead of releasing her, he only grunted, then laughed and tightened his hold.

"Come," he said, and swept her off her feet, cradling her against his chest. "There have been enough words between us this evening. I am a warrior, Lianna, a brute and a barbarian, as you say—and for a man like me, words are of little use. To stay alive, I must act."

He set her down upon the bed, not ungently, but neither did he give her a chance to roll away. Even as she tried to bolt, he pinioned her once again, clasping her wrists above her head, gazing into her eyes with unmistakable determination.

"You have every right," Lianna said between gritted teeth. "So do what you will. For Penmarren's sake, I gladly sacrifice myself to your base needs, your low animal . . ."

She made a moaning sound deep in her throat as his mouth came down upon hers and incinerated her words. And not only her words. Her bones, her blood, her soul. The kiss was deep, roaringly hot, vanquishing.

His mouth worked clever magic. His body pressed her down, down into the velvet covers. And her heart soared as never before when his hands roved over her with strokes of unexpected gentleness.

As if drawn onto a battlefield, Lianna found herself waging a war of heat and desire. Determined to feel nothing, to want nothing from him but to be finished with him and left alone, she found herself swiftly caught up in a maelstrom of emotions so stormy and riotous she could scarcely think. Her arms flung around his neck, she pulled him close, closer, and as his tongue thrust boldly into her mouth, she quivered as if he'd shot an arrow through her. She was kissing him back before she knew what had happened, writhing beneath him, not to escape but to satisfy an exquisite urge that grew more insistent with every touch.

"So beautiful." His lips scorched lightly along her throat. She trembled. "Let me look at you, Lianna." His voice was excitingly deep. "Let me love you."

He leaned back slowly and she sat up, her breath coming in shallow gasps. They gazed into each other's eyes, neither of them able to look away. "I want to see all of you," he said huskily and instead of wishing to flee from those gleaming eyes, Lianna angled forward as he touched a hand to the neckline of her delicate gown.

She shivered as he removed the ivory gown. The warm light of his eyes pleased her, and experimentally, she tossed her head, letting her long sable curls swirl around her shoulders and over her breasts. To her delight, a muscle clenched in Ambrose's jaw, and his eyes darkened to the color of smoke.

"Your turn," she heard herself whisper, amazed by her own boldness. She reached for his tunic and removed it, then gazed at him in wonder.

He was splendid. So splendid. All steel and bronzed muscle, his stomach flat, his chest broad and powerful, furred with soft, dark hair that invited her fingers to touch it.

But even as she did so, she realized that his warrior's patience was wearing thin. He made a growling sound deep in his throat and snatched her to him, tangling his hands in her hair, pressing his mouth against her breast.

Her startled gasp quickly turned to a moan of dizzy pleasure. Sweet sensations such as she had never known swept through her as he laid her down among the silk and velvet pillows and with his roughened hands and seeking mouth set about exploring every tingling inch of her.

Her breasts ached as his palms rubbed against them, building to a slow torment. How could such strength be curbed into such tantalizing gentleness? she wondered as thought buckled beneath waves of pure, sleek pleasure. Pulling him down upon her, closer, ever closer, Lianna pressed wild kisses against his flesh. Reason, time, dignity vanished. There were only Ambrose and her—the two of them alone in the whole wide world, only passion and fire and bliss so sweet her blood sang with it.

Her throat quivered as he stroked it. Gently, surely. Seductively. Flames licked through her. Lianna clutched at him, her own hunger building, building to a consuming arc of fire. The length of her body grew aroused and torturously sensitive as he rained moist, hot kisses upon all its secret places, and she cried out, begging him wordlessly, trem-blingly, to fulfill the promise of those kisses, to relieve the almost painful ache that had begun to rock her with prim-itive need and longing.

He laughed low in his throat and continued to torment her with knowing hands and ruthless mouth. He held her, opened her, took her, inch by inch conquering her body, melting her defenses, storming her soul.

There upon the velvet-covered bed, by firelight and moonlight and starlight, they discovered each other, prin-cess and warrior. They were locked in a sweet, rough battle that was as ancient as the earth and from which there was no retreat.

They waged the battle long and hard into the night—until victory claimed them—a fierce, wild victory sweet-ened with joy. Lianna felt herself exploding again and again, brilliant colors and sensations tearing through her, Ambrose's strong arms and hard thighs clenched her, hold-ing her earthbound while her senses soared and her heart throbbed at his every touch, kiss, and thrust.

He drove her to the brink of madness and sent her top-pling over. She set him afire as he'd never been afire before. He buried his face in her hair, plunged inside her and stormed every battlement. Bodies linked, hearts racing, blood pounding, they wrested shattering fulfillment from each other's arms.

Outside the castle walls, the moon sailed across the sky, the stars winked and glowed. Within Lianna's bedchamber, the fire in the hearth gilded their sweat-slicked skin with palest gold. Spent and shaken, they lay together across the bed, all in a heap, and at last—at long, long last—at peace.

6

CALM AND LIANNA'S senses slowly returned. She became aware that she was entangled with Ambrose, arms and legs entwined, linked, touching so intimately that it was no wonder she still felt the flush of heat.

She felt no urge to move or escape. This alarmed her, and she lifted a hand to her heart. What in heaven's name had come over her?

She had lost her mind, become crazed. Over a *barbarian*.

This wasn't the way it was supposed to happen. She was supposed to have given herself to him with reluctance and silent revulsion. She was not supposed to have enjoyed even one moment of it.

But she had thrown herself into their union with such passionate desire—no, *need*—that a pink blush stole over her naked form as she remembered it.

You hate this man. You loathe him. He forced you to this marriage, he is a bloodthirsty bastard who takes what he wants and lives by the sword and . . .

He made you feel more alive than you ever have before. He made you forget you're a princess and feel like a woman. He made you want him with all of your soul, want him so deeply and powerfully that you gave yourself to him, to this enemy, with abandon—and, may the angels save you—with joy.

She swallowed a cry in her throat and slid off the bed, extricating herself carefully from Ambrose's heavy limbs. Shivering, for the fire had died down, she pulled on her sleeping gown and then lifted her cloak from its peg and wrapped it around her. The star-brooch glinted at her shoulder as she crept to the window and stared out at the purple sky.

She wanted to hate him, this man who had swept her from her home and brought her to this accursed castle. But he was not what she had expected. She remembered how he had laughed at her when she'd fallen off the bed in the inn. The way he'd fought the men who would have harmed her in the forest, killing them with single-minded fury. The way he'd plundered her mouth with sweet kisses and awakened her body to glorious pleasure as they tossed upon the bed like cresting waves across a burning sea.

Her wish—if she had but seen a falling star—would have been to touch his heart. But, heaven help her, he had touched hers.

If she wasn't careful—most careful—she would find herself in love with him.

"No," Lianna whispered, scarcely realizing that she spoke aloud until the next moment, when she heard his voice beside her.

"No, what, Princess?"

How long had she been gazing at nothingness, lost in dreamy thought? She'd never even heard him rouse himself from the bed or don his tunic. As she glanced up at him, so darkly handsome in the dim room, her heart ached, and she searched his somber face for some of the same emotions that she felt.

But she found none. Ambrose looked like the fierce warrior he was—strong, cold, aloof. And in a hurry to be gone.

"I was thinking aloud." Her reply was soft, and she knew that a ridiculous blush was staining her cheeks.

"Oh?" For an instant she thought he was trying to search her mind, as she sought to search his. His gaze settled on her, warming, but then, just as quickly, it grew cool.

"You should return to the bed. The air is chill."

Instead of obeying him, she merely pulled the cloak closer around her.

"Stubborn as always, I see."

He spoke evenly, yet he found himself exerting every measure of self-discipline he possessed to steel himself against the beauty that radiated from her. It smote his heart to gaze at her and remember the feel of her in his arms, the sweet, enticing warmth of her beneath him, the scent of roses and woman that had filled his nostrils as he loved her. If he was not careful, he thought in alarm, he would find himself thinking of her when he had no business to be thinking of anything but the matters at hand. Whether fighting or leading war councils, he could not afford to be distracted by thoughts of a woman—any woman, even one as spectacular as this one.

"I must leave you," he said curtly. If he didn't leave soon, he would carry her to that bed and make love to her again. And again. By all that was holy, he wanted to do just that. "William is to ride out on a scouting mission at first light, and I have need to speak with him before he goes."

Then his gaze fell upon the roots and plants protruding from the pocket of her cloak. Frowning, he snatched them before Lianna could protest.

"There is a crone in the village who knows of the healing arts. She will tell me if these are to be used solely in innocent medicines—or if they could be used for ill purposes as well."

"So you doubt my word?"

"I doubt everyone's word, lady. It is why I still live today."

They had made love to each other in that bed, kissed, touched, held each other in the most intimate of ways, and he doubted her word over a simple matter of herbs?

"What did she do with her plants and herbs, Ambrose?" she asked quietly, her dark hair swaying back from her face as she lifted her eyes to his. "Your first wife—did she try to poison you?"

Anger pulsed through his veins. He set the plants down upon a low table. "How do you know about my wife's dabblings?"

"So it's true, then? Mine was only a guess, since you are so wary of that which I've gathered. But . . ." Lianna took a deep breath. "Is that why you killed her?" she continued, as steadily as she could. Her eyes were glued to his face. "Because she tried to poison you?"

His hands tightened into fists. "So you think it still," he said, his voice low, harsh. "Even after—"

He broke off, his mouth white with anger. Had he been about to say "even after last night"? Lianna would never know, for instead of completing the sentence, he seized her arm.

"You must fear me, then." Granite eyes pierced her. "For if it were true, I could kill you as well. As easily as a hawk swallows a mouse."

"You're trying to frighten me." Lianna spoke calmly, but the slight quaver in her voice gave her away.

"Do you know how she died?" Ambrose asked brutally. "She fell—from the parapet in my bedchamber."

"Fell?" It was a whisper. "Or was pushed?"

"What do you think?"

She stared into that stern, hard face, with its harsh lines and the dark stubble across his jaw. Studying the gray shards of his eyes, she remembered how tender had been his kisses in the night, the care he had taken not to hurt her.

"She fell." The words came from her in a cool, soft breath, edged with certainty.

Ambrose slowly nodded. The tension went out of his shoulders, and a flicker of relief lightened those penetrating eyes.

"Actually," he said, "she jumped."

"Jumped?"

"Madeline became so caught up in her potions and strange medicines—trying to ensure that she would bear my child—that she grew desperate." He sighed, released her arm, and raked a hand through his hair. "Never mind. It doesn't matter."

"Yes, it does matter. Please tell me."

He hesitated, but the urgency in her gaze, and something in her voice, made him sigh again and lead her to the gold-cushioned bench beneath the window. They sat side by side, and as the candles sputtered low, casting pale, glimmering shadows across their faces, he spoke to her in a low, grim tone.

"We were not often together in the three brief months of our marriage. I was called away to battle more than I was home. The nights we spent together were rare and did not result immediately in prospects for a future heir. Madeline was impatient, then she became distressed." Ambrose shook his head. "Her women told me later, when I questioned them, that it was all she could think about, talk about. Our marriage had been arranged, of course, like yours and mine. But unlike you, Lianna, she had been eager for it. She was a quiet, fragile-looking thing, but she was ambitious. She sought the power and glory of being duchess of such a great kingdom as Blackenstar, and she wanted to ensure her position by giving me an heir."

"I understand," Lianna said softly. "Go on." Without thinking, she reached out and touched his hand.

Ambrose jumped as if she'd bitten him, then glanced at her sympathetic face. Slowly he twined his fingers through hers and continued. "The sooner the better, that is how Madeline felt. But when this didn't happen . . ." His mouth twisted. "She sought out the crone in the village who had knowledge of potions that could help a woman in this matter. And she tried them—but to no avail. Then"—his voice hardened—"according to her women, she heard of a gypsy band passing through the village, and she had them brought to her. Madeline questioned one of the gypsy women—all this while I was away fighting my eldest half brother,

Eoric,'' he added darkly, ''and though she was supposedly warned of possible ill effects, she mixed a potion meant to ensure that she would be able to beget a child. But the effects of this potion were powerful—and immediate.''

A silence fell in which the only sounds were the low hiss and sputter of the dying candles. Lianna held her breath, waiting for him to continue. He did, gazing not at her but at the few glinting embers that remained of the fire.

''Madeline became crazed. She ran about, blathering, shrieking, seeing things that were not there. She needed to fly, she said, to get away, and she ran to the parapet. To fly, she screamed. Beorn was here, and even he could not stop her in time . . .''

He broke off.

Lianna squeezed his hand. ''I'm sorry,'' she whispered.

''I didn't love her.'' Ambrose shrugged his massive shoulders. ''As I said, I arranged the marriage much as I did ours. Her father was a count—she was of good stock, wealthy, a fine match—and the count's lands bordered the farthest tip of my southern border. That increased the security of Blackenstar, at least in one tiny corner of this great meandering land. I wanted the marriage for that reason, and though I barely knew her, I would have given my life to protect her.'' He spoke fiercely. ''She was *mine* to protect, like Blackenstar, like this keep.''

Suddenly he surged to his feet and stalked across the chamber.

''Never have I known peace in my own land, Lianna. *Never.*'' He spun about and returned to loom over her. ''Ever since I was a boy, I've had to fight, fight with my half brothers and my cousins over every scrap of food. I fought with them over which horse I'd be riding, which pallet I'd sleep upon, which regiment I'd have the right to lead. We were raised like a pack of dogs—my father encouraged us to hate each other, distrust each other, fight each other, plot against each other—always with the doctrine drummed into our heads that only the strongest can lead, and even from the first, deep down, we all knew we were really fighting over who would one day rule Blackenstar.''

Silent, horrified, Lianna watched his face. She who had grown up under the shadow of her mother's disapproval, yet with every luxury granted her, and those around her who cared for her every wish, tried to imagine the household he described. Her pity grew as his story continued.

"My mother died when I was five. I was the youngest and the smallest. If I hadn't become the toughest I would surely have starved. I very nearly did. But I learned to fight- -oh, yes, I learned it well. Eventually, when my father was killed in battle and Blackenstar went up for grabs, slices of land being tussled over like meaty bones, I went to war with each of my brothers. And they with me.''

"And you won."

He nodded grimly. "So far. But Kenneth and Duncan still have formidable armies and greedy hearts. They are not satisfied with the lands I granted them when we made peace. They will attack again—unless I am so strong, so firmly entrenched as the duke of Blackenstar that they see no hope whatever in challenging me.''

"And that," Lianna spoke softly, "is why you married me.''

She pulled the cloak more tightly around her again, for it was not yet dawn and the room was still chilly.

"If your wife is royal, as royal as can be," she went on quietly, "and you are a strong ruler and fighter, as strong as can be, then few men will question your ability or authority. Or your heir's," she added, and saw him nod.

"You are wise as well as beautiful, Lianna. Yes, it is of my heir that I think. I'd never want my child to go through what I have—forced to fight continuously for what is his, never knowing a time of peace in which to build and let the land and the people prosper. My people have already endured year after year of turmoil and war.''

He reached out an arm and pulled her to her feet, his eyes riveted on hers. "With you by my side, no one will dare question me. I'll wear the mantle of the warrior duke, the Barbarian, and fight all I must, but I hope that by the time my son is grown, he can turn his attention to making the land and the people—and the House of Blackenstar—great and prosperous. And peaceful. I might be a bastard, but my son will be a true-born ruler of men, descended from a line of kings. Then I can end this damned curse—''

"Curse? So there is a curse?"

"Surely you know the tale."

A shiver danced down her spine. "Well, I knew the rumors. And then I felt it—I felt it in the walls the first moment I set foot inside the keep."

His eyes glittered. "They say that Morgan le Fey cursed the keep in a fit of rage after Merlin himself paid her a visit here—and warned her to keep her evil magic far from King Arthur. I don't say that I believe it, but there does seem to be something, something that prevents Blackenstar from ever knowing peace, something that keeps us in turmoil, always fighting, with those of us who share the same blood remaining enemies instead of becoming allies."

Faintly her grandmother's voice whispered in her head, pure and musical as the notes of a harp: *Comes the night of a falling star . . .*

"I must go." Abruptly the intimate mood was gone. Dawn was breaking over the mountains of Blackenstar, delicate streaks of lilac and peach hazed with gold lightening the horizon. Banishing the stars. And Ambrose was no more the bold lover, nor the surprising confidant. He was all warrior. He released her arm, scowling, and swung toward the door.

"Beorn will guard you henceforth."

"I don't care for Beorn and I don't need a guard."

"Would that that were true." Ambrose eyed her from the door. "If in the following days you cause no further trouble, I'll allow you to send for your ladies-in-waiting and will provide an escort for them."

He opened the door, then suddenly remembered the plants. He stalked to the low table where he'd set them and stared down at them as Lianna watched, her stomach clenching.

Then, without a word, he spun about and left.

Was this a sign of trust? Lianna wondered, as she gazed after him in confusion. Had something changed between them?

Everything had changed between them.

Everything she thought and felt about Ambrose the Barbarian, and about Blackenstar, was not as it had been before.

Except for one thing.

Constantine was still coming—to destroy this keep and the duke who had spent his whole life fighting for it.

And she must stand by and watch.

7

LIANNA SPENT THE next few days in a state of wonder, doubt, and bewilderment. Each time she saw Ambrose, her pulse quickened, her heart leapt. How could this be?

Tormented, she tried to avoid him. She visited the village—accompanied by and closely watched by Beorn, per Ambrose's orders—where all the people she encountered watched her in awe, and she found that contrary to hating and fearing Ambrose, the people there respected him and wished him well on his marriage.

"Now, if Master Eoric had become duke of Blackenstar, we'd be in a sad pickle," one old woman huffed as she leaned on a rough bark stick. "He was always a vicious boy. But Duke Ambrose, though he be as fierce in battle as they come, is fair and has a care for the rest of us. I hope you give him many fine sons, my lady," she told Lianna before bowing past and going on her way.

In the keep, preparations began for a great feast. Ambrose wished to celebrate their marriage with a grand ball and had invited all the nobles, gentry, and villagers to join in the festivities. The serving maids scurried this way and that, polishing, scrubbing, airing, dusting, and in the kitchens the cook and Marthe and countless others toiled night and day.

Lianna supervised and approved all of the food for the feast—there would be mutton and venison and sauced duckling, sweetmeats, and honey cakes and fruit, and dark, soft bread and silver goblets brimming with spiced wine.

She managed to see little of Ambrose during the days and found her heart heavy for it. But each midnight, when the stars glimmered and the silver moon sailed across the tranquil sky, he came to her chambers. Always there was that strange distance between them, the moments of unease and jousting with their words, and then they would come together, and he would kiss her, touch her hair with gentle fingers, and it would all begin again—the strange magic he worked on her, the undoing of all her resolve to despise him. Her heart opened like a flower and her body burned at his touch, and she couldn't hate him. And she was certain from the way he held her, stroked her, gazed at her with those keen eyes, that he did not in the least hate her.

So she found that though she did not hate him, *could* not hate him, she couldn't love him either, Lianna told herself on the fourth morning as she swallowed a crust of bread, nibbled at a bit of cake, and turned her attention to dressing for the day.

He was known far and wide as a ruthless enemy, she reminded herself, a fierce warrior who showed no mercy, a bloodthirsty fiend feared by the weak and the powerful alike.

Yet now she knew that the rumors were not all to be believed, that Ambrose fought only to hold the vast kingdom that was his, that he was as much a victim of his enemies as her father had been of Ambrose himself.

And then, the day before the ball, the moment she had begun to dread arrived.

The message came.

It came as Marthe was dressing her hair for dinner, coiling it into a tight coronet atop her head. Lianna glanced up at the knock upon the door, and when a towheaded page entered, he bowed low.

"My lady, two knights have arrived from the court of King Penmarren. One of them wishes to present himself before you. The duke received him before riding out to the hunt, and he has given leave. The knight bade me tell you he brings news of your father and of your homeland and begs for an audience."

Her heart stopped. Lianna stared at the youth, unable to utter a word.

"My lady?"

"Yes, yes. I will see him. Tell him I shall meet with him in the garden." Lianna jumped up from the velvet bench before Marthe could wind the gold ribbons through her hair. With her amber silk gown rustling, she snatched her cloak from its peg and rushed to the door, then reminded herself that she was a princess and a duchess and she should walk with dignity and grace. It had been many years since she had forgotten that lesson.

Ambrose, what have you wrought? she thought in frustration. She deliberately slowed her steps and straightened her shoulders, aware that Beorn, who had been stationed near her door, followed at a discreet distance.

But she was bursting with impatience by the time she reached the great hall. She headed toward the corridor that led to the kitchens and the garden, but was stopped by the peddler and his wife, who called to her when she would have hurried past.

Despite her impatience, she paused to greet them, noting that the man was nearly well and would be able to travel soon.

"Bless you, my lady." The woman curtsied low before her, but Lianna raised her, smiled, and wished them good health.

She reached the garden at last, hoping that here at least she would have an opportunity to talk with the knight in private. Beorn would be near, but she would request him to stand back a little distance. So long as he saw that she could not flee into the woods or toward some possible danger, he would not impose himself closer. Or so she hoped. It seemed to her that Beorn disliked her as much as she disliked him. So he would guard her, but from afar.

The winter garden was gloomy and gray—the stone benches, urns empty of blooms, the shrubs and trees naked and shivering in the light wind that blew down from the north. Beyond and to her right, the sea churned and crested and roared, and the salt tang of it filled her nostrils as she wandered the pathways, searching for her father's man.

He appeared from down a tree-lined path. Sir Gryford had guarded her father's litter when last he had been carried into battle. Middle-aged, paunchy now, and dark-bearded, he came toward her, limping slightly from a wound he had suffered in that same battle.

"My lady, it gives me joy to see you are well." He knelt and kissed her hand, but Lianna quickly raised him. She searched his face. Even here, where they seemed to be alone, she knew they could not speak freely.

To be overheard would spell disaster—and certain death.

"My father—is he well? And Meeg?"

He assured her of their good health and good wishes. "And Constantine, my cousin?" Lianna asked with as much casualness as she could muster.

She held her breath waiting for his reply.

"He is well and strong. He has returned from his journey and is eager to serve your father in every way."

"How good of him." Lianna clutched her cloak more tightly around her as her blood turned to ice. Constantine was back, and Gryford had come to tell her that the attack was imminent.

"Let us . . . walk a little through the garden," she managed to say through trembling lips, and then glanced over at Beorn, who stood watching from beneath the bare branches of an ancient, gnarled tree.

"I am well guarded by my father's man—and cannot possibly escape the gates," she said to Beorn. "You needn't follow me like a nursemaid if there is other business you might attend to."

She expected him to assert his orders to stay close by her at all times, but to her surprise, he saluted. ''Aye, my lady, there is a matter I need to see about, and you're in no danger here. The duke won't mind if I loosen the leash just for a little while. But take care—if you play any tricks, it will come down on both of our heads.'' A grin spread across his scarred, fleshy face, and then he turned and stalked back toward the bailey with swift strides.

''My lady, come, let us walk. This way.'' Gryford gripped her arm and began leading her purposefully toward the rocky path that wound out of the garden, toward the craggy cliffs and paths that bordered the sea.

She followed silently, her heart tight in her chest. All she could think was that Constantine was coming and battle was near, and a vision of Ambrose fighting that massive army within the borders of his precious Blackenstar weighed upon her like a boulder.

But her thoughts were interrupted when Gryford suddenly veered from the path and led her higher, toward the towering cliff that overlooked that dangerous winter sea.

''Quick, my lady. This way. Ahead, past those trees, behind the rocks, there is Emmett with our horses. Two horses, his and mine. I'll stay behind—he is to take you at once to Constantine.''

Lianna heard a sound behind her and looked back in alarm, but saw nothing, no one, except a crow lift from the branch of a furze bush and soar toward the tower of the keep.

''But what of you, Sir Gryford?'' she asked as she breathlessly picked her way up a rocky path tangled with dead brush and stones.

''I'll hide myself until the battle commences and I can serve your father and Constantine from here within the keep. Don't you fret about me, Princess—it's you we must get safe away, lest the Barbarian use you as a hostage once he learns what is afoot.''

He's not a barbarian, she wanted to cry, but she held her tongue. ''Tell me, Sir Gryford, where am I to meet

Constantine? And when—and where—is he planning to stage the attack?''

''He is marching on Blackenstar even as we speak. He will await you on the Hill of Rivalen to take you into safety. If all goes as planned, the battle will commence tomorrow at dawn.''

Dawn. Only this very dawn, she had been lying in Ambrose's arms while his lips trailed kisses across her shoulder. Tomorrow, he would be at war with her cousin and her father. The keep would be under siege.

''No. *No!*''

''What, my lady? What is amiss?'' The aging knight was as out of breath as she. They paused at the crest of a cliff that overlooked the wild sea, and he turned to her, studying her drawn, pale face, the wide, panicked eyes. ''Do not fear, Princess. You will be far and away—safe from the battle,'' he assured her.

''I don't want a battle, Sir Gryford. There must not be any attack. I must go to Constantine and stop him!''

''Stop him?'' Sir Gryford gaped at her, thunderstruck. ''But the Barbarian took you from Penmarren, forced you to—''

''I won't leave him. I won't have him fighting Constantine or my father or anyone!'' *I love him,* she thought, but she bit back the words. How could she tell Sir Gryford this when she had not yet told Ambrose? She had only just discovered it herself.

''Come, we must hurry and reach Constantine before Ambrose discovers something.'' Frantic, she grasped his arm. ''He has spies everywhere, and if he were to learn of this, he would be certain I had betrayed him—''

Suddenly a tall figure sprang out from the rocks behind her, knocking her aside. With a cry, Lianna found herself sprawled across the rough path, and then she saw Beorn hurling himself straight at Sir Gryford. The knight never had a chance. Beorn drove a knife through his heart as Lianna screamed. The sound echoed round and round, and before it had faded, Beorn yanked his knife out and dragged the knight to the precipice of the cliff. As Lianna watched in frozen horror, he threw Sir Gryford into the icy green waters far below.

Stunned and sick, Lianna struggled to her knees. Beorn spun back from the edge of the cliff and came toward her, his face wearing a triumphant sneer.

"*That* takes care of *that*, my lady," he said pleasantly. He was deadly calm, scarcely out of breath. The sun glinted off his bright gold hair. "Now it's time to take care of you."

Marthe's scream was a hoarse, rusty sound that grated through every corner of the kitchen. The peddler and his wife, eating bread and cheese at the table, stared in terror at the serving woman who stood at the door, her mouth open, and terrible low keening sounds emerging as though she were gazing at the devil. Half a dozen other servants stood rooted to the spot, petrified that the woman who had never uttered so much as a whisper had let out that blood-curdling scream.

The peddler's wife was the only one to move. She rushed to the door. "What? What is it?" she demanded.

Marthe lifted an arm and pointed.

When the woman looked up, she could just make out the rocky outcropping where someone—a dark-haired woman in blue—lay sprawled upon the ground. And at the same time, she saw a huge broad-shouldered man toss another man into the sea.

"It's my lady! That's her—up there!" she shrieked.

A commotion began in the kitchen, an uproar of shouts, prayers, questions—with everyone shoving toward the door. Suddenly Duke Ambrose strode into their midst.

"What goes on here?"

"My lord!" The peddler's wife stumbled toward him and fell to her knees. "I beg you—my lady is in danger!"

"What are you talking about, woman? Do you mean my wife?" Ambrose grabbed her arm and dragged her to her feet. "Where? Where is Lianna?"

"Upon the . . . ground . . . my lord." It was Marthe who answered him, slowly, in a rasping whisper, each word a struggle. He turned in shock to stare at her. "The . . . cliff—up there . . . a man . . . *hurt* her. He . . . killed the man . . . threw him over . . ."

Ambrose's skin turned ashen. Fear churned through him, stronger than any emotion he'd ever known. "Where, Marthe? Show me where, damn it!"

The peddler's wife rushed back to the doorway. "There—she was there! You see? The gray rocks, above the gardens—I saw it, too—the man who threw the other into the sea—"

She broke off, trembling, lifting terrified eyes to the duke.

Ambrose's keen stare raked the cliffside. His blood froze in his veins. No one was there.

8

"Y OU'RE MAD."

"Mad, is it? Think what you want, Princess. I know exactly what I'm doing."

Beorn suddenly dragged her off the path he'd taken and pushed her across a small ledge toward what she saw was the entrance to a cave.

"This is where you'll be staying until all the fighting's done. Then the new duke of Blackenstar will be back to claim you." His mouth curled into a smile. "As a royal bride, you'll serve me every bit as well as you did Ambrose."

"You think that *you* are going to become the new duke of Blackenstar?" Lianna's throat closed with horror. "You mean to kill Ambrose, don't you?" she whispered, a sick panic washing through her.

"I wouldn't put that fine a point on it," Beorn growled. "I only mean to see to it that he dies in this battle with Constantine—one way or another. Ah, yes, my lady." Beorn's lips curled into an ugly smile. "I followed you and that old knight, heard most every word. This attack planned

160

by Prince Constantine—it'll serve me. Aye, it'll serve me damned well."

"Traitor," she whispered, her fists clenching at her sides.

Beorn shrugged. "It's his own fault—naming William captain-of-arms instead of me. He granted William land and a title. Not me. I've served him nearly thrice as long, and this is the way I'm rewarded? Assigned to protect both of his wives, a lady's guard." He snorted contemptuously, but beneath the scorn there was raw fury blazing in his eyes.

Her arms were bruised where he had grabbed her, held her helpless as he'd forced her away from the cliff and along another twisted path that wound back into the mountain along the coast and near the cave. If only she could get past him, back to the path. She could scream, try to rouse the attention of the guards, or someone at the castle, though the roar of the sea and the squawking of the crows might well drown out her cry. But as Beorn pulled a length of rope from the pocket of his heavy green cloak, she shrank back.

"You can't tie me up and leave me here, cave or no. I'll freeze!"

"That's a chance we'll have to take, won't we, my lady?"

He advanced on her.

"Why?" Lianna forced herself to hold her ground, to stand firm as he approached, swaggering a little in his eagerness.

"Why must you betray Ambrose in this way? If you want recognition for all of your service, I can help you. I'll speak to Ambrose on your behalf. He'll listen to me."

"Aye, he'll listen to you. He has a soft spot for you, that he does." The gold-haired soldier nodded, his voice thick with contempt. "Not like that other one, the poor stupid wench."

"Madeline?"

"It's her fault, all this." Beorn grimaced. "If she hadn't taken those potions and gone mad like she did—trying to fly off the parapet—I'd have been captain-of-arms instead of William. Ambrose held me accountable for her dying.

He didn't say it." His eyes glittered. Black rage thrummed through his voice. "But I know he did."

"That's not true—he would have told you if it were. He thinks highly of you. He set you to guard me. He wouldn't have entrusted you with the care of another wife if he didn't trust you. After all, I escaped Sir William only days ago. He has not been faulted—"

"You didn't die after escaping the guard of Sir William," Beorn snarled. "If you had, it would have gone badly for him."

"But now . . . if I disappear," Lianna rushed on desperately, "Ambrose will hold you responsible once again. You were set to guard me today. He'll question you. You can't possibly get away with—"

"I'll tell him that your father's men overpowered me and ran off with you. By then, word of the coming attack might well have reached him, and he'll realize you betrayed him."

"I haven't!"

Beorn continued as though she hadn't spoken. "He won't want you back, my lady," he said softly. "He'll want you dead. Along with Constantine—and your father. Ambrose doesn't like betrayal." His green eyes shone. "You ought to be glad. It will make Constantine's job easier for it. Ambrose never was one to let himself get tied in knots over a woman, not him—not even when Madeline died, much as he regretted that. But he will, I would wager, get tied in knots over you. He'll be distracted in battle, as he's never been before. And I'll see to it that he finds himself in harm's way, with men loyal to me surrounding him, men who will let him be outnumbered and fall."

"How can you hate him so?"

"I didn't always hate him," Beorn told her, lifting the rope, stepping closer. "I admired him. Until he promoted William over me. Until he went soft—over you."

Suddenly he ripped the star-brooch off her cloak and clenched it in his fist. "He wore this always. *Always.* A symbol of Blackenstar. Until he brought you here. When he gave you this brooch, as a symbol that you were under his protection, I knew something had changed with him. He never gave it to Duchess Madeline. He cared for you even then, when you first reached Blackenstar. More so now. I've seen it when he looks at you. You are his weakness. Now you are my hostage.'' His lip curled. ''And soon you'll be my bride. You, my lady, will help me forge a treaty with Constantine and with Penmarren, and then you will remain by my side, adding legitimacy to my reign.''

Lianna snatched the brooch back from him, holding it tight within her hand. ''I'd rather jump into the sea and sink beside Sir Gryford than help you in any way!''

''No, my lady, you would not. For if you don't cooperate with me, your precious father will die. And that nurse you're so fond of. I have men in place inside Penmarren even now,'' he sneered. ''On my orders they'll kill those you hold dear. Only if you do my bidding will they be safe.''

A red fog swirled before her eyes. She struggled to remain calm, to think clearly. ''Monster!'' she gasped. Her hand plunged into her cloak pocket for her dagger, but Beorn only laughed aloud. ''Drop it to the ground,'' he ordered. ''If you don't obey me, I'll send word for those you love to be killed.''

She gripped it still.

''Drop it now.'' His scarred face flushed. ''The duke might have patience for you, Princess, but I do not. If you don't value their lives . . .'' He shrugged.

Biting back a sob, Lianna dropped the dagger. It clattered down among the rocks.

Suddenly there was a great noise below. Horses, shouts.

Then Ambrose's voice rang out—he sounded as if he were on a path nearby, just below the cave.

''Lianna!'' The urgency of his tone sent a sharp wave of love through her. ''Lianna—answer me!''

In a flash, Beorn had her imprisoned, his huge hand pressed against her mouth, preventing her from crying out, while his other arm clamped her body to his. Uselessly she struggled to free herself, but was unable to budge him.

"Duchess Lianna!" Another voice called out, more distant.

And another. "Are you hurt? Duchess Lianna!"

The shouts of Ambrose's knights drifted to her above the frenzied roar of the sea, and tears stung her eyes at her helplessness to answer.

Then Ambrose's voice came again—he sounded as if he were now directly below the ledge, on the path that wound around the cliff.

"Lianna!"

She heard the fear, the desperation underlying his commanding tone, and her heart broke in two.

Suddenly she remembered the star-brooch clenched in her fist. With all her strength she hurled it toward the tip of the ledge that overhung the path. It struck a rock, rolled, then tumbled over the edge, glittering in open space for one heart-stopping moment before it disappeared from sight.

Ambrose heard a slight clatter and glanced up. A small glimmering rock hurtled down toward him. On instinct, his arm shot out and caught the shining stone.

Only it wasn't a stone. It was a star. The star-brooch he had given to Lianna.

His mouth grim, he wheeled his destrier toward the path leading to the upper ledge, dropping the brooch into his pocket.

Sounds of a scuffle reached him as he drew near, and he spurred the destrier on. Reaching the path, he saw Lianna struggling mightily as Beorn attempted to drag her into a cave.

"Release her!" He was already swinging out of the saddle, striding toward them. "What the devil are you doing, Beorn? You were set to guard her, not to—"

Only then did he see the stark terror upon Lianna's face.

"What have you done to her?" Ambrose's stride quickened. His eyes were dark as thunder. "If you've hurt her, I'll kill you."

But before he could reach them and tear Lianna from the soldier's grasp, Beorn hurled the woman away, straight at

Ambrose. Ambrose caught her and held her steady.

"You dare treat my bride this way? Beorn, have you gone mad?"

He glanced down at Lianna, trembling like a spring leaf in his arms. "Whatever has happened," he said in a quiet, soothing tone, "I will make him pay. Stand aside now while I deal with him—"

He broke off as he saw that Beorn had drawn his sword. With his face taut and determined, the gold-haired soldier advanced.

"Deal with me, Ambrose? You think *you* shall deal with me? I, my lord duke, am going to deal with *you*. I've been wanting to do this ever since you passed me over for captain-of-arms. This isn't exactly the way I had planned things, but it will give me great pleasure to run you through here and now."

Ambrose thrust Lianna behind him and regarded the other man with steely eyes. "So you were the traitor. I thought of others, Beorn. Never you." His sigh was heavy. "You alerted Sandar when I went to Penmarren. You told him how my troops were dispersed, where and when we might be vulnerable to attack. Tell me, what did he promise you?"

"He promised me captain-of-arms of his whole army, for one thing—but that's not all. The kingdom of Pye for my own!" Beorn bragged.

"Too bad he failed. But even if he hadn't, you're not going to be alive long enough to have enjoyed any of it."

"Don't count on that." Beorn gripped his sword tighter. "I am a match for you, whether you know it or not. I know your skill, your great skill," he mocked, "and I'm not afraid to fight you. You'll be afraid before we're done. But first there is something you should know," he added slyly. "Your lovely bride has been conspiring with your enemies. Even now an army is marching on Blackenstar."

"No!" Stepping up beside Ambrose, Lianna clutched at his cloak. "I did not conspire! Not . . . exactly. I can explain . . ."

She broke off, her heart sinking at the expression on his

face. Shock. Pain. And then a coldness unlike anything she had ever seen. His gaze flicked back and forth between her and Beorn, sharp as a hawk.

"Ambrose, let me but explain," she begged. "There is not much time."

"That's true. Even as we speak, her cousin, Prince Constantine of Wyborn, is coming to rescue her from the barbarian duke of Blackenstar!" Beorn's mouth twisted. "She would see you dead. And now, yes, indeed she will—but not at Constantine's hand. At mine!"

He lunged forward so swiftly that Lianna screamed.

In a blink Ambrose thrust her aside and drew his sword. Even as Beorn closed in, Ambrose swung the glittering blade. The swords clashed. Beorn laughed.

Lianna gasped as she watched Ambrose cut his sword again, even more fiercely, at the soldier.

They fought ruthlessly. Single-mindedly. Grunting, dodging, charging, parrying with blinding speed. The blades glittered in the sunlight, and Lianna watched in horror as Beorn's thrust nearly went home, and then Ambrose drove forward with impossible strength and dizzying speed, and only narrowly missed running the gold-haired soldier through.

The sun dipped and faded in the graying winter sky, the crows flapped their great black wings and squawked, and the two men struggled and grunted and circled one another on the rocky ledge high above the sea. Ambrose fought with savage, dazzling skill and a strength that would have terrified any other man, while Beorn thrust and parried with a rough-edged skill every bit as ruthless and unrelenting.

It ended as suddenly as it had begun. A mighty thrust, a groan, blood spurting like a fountain. Beorn toppled over, sprawling across the ledge, his green eyes staring sightlessly toward the heavens as Ambrose slid his bloodied sword out of his enemy's chest.

Slowly Ambrose turned to Lianna.

"You're hurt." She started toward him, distraught by the blood staining his cloak, but he pushed her away.

"Is it true, Lianna? What he said? Did you conspire against me?"

"Yes." There was a dull roaring in her ears. A crushing anguish in her heart. Never had she seen such pain as she saw now upon his lean, handsome face. "But it isn't what you think," she rushed on, her voice trembling. "I knew that Constantine was raising an army . . ."

"*Duke Ambrose!*" A flame-haired knight on a gray horse charged into the clearing. "A scout has just ridden in from the west country. A great army is on the march—making its way, he believes, toward the Hill of Rivalen. A thousand men, armed to the hilt, with giant horses and—"

The knight broke off, staring in stupefaction at Beorn's bloodied form and then at the tall, hard-eyed duke.

"Call every man to arms. We will assemble at Lansdowne Point and stop them there. Send word to Masson in the south and to the troops quartered in the Low Country." Ambrose fired off his orders in a tone of deadly calm. "We ride within the hour."

He wiped his bloodied sword on his cloak. When the man continued to stare at him as if dazed, Ambrose shouted, "Ride, man! Ride!"

The knight disappeared in a spray of small stones, and Ambrose returned the sword to its scabbard and silently mounted his horse. Her heart breaking into a thousand pieces at the sight of his grim, weary face, the heaviness of his shoulders, Lianna stumbled forward.

"Wait. Ambrose, please. Wait! I can explain."

"Explain? There is no need. You have what you want, Princess. This might well mean the destruction of the House of Blackenstar. You can go home to Penmarren and leave us to be picked apart by the crows and whatever other scavengers happen by. But I vow it will not happen while I still breathe," he growled, a terrible icy fury claiming his features.

A sob broke from Lianna, but Ambrose wheeled his horse away, and even as the horn sounded from far below, trumpeting the alarm, and the clamor to arms began in the bailey and all through the keep, he charged down the path toward the soldiers gathering in the yard. It was her last glimpse of him—a tall, strapping giant sitting straight in the saddle, galloping away from her and toward the coming battle.

9

"HELP ME, SIR Emmett! Quick, help me to mount that horse!"

Lianna flew toward the young knight from her father's court as he stared at her in astonishment, scarcely recognizing the dignified princess he had known in Penmarren. Her hair had tumbled down from its stiff coronet, her face was streaked with tears and dirt, and the hem of her gown was torn.

"Princess Lianna—what are you doing—"

"Help me!" Lianna commanded as she skidded to a halt before Sir Gryford's dun. Frantic, she sprang into the saddle with the knight's assistance and spurred the horse forward, leaving the stunned knight to vault onto his mount and follow as best he could.

"But where is Sir Gryford?" he called after her.

"Dead," Lianna called back. "Dead!"

It was a blur to her, the mad dash down the perilous slopes, across the bailey, through the gates. The gates had already been raised while Ambrose's men hoisted their

169

banners, gathered their armor, and prepared to ride out, and the guards manning the portcullis merely stared in shock at the princess and the knight who flew after her.

Back in the courtyard, Ambrose stared after the dark-haired girl on the huge destrier as she galloped like the wind away from the keep.

His eyes followed her, wasting precious seconds as he memorized that slim, lovely figure riding hard as a soldier on an urgent mission.

A terrible pain assailed him, a pain unlike any he had ever known. Only his tremendous self-discipline overcame the grief that rent him, and he tore his gaze from his fleeing bride at last and turned his attention to the men under his command.

"To Lansdowne Point!" he shouted. The world was a bleak, ugly, faithless place, but he could not escape his duty. Or his fate.

He spurred his destrier toward the gate as horses sidled, banners lifted, swords smote the air, and with one shout, one voice that roared through woods and cliffs alike, his men surged in a faceless sea behind him.

It was nightfall when Lianna and Sir Emmett neared the Hill of Rivalen. She was by now too weary and weak even to glance at her surroundings, and she heard as if from a great distance her companion whistle, then whistle again. As if conjured up from the very air, a troop of ten men materialized through the trees, closing around them.

"The princess of Penmarren seeks the refuge of her cousin, Prince Constantine," the young knight barked to the fierce, heavy-bearded men.

Warriors, Lianna noted with a shiver. They had the tough and seasoned look of formidable men, a true match for even Ambrose's experienced troops. Her throat was thick with silent sobs, her heart heavy as the darkening sky.

She was escorted to a tent at the crest of the hill and ushered inside.

Constantine, golden-haired, strong, fit, and handsome, hurried to embrace her.

"Cousin! I am sorry to see you looking so weary. Are you ill? You're shaking," he said sharply. "You must be starved. There's bread and soup . . ."

"No, Constantine, nothing. I want nothing—only your ear. You must listen to me!"

"Yes, Lianna, I shall. But first you must sit. And eat. You're trembling."

He drew her in, tried to pour her wine and offered her bread, but Lianna clutched at his tunic and demanded that he be silent.

"There is no time. You must call off this battle. And come with me now to find Ambrose—to help me explain."

Constantine's thin face puckered in concern. "Have you gone mad, Lianna? Yes, I shall find Ambrose. At dawn. We will converge, his army and mine, and I will teach him not to threaten my uncle and steal my cousin . . ."

"No." Through a swimming weariness and despair, Lianna's determination rose. She pushed her wild hair out of her eyes and seized Constantine's arm. "No, no battle! I don't want this war. I don't want to return to Penmarren. I love Ambrose." The words rushed out, frantic and fevered. "I love him, do you hear me? You must come with me—not to fight him—but to make peace!"

Constantine stared down at her pale, desperate face, stunned into silence.

"Peace? With the Barbarian?" he asked at last, incredulously, and then caught her as she swooned, falling straight into his arms.

In the thickest, blackest hours of the night, the small party reached the pass that led to Lansdowne Point. Once they had traveled the narrow pathway cutting through the hillside, they would come to an open plain in sight of where Ambrose's men were encamped.

There were few sounds, save the hooting of an owl and the scurrying of unseen creatures in the dense brush. A light snow began to fall as Lianna and Constantine, Sir Emmett, and five of Constantine's soldiers rode silently along the narrow track beneath moon and stars.

It was just as they emerged upon the plain that the night exploded with the sounds of charging horses, and danger suddenly vibrated through the frosty air.

A dozen men surrounded them, swords drawn, glistening in the silvered moonlight. Drawing in her breath, Lianna found herself gazing into her husband's cold, furious face.

"Ambrose," she managed to whisper, a catch in her throat.

Constantine had forced her to eat a few morsels before they'd departed, but the strain and exertion of the day and the long, arduous hours in the saddle had left her weak and aching.

But there was hope and determination in her face when she gazed across her horse's graceful head at the tall warrior before her, sitting his destrier with such unconscious grace.

"I must speak to you."

"There is nothing for either of us to say." He spoke over his shoulder then to William, one of the dozen knights. "Take this woman to the camp and guard her well. She is my hostage now."

But before William could spur his mount forward, Lianna slipped down from the saddle and ran toward Ambrose's destrier.

"My lord, I won't go with him. I must speak with you—alone. We come in peace—"

"Peace!" He gave a fierce bark of laughter.

"William, take her away from here before I can no longer be responsible for what I do. I can't bear the sight of her!"

The words cut her to the quick, and Lianna choked back a cry. Her eyes pleading, she reached up to try to touch him, implore him, but he wheeled his horse away from her so abruptly that she stumbled.

Instantly Constantine vaulted from his saddle and was at her side. "You *are* nothing but a damned barbarian," he said to Ambrose as he steadied Lianna, slipping an arm around her waist. "I told her it was no use trying to—"

Before he could finish, Ambrose had leapt to the ground,

grabbed him by the throat, and shoved him up against a tree.

"My only question is should I kill you here and now, or wait until full battle begins." His voice was a murderous snarl. Suddenly the tip of his sword pressed ever so lightly against the prince's throat.

"Ambrose—no!" In vain Lianna tried to pull him off Constantine, but she may as well have tried to uproot an oak. "Listen to me. He comes in peace! Please, if you'd only listen to me—"

But even as she tried to pull Ambrose off Constantine, her cousin suddenly shoved him back with a flashing burst of strength. The next instant, Constantine's sword hissed out, and the two men faced each other, both of them white-lipped with fury. Every man present drew his sword and eyed his enemy.

An eerie silence filled the air. Lianna's heart thudded as the twin scents of danger and death wafted about her.

One last time she tried to reach the man who held her heart, who owned it forever, if only he knew.

"Ambrose, stop being . . . such a fool. I never wanted . . . this. I knew about the army, yes, but that was *before*. Before I came to Blackenstar, before I fell in love with you—I wish you could only know how much I love you . . ."

He spun toward her, a stunned expression in his eyes. But at that same instant Constantine lunged, his sword swinging in a deadly arc straight at Ambrose.

"No!" Seeing the danger, Lianna hurled herself forward, knowing only that she had to protect Ambrose from the deadly blow. Constantine cursed and tried to turn aside the thrust, but the blade slashed through her cloak, and she gasped as the point pierced her flesh.

Lianna went down in a heap, darkness swimming before her dazed eyes. Pain burned at her shoulder, and warm, sticky blood flowed down her arm, soaking her gown and cloak.

"By all the saints! Lianna! Lianna, no!" Ambrose swept her up from the stony earth and cradled her like a doll in his arms. As long as he lived he would never forget the sight of her taking the blow that had been intended for him. Her face was still and white, whiter even than the snow that fell so lightly, like wisps of lace, melting upon her cheeks and eyelashes.

Constantine stood frozen. The sword fell from his numb hand. "Cousin!" His blue eyes blazed with a stark fear. "May the devil strike me blind, I never meant to hurt you."

"Of course . . . you didn't. My father . . . would be most . . . displeased," she managed to mutter with a bleary smile, but her glazed eyes were trying to focus upon Ambrose, upon his handsome face, ashen now in the starlight, his gray eyes studying her with undisguised fear and shock.

"Don't worry, my . . . lord . . . my . . . love. It is . . . nothing . . . it would take more than a simple wound to make me leave you," she whispered, and, reaching up, gently touched his beloved face.

Ambrose couldn't speak. Tears scratched at his eyes. Still cradling her, he tore off her cloak and tossed it on the ground, then carefully lowered her upon it. He ripped her gown at the shoulder to reveal the wound, and his shoulders sagged with relief as he saw that it wasn't deep, certainly not fatal. As Constantine came forward to clutch Lianna's hand, Ambrose ripped a wide strip from his own cloak and began to bind up the wound, as gently as he could, despite her slight moans and grimaces.

"We came here . . . Constantine and I . . . to stop the battle . . ."

"Quiet. Don't try to talk now. Save your strength."

Lianna felt herself sinking into dizziness and a thin, dark fog. The wound, the shock of it—added to her weariness from the grueling ride and her tormented heart—was exacting a toll. She felt herself weakening, slipping away. She fought to focus upon Ambrose's face.

"Listen to me . . ."

"No. Be silent. It doesn't matter, Lianna."

"Constantine, tell him . . ." she begged, even as she closed her eyes, letting the heavy blackness take her.

Dimly, through her faint, she heard Constantine begin to

tell Ambrose that they had indeed come in peace, that Lianna had ridden to the army's encampment and begged Constantine to call off the attack.

"She convinced me that she wants to remain with you. To remain the duchess of Blackenstar. I had gathered an army to rescue her, but she would barely take time to eat a single bite of bread—that though she was weary of riding all through the afternoon and evening. She wanted only to bring me to you . . . to explain to you . . ."

His words rose, fell, faded. In their place came the fairy song. Her grandmother's voice. The faint tinkle of the lost spell.

> *Catch yourself a falling star*
> *And love will blossom where you are*
> *Watch 'til dawn's new sun peeks through.*

"William, prepare a litter." Ambrose's voice broke through, sending the pieces of the spell spinning into murk once more, just as she was about to grasp them all. "We'll take her back to my tent."

"*No.*" Half sitting up, Lianna forced her eyes to open and clutched at his arm. "We must stay here. *Here.* 'Til dawn."

"Lianna, let him take you into the tent. You'll be warm, there are blankets—" Constantine began, but she shook her head weakly. Her gaze was locked upon Ambrose.

"Did you catch . . . the falling star?" she whispered.

He looked puzzled a moment, then suddenly nodded. "The star-brooch. You threw it to get my attention." He dug it out of the pocket of his cloak and stared at it. *Catch a falling star.* He shook his head and wrapped her cloak back around her, fastening the brooch in place once more. He lifted her so that she was nestled against him, his strong arms enfolding her. "It is safe. And so are you. Or you will be, once we get you out of this cold."

"No. We must stay . . .'til dawn. The spell . . . I feel it, Ambrose. My grandmother's spell. It is coming back to me . . . all of it. But we cannot leave here now, we must watch for . . . *there it is!*''

Ambrose followed her joyful gaze and saw, in a dazzling sweep of white, the shooting star that blazed through the blackness above and danced in a flash across the midnight sky.

"Comes the night of a falling star," she murmured, placing her hand upon his chest, "send a heart's wish from afar. Then a kiss of love that's true . . . will banish evil's curse from you."

The words tumbled out softly, pure and sweet and true as new snow. Ambrose drew her closer. He didn't fully understand, he only knew that this sable-haired princess had tried to save his life, that she was gazing at him with love glowing from her beautiful eyes. And he knew he couldn't go on for a single day without her.

"A kiss of love that's true," he repeated, and thinking of how close he'd come to losing her, he tightened his arms and leaned his head down toward hers.

The kiss was deep, sweet, and gentle as the dawn. All the coldness vanished. Pure warmth flowed between them, heat and light and tenderness that brought the sheen of tears to her eyes.

"A kiss of love that's true . . . will banish evil's curse from you," Lianna repeated the spell against the warm slant of his mouth.

They stayed there throughout the long, chill hours of the night. The soldiers brought blankets, and Constantine built a fire, and then all of Blackenstar's knights retreated. Constantine and his party went with them, leaving Ambrose and Lianna there upon the plain, with the moon and the stars as their companions, snuggled together while the hours tiptoed toward the dawn.

Early morning came at last, naked and sweet and golden against a shimmering lilac sky, and they watched it together, snug in each other's arms.

As Lianna gazed at the peaceful glow of color in the sky, as the chill of night faded and the new day began, the words came to her, softly, easily, every single one of them.

Breathlessly she murmured them, her eyes fixed upon the sun.

> *Comes the night of a falling star*
> *Send a heart's wish from afar.*
> *Then a kiss of love that's true*
> *Will banish evil's curse from you.*
> *Catch yourself a falling star*
> *And love will blossom where you are.*
> *Watch 'til dawn's new sun peeks through*
> *And all your dreams will fair come true.*

She closed her eyes and saw her grandmother's face, smiling, smiling.

The spell was complete.

"My heart's wish," she said, reaching up to stroke Ambrose's jaw. "I spoke it last night—that you should only know how much I love you. I didn't want to . . . but I gave you my heart, Ambrose the Barbarian. It is yours."

"And I give you mine, my beautiful, brave, and very stubborn princess. My heart, my life, my love. Forever."

A great rushing, flapping noise split the silence of the dawn, and, glancing up, they saw the sky grow black with crows. They swooped and darted, cawing and squawking, then wheeled away to the west, flying straight and fast and furious, leaving behind them an even deeper silence.

"The crows are gone from the keep." Lianna spoke with quiet certainty. "The curse is lifted."

"I hope that means we can leave this place now." He grunted and stroked a finger along the curve of her cheek. "Your shoulder must be throbbing. You must be cold, sore, hungry. Ready or not, Princess, I'm taking you home."

"Home." Lianna laughed as he lifted her in his arms. The twinge in her shoulder was nothing. Compared to the joy in her heart, it was nothing at all.

She thought of the keep that had so alarmed her at first, the place where she now wanted most to be. Alone in her sweet-scented chamber, with a blazing fire and the deep featherbed—and Ambrose. The two of them—safe, together.

She knew that a chance for peace now would grow across the land.

"Yes, my darling barbarian." Smiling, she wrapped her good arm around his neck as he began to carry her toward the camp and the horses and the men stirring from their sleep. "Let us go—*home.*"

EPILOGUE

"WHAT I DON'T understand is why this place is called Crow's Keep." Meeg glanced up from the five-month-old baby boy dozing in her arms and peered from Lianna's glowing face to Ambrose's beaming one. "I've seen larks, and doves, and gulls aplenty, but not a single crow in the fortnight we've been here."

"They're gone, banished—like all the other dark and ugly things in my life." It was Ambrose who replied. As he spoke, he leaned down and stroked a finger across the baby's cheek. His smile deepened as he stared at the dark fuzz of hair upon the boy's head and studied his peacefully closed eyes. "Thanks to this little fellow's mother."

King Penmarren's lips twitched in satisfaction. Constantine lifted his fair brows and smiled. But it was Lianna's laughter that rang like soft golden bells through the sun-drenched castle garden.

"It was nothing, my lord," she retorted. And turning to Meeg, she said in a loud whisper, "He must want something from me. Whenever it is so, he resorts to flattery. In the year and a half we have been wed, I've learned all his strategies.''

''All his strategies, eh?'' King Penmarren leaned back in the deep-cushioned chair that had been brought out to the garden for him, a twin of the one in which Meeg sat cradling the future duke of Blackenstar. The fragrance of a thousand flowers filled the air. ''So great and renowned a warrior must have many strategies, my dear. How clever of you to have learned them all.''

''Not all.'' Ambrose suddenly tugged Lianna from the stone bench upon which she sat and pulled her into his arms. ''Would you like me to demonstrate some you have not yet learned?'' he asked in a low, silky voice directly in her ear.

''Why, yes. But later, my lord.'' Her violet eyes sparkled. ''This is hardly the time or place. We have guests.''

''Family,'' he corrected her. ''Not guests. They won't mind excusing us. We have much to discuss—the entertainment for the banquet tomorrow. Jugglers or musicians. These things call for decisions.'' He wrapped an arm around Lianna's waist and glanced at each person in the garden. All chuckled and assured him that they were perfectly content to see him and Lianna excused.

''What more could we want now?'' Meeg shifted the baby in her arms as Marthe entered the garden with a golden tray of refreshments, which she set down upon a carved stone table. '' 'Tis a beautiful day, like the May days of my girlhood. We have wine and cake and grapes. And I have this beautiful little one in my arms—happy and healthy.'' Her sigh of contentment was mirrored by the grateful tears that shone in her eyes. ''All is well. Never did I think it would turn out this way!''

Lianna slipped free of Ambrose and went to her and kissed her cheek, as she had that long-ago night when she'd been taken from Penmarren as a most reluctant bride.

''Never did I think so either,'' she murmured.

''Will that be all, my lady?'' Marthe curtsied.

''Yes, Marthe. Thank you.'' Ever since the day that Beorn had killed poor Sir Gryford and tried to murder Ambrose, Marthe had found herself once more able to speak. The shock of seeing Lianna in danger had somehow shaken her out of her silent state, and though she remained for the most part quiet as a moth, she did speak now and then, especially to Lianna, to whom she had become wholly devoted.

As Marthe wove her way back toward the castle, Lianna bent her head and gave her son a kiss. "Now I believe it is my turn," Ambrose chuckled, and she rose to go eagerly into his arms.

"So that is what you wanted." Rising up on tiptoe, she brushed a kiss across his jaw.

"There. Will that serve, my lord?" she asked softly.

"For now." He took her arm and began leading her toward one of the peach-tree-lined paths that wound beneath the cliffs, away from the others, who were enjoying the May sunshine and the sweet profusion of flowers. "Constantine, will you be jousting in the tournament tomorrow?" he asked, as they passed the prince of Wyborn.

"That I will. Lady Else has been so kind as to give me her handkerchief as a token."

"Well done." Ambrose grinned. "And I suspect Sir William will have a token from the fair Lady Kira," he added as Sir William and Kira appeared on the path above, strolling together beneath the trees.

Lianna's ladies-in-waiting, Else, Kira, and Gwenlyn had all come to Blackenstar shortly before she learned she was with child and had been attending her ever since. But she would soon need to choose some new ladies-in-waiting. Gwenlyn had already been pledged to marry one of Ambrose's knights, and it appeared that Else and Kira would soon both be wed as well.

Something in the air at Crow's Keep—ever since the curse was broken—seemed to make love flourish.

At least, Lianna thought, it had been so for her and her Barbarian Duke.

As Ambrose led her to a secluded clearing that dipped off the path, out of the sight and earshot of those in the garden, she reflected on her life as the duchess of Blackenstar.

Not only had love flourished here at the castle, but peace had settled like a silken coverlet across the land. Those aligned with Beorn had been found and dealt with. The borders were secure, and Ambrose's enemies had turned their thoughts elsewhere, cowed by the strength of his new alliances.

And since little Rowan had been born, an air of laughter and contentment had seemed to shimmer right off the ancient stone walls of the castle—a joy almost tangible, for all to see.

The night of the falling star had brought the granting of all her wishes—hers and Ambrose's both.

"Now," Ambrose said, and touched the star-brooch that glittered at the shoulder of her topaz silk gown, "what do you say to jugglers first and musicians second?"

"I think musicians first and jugglers second," Lianna teased, then drew in her breath as his arms slipped around her waist, drawing her so close she could feel the strong, steady beating of his heart.

As always, her own heart began to thud in anticipation.

"As you wish, Princess," he murmured and cupped her face in his hand.

"If this is your strategy, my lord, to accede to all my desires in order to win my favor, and to flatter me and to . . ."

He brought his mouth down on hers and kissed her thoroughly.

"And to kiss me until I can't think straight . . ." she gasped.

Ambrose ruthlessly kissed her again. "That is my strategy exactly," he said.

"Then let me advise you." Lianna pulled his head down to hers and kissed him ardently, her mouth soft and pliant and eager upon his. Joy and love rose like soaring doves in her heart and shone from her eyes. "Proceed according to your battle plan, my lord. It is working splendidly."

THE CURSE OF
CASTLE CLOUGH

★

Ruth Ryan Langan

For Nora, Marianne, and Jill—true friends
And for Tom—best friend and love of my life

Prologue

Castle Clough, the Scottish Highlands

"Griff." Slightly out of breath, Lord Robert Cameron paused in the doorway of his father's library. Not his father's, he mentally corrected himself. It was his library now. As it had done for hundreds of years, everything at Castle Clough had once again passed from father to son. The land, the buildings, and everything in them. "I was busy with the herd when I got the message that you'd driven up from Edinburgh."

"Still playing the part of a gentleman farmer, I see." Griffin Mackenzie looked up from the ledgers he'd spread open across the desk and shot a challenging look at his former brother-in-law.

"I'm proud of the herds I've developed, Griff. They're the finest in Scotland. Maybe in the world. Now," Rob said tiredly, "I was in the middle of an important test. What is it you wanted to see me about?"

"It's about these." Griffin Mackenzie waved a hand over the ledgers. In his mid-sixties, he was thirty years Rob's senior. He was still a handsome man, with smooth, even features and dark hair graying at the temples. Over the years he had parlayed his knowledge of finance into one of Scotland's largest fortunes. He wore his success as easily as the perfectly tailored Saville Row suit and Italian leather shoes.

"What about them?" Lord Cameron crossed to the desk and glowered at the man who had dared to invade his private sanctum while he'd been busy in the fields.

"You'll find them interesting reading, Rob." Griff walked around the desk, then settled himself into a chair and stretched out his legs.

"All right, Griff." Rob crossed his arms over his chest. "You look far too smug to be here with good news. Why don't you tell me what I'll find."

"You'll find that your father's . . . vices were extremely costly."

Rob tensed. He knew all about his father's drinking, gambling, womanizing. "How costly?"

"More than fifteen million pounds."

Stunned, Rob sank down onto the desk chair and stared blindly at the ledgers. "And how would you know all this?"

"Because he came to me for the money."

"Which you were only too happy to lend him."

"I was, indeed." Griff's eyes glittered. He leaned forward, lowering his voice for emphasis. "You'll find that the documents your father signed are all legal and binding. If you can't repay the loans by month's end, the entire estate becomes my property."

Rob clenched a fist atop the ledger. "You know I can't raise that kind of money in only a few weeks' time."

Griff sat back and picked a piece of lint off his cuff. "A pity. But it should be some consolation that Castle Clough and all the surrounding land will still be in the family, in a manner of speaking."

"You aren't family, Griff. And you never were."

"I was married to your sister."

"And we all know why you married her." Rob's eyes narrowed. "I never realized until this moment just how much you resented me."

"I don't resent you, Rob." Griff closed his hands around the lions' heads carved into the arms of the chair, worn smooth by use over the centuries. The piece would be a fine addition to his office in Edinburgh. "I pity you. You had the misfortune of being born to a weakling father, who could never resist the lure of slow horses and fast women. He didn't deserve Castle Clough. You probably do, but now you'll never have it. It will all be mine."

"You said I have until the end of the month."

"I did. But don't get your hopes up." Griff smiled, though his eyes remained cold. "There isn't a bank in Scotland that will lend you a dime. Those I don't own outright, I control through stock or personal friendship. They'll do as I tell them."

"Then I'll sell everything." Rob glanced around at the elaborate coat of arms hanging over the fireplace. At the paintings, several of which were priceless and had been in the family for generations. "If I have to, I'll sell them for a fraction of what they're worth."

"I don't believe you." Griff leapt to his feet and stood facing him. "You love these things too much to sell them. It would kill you to part with them."

"I do love them. Not for their dollar value, as you do, but because they've been in my family for centuries. But I'd rather give them away than see them in your hands."

"Go ahead, then. Do what you please. But know this. When I take possession of Castle Clough, I'll retaliate by making the sale of your beloved cattle my first priority. Better yet, I'll have them all slaughtered."

He had the satisfaction of seeing Rob's face drain of all color. "And your pathetic staff will be out on the street. At their age, I doubt there'll be much demand for their services."

"You really are a bastard, Griff."

"A very rich one. And about to become much richer."
He sauntered to the door, then turned for one last thrust of
the knife. "I'll see you in a couple of weeks, Rob, old boy.
Have the keys to the estate ready to hand over."

1

"THERE IT IS, miss." The driver of the aged Rolls pointed to a break in the trees.

Estelle Sinclair leaned forward from her position in the backseat. At first all she could see was the curtain of rain that had been falling for the past hour or more. Suddenly lightning sliced the sky, revealing ancient turrets. The castle itself was hidden from view behind tall hedgerows and scattered woods. Then, as the car rounded a curve, she caught her breath at the sight of Castle Clough. She could see why it was often called the castle in the clouds. It was situated high on a hill, overlooking green, rolling meadows dotted with sheep. Despite the rain, the lovely pastoral setting made Estelle sigh with pleasure. At last she would see for herself the place she had been researching nonstop in her New York offices for the past four days.

Her heart raced at the rugged beauty of the Scottish Highlands. On the long drive from Glasgow she had seen the gradual changes, from long, lonely glens and open farmlands to craggy mountain peaks and wild, rushing streams. She had nearly wept at the sight of heather hills and cool, lovely lochs half hidden in dense woodlands and steep-sided glens.

The castle suited its rugged surroundings. With the mist-shrouded Highland forest behind it, it loomed like a fortress, dark and forbidding. The ancient stones had weathered to a dull gray. Though the towers were now empty, Estelle could imagine how they must have looked filled with Highland warriors holding their swords aloft, standing their ground against invading armies.

"Is this your first visit to the castle, miss?" The driver studied her in the rearview mirror as he swung the car through the open gates and up the wide, curving ribbon of drive.

"Yes." She met his eyes in the mirror and saw them narrow with speculation.

With a frown he brought the car to a stop and stepped out, then opened her door and offered his hand.

She accepted his help and stood admiring the ornate front entrance while he began removing her luggage from the trunk. He struggled under the weight of her first oversized suitcase and led the way up the wide stone steps.

Before he could lift the heavy brass knocker, the front door was thrown open and a tall stick of a man in a dark suit, crisp white shirt, and perfectly knotted tie stood glowering at them.

"What's this now, Angus?" he demanded.

The driver nodded toward Estelle. "The lass says she's here at the lord's request, Desmond."

Estelle stepped forward, eager to explain. "I'm Estelle Sinclair, with Smythe-VanPell Auction House in New York."

The older man looked down his nose. "We were told to expect you yesterday."

"Oh, dear. My original flight was delayed, and then I missed my connection. I see you haven't received the communication from New York about the change in plans."

Her driver reached into his pocket and produced an envelope. "I'll bet that's what this is, Desmond. I was told to deliver it with all haste."

"All haste, is it?" With a look of censure in the driver's direction, the man in the doorway tore open the envelope and read, then nodded.

When he spoke, his tone became brisk and business-like. "Come in, Professor Sinclair. Welcome to Castle Clough. My name is Desmond Snow." He turned to the driver. "Angus, you may leave the bags here. I'll see that they're taken to the professor's rooms."

Angus looked relieved as he backed away from the door and hurriedly retrieved the other bags.

As he set them down, he leaned close to whisper, "Be warned, miss. There are those, myself included, who would never dare set foot inside this place. There's a curse on it."

He looked up to see Desmond staring holes through him. He hurried back to the car. Within minutes he was driving away, the wheels of the car spewing gravel in his haste to depart.

Estelle looked after him thoughtfully. She'd read of the ancient curse of Castle Clough. Something about all the women dying young. But it was nothing more than an old wives' tale. It was difficult to believe that in this enlight-ened age people would still fret over such a thing.

Desmond stood aside, beckoning her in. "I'll show you to your room and see that you're given some tea and a bite to eat. I'm sure you'll want some time to rest after your long journey."

"Thank you. But I'd really like to see Lord Cameron. I'm eager to get started on my work here."

"I'm afraid that isn't possible right now, Professor Sin-clair." His tone was brusque. "Lord Cameron is in a most important meeting. But I'll inform his lordship that you've arrived."

He led the way up a wide, curving staircase. Estelle couldn't help darting glances of admiration as she followed. The highly polished balustrade was hand-carved mahogany, each step of the staircase a slab of gold-veined marble. A chandelier was suspended on silver chains from four stories above. After a cursory glance, she estimated it to be the finest crystal, several hundred years old. The soaring walls were softened with ancient tapestries whose symbols of lions and stags and warriors may have faded through the centuries but were still excellent examples of superb craftsmanship.

Along the hallway leading to her room were portraits of lavishly dressed women and darkly handsome men. She had the odd feeling that they watched as she passed by.

Desmond opened a set of double doors, then stood back, allowing Estelle to precede him. Inside was a sitting room, with a mix of seventeenth- and eighteenth-century furnishings in remarkable condition. The room smelled of beeswax and ammonia, attesting to the fact that it had been thoroughly cleaned in preparation for her arrival.

"It's a bit drafty, with all this rain. If we had known . . ." He stopped and cleared his throat. It wasn't his place to criticize a guest's late arrival. "I'll have one of the lads sent up to start a fire." Desmond opened another door revealing a bedroom fit for a queen, with a huge four-poster bed decked with peach-and-white-silk bed hangings and an ivory comfortor adorned with what Estelle recognized as the Cameron crest.

He stood aside as she slowly circled the room, touching a hand to the silk hangings, pausing to study the signature on the painting that hung over a Louis XIV desk.

"I hope you'll be comfortable here, Professor Sinclair."

Despite his words, Estelle had the distinct impression that this man wasn't as much concerned with her comfort as with her untimely arrival. "Thank you, Desmond. I'm sure I will be."

She waited until he left. As soon as the door closed behind him, she kicked off her shoes and began slowly circling the room again, pausing to touch, to examine, to admire.

What a treasure trove. For someone like Estelle, who had spent years studying Scottish antiquities, this was the opportunity of a lifetime. She spread her arms wide and danced around and around before dropping onto a sixteenth-century chaise to catch her breath. Despite the less-than-cordial welcome, nothing could dampen her excitement at being here. And, she reminded herself, perhaps Desmond Snow was merely annoyed at being caught unawares. If he was in charge of the household staff, he probably took his duties very seriously.

Still . . . she considered her surroundings further. How could anyone remain annoyed at anything for any length of time in a place as regal as this?

At a soft tap on the door she looked up. Before she could cross to the sitting room, the door was opened and a brawny young man entered, carrying an armload of wood. Though such a burden would stagger most men, this lad carried the logs as though they weighed no more than a feather.

He looked at her, then quickly away. But in that moment she caught sight of his eyes. They had a strange, vacant stare.

He crossed the room to the fireplace, where he knelt on the hearth and deposited his burden.

Behind him trailed a boy of about twelve or thirteen. "Good afternoon, miss." The boy's cheeks turned a becoming shade of pink when he caught sight of Estelle in the doorway. "Desmond sent us up to start a fire and see to your comfort."

"Thank you." Estelle watched as the older lad carefully arranged the logs, then held a match to the kindling. His movements were slow and deliberate. Like someone who was sleepwalking. "My name is Estelle Sinclair. What's yours?"

"I'm Arley Barclay. And this is my brother, Fergus."

"It's very nice to meet both of you. Do you live here at Castle Clough?"

The younger boy laughed. "Oh, no, ma'am. We live in the village you can see from the window. Just down that winding road a bit. Dunfield, it's called. I help out here after school and on weekends. Fergus doesn't go to school, so he's here most every day." He studied the newcomer. "Will you be staying here long?"

Estelle shrugged. "I don't know yet. That depends on

Lord Cameron, and how satisfied he is with my work."
She sighed. "Though it will seem more like a holiday, living and working in such a beautiful place as this."

The boy and his brother exchanged quick looks, before glancing away. Estelle felt a shiver along her spine. Just a quick tremor. But it left her with an uneasy feeling. As though these two shared a secret. A not very pleasant one.

Satisfied with the fire, Fergus lumbered out of the room and returned minutes later, handling Estelle's bags the same way he'd handled the logs. As though they weighed nothing at all.

"Bring them in here, Fergus," Arley called, leading the way to the bedroom.

When the luggage had been deposited on a long wooden bench, Fergus gave a nod of his head, then left the room.

Estelle stared after him. "Can he speak?"

His brother nodded. "Sometimes. A few words, though not many. Mostly he just lives in his own world." He seemed eager to change the subject. "Desmond told me to see to your things, Professor. Do I have your permission to unpack your bags and hang your clothes in the wardrobe?"

"Of course. Thank you, Arley. But just the larger case. The smaller one contains personal items. I'll unpack them later. I'll just take this and go over some of my notes." Estelle picked up her briefcase and carried it to the sitting room, settling herself on a sofa in front of the fire.

Just as she sat down, another knock heralded the arrival of a stone-faced man carrying a silver tray.

"You'd be Professor Sinclair," the man said as he set the tray on the table next to the sofa. He was a big man, with broad shoulders and large, work-worn hands. His white hair had been cut razor-sharp, adding to the harshness of his stern, narrow face. There was a look of tension about him in his stiffly held arms, in his brown eyes, which peered unblinking, and in his mouth, which turned down into a hard, tight frown.

"I'm Alfred Snow, Desmond's brother and the cook here at Castle Clough for more than forty years."

"It's nice to meet you, Alfred. I envy you living and working in such a beautiful place."

"Huh." That was the only acknowledgment the man made. But his frown, Estelle noted, deepened. "I hope this will hold you until dinner." Alfred lifted the linen covering to reveal a pot of tea, a tray of little sandwiches, and a lovely arrangement of sliced fruit.

"Oh, Alfred, that's more than enough. Thank you."

Estelle's smile elicited no matching response from the cook.

"I wonder if I might have a chance to meet Lord Cameron before dinner."

Alfred's lips thinned. "His lordship's still locked away in his meeting."

Just as he said that, a man poked his head in the doorway bellowing, "Alfred, where the hell is . . . ?"

He stared at Estelle, who jumped up and stared back at him. She had a quick impression of dark, flashing eyes, thick black hair, and a face that might have been handsome if not for the scowl that marred its features.

She knew from photographs she'd seen in her research that this was the new Lord Cameron. In his university days he'd been part of the wealthy and titled, following the sun and the parties around Europe. Now in his mid-thirties, he it was rumored to have rediscovered his roots and had returned to Scotland to raise prize cattle and carry on research in veterinary medicine.

His photographs hadn't done him justice. They didn't reveal the cleft in that strong jaw or the hint of danger that flashed in his eyes.

For several seconds he merely stared at her.

Alfred Snow said dryly, "Lord Cameron, this is Professor Sinclair."

The man frowned, running a hand through his hair in frustration. "Desmond should have told me the professor had arrived."

The cook gave a negligent shrug of his shoulders. "You were meeting with the bankers and told him not to disturb you for any reason."

"Yes. Well. I must return to the meeting. I just broke away for a moment." He recovered his wits and strode closer, extending his hand. "Welcome to Castle Clough, Professor Sinclair. Or should I call you Doctor Sinclair?"

He was tall, well over six feet. Estelle's own five-and-a-half-foot stature seemed small by comparison. When she placed her hand in his she felt a rush of heat and blamed it on their proximity to the fire. Or perhaps it was the anger she could sense in him. Anger mixed with frustration. "Those are such stuffy titles. I much prefer Estelle."

"Estelle." If he had any reaction of his own to her touch, he gave no indication. If anything, his frown became more pronounced. He dropped his hand to his side. Curled it into a fist. "My family and friends call me Rob. I prefer it to Lord Cameron."

"I'll remember." Estelle tried a smile, hoping it might put him at ease. "Now that you're here, perhaps we could talk about some of the things I'll be doing."

"I'm a bit . . . rushed at the moment." He bit off the words with a trace of annoyance. "Perhaps you could join me for dinner, and we can talk then."

Stung by his dismissal, she merely nodded. "Of course."

He seemed not to notice as he turned to his cook. "I'm looking for Fergus."

"This time of day he'd be hauling logs for the fire. I'll fetch him."

"Fine. Tell him to go up to my uncle at once. Until dinner, then, Profes—Estelle." Without a backward glance he strode out of the room.

Alfred Snow waited until he was out of earshot, then said dryly, "His lordship has a bit on his mind these days." He paused in the doorway between the sitting room and the bedroom, watching Arley hanging clothes in the wardrobe. Satisfied that the orders were being followed, he nodded to Estelle, then exited the suite, closing the door firmly behind him.

Estelle dropped down onto the sofa and stared into the flames of the fire. The notes from her briefcase lay forgotten on the coffee table. The tea and sandwiches no longer held any temptation. She'd arrived at Castle Clough as eager as a child at Christmas. This had seemed like the offer of a lifetime. A chance to see for herself all the lovely things that, until now, had never been viewed by anyone outside the Cameron family.

Now she was feeling more than a little uneasy. As though everyone around her knew a secret. A secret they had no intention of sharing with her.

What a strange reception.

Lord Cameron was either rude or distracted. She had, after all, dropped everything to come clear across the ocean at his invitation. Yet he couldn't even give her a moment of his time.

As for Desmond and Alfred Snow, they looked at her as though she were intruding on their turf.

Arley and Fergus seemed nice enough. But even they gave the impression of knowing something that she didn't.

She slipped off her shoes and curled up in a corner of the sofa, closing her eyes as weariness overtook her.

She hoped it was just the exhaustion of the overseas flight and the long drive from the airport. But she had the distinct feeling that something was very wrong here. Something dark and sinister was in the wind. And like Alice, she had fallen down a long, dark tunnel into a strange, alien world.

2

"WE'VE GONE OVER all the documents, Lord Cameron." Gordon MacKinnon was as round as he was tall, with soft, pudgy fingers, the nails carefully manicured. He sat hunched over the desk, tracing a finger around the rim of the bulging folder crammed with papers. "Each bank draught was signed by your father and properly witnessed."

"And the time limit? Is there any legal way to extend it?" Lord Cameron stared into MacKinnon's sad, hound-dog eyes.

"Perhaps . . ." The man shrugged and glanced around at the other men seated in the library, seeking their agreement. "Perhaps if you were to go to Griffin Mackenzie and ask for an extension . . ."

"He has already made it clear that it's out of the question. What about a loan? The estate is showing a profit. Certainly this house, and especially the land, can be used as collateral."

Bank vice president Maxwell answered in a gravel voice that grated like nails on a blackboard. "Your father already used the land and castle as collateral, your lordship, when he went to Griffin Mackenzie for money to finance his . . . various endeavors.''

Lord Cameron rounded on him, but before he could open his mouth to protest, Gordon MacKinnon interrupted. ''Maxwell doesn't mean to malign your father's reputation, your lordship.'' His voice was calm, soothing. ''He's just stating the facts, the same as the rest of us.''

''I know, Gordon. I know.'' Lord Cameron ran a hand through his hair as he studied the bank officials, all dressed in identical dark suits and crisp white shirts. His own scuffed boots and slightly frayed cuffs attested to the fact that he'd been working in the fields until their arrival. He had to keep working. It was the only way to hold on to his sanity.

''The fact is,'' Gordon MacKinnon said softly, ''your father, for whatever reason, chose to plunge his estates deeply into debt. We're not here to cast blame. We're here at your request, to help you find a way to hang on to your inheritance.''

The others nodded their agreement.

Lord Cameron lowered his voice. ''Thank you, Gordon. I appreciate that. But if the bank will extend the notes, I may have a way. I've sent for an expert on antiquities from Smythe-VanPell Auction House in New York. I'm told they're the best in the business. When Professor Sinclair has finished cataloguing the assets, I'll agree to a sale.''

The bankers' eyes widened in disbelief.

MacKinnon spoke for all of them. ''You refused to allow public tours of the castle, and you rejected out of hand the idea of turning it into an exclusive hotel. And now you're saying you'd strip Castle Clough of all its priceless antiques?''

''What choice do I have? I'd rather sell every piece of furniture, every rug and wall hanging, before I'd turn my home into something no better than a tourist trap or a cheap motel.''

''Hardly cheap.'' MacKinnon glanced at the others.

"People pay very good money to sleep in a castle. Especially one that's known to be haunted."

Annoyed, Lord Cameron walked to his desk and stared morosely at the thick file detailing the debt left by his father.

Gordon MacKinnon watched for several minutes before clearing his throat. "I know this is painful, your lordship. But Griffin Mackenzie is a very wealthy and powerful man."

"And you have no intention of going against his wishes."

MacKinnon pursed his lips. "Perhaps Griffin Mackenzie is just what Castle Clough needs. He can give the land and buildings the infusion of cash they need to properly represent our country in the next millennium. And at least it will stay in the family, so to speak. After all, he was once your brother-in-law. What is even more important, it will keep your family name free of scandal. The press need never hear of it. Your father's reputation need never be tarnished by rumors of debt and doubt."

He could see he'd struck a nerve. Lord Cameron winced and sank down into his chair.

Gordon MacKinnon pressed the issue. "I hope you'll give this matter your utmost consideration, your lordship. Griffin Mackenzie is the one man in Scotland who has enough influence to see that there's never a hint of scandal about this."

He paused dramatically before glancing at the others. "Gentlemen, I believe Lord Cameron has enough on his mind for one day."

The men got to their feet and shuffled toward the door.

A scowling Desmond Snow stood just outside the closed doors of the library, waiting to escort them to their waiting car and driver.

As Gordon MacKinnon took his leave, he turned and said softly, "When you've had time to think this over, I think you'll realize that Griffin Mackenzie is your best—your only—solution, your lordship."

● ● ●

"Ah, Professor Sinclair." Desmond Snow stood at the foot of the stairs, glancing at his watch as Estelle descended. "You're right on time. His lordship admires punctuality."

"So do I." She managed a smile. The nap had refreshed her. That and a long, scented bath. She had put aside her earlier fears, dismissing them as nerves. She'd dressed in a simple navy blazer over a navy wool dress and had pinned her hair into a no-nonsense knot at her nape. Perched on her nose were round glasses. On her feet were sensible pumps.

"If you'll follow me, I'll take you to the dining hall." Desmond led the way, with Estelle trailing behind.

He opened double doors and stepped inside. "Professor Sinclair is here, your lordship."

Estelle paused in the doorway. The room was enormous. Dark wood paneling, with great stone fireplaces on either end. In the middle of the room was a table massive enough to seat at least twenty or thirty people. It appeared incongruous with only three table settings at one end.

Lord Cameron had been staring into the flames. He turned to greet her, and she was struck by the look in his eyes. Sadness, she thought. Or worse, the very depths of sorrow. Then he blinked, and the look was gone.

He held out a hand in greeting. "Come and warm yourself by the fire. Will you have some wine?"

"Yes, thank you." She could feel such strength in his fingers as they closed around hers. It would seem that Lord Cameron was powerful not just in terms of wealth and social standing, but in physical condition as well. It was surprising, considering his life of ease. Perhaps, she thought, in recent years he had discovered the value of hard physical work. Or maybe he simply worked out with a trainer. Whatever his regimen, it seemed to suit him.

She took the seat he indicated, sinking comfortably into the oversize masculine wing chair. She glanced at an ancient sword, its jeweled hilt winking in the firelight. This man looked strong enough, and dangerous enough, to make use of it.

He handed her a glass of white wine. "How are your accommodations?"

"Just fine." She sipped. "Actually, they're better than fine. The suite is lovely. And finding myself surrounded by so many beautiful antiques is sheer bliss."

When he merely looked at her, she flushed and added, "As you know, my specialty at Smythe-VanPell is Scottish antiquities. Now that they're all around me, I can't help cataloguing them in my mind."

"I see." He nodded and settled himself into the chair across from her. "I suppose even when you're not working, you actually are, in a way."

"Exactly." She smiled, reminding herself to relax. There was something about this man that made it difficult. Perhaps it was those dark, piercing eyes, staring at her as though she were under a microscope. Or the tight set of his mouth, making her think he was wishing he could be anywhere but here.

He was distracted, she realized. Forced to be here while his mind was on other things. Or perhaps other, more interesting people.

He sipped his wine. "About this . . . cataloguing. Is it something you can do quickly? Or does it require a great deal of testing?"

"It takes a great deal of time and study and testing to determine the value and authenticity of most antiques. But I can often tell at a glance if certain items are worth the time involved. That sword, for instance. Though I'd have to examine it more closely, I'd estimate it to be from the fifteenth century."

He arched a brow, the only indication that she was correct. "Can you do the testing here? Or would you need to ship the items back to New York?"

"I'm qualified to do most of the work here, if you prefer. If I find anything questionable, I'll recommend that it be shipped to New York for further tests."

"I see." He looked up when Desmond entered.

Behind him was the lad Fergus, wheeling a chair. As he got closer, Estelle could see an old man huddled beneath a plaid blanket. A thatch of white hair topped a face that was deeply lined.

"Uncle Charles." At once Lord Cameron's tone softened, as did his eyes. "Thank you, Fergus." He dismissed the lad and wheeled the chair himself until it was positioned close to the fire. Then he knelt beside it and said, "We have a guest. This is Estelle Sinclair, from Smythe-VanPell Auction House in New York. Estelle, this is my uncle, Sir Charles Cameron."

"Sir Charles." Estelle offered her hand, and he accepted it, drawing her closer as he studied her.

"Did I read that you are a professor and that you earned your doctorate in Scottish antiquities?" Despite his age and infirmity, the old man's eyes were blackbird-sharp, as young and inquisitive as a child's.

Estelle smiled. "Guilty as charged."

He arched a shaggy white eyebrow. "In my day we never had any doctors or professors who looked like you, Dr. Sinclair." He glanced at his nephew. "Our expert isn't at all what we were expecting, is she, Rob?"

"Not at all." In fact, the picture he'd had in his mind was of someone old and doddering, and a bit eccentric. But there was no question of this woman's credentials. She had come highly recommended.

Rob stood to one side, watching the interaction between this stranger and his uncle. Charles had a way with people. He could cut through the walls they built around themselves and lay them bare, or draw them into the circle of his friendship in the blink of an eye. He'd always trusted the old man's instincts. "By the way, Uncle Charles, she prefers to be called Estelle."

"Estelle." The old man looked down at the hand resting in his. "Did you know that your name means 'star'?"

She nodded and gave him a smile before withdrawing her hand from his grasp. "Are you interested in names, Sir Charles?"

"I'm interested in anything and everything, my dear, no matter how trivial. It's always been my blessing and my curse."

He accepted a glass from his nephew and sipped, then nodded. "Scotch. Neat. Excellent, Rob. You never forget."

Lord Cameron winked at his uncle, then turned to their guest. "I'll need you to start first thing in the morning. Tell me what you'll need, and I'll see that young Fergus makes it available."

"The first thing I'll need is a workroom, big enough to set up some tables where I can examine the artifacts."

"A workroom . . ." He paused a moment, deep in thought. "Since time is of the essence, I'd hoped you could merely walk through each room and tag those items that are most valuable. As I explained to the director of Smythe-VanPell, I must complete the sale before the end of the month. In fact, in order to assure that I have the money in time, I'd prefer that the sale begin within the next few days."

She took a deep breath, choosing her words carefully. "I must caution you that you'll receive far less for these items if you sell them quickly, without a chance to have competitors bidding against one another. If you would allow our staff to take a year . . ."

"It's out of the question. Can you choose the most valuable items for quick sale?"

She nodded. "I can. I've brought along my computer and a digital camera, so I can take photos of the items you wish to sell, and send them to prospective buyers over the Internet. The buyers can respond in the same manner. But in order to authenticate each item, I'll still need a place where I can do a thorough examination. I suggest someplace where I won't be in the way. I will need a phone line for my computer's modem. And plenty of good natural light."

"How about the old playroom, Rob?"

"I don't think . . ."

Seeing that his nephew was about to refuse, the old man added, "It's big enough to set up several tables. A phone line was added years ago. It has those big windows. And it's certainly out of the way."

Lord Cameron started to shake his head, then gave a

grudging nod of approval before turning to his guest. "It's in the west wing, where it would get the benefit of afternoon light."

"Excellent." Estelle brightened. "Do you suppose I could see the room after dinner?"

"Of course. I'll take you there myself." He looked up as Desmond knocked and entered. "Is dinner ready, Desmond?"

"It is, your lordship."

"Tell Alfred he may begin serving." Rob wheeled his uncle's chair to the table, positioning it on one side, then holding the chair across from it for Estelle.

When they were seated, Alfred Snow entered, followed by Arley, who was pushing a serving cart laden with silver dishes.

They began with a clear broth to which spring vegetables had been added. Estelle felt her mood lighten considerably as she tasted it. Like the wine, the food was proving to be delicious.

Charles glanced at his nephew. "You're not eating, Rob?"

"Yes. Of course." Lord Cameron forced his attention to the food and made an effort to look enthusiastic.

Satisfied, the old man glanced at Estelle. "How is it that an American is an expert in Scottish antiquities, my dear?"

She smiled and lifted her wineglass. "It's all I ever heard from my aunt." The thought of her Aunt Rose brought a mist to her eyes. "After the death of my parents, she took me in and raised me as her own."

"It's what family does, my dear." Charles sipped his Scotch, watching her over the rim of his glass.

His nephew did the same.

She found the effect disconcerting.

"That's true. But it was quite a sacrifice on my aunt's part. She was single, with a challenging career. In retrospect I realize that she was passed up for promotions because of the demands of a child. Her private life suffered as well. She never married."

"All the more reason why she would have appreciated

having you in her life,'' Charles said softly. ''I'm sure she was very proud of your accomplishments.''

''I hope so. She spoke so lovingly about Scotland that when it came time for me to choose a course of study at the university, I never had any doubt what it would be.''

Charles lifted a brow. ''I'm surprised your aunt didn't accompany you on this trip.''

''It would have been my fondest wish to bring her. She . . .'' Estelle carefully controlled her tone. ''She died last year after a long illness.''

''I'm sorry, my dear.'' Charles reached across the table and squeezed her hand.

''I have a confession to make.'' She managed a shaky smile, grateful for his kindness. ''When your nephew's letter came to the firm seeking our advice, I couldn't help thinking it had been guided by my aunt's hand.''

''That's a lovely thought.'' The old man winked. ''I've always believed in spirits myself.'' He turned to his nephew. ''With good reason, wouldn't you say, Rob?''

Lord Cameron seemed relieved when the cook interrupted at that very moment, directing the serving of the main course. With a sigh the old man set about devouring a meal of succulent roast beef and potatoes, with biscuits warm from the oven.

''Alfred,'' he said between bites, ''as always, you've prepared an outstanding meal.''

''Thank you.'' Though he didn't smile, the cook did manage to nod his head before taking his leave.

A short time later he returned with crystal bowls of creamy caramel pudding and a platter of shortbread, as well as a pot of strong, hot tea. With an economy of movement he filled their cups, then nodded once more before exiting the room.

As if by magic, the moment their desserts were finished, Arley slipped silently into the room to retrieve their empty dishes. Estelle found herself wondering if the servants stood at attention just outside the door, counting the minutes between each course. The thought had the corners of her lips quivering with suppressed laughter.

When Desmond entered the dining hall, Charles motioned toward his empty glass. "I'll have another Scotch, Desmond."

The butler shook his head. "You know Dr. MacCallum left orders that you were to have no more than one a day, Sir Charles."

The old man scowled. "The bloody doctor probably has two or three drinks a night. But who's to tell him otherwise?" He waved a hand to his nephew. "I'd like to sit by the fire now. I'm beginning to feel a chill."

As his wheelchair was being pushed across the room, he said, "Didn't you say you'd like a drink, Rob?"

"Aye." Lord Cameron kept a perfectly straight face as he turned to their guest. "And you, Estelle?"

"No, thank you."

Lord Cameron nodded toward the butler. "I'll have a drink, Desmond. Scotch. Neat."

Desmond walked to a cabinet and opened the glass doors, pouring a generous drink into a tumbler, which he placed on a silver tray.

"Thank you, Desmond." Lord Cameron accepted the drink and waited until the butler left the room. Then he placed it on a table beside his uncle's wheelchair.

He turned to Estelle. "Perhaps you'd like to see the workroom."

"Yes, of course. I'd like that."

"Uncle Charles, would you like to accompany us?"

The old man waved him away. "It's far too chilly on that side of the castle. I'll just wait for you here by the fire."

Lord Cameron led the way across the room. While he was opening the door, Estelle turned in time to see his uncle lift the tumbler to his mouth and sigh with pleasure. When he caught sight of her watching him, he gave her an impish wink.

As Lord Cameron walked along a dimly lit corridor, he muttered, "I suppose you think I'm making light of the doctor's orders. But that little glass of whiskey is one of the few things my uncle actually looks forward to these days."

"There's no need to explain. I understand completely. My aunt had a fondness for chocolate. Near the end, when the medicines had stolen her appetite, those little nighttime chocolate treats were often the only things she had to look forward to. It gave me such pleasure to be able to do something, no matter how simple, to ease her burden."

He paused a moment, staring at her in that way that made her uncomfortable. "Yes. I suppose that's it. There's so little I can do for my uncle. And it gives him such pleasure to think he's getting away with something. Desmond is in on it, of course. But it would spoil my uncle's fun if he were to guess that. And so Desmond plays his part, and I play mine."

As he turned and continued down the hallway, Estelle found herself wondering about this dour man. A man of such contradictions. Despite the fact that he'd offered a less than cordial welcome and had seemed thoroughly distracted throughout their meal, it was clear that he had a soft spot in his heart for his aged uncle. She was touched by the charade he and his butler were willing to play for the sake of one old man.

After many twists and turns along several different hallways, they paused outside a heavy oak door. Lord Cameron produced a set of keys from his pocket and unlocked it. The hinges creaked as he forced it open. Estelle waited while he switched on the lights, then stepped inside and looked around.

Like all the rooms in the castle, this one was oversized, with massive fireplaces on either end. The outer wall had three floor-to-ceiling windows that would allow a flow of natural light. In the darkness all that she could see beyond them was the tall spires of trees and the soft glow of moonlight.

The floors were covered with a layer of dust, but it appeared that they were made of wood. In one corner was a lovely Oriental rug that Estelle estimated to be at least two hundred years old. In front of the fireplace stood an ancient cradle, still draped in dusty fabric that looked fragile enough to shred if it were touched.

Across the room were toys that would have been modern several generations ago. A hand-carved rocking horse. A wooden wheelbarrow. A wagon, with smooth wooden wheels.

On one wall hung a child's sword, an exact replica of the one hanging in the great dining hall.

She began to circle the room, pausing to touch the dusty cradle, the wooden toys. "Did you play here as a boy?"

"Aye. Often. It was my refuge."

She found herself wondering what a boy of wealth and privilege could possibly need with a place of refuge. Perhaps he merely wanted to escape from a world of adults to one of childish pleasures.

She took some mental measurements, then nodded. "This room is more than adequate for my needs. If you can find a couple of tables . . ." She turned.

Lord Cameron was standing at the window, staring into the darkness. As though, she thought, searching for something just beyond the circle of light.

With an effort he pulled himself back. "I'll have Fergus see to them first thing in the morning. Now, if you don't mind, I think we should get back to my uncle."

"Yes, of course." She followed him out the door and back along the darkened hallways.

"Ah. There you are." Charles looked up with relief when they entered. "I was beginning to think you'd forgotten me."

"Not a chance." Lord Cameron smiled and hurried to his uncle's side. "Are you ready to turn in?"

"More than ready. I don't know whether to credit the whiskey or the warmth of the fire." He caught Estelle's hand. "Or maybe the lovely company. At any rate, I'm warm and content and eager for my bed. I should think you would be as well, my dear, after your long journey."

"Like you, Sir Charles, I need no coaxing tonight," she said with a laugh.

They looked up when Desmond entered. "Will there be

anything else before I retire, your lordship?''

Lord Cameron nodded. ''You can accompany my uncle up to bed.''

''What about you, Rob?'' Charles asked.

''I have some bookkeeping to do.''

''Give it a rest, Rob,'' the old man muttered.

His nephew's tone held a note of weariness. ''How I'd like to. But I can't keep avoiding it.'' He turned to Estelle. ''Good night. I hope you'll be comfortable here at Castle Clough.''

''I'm sure I will be.''

She followed Desmond, who pushed the wheelchair out the door. At the bottom of the stairs young Fergus lifted the old man out of his chair and began to carry him up the steps. Halfway up, Estelle turned to see Lord Cameron striding down the hallway.

He looked, she thought, like a man who was going to his own hanging.

3

Rob sat at the desk that had once belonged to his father, his grandfather, and his great-grandfather, and worked on the rows of numbers. The fire burned low in the grate. A tumbler of whiskey rested untouched on the desktop. A clock on the mantel chimed the hour. Two o'clock.

He looked up, running a hand through his hair in frustration. He was weary beyond belief. But he knew that if he were to go up to his room, sleep would elude him. He was too tense. There was too much at stake here.

How could his father have plunged the estate so deeply into debt? It didn't seem possible. And yet the figures didn't lie. There were the bank notes, all properly signed and witnessed, using Castle Clough and the surrounding land as collateral. Fifteen million pounds borrowed, and none of it repaid.

At the thought of what he could do with that much money he had to close his eyes against the pain. The improvements to the castle. The additions to the barns. As well as to the herd. More aid to the villagers who had lived for generations in the shadow of this place.

Instead, his father had squandered his family's birthright on his own weaknesses.

Rob picked up the tumbler and crossed to the fireplace, staring into the glowing embers. Time was running out. It seemed impossible to believe that something that had been in the Cameron family for more than four hundred years was about to be lost forever.

With a muttered oath he lifted the tumbler to his lips and drained it. He thought fleetingly about tossing it against the hearth, and having the satisfaction of seeing it smashed to bits. Then he reminded himself that it was Baccarat crystal. Like everything else in the castle, it would fetch a good price at auction. He could no longer afford to indulge himself. Even in a fit of temper.

He was about to set it on the desk when he heard a sound and turned toward the door. He saw a flutter of white as someone hurried past. Curious, he walked to the doorway and watched as the door to the butler's pantry closed.

With the tumbler still in his hand he made his way to the kitchen. "Alfred, while you're up, do you suppose you could . . . ?" His voice trailed off as he caught sight of Estelle. She had opened the refrigerator door and was pouring a glass of milk. She turned, and the light from the interior illuminated her eyes, wide with alarm.

"Your lordship . . . Rob. I'm sorry. I thought by now everyone was asleep."

"It's quite all right." Intrigued, he stepped closer. She didn't look anything like the woman he'd met earlier. That woman wore her hair in a plain bun and hid behind owlish glasses. Now her hair fell in wild disarray around her face and shoulders. And what glorious hair. It was a tangle of red-gold strands that would rival autumn leaves. Her face, without a trace of makeup, was absolutely stunning. All flawless, porcelain skin and the sort of high cheekbones a model would kill for.

He watched while she replaced the container of milk in the refrigerator. Then, needing something to do, he opened a cupboard and poured himself another drink. "Can't sleep?"

She shook her head, causing her hair to kiss her cheeks in a most provocative way. He had to curl his hand into a fist to keep from touching it.

"It's probably jet lag. I was exhausted a few hours ago. Now I'm wide awake."

"You'll be fine after a day or two." He took a sip of whiskey to soothe his parched throat. Up close, despite the modest terry robe, he could see the dark cleft between her breasts.

"I'm sure I will." She drank her milk, feeling distinctly uneasy at this nighttime encounter. She'd been as quiet as a mouse, hoping she could slip downstairs without disturbing the household.

She rinsed the glass, then turned and found him staring at her in a way that spread heat through her like slow, liquid fire.

"I'll say good night now."

"I was just going up." He tossed back the rest of his drink, then set the empty tumbler beside hers.

In silence they climbed the stairs. The only illumination came from torchères spaced evenly along the hallway.

At the door to her suite she reached for the knob, only to find his hand already there. At the touch of him she pulled away as though burned, then regretted her action when she looked up to see him watching her with a strange, knowing smile.

She swallowed and forced herself to meet his eyes. "Good night . . . Rob."

"Good night, Estelle. Pleasant dreams."

When the door closed, he continued on to his room, lost in thought. He ought to be grateful for this unexpected nighttime encounter. Up close, the good professor smelled like a field of wildflowers and had a touch that was as potent as a kick from an angry heifer. In a matter of minutes she'd managed to wipe all unpleasant thoughts from his mind.

He prayed the lovely image would last long enough to grant him at least a few hours of sleep.

Estelle awoke and lay very still, struggling to remember where she was. Then she smiled as sunlight peeked around the edges of the draperies and spilled across the bed.

Excitement rippled through her at the thought of what she was about to do. For the next few weeks she would be privileged to touch and feel and examine at length objects that had never been seen outside these castle walls. The Cameron family heirlooms had never before been catalogued. They were a collector's dream.

The unexpected encounter with the lord of the manor had threatened to rob her of precious sleep, but exhaustion had won. Now, too eager to remain in bed, she tossed aside the covers and made her way to the shower. A short time later, dressed in comfortable charcoal wool slacks and sweater, she descended the stairs, clutching her briefcase. Though the castle was still in darkness, she followed the sounds of activity until she found the huge butler's pantry, where Alfred and Desmond Snow were already hard at work.

They looked up in surprise. Though they appeared startled, they quickly composed themselves.

Alfred glowered, while Desmond, the more diplomatic of the two, managed to call out, without too much enthusiasm, "Good morning, miss." He indicated the dining hall. "Fergus has just started a fire. His lordship and Sir Charles won't be downstairs for a bit yet, but you're welcome to wait in there, and I'll bring you whatever you'd like."

"Thank you, Desmond. But all I'd like is some coffee. I'll take it with me to my new workroom."

"Yes, miss." He and his brother exchanged a look before he said, "Fergus has already set up the tables you requested. If you wish to go ahead, I'll be along shortly with your coffee."

"Thank you. I'd like that." Her wide smile betrayed her delight. "I can't wait to get started."

She followed the twists and turns of the hallways, hoping

she could remember the way. When she finally stepped inside the old playroom, she was surprised at the transformation. The floors had been swept clean, and the dust and cobwebs removed. A fire blazed at either end of the big room. In the middle were three long tables, spaced several feet apart.

She set her briefcase on the first table and removed pens, notebooks, and a handful of reference books. Then she opened her computer, plugging in the modem before turning it on.

She looked up when Desmond approached, carrying a silver tray covered with a linen cloth.

He set it in front of her and removed the cloth to reveal a carafe of coffee and a china cup, as well as cream and sugar and a plate of freshly baked scones and a little pot of jam.

"Would you like anything else, miss?"

"Oh, no, Desmond. This looks wonderful. Thank you."

"You're welcome." He took a step back, then glanced around. "What made you choose this room for your work?"

"Hmmm?" She poured coffee, then looked up. "I believe it was Sir Charles who suggested it."

"I see." He nodded, then continued looking around, as though in search of something. "If you should find it . . . not to your liking, I'd be happy to have Fergus set you up in some other room in the castle, miss."

"Thank you, Desmond. I'm sure this will be just fine. When Fergus has finished his morning chores, would you mind sending him here? Lord Cameron said that whenever you can spare the lad, he could help me by carting some of the heavier artifacts."

"Aye, miss. I'll send him right along. Which room will you be starting in?"

"Lord Cameron suggested I start with the rooms in the north tower, which haven't been used for years."

"Very good. Fergus can show you the way."

When he was gone, Estelle sipped her coffee and broke off a piece of scone, nibbling as she walked to the floor-to-ceiling windows. In the morning sunlight the view was breathtaking. The rain had washed the land clean, revealing undulating hills of deep green and, on the distant meadow, a carpet of heather. Beyond that was forest, wild and tangled, and falling from a high peak, a waterfall that tumbled into a loch far below.

What would it be like, she wondered, to awake to this each morning and know that everything, as far as the eye could see, was yours? What would it do to a man? Would he simply take it all for granted, as a king surveying his kingdom? Would it make him hungry for more? Or would he be content and wish nothing more than to remain here forever?

Though she heard not a sound, she sensed that she was no longer alone. Turning, she found Fergus standing in the doorway, watching her.

"Good morning, Fergus." She offered a friendly smile. "Have you finished with your morning chores?"

He nodded.

"Good. Lord Cameron suggested I start with the north tower. Would you mind showing me the way?"

He turned and started down a corridor. Estelle set down her cup and followed. She had no trouble keeping up with him. Despite his size and strength, he moved at a snail's pace.

Finally he paused and pulled open a door, then stood aside, allowing her to enter first. What she saw took her breath away.

It was a lady's boudoir, with a satin-covered bed and bed hangings and a matching chaise.

"Oh, this is just perfect." Estelle slowly circled the room, noting the crystal lamps, the mirrored tray on which rested a comb and brush of hammered gold. There were paintings hanging on the walls in soft pastels, statues in corners and on pedestals that appeared to be made of marble and jade, and pretty little boxes encrusted with semiprecious jewels.

She worked quickly, tagging those pieces she considered most important. "If you can bring these tagged items to my workroom, Fergus, I'd be most grateful. But I must caution you to be very careful. If they should be damaged, their value could be lost."

The lad nodded and lumbered forward, plucking two crystal lamps from a dressing table. Estelle continued on to the rest of the rooms in the north wing, delighted with the treasures she found in each. Then, while Fergus made dozens of trips back and forth from the various rooms, she settled down to begin the task of examining each piece and photographing it in anticipation of the sale.

As she picked up the first piece, the brush of hammered gold, she had to swallow the lump in her throat. It was true that the gold alone was worth a fortune. But what meant even more to her was the fact that it had been here, in this very place, for hundreds of years. How many women had held this in their hands and run it through their hair? Had a man commissioned this for his lover? His wife? Perhaps on their wedding day?

"Good. I see you've started."

At the sound of Lord Cameron's voice, she looked up sharply, the spell broken. "Yes. I . . . was just examining this brush."

"So I see." He'd seen much more. He'd been standing there for several minutes, watching her without her knowledge. It had given him a chance to really look at her. In the morning sunlight she appeared as clean and fresh as the flowers blooming in the meadow. Everything about her was so neat and tidy. Her hair was pulled back into a knot, without a single strand out of place. She had slipped on those round glasses, which only added to her prim and proper schoolmarm look. A look he found most appealing. She had rare beauty. A lovely oval face. High cheekbones. A perfectly sculpted mouth. The sight of it made his throat go dry, and he remembered their nighttime encounter with gratitude. It had caused him to see her in a way he couldn't forget.

She held up the brush. "I would advise you not to sell this to the first bidder. It's worth a fortune."

He walked closer and took it from her hand. At once he

felt the jolt and could see in his mind's eye the vision of his ancestor running it through a woman's hair. It had been part of their courtship ritual. The man had taken the pins out of the woman's hair, then had worked the brush through the long waves, all the while watching the reflection of her eyes in the mirror of the dressing table.

Rob blinked. The vision left him shaken. He managed to keep his voice unemotional. "It looks quite old."

"At least two hundred years. Maybe more. Do you know anything about it?"

He shook his head. "Afraid not. My sister, Patience, probably would have known. I'm told she made a detailed history of the place. It was the great passion of her life."

"How wonderful. Perhaps she'd be willing to help me."

"My sister died when I was just an infant."

"I'm sorry. Are there any other brothers or sisters?"

He shook his head. "Just the two of us. Patience was already married when I was born. Needless to say, I was quite a surprise to my parents, and to my sister. She died shortly after I was born. The child she was carrying died as well."

"How terrible for her husband."

His tone was dry. "He managed to survive. It was much harder on my parents. My mother never got over it. She died a few months later, leaving my father in a state of shock."

Estelle thought about the curse. No wonder that even today people believed such a thing. This story only added another layer to the myth.

"After my mother's death I'm not certain that the family could have held together without Uncle Charles, who is my father's younger brother. He pulled my father through a very rough time. As for me, it was always Uncle Charles that I turned to in times of trouble."

"Then I can see why you love him so."

"Aye." Up close, the round glasses seemed to magnify her eyes. Last night he'd thought they were blue. But he could see now that they were more green than blue. And her hair looked like fire in the sunlight. He itched to touch it. He had the most unreasonable urge to take the pins out of it and watch it tumble about her shoulders. And an even more unreasonable urge to kiss her. He stared at her mouth, mesmerized by the thought of those full, ripe lips crushed beneath his.

It was the brush, he thought. Just holding it had given him all sorts of fanciful ideas. He handed it back to her. "We'll be having breakfast when Uncle Charles comes down in an hour or so. I hope you'll join us."

"Thank you. I'm sure that by then I'll have worked up an appetite."

He nodded. "I'll send someone to fetch you."

As he walked away he passed Fergus, who carried a marble statue that would have staggered most men. He watched as the lad set it down on the table.

"My uncle has need of you now, Fergus."

The lad nodded before lumbering away.

For a moment longer Rob paused, watching as Estelle carefully examined the gold brush, then bent toward her computer to enter her remarks.

He had told her, in the space of a few seconds, more than he'd ever told anyone about his family. And though he'd revealed few secrets, he was surprised by even those simple admissions.

He turned away and found, to his amazement, that his hands were actually trembling.

He'd have to see to it that he got more rest in the nights to come. What else but a lack of sleep could explain his strange reaction to this woman? As for the vision of the brush, that was a bit easier. It was merely the strain of knowing that he would have to dispose of everything he'd ever loved in order that his father's reputation could remain untarnished.

Still, he would have to take pains to keep his distance in the days to come. He needed to focus all his attention on the problem at hand. The last thing he needed was a distraction. Especially one as tempting as Estelle Sinclair.

4

ESTELLE SLOWLY LIFTED her head and studied Lord Cameron's back as he walked away. She let out her breath on a long, slow sigh of relief. Whenever he got too close, she had to struggle with the most unnerving sensations. She couldn't explain them. But she would have sworn that for one breathless moment he'd been about to kiss her.

Ridiculous. They had known each other less than twenty-four hours. He barely acknowledged her presence in his home. And yet she couldn't shake the feeling.

He had the most incredible eyes. Eyes that seemed to see clear through her. And he exuded strength. Not just physical strength, though that was apparent in the width of his shoulders, in the bulge of muscles that the sleeves of his sweater couldn't camouflage. This was an inner strength. She could sense in him an iron will and, despite his cultured manners, a keen edge of danger. He wouldn't be a man to cross.

"So. Have ye come to play, then?"

At the childish burr, Estelle glanced around. The boy was standing in a corner of the room, his face half hidden in shadow.

"I didn't hear you come in. How long have you been here?"

"Long enough to know ye're alone. I waited for the others to leave."

"Why? Are you shy around people?"

He laughed, a clear sound like the tinkling of a bell. "Ye might say that."

"What's your name?"

"Jamie."

She pushed back her chair and crossed to him, holding out her hand. "Hello, Jamie. My name is Estelle."

"I know." He placed his small hand in hers, and she felt a shimmer of heat.

She crouched down, studying him intently. "What an adorable costume." She ran a finger along the soft fabric of the wide-sleeved shirt, tucked into the waist of satin knee britches. On his feet were high stockings peeking out above well-worn boots. "Are you practicing for a play?"

"What's a play?"

"Make-believe. Acting."

"Ach. Nay. These are my clothes."

"I see. I'll bet you found them in a trunk. Are you someone's grandson? Alfred's or Desmond's?"

"They've no family save the Camerons. That's why they're so sad. They fear they're about to lose the only home and family they've ever known."

"Why would they think that?"

"Because Lord Cameron is on the verge of losing everything he loves."

"What nonsense. Jamie, why would you say such a thing? Look around you. Why, he must be worth millions."

The boy stared up at her. "Ye dinna know? That's why ye're here, Estelle Sinclair. To prepare for sale the things that are most valuable, in order to keep Castle Clough from falling into the wrong hands."

She sat back on her heels, alarmed at what she was hearing. "I'm sure you're mistaken, Jamie. I think Lord Cameron merely wants to be rid of some of the things that are gathering dust."

"Why would ye think that?"

"He made it clear that he disdains his title. I assume he thinks even less of his family possessions."

"Then ye dunna know him at all. He rejects his title because of what it did to his father. And because he fears it will set him apart from others. He's a man of the soil. A man of this land. He's very good at hiding his true feelings. But his heart is breaking at what he's about to do."

"How would a boy like you know so much?"

He gave her a strange, knowing look. "I hear things."

"How?"

His lips split into an impish grin that tugged at her heart. "Most people canna see me. So they speak freely when I'm around."

"Really?" She was laughing now. This boy was delightful. "Do you make yourself invisible?"

"Aye."

"Professor Sinclair."

At the sound of Desmond's voice she looked up, then got to her feet.

"Lord Cameron wishes you to join him and his uncle for a morning meal."

"Thank you, Desmond. I'd like to bring..." She turned. Jamie was gone. She turned a complete circle, then circled again, glancing over her shoulder as she did. But he was nowhere to be seen.

"Yes, miss?" Desmond stood in the doorway, looking puzzled.

"Nothing. Thank you. Tell Lord Cameron I'll be there shortly."

"Yes, miss." The butler walked away.

When he was gone, Jamie gave his little laugh. Estelle turned to find him standing exactly where she'd last seen him.

"What sort of trick is this?" She wasn't so much frightened as she was annoyed. How had she overlooked him?

"I told ye. I can make myself disappear whenever I choose. For I only permit certain people to see me."

"Is that so? Then why me, Jamie? Why have you decided to let me see you?"

"I need . . . I need someone I can trust. And I think . . . Tell me. Can I trust ye, Estelle Sinclair?"

"That depends."

"On what?"

"On whether there will be any more tricks like that. Whatever you're doing, I want you to stop."

For a moment a look of contrition came over him. He folded his hands behind his back and hung his head. Then, just as quickly, the mood was gone, and he brightened. "Oh. Ye sound just like my mother. I knew I could trust ye." He surprised her by wrapping his arms around her neck and giving her a fierce hug.

"What was that for?"

"For scolding me. It's been ever so long since I've had anyone scold me. I've missed that. I have to go now. But I'll be back."

Estelle started toward the door. "I'll walk with you. I have to join Lord Cameron and his uncle for breakfast."

At the door she turned, expecting him to be trailing behind her. Instead, the room was empty. Though she peered into every corner, there was no denying that Jamie was gone and she was alone.

Puzzled, and more alarmed than she cared to admit, she made her way quickly to the dining hall, determined to tell no one of this. If Lord Cameron should find out, he might dismiss her on the spot, claiming she'd lost her mind.

"Ah, here she is, Rob." Sir Charles looked up from the table and smiled as Estelle hurried across the room. "We were just speculating on what was keeping you."

"I got a little busy." She accepted the chair Rob offered and waited to speak until he took his place at the head of the table. She continued to hold her silence while Alfred Snow served her plate.

Sir Charles cleared his throat. "Are you finding everything you need, my dear?"

"Yes, thank you. And I'm grateful that you could spare Fergus. He's very helpful."

Charles glanced at his nephew. "The lad has the strength of a bull and the heart of a warrior."

Estelle sipped her tea. "Why doesn't he speak?"

"He will when he has something to say."

She looked up. "You've heard him?"

"Once or twice." Charles dug into his eggs with a sigh of pleasure. Eating was one of the few things he could still enjoy. "Actually, Rob has heard him more often than anyone."

"He speaks to you?" Estelle turned to Lord Cameron.

He nodded. "When it's necessary."

Charles spread jam on a scone and popped it into his mouth. "How long do you think it will take to prepare everything for sale, my dear?"

"I'll try to complete a walk-through of the entire castle by the end of the week, tagging those items that I think will bring the highest offers." She turned to Rob. "As I explained, they won't bring nearly the money you'd get if you could circulate a catalogue that would stimulate excitement and then offer them at auction a year from now. Dealers from all over the world would be bidding against each other for such treasures."

She saw the pained expression on his face before he composed himself. In that moment, she knew that Jamie had been correct.

She noticed that he hadn't touched a bite of his meal. She realized she'd lost her own appetite as well. Suddenly she felt compelled to get back to work.

She looked up. "Would you be offended if I return to my workroom now?"

"Without eating?" Sir Charles looked up in surprise.

Rob shot a glance at his uncle, then shook his head. "Of course not. I have little appetite myself. I understand how compelling work can be."

Rob watched her until she had left the dining hall. Then

he turned to his uncle. "Griff is stopping by this afternoon."

The old man's mouth turned down in a frown. "So he can gloat?"

"Most likely. But I'm in no position to refuse, especially since he claims to know a way to save Father's reputation."

"Griffin Mackenzie never gave a thought to my brother's reputation while he was alive. Why would he care about his good name now?"

"Maybe because it will reflect badly on him as well. After all, Uncle Charles, he was once married to Patience."

"A mistake your sister lived to regret."

"You don't know that for a fact. You told me that she never said she was unhappy."

"She didn't have to. Every time I saw her I could read the misery in her eyes."

"Then why did she choose to start a family with him?"

"I've asked myself that. Maybe for the same reason your heritage will soon become Griff's prized possession."

"Are you saying he bullied Patience into conceiving a child?"

The old man shrugged. "Griffin Mackenzie has made a study of people's weaknesses. It's what has earned him millions. He knows what buttons to push. He knows, for instance, that you would never sell Castle Clough. So he had to get to your father before he died. I'd be willing to bet any amount of money that he dangled his fortune in front of your father's eyes, and in a moment of weakness, the wheels were set into motion that have now brought us to the brink of disaster."

Rob pushed away from the table. "For now, Griff is the only player in the game. I have no choice but to listen to his latest offer."

"Aye." The old man clasped his hands in his lap. "Just promise me one thing. Promise you won't sign anything."

Rob touched a hand to his uncle's shoulder. "You know me better than that."

As he strode away, the old man brooded. When Fergus came to take him to his room, he said, "Not yet, lad. I'd like to take a turn around the gardens. Maybe the sunlight will be just the thing to cheer me up a bit.''

Once outside, the old man huddled beneath his plaid blanket and dreamed of younger, happier times, when he'd raced across these lawns with all the grace and speed of a gazelle. He'd done so much in his youth. Lived. Loved. And lost. Then he thought of the bleak future looming on the horizon for his nephew, and lifted his face to the sun, struggling to dispel the chill that seemed to have penetrated his very bones.

He looked up to see Estelle in her workroom, head bent, eyes downcast, as she studied the object in her hands. There was something about the lass that tugged at him. It wasn't just the auburn hair and green eyes, though he'd always had a weakness for green-eyed redheads. There was a sweetness about her. A simple artlessness that was most appealing. Beyond her titles and degrees, he felt quite certain that she had a genuine love for this land and its artifacts.

Perhaps he would just drop by her workroom and spend a few pleasant moments before retiring to his room.

He turned to Fergus, who stood silently behind the wheelchair, staring off into space. ''I believe I'd like to go inside now, lad. And if you'd be good enough to take me to our young lady's workroom, I'd be grateful.''

Fergus pushed the old man's chair effortlessly across the lawn and into the castle.

''Sir Charles.'' Estelle looked up from her work and smiled in welcome. ''How nice to see you.''

''You don't mind that I'm interrupting your work?''

''I can't think of a nicer interruption.''

The old man signaled for Fergus to push him closer. When his chair was parked beside her table, Charles waved the boy away. ''Come back in an hour, lad. Oh, and you might ask Arley to bring us some tea.''

Fergus nodded before lumbering off.

''This is lovely.'' Charles picked up the jeweled box Estelle had been inspecting. ''I remember seeing this once when I was a lad. I believe it was in my mother's reading room. It held notepaper and a lovely crystal inkwell.''

Estelle shook her head in amazement. ''Even after all my years of study, I find it hard to believe that there are people who actually grew up surrounded by such beauty.''

''And we've taken it for granted all these years. We were quite spoiled, I fear. We wanted for nothing. Toys. Clothes. Amusements. My parents lavished my brother and me with love and attention as well. In our youth our father took us all across the Highlands, hunting and fishing. Even when we went off to university, we were always eager to return home.''

''I can see why. It's so lovely here.'' She accepted the jewel-encrusted box from his hands and set it aside. ''Did you ever marry, Sir Charles?''

He shook his head. ''There was a special young woman. We met at the University of Edinburgh, where I was teaching a class and she was working on her degree. We knew from the first that we were fated to be together.'' His eyes glowed with the memory. ''I can't remember a happier time.''

''What happened? Why didn't the two of you marry?''

''The time was wrong for both of us. She had obligations and was forced to leave the university. At the same time, my brother's wife died, and I realized he wasn't able to cope with the responsibility of raising little Rob alone. Maybe it's because my brother, Robert, was so spoiled as a child. Or maybe he was just born with a selfish streak. For whatever reason, he seemed unable to conquer his weaknesses. So I came back to Castle Clough to help in whatever way I could, thinking I could pursue my own happiness later.'' His voice lowered. ''But the years have a way of slipping by. When I tried to reestablish contact with the woman I loved and lost, my letters were returned. I suppose she grew weary of waiting for me and married someone else. I couldn't blame her. She had a right to happiness. But it taught me a painful lesson. We have but one chance in this world. We must seize it with both hands and live life to the fullest, or the opportunity for happiness could be gone forever.''

Estelle placed a hand over his. "I'm sorry, Sir Charles. Sorry that you lost her. And sorry that I asked such a personal question. I had no right to open up an old wound."

"Nonsense. It all happened a long time ago. I'm resigned to the fact that I can't go back and change a thing. So I'll not waste time on regrets."

"My aunt used to say that very thing." Estelle smiled. "You would have liked her. She had this childlike sense of wonder about things. She was curious, inquisitive, inventive. When I was very young, I used to wonder why I'd had to lose my parents. But as I grew older, I realized that I wouldn't trade a single minute of my time with my aunt. And I think . . ." She paused for a moment, wondering if she ought to be so bold. Then she plunged ahead. "I think it's the same for your nephew. Though he appears to have been a loving son, he truly loves you as well. He understands the sacrifice you made for him and loves you for it."

The old man cleared his throat. "Thank you, my dear. I can't think of a higher compliment."

They both looked up as Arley entered, carrying a silver tray. He set it on the table and removed a linen cloth to reveal a pot of tea and a plate of biscuits.

"Will I pour, Sir Charles?" the lad asked.

"Yes. Thank you, Arley." Charles accepted a cup of strong, hot tea and waited until Estelle lifted hers.

"How was school today, lad?"

"Fine, sir. But I was delayed by soccer practice, and Desmond isn't happy with me. I've left too many chores undone."

"Then I'll not keep you. You wouldn't want to make Desmond angry."

"No, sir." With a laugh the boy sprinted away.

"He's sweet." Estelle watched as he disappeared down the hall.

"Aye. His grandfather worked here at the castle when I was a lad. That makes him part of our family. And when he and Fergus lost their father, Rob insisted that we hire them so that they could help their mother a bit. He pays the lads far more than they could earn working in the village. Probably more than they're worth to Desmond. But it helps in two ways. It gives them spending money, and it eases Desmond's burden, now that he's getting up in years." He grinned. "Not that I'd ever say that in his hearing, you understand. Desmond and his brother, Alfred, are very proud men. They'd not likely enjoy being reminded of their age. But they've spent their whole lives in service to our family. They deserve some help as they grow older."

She thought of the things Jamie had told her. No wonder Desmond and Alfred looked so unhappy. They were in peril of losing the only security they'd ever had.

"What about Fergus?" Estelle asked. "Is there a story behind his infirmity as well?"

"Ah. The poor lad." Sir Charles sipped his tea for a moment. His eyes grew somber. "Aye, a sad story. Fergus was hunting in the Highlands with his father just four short years ago, when he was twelve. They had no way of knowing that a company had come in to cull dead trees from the forest. Too late they heard a shout and realized a tree was falling toward them. They tried running to safety, but it was too late. The tree fell on both of them, grazing the lad's head, crushing his father. When the woodcutters arrived on the scene, they found Fergus lifting the tree in an effort to save his father. They came to his assistance and claimed it took four of them to do what the lad had done alone. But his superhuman effort was too late to save his father's life." He tapped a finger on the arm of his chair. His voice lowered to a whisper. "The accident left the lad damaged as well. Some in the village think he's addled. But it isn't so. He's just a bit slower now. Head injuries do that, you see."

"And your nephew hired him because no one else would."

"Aye." He looked up when he heard the slow shuffle that signaled the arrival of the one they were discussing. "Here you are, lad. Right on time. I believe I'd like to go up to my room now and have a rest."

The young giant crossed the room and nodded to Estelle,

then took up his position behind the wheelchair.

Sir Charles patted her hand. "Thank you for giving an old man the gift of your valuable time, my dear. You've helped the hour pass very pleasantly."

"It was my pleasure, Sir Charles. I hope you'll drop by and visit often."

"I'd like that." He lifted his hand in a salute, as Fergus pushed his chair out of the room.

When she was alone, Estelle sat for a moment, staring out the window and thinking over all that she'd heard.

Lord Rob Cameron, it would seem, wasn't at all the dour, unemotional man she'd first thought him to be. He was kind and compassionate. And she was beginning to care about him, and his trouble, more than she wanted to admit. That fact disturbed her. After all, her job was to evaluate and prepare the artifacts for auction. She had always prided herself on her professionalism, which dictated that she had no right to become emotionally involved—with either the sale or the seller.

She pushed aside the troubling thoughts and returned to her work, more aware than ever that time was of the essence.

5

"ACH. WHAT'S THIS NOW?"

At the childish voice Estelle turned.

Jamie's head popped up from behind a marble pedestal. "I remember hiding behind this and watching while my little brother searched everywhere for me."

"You have a little brother?"

"I did. Once. He's gone now."

"Gone where?"

"Home." His voice grew sad and distant. "They've all gone home. All but me."

The look in his eyes nearly broke her heart. A shiver passed through her. This boy didn't appear to be ethereal. There was no puff of smoke. No passing through walls. He simply appeared and disappeared. And he seemed as much flesh and blood as she. But she knew without a doubt that he was from a spirit world. It all fit. The odd-looking clothes. The ancient manner of speech. The ability to come and go at will.

Sweet heaven, she hoped she wasn't losing her mind.

Still, she had to risk it. She had to verify what she suspected. "Why can't you go home with them, Jamie?"

He paused a moment, looking perplexed. "There's something I have to do. Something I promised. And until I get it right, I can't leave here. It's been such a long time. And I really do want to be with them. I get so lonely sometimes. It's been years since there were any children to play with." Suddenly he brightened. "But now ye're here. And I've found a new friend. Ye promised ye'd be my friend, Estelle."

"Yes, I did."

He pulled himself on top of the pedestal and posed, his arms over his head. "Do I remind ye of that statue?"

Estelle couldn't help laughing. He was an adorable imp. She nodded. "You do indeed. But the statue is prettier."

"I should hope so. I have na wish to be pretty like my mother. I want to be strong and handsome like my father." He hopped down and walked closer to the table, running his hand over the objects that had been neatly tagged. "These won't bring enough, ye know, to save Castle Clough from foreclosure."

"How much will it take?"

"Fifteen million pounds."

"Fifteen million . . ." She pressed a hand to her mouth.

"Aye. Poor Rob. When the news gets out, his father's name will be ruined, and all the generations of Camerons to come will bear the shame."

"Is there any other way to save his estate besides selling everything he loves?"

The boy shot her a quick grin. "I was hoping ye'd ask, Estelle. Ye see, my powers are limited. But if ye were to join forces wi' me, maybe together we could do what neither of us can do alone."

"Your powers . . ." Estelle decided to keep her thoughts to herself. But the idea of one woman and a child—who may or may not be a . . . ghost—solving this crisis was simply too much. She shook her head in denial. "I've wasted enough time, Jamie. I must get back to work. But while I do, why don't you tell me how you happen to be here while the rest of your family is . . . gone.''

"Aye. Ye wouldna have heard." He clasped his hands behind his back and began to stride around the room. "The castle was under siege. It was a terrible battle, made all the worse because it was with family, in a way."

"In a way?" She looked up.

"Aye. The warrior Donan was wed to my father's sister. But he had long coveted Castle Clough and the treasure it held." He glanced over. "Ye've heard of the Star of Scotland?"

Estelle's eyes widened. "Of course. It's the mythical star-shaped diamond said to have been worn by the first laird of Castle Clough in the thirteen hundreds. But there has never been any documentation to prove its existence. Scholars have declared it nothing more than a legend."

"A legend, is it? If that's true, then I've seen this legend. And held it in my hands."

Estelle lowered the magnifying glass she'd been using and turned to stare at him. "You're having fun with me now, aren't you, Jamie?"

"Nay." Agitated, he hopped up on the end of the table and began to walk along the edge, waving his hands like a tightrope performer. "My father presented it to my mother on the day they wed. It sat in a special place on her dressing table as a symbol of their love."

"What happened to it? Was it stolen during the siege?"

"I think so. I canna remember. I've tried so many times to recall. But the memory is gone. I remember . . ." He paused, staring out the window into the afternoon sunlight.

"What do you remember, Jamie?"

"I remember my mother telling me that Donan knew about the curse of Castle Clough." He looked up. "Surely ye've heard of it as well?"

She nodded. "All the Cameron women are doomed to die young."

"Nay. That's not the curse."

"It isn't?"

He shook his head. "The curse is this: Cameron men,

when they love, love so deeply that they can give their hearts but once in a lifetime. If a Cameron should try for more than one love, his fortune, and his very life, will fail.''

"That would explain what happened to Rob's father."

"Aye. He was brokenhearted over the death of both his daughter and his wife. He spent a lifetime trying to love again. But all he did was lose everything. And so it was, from the beginning of the clan. The enemies of the Camerons, knowing of the curse, use it to their advantage.''

"How?"

"By threatening the life of the woman. They know a Cameron warrior would rather die than sacrifice the one he loves. My mother, realizing Donan intended to use her to snare my father, sent me to fetch the Star of Scotland and bring it to her in the great hall. She hoped to use it to bargain for my father's life. She told me I must not tarry, for Donan was a man of little patience.''

"Did you do as she asked?''

"I tried. I remember racing along the long, dark hallways, the jewel in my hand. But then I heard a cry. It was my little brother. And as a warrior in training, I knew that I must save his life, even if it meant sacrificing my own. So I ran down to the playroom to save him. But it was too late. One of Donan's warriors had already come upon him and was laughing as he carried him away.''

"Oh, Jamie! What did you do then?"

"I was torn between saving my brother and doing as my mother asked. I had my dirk at my waist and was skilled in its use. So I unsheathed it and followed the one who had my little brother. When I was close enough, I hurled it at him. But at the last moment he turned, and instead of inflicting a mortal wound, it merely pierced his shoulder, enraging him. In his anger he ran my little brother through with his sword, then came after me.''

Estelle covered her mouth to keep from crying out.

"I knew then that I had squandered my chance to save not only my little brother but my father and mother as well. I started running toward the great hall, desperate to make up for the time I'd lost. I heard the pounding of feet behind me, and knew that Donan's warrior was still there. I felt the bitter sting of a sword and knew that I'd been mortally wounded. But as I fell I managed to trip him, and he fell forward, impaling himself on his own sword. He landed on top of me, and I feared I was goin' to die. But at last I managed to drag myself free. I crawled away and hid, for the castle was alive with warriors.''

Estelle glanced around. "Where did you hide?"

He pointed to the far wall. "There were some loose bricks there, where my brother and I used to play. I slipped inside. I must have been very weak. I don't remember much, except the sound of fighting that seemed to go on for hours, or perhaps days. Finally, when there was only silence, I slipped out of my hiding place and went in search of my family.''

He slumped down on the edge of the table and sat staring into space.

Estelle walked over and wrapped her arms around him. "It must have been horrible, Jamie."

"Aye." His voice was muffled against her shoulder. "There was blood everywhere. Many of the rooms were smoldering, for our enemies had vowed to burn the castle to the ground.''

"And your family?"

"They were all . . . dead. My father. My mother. My little brother.''

"What about you, Jamie?"

She felt the shimmer of heat before he said softly, "Aye. At least I thought I was dead. I could see my body there in the hiding place. But even after it was nothing more than dust, I was still here. And here I remain, sleeping in that same hiding place for all this time.''

"I can't see it."

"About a hundred years ago the castle was remodeled. These walls were covered over with expensive panels of mahogany. So I simply pass through each night and return to my old place.''

"But you can't . . . go home?"

He shook his head. "There's something I still must do."

He pushed a little away and stared deeply into her eyes. "But I dunna know what it is. And I'm so weary. I just want to go home."

She picked him up and gently kissed his tearstained cheeks. "You will, Jamie."

"Do you think so?"

"I do. If there's any way I can help, I will. I promise." It occurred to her that, though he was hundreds of years old, his heart and soul were still those of a little boy. A very sad, very homesick little boy.

"What about the Star of Scotland, Jamie?"

He shook his head sadly. "I dunna know. It was my intention to hide it, to keep it safe. But I cannot remember. Perhaps I dropped it in my haste. Someone may have found it and carried it away. It was all so long ago."

They looked up at the sound of a deep voice from the doorway. "So. This is the professor of antiquities who is going to be Rob's savior."

Estelle felt the sudden chill and realized that Jamie had disappeared.

She crossed the room and extended her hand. "I'm Estelle Sinclair."

"I'm Griffin Mackenzie." He closed his other hand over hers, holding her when she tried to pull away. "Since I hold the mortgage on Castle Clough, I thought I'd take a look at your work and see just what you've uncovered."

She saw his greedy gaze sweep the paintings, the statuary, the gold and jewel-encrusted items.

"Such a pity that Rob will have to let go of some of his family treasures. I told him that if he really cares about such things, he should simply let them all remain within the castle walls. At least then they'll be here for future generations to enjoy."

"How generous of you." Estelle couldn't keep the ice from her tone. "Perhaps you'd be generous enough to extend the deadline. Then he could remain here where he belongs, surrounded by the things he loves."

At her boldness he gave her a long, slow, insolent look, then threw back his head and chuckled. "A word of warning, Professor. You're beginning to sound as though this has become a personal battle. There are those who might say you've overstepped your professional bounds.''

''I don't live my life considering what others say, Mr. Mackenzie. Now if you'll excuse me, I have work to do.''

''By all means, Professor. Please get back to it. After all, it's for my benefit as well as Rob's. Within a matter of a few weeks, all this will be mine.''

Estelle watched as he sauntered out of the room. She looked down to find Jamie hiding behind her skirt. On his face was a look of pure terror.

''It's Donan. Come back to pillage.''

''Nonsense. He said his name is Griffin Mackenzie.''

''Aye. The name may have changed through the centuries, but his heart is still evil. I know this man. The same eyes. The same heart.'' He looked up at her. ''Did ye know that he was once married to Lord Cameron's sister?''

''Patience?''

''Aye. When he married her, he thought he was marrying an only child who would one day inherit all this. The arrival of Rob, so many years after his sister, caught everyone by surprise. By that time Patience had already told her family of her expected baby. As I recall, when Mackenzie learned that her parents would be having a baby of their own, he wasna happy. He suggested that his mother-in-law was too old to give birth to a healthy child. He even went so far as to give his father-in-law a list of doctors, in case there were any second thoughts.''

''Obviously they didn't take him up on the offer.''

The lad nodded. ''But consider this. Shortly after Rob was born, Patience suffered a terrible accident, and she was found dead. The babe she was carrying died as well.''

''Are you suggesting that her death wasn't an accident?''

Jamie shrugged. ''There was speculation that the marriage hadna been a love match. Now that there was an heir apparent to Castle Clough, Griffin Mackenzie had no need of a wife, or her child, for they could do him no good.''

''You're frightening me, Jamie. Do you really believe he has waited all this time to steal the Cameron inheritance?''

"Ye tell me. Do ye think these things only happened hundreds of years ago? Or do ye believe that even today greed can drive a man to madness?"

Jamie's voice trembled. "For years, Donan was consumed with jealousy, until it drove him to kill all who stood in his way. For years, Griffin Mackenzie has coveted Castle Clough but has kept his distance. But a greedy man knows how to bide his time and how to use the weakness of others for his own benefit."

Estelle shivered. The boy made sense. But it wasn't her battle. She had been brought here for one thing.

To get her mind off her troubling thoughts, she forced herself to return to her work, picking up an ancient jewel-handled sword.

Jamie hopped up on the end of the table and began walking along the edge, staring at the sword as he did. "That belonged to my father, ye know. And one day it was to have been mine."

Hearing the pain in his voice, Estelle said, "I'm sorry, Jamie. I hate it that you and Rob must part with such special treasures. But he is . . ." She glanced up in alarm. "Be careful, Jamie. You're going to fall."

"Not a chance of it. It was always my little brother who couldna balance . . ."

Before he could finish the sentence he tumbled headfirst. Estelle scooped him up and hugged him fiercely. "Are you hurt? Are you bleeding?"

"Nay." He looked up and, seeing her concern, wrapped his arms around her neck. "Oh, it's been so long since anyone worried about me. You see? You're just like my mother."

She carried him back to her chair and sat down, cuddling him on her lap.

He snuggled against her for a moment, clinging to the warmth of her. "When you hold me like this, I see my mother's face. I even smell her." He reached up and touched her head. "But your hair is all wrong. Why do you wear it like this, Estelle? It should be all soft and loose." He pulled a strand out of the neat knot.

"Jamie, stop that."

Just as she reached a hand to his, a stern voice from the doorway had her stiffening in surprise. "So. The job has you talking to yourself already?"

She looked up.

Lord Cameron was walking toward her, looking at her in the strangest way.

"I was just . . ." She glanced down and saw Jamie grinning up at her. "Jamie and I were . . ."

At that moment she felt a cool breeze and realized that her arms were empty. Jamie had fled.

Rob crossed the room until he was standing directly in front of her. "Say that again."

She got to her feet. "It was nothing." She shook head, trying to pull herself together.

"You said 'Jamie.' Have you seen him?"

"Don't be sill . . ." She stopped. Started over. "You . . . know of him?"

He arched a brow. "Then you have seen him."

She swallowed and lifted her chin. "Yes, I've seen him. And I'm not crazy."

He smiled then, and she was amazed at the transformation. His eyes crinkled at the corners. His lips curved in the most enticing manner. He threw back his head and roared. "Believe me, Estelle. You're not crazy. I've seen him, too. Though I have to admit it's been years now. When I was a lad, Jamie was my playmate."

"Truly? You're not making that up?"

He nodded. "Jamie was my friend. My only friend when I was very young, and alone in this house with a father who hardly knew I existed. Jamie and I had some amazing experiences together." He shook his head, remembering. "I can't tell you how many times he got me into trouble."

"I can imagine. He's quite a little scamp. In fact, he was the one who tugged my hair loose just now."

She lifted a hand to push her hair back, but Rob closed a hand over hers, stilling her movement. "Don't. I like it better this way."

Estelle's eyes widened. At the mere touch of him, she

experienced a rush of heat that left her trembling.

"I'd like it even better if you'd let me do this." Rob reached up and removed the pins from her hair, watching through narrowed eyes as the rich red waves tumbled about her shoulders. It was as though he'd been cast under some sort of spell. And he thought fleetingly that Jamie might be the cause of it. Still, the scene when he'd held the brush flashed through his mind once more, conjuring an image he couldn't forget.

It seemed the most natural thing in the world to plunge his fingers into the tangles. He drew her head back and stared into her eyes. Saw them widen with surprise, then slowly heat as she realized his intentions. He lowered his gaze to her lips and tested himself for just a moment, holding back until he could almost taste them. Then he could wait no longer. Moving as slowly as though in a dream, he fitted his mouth to hers, and on a sigh he drank in the sweet, clean taste of her.

At that first contact Estelle felt the floor dip and tilt dangerously, and her hands reached out, clutching blindly at his waist. Though she tried not to react, she couldn't help the way her breath hitched, then released in a long, slow sigh. She could feel her pulse rate speed up and her blood begin to heat. Though she thought about resisting, she was afraid to move. Afraid that if she did, she would shatter like crystal. And so she stood, absorbing the most delicious sensations.

As he took the kiss deeper, all thought fled. All she could do was hold on while he took her on a roller-coaster ride of emotions.

He'd never met anyone quite so exciting to watch. He kept his eyes open, loving the way she responded to that simple kiss. Color flooded her cheeks. Her lashes fluttered, then lowered.

He changed the angle, keeping his mouth on hers, and found himself deeply aroused by the touch of her hands at his waist. The thought of them touching him everywhere aroused him even more. Though he was tempted to crush her to him and take what he wanted, he forced himself to go slowly, allowing the merest stroke of his hand along her spine. Her little shiver of delight only excited him more.

It took all his willpower to pull back. "I was tempted to blame this on Jamie. He was always getting me to do things I wanted to do, but was too cowardly to try." He smiled then, and there was an edge of danger in it. "But that would be a lie. This wasn't Jamie's doing. It was all mine." He tilted her chin, lifting her face to his, and brushed a light, butterfly kiss over her lips. "And you'd best be warned, Estelle. Given the chance, I'll do it again."

"Don't I have anything to say about that?"

He chuckled. "I didn't see you resist."

She felt the heat stain her cheeks. There was no denying the truth of what he'd said. Not only had she not resisted, but she had fully participated. And judging by the way her body was continuing to vibrate, she would gladly do it again.

"I wish I didn't have to leave to meet someone." Because his hands were shaking, he tucked them into his pockets and took another step back. It was dangerous standing too close to her. "Why don't you join my uncle and me in the library at six for drinks?"

"I . . . Yes. All right."

"Until then." He was, he realized, already looking forward to it.

He turned away and caught sight of Griffin Mackenzie standing in the doorway. When he realized what Griff had witnessed, his smile instantly disappeared.

Without a backward glance he stormed away.

6

"GOOD EVENING, MY DEAR." Sir Charles looked up from his position beside the fire. "You look lovely tonight." He glanced at his nephew. "Doesn't she, Rob?"

"Aye." Rob's eyes darkened as he studied her.

Estelle braced herself before meeting Rob's gaze. Ever since their kiss, she'd been fretting over how she would react in his presence.

"Wine?" Rob handed her a fluted glass, and as their fingers brushed, he felt a rush of heat that left him shaken. He tempted himself further by placing a hand beneath her elbow as he led her to a chair beside his uncle.

She felt heat stain her cheeks. She'd taken pains to look just right this evening. The dress was a vibrant shade of body-skimming green silk. At her throat was a single strand of pearls, a gift from her aunt. On a whim she'd brushed her hair long and flowing, but now she wished she had pinned it up. She suddenly felt silly and frivolous.

"My nephew was just telling me that you've met Jamie."

"I . . . Yes." What was happening to her? She was an intelligent, sensible woman who had slowly worked her way into a position of respect and authority in one of the finest auction houses in the world. She held art history degrees from two universities and was regarded as one of the most knowledgeable curators of Scottish artifacts. In less than two days, however, she had compromised her position by shamelessly flirting, and worse, was openly admitting to seeing and talking to a ghost in her workroom.

"I remember him as being such fun."

"Are you telling me that you've met him also, Sir Charles?"

"Of course. All the Camerons have met the lad, since his . . . demise in 1620."

"Have others outside the family seen him?"

Charles shrugged. "Only if he wants them to. Through the centuries there have been dozens of reported sightings. He's become an accepted member of the family."

"He told me the rest of his family has gone home. Why does he stay? Why doesn't he . . . join them?"

The old man shook his head. "I don't really know. It seems there's something he feels he must do before he can enjoy his eternal rest."

"He mentioned the Star of Scotland. Have you heard of it?"

"Of course. It was rumored to have been an important piece of Cameron history. But there are no paintings of it, no sketches, no written history of it. All we have is word of mouth handed down through the centuries. It appears to be more fiction than fact."

Estelle sipped her wine, considering what she was about to say. Then, after taking a deep breath, she turned to Rob. "Jamie told me that you've only agreed to auction off your belongings because you're about to lose Castle Clough. Is that true?"

His hand tightened on the glass, the only indication of his pain. "It is."

"I'm sorry. I can't even imagine what it must feel like to have to give up something this beautiful."

"It isn't only the beauty of Castle Clough that I'll lose. It's the land that has been in my family for generations. And the pleasure I take from my work."

"Not to mention," his uncle added, "all the people who live here and in Dunfield who depend on Rob to see them through the hard times. It's been a tradition for the Cameron family, one we take very seriously."

Now Estelle understood the sadness she could sense in Desmond and Alfred Snow, and Arley and Fergus Barclay. Then she thought about what Jamie had told her of the man who held the mortgage. "Jamie said that Griffin Mackenzie has long coveted your land."

"Aye." As always, when Rob's temper grew, his burr thickened.

Estelle knew that if she but closed her eyes, she could imagine Rob Cameron as a warrior of old, sword lifted, ready to do battle with his enemy.

She leaned forward. "There has to be a way to stop him from taking what is rightfully yours, Rob."

"Don't you think I've tried to find a way?" He stood and walked to the fireplace, resting a closed fist on the mantel. "I've been to every banker. I've had lawyers going over the documents, looking for a loophole. Griff was clever. Everything is legal and binding. And in just a few weeks, unless I find a pot of gold, everything I've ever loved will be his."

Estelle could hear the pain in his voice, could actually feel the sorrow he was feeling. It pierced her heart like a knife. She set down her drink and clasped her hands in her lap. "It isn't fair."

Rob stopped his pacing to look at her. On his lips was a heart-stopping smile. "No one ever promised that life would be fair."

Their gazes met and held.

"Jamie said that if we work together we may yet thwart our enemy."

"Ah. So now it's become your fight, too?"

Sir Charles sat in his wheelchair, sipping his drink and watching the interaction between his nephew and this young woman. Though he was certain they weren't aware of it as yet, he could sense a depth of feeling that went far beyond that of employer and employee.

Despite the seriousness of the situation, he felt a sudden lightness around his heart. It had long been his wish that Rob would meet someone worthy of him. Someone who would cherish his way of life and help preserve it. Who better than this woman, who had made a career of studying the very things Rob most loved in this world?

Maybe, he thought with a smile, there was more going on here than met the eye.

He cleared his throat, and the two young people looked his way. "It has often been my experience that out of even the most wretched of circumstances, much good can come." He gave them the benefit of his smile. "Who knows? Perhaps if we all work together, we may yet come up with a way to save Castle Clough."

"Miss?"

Estelle looked up from her work to find Arley standing in the doorway. "Yes, Arley. Come in."

"Sir Charles asked if you would deliver this to Lord Cameron." He held out an envelope.

She accepted it, noting that though it was sealed, it bore no markings. "Deliver it? Where is Lord Cameron?"

"Out in the field, miss. Working with the herd."

"Is it far?"

"No more than a kilometer."

"Is Fergus too busy to go?"

The lad shrugged. "I don't know, miss. I only know that Sir Charles asked that you deliver it."

She sighed. In the past few days she'd been given half a dozen such assignments by his uncle. Take this to Rob in the library. Take that to him in the dining room. Now she was being sent out to the field. At this rate, she'd never get her work done.

"All right, Arley. Tell Sir Charles that I'll see to it right away." She turned away and picked up a tweed jacket. Though the sun was shining, the air had a bite to it.

As she started off across the field, her spirits lifted. For days now she hadn't seen Jamie. In fact, she'd stopped looking for him. At first she'd missed his silly pranks. But now she was beginning to believe that he didn't exist at all. It was simply the sort of hysteria brought on by the power of suggestion. She'd read of the curse of Castle Clough, and because she'd misunderstood it, she'd simply conjured an image of a young ghost because . . . well, because all castles ought to have one.

There now. She felt better already. She was back to her old sane, sensible self.

As she came up over a curving meadow, she caught sight of Rob walking toward her. Slung over his shoulders was a newborn calf.

At the sight of him, tall and rugged, his dark hair mussed, his big hands holding the animal gently, her heart did somersaults.

"Estelle." He broke into a wide smile. "What brings you out here?"

"A message from your uncle."

He accepted the envelope and stuck it in his pocket.

"Who is this?" She reached up to stroke the velvet nose of the sleepy-eyed animal.

"This little guy's just a few hours old. The poor little thing will have to be hand-fed for a day while I treat an infection in his mother." He motioned behind him, and Estelle caught sight of a field hand leading a cow.

"Does he have a name?"

He shook his head and started toward the barn in the distance. "Not yet. Maybe you'd like to give him one."

Estelle kept pace beside him. "I've never named a calf. Tell me a little about him."

"His father is Brawny of Clough. One of the finest bulls in all of Scotland." Rob stepped out of the sunshine and into the darkness of the barn, strolling past several stalls before pausing before an open door. Inside, in a bed of straw, he gently settled the tiny animal and covered it with a blanket.

"And his mother?" Estelle knelt beside the calf and continued to soothe and stroke, while Rob filled a bottle with formula.

"A bonny heifer. This is her first birthing, and she came through it admirably."

He handed her the bottle, and she laughed with delight when the calf fastened onto it and began to drink. But she felt suddenly light-headed when she looked up to see Rob toss aside his shirt and plunge his hands into a bucket of water.

At the sight of his hard, muscled back, her throat went dry. When he turned, she could hardly tear her gaze away from the hair-roughened chest, the flat, trim stomach. The muscles of his arms bunched and tightened as he reached for a towel and dried himself before pulling on a clean shirt.

It seemed incongruous that all morning she had photographed priceless artifacts with a digital camera, sending the images over the Internet to prospective buyers, and now she was kneeling in a barn with a newborn calf, fighting the most primitive of all urges.

She looked down at the calf. "Oh, look, Rob. Look how bold he is."

"Is that his name, then?"

She arched a brow, considering. Pleased, she nodded. "He is bold. It suits him."

When the calf had emptied the bottle, Rob picked him up and gently draped him around his shoulders. "Come on, Bold. I'll take you to your mother."

With Estelle following, he carried the calf to another stall, where the mother stood waiting. As soon as he deposited the calf in the straw, its mother began nuzzling and coaxing, until the calf was standing beside her.

"Oh, Rob, aren't they beautiful?"

"Aye. But here in Scotland we say 'bonny.' "

"Bonny. Aye," she said, imitating his burr. "Mother and son are indeed a bonny pair."

He stood beside her, his foot resting on the crossed bar of the stall. For some reason he couldn't quite fathom, his heart swelled with pleasure. There was nothing she could have said that would have pleased him more.

She glanced at her watch. ''I'd better get back. I'm neglecting my work.''

''Wait.'' He pulled her close and brushed his lips over hers. It was the merest touch of mouth to mouth, but it had her blood running hot.

She savored the moment, loving the press of his hard, muscled body against hers, and the feel of his big hands moving along her spine. She realized that she would like nothing more than the pleasure of staying just so, with his breath warm against her cheek, and his firm, clever lips nuzzling hers.

''Until tonight, Estelle.'' He tucked her hair behind her ear, allowing his hand to linger a moment.

As she walked away, Rob tore open the envelope she'd given him. He read his uncle's familiar scrawl, then threw back his head and roared with laughter.

The old codger was playing matchmaker. He'd admitted as much in his note. He'd sent her out here for no other reason than to throw them together. And he'd added as an afterthought that he hoped his nephew would be sufficiently grateful for the favor.

He was, Rob realized. While everything around him was falling apart, while his whole world as he'd known it was shattering beyond repair, he was foolishly, and completely, losing his heart.

Estelle entered the dining hall and glanced around in surprise. Rob wasn't there. Sir Charles was sitting alone before the fire.

She felt a wave of bitter disappointment. She'd taken such pains with her dress. It was a soft white wool, with long, tapered sleeves and scooped neckline. She'd waged an argument with herself before deciding to pin up her hair in a neat knot. That way, she reasoned, she wouldn't look too fussy. Or too overtly sexy.

''Rob is late tonight, I see.'' She crossed the room and offered her hand to Sir Charles. Instead of squeezing it, he lifted it to his lips.

"He sent word that he'll be spending the night in the barn."

"Oh, no. Don't tell me there's something wrong with Bold."

"Bold?"

"Did he mention a calf, Sir Charles?"

"A calf?" The old man shrugged. "I believe he did. Something about keeping an eye on him . . ."

"Oh, Sir Charles. Would you mind terribly if I went to the barn to see for myself? I hate to abandon you, but this is the first calf I've ever named. He's very special to me. And if there's something wrong . . ."

"But of course you must go, my dear. I insist. Here." He lifted the soft plaid blanket that covered his lap and handed it to her. "Drape this around your shoulders to ward off the night air." Then he beckoned to Desmond. "Have you the basket of supper Alfred fixed for my nephew?"

"Aye." The old man lifted a basket from the table. With a slight bow he handed it to Estelle.

"Thank you, Desmond. Sir Charles, I won't be long."

"Now you musn't race back on my account. In fact, I'm feeling rather weary. I'll probably go up to my room any minute now and take my supper in bed. So take your time, my dear. Stay with my nephew a while so he won't be lonely out there in the night."

She started off, then thought better of it and returned to brush a kiss over his cheek. "Thank you, Sir Charles."

As she dashed out of the room, the old man touched a finger to the spot, then glanced at Desmond with a devilish smile. "You had Alfred add a second supper to that basket as I requested?"

"Aye, Sir Charles."

"Good. Good." The old man rubbed his hands together gleefully. "Now, if my nephew can resist all that, he's not the man I think he is."

The two old men shared a chuckle. Then, as he did every night, Desmond poured Scotch into a tumbler, set it beside Sir Charles, and went out, leaving him to his fire, his drink, and his memories.

7

"R_{OB}."

At the sound of Estelle's voice, Rob turned to see her standing in the doorway of the barn, trying to locate him in the darkness.

"In here." He lifted a lantern from a hook and started toward her.

She raced forward, meeting him halfway. "Has something happened to Bold?"

"No. He's fine. Why?"

"Your uncle said . . ."

"My uncle." A flicker of a smile touched the corners of his lips. "I should have known. Bless his conniving old heart." He caught her arm and led her toward the stall. "I just wanted to stay here a while so I could keep an eye on mother and son." He held the lantern aloft so she could see for herself that the cow and calf were indeed fine.

"Oh, I'm so relieved." She set aside the basket and leaned on the rail, watching as the cow nuzzled her calf. "When Sir Charles said you'd be spending the night out here, I was certain something had gone terribly wrong."

"Spending the night, am I?" He hadn't planned on it, but suddenly it seemed like a fine idea. As long as he didn't have to spend it alone. "And you rushed out to keep me company."

"Yes." She glanced over and realized he was studying her with a strange, intense look on his face. "What is it? What's wrong?"

"Wrong?" He touched a hand to her cheek. "Nothing is wrong, Estelle. In fact, everything is so right. Especially where you're concerned. The way you look. So intriguing. One minute the prim professor. The next, a tempting little seductress." He drew her close and pressed his face to her hair, breathing her in. "The way you smell. Fresh and clean, like a field of wildflowers." He ran his hands down her back, sending little tremors along her spine. "The way you're willing to fight for me." He chuckled, and the sound sent a thrill racing through her. "I can almost see you marching headlong into battle, sword at the ready, determined to fight for what you believe in."

She'd never known such amazing sensations. Icy tingles and shimmering heat. Fear and longing and a strange sense that everything in her life was about to change. And though it frightened her more than she cared to admit, there was a sense of anticipation, of wild exhilaration, as well. "I would fight for you, Rob, if only I knew how."

"I know that. And I find it so . . . endearing." He caught a tangle of her hair and watched as the strands sifted through his fingers.

She felt the breath hitch in her throat and knew with absolute certainty that he was going to kiss her. Knew also that she wanted him to. Desperately. Still, she was torn between desire and a need to run back to the castle, where she knew she could be safe from her own weakness.

"You're so soft, Estelle. Everything about you is soft." He seemed fascinated by her pale skin, peeking out from beneath the cover of a blanket she wore like a shawl. With his eyes on hers, he ran a fingertip along her exposed skin, from her neck to her shoulder.

She shivered and started to draw the blanket tighter around her. But her fingers fumbled, and it fell to the straw at their feet.

"You look like an angel. My angel. Come to save me." He lowered his head, running wet, nibbling kisses along the sensitive hollow between her neck and shoulder until she moaned and pushed away a little.

Her eyes suddenly looked too big. She opened her mouth to speak, but no words came out.

"What's wrong, angel?" He smiled. But he seemed more dangerous than amused.

"I'm afraid."

"Of me?"

"No." She struggled to speak over the knot of fear that clogged her throat. "Of me. Of the things I'm feeling."

"Ah." There was a gleam in his eye as he lifted a hand to her cheek. "An honest woman. I'd expected as much." He stared down into her eyes before saying softly, "I have to kiss you, Estelle."

His arms came around her, drawing her close against his chest. His mouth hovered over hers for a moment, and she felt the jittery thrill of anticipation. Then his lips covered hers in a kiss that drained her even as it filled her.

As he took the kiss deeper, his tongue darted between her lips, dueling with hers, mating, while his hands moved seductively across her shoulders, down her arms. On a moan of pleasure he backed her up against the rough wood of an empty stall and continued raining kisses over her eyes, her nose, her cheek.

She was so hot she was melting. Each touch of his hands, each press of his lips, made her blood heat more.

At the whimpering, sighing sounds she made his blood pumped furiously. He could hardly see through the dark mist of desire that nearly blinded him. He couldn't remember ever wanting anything or anyone so desperately.

"Stay with me, Estelle." He spoke the words inside her mouth. "Stay the night."

"No. Wait. I musn't." She put a hand to his chest, struggling to think. But all she could think of was him. The way his eyes, hot with desire, met hers. The way those big, work-worn hands moved over her. All she could taste was him. A dark, mysterious taste that was like no other. And the need for him. Pulling at her. Tugging at her. Making her weak with the wanting.

"I can't wait. I don't want to." He dragged her close and kissed her again, until she was breathless. "You don't want to. Admit it."

At that she went deathly quiet.

He pressed his advantage. "If you tell me to stop, I will, though I swear it'll kill me. Tell me, Estelle. Tell me to stop. Tell me you don't want this, too."

She could feel the pounding of his heart against her palm. It was as wild, as erratic, as her own. He wanted her. Wanted her. The knowledge bloomed inside her heart until it felt as though it would explode. And the truth was, she wanted him. Desperately.

In the silence of the night he waited for her answer. Everything depended on her next words.

She let out a long, deep sigh. "I can't tell you I don't want this. It would be a lie."

He reminded himself to breathe. For the first time the tension left his voice, smoothed it out with a smile. "Thank heaven." He lowered his mouth to hers, avid, hungry. And he feasted.

She'd never had a man taste her like this, as though she were a banquet. He lingered over her lips, drawing out every drop of flavor, before moving on to nibble her jaw, and then lower, running hot, wet kisses down the long column of her throat.

"Oh, Rob." The words were more a sigh than a whisper.

His mouth found hers again, and he kissed her until they were both breathless.

With a moan of sheer pleasure she wrapped herself around him, returning his kisses with such fervor, she couldn't quite believe what she was doing. She'd never before thought of herself as greedy. But she wanted to touch, to taste, to savor every kiss, every jolt, every sweet sensation.

The purely male flavor of him poured through her, leaving her giddy with delight. In her prim, practical world there had been so little time to indulge herself. Instead of dinners and dates there had been field trips and seminars. Instead of flowers and candy there had been theses and exams. But now—now, she could indulge her woman's heart. With Rob, she could have what her heart desired. It was all here for the taking, in this man. This moment. And this, this taste, was only the beginning.

Her fingers fumbled with the buttons of his shirt. She could hardly wait to feel that hard, muscled flesh she'd seen earlier today. She slid the shirt off his shoulders and allowed her hands to splay across his chest, loving the ripple of muscle beneath her palms.

She felt the coolness of the night air as his fingers lowered the zipper of her dress. It slid off her shoulders to pool at her feet.

"Why, Estelle." His voice was warm with laughter as he realized that she was wearing nothing beneath it. "Who would have thought it of you?"

She found herself laughing with him, and marveling at the fact that they could laugh at a time like this. "I think I'll have to lay the blame at your feet, Rob. You make me feel like a woman."

"You are a woman. A beautiful . . ." He ran soft, nibbling kisses across her shoulder. ". . . desirable . . ." He brought his mouth lower, to her collarbone. ". . . absolutely fantastic woman." With a growl in his throat that sounded more animal than human, he closed his mouth around one erect nipple.

The jolt shuddered through her, and she struggled against a tidal wave of feelings that threatened to swamp her. All she could do was hang on as wave after wave assaulted her, leaving her trembling with weakness.

Each tug of his mouth, each clever flick of his tongue, had her climbing higher, then higher still, until she wondered how she could possibly survive any more.

She clung to him, weak and boneless, afraid that at any moment her legs would refuse to support her. Sensing her need, he lowered her to the blanket, then stretched out beside her.

Despite the coolness of the night air, her flesh was hot and damp, and quivering beneath the clever ministrations of his big, calloused hands.

He couldn't get enough of this soft, soft skin. Never in his life had he felt so thoroughly aroused. He had to struggle against the raging desire to take her quickly. Needs pulsed and throbbed, threatening to explode. But still he held back, wanting more. Wanting all.

"Rob, I . . ." She suddenly stiffened as, with just his tongue, he sent her soaring. It was the most incredible feeling in the world, and all she could do was fist her hands in the blanket beneath her, feeling the straw shift and move as she reached the first crest.

This was how he'd wanted her. Writhing beneath him, her eyes huge, her heart hammering. And his name on her lips. Only his.

"Rob, please. I need you to . . ."

"Shhh." With a hot, hungry kiss he stilled her words. "I know, love. I can't wait any longer either." He levered himself above her, fighting the urge to devour her.

As he entered her, she wrapped herself around him and began to move with him, climbing higher, faster, than either of them could have ever imagined.

Where had this strength come from? This intense energy? It nearly consumed them with its heat.

They moved together, hearts hammering, lungs straining, as they climbed higher and higher until they reached the moon. And shattered in an explosion of stars.

"You actually brought supper?" Rob lounged against the rough wooden boards of the empty stall while Estelle opened the basket and removed a chilled bottle of champagne, along with caviar and toast points, rare roast beef nestled in flaky rolls, and exquisite little fruit tarts.

"I see my uncle thought of everything." Rob couldn't help laughing.

"He said Alfred had prepared it for you. But there's enough here to feed half the town."

"The old scoundrel had it all planned."

Estelle's head came up sharply. "Are you saying he knew that I'd . . . that we'd . . . ?"

Rob kissed her before spreading caviar on a sliver of toast. "He couldn't know for certain. But I'm sure he was hoping."

Seeing the flush on her cheeks, he fed her, then filled two fluted glasses with champagne and handed one to her before sipping. He crossed one bare foot over the other and studied her by the light of the lantern.

She was wearing his shirt. Unbuttoned, it fell open, revealing pale, creamy breasts. Her hair tumbled about her face and shoulders in a riot of tangles.

She laughed, then a moment later found to her embarrassment that her eyes were swimming.

"What's this?" He wrapped an arm around her shoulders and drew her close, kissing away her tears. "Regrets?"

"Never." She shook her head, struggling for composure. "It's just that I've never experienced anything quite like this. Or experienced anyone quite like you."

"I could say the same about you." He traced his index finger around the outline of her lips. "You're the only bright spot in my life right now, Estelle."

She sighed. "I hate what's being done to you. It's so unfair. I feel so helpless."

"Helpless? You?" He nuzzled her cheek and lightly nipped at her earlobe. "There's such strength in you. I sensed it the first time I saw you."

"Did you?" She turned to face him, her eyes shiny-bright in the light of the lantern. "I figured, the first time we met, you never even noticed me."

He chuckled, remembering. "I'd been meeting with the bankers. They'd refused to offer me any shred of hope. Then I came upstairs, in search of Fergus, and found you, looking all neat and buttoned up. For hours after the bankers were gone, I was still seeing you in my mind. And hearing your voice. And smelling your subtle perfume."

"Amazing. I'd have never guessed. Jamie told me you're very good at hiding your feelings."

"What else did that little rascal tell you?"

"That he's lonely because there are no more children to play with. And that I remind him of his mother."

"You definitely do not remind me of my mother. Especially in that shirt. I've decided I like it better on you." He brushed his lips over hers, then spread more caviar, handing a piece of toast to her, then tasting his own.

She stared into her glass. "Something Jamie said keeps nagging at my mind."

"What's that?"

"When Castle Clough was under siege, he was told to fetch the Star of Scotland, in the hope that it could be exchanged for the lives of his parents. He was mortally wounded and doesn't recall much after that."

"So?"

"I know that the odds are very good that the Star was actually stolen during the siege. But, Rob, what if it wasn't? What if it's still hidden somewhere here in the castle?"

"Impossible. This old place has gone through extensive remodeling throughout the centuries. Someone would have come across it."

"But what if no one did? What would such a thing be worth today?"

"The Star of Scotland?" He shook his head, considering. "Absolutely priceless."

"If it were found here in Castle Clough, who would own it?"

He shrugged. "I suppose it could legally be claimed by the Cameron clan. But something that historic, that special, should rightly be put on public display, so that it could be viewed by all the people."

"If you were to own such a treasure, and you offered it to the government, wouldn't they, in turn, see that your father's debt was paid in full?"

He caught a strand of her hair and wrapped it around his finger. "That's a lovely fantasy, Estelle Sinclair, but a fantasy all the same." Then he drew her close for a long, slow kiss that heated his blood and started his heart racing again. "This, on the other hand, is real. And now that I've regained my strength, I'd like to go for seconds, if you don't mind."

Her own heart was behaving like a runaway train. Against his lips, she whispered, "That's a lovely, bonny thought, your lordship. I don't mind in the least."

And then there was no need for words, as they lost themselves in a world of soft sighs and long, lingering kisses. A world reserved for lovers.

8

"Ah, here's our lass now." Sir Charles looked up from his breakfast as Estelle rushed in.

Fresh from the shower, she wore creamy wool slacks and a cream-colored turtleneck. Her hair was still damp and curling around a face that was flushed with embarrassment.

She and Rob had sneaked into the castle like two errant children, their clothes in disarray, bits of straw stuck in their hair. The first person they'd run into had been Desmond. Though he spoke not a word, Estelle had seen the flicker of emotion in his eyes as he stiffened his spine, then continued on his way.

By now, she was certain the entire castle knew that she and Rob had spent the night together in the barn. And she could tell, by the gleam in Sir Charles's eye, that he was delighted with the part he'd played in all this.

"Well, my dear. You look as rested as Rob. Come. Join us."

"I . . . really can't stay." She brushed a kiss over the old man's cheek, then took the chair Rob held for her. As she sat, he pressed a hand to her shoulder, allowing it to linger a moment before returning to the head of the table.

"Coffee, miss?" Desmond paused beside her.

"Yes. Thank you." She lifted her cup and sipped, aware that all three men were watching her.

"Now, tell us why you can't stay for breakfast." Sir Charles broke open a scone and smothered it with jelly.

"I've been checking my E-mail. The offers are starting to pour in on the items we've offered for sale. There's no time to waste. The deadline is almost upon us."

"Us." Sir Charles smiled. "I like the sound of that."

"I just meant . . ." She glanced up to see Rob sharing a grin with his uncle.

"Eggs, miss?" Alfred paused beside her and held out a steaming platter.

When she started to refuse, he spooned some onto her plate, then moved to stand beside Rob, and then Sir Charles. Without a word he returned to the kitchen, with Desmond following.

"Well." Sir Charles glanced at Rob, then at Estelle. "I'd say you've just been paid the highest of compliments, my dear. Alfred has rarely, if ever, taken the liberty of serving someone's plate. He must think you are special indeed."

She ducked her head, avoiding his eyes. "I can't imagine why."

"I'd say it's because he admires the way you're fighting to save this old place. It's something we all admire, my dear."

"I just wish I could do more." She ate a few bites, then pushed away from the table. "I'm sorry. I'd love to stay. But I have to get to the workroom and check my computer." She turned to Rob, and for a moment their eyes met and held. "I'll inform you of the first offers as soon as they're tallied."

He nodded, then surprised her by catching her hand and pressing it to his lips before releasing it. "I'll come by your workroom later."

When she was gone, he turned to his uncle. "I see the

grapevine has already begun buzzing about my nighttime activities.''

"I don't know what you mean." The old man seemed particularly intent upon sprinkling salt and pepper on his eggs.

"You old rascal. You're worse than Jamie."

Sir Charles looked up. His face broke into a wide smile. "Am I really?"

"Stop being so pleased with yourself."

"Have I reason to be?"

Rob threw back his head and roared with laughter. "I should be the one who's pleased. I can't remember when I've spent a more fascinating night. Or beheld a more beautiful sunrise."

"Then I'm happy for you." Sir Charles looked across the table at his nephew and smiled. "When you reach my age you realize what really matters most in this brief time on earth. Family. Honor. Love." He put a hand over Rob's and squeezed. "If a man should have all three, he is indeed blessed."

He beckoned to Fergus, who stood waiting in the doorway. "Come, lad. I think I'd like to take a turn around the gardens."

Rob waited until he was alone, then stood and walked to the windows, staring out at the stark, rugged Highlands. His uncle's words played through his mind. *Family. Honor. Love.* It was all that had ever mattered to him. His father had denied him the first, though his uncle had more than made up for it. As for honor, though he'd had his share of setbacks, he'd tried to lead an honorable life. And now, because of his father's weakness, even that might be sullied. As for the last, he'd feared it would forever elude him. Until Estelle. What a special gift she was.

With a sigh he turned away and headed toward her workroom, to face the figures that would determine his future.

"How are the numbers?" Rob paused in the doorway and watched as Estelle's fingers flew over the keyboard of her computer.

She looked up. ''Not as high as I'd hoped. If only we had time for a bidding war.''

He crossed the room and paused behind her. With his hands on her shoulders he pressed his lips to her temple. ''I agree with what my uncle said. I like the sound of 'we.' I'm so glad you're on my side.''

She closed one hand over his, then pointed to the computer screen. ''Here are the latest offers.''

She scrolled slowly, so that he could read the numbers. A quick tally told him they were far short of the amount needed.

''Add the paintings,'' he said tiredly. ''And anything else that can interest a buyer.''

''I've had a request for personal items from an American collector. He . . . mentioned a particular interest in your ancestors' sword and in the trunkful of clothes I found in the tower.''

She saw the way his eyes darkened before he nodded. ''All right. Have him make an offer.''

''Oh, Rob.'' She stood and wrapped her arms around his neck. ''I hate that this is happening to you.''

''So do I. But it can't be avoided any longer.'' He kissed her, lingering over her lips, taking comfort in her warmth. ''I'll be in the library, going over the papers. I expect that I'll be hearing from Griff before the day is over.''

''My, my.'' At Griff's deep voice from the doorway their heads came up sharply. ''Now isn't this a tender scene.''

Rob stepped forward, placing himself in front of Estelle, as though to keep her out of harm's way. Once again she was reminded of an ancient warrior. ''Why didn't you allow Desmond to announce you?''

Griff's tone sharpened with anger. ''Don't play lord of the manor with me, Rob, old boy. I don't need to be announced like some mere visitor. Soon this will all be mine.'' He stared beyond Rob to the woman who stood just behind him. ''Tell me, Professor. Have you managed to lure enough fools into bidding on these pathetic relics?''

She tucked her hand into Rob's, sharing her strength,

while drawing on his. "I don't report to you, Mr. Mackenzie. I work for Rob."

"Work for him? Is that what they call it these days?" He gave a short laugh. "Too bad you've chosen the losing side in this battle, Professor. I could have made your life extremely comfortable." His smile faded when he focused on Rob. "I'll wait for you in the library. I have an offer that might interest you."

"You have nothing that would interest me, Griff. If you want to talk, call my lawyer."

Mackenzie's eyes glittered with a dangerous light. "If you know what's good for you, you'll listen to what I have to say."

He spun on his heel and stormed away.

When they were alone, Estelle clutched Rob's hand. "Don't go. I don't trust him. I truly believe he could become violent. I can see it in his eyes."

He squeezed her hand, then brushed a kiss over the worried frown that marred her forehead. "Relax, love. Talk is cheap. It won't cost me anything to listen."

She watched as he exited the workroom. As she returned to the computer she couldn't shake the feeling of impending doom.

By late afternoon Estelle had tallied the final numbers, then printed them out. The thought of presenting them to Rob weighed heavily upon her heart. Even with the addition of the paintings and personal items, they were short of their goal. Which meant Rob would have to consider selling his herd.

She knew, from all she'd heard and observed, that the herd was much more than just his livelihood. It was his pride. His passion. It would be the cruelest loss of all.

"Bad news, Professor?" Griff stood in the doorway. On his face was a look of triumph.

Estelle took the papers out of the printer and clutched them to her, determined that he wouldn't see them.

"What's this? Secrets?" Griff was across the room in seconds. "So, Professor, what's the verdict?"

"You'll have to ask Lord Cameron."

"I'm asking you."

She started past him, but his hand shot out, stopping her in midstride. "Maybe you don't understand, Professor. I want that report."

She stared at his offending fingers, pressing painfully on her flesh. "You have no right to it."

"No right?" His voice was low with anger. "Don't you talk to me about rights. Do you know what it's like to have to claw and scratch your way out of the very bottom of a filthy hole, only to learn when you reach the top that there are others who will be allowed to push you aside? Not because they're smarter, or more clever, but because they were born to wealth. Born to it. And that gives them the right to fancy titles and special privileges the rest of us will never have. While I was still scrambling for my first dollar, Rob Cameron was sailing on fancy yachts and partying with royalty. Then, when he tired of that life, he came home to play the part of a country gentleman, reaping honors from his country for his precious herd of cattle. Well, he's about to get a taste of the cold, hard facts of reality. Now I'm the one with the money. And the power. And soon I'll have what should have been mine in the first place, if only he hadn't been born."

"So it's true that you resent him for simply being born."

"I hate him with every fiber of my being. And when I'm through with him, he will wish he had never been born." Griff tore the papers out of Estelle's hand and read the figures, then threw back his head and laughed. "Here." He shoved them at her, then turned away. "I've seen enough to know that by midnight tomorrow Castle Clough will be mine."

"Jamie." With Rob watching from the doorway, Estelle walked slowly around the workroom, calling softly, "Jamie, please come out."

After several minutes Rob shook his head. "I've told you, love. It's no use. No one has ever been able to entice

Jamie to show himself. He only comes out when he wishes.''

''Jamie.'' Estelle lowered her voice. ''I know you're frightened of Griffin Mackenzie. I know he's the reason you disappear. But he isn't here now. There's no one here who will harm you. And we need you. Please show yourself.''

In the silence that followed, she closed her eyes, wishing with all her heart that she could coax the lad to come out. When the room remained empty, she turned away in defeat.

Rob held out his hand, and she started toward him.

''Did ye come to play, then?''

At the sound of Jamie's voice she spun around. A smile lit her eyes. ''Oh, Jamie, I knew you'd come.''

''Ye woke me, Estelle Sinclair. I was havin' a lovely nap. Now are we goin' to play?''

She glanced at Rob, then nodded. ''Yes, Jamie. I have a wonderful game planned.''

''A game, ye say?''

Estelle nodded. ''That is, if you're willing to allow some others to see you.''

''Others?'' He backed up, looking alarmed.

''It's only Desmond and Alfred and Fergus.''

''They're not of the Cameron clan. I canna do it.''

''I'm not a Cameron either, Jamie. But you let me see you.''

''That's different. Ye remind me of my mother.''

''And what about the strangers who've seen you over the centuries? Not all of them were Camerons.''

''Aye. I did it to frighten them. Because I was tired of bein' alone.'' He paused, considering. ''What's this game we're to play?''

''Come here, Jamie.''

She took a seat at the worktable, and the lad climbed up on her lap.

''From what you've told me, I have some doubts about what really happened that day of the siege. I believe you may have managed to hold on to the Star of Scotland after you were wounded.''

"What makes you think that?"

"Because you're still here. And you're a clever, feisty lad. What if, before you . . . gave in to the seriousness of your wound, you had the presence of mind to hide it?"

"I dunna know. I canna remember. Is that what ye want, Estelle? Do ye wish to search for the Star?"

She nodded.

"But why? I've had hundreds of years to try and I've never found it. What makes ye think we'll succeed tonight, when we've never done so before?"

"I don't know, Jamie." She tousled his hair and pressed a kiss to his temple. "Maybe because there's so much at stake. If we don't find the Star of Scotland tonight, Castle Clough will pass from your clan's hands into the hands of your enemy tomorrow. I thought that, with your help, I'd have Desmond and Alfred and Fergus work with us to rip apart some of the walls around the area where you sleep. Are you willing to try?"

He looked up into her eyes, then glanced at the man in the doorway. In a voice meant for her ears alone, he whispered, "Ye love him, don't ye, Estelle?"

She nodded. "With all my heart."

He pushed free of her embrace and slid to the floor, then took several steps across the room.

She sighed, wondering why she'd ever thought he would agree to her plan. But as she stood up, preparing to leave, he turned toward her.

"All right," he said softly. "Call in the others. But they'd better not laugh at me."

9

"THIS WAS WHERE I woke up after the siege." Jamie knocked on the wall, and the others could hear the hollow sound, revealing a hole behind it.

True to her word, Estelle had cautioned the others not to react with fear or humor when they first caught sight of Jamie. Desmond had maintained his usual stony expression, showing absolutely no emotion. Alfred's scowl had deepened as he'd studied the lad's strange clothes and heard his ancient manner of speech. But Fergus had surprised them all by his smiling acceptance of this stranger. It was as though he knew instinctively that Jamie was a friend. He knelt and offered his hand. And with a matching smile, Jamie accepted the handshake.

Sir Charles joined in by calling encouragement from the doorway, where his wheelchair had been parked out of the way. With crowbars and handsaws and assorted other tools, they began an assault on the walls, tearing the lovely mahogany away, to reveal ancient stone and brick.

At first they were infused with excitement as they peeled

away the wood. The keen edge of anticipation kept the adrenaline pumping as they pulled aside every loose stone and brick and piece of mortar, searching every crack and crevice that might serve as a hiding place for the jewel.

Shortly after midnight Rob noticed that his uncle had fallen asleep in his wheelchair.

"Fergus," he called softly.

The lad looked up.

"Take my uncle upstairs and see him safely to his bed."

The young giant set aside his tools and hurried to do the lord's bidding.

Half an hour later Rob touched a hand to Desmond's shoulder. "Desmond, you and your brother have done all you can. Go to bed now."

"An hour more, your lordship."

"No." Rob shook his head. "Fergus and I will search a while yet. But the hour is late. You need your rest."

Reluctantly the two old men turned away and went off to their beds.

Fergus, who had returned, surveyed the damage, then picked up a crowbar and attacked the last section of wall. Several hours later he slumped down in a corner of the room, his head nodding. Rob covered him with a blanket and left him sleeping, then walked over to Estelle and Jamie, who were digging in the rubble.

"It's no use," he muttered.

Estelle continued working.

He felt a sense of sadness tinged with respect when he looked at her. Her clothes, her hair, were covered with dust. Her nails were torn and ragged.

With an oath he hauled her to her feet. "It's over, Estelle. It was a lovely dream, but it isn't meant to be. Now it's time to admit defeat."

"I won't. I can't. You can't either, Rob. You can't let everything you love fall into Griffin Mackenzie's hands."

He touched a hand to her hair. "Not everything I love will be his."

For the space of a heartbeat she didn't understand. Then,

as the knowledge of what he'd said penetrated, she started to weep.

He pulled her into his arms and pressed his face to her hair. "I do love this place. And all the things in it. But they're not nearly as important as you've become to me, Estelle. Don't you see? Griff will have only things. But I'll have the memory of what we shared here." He lifted her chin and brushed a kiss over her lips. "And in the end Griff will have nothing. And I'll have everything."

As Jamie watched, he was overcome with bittersweet memories. Of a father and mother who had loved each other just this way. Who had bravely faced the inevitable with the same courage, the same stoic determination.

"Is that it, then?" he whispered.

"Aye." Rob looked at Estelle.

They both turned to Jamie and held out their arms, and the lad allowed himself to be drawn into their embrace. For just a moment, as he squeezed his eyes tightly shut, he was almost able to imagine he was being held by his own father and mother.

But then he opened his eyes and knew he was still here. Trapped between heaven and earth.

"Don't look so sad, Jamie." Estelle kissed his tears-stained cheeks. "If you wish, we'll keep on searching."

Rob shook his head. "You're exhausted. We all are. Go up and shower, and try to get some sleep."

"What about you?" She studied the weary look in his eyes, the dark stubble of beard, the slump of his shoulders. Though he had tried to keep her spirits up, his own were battered.

"I've told the bankers to be here at nine. The mayor of Dunfield, as well as the council and police chief, were included, since it will affect all of them. We'll formally sign the documents and turn over everything to Griff."

At the very mention of that, Estelle saw Jamie shimmer, then disappear. With a sigh of defeat she linked her fingers through Rob's and together they walked out of the room.

● ● ●

Estelle passed a hand over her eyes in a gesture of weariness as she climbed the stairs to her room. What a fool she'd been. She'd honestly believed that somewhere in that old playroom they would find the mythical Star of Scotland. She'd hoped that peeling away the wood and revealing the original walls might at least trigger some glimmer of memory in Jamie's subconscious.

What had happened during that terrible siege? Had Jamie panicked as he believed? Not that it was anything to be ashamed of. He was only a lad. And he'd loved his mother and father and little brother so deeply. It must have been a nightmarish ordeal for him. Still, the fact that he was still here seemed somehow connected to his actions on that fateful day.

She passed the portrait of his parents and paused. She could see why he was reminded of his mother whenever he looked at her. Like the woman in the portrait, she had the same auburn hair, the same green eyes.

She studied the lovely, flowing gown with long, tapered sleeves and a high circlet of lace at the throat. There had been dozens of such gowns in the trunks stored in the tower room.

Suddenly she had a flash of insight. Could it possibly work? She shook her head. It might prove to be just another dead end. But it was worth a try.

Her exhaustion dissolved as she raced along the hallway, taking the steps to the tower two at a time.

Estelle studied herself in the mirror, fussing with her hair until she was satisfied that it closely resembled the hair of the woman in the portrait. Then she stepped back to view the gown. The fabric was so fragile the seams were coming apart. But the neckline was the same, with a high, tight circlet of lace at the throat and long tapered sleeves edged with matching lace at the cuffs. The fact that the skirt was so long she was tripping over it didn't matter.

She caught the skirt in her hands and descended the stairs.

When she entered the playroom, she was surprised to see

that Fergus had already swept up the debris. It lay in several piles of wood and sawdust and broken bricks and mortar, to be carted away later.

A second pile of dust-covered toys lay nearby. The wooden rocking horse. The child's sword.

By now, she surmised, Fergus would be upstairs, helping Sir Charles to dress and prepare for the dreadful day ahead. And Rob. Rob would be facing his bleak future the same way he faced everything. With courage and dignity.

"Jamie." She walked to the middle of the room and slowly circled. "Jamie. Please come out. I need you."

Out of the corner of her eye she saw a movement and turned to see the little boy, his hand over his mouth, yawning loudly. He blinked, then, seeing her, opened his eyes wide.

"Mother. Ye've come for me."

"Aye." She swallowed, fighting a wave of guilt. It was a sign of her desperation that though what she was doing might save Rob, it would be seen as nothing but a cruel hoax by this tenderhearted lad.

"I knew ye'd come one day. Are we goin' home now?"

"Not yet, Jamie lad." She clutched her hands together tightly, so afraid her voice would break and give her away. "First you must prove yourself worthy."

"I will, Mother. I'll do anything. Just tell me what I must do."

"You must bring me the Star of Scotland, my son."

"But I dunna know where it is."

"Close your eyes, Jamie. Then search your mind. Think back. I know you'll remember."

Just as he did, a voice from the doorway startled her.

"What's this?" Griff stared around with a look of puzzlement. Then, as he saw the devastation to the room, the realization dawned. "You knew."

"Knew what?" Estelle stared at him blankly.

"I thought I was the only one who had the complete history of Castle Clough. Patience swore to me that she hadn't told a soul about her discovery."

"Discovery?"

"Don't act so innocent, Professor. Obviously you uncovered the same facts that my late wife did."

"Yes. Of course. The facts." Though she hadn't a clue, she struggled to keep her features composed.

"Patience believed, from her research, that since the Star of Scotland has never surfaced, it has to be still hidden somewhere in this room. It was the last place the ghost had been."

"Ghost? Are you saying there's a ghost in Castle Clough?"

He seemed to notice her odd costume for the first time. In quick strides he crossed the room and caught her by the arm. "What game are you playing now, Professor?"

She tried to pull away. "I don't know what you mean."

"You know entirely too much. I was certain of it when I first met you. And I knew, even then, that I should have had you . . . eliminated, before you went any further."

"Let go of me, Mr. Mackenzie."

"Not this time, Professor. You've found the Star of Scotland, haven't you?" He plucked a small, thin object from his pocket. When he touched a finger to a button, it opened to reveal a razor-sharp blade. "If you value your life, you'll give it to me. Now." He pressed the blade to her throat.

"Is this what you did to your wife?"

He laughed, a high-pitched sound that scraped her nerves. "It wouldn't do to have the wife of the very successful Griffin Mackenzie found with her throat slit. I merely broke her lovely neck, then pushed her down a flight of stairs. It was neat and quick and final."

The ease with which he described such a gruesome event made her shudder. "And how will you explain this?"

"Easy enough. A thief. One who saw the signs of digging for treasure and decided to help himself. The authorities will be convinced when they see these piles of rubble. You surprised him, and he was forced to kill you before fleeing." He pressed the blade until he drew a thin line of blood. "Now give me the Star of Scotland, Professor. Or do you think it's worth dying for?"

"Nay." Jamie appeared in a shimmer of heat. "Dinna harm my mother."

"What this?" Griff shook his head and tightened his grasp on Estelle. "What sort of trick are you playing?"

"It's no trick!" the boy cried. "Unhand my mother, and I'll give ye what ye seek."

Griff's eyes narrowed in anger. "I don't know who or what you are, but I'm not stupid enough to do what you ask. First you'll produce the Star of Scotland. Then I'll let go of the woman."

"All right, then." With tears nearly blinding him, Jamie raced across the room and picked up the child's sword from a pile of rubble.

"You think you'll fight me with that toy?" Griff threw back his head and laughed.

"Nay." Jamie grasped the sword by the blade and pointed to the jeweled hilt. There, in the center, was a star-shaped diamond the size of a walnut.

Griff's eyes widened as the truth dawned. Through all the centuries, everyone had looked for the treasure in some secret place. But all this time it had been in plain view, and never once had anyone recognized it for what it was.

"Oh, Jamie!" Estelle could hardly believe her eyes. "You finally remembered."

"Aye, Mother. All these years it had been wiped from my mind, but seeing you again gave me back my memory." He dug his chubby fingers into the hilt until the jewel slipped free and dropped into his palm. Then he walked toward Griff, with his hand outstretched. "Here's what you want. Now release my mother."

"Gladly." Griff shoved her roughly aside and reached for the jewel. As he did, Jamie reached up with his other hand, thrusting a dagger into Griff's stomach.

For a moment the man was too stunned to react. Then, enraged and in pain, he brought his hand out in a wide arc, intent upon slashing Estelle.

"Nay!" With a cry Jamie pushed her aside, taking the blow meant for her.

The force of it sent him staggering backward, the knife buried deep in his small chest.

"Oh, no! Jamie, no!" Estelle dropped to the floor, cradling the boy's head in her lap.

"Now I'll just take what's mine," Griff muttered as he started toward them.

"The only thing that's yours is a future in prison, Griff." The sound of Rob's voice stopped his old enemy in his tracks.

When he looked up, Griff saw Rob standing in the doorway, holding his ancestor's jeweled sword.

"Do you think you're man enough to use that?" Griff challenged.

Rob's voice was pure ice as he stepped closer, lifting the sword as he did. "There's only one way to find out."

Griff glanced beyond him to the doorway and realized that they weren't alone. Crowding in behind Sir Charles and Fergus were Desmond and Alfred, half a dozen bankers, and the mayor and police chief of the nearby village of Dunfield.

Knowing he was defeated, Griff lifted his hands in surrender.

At once the police chief strode forward and secured his hands with handcuffs.

"It was self-defense." Griff's voice rang with authority. "I'll never be convicted. It's obvious this woman is crazy. You can tell by her ridiculous costume. She attacked me when I walked in."

"Jamie is dying!" she cried, "and this is the man who inflicted the fatal wound." But she knew by the puzzled looks on the faces of the strangers in the doorway that they couldn't see the lad.

Griff shot her a look of triumph. "You see? She's absolutely mad."

"Rob." She turned to him in desperation. "Griffin Mackenzie confessed to killing your sister."

With a cry of rage Rob grabbed the front of Griff's shirt and aimed his sword at his heart.

"Please, your lordship," the chief said sternly. "Let the authorities handle this."

"Aye." With a long, slow hiss of anger Rob leaned close to whisper, "I wish you had given me the satisfaction of avenging my sister's death. But at least I know you'll pay, Griff. For the rest of your miserable life."

He tossed the sword aside and knelt beside Estelle, watching helplessly as she stroked the lad's cheek.

"Hold on, Jamie," she whispered through her tears. "You were so brave."

She looked up at Rob. "This is all my fault. I tricked him into believing I was his mother so that it would jog his memory about the jewel. But I never intended this. He took the blow meant for me."

Rob wrapped an arm around her shoulders. Against her temple he murmured, "Don't you see? It's what he wanted to do that first time, and couldn't. Now he's had his chance to get it right."

Her eyes widened as she realized the truth of it. And then, as they both watched, Jamie's eyes opened, and he smiled. "This is for you, Lord Cameron. And for all the Camerons through the centuries. Guard it well." He handed him the Star of Scotland. Then he looked over, and his smile grew radiant. "There you are, Mother. I've been waiting so long."

At first Estelle struggled with guilt, thinking she had once again deceived the poor lad. Then she realized that he wasn't looking at her. He was looking just beyond her. She turned to see a shimmer of light. And then, still smiling, Jamie began to glow, brighter and brighter, until the light was so brilliant that she and Rob had to shield their eyes.

"Are we going home now?" Jamie whispered.

There was a sound like the rushing of wind, and then the room went eerily silent.

While the others looked on without comprehension, Rob helped Estelle to her feet, then drew her into his arms, where she wept uncontrollably.

Epilogue

THE HOUSE WAS strangely silent. For a while the grounds of Castle Clough had been turned into a media circus as news photographers vied for glimpses of the notorious Griffin Mackenzie being led away. The authorities had conducted endless hours of interviews. A score of security officials from the government had already taken the Star of Scotland to a safe place, until the government could work out with Lord Cameron the details of its future. Though all agreed that the priceless treasure was the property of the Cameron clan, Rob had generously suggested that it was too important to be locked away in a vault. In time it would be put on view, presumably in a public building, for the whole world to admire.

Even now Rob and his lawyers were in the library meeting with representatives of both the government and the bank, and historians from several museums, reviewing the legalities involved.

Estelle folded the ivory wool dress and set it in her suitcase. She thought of the night she had worn it, then turned toward the window, deep in thought. Who would have ever believed that a few short weeks in Scotland would change her life so dramatically? She had lost her heart and for a while thought she was losing her mind. She would never see life in quite the same narrow way again.

Upon hearing the knock on the door she looked up.

Fergus entered, carrying an armload of logs. Without a word he bent and tended the fire, then stood, wiping his hands on his pants.

"Thank you, Fergus." She managed a smile. "I'll be finished packing soon. I'm expecting a car and driver within the hour. Could you come back shortly and carry my luggage downstairs?"

He nodded, then walked out of the room.

A few minutes later Estelle heard a knock at the door and hurried over. Sir Charles was seated in his wheelchair, with Fergus behind him.

"May I come in, my dear?"

"Of course, Sir Charles." She held the door while Fergus pushed him across the threshold.

Once inside, he waved the lad away.

"So." He glanced at her luggage. "It's as Fergus told me. You're leaving."

She nodded, no longer curious as to how the lad communicated. Perhaps he spoke. Maybe he used sign language. It wouldn't surprise her if he simply transferred his thoughts to others. Here in this fanciful place, anything was possible. "My work here is over, Sir Charles."

"Is it?" He pushed on the wheels of his chair, propelling himself around the room. "What about Rob?" He turned his head to study her carefully. "Do you love him?"

She swallowed. "Yes, but . . ."

"Do you think he loves you?"

"I think . . ." She chose her words carefully. "I think, now that his debt has been cleared, he will want some time to himself. Time to think about the future. As for me, it's time I got back to New York. To reality." A reality that didn't include life in a castle with a wealthy, handsome

Highland lord. That was for novels. It didn't happen in real life. Like everyone and everything else in this place, she had simply fallen under a spell.

"Ah, yes. New York. I'm sure one must be strong and . . . firmly grounded to survive there."

"Exactly. After a lifetime there, I know a little about survival."

He smiled then and halted his chair in front of her dresser. For long moments he stared at the framed picture of a young Estelle with a beautiful, auburn-haired woman. His smile faded, and he plucked the photo from her dresser.

She saw him trace his finger over the woman in the picture. "What are you doing, Sir Charles?"

"Remembering." He looked up. "I should have known. You look like her, you know."

"My aunt?"

"Aye. Rose. I wasn't certain, of course. You'd never told me her name. But the moment I saw you, I thought it was a possibility."

"I don't understand . . ."

"I told you I was in love once, and for that one brief summer, I was deliriously happy. But events happened that changed the course of both our lives forever. Her sister and brother-in-law died, and there was a child to raise. And my own family was in need of me."

Estelle's mouth dropped open, but no words came out. Finally she managed to whisper, "You and Aunt Rose?"

"Aye, lass. Did she never speak of it?"

Estelle shook her head. "She said only that she had loved once, and it was enough to sustain her for a lifetime. I always thought it too painful for her to talk about. But I never dreamed . . ."

"It was the same for me. It's the curse of Castle Clough, my dear. Cameron men love too deeply. They give their hearts but once. And that one woman is loved with a depth of passion that is all-consuming. So you see, when you wondered aloud if your aunt had a hand in getting you here, you now have the answer. You were meant to be here. With Rob." He pressed the photo to his heart. "And I was meant to learn the truth. My beloved Rose never married another. She went to her grave loving only me. Which means that if we couldn't be together in this life, we will surely be together in the next." He looked up at Estelle. "Do you know what love, true love, really means?"

"I think I do."

"If you do, you must know that Rob is under the same curse. If you go, you'll condemn him to a life of loneliness. Is that what you want?"

"I want . . . I want to do what's right. I want to give Rob a chance to enjoy this new freedom. I want . . ." She was too overcome to speak. All she could do was shake her head. Suddenly chilled to the bone, she went to the fireplace and stood staring into the flames.

She didn't know how long she stood there. But when she turned, Sir Charles was gone. And Rob was standing behind her.

"Estelle." He saw the pain and confusion in her eyes and clenched a fist at his side. "I wanted to come to you sooner." He ran a hand through his hair in frustration. "So many demands on my time. So many interruptions. But all I really wanted was to be here with you. I can see that you've been deeply disturbed by all that has happened. For that I'm truly sorry."

She turned back to stare at the flames. "It really happened, didn't it, Rob? Even though the others swore they didn't see or hear any of it, we didn't just dream it, did we?"

"It truly happened. Jamie's gone, love. Our little scamp has finally gone home. And though I'm happy for him, I'll miss him."

When she started to weep silently, he drew her close. Against her hair he whispered, "Maybe we'll be blessed with a little scamp of our own. That is, if you'd be willing to uproot yourself and make your life with a country farmer in this lonely, out-of-the-way village in the middle of the Highlands."

"How can you . . ." She tried to laugh, but it came out in a sob. ". . . be so sure? After all we've been through?"

"I've never been so sure of anything in my life. And though the time isn't right, and the setting isn't romantic, I'm humbly asking you to marry me."

"Oh, Rob." She offered her lips, and he kissed her with such tenderness, she felt her heart nearly break. "I don't need sweet words or romantic settings. What you've just described sounds like pure heaven. I can't think of anything I'd rather do than spend the rest of my life here in this magical, wonderful place with you."

"Estelle. My little star. I love you desperately." He pressed slow, deliberate kisses on each of her eyelids, her cheeks, the tip of her nose. "I couldn't bear to spend even one night without you. If you agree, I'll have the mayor of Dunfield do the honors tomorrow."

She wrapped her arms around his neck and gave a little laugh of pure delight. Then she caught his hand. "Come on, Rob. We'll go and tell your uncle. He'll be so happy."

"In a while, love." He lifted a hand to the buttons of her prim, high-necked blouse and slowly unfastened each one before pressing his lips to the hollow of her throat. "But first I just want to love you. The way all the Camerons have loved their women, from the beginning of time."

As she lost herself in his kisses, Estelle found herself blessing the one who had put such a tantalizing curse on Castle Clough. Because of it, she would one day die the happiest of women. But not young, she vowed. For that wasn't a part of the curse at all. The curse was love. Enough love to last a lifetime and beyond. Or at least until they had filled these lonely rooms with enough Camerons to carry on the tradition for generations to come.

STARRY, STARRY NIGHT

★

Marianne Willman

For my sisters, Jane Clark, Elizabeth Clancy-Brown, and
Lowell Montgomery Clark

For my other sisters—Nora Roberts, Ruth Ryan Langan,
Jill Gregory, Karen Katz, and Laura Sparrow

And for every dreamer who ever hoped and wished upon a star

1

Cornwall

Lɪʟʏ Kᴇɴᴅᴀʟʟ ᴡᴀs lost.

What had been a pleasant evening walk between the dramatic Cornish cliffs and the dark, foaming waves had become a dangerous venture. She'd strayed too far.

One moment the evening sky was a Van Gogh painting, all sapphire depths and bright, swirling stars. The next it was a blank gray canvas, as the fog came sweeping in from the bay. The sparkling indigo sea had vanished, and the craggy walls of lichen-covered rock had as well. It had seemed to happen in a literal blink of the eye.

And in the same time span, she had transformed herself from a sophisticated American traveler into a silly tourist caricature.

Somewhere behind her, the picturesque village with its narrow houses tiled in colorful slate and steep, cobbled streets was nestled cozily against a sharp upthrust of land.

Somewhere ahead—not too far, Lily prayed—lay the gentle slope up from the bay and along the strand to the lovely old hotel where she was staying. Exactly where, was the question. And the way back was strewn with great boulders and slippery, ankle-twisting stones.

Taking the shortcut along the base of the cliffs had been a miscalculation. A bad one. In fact, she thought distractedly, this whole trip was turning out to be a huge mistake.

She wished she were back home in her apartment in Washington, D.C., curled up in her fuzzy robe, watching an old movie on video. She would even trade her present adventure in for her familiar workaday world of fluorescent lights and gray filing cabinets, beige computers and worn metal desks.

But lately she had been feeling just as lost there, as if she were being smothered by layers of rules and protocol. The offer of promotion into the ranks of upper management had thrown her into a panic.

"My advice to you, Miss Kendall," her supervisor had told her, "is to take all your accumulated vacation days. Rethink your priorities. If you turn down this promotion, then they are certainly not here at the Department of Transportation."

This wild Cornish coast was as far removed from Washington's corridors of power as anything could be. The heavy mist clung to Lily, slid over her skin like a cool caress as she worked her way across the slippery strand. The breeze teased wisps out of her long blond braid as she struggled to get her bearings—a task that was increasingly impossible in the distorting layers of thickening fog.

Her supervisor's words had shaken her. She'd envisioned herself years from now, her identity gone, fossilized in the artificial world of work and career. How had she gotten so far from the dreams she'd woven for herself in college?

The decision of where to go to do this rethinking of priorities hadn't been difficult. Caribbean beaches seemed to be made for honeymooning couples, and the idea of joining a tour group lacked appeal. Her mother's ancestors had come from Cornwall. With its fantastic nineteenth-century bridge spanning the Tamar, its legends of Ygraine, King Arthur, and Merlin, that westernmost tip of Great Britain had always called to her—and how could she resist exploring a place with quaint names like Lostwithiel, Rump's Point, Land's End, and Mousehole?

She now stood on a shingle beach in a foreign country, lost, with an impenetrable mist rising like ancient wraiths around her.

Lily forced herself to listen. She could hear the sound of the waves rolling in to her right, could sense the massive bulk of the granite headland to her left, from the echoes bouncing back. A strange yearning filled her, a deep and terrible loneliness, as if she were the last person on the face of the earth. Wrapping her arms around herself for warmth, she headed in the direction that she thought led to the granite base of the cliffs.

The fog thickened and took on the texture and density of a damp wool sock. She was cold, cocooned in a narrow, alien world that was devoid of shape and color. The sound of her footsteps on the shingle beach was muffled, swallowed up by the thickening atmosphere. The sound of the wind was like a chorus of whispers, filled with a desperate, infinite longing. A shiver danced up her back.

Lily knew she had no business taking unknown routes in an unfamiliar landscape. She was a city girl, born and bred to concrete, asphalt, and taxis, to museums and theaters and high-rise apartments, and Chinese takeout on the corner. But hadn't that been part of the reason she'd come here to Cornwall, because it was far removed from her workaday life and totally different?

"Picturesque, and very restful," the travel agent had told her. "Calm."

A slimy tendril of seaweed snaked around Lily's bare ankle, and she yelped in alarm. "Calm, my ass!"

She kicked the attacking weed away. No need to panic. She was an intelligent and resourceful adult—and, she tried to tell herself, she was having an adventure. "I'll laugh at myself in the morning!"

The sound of her own voice was so comforting that Lily

almost convinced herself. Then another cold wave crashed against the shore, stronger than the last. It came hissing through the shingle as if it were alive, tugging at her ankles, urging her to follow it home to the sea.

Her canvas summer shoes filled with water, and before she could take them off to shake it out, another wave came swirling in. The sand sucked at her feet, and the cold water stung her bare legs. The lower half of her expensive embroidered linen dress was soaked and dripping. This wasn't the pleasant bay she'd seen in the brochures. Not by a long shot.

Squelching along in her sodden shoes, Lily moved up the beach toward the relative safety of the bluffs. Anything to get away from the increasing roar of the waves, the reach of the hungry sea.

All she had to do now was find the base of the cliffs and follow the headland around to the other side—without breaking a leg, getting caught by the tide, or succumbing to hypothermia.

Her right foot skittered on something slimy, and she recoiled. God only knew what disgusting things the waves might have cast up! Another wave slammed up the steep shore, and she lost her footing. The swirling, foaming water undercut the rocks beneath her feet.

One moment she was fighting to keep her balance, the next she was caught in a cold, salty wall of water, being sucked out toward the blackness of the bay.

Gut-wrenching fear gripped Rees Tregarrick as he braved the strong wind. No one from the village was fool enough to stray past Yearning Head by night. But there was a woman down at the base of the cliffs, picking her way through rocks as if she were out on a Sunday shell-gathering expedition.

He knew, beyond a doubt, that it was the woman who haunted his dreams. Whether ghost or reality, he had to know. If she was real, her danger was acute.

Atop the headland, the sky was unusually clear and filled with the largest, most scintillating stars he'd ever seen—

even at sea. The stars had drawn him out of the house toward the cliff's very edge. He hadn't gone there in the three years of his recuperation. Of his self-imposed sentence and exile. The house was his world. The sea—once his mistress, his lover—formed the bars of his invisible prison, locking him away on land.

But tonight he'd been drawn to the headland. No, had almost been forced here. While his mind was filled with tortured thoughts of loneliness and death . . . of Catherine . . . *she* had come lightly down the shingle beach, lost and out of her element, like a sea-maiden cast up from the waves onto the shore.

It was still a long way to the stairs carved into the granite of the headland. His stomach clenched. Would he get there in time, or would she be washed out with the undertow before his very eyes? He didn't think he could bear to see her white body thrown against the rocks. The urge to flee back to the safety of the house was almost as potent as the urge to save her.

Rees Tregarrick stumbled and cursed his way through the dark, wondering if he would be in time to rescue her from the cold, dark sea.

Lily's skirt snagged on the edge of a rock, and she wedged herself against it with all her might. When the wave retreated, she struggled to her feet again, barely managing to keep her shoes from being washed away.

Shivering in her light dress, chest heaving with exertion and fear, she scrambled away from the bay. Her situation was desperate, and she prayed to find her way safely back to the resort. Instead of a prayer, a jingle she'd learned in her grade-school days floated into Lily's mind:

> *Little star, do not hide*
> *Please come out and be my guide.*
> *Through rain and snow and darkest night,*
> *Guide me with your shining light.*

Lily lifted her eyes . . . and *there it was!*
It was incredible, the largest star she'd ever seen. And

the only one visible through the shifting layers of fog overhead. Instinct urged her to follow it, and she obeyed. With
every step the light led her farther away from the restless
murmur of the sea.

Thank God!

The nearer she got to the cliffs, the thinner the fog grew,
until it shredded on the rocks like old lace. She had never
realized that the air could have so many different shapes
and textures.

She was still disoriented, but the star led Lily on, away
from the increasing roar of the waves. Now and again the
star vanished behind the prowlike outthrust of the headland.
Each time, her heart turned over. She was terribly afraid
that she would lose sight of it for good.

A few more feet, and suddenly she stopped dead. This
couldn't be right. It seemed the star was leading her back
toward the water now. That felt wrong at best, and dangerous at worst. She hesitated. Foolish to trust her life to a
light that could be far out at sea for all she knew. Changing
her direction, she turned back toward the cliffs. She hadn't
gone ten feet when she heard a voice carried on the wind:

"Not that way! Tack around to your former position."

Lily was startled. The voice was deep, male, and urgent.
"What? Where are you?"

*"Damn it, keep moving toward the headland! The tide
is about to rush in. Hurry, or you'll be swept away!"*

The tide? *Jesus!* Her teeth chattered in fright and cold.
"Where are you? I can't see you."

*"Waste no time talking! Keep bearing to port, lass. No,
damn your eyes! That's starboard. Turn to your left! Ah,
that's right! Hurry now."*

The urgency in the man's voice spurred Lily to action.
She had to trust him. She could hear the waves roaring as
they smashed against the rocky shelf just past the headland.
Not much time! Dashing over the loose shingle, she turned
her ankle and swore as a line of fire seared up her leg.

"Come on, lass. You can do it!"

Half hopping, half sliding, and swearing fully, Lily followed the voice. The fog was thinning now, and she could

see the dark waves coming, row on row, against the foot of the cliffs ahead. She knew without looking back that the way behind her was already under water. Too late!

"Oh, God!"

"You're there! You've made it! Only another step . . ."

Lily stumbled over a snag of driftwood and pitched forward. Her hand touched something cold and scaly, and recoiled instinctively. Then she realized it was only a rusty metal handrail. There were stairs leading up, barely visible in the mist, and burning like a beacon above them was that single scintillating star.

Catching the rail, she hauled herself up the steps as quickly as her numbed feet would go. They were rough, carved from the cliff itself, but felt wonderfully solid after the shifting surface of the beach. The sea thundered up behind her, and she felt the wave break against the bottom step in a cold spray. Fear gave her the strength to bolt up the next steps. She was almost at the top when she heard the roar of an incoming wave, louder and higher than the last.

Despair and disbelief rattled her: *Jesus! I'm not going to make it!*

A hand reached out to grasp her arm roughly. "Easy, there, lass. I've got you!"

Now a second hand grasped her other wrist, pulling her off her feet and up against the slick granite surface of the rock. Her rescuer let one hand go free. Lily dangled helplessly, a sob lodged like a bone in her throat. The misty world reeled in a haze of vertigo. She smelled wet wool and male sweat. Then a strong arm wrapped tightly about her waist, and she was half hauled, half carried up and over to the top of the cliff.

She sat against a rock, gasping for breath, her fingers digging into the wet grasses. A hand brushed her cheek. "It's all right, lass. I wasn't sure for a moment if you'd make it free of the waves. But you managed . . . barely."

She was tired and weak with reaction. "Why didn't you help me sooner, instead of just shouting at me?"

"I would have, if I could."

For just a moment the fog swirled and shifted. She had a fleeting glimpse of a man in his prime bending over her: thick, dark hair, hawklike features, a firm, sensual mouth. He was dressed in a heavy fisherman's sweater of ivory wool and leaned on a crutch.

"Oh, God! I didn't know . . . I'm sorry!"

His voice was curt. "No more sorry than I. Come with me. Don't dawdle."

Lily was too cold and wet and frightened to argue.

She didn't even ask where they were headed. At the moment she would have cheerfully gone off with Norman Bates, Freddy Krueger, and the entire cast of a Hollywood horror film.

"Wait!" He stripped off his heavy sweater, then pulled it over hers. It came past down her knees. As Lily snuggled into the warm wool, the cold bite of the wind eased.

"Come along. We'll get you to shelter."

Her rescuer was strong, despite his limp, and his hand on her arm urged her forward with each flagging step. Shock and cold had taken a toll on her energy, and she stumbled on her injured ankle, but he covered the ground without a misstep.

"How can you see where we're going in this fog?"

"Fog?" He gave her a curious look, then shook his head. "I know every inch of this godforsaken place," he said, propelling her onward.

They passed through an iron gate set in a lichened granite wall. Once they were through it, the fog dissipated like magic. It was only then that Lily saw the lighted windows of a Victorian facade. Like the village houses, it was made of local granite and slate; but the lines were softened by porches and bays, gables and spires, and gracefully curved towers.

Light spilled from the far turret's beautiful and unusual window. Myriad triangles of golden glass radiated from a central diamond-shaped pane. It glowed in the misty haze, looking for all the world, Lily thought, like something from a Christmas card.

"The star!" she exclaimed. "I saw it from below. I thought it was real!"

He didn't answer.

Lightning shattered the blackness in the distance, illuminating the roiling clouds with orange light. It was a startling sight, as if the night had cracked open, revealing hints of a molten sky. He stopped in midstride and tipped his head back defiantly. Another flash of lightning was reflected in his eyes. Lily thought he swore beneath his breath, but the wind snatched away the words.

His grip tightened on her elbow, and he guided her purposefully toward the house. Lily's ankle felt better, but she still had to hurry to keep pace.

She had her bearings now. The cliff road picked up at the end of the narrow drive. Just down the steep hill and around the bend, the village of St. Dunstan clung to the granite shore. But—shouldn't the red lights on the steel communications antenna above the harbor be visible from here?

With every step removed from danger, her survival instincts came more to the fore. There was no reason she couldn't continue on to her hotel. Even if the threatening rain did materialize, she would be no wetter than she was now, and the brisk walk would warm her.

She hadn't lived most of her life in Washington, D.C., without picking up a certain degree of cynicism: Compounding one mistake with another wasn't very wise. Her companion had rescued her, yes, but he was still a complete stranger.

They were almost to the porch when she pulled away. "Words are inadequate, but—thank you. I'm five minutes from my hotel. If you'd be kind enough to let me keep your sweater until morning, I'll be on my way," she said firmly.

"Don't be more daft than you've already proved!" he said sharply. "You'd not get far in this weather."

On the heels of his words a hard rain came rattling out of the night, and the wind tore through the trees. A scattering of twigs and dried leaves blew across the cobbles.

He brought her up to the door and turned the handle. It swung wide to reveal a paneled hall with a grand, winding staircase at one side and a thin woman in a dark dress standing anxiously at its foot.

When she saw them she went paper-white, and put a hand over her heart. "Captain Tregarrick!"

Lily was aware of how she must look, with water dripping from her hair and her dress plastered against her body. She started to shiver violently.

"The little fool was caught below the cliffs and almost washed away," he said harshly.

Without another word, the man the other woman had called Captain Tregarrick ushered Lily through the reception hall toward the stairs, past paintings in heavy frames and beneath the light of twin lamps.

The woman gathered her scattered wits. "What a start you gave me! I thought . . . Well, never mind what I thought. Thank the good Lord, you reached the poor girl in time!"

She hurried to Lily's side. "Come in, come in, poor dear. We'll have you set to rights before you know it."

"Where do you want her, Mrs. Penhale?"

"In the kitchen, of course. It's warmest there, and I've a kettle already on the boil."

There was something about the woman, with her welcoming blue eyes and concerned expression, that eased Lily's fears. No harm would come to her here.

As they passed the japanned sideboard by the staircase, she had her first good look at her rescuer in the warm light of the oil lamps. Mist beaded his thick, dark hair and clung to his lashes. His straight brows were drawn into a scowl above an aquiline nose, and he had the stubborn jaw and firm mouth of a pirate-hero from an old MGM swashbuckler.

He tossed his crutch onto a satin settee and snatched up a blackthorn cane from the large majolica vase used as an umbrella holder. Every movement was swift and economical.

Lily studied him. *Lean and stern as the granite cliffs of*

the headland, she thought. His hard-muscled body, beneath the rain-smoothed striped cotton shirt, seemed carved of the same material.

He was, Lily thought, quite simply the best-looking man she'd ever seen.

And, apparently, the angriest. That much was evident in the harsh lines that bracketed his eyes and mouth. He hadn't once looked squarely at her. Outside, those eyes had seemed darker than the night around them. But they weren't black at all. His irises were dark gray and blue flecked with white, like a wind-chased sea. She could sense, more than see, the bitter emotion that flickered in their fathomless depths.

"See to her needs," he told the woman brusquely. "Keep her out of my sight."

With those kind words of welcome, he handed Lily over into Mrs. Penhale's care.

2

W︎ITHOUT SO MUCH as a good-bye, Captain Tregarrick vanished through the open door into what appeared to be a cozy study, and shut it behind him. The room seemed vastly emptier without his dominating presence.

Then Lily was whisked away toward the back of the house and through a green baize door. "Is he always so outgoing and friendly?" she asked, barely reining in her sarcasm.

"You'll not mind his ways," the woman said as they entered the warm kitchen. "The captain is not used to having strangers about. Nor has he ever been one to pass the time of day. Comes of being off to sea, no doubt. Grew up on the bay, he did, sailing his little boat from the time he was a lad."

The housekeeper plucked a colorful quilt from the back of a painted rocker and clucked over Lily like a hen with one chick. "Poor lamb, let's get you warm. Sit here, by the fire."

The kitchen was all whitewashed stone, scrubbed pine, and shining pots and pans. A fat lamp with a white opal-glass shade hung over the table. The heat of an ancient cooker—enameled a stunningly bright yellow—made the big room cheerful and as warm as toast.

The housekeeper dipped out a hearty serving of soup and took a thick slice from a crusty loaf of bread. "Eat up, while I serve the tea."

She smiled as she poured a generous splash of liquid from an amber bottle into the stout china mug. "You're new to St. Dunstan, Miss . . . ?" The woman managed to make the question seem like a friendly comment.

"Yes. I'm Lily Kendall. I'm staying at the Castle Inn."

"And I am Mrs. Penhale. I keep house for Captain Tregarrick."

"It's a big house to keep!" Lily said, stirring sugar into the tea. In its day, the mansion would have been filled with housemaids and parlormaids and scullery girls. "It must be difficult to manage such a large place these days."

"Oh, aye. It's been hard since the missus was lost, and I feared for him," Mrs. Penhale said, leaving Lily more than a little confused. "You finish that up, and I'll just have a word with the captain."

"Of course."

Lily wondered if Captain Tregarrick had suffered his injury in service to his country or if there was a more mundane reason. Now that the adrenaline rush of danger had waned, the warmth of the room and the tot of brandy in the tea lulled her senses. She had such a cozy, contented feeling that she didn't want to stir. Certainly not to go back out in the fog and rain. By the time the housekeeper returned, she was nodding.

"It's all settled," Mrs. Penhale announced. "Mr. Tregarrick has sent word down to the inn. You'll spend the night here, snug and safe, and Jem will drive you down on the morrow."

Lily didn't resist. "Thank you, Mrs. Penhale. And please thank Mr. Tregarrick."

The strangeness of the situation took on a surreal atmosphere. *I am having an adventure!* Lily told herself, and was glad that years of rigid routine hadn't rotted away her ability to sit back and enjoy the unexpected. More than ever, she was glad she'd taken a leave and come to Cornwall. Everything about it was so vastly different from anything she knew at home.

And now the fog, the threatening tide, and the handsome, brooding master of the manor only added to her wonderful sense of unreality.

Or perhaps, she thought belatedly, *it's the brandy.*

In any case, she wasn't about to turn down an offer to spend a night in this marvelous house. And, truth to tell, she was hoping for another encounter with the handsome and taciturn Mr. Tregarrick. *Just to thank him,* she told herself. *That's all.*

The housekeeper took a small lamp and led her up the staircase and down a hall. Lily caught a glimpse of herself in the mirror behind the desk, her blond hair turned mousebrown with dampness, her fair skin several shades paler with exhaustion. At the sight, she cringed. "Drowned rat" would be too kind a description.

"I've put you in the Green Chamber," Mrs. Penhale said. "It's at the end of the hall. There's a fire laid, and to my fancy, it's the prettiest bedchamber of the lot."

Lily looked around. "Where is the big window that looks like a star?"

Mrs. Penhale stopped short and turned to her. "It's at the far end of the corridor and up the winding stairs. But please . . . don't think of going up there, lass. Mr. Tregarrick doesn't allow it."

"Why?" Lily smiled. "Is it haunted?"

"Only by him," the housekeeper said sadly. "Ah, lass, only by him."

She started off again, and Lily had to hurry to keep up with her.

Rees Tregarrick paced the floor of the study. He had been almost happy in his isolation. One by one he'd learned to wind his strong emotions down, furling them like unneeded sails. He'd vowed he would stay at Star House until Catherine sent him a sign that she forgave him. In three years no sign had come.

Until tonight.

It had come with the storm and wind and near violence, in the person of a small, blond-tressed woman, with a heart-shaped face and a softly rounded body. The question was, What was he meant to do? He stared out the window at the slashing rain.

After Mrs. Penhale went off, Lily lay beneath the down comforter in the Green Chamber, in the flannel nightgown the housekeeper had provided. Warmth seeped into her bones as she watched the small flames of the banked fire contentedly. She couldn't think of a cozier place to be on a night of such wind and rain. The windows rattled in the gale, but the room was exquisite, far nicer than the one she'd taken at the Castle Inn. Light flickered on the white-painted woodwork and the walls hung with pale silk in green and rose to match the bed hangings.

The soft linen pillowcase was edged with crocheted lace and carried faint scents of sun-washed air, of sea lavender and lemon verbena. Lily imagined Mrs. Penhale gathering herbs and flowers from an old-fashioned garden and making little sachets to tuck among the household linens. *As if she'd have time, with this big house to look after!*

There was something to be said for the slower pace of the days gone by, Lily thought. In this old house the past seemed very real, just as it did in the village. She wished she could see the rest of the house, but doubted that the taciturn Mr. Tregarrick would invite her back for a guided tour.

An odd man, her rescuer. There was no doubt in Lily's mind that he'd saved her life. And then, after bringing her home, he'd casually dumped her on Mrs. Penhale, as if she were a bedraggled stray kitten he'd found shivering in the rain. A strange man.

An interesting man.

She wondered what had happened to him. Not whatever it was that had made the crutch and cane necessary, but whatever it was that had made his eyes so dark and angry. Even now she could vividly recall the restless energy he radiated. Walking beside him had been like standing beneath a high-tension wire. Every cell in her body had been aware of every cell in his.

She had to admit that she hoped she would see him in the morning, and at the thought she felt her heart speed up just a little. No doubt about it, Captain Tregarrick was the kind of man to get a woman's juices flowing.

A log popped in the fireplace, sending a shower of sparks up the chimney. As she waited for Mrs. Penhale's promised return, Lily watched the flames. The peaceful atmosphere of the room fell over her like an enchantment. No ringing phones and faxes, no clacking printers. No muffled sounds of television from some neighboring apartment. Only the wind, the fire, and the settling of the house.

It was like stepping back in time. Surely, she thought, the place had looked much the same: candles in ormolu sconces bracketing the mirror above the fireplace, a tufted velvet slipper chair, even a needlepoint footstool with small gilt feet. It was, Lily decided contentedly, exactly like something out of *Jane Eyre*.

All it lacked was a madwoman, howling in the attic.

She slid softly into dreams—and was rudely awakened by the fearsome sound of a woman's screams.

3

LILY BOLTED UPRIGHT. The sun was up—had been for some time—and the door to the corridor was open. A girl in a red sweater and jeans stood just inside the threshold. Her eyes showed white around the irises, and she was shouting down the house as if she was demented.

The sound of running feet came from beyond the door. Lily heaved a sigh of relief. Help was on the way.

"What's all this, Portia? Found a mouse in the mattress or the moth in the carpet?" a male voice said.

A young man with reddish hair appeared beyond the young woman's shoulder. "What in bloody hell . . . !"

The girl had stopped screaming. She took a deep breath. "Sorry, James. I thought for a moment that she was a ghost."

"Catherine T.? She does have a bit of the look of her, doesn't she? Well, go down and ring up Constable Polkenny. Tell him we've got an intruder on our hands."

He pushed past the girl in the red sweater and faced Lily,

arms akimbo. "What the bloody hell do you think you're doing?" he said.

Lily glared at him. "I *was* sleeping!"

"I can see that." He moved closer.

Lily edged to the far side of the bed. "Good. Now, would you please go away?"

"Aye, I will. And bring the constable back with me. Then we'll see how that sits with you."

She frowned and pushed back her hair. "Is everyone under this roof, except for Mrs. Penhale, stark raving mad?"

A thought hit her belatedly. Mr. Tregarrick had seemed more than a little odd last evening. Perhaps she'd just committed a terrible gaffe.

Lily edged to the far side of the bed, in case she had to make a bolt for it. "Ah, this . . . er, isn't a sort of place for . . . I mean a . . . *a rest home?*"

James gaped at her. "No," he said. "It's a bloody museum."

It was Lily's turn to stare. "Oh!"

Small wonder that everything looked so authentic. She tucked a strand of hair behind her ear. "How peculiar. I didn't know! When Mr. Tregarrick brought me here last night, it never occurred to me that this wasn't a private home. And evidently no one told you that I was here."

James was regarding her oddly. He backed away toward the door. The girl he'd called Portia was still standing there, frowning at Lily. The young man scratched his chin thoughtfully. "Mr. Tregarrick."

"He rescued me on the headland last night. Saved my life, really. I was almost washed out to sea by the tide."

James turned his head to Portia, but his eyes never left Lily's face. "You had better ring up Dr. Landry as well."

"Look," Lily said, "I'm fine. I don't need a doctor. I need my clothes. The housekeeper took them to dry—Mrs. Penhale said she'd hang them in the kitchen by the stove." She saw the blank looks on their faces. "Mrs. Penhale, the housekeeper."

Portia hadn't moved an inch. She put her hands on her

hips. "There is no Mrs. Penhale here, although there was once, a long time ago. I have her receipt books. And as for your Captain Tregarrick, there's been no one by that name under this roof in almost a hundred years."

Lily was dressed and sitting on the edge of the bed when the doctor arrived. Portia had brought her scalding-hot black coffee and shared the last stale donuts in a bakery box with her while they waited.

James had found Lily's clothes in the kitchen, just as she'd said, neatly pegged out on a line stretched across the room. Her shoes had gone missing, and Portia had obligingly fetched a pair of rubber thong sandals from a service closet.

"I got them at a jumble sale and wear them when I hose down the terrace," she said. "Or when I'm pottering about my grandmother's garden, at Old Cross Farm. You can drop them back here anytime. Just leave them on the side porch if I've locked the place up."

Lily sipped her coffee. "You take care of the museum, then?"

Portia smiled, looking younger than the twenty-two years she'd claimed. "I'm the curator. I've a degree from university, but in reality I do a bit of everything: keep the catalogues up-to-date, dust the knickknacks and hoover the carpets, schedule group tours, and generally see that everything is kept shipshape and in good preservation."

"That's a weighty responsibility."

The girl dimpled. "It's a family tradition, you might say. Ah, there's the doctor now. He's got an ancient Morris-Mini and you can hear him come sputtering halfway up the hill from St. Dunstan."

A short time later he came up the stairs and into the Green Chamber. Dr. Landry was a kindly-looking man, with a thick thatch of silver hair and a military moustache. Lily let him give her a brief examination. The situation had her baffled.

"Ticker working, lungs clear, oriented to person, place,

and time," he announced. "Although I gather that time was rather out of whack for you earlier."

"It seemed so real," she told him a little shakily. "I would have *sworn* that it was!"

"Let me see. Ah, you've quite a knot here," he said, probing the side of Lily's head. "My guess is that it took quite a blow to put it there."

"It must have happened when I lost my footing in the waves. I did a foolish thing," she told him. "I went walking along the strand and got lost in the fog."

He tugged at his silver moustache. "At Yearning Head?"

"Is that what it's called? How peculiar."

"The maps call the headland Dunstan's Head. No one here calls it that, though. It's been Yearning Head as long as any can remember. Some say it's because the waves sound like lovers' mingled sighs; others who've tarried there claim that they were filled with a great longing, like a terrible loneliness, when the wind blows in and the tide is just right. The old-age pensioners say that if you yearn for something hard enough there, it will come to be."

Lily remembered the strange feelings that had swept through her. "It is a beautiful spot, but very eerie."

"Yes. A dangerous one, too. You were fortunate. It was high tide last night. Others have been less so, and were washed out to sea."

Lily shivered. "And I would have been another, if not for Captain Tregarrick . . . uh, rather, for the man who saved me, whatever his name. He saw me from the cliff and guided me to the stairs carved into it, just in the nick of time. I would never have found them on my own."

From the corner of her eye, she saw the doctor give her the same long, assessing look that James had. "Tell me about the man you called Captain Tregarrick. Could you describe him to me?"

Lily closed her eyes and conjured up his image. "He's tall. Strong. Dark-haired, with a patrician nose and a stubborn-looking jaw. Oh, and his eyes! I thought they were black at first, but in the lamplight I could see they were as many shifting shades of blue and gray as the waters of the bay.''

"A poetic description." Landry cocked his head. "Many artists come to St. Dunstan to paint the views. Are you perhaps among them?''

Lily shook her head. "When I was in college I wanted to paint . . ." She broke off.

"Ah, now that's interesting. Not to *be* a painter, but 'to paint.' Your choice of words tells me that painting is something with a great deal of meaning for you—yet you say you became a design engineer. Tell me, do you paint now?''

"No."

"Will you tell me why?''

"I tried. I haven't the talent for it." She frowned. "It never came out the way I intended it.''

"You're a perfectionist, then.''

"That isn't the reason I forsook my canvases." She laughed. "It was my stunning lack of talent. I wanted to be a dashing artist, blending shapes and colors with abandon and genius. Unfortunately I can only copy what I see, like a camera. But not nearly as well!''

A gleam came into Dr. Landry's eye. "Tell me, was your hotel room furnished with local brochures?''

"There were some in the desk." She shrugged. "I glanced at a few and put them back. I wasn't interested in doing the usual 'touristy' things.''

"I believe the mystery is solved, young lady. Come along to the drawing room with me, and you'll understand what I mean.''

He escorted Lily down to the ground floor and through a set of high pocket doors. She wondered how she had missed the strategically placed velvet ropes that kept people from getting too close to the matching Oriental cabinets in the main hall, or the sign welcoming visitors to Star House. Gently she touched the bump at the back of her head. It *was* quite a knot. It seemed less real than her invented memories of the previous night.

The doctor escorted her to a sunny parlor with white

wainscoting and pale blue walls. It had elegant proportions, with long windows on two sides and a fireplace at the far end. Dr. Landry indicated the portrait over the mantel.

"Is there any resemblance to your mysterious rescuer?"

Lily's jaw dropped. She frowned up at the painting. The frame was formal and unfamiliar, but the pose and the subject were not. The dark-haired man in the painting wore a thick ivory fisherman's sweater, like the one she had worn last night. His head and upper torso were depicted against a background of blue sky and a bluer sea. She recognized St. Dunstan Bay, obviously in another century, its surface dotted with assorted sailing ships.

Whatever the portrait's age, the man who had sat for it was almost an exact double of the man who had rescued Lily on the cliff.

"They could be twins," she said slowly. "Except for his eyes. They're the same dark blue and gray, with those little flecks of white, but the expression in them is totally different."

"What do you mean?"

"The man in this portrait is young and happy and carefree. The one I met was older. Stern and bitter." Lily stopped and reconsidered. "No, I think I used the wrong words. Perhaps 'burdened' is a better choice. As if the weight of the world had come crashing down on him."

"That painting," Dr. Landry told her, "is of Rees Tregarrick. He captained his own clipper ship and made a fortune in the China trade. He's the most well-known citizen of St. Dunstan, having contributed generously to the village. His picture is found on the cover of local tourist guides, as well as several area businesses."

"I hadn't noticed."

"Perhaps not consciously. But without realizing it, you had seen his face before. The artist in you took note. Later, when you injured yourself and stumbled upon the museum, his image was already impressed on your brain. Exhaustion and that bump to your head did the rest."

Lily's eyes were still on the portrait. It drew her against her will. She seemed unable to look away. "Is that a polite way of pretending you *don't* think I'm insane?''

Landry laughed. ''People who are truly mad don't seem to be aware of it. They usually think they're perfectly normal. If need be, I'll attest that you're as sharp as I am, Miss Kendall.''

Lily smiled back. ''I'll take a census of local opinion, then, before committing myself.''

He roared at that. ''I'm afraid you'll find it sharply divided. I'm considered one of the local eccentrics,'' he told her. ''I'm on my way to Penzance. May I give you a lift back to your hotel?''

''Yes, thank you.'' With a long glance at the painting, Lily allowed the doctor to escort her to the door.

The painted lapis-blue eyes seemed to follow her with their gaze. She felt self-conscious, as if he were actually there, watching her leave the room. What a powerful man Rees Tregarrick must have been, Lily thought, that even a painting of him could stir up something in her soul!

Portia and James were out on the porch, examining a loose railing, and waved cheerily as Lily and the doctor drove off down the steep and winding hill.

Dr. Landry pointed out a few places of local interest as his ancient car puttered down the cobbled streets. There were artists painting, their easels atop the granite wall. The view was breathtaking, overlooking the dull green and navy and cinnamon-colored slate roofs of the village, and the sparkling turquoise variations of the harbor beyond.

This, Lily told herself, *is the calm, picturesque place I wanted.* There was plenty to explore, while managing to stay away from isolated stretches of beach. And yet she knew she would go out to Yearning Head again. It called to something wild and lonely in her blood.

The car stopped for a fat tabby chasing a yapping terrier, then turned at a corner. The window of a small antiques shop displayed tin soldiers and Staffordshire pugs, and pair of striking blue-and-white vases.

''Those vases might have come over with Captain Tregarrick,'' Dr. Landry said. ''He imported a great quantity of fine porcelainware.''

But it wasn't the vases that had caught Lily's attention. "I thought there was a tea shop on this corner. I must be turned around."

Her companion glanced at her. "Are you sure you've never been to St. Dunstan before? There was a family-run tea shop there for generations. It went out of business when I was a lad, after old Miss Truro passed on."

"I suppose I might have heard it mentioned," Lily said doubtfully. But in her mind's eye she could envision lace curtains at the window, and a cozy tearoom done up in mauve-and-green chintz. Even a verdigris grasshopper on the ledge above the slate fireplace.

In less than five minutes she was standing in front of her hotel overlooking the harbor. Lily leaned down to the open window of the car and expressed her thanks to the doctor. "I know now that I imagined the entire episode," she added, "but I have to tell you that it still seems very real in my mind."

Dr. Landry smiled. "The human brain is capable of creating the glories of the Sistine Chapel, or sending men to walk upon the moon, Miss Kendall. It's small wonder, then, that it can make a dream seem like reality—often down to the finest details, no matter how seemingly bizarre."

"That's very true," she answered, shaking her head. "Right down to the crutch he leaned on!" She gave a little wave and started toward the door.

"Wait!" Dr. Landry called after her. "How did you know about Captain Tregarrick's injury?"

He was certain that there was nothing in the tourist literature about the tragic misfortune that had injured the captain and killed poor young Catherine Tregarrick.

It was too late. Lily had already vanished inside the Castle Inn. The doctor was still wondering about it when he passed the antiques shop on the corner, where the Grasshopper on the Hearth Tearoom had stood in his youth.

4

LILY WENT UP to her demi-suite with its papered walls, chintz curtains, and Victorian walnut furnishings. At least here nothing had changed. After a hot shower and shampoo, she put on a floaty dress of white cotton eyelet, threaded with blue ribbon.

The summer shorts and her jeans were still neatly folded in the drawer, untouched since her arrival. Somehow they didn't seem appropriate to the village of St. Dunstan. She felt cooler and more comfortable in the long, retro dresses that swirled around her slim ankles.

Only when she'd bound her long hair up into an old-fashioned coronet did she dare to lift the lid of the antique desk and remove the handful of pamphlets that discreetly touted the local wonders. Her fingers were unsteady as she spread them out on the desktop.

There were brochures of St. Dunstan village and other points of interest throughout the Cornish countryside: deserted tin mines, medieval monk's towers, rings of prehistoric standing stones, and the man-made moonscapes of white china clay.

There was nothing at all about Star House or Captain Rees Tregarrick.

Lily noticed the edge of a glossy leaflet peeking out from beneath the brown paisley lining paper. The front showed the slate-and-granite Victorian manor she'd seen through the fog, with gables and turrets and great starburst window. "Visit the Star House Museum." it read, "and take a Journey to the Untouched Past."

"Well, I certainly did that!" Lily turned it over.

Her heart gave a lurch that was not entirely unpleasant. There he was again, Captain Rees Tregarrick, in all his masculine splendor. The reproduction of a full-length sepia photograph was almost an exact likeness of the man she remembered . . . or had dreamed up—the wide brow, the strong jaw and aquiline nose, the firm, sensual mouth.

Again, only the eyes were different. There was no anger in them. And, Lily noticed, no crutch or blackthorn cane braced against his side.

She started to slip it back into the desk, then paused. Instead she tucked it into her purse.

Dr. Landry had recommended a nap: "Mother Nature's cure-all." But the sun was out, the sky a brilliant blue, and Lily felt absolutely wonderful. She hadn't come to Cornwall to nap, and her stomach was protesting its lack of lunch. Slicking pink gloss over her lips, she went down to the spacious dining room, with its rock-walled fireplace and tall windows overlooking the sea. It was still early, and only a handful of others were there.

"Good afternoon, Miss Kendall. Your usual place?" the hostess asked.

Lily hesitated. For the past four days she'd requested a seat in the sunny bay with the morning paper, and a view of the picturesque village. *Dear God, I've become such a creature of habit!*

She'd been running on the Washington gerbil wheel too long. She was in danger of making routine her god, change her enemy. No, worse, God help her! She was in imminent danger of becoming a career bureaucrat. And that wasn't the real Lily Kendall. Not really.

Was it?

She smiled at the hostess. "I think I'll change my routine today. I'd like a table with a view of the sea." *Of the headland.*

She didn't say it aloud, but she was given a table with a partial view of the harbor and beyond, the dark granite cliffs of Yearning Head. The sea was all slick, blue Bristol glass, rimmed with crystalline spray.

Star House was hidden by the headland's sharp uplift of terrain, and a frieze of stunted trees, bent sharply by the prevailing winds. Lily was almost glad of it. Despite Dr. Landry's explanation, she felt uneasy.

Portia had told her that the star-shaped window was no longer lit at night, to guide the ships home to port. "Cost, you know." But Lily could not deny the bone-deep belief that she'd seen the star guiding her to safety and heard Rees Tregarrick's rich, resonant voice leading her toward the granite sea-stairs.

Felt the warm, very human touch of his strong hand on her arm.

There she'd admitted it.

"Oh, I beg your pardon." She realized the hostess was holding out the handwritten menu. Lily took it and set it aside.

"Tell me," she asked, "have you ever been up to the Star House Museum?"

"My goodness, yes. I'm not from St. Dunstan, you know. I'm at university, and they take me on here for the summers. I visit the museum at least twice each season. You really should tour Star House. It's a fascinating place. Millions of pounds' worth of wonderful things."

Lily was surprised. "I thought it was just a restored manor. What kind of museum is it?"

"Oh, all sorts of treasures! Lovely Chinese porcelain and Indian furniture that Captain Tregarrick brought back from his voyages. Venetian glass, trinket boxes covered with semiprecious stones and mother-of-pearl, and snuff bottles carved out of amethyst and opal. My favorite is the Jade Room. It used to be the library.''

Lily remembered a glimpse of pale yellow jade when Captain Tregarrick had vanished into his study. But it was all fading, running together, exactly ike fragments of the dream that Dr. Landry had called it.

An elderly couple entered the dining room, and the hostess edged away from Lily with a polite murmur. ''If you go,'' she said over her shoulder, ''look out for the engravings done by Mrs. Tregarrick. She was a noted botanist— quite famous in her day.''

Lily hunched forward, as if a fist had punched her in the stomach. That's exactly how it felt. *Of course there was a wife in it somewhere.* Hadn't she come reeling off her last failed romance with the same discovery?

It took Lily a minute to recover. She'd felt as if all the breath had gone out of her. *Which is utterly ridiculous,* she told herself. *Why be upset over something that happened to a man who who lived almost a hundred years ago?*

She finished her meal and went out into the sunlight, strolling past shopfronts brimming with geraniums, up past the slate-and-granite houses, where the ubiquitous hydrangeas of Cornwall bloomed blue, and pink, and lavender in prodigal beauty. Ignoring a crowd waiting to get into the St. Dunstan Tin Museum, with its working model of the old mine that had gone out into the bay, far below the seabed, she turned south as if pulled by a magnet.

She climbed the cobblestones until she was high above the village, with the sea spreading out like a swath of crimped blue satin. Sequins of light glittered through the spume of brilliants the waves dashed up. Lily had never seen it look more beautiful. She stopped at the granite wall above the village, to watch the seabirds skim over the waves. Higher still, the dark bulk of Yearning Head towered over the cresting waves, drawing her back.

Rees Tregarrick stood at the star window and looked out at the headland. She was still there. Although the tree hid her from clear view, he could see the ends of her long blond hair, and the thin white of her skirt billowing in the breeze.

She had never appeared to him by daylight before. It had always been in starlight or moonlight that he'd seen her moving across the headland, or walking the strand below the cliffs, with her fair hair streaming out like satin ribbons.

He'd never managed to get close to her. Usually by the time he reached the front door she was gone. Then, lately, he'd been able to cross half the distance to the cliff's edge before she vanished.

Until last night.

He turned away from the window. *Until last night.* Those were the critical words. Until then, he'd turned his back on the sea and walled himself away in the house. His emotions had been as dead as poor Catherine. And then *she* had come, stirring up terrible memories, this mysterious woman who haunted his nights. His dreams. Terrible longings that had kept him awake till dawn. She hadn't had a stitch on beneath her summer frock, he was sure of it. *God in heaven, I am a man. And a lonely one, at that.*

Perhaps the sea had sent her to torment him, to lure him back to it. Why else had she vanished without a trace in the night? Cursing beneath his breath, Rees Tregarrick turned away from the window.

Lily had unplaited her hair and let the wind blow through it. The rubber thong sandals that Portia had loaned her were still in the canvas bag by her side, along with a notepad, a new copy of *People,* and the paperback of a favorite by Mary Stewart that she'd picked up on her way.

Lily had made no attempt to return the sandals, nor had she bothered to even skim the magazine's table of contents. She took out a pencil and sketched one of the flowers growing in the protection of a stunted tree. The rough bark made a pleasing contrast with the soft-textured pink petals of the blossom. Quite lifelike, she decided.

Soon, though, even the drawing palled. The breeze sighed, filled with invisible yearnings longing to be made real. Lily closed up the notebook and looked out over the sea.

The light was changing. The view had been like an Impressionist painting, myriad dots of color blending into one another. Now it was bold and crisp, each in-rushing wave distinct from the others. With the sun turning the air all crystal and gold, she was content to sit beneath one of the wind-gnarled trees. And wait.

She'd been waiting for some time when she felt his presence. Suddenly the light shifted, became clearer. The scent of some unfamiliar, exotic flower filled the air.

Lily didn't look up. She was afraid to.

She'd known that he would come. Known it deep in her bones.

Out of the corner of her eye she could see his boot, with grains of sand and a blade of fresh green grass clinging to it.

"Go away," she said. "You're not real."

"Oh, I'm real enough," Tregarrick responded. "Too damned real for my own good. It's you who are the ghost."

She looked up at that. "A ghost?"

He stared out past her, to the restless sea. The same aspects, changeable and fathomless, were reflected in his eyes. "Aye. You come and go like the moon through clouds, vanish like the mist."

"I've only been here once before. Last night, when you rescued me."

"Ah, no. I've watched you a hundred times before. I know the way your hair turns color in the light, and the whiteness of your skin beneath that dress."

He turned his head then and faced her fully. Her heart thudded painfully. Above the knitted fisherman's sweater his face, so handsome and intense, robbed Lily of breath.

"It's been more than a year since I had the first sight of you," he told her. "At the time I thought you were . . . someone else." A muscle ticked at his jaw. "Tell me, for God's sake! Why are *you* haunting me? If it were Catherine now, I could understand . . ."

He uttered a muffled oath and moved a little away. Lily watched him. The wind ruffled his thick, dark hair, the same as it did hers. His shadow fell across the tree's knotty roots, just as did hers. Surely there was a mistake somewhere. He was as real as she. Lily rose to her feet.

"You *are* Captain Rees Tregarrick? The man who built Star House?" she asked. She was surprised her voice remained so steady.

"Aye, lass." He looked back at her, frowning. "Why do I think I know you? We've never met in this life."

"No."

And yet she had the same feeling as he. The crosswinds blew against the headland, and the soulful sound of the sea echoed up to them, like the murmuring of lovers. The air seemed to thicken, steeped with the echoes of old and powerful emotions.

Shivers ran up the back of her bare arms. Tentatively Lily reached out and touched his sleeve. Woolly, soft, and very real. As were the steely muscles of his arm beneath it.

"It's summer," she said, feeling the warm breeze against her face. "Aren't you warm in such a heavy sweater?"

He shook his head. Leaves skittered past his boot. "It's autumn," he told her. "You should be shivering with cold in your light frock. You'll catch a death of a chill."

Lily smiled. "Not if I'm a ghost . . ."

For a moment the air rippled between them. It was like looking down into the sunny tide pools of the bay as a light breeze ruffled the water over the rocks and moss and tiny scattered shells. She expected him to thin and disappear like fog in sunlight. The shimmer steadied, hardened.

He was still there.

Rees Tregarrick caught her hand in his, as if he were afraid she would run away. Or vanish like sea spray, among the sunbeams.

"Who are you?" he said. "*What* are you?"

Lily's breath snagged in her throat. "A woman," she whispered. "Just a woman."

5

Rees Tregarrick looked down at Lily with an enigmatic expression. "A woman."

The wind whipped her hair around them like a cloak. Without warning, he pulled her into his arms. She trembled in his embrace, as his hand splayed against her back. Her breasts pressed against him as he smoothed the light fabric of her dress down the gentle curve of her spine, along the lush curve of her waist and hip. His breath came quicker.

"You feel like a woman." His bent his head until his cheek grazed the top of her head. Lily heard him inhale. "You smell like a woman."

Then she was pulled tight against his chest, and his mouth came down on hers, warm and firm and incredibly sensual.

She was intensely aware of everything about Rees Tregarrick, from the scent of cedar on his clothes to the strength of his fingers against her back, the roughness of his jaw against her cheek. She clung to him while the world spun and rocked around her. Surely she was dreaming.

His mere nearness had triggered something between them. Now the heat of his hard body against hers was like an elemental force of nature, molding them together. Melding past and present, hinting of future pleasures, delicious and dark, and well beyond her own experience.

That first, hard kiss gave way to another, softer and yet more demanding. A shiver ran through her. As his embrace tightened, he took the kiss deeper, wilder. And she responded totally to the moment.

To him.

He broke the kiss and looked down at her. His eyes looked dazed and heavy with need. "Ah, God Almighty, but you taste like a woman!"

"I told you that."

"Yes." He wound his fingers into her hair, lacing them through it. "But I know I'm dreaming." He tilted her chin up until her eyes locked with his. The tip of his thumb grazed her full lower lip, and his eyes were dark as the sea.

"I'm real."

Rees shook his head. "You're a mirage. Or, if you truly are the woman who has been haunting my sleep, prove it. Make my dream come true. For the love of God, put an end to the curse, and to my hellish loneliness!"

How could she refuse his plea, especially when it was exactly what she craved herself? Lily stepped up on her tiptoes, and touched his mouth with her own. His lips were firm, then softened. He wrapped her close in his arms and kissed her again.

Lily had never been kissed so thoroughly, so passionately. It was a lost art, she thought weakly, a kiss for its own sake. Uncalculated and not a mere hasty prelude to something more. It was like an exotic drug in her blood. She wanted him with an ardor she had never known. Wanted him fully and completely.

Wanted him *now*.

His hand brushed her breast. She felt her body go liquid at its core as she leaned into him, and felt the potency of his response. Her fingers twined in his hair, pulling his mouth closer, drinking deep.

The textures of his mouth, the touch of his tongue were so real, yet she knew it was utterly impossible. *This can't be happening. It's a dream. I've fallen asleep beneath the tree,* she told herself, *and I'm dreaming.*

But his mouth was hot on hers, no less real than her own. His tongue followed the curve of her lower lip, and she sighed as it slid between her teeth. Her entire body shuddered with pleasure as something untamed and dark inside her responded. His leg nudged hers apart, and he pulled her closer, tighter, until she moved restlessly against him.

If this is a dream, Lily thought, *don't let me awaken.*

Her heart pounded against his chest, and she could feel the rough texture of his sweater against her straining breasts. His hand cupped one, weighing it gently against his palm. The tip contracted, hardened as he caressed it with his long fingers, and circled it with his thumb. She gave a tiny cry of eagerness, offering herself to his questing hand.

His skin was hot against hers, as he pushed down the strap of her summer dress and tugged it low. All the while his mouth worked against her, nibbling at her lips gently, then pressing them hard against her teeth until she reeled and ached with need. He was like the sea, relentlessly eroding her ability to think. She could only feel.

It was enough.

He worked the other strap down her shoulder, and they both shivered when it broke free in his hand. His lips moved from the corner of her mouth and down her arching throat. Over the delicate hollow at its base, and along her bare shoulder. Tasting. Teasing. Taunting.

Then he bent her back along his arm, and his lips touched her breast. So light, so light, it was like the brush of a butterfly's wing. The sensation was exquisite. Her body tingled with anticipation. Then he took the tip into his mouth and tugged, hard. There was nothing in the world but the cool kiss of the wind along her naked flesh, the heat of his hungry mouth upon her breast.

Lily lost control. Without warning she was thrown up and over the edge of reason. All conscious thought was washed away, overcome by waves of cresting desire.

He held her close until it passed, murmuring words in an unknown language against her flesh. When it was over, she lay limp in his arms. Lily felt shattered. And he hadn't really touched her. Not yet. Not the way she ached for him to do.

He lowered her to the sun-warmed ground, out of the breath of the wind. He didn't speak, but pressed a soft kiss against her throat. His hand kneaded her breasts gently, while he kissed his way back up to her lips. He kissed her deeply, plundering her mouth with his tongue until she was eager and wanton with desire.

Only then did he look down at her. His stern, masculine beauty struck her like an arrow to the heart—a sharp, sweet piercing surely as fatal to her peace of mind as any shaft of feathered wood. His eyes were ablaze with need that found an answering echo inside her.

Lily's lips were swollen from his kisses, and her breasts ached to feel his mouth once more. She touched his face, cradling the side of it with her hand. So real, so solid. She traced his lips with her fingertip, and he closed his eyes until she was done.

"Are you a witch?" he whispered, frowning down at her. "A creature sent by the sea to lure me back into her clutches?"

She could have wept with need and tenderness. "Only a woman," she said, trailing a hand along his jaw. "And who are you?"

He laughed without mirth. "Only a man. One you have driven half mad with desire."

"Then take me." She stretched her arms above her head, offering her breasts to his seeking mouth. "Make love to me. Even if this is nothing but a dream."

"If this is the dream, then I am the dreamer," he said, his voice rough with passion. "I have waited months to know the end of it.'' He caught her hands and kissed her fingers. ''And I intend to make it end my way! Don't vanish on me now, woman, or I swear to God I'll go mad!''

Another ripple shuddered through the air, as dazzling as sunlight. Lily was afraid that it was he who would vanish, that she'd awake and find herself back at her hotel—or worse, back in her lonely apartment.

But, no, she was still dreaming. With her head turned seaward as he kissed her throat, she watched a freighter fade and wink out on the horizon. The newer houses high above St. Dunstan were gone, as if they never were and the bright blue bay was covered with sailing ships, their acres of white canvas billowing in the wind like cumulus clouds. It had to be a dream . . .

Yet he was so real, so ardent. He kissed her breasts, and the touch of his mouth was more genuine than the earth beneath her, or the twisted, sunlit branches above. Heat built up inside her, spreading through her limbs like warm honey.

''Hurry,'' she whispered. ''Oh, hurry!''

He pulled his sweater off, and the sun gleamed on hard muscles sculpted by the rigors of the sea. Lily laughed in delight and ran her fingertips through the crisp hairs on his chest, watching his face flood with desire.

Stripping off the rest of his clothes, he slid her skirt slowly up her legs, caressing her skin as he worked it higher. ''No stockings,'' he said, as if to himself. ''No corset and no garters. Nothing but beautiful woman beneath this flimsy frock.''

He shook his head wonderingly at her skimpy lace bikini panties, then tried to tug them down. Lily lifted her hips, and the fragile lace tore in his hands. She was free, naked and warm beneath him. He covered her with his length and lay still, breathing hard, like a long-distance runner. Waves of pleasure rolled over her, and he caught her in his arms as she trembled beneath him.

His chest rose and fell, and its mat of hairs tantalized her nipples, bringing them erect. He tightened his embrace and groaned. ''Sweet vision, if you vanish now, I'll never find you again. And I will be doomed, lost forever in my lonely hell.''

Instead of answering, she brought his head down to her breast and arched against him. As he took the velvety tip into his mouth, teased it with his firm lips, she shifted her legs apart. He was hard and ready, and she couldn't wait any longer. The fear that she was dreaming, that he would disappear stabbed at her. *At least give me this*, she thought. This one moment of perfect joy.

She moved against him with a small, sharp thrust of her hips. A tremor shook his big frame, and he groaned again. ''So impatient, love?''

''Yes.'' And so afraid to wake up and find herself alone. That the lover of her dreams was only, after all, a dream-lover. She moved against him, watching desire chase the shadows of pain from his face. ''Love me, Rees. Now.''

He touched her, felt her hips shift up to meet his questing fingers. She was slick and ready, and he could no longer hold back. He took her boldly, lustily, as he sensed she wanted. Lily's breath hitched in her throat. Their joining was as ruthlessly fierce and beautiful as the land around them. Elemental as the sun and wind, powerful as the pounding of the sea.

When the moment came, intense almost beyond bearing, they rode it together, like hawks rising on the wind. Sensations poured through Lily, bright and dark, as he carried her up with him toward the sky. With every thrust her body arched to meet his, taking and demanding more. Then they were free-falling through space, and only his embrace kept her safe until they drifted gently back to earth.

Later she lay cradled in his arms with her hair splayed out over his naked chest, like a shawl of spun gold. She curled into the warmth of his body, afraid to move or speak. Afraid he would melt away beneath her like the mist rising through the trees. It would storm soon. She could feel the excitement of it in the air.

And what then?

As Lily lifted her face and looked down at him, he shimmered like a mirage before her eyes; but he was real and solid in her arms. She could feel the steady thrum of his heart against her ribs. All the tension was gone from his face. He looked younger, and so handsome and radiant she felt her heart might break.

He opened his eyes and smiled at her. "The sea gives and the sea takes away," he said slowly. "I asked for a sign of forgiveness . . . and you came to me, out of the fog and mist. I thought it was a trick of fate. I was afraid to trust that you were real." His hand closed on her bare breast. "But you are."

Leaning down, he kissed it, laved it with his tongue while she took in a deep, shuddering breath. No one had ever made love to her like this. She hadn't known . . . hadn't dreamed it could be so beautiful and so savage, so primal, yet so exquisitely tender. She kissed his shoulder, nipped the bronzed skin with its heady taste of salt and sweat and man.

His mouth moved lower, grazing the cleft between her breasts, moving down along her ribs. He planted kisses down the length of her, over the soft curve of her hip and the gentle swell of her belly, tasting her as he went. His lips brought trails of fire down her thigh, all the way to the delicate arch of her foot. And then he started to work his way up.

He bent his dark head and touched her with his mouth. She shivered beneath him, barely able to stand the deliciously intense sensations evoked by his darting tongue. A force was building in her, so hot and powerful she couldn't contain it. Passion exploded through her, pouring like liquid flame along her limbs. She bucked and shuddered against him, and then her blood was a bright torrent of sparks, racing hotly through her veins, melting any last remnants of her reserve.

He held her tightly until it was over, his hands cupping her possessively. When it was done she was deliciously weak and dizzy and spent. Her whole body seemed swollen with womanly response, ripe to bursting.

"Did you like that, love?" he murmured against her temple, as he pressed his mouth against her hair. "I knew you would. You've a fire in you that matches mine. It can't be quenched.'' His mouth slid down the curve of her jaw. "It must be fed!''

Before she could speak, he twisted around and pinned her with his weight and kissed her. Sweet languor flowed through her, filled her with delight. The flame of need ignited once again. Lord, how she wanted him. Wanted to ease whatever sorrows had haunted him and banish them forever. His hand moved between her legs, and she shivered in delight and anticipation. Every atom of her body longed for him.

"Slowly this time,'' he told her. "So that I can learn every inch of you, what you like and don't like. So that I can match the heat of your passions with my own.''

"Impossible.'' She laughed against his shoulder. She was on fire with need for him, burning with a wild, sexual hunger. "But try.''

He took his time, exploring her body as he had promised. Memorizing every intimate curve and texture, making love to her with his eyes and his hands. Bringing her to the crest once more through sensual anticipation and his own passionate will. His fingers plunged deep, and she arched up off the ground, in pleasure so intense she was mindless with it. Again and again he brought her there and over, until she clung to his wrist to make him stop.

"Take me again,'' she said huskily. "As hard and wild as you please.''

And he did, riding her through the bright fields of passion until they were both gasping for air, locked in each other's arms. Lily closed her eyes, inhaling the wonderful masculine scent of him, satiated and replete. She started to drift to sleep, lulled by the sounds of his breathing and the singing of the birds that had settled back in the trees.

Then a metallic *thunk* carried from somewhere in the distance. Lily's eyes flew open. Rees was still there. She could see his face alight with emotion as he gazed down at her, feel his weight pressing her down into the grass, the thrum of his heart beating in time to hers. But when she tried to tighten her embrace, her arms closed on empty air.

She could still feel the pressure of his magnificent body, its radiant warmth, and the hard, protective circle of his arms about her shoulders; but the air shimmered, and she could see the wavery sky, the tremor of the high cirrus clouds through him, as if he were made of pebbled glass. In a moment he was gone, as if he'd never been.

"No!" The cry was ripped from her throat. Lily didn't want the dream to end. She couldn't bear it.

But as she sat up, the evidence was still there. The mark of his teeth on her skin. The taste of his mouth on hers. The sweet stickiness between her thighs. Even a few woolly threads of his sweater clinging to the bracken. But that was all.

"Miss Kendall?"

Lily heard her name called, and scrambled to cover herself. *Dr. Landry!* She pushed her skirt down and pulled up the straps of her bodice. Her breasts felt swollen and ached with tenderness from Rees's kisses. She glanced around for her lace panties, but they were gone, heaven knew where.

As she tried to loop her long hair back, Dr. Landry came around the line of stunted trees. "Ah, so it is you. Portia thought she'd spotted you out here earlier."

Lily wondered if he could see the wild beating of the pulse at her throat. "I came to bring her sandals back, and was seduced by the view." *Close enough,* she told herself.

"Yes, it's quite splendid, isn't it?" He leaned against the trunk. "Voices carry a long way. I thought I heard you talking to someone. Another tourist, perhaps."

Lily wrapped her arms around her shoulders to hide the red marks of Rees Tregarrick's hands on her upper arms. "I was singing," she said. That wasn't entirely untrue.

He leaned down and retrieved her fallen notebook. It fell open to her drawing, and Dr. Landry paused to examine it. "That's very well done! Have you ever given thought to becoming an illustrator?"

Lily shook her head. "It never crossed my mind. At any rate, it's too late for me to change careers."

"It's never too late," he told her, handing over the notebook. "You have a true talent, Miss Kendall. Don't dismiss it so lightly. I'm on my way to family gathering in St. Just. May I offer you a lift back to the village?"

"No, thank you. After I return Portia's shoes, I thought perhaps I'd take the tour."

"You'll find it worth your while. Captain Tregarrick brought back some wonderful treasures from his trips abroad."

When she was gone, Dr. Landry turned away from the sparkling bay and stared out over the placid farmland behind Yearning Head, the fields green and gold between their low rock walls. Some of those same fields were ancient, had been tamed and tilled since the Bronze Age. What a contrast they made with the bay, where the sea and land met violently, locked in eternal conflict.

Some people were like that restless seascape, mutable, shifting from moment to moment. Others were like the fields, neat and cultivated and all of a piece. Like Lily Kendall. At least on the surface. But what was she really like? People wore so many masks these days, it was difficult to tell.

Dr. Landry sighed. He was concerned about Miss Kendall, yet he couldn't say why. She'd gotten over that knock on her head without any untoward effects as far as he could tell. She seemed perfectly normal and levelheaded. But beneath the most placid of landscapes, volcanoes sometimes came bursting up through the earth.

He laughed at his wild fancy. "Too many National Geographic specials on the BBC," he told himself. Lily Kendall would be just fine. Meanwhile, a wonderful dinner awaited him at a restaurant in St. Just.

As he turned to make his way back to where he'd parked his battered mini, the wind blew across the headland, full of silent, urgent longings so keen that even a staid man of science could feel them. He stopped in his tracks.

The sun shone bright around him, and the air seemed

rich with the unmistakable scent of exotic blooms and recent lovemaking. Landry shook his head. ''I'm imagining
things,'' he said.

Jingling his keys, he took a few steps toward the car.
Something crackled beneath his shoe. He looked down to
see what it was: a wisp of torn lace, and a handful of drying
leaves, looking as if they had been just been blown fresh
from some autumn garden.

6

"THIS IS CATHERINE, the first Mrs. Tregarrick," Portia said in her brisk, tour-guide mode. She'd set aside cataloguing the contents of various boxes from the attic to show Lily around. "The portrait was painted shortly before her death."

Lily was shocked. "She was very young!"

"Eighteen years and two months."

She didn't want to ask, but had to. "How did she die? Childbirth?"

Portia looked uncomfortable. "I suppose you'll have heard the gossip. Some people say she threw herself down the sea stairs carved into the cliff. Others say she was pushed."

"By whom?"

"Her husband, of course. Captain Rees Tregarrick."

Lily gasped. "And do they say why?"

Portia went on to another portrait, which showed Rees Tregarrick in formal attire. "Look at him. He was an adventurer. They say he wanted to live in the Sandwich Islands—Hawaii, one of your states now—but she refused to go.''

Portia smiled up at his likeness and dimpled. "What a fool. If he wasn't my own great-great-something grandfather, I'd have gone off with him in a trice."

Lily blinked. "You're a descendant?"

"Not of Catherine Tregarrick. Of his second marriage."

Again Lily felt that blow to her stomach. *Two wives in your life*, she said silently. *Did you love them both?*

She looked up at his painting, and those lapis eyes seemed to bore into hers. There were the lips that had crushed her own, that had suckled her breasts and driven her half mad with desire. And those were the skilled hands that had stroked her flesh, alternately soothing and inflaming her. She would swear it on her life.

I'm going insane, she thought with a sudden sense of panic. But her glance caught her trapped reflection in the mirror above the side table. Even with the strap of her dress in place, she could see the reddened place where his teeth had nipped. There was a small bruise on her inner arm where his thumb had pressed, and her body still tingled with satisfaction from his lovemaking.

Somehow, under Yearning Head's strange spell, Rees Tregarrick had crossed over from his time to hers and made love to her beneath the trees. She was as certain of it as she was of her own identity.

Curiosity warred with jealousy that she knew was totally ridiculous. "Where is the portrait of the second Mrs. Tregarrick?"

"None are known to exist," Portia said wistfully. "Neither paintings nor photographs. I should have liked to have known how she looked. If we might share some family resemblance, you know."

Lily turned away. "The people in the village say this house is haunted. Is it Catherine Tregarrick who walks about, rattling her chains?"

Portia looked offended. "There are two ghosts, although I've seen neither one. The first is a 'woman in white' who is seen up on the headland. The other is Captain Tregarrick himself. James saw him once, standing at the star window, looking out to sea. He said he looked terribly sad—and rather angry.''

"Yes," Lily murmured. "That is how I first saw him."

"I beg your pardon?"

"Um . . ." Lily recovered quickly. "When I saw his photograph in the study, I mean. Could I see the star window? It intrigues me."

"It's really off-limits to visitors just now," Portia said, "but since there is only you today . . ."

She led Lily through a pair of wine velvet portieres and into another parlor. "This was the ladies' parlor." They went into a charming, sunlit room and finally up a flight of stairs. The window was in a turret at the very top.

Lily was amazed. The star window was much larger than she'd thought. Taller and wider than the stained glass windows in St. Dunstan's Church. It was a work of true genius. It gave the impression of being in three dimensions because of the masterful arrangement. The outer rectangle was formed of various shades of dark blue glass, the star inside composed of dozens of triangles of brilliant stained glass in bright yellow, shining gold, and rich, mellow amber. It was breathtaking, a magnificent work of art.

"Why here, away from the main living area?" Lily asked. "Surely they would have enjoyed it more in a place they would pass by frequently."

"There used to be a triple lantern hanging in front of the star, to light it in the night. It was a beacon," Portia explained, "a sign that could be seen far out at sea, welcoming Rees Tregarrick home. Guiding him to the harbor side of St. Petroc's Cathedral—that's what we call those sharp, toothy rocks that rise up out of nowhere past Yearning Head."

Lily remembered seeing the formation from the headland, protruding from the waters like a great granite claw.

The colors of the window fell across Portia's face. "On the day Catherine Tregarrick died, her husband's ship had been expected to make harbor for several days. The man at the helm always looked for the star window. Steering between Yearning Head and Tregarrick's Star, the pilot would know he was in safe waters, you see.''

She turned to Lily. ''For some reason the lamps were unlit that night. The pilot said the beacon at Star House went out suddenly, and he lost his bearings. *Tregarrick's Star* was almost lost in the mist and rain. It came too close to St. Petroc's Cathedral and was almost dashed to pieces on the sharp rocks. It nearly capsized when they brought her about. Two men were lost overboard, dashed against the rocks.''

''How horrible!''

''Yes, and senseless,'' Portia added.

''But why wasn't the window lit up?''

''No one knows. Perhaps the wind blew the flames out. Or a jealous rival might have paid someone to sabotage it. The competition for the China trade was fierce. The servants reported that Captain Tregarrick reached home the next morning in a terrible fury. He blamed Catherine for not making sure the Star Window was well lit. There was a frightful row. Catherine ran out of the house, with Captain Tregarrick hot on her heels. Later the servants heard a woman's scream, and they ran out of the house. A fog had rolled in from the Atlantic. There was no sign Catherine or Rees Tregarrick. They'd ventured too near the cliffs, and weren't found for some time.''

Lily listened, appalled. So that was how he sustained his injury! ''What happened then?'' She was almost afraid to know.

''Rees Tregarrick was on the sea-stairs with his leg badly broken and his face raked raw along one side . . . as if by a woman's fingernails. Catherine was on the strand. By the time they reached her, she was beyond human help.''

''How very sad.'' Lily remembered the broken way Rees had uttered Catherine's name. ''How did they fall?''

Portia looked away. ''Captain Tregarrick claimed that his wife was suicidal. That she intended to jump from the headland, and that he tried to save her, but she fell to her death. He fell in the struggle to aid her. With Catherine dead, of course, there was no one to say any different.''

Something in the young woman's voice arrested Lily. "I see. And so a taint was attached to his name." She couldn't believe that he had murdered his wife. "I don't understand why he was blamed."

"It was an unhappy marriage," Portia said. "He wanted her to go to sea with him, as was frequently the custom. Unlike the second Mrs. T., Catherine hated the sea, hated Cornwall. She refused."

"Then why did she marry him in the first place?"

Portia laughed. "You've seen his portrait. Quite a man, I would say! Catherine was pretty and spoiled, and she set her cap for him. According to her diary, she was determined to make a splash in London society, and completely sure of her powers to persuade him to her will. Of course, his business brought them here."

"Quite a shock after London," Lily said.

"Oh, yes."

"He isn't a murderer," Lily said vehemently. "I am sure of it."

Portia slanted a look at her. "You've become his defender. Perhaps I should tell you the rest: Some say that Catherine was still clinging to life when they found her, bleeding and broken on the rocks. That she blamed her husband, and died with a curse on her lips."

Lily shrugged off the shiver she felt; but as they continued on the tour, she remembered Rees's words, how he had begged Catherine for a sign of her forgiveness. It went against her every instinct; but the knowledge weighed on her like a pall of lead.

They came upon James near the servants' stair, humping a large trunk down the worn treads. Light gleamed dully from the tarnished brass studs and double locks. He set it down on the carpet, dusting his hands of the stray webs that clung to old leather.

"This is the last of that lot beneath the north eaves. Shall I take it into your workroom?"

Portia looked it over. "Good quality. Look at that elaborate tin stamping. It doesn't appear to be an item one of the maids could have afforded. Perhaps it belonged to an upper servant." Her eyes lit. "Or even a member of the family. Wouldn't it be wonderful if we found a photograph of the second Mrs. Tregarrick? There *must* be one somewhere."

"There's only one way to find out," James said, leaning against the carved newel post. "It awaits your pleasure, my lady."

Portia's face shone with excitement. "You never know what you might find—clothes, or letters and documents that might shed more light on the Tregarricks. One old valise was packed with remnants of a wonderful Oriental brocade, embroidered with gold thread. I've displayed some fans against a piece of it, in the case in the ladies' parlor."

Lily caught her breath. For a moment James and Portia, the stairwell and the leather trunk, were overlaid with the image of shelves filled with rich silks and satins in every color known. She could smell incense and flowering plum outside the window.

She could see Rees Tregarrick nodding at the Chinese merchant, and turning to smile at her. So real she could reach out and touch his face.

The vision vanished, and Lily swallowed, hard.

Portia hadn't noticed anything unusual. She twisted the hitch that held the lid closed, and opened the trunk. Cedar and lavender filled the air, along with a scent of must. The inside held a woman's summer garments—tucked and frilled white organza and finely embroidered lawn—all neatly packed away in layers of silver paper. But on the very top, placed exactly in the center, were a pair of very modern-looking woman's canvas summer shoes.

Portia snatched them. "How on earth . . . ?"

"How did they get into the trunk?" Lily exclaimed, recognizing her missing shoes.

"Don't be daft, the both of you." James put his hands on his hips. "There's nothing hocus-pocus about them. They had rubber-soled shoes like that for beachwear in Victorian times."

"No, I don't think they had Keds back then," Lily said quietly, pointing to the inner markings. "They're mine.

There's the place where I snagged the toe when I was almost caught by the tide. But I swear I have no idea how they came to be there.''

The air shimmered in front of Lily. For a disorienting moment she found herself in two places: She was standing at the foot of the staircase with Portia and James, staring at her shoes—and at the same time she was in a huge bedchamber, laughing as she slipped them atop the items in the trunk. There was a soft rushing sound in her ears, like the flow of fast water over smooth stones. She had to put her hand on the stair rail to keep her balance.

Portia shook her head. ''How do you explain the cobwebs over the lock?''

James made a sound of disgust. ''A busy spider. Nothing more.'' Portia glanced from the shoes to Lily, and gasped.

''What, have you been bitten, then?'' James took her hand in his and examined it anxiously. ''No. It wasn't that,'' Portia said shakily. ''When I looked at Miss Kendall just then . . .'' She paused and rubbed her eyes. ''For a moment I thought . . .'' She gave Lily an apologetic smile. ''I swear that it looked as if you had become transparent.''

''You need a vacation,'' James said, scowling. ''And no more episodes of *Twilight Zone* on the telly or reading those reincarnation books old Mrs. Polgelly sells to the tourist trade.''

He took the canvas sandals from her and handed them firmly to Lily. ''As to the shoes, you must have wandered into the attic that night, Miss Kendall, and left us a souvenir of your visit.''

''I suppose I could have,'' Lily said without conviction. ''I don't recall doing it, though.''

Portia bit her lip. She was still pale and agitated. ''If I didn't know better, I'd swear that trunk hadn't been opened in a hundred years.''

7

LILY RETURNED TO St. Dunstan after spending more time at the museum, staring at the paintings and photographs of Rees Tregarrick. As she wound her way down, her chance meeting with him on the headland seemed like a strangely vivid, erotic dream.

She wondered again if that was what it had been. Every time she did, she stopped to examine the small bruise his thumb had made on the inner side of her wrist, and the love-bite beneath the strap of her dress. He'd been real enough to leave them both.

Or perhaps I am imagining them as well, she thought with a tiny flutter of unease. She rejected it. Even in her wildest imagination, she could not have invented a man like Rees Tregarrick, or the marvelous things he had done to her as they made love.

The village was bathed in pale shades of muted gray and blue. *Like a Vermeer,* she thought, *but without the tranquillity.* She made her way down the steep, cobbled High

Street, past a few chattering tourists and the ubiquitous artists busily painting the view out over the quaint rooftops
to the sparkling turquoise bay. Beyond the Atlantic
stretched to the horizon like striped satin in tones of blue
and gray.

Since talking to Dr. Landry, she'd been thinking about
her love of art and painting. About how she'd turned her
back on it in despair when she realized she hadn't the talent
to take the visions from her mind and put them on canvas
to share with others. She'd gone into a field that was all
ruled lines and by-the-numbers regulations, a discipline
where everything was precise to the last degree. It was the
antithesis of everything she had once wanted. Small wonder
that she now felt so stifled.

And since Rees Tregarrick had touched her, bringing her
body alive with sensations she hadn't known existed, she
realized how barren her life had become. This trip to Cornwall had forever changed her.

A hard rain pelted down all afternoon and didn't let up
for two days. While the other tourists flocked to the local
cinema and the Tin Museum, or sat around the fire in the
quiet lounge over cards, she kept to her room. Except for
a brief courtesy call by Dr. Landry, she hadn't seen anyone
but the maid and the waiters from room service.

With her face against the cool panes, her body on fire
with need, she watched the gray silk rain and thought of
nothing but Rees Tregarrick.

He came to her in dreams, as she lay in the high tester
bed, bringing every inch of her alive and glowing. In
dreams her breasts tingled to his touch and ached for his
kisses. Time and again, her dream-lover brought her gasping to the edge between anguish and glory, and she would
awaken in the lavender dimness, sweaty and tangled in the
sheets, groaning with loss as the image of Rees Tregarrick's
strong, hard body and the lingering sensation of his strong
embrace faded from her mind.

The phone rang, startling her. It was the front desk.
"You haven't been down since early yesterday, Miss Ken-

dall," the head clerk said. "I took it upon myself to make sure that you're not ill . . . ?"

"Thank you, no." Lily tried to think of an excuse. "I've been catching up on my sleep and my reading, enjoying the quiet of the suite."

"Very good. If you require anything you have only to ask."

Lily replaced the phone and sat up. The clerk had sounded relieved. She wondered if the maid had said something about the way she sat at the window, staring over the cobbled waterfront to the gray, wind-ripped bay. Perhaps this was how Catherine Tregarrick had waited for him to come home from the sea, watching for him to make safe harbor.

She must have loved him when she married him, Lily thought. *Any woman in her right mind would have fallen in love with him.* Yet it must have been lonely for a young girl left behind, even by her own choice, while her husband sailed the oceans. *"She should have gone with you,"* Lily murmured to the falling rain. *"I would have."*

She wished she knew more about both of them. Rees Tregarrick was a powerful lover—could a man capable of such intense passion be capable of other, more violent emotions? A chill ran through Lily. She wrapped her arms around herself. She wanted to see Rees Tregarrick again. To ask him about Catherine. To have him take her into his arms and kiss away that very faint, lingering shadow of doubt.

Pacing the carpet before the windows that overlooked the harbor, Lily wept and cursed the rain.

The sun came out on the third afternoon, and St. Dunstan village bloomed once again with nasturtium and giant hydrangea, tourists in shorts with cameras slung about their necks, and artists dabbling in oils and pastels and watercolors along the quay. Her heart in her throat, Lily dressed eagerly, carefully, as if for a bridegroom. She'd done a lot of reading. A lot of thinking. She thought that she had finally figured out what she must do.

Leaving the hotel that had been both sanctuary and prison, Lily walked past the greengrocers and tea room to a little stationery store run by Mrs. Polgelly. It was a fascinating little hole in the wall, filled with postcards, artists' supplies, and souvenir books on one side, the latest magazines and paperback fiction, some old favorites, and a section of New Age books, crystals, tarot cards, and pamphlets on the other.

The rest was given over to everything from paperweights hewn from the local granite to miniature teapots and hand-embroidered tea towels. The proprietor bustled over and assessed Lily from head to toe.

"Visiting relations in St. Dunstan, are you?" she asked.

"No, just a tourist, I'm afraid."

"Ah, but you've Cornish blood, aye, and it's brought you back." The old woman fixed her with a bright blue gaze. "You've the look of the old Trelawnys about you. They have the farm up beyond Yearning Head. They've been at Old Cross Farm these three hundred years and more. Young Miss Portia who runs the Starr House Museum lives there." She wrapped Lily's purchases—a sketchbook and drawing pencils—nodding in satisfaction. "You've Trelawny blood. I'm never wrong, you know."

Bemused, Lily went out and started the long climb up the zig-zag street toward the headland. Could it be true that she and Portia Trelawny were some sort of distant cousins? That might explain her feelings of belonging in Cornwall, her sense of having come home. Or perhaps it was only Rees Tregarrick who made her feel that way. The nearer she got, the harder her heart beat with anticipation. Her excitement at the thought of seeing Rees Tregarrick again made her tremble inside. Whether he was man, or ghost, or illusion, she longed for him with such intensity it was a physical ache.

She sat beneath the same tree where he had come to her before and waited. Time passed, marked by the scudding clouds and the angle of the westering sun, but she felt no presence. She remained alone.

Lily tried to sketch the view, but her hands shook too

much, and her perspective was abominable. The vast expanse of the headland was empty. The wind soughed through the line of twisted trees, sounding like a woman's muffled sobs. There was nothing there but sea and sky, and the strange, intense longing that swirled through the very air along the headland. It seemed to emanate from the violent meeting of stern, unyielding granite and insistent, lapis sea.

Like doomed lovers. Lily thought, watching the waves. *Always meeting in passion, never able to hold on to the moment . . . or each other.*

Finally she gave up trying to sketch the wild Atlantic, rushing to engulf the great granite rock formation offshore that the locals called St. Petroc's Cathedral. Her waves were lumpy, not liquid, and her rendering of the delicate salt spume looked as thick as frosting on a cake. It was too much for her minor skills, she realized.

Setting her sights on something less grand, she concentrated on the wildflowers that dotted the grassy slope and clung to the lichened rocks. The colored pencils filled in the shadows and highlights as the flowers came to life on her page, but there was nothing else that stirred around her.

The sun lowered over the water, gilding the rocks and turning the wave-tossed sea to a cauldron of gold, and still Rees didn't come. Disheartened, Lily packed up her things and went back to the hotel.

Every morning for four more days, she went out to Yearning Head and spent the hours sketching the odd shapes of the wind-sculpted trees and the wildflowers that dotted the rugged headland. Every evening she returned to her hotel room with nothing but pages of carefully tinted sketches to show for her vigil, and a heart filled with aching disappointment.

By week's end she was anxious and out of sorts. Only three days of vacation left, and then she had to leave. How far away her life in the States seemed! How infinitely lonely. Once more she went along the strand and climbed the granite steps while the wind plucked at her skirts and pulled her hair loose from its clips.

She stood on the headland and lifted her face to the wind. "Where are you?" she cried softly. "Why won't you come to me, Rees Tregarrick?"

The sun warmed her face, a breeze kissed her mouth, but that was all. The doubts that had been growing in her heart loomed large. Perhaps Dr. Landry was right. Her loneliness and romantic imagination, compounded by a blow to the head, had conjured up what was nothing more than a vivid hallucination.

But, oh, the pressure of his hot mouth on hers, the feel of his warm hands upon her naked body, had been so wonderfully real.

Lily sat on the headland until well past dinnertime, and finally came to a decision. There was no use pining away over a man who'd lived a hundred years ago—and she couldn't face the boredom of returning to her job with the Department of Transportation. Not just yet.

She would wire her supervisor and request a leave of absence. Then she'd pack up and leave St. Dunstan, hoping her experiences would fade in time from sharp loss to a happily remembered dream. The world was full of other places to visit: Rome and Athens, Cairo and Capetown, Jakarta and Hong Kong. She would see them all. When her leave was up, she would know what to do about reshaping her life. One thing was sure, she wouldn't continue on the same worn path she'd been treading for years.

That decision made, Lily was still reluctant to leave Cornwall behind. She knew, with overwhelming sadness, that once she left she would never come back to St. Dunstan.

Two nights before she was to leave Cornwall, Rees came to Lily in her dreams once more, handsome and virile as before. She reached out to him, but he vanished into the gathering fog. The scene shifted in the strange way of dreams. Lily stood on the headland, wind whipping her hair against her face, while he watched her from the star window, his fists beating soundlessly against the stained-glass panes.

She wakened, drenched in sweat, heart fluttering with fear. And with hope. Lily lay awake till dawn, thinking. In the end, there was no real decision to be made. She knew what she must do.

On her last day in the village, Lily stayed in her room, packing. A quick call to the airline confirmed her flight home. She tucked in two of the sketchbooks she'd filled with her drawings, and placed the souvenirs she'd bought in her carry-on. Ignoring her half-finished letter to a friend on the desktop, she shot several pictures of her room with the new camera she'd bought in the little town. It was late in the day when she set out on a final pilgrimage to Yearning Head.

She walked briskly along the High Street and made her way to the strand. She reached the base of the cliffs as the sky turned from gold and pink to lavender. Twilight closed in, but she was not afraid. The water had gone out in the bay and shimmered in the distance like gray, watered silk. Lily couldn't help remembering her frantic scramble in the fog, racing the rising tide. The bright, burning star that had guided her footsteps.

The voice—*his* voice, calling her to safety. *Oh, Rees, my love!*

She smiled at the rich life of the tide pools, the colorful clumps of barnacles and limpets exposed on the rocks by the retreating waves.

"Good-bye," she said softly to the tide pool, and the silvery sea, and the great craggy bulk of Yearning Head.

As she rounded a jutting rock, her foot slipped on the loose shingle, and she went sprawling. Her sketchbook flew out of her hand. Lily ignored it. Before she could get to her feet, the air darkened and shimmered, and she knew. He was waiting for her at the head of the stairs.

She made the climb eagerly, grasping the rough railing to pull herself higher. When she reached the top of Yearning Head, there was nothing but a wide sweep of wind-bent grasses, the stunted trees to one side and the graceful lines of Star House against the rapidly darkening sky.

The wind grew chill, and she wrapped her arms around herself for warmth as night fell. Stars spangled the firmament, but the mansion's tower was a black bulk rising up like a threat, its great stained-glass window blank and unlit.

Lily lifted her arms to the sky. Love and a fierce longing flowed from her like an invisible force. The air crackled with tension.

"*Damn* you, Rees Tregarrick! Come to me. Come to me!"

The wind snatched her voice, carrying it inland, yet it seemed to echo from behind her, from the granite mass of Yearning Head. As those lonely echoes faded, a faint light bloomed in the tower, grew and blossomed before her eyes. Lily held her breath, afraid to move. Then the great star window lit the night, blazing in all its golden glory. "*Rees!*" she whispered.

And suddenly, miraculously, *he* was there.

He stood a little away. He looked older, and his cane was gone. His jaw was so hard, his eyes so angry that it frightened her a little. Was this how Catherine Tregarrick had seen him that fatal night? But, no, whatever it was that sparked in the depths of his eyes, she knew beyond doubt that he would never harm her.

"Rees!" She held out her arms to him, but his own stayed at his side.

"What do you want of me, woman?"

The harshness of his voice stung her. Lily went toward him despite it. All the longing in her soul welled up, compelling her to go to him.

He was no hallucination. He cast a shadow in the lowering sun, and she could smell his scent of cedar, see a few small whiskers he'd missed in shaving along his squared jaw. Her fingers itched to touch him, to reassure herself that he was really there. She restrained herself with difficulty.

"I've been waiting for you," she told him. "Calling for you."

He sighed. "I heard you tonight, in every sigh of the wind. Why are you tormenting me, woman? For the love of God, go away! Go back to wherever you came from and leave me in peace!"

8

Lɪʟʏ's ᴇʏᴇs ᴡᴇɴᴛ wide in surprise. "*I*, tormenting *you*? The shoe is on the other foot. You came to me, made love to me! And then you went away!"

He recoiled as if she'd slapped him. "A year and more has passed since then! I went out to the headland each day, for months afterward, searching for you. Waiting for you." He laughed bitterly. "I wanted to call out to you . . . and realized that I didn't even know your name."

Lily frowned. "Is it still autumn?"

"Spring," he replied. "Just after Easter week."

"It is still summer," she said slowly. "Only three days have passed since we met."

"Ridiculous!"

"What year is this?"

He looked confused. "What year? Why, it's the year of Our Lord 1881."

"Not in my world," Lily said quietly. She knelt and retrieved her handbag, pulled out the calendar in her wallet, and silently handed it to him.

"This is dated far into the next century!" he exclaimed.

Reaching in again, she took out several other items: a ballpoint pen, a credit card with a hologram on the front, a solar calculator, and showed him how they worked. He scanned her driver's license, her other I.D., and watched the hologram on the credit card change with the flick of his wrist.

His jaw tightened. "Are you saying that you are not a ghost, but a visitor come from the future? Like something out of Jules Verne?"

"Not exactly." Lily bit her lip. It was so difficult to explain. "I live in the future, yes. But it is you who have come to me, out of the past."

He touched her face. Her mouth. His long fingers outlined the contours of her lips until they trembled. "You are no illusion." His eyes darkened with desire. "And whatever—whoever—you are, Lily Kendall, you still make my blood run hot!" His hand dropped to his side. "Go away. Go back to wherever you come from and forget me. Perhaps that will end this curse."

"Why is it a curse?" she cried. "Are you afraid to love again? I'll stay with you, here in your time, if that is what you want. I don't know how, but I'll find a way!"

His face and voice were impassioned. "I can't ask that of you. It would destroy you, as it did Catherine. I took her away, out of her element, and she was driven mad because of it. I'm burdened with enough guilt for that."

Lily moved closer, so close that his breath stirred her hair. "I'm not Catherine. She was a mere girl. I am a woman. I'm stronger. And I want you, Rees Tregarrick! Not your position or your wealth. Only *you*."

She moved into his arms, pliant as a willow. With an anguished growl, he scooped her up. His kiss was as wild and defiant as the elements. She opened her mouth to him, sighing with relief. He wanted her, too. Lily's arms wound round his neck.

"I will never let you go," she whispered against his broad chest.

His limp was no impediment as he carried her down the grassy slope toward the house.

"No," Lily whispered against his cheek. "Portia and James are there."

"And who the devil are *they*?" Rees asked. "I tell you, there is no one at home today. It's St. Dunstan's fair, and all the servants have gone down to the village, even Mrs. Penhale."

When they reached the house, he kicked the door open and carried her inside. He mounted the stairs as if she were weightless in his arms. Lily barely had time to see that there were no velvet ropes before the cabinets, no advertising flyers on the table or blue-and-white vases by the parlor doors. The whole house was subtly different—but Rees Tregarrick was the same.

He pushed the door to the master suite open with his shoulder. "Not here," Lily murmured. "Not in her bed."

"Catherine never slept here," he whispered hotly. "I went to her. But you, Lily Kendall—I will make love to you here, as I've dreamed I have for so long."

And he did. His hands were rough as he stripped away her clothes, but gentle on her naked flesh. "I've aged three years, and you not a single day," he said. "Your breasts are as firm and high, your face as unlined as it was the day we met."

Lily noticed the faint sprinkling of silver at his temples. She ran her fingers through his hair, locked them into it and pulled his face down to hers. Her eyes were as fierce as her emotions.

"If this is all we ever have, we'll make the best of it! Love me, Rees Tregarrick, for I love you with every atom of my heart and soul."

This time they didn't bother with preliminaries. They were both more than ready. He slid inside her as if their bodies had been designed solely for one another. For a moment he just held her close to his heart.

"I'm so afraid you'll vanish again."

The moment the words were said, she felt a strange rushing sensation, as if she were being pulled backward through the air. She fought it and clung to him with all her might. Lily knew with terrible fear that if they were separated this time, they would never find one another again. Never in all eternity. And they would both be lost.

"Take me, Rees. Take me!"

As he lunged against her, the air shimmered. His voice was urgent, as if he shared her fear. "I love you, Lily Kendall. Love you with all my heart and soul."

She wrapped her legs around him, welcoming him, and he plunged deep. As their bodies joined, the air shimmered once more, fractured into shards of gold and rose and bright, electric blue.

She closed her eyes against the whirling colors, blocking out everything but Rees Tregarrick . . . the masculine smell of his body, the strength of his arms, the potency of his virile, male passion. Sliding his hands beneath her, he lifted Lily higher, thrusting harder, faster, with every beat of their hearts. They were flying like seabirds again, swooping over the brilliant sea, soaring up together over the bay and into the fiery sun.

He pushed her harder, and higher. "Don't leave me, Lily," he whispered against her ear. "Never leave me! Swear it!"

Lily felt the tension crackling in the air around them. She knew, without a doubt, that she had come to a crossroad in time. Once the decision was made, there would be no going back. Literally.

She arched up into him, taking him deep, and kissed his firm mouth. "Rees Tregarrick, I swear that if it is in my power, I will never leave you."

He filled her completely, claiming her as his own with every powerful stroke. The air shimmered once more, and although the sun shone outside the windows, a mighty crack of thunder rent the air. The lovers didn't care. Lost in each other, they rode the currents of desire higher and higher, until their wings were singed with the heat of their passion, and they fell spiraling back to earth, together.

He worshiped her with his body, grazing her skin with his lips, from the soft curve of her throat to the firm upthrust of her breasts and down to her thighs. He savored the taste of her, the scent of her, and brought her arching up into glory again and again.

Afterward, Lily lay in his arms, her head against his shoulder. "Tell me about Catherine. But only if it is not too painful."

"No." He sighed. "That wound is an old scar now. What is there to tell? She was young and beautiful, and I loved her despite her flaws, with all the ardor of a young man in his first infatuation. She was also selfish and shallow, but I was too head-over-heels to realize it. Catherine married me with no intention of settling at Star House. I didn't know that. I built it for her."

"Oh, Rees!" Lily heard only ghosts of the old pain in his voice, but the bewilderment was still there. She pressed a kiss against his shoulder.

"Were you never happy together?"

"It was all a sham. I think she was one of those women who loved herself so well, she had no love left for anyone else. But I was besotted. When she refused to go to sea with me, I brought her back all the treasures of the earth that I could find, hoping, I suppose, to buy her love. She didn't want them. And she didn't want me."

"She was a fool."

"Only young and ambitious. She wanted to be a dashing young London hostess, to spend her life at parties and balls, dancing away the hours. I was to be her tool, my wealth her entrée into the world she coveted."

He rolled onto his back and stared up at the ceiling. Lily ran her hands across the sculpted muscles of his chest, offering comfort. "You needn't tell me any more."

A long sigh answered her in the gathering darkness. "Some say I killed her, Lily."

"Yes, I know. I have never believed it."

He rolled over and took her face between his hands. "You should know this, then. I could have killed her when I learned what she had done! It was Catherine who snuffed out the lamps that lit the star window and sent the *Tregarrick's Star* onto the rocks."

"Dear God, why?"

"To rid herself of me!" The words were wrung from him. "So that she might return to London a wealthy widow and lose herself in a round of balls and mindless pleasures. For that I lost two men! Two good men, with wives and children in St. Dunstan. When she told me what she had done, I wanted to kill her, Lily! I wanted to throttle her with my bare hands!"

"But you didn't. You didn't!" She pulled him down and kissed him fiercely.

He laughed, with only a trace of bitterness now. "No. She ran out onto the headland, and I ran after her, thinking she meant to fling herself into the sea. Fool that I was! Instead, Catherine tried to trip me. She was insane with rage and thwarted ambitions. She meant for me to die that night, but she lost her footing. I tried to save her, and we both went tumbling down the sea-stairs."

His voice grew low and bleak. "She cursed me as she lay dying. 'May you never have a happy moment again, Rees Tregarrick, until you find a woman fool enough to give up everything else for love of you!' "

Lily kissed his chest, moved her lips teasingly over the crisp hair, and touched his nipple. "You've found her," she said, sliding atop him. "I will go where you go, live where you live. And," she said, as his body responded, "I will love you body and soul."

She straddled Rees and slipped down onto him, sheathing him inside her until he groaned and reached out to her. "Oh, Lily, I was such an imbecile. I never knew what love was until I met you. These past three years have been a lover's hell, waiting for you to appear again. Wondering if you ever would—or if I had conjured you up out of my loneliness."

"We'll make it paradise," she promised.

Placing his hands on her waist, he pulled her down, hard, and thrust his hips up to meet hers. She met him, jolt for jolt, her back arched and her head thrown back, reveling in the pleasure that she gave and took. The last fading light of the setting sun gilded the outlines of his splendid body, tipped her breasts with gold. As she cried out in sudden passion, he sat up, rolled her over, and took her with a fierce possessiveness that left them both spent.

Rees looked down into her eyes. "Lily, my love, my heart, will you come away with me? Will you leave this place behind and sail away with me?"

She smiled up into his beloved face. "Rees Tregarrick, I will sail with you to the ends of the earth."

9

Dr. LANDRY CLIMBED out of his ancient automobile, feeling that he was on a fool's errand. For a moment he almost wanted to turn around and leave. It had been an exhausting morning, and he didn't want any more disappointments. But the note from Lily Kendall crinkled in his inner jacket pocket.

She hadn't signed it, but he recognized her writing from the postcards, and the woman who had left the note with his receptionist matched her description perfectly. Only a few sentences were penned on the neatly folded sheet:

> *Don't worry about me. I'm well and happy and more alive than I've ever been! Look behind the lining of the trunk that Portia opened at the Star House Museum while I was there—she'll know which one—and you'll understand.*

She'd vanished three nights ago, after having been seen walking briskly toward Yearning Head, her tote bag of sketching materials over one arm. Her ruined camera and rain-soaked handbag had been found among the rocks just above the tide line, along with the battered thermos from her picnic lunch.

As he would tell the coroner's jury, Miss Lily Kendall had evidenced no suicidal tendencies, as was shown by the letter she'd left half finished on her hotel desk, and the expensive new camera she'd purchased only the day before. She had confirmed her return ticket with the airlines.

The verdict would be only a formality: Miss Lily Kendall had been caught in the sudden squall that had blown up with unusual suddenness and been swept out to sea by the high tide. Like those previously lost on the beach at Yearning Head, no trace of her was likely to ever be found. A terrible tragedy.

And yet . . . The words of her note echoed through his head: *Don't worry. . . . I'm . . . more alive than I have ever been!* Somehow he felt it must be true.

Dr. Landry straightened his shoulders. He was wise enough to know that he didn't have the answers to half the questions that life posed. He was a man of science, never happy unless he'd investigated every avenue of inquiry.

Even if it turned out that he could never make the truth public, he had to find out for his own peace of mind.

He crossed the gravel car park and went through the side door into the museum, where he was one of the trustees. Portia looked up, surprised to see him. "Miss Kendall told me that you opened a trunk when she was here last. I have a particular interest in seeing it, if I may?"

"Of course." Sighing, Portia picked up her ring of keys. "I keep hoping we'll learn she went off to visit some other place and forgot to leave word."

The doctor avoided her eyes. "I don't think she's the kind of woman not to leave word."

"No, I suppose not." Handing him the key to the chest, she went back to her task of sorting out catalogue cards and entering them in her notebook computer.

The doctor passed through the door and into the museum's storeroom. The old trunk with the embossed tin panels was against the far wall with other items to be cataloged and photographed. Light from the partially shaded window behind it made it seem to glow. *I'm getting fanciful in my old age,* he told himself.

Look inside the lining, Lily's Kendall's note said. Turning the trunk carefully toward the window, he unlocked it. He found the small book nested inside the white organza folds: *Unique Flora and Fauna of the Sandwich Islands,* written and illustrated by Mrs. Lily Kendall Tregarrick. It shook him profoundly.

Opening the pages, he admired the beautiful renderings of birds and flowers in the engravings—each one so perfectly precise and lifelike that it might have been taken with a camera. "So, you found your talent, after all," he murmured.

Landry ran his sensitive fingertips along the top lining. Instead of a fine, smooth finish, the chest had a thin, rough edge on one side of the floral panel. His heart gave a leap of excitement.

He hunkered down and pulled out his pocketknife. Sliding the thin tip behind the liner, he worked it loose. There were only six tiny nails holding the panel in place. He popped the last one out and jumped as an envelope fell out from behind it and landed facedown inside the chest.

When he turned it over, his hands shook just a little, as he recognized his own name printed neatly in faded ink across the front of it. The envelope was heavy. There seemed to be a lot of papers in it, or perhaps old photographs.

Ah, yes. He pulled out a yellowed marriage certificate, two birth records, a slim diary, and an ornate cardboard frame, such as Victorian photographers had used. There were several very like it in his collection of family memorabilia.

It opened like a book. Inside were the ornate silver-stamped name of a photographer in Honolulu, and two sepia-toned photographs. One showed a dashing man and a radiant woman, holding a bridal bouquet. The second was a family grouping: the same couple, this time with two children.

To Dr. Landry, the baby looked like any other baby of three or four months, but the pretty toddler, with her wide eyes, deep dimples, and glossy ringlets, bore a startling resemblance to Portia Trelawny.

He smiled as he looked over at the wedding portrait again. The man's arm was around his bride with proud protectiveness. A happy bridegroom—Captain Tregarrick, certainly, but not the stern, unhappy man in the museum's portrait. Despite the hint of gray at his temples in the photograph, Tregarrick looked joyful, and carefree, and, Dr. Landry thought, almost amazed to find himself so.

And Lily Kendall—for despite the old-fashioned gown and hairdo and jewelry, he had no doubt at all that the woman with Tregarrick was truly she—how beautiful, how joyous her face was, with love and contentment shining from it like the sun!

Landry shook his head and smiled back. She had been right after all—and she had found her Rees Tregarrick, despite the span of generations that had separated them. His hands shook, just a little, but his world was shaken even more. Somehow Lily Kendall had managed to go back in time.

Ordinary logic had no rational explanation. He certainly had none himself. Perhaps quantum physics had the answer, and time and the universe were composed of a magical fabric, where every moment touched and blended into every other. Perhaps Yearning Head was one of those places where it was possible to step from one world into another.

Or perhaps, he told himself, he was mad as the proverbial hatter.

But no, here was Lily Kendall, in the portrait she had purposely hidden away a hundred years ago, for him to find today. Lily Kendall looking, as she had promised, happy and well and more alive than ever before.

Dr. Landry wiped his eyes. "Sentimental old fool," he muttered, and blew his nose in his linen handkerchief.

A small piece of yellow paper was tucked behind the

family grouping. The doctor pulled it out and read the words written in Lily's unmistakable handwriting:

Dear Dr. Landry,
I thought perhaps Portia would like to know how much she takes after her great-grandmother—even to the dimples!

There was no name, only the simple initial "L."

The tropical sun was clear and golden as the small sailboat cleaved the shining waves. The man at the tiller lifted his arm. "Look there, darling! A pod of whales!"

"Where, Rees?" As the prow knifed through the warm, tropical waters, Lily shaded her eyes from the bright sun and gazed out over the dancing waves.

"Oh! I see them now."

The sleek backs of the ocean giants glistened as the waves foamed and washed over them, darker shapes against the myriad blues and grays of the sea. One burst upward in a flash of strength and joy, then splashed back into the sea in a rainbow spray. A moment later she saw the misted-feather plume of its spouting.

"Can we get closer, Rees?"

He smiled at her from his place at the tiller, his eyes darker blue than the Pacific waters, his teeth white against his tanned skin. "As close as is safe. I'll not take any chances with you, my love."

Or the baby to come, Lily thought, smiling to herself. She hadn't told him yet. She wanted to be sure—but in her heart she already was. It would be a daughter, the first of the two children that she would bear him. Their son would be named Rees, like his father. But this one would be a girl, blond and dimpled, with laughing blue eyes. Her name would be Portia, of course. That was the name Lily had read in the records at the Star House Museum.

The small sailboat cut through the sparkling sapphire waters. Lily turned her face up to the warm December sun. Rising up in the distance, were the emerald-green humps of the Sandwich Islands, where they now made their permanent home.

In the eighteen months since their marriage, they had sailed to exotic ports of call, but now they had come back to Lahaina. If she strained her eyes, she could almost make out the white pillars of their home in the lush green hills above the town.

With the glorious flowers and balmy air, it was strange to think that it would be Christmas in little more than a week; but here everything was different—just as she was, since falling in love with Rees Tregarrick. Every day her love for him grew deeper, more boundless than the oceans they had roamed.

She glanced up at him, tall and tanned, against the azure sky. How handsome he looked in his white shirt, with the neck open at his strong throat and the sleeves rolled up against his sinewy arms. Lily's heart swelled with love for her husband. With gratitude to him, for the joy and love he gave her—and to fate, for enabling her to turn his life around as well.

It felt odd to know the outcome of their love story. That she and Rees would grow old together, surrounded by their children and grandchildren—and that someday, some of their descendants would return to Cornwall and St. Dunstan, and settle down in the little village whose cobbled streets and seaswept vistas she knew so well. To know that one of their granddaughters would marry Pen Trelawny, of Old Cross Farm, and their line would produce the eager young Portia Trelawny who ran the Star House Museum. A cousin would wed a Scots-Irish American named Malcolm Kendall and move to Arlington. But all that was still to come.

It would be many years, many generations until the circle of time, of fate, would be complete.

At the moment Lily was far more interested in the present than the past or future. They watched the whales at play for a while, and then Rees set their sail for a small and private island that they had made their own secret trysting place. He cut through the opening in the reef and dropped anchor in the sheltered lagoon.

The sands were white as sugar, the foliage as bright as the emeralds in Lily's wedding ring. Beyond them a crystal waterfall poured over a verdant green ledge like a veil of spangled tulle. Flowers garlanded the open-air bower Rees had built for her with his own hands, and tiny jeweled birds flitted past purple plumeria and deep crimson hibiscus, and the startling scarlet red of the high poinsettia hedges.

Lily knew she would never become jaded to the beauty of her adopted homeland. Or to her feelings for Rees. The how and why of their meeting was something they never discussed any longer. It was beyond their fragile human understanding.

Perhaps there were times—and places—Lily thought, when the barriers between past and present touched and mingled, like tendrils of fog melting into one another. Perhaps she and Reese had met on Yearning Head at such a magical moment.

Or perhaps the old St. Dunstan legend was true that, if someone longed for something with all their heart and wished for it in the crosswinds at Yearning Head, the wish would be granted. Theirs certainly had. Lily and Rees took it for what it was—a gift.

He made love to her in the bower, with dappled sunlight kissing their bodies and the music of the waves against the reef. He cupped her breasts in his hands and showered her face with heated kisses. His eyes shone bluer than the sun-tossed sea and as clear of the shadows that had haunted them.

He touched her cheek. "No regrets, Lily?"

"Not a one."

Rees kissed her hand. "Every morning and every night, I thank God for sending you to me. I don't understand how it came about." His fingers stroked her skin. "I don't care. It's enough to know you are here with me now."

"And to think you tried to send me away." She laughed softly.

"I was a fool," he said, pressing his mouth against her

breast, teasing the tender tip until she groaned and shifted beneath him.

"I wouldn't have gone," she told him as he slid his hand between her legs. She gasped in a deep breath. A single stroke of his thumb had her quivering with need. "Nothing you could have said or done, Rees Tregarrick, would have rid you of me. We are fated to be together."

The western sky turned to gold. The perfumed breeze caressed their bodies, as Lily and her beloved sipped wine and watched the tropical sun make its sudden plunge below the horizon. Stars sprang out against the velvet night. Huge, swirling globes of light, against a dome of sky like a hollowed-out sapphire. The sea glittered darkly around them, while night birds called and the surf murmured a soft lullaby. *Not a Van Gogh canvas.* Lily told herself, *but a painting by Gauguin. Paradise before the Fall.*

Setting down her crystal wineglass, she wound her arms around Rees's strong neck and arched herself against him. "Make love to me, darling."

His embrace tightened. "All night long, if you desire."

And he did, with all the skill and ardor he possessed. Afterward Lily smiled as she lay cradled in Rees's arms, sheltered and warmed by the heat of his body. He returned her smile and followed it with a passionate kiss.

"I love you, Lily Tregarrick."

"I love you more."

"Impossible!" he whispered, kissing her temple, her cheek, her soft and rosy lips.

The loneliness and sorrows of the past had been banished forever. Heart to heart, soul to soul, they celebrated their deepening love and joy in one another, all through the starry, starry night.

BIRTHRIGHT

Nora Roberts

When five-thousand-year-old bones are
found at a construction site in the small town
of Woodsboro, the news draws archaeologist
Callie Dunbrook out of her sabbatical
and into a whirlwind of
adventure, danger, and romance.

0-399-14984-8

NORTON HISTORY OF SCIENCE
GENERAL EDITOR: ROY PORTER

already published:

Environmental Sciences   PETER J. BOWLER
Chemistry   W. H. BROCK

forthcoming:

Technology   DONALD CARDWELL
Mathematics   IVOR GRATTAN–GUINNESS
Physics   RUSSELL MACCORMMACH
Astronomy   JOHN NORTH
Biology   ROBERT OLBY
Medicine   ROY PORTER
Science in Society
LEWIS PYENSON & SUSAN SHEETS–PYENSON
Human Sciences   ROGER SMITH

'Chemical Industry, Upheld by Pure Science Sustains the
Production of Man's Necessities', frontispiece to A. Cressy
Morrison, *Man in A Chemical World: the service of chemical industry*
(London & New York: Scribner's, 1937)
Reproduced courtesy of Scribner's, Collier Macmillan, New York

NORTON HISTORY OF SCIENCE
(Editor: Roy Porter)

THE NORTON HISTORY OF
CHEMISTRY

William H. Brock

W·W· Norton & Company
New York   London

Library of Congress Cataloging-in-Publication Data
Brock, William H.
    [Fontana history of chemistry]
    The Norton history of chemistry / William H.
Brock. — 1st American ed.
        p.   cm. — (Norton history of science)
    Originally published in UK under the title: The
Fontana history of chemistry.
    Includes bibliographical references and index.
    1. Chemistry—History.   I. Title.   II. Series.
QD11.B76   1993
540'.9—dc20   93–19054

ISBN 0-393-03536-0   (cl)
ISBN 0-393-31043-4   (pa)

W. W. Norton & Company, Inc.
500 Fifth Avenue, New York, N.Y. 10110
W. W. Norton & Company Ltd.
10 Coptic Street, London WC1A 1PU

4 5 6 7 8 9 0

PREFACE TO
THE NORTON HISTORY OF SCIENCE

Academic study of the history of science has advanced
dramatically, in depth and sophistication, during the last
generation. More people than ever are taking courses in the
history of science at all levels, from the specialized degree
to the introductory survey; and, with science playing an
ever more crucial part in our lives, its history commands
an influential place in the media and in the public eye.

Over the past two decades particularly, scholars have
developed major new interpretations of science's history.
The great bulk of such work, however, has been published
in detailed research monographs and learned periodicals,
and has remained hard of access, hard to interpret. Pressures
of specialization have meant that few survey works have
been written that have synthesized detailed research and
brought out wider significance.

It is to rectify this situation that the Norton History
of Science has been set up. Each of these wide-ranging
volumes examines the history, from its roots to the present,
of a particular field of science. Targeted at students and the
general educated reader, their aim is to communicate, in
simple and direct language intelligible to non-specialists,
well-digested and vivid accounts of scientific theory and
practice as viewed by the best modern scholarship. The most
eminent scholars in the discipline, academics well-known
for their skills as communicators, have been commissioned.

The volumes in this series survey the field and offer
powerful overviews. They are intended to be interpretative,
though not primarily polemical. They do not pretend to
a timeless, definitive quality or suppress differences of

viewpoint, but are meant to be books of and for their time; their authors offer their own interpretations of contested issues as part of a wider, unified story and a coherent outlook.

Carefully avoiding a dreary recitation of facts, each volume develops a sufficient framework of basic information to ensure that the beginner finds his or her feet and to enable student readers to use such books as their prime course-book. They rely upon chronology as an organizing framework, while stressing the importance of themes, and avoiding the narrowness of anachronistic 'tunnel history'. They incorporate the best up-to-the-minute research, but within a larger framework of analysis and without the need for a clutter of footnotes – though an attractive feature of the volumes is their substantial bibliographical essays. Authors have been given space to amplify their arguments and to make the personalities and problems come alive. Each volume is self-contained, though authors have collaborated with each other and a certain degree of cross-referencing is indicated. Each volume covers the whole chronological span of the science in question. The prime focus is upon Western science, but other scientific traditions are discussed where relevant.

This series, it is hoped, will become the key synthesis of the history of science for the next generation, interpreting the history of science for scientists, historians and the general public living in a uniquely science-oriented epoch.

ROY PORTER
Series Editor

CONTENTS

ILLUSTRATIONS

ACKNOWLEDGEMENTS

The Norton History of Chemistry was begun during a period of study leave from the University of Leicester that was spent as a Visiting Fellow in the Department of History and Philosophy of Science at the University of Melbourne from September to December 1989. I am grateful to Professor R. W. Home, and to the Master of Ormond College, Melbourne, for their hospitality and shared scholarship. The bulk of the text was written while I held the 1990–91 Edelstein International Fellowship in the History of Chemical Sciences and Technology at the Arnold and Mabel Beckman Center for the History of Chemistry in Philadelphia. The Center and its associated libraries provide excellent facilities and resources for anyone engaged on research in the history of chemistry. I therefore owe a debt of gratitude to Dr Sydney Edelstein, Professor Arnold Thackray, Professor Emeritus Charles Price, Dr Larry Friedman, Dr O. Theodor Benfey and all the other Beckman staff for making my stay in America so happy and productive. My predecessor as Edelstein Fellow, Professor Seymour H. Mauskopf of Duke University, helped in many ways to make my stay in America a great pleasure. My thanks are also due to the University of Leicester and my colleagues in the Department of History for allowing me effectively over a year's leave of absence from teaching and administration. Rose Canteve and Lisa Kazanjian in Philadelphia and Drs J. G. Smith and D. L. Wykes in Leicester kindly rescued me whenever I was in difficulties with word processing. Angela Chorley and Julie Bowles of Leicester's Graphic Design Service kindly prepared the artwork. Finally, I should like to thank Roy Porter for his enthusiasm and advice.

BIBLIOGRAPHICAL NOTE

So as not to encumber the book with footnotes, I have employed the simple device of indicating the source of a quotation by a superscript number. These sources will be found in the relevant notes section (often briefly) and more details are given in the bibliographical essay, which not only provides an up-to-date guide to the published literature, but is also my acknowledgement to the hundreds of historians whose work has guided me in writing this book. For historical convenience, trivial rather than systematic (IUPAC) names are used for inorganic compounds, viz. 'alum' rather than 'aluminium potassium sulphate-12-water'. In the case of organic compounds, systematic names are used only for more complex compounds.

INTRODUCTION

That all plants immediately and substantially stem from the element water alone I have learnt from the following experiment. I took an earthern vessel in which I placed two hundred pounds of earth dried in an oven, and watered with rain water. I planted in it the stem of a willow tree weighing five pounds. Five years later it had developed a tree weighing one hundred and sixty-nine pounds and about three ounces. Nothing but rain (or distilled water) had been added. The large vessel was placed in earth and covered by an iron lid with a tin-surface that was pierced with many holes. I have not weighed the leaves that came off in the four autumn seasons. Finally I dried the earth in the vessel again and found the same two hundred pounds of it diminished by about two ounces. Hence one hundred and sixty-four pounds of wood, bark and roots had come up from water alone.

(JOAN-BAPTISTA VAN HELMONT, 1648)

Helmont's arresting experiment and conclusion capture the essence of the problem of chemical change. How and why do water and air 'become' the material of a tree – or, if that sounds too biochemical, how and why do hydrogen and oxygen become water? How does brute matter assume an ordered and often symmetrical solid form in the non-living world? Helmont's experiment also raises the issue of the balance between qualitative and quantitative reasoning in the history of chemistry. Helmont's observations are impeccably quantitative and yet, because he ignored the possible role of air in the reaction he was studying, and since he knew nothing of the hidden variables of nutrients dissolved in the water or of the role of the sun in providing the energy of photosynthesis, his reasoning was to prove qualitatively fallacious.

Chemistry is best defined as the science that deals with the properties and reactions of different kinds of matter. Historically, it arose from a constellation of interests: the empirically based technologies of early metallurgists, brewers, dyers, tanners, calciners and pharmacists; the speculative Greek philosophers' concern whether brute matter was invariant or transformable; the alchemists' real or symbolic attempts to achieve the transmutation of base metals into gold; and the iatrochemists' interest in the chemistry and pathology of animal and human functions. Partly because of the sheer complexity of chemical phenomena, the absence of criteria and standards of purity, and uncertainty over the definition and identification of elements (the building blocks of the chemical tree), but above all because of the lack of a concept of the gaseous state of matter, chemistry remained a rambling, puzzling and chaotic area of natural philosophy until the middle of the eighteenth century. The development of gas chemistry after 1740 gave the subject fresh empirical and conceptual foundations, which permitted explanations of reactions in terms of atoms and elements to be given.

Using inorganic, or mineral, chemistry as its paradigm, nineteenth-century chemists created organic chemistry, from which emerged the fruitful ideas of valency and structure; while the advent of the periodic law in the 1870s finally provided chemists with a comprehensive classificatory system of elements and a logical, non-historically based method for teaching the subject. By the 1880s, physics and chemistry were drawing closer together in the sub-discipline of physical chemistry. Finally, the discovery of the electron in 1897 enabled twentieth-century chemists to solve the fundamental problems of chemical affinity and reactivity, and to address the issue of reaction mechanisms – to the profit of the better understanding of synthetic pathways and the expansion of the chemical and pharmaceutical industries.

Returning to Helmont's tree, an arboreal image and metaphor can be usefully deployed. The historical roots of chemistry were many, but produced no sturdy growth until the eighteenth century. In this healthy state, branching into the sub-disciplines of inorganic, organic and physical chemistry occurred during the nineteenth century, with further, more complex branching in the twentieth century as instrumental techniques of analysis became ever more sophisticated and powerful. Growth was, however, dependent upon social and environmental conditions that either nurtured or withered particular theories and experimental techniques.

Although conceived as a work of synthesis for the 1990s (there has been no extensive one-volume history of chemistry published since that of Aaron Ihde in 1964), *The Norton History of Chemistry* draws extensively upon some of the themes and personalities treated in my own research as well as upon the post-war work of other historians of chemistry. Gone are the days of Kopp and Partington, when a history of chemistry could be allowed to unfold slowly in four magisterial and detailed volumes. My volume is designed to be neither a complete nor a detailed narrative; nor is it a work of reference like James R. Partington's *History of Chemistry*, to which I, like all historians of chemistry, remain profoundly indebted. I am particularly conscious, for example, of ignoring developments such as photography (that most chemical of nineteenth-century arts), spectroscopy, Russian chemistry, or the emergence of ideas concerning atomic structure. In some cases, as with the omission of any emphasis on the role of Avogadro's hypothesis in the nineteenth-century determination of atomic and molecular weights, the lacuna is justified historiographically; in other cases, as with my muted references to the roles of rhetoric and language in chemistry, it was a decision not to introduce a contemporary historiographic fashion in a book largely dedicated to a readership of chemists and science students.

In yet other cases, choices of subject matter, and therefore of omission, have stemmed from the decision to structure chapters around seminal texts, their writers and the schools of chemists associated with them. This principle of organization has been freely borrowed from Derek Gjertsen's *The Classics of Science* (New York: Lilian Barber, 1984) and a book edited by Jack Meadows, *The History of Scientific Development* (Oxford: Phaidon, 1987), with which I was associated. To use a metaphor from organic chemistry, the book is arranged around textual types, each title standing symbolically for a paradigm, a theoretical, instrumental or organizational change or development that seems significant to the historian of chemistry. I have tried to lay equal emphasis upon the practical (analytical) nature of past chemistry as much as on its theoretical content, and, although it would have taken a volume in itself to analyse the development of industrial chemistry, I have tried to provide the reader with an inkling of the application of chemistry. Wherever possible I have stressed the significance of chemistry for the development of other areas of science, and I have noted some of the false steps and blind alleys of past chemistry as much as the developments that still remain part of the scientific record. Echoing Ihde's incisive treatment, *The Norton History of Chemistry* also provides a generous treatment of twentieth-century chemistry – albeit within the constraints of my chosen themes and typologies. I have tried wherever possible to illustrate the international nature of the chemical enterprise since the seventeenth century.

Helmont's tree leads us both backwards and forwards in time – forwards to when evidence accrued that air (and gases) did participate in chemical change, and backwards to the ancient traditions of elements and of transmutation that Helmut had inherited. The book opens with the roots of chemistry and the social, economic and religious environments that promoted it before the time of Helmont. In particular, the opening chapter examines early chemical technologies and their rationalization by Greek philosophers in theories of elements or, more iconoclastically, in terms of corpuscules and atoms. The tree enters here again, for one of the perennial proofs for the existence of elements and for their number was the destructive distillation of wood by fire – an important phenomenon empirically (for it was the model for distillation techniques generally) and cognitively because it was the basis of the concepts of analysis and synthesis. Chemistry was, and is, concerned with the analysis of substances into their elements and the synthesis of substances from their elements or immediate principles.

The possibility of manipulating elementary matter into substances of commercial or – at the extreme – of spiritually uplifting value, such as silver and gold or an elixir of life, led to alchemy. The latter's origin, as well as its formal connections with chemistry, are complex and even contentious. However, our contemporary demand for science to have empirical validation, as well as our respect for the technological manipulation of Nature's resources for the benefit of humankind, can be traced back to the philosophical spirit of enquiry that underpinned alchemical investigations. And it goes without saying that alchemy provided early chemistry with much of its apparatus and manipulative techniques, as well as the idea of a formal symbolic language for practitioners of the art.

Each of the sciences, no doubt, has its own difficulties and peculiarities when it comes to presenting its historical development to a diverse audience of professional historians, scientists, students and laypersons; but chemistry, like mathematics, possesses a particularly intimidating obstacle in its language and symbolism, which potentially obscures what are usually quite simple theoretical ideas and experimental techniques. As William Crookes noted in

1865 when reviewing a book on stuttering that had been inappropriately sent to *Chemical News* for review:

> Chemists do not usually stutter. It would be very awkward if they did, seeing that they have at times to get out such words as methylethylamylophenylium.

However, if (as Peter Morris has noted) the historian avoids chemical detail and language, the scientific story become exigious and almost trivial. For this reason, while the first twelve chapters should present little difficulty to a sophisticated general reader, I have not hesitated to use technical language in the five chapters that are devoted to twentieth-century chemistry. Because this is a history, and not a textbook, of chemistry, I have not defined and explained symbols, equations and technical vocabulary. These chapters will present little difficulty to readers who have a secondary or high-school foundation in chemistry (and will have the privilege of being critical of my treatment). At the same time, it is to be hoped that there is sufficient of a human interest story in the intellectual and experimental worlds of Pauling, Ingold, Nyholm, Woodward and the other giants of twentieth-century chemistry, to propel the non-chemical reader towards the final pages.

The history of chemistry has served and continues to serve many purposes: didactic and pedagogic, professional and defensive, patriotic and nationalistic, liberalizing and humanizing. As I write, especially in America, where words like 'chemical', 'synthetic' and 'additive' have unfortunately become associated with the pollution, poisoning and disasters caused by humans, the history of chemistry has come to be seen by leaders of chemical industry and educators as a possible way of revaluing chemical currency: that is, of demonstrating not only the ways in which chemistry plays a fundamental role in nature and our understanding of cosmic processes, but also how it is essential to the economy of twentieth-century societies. In other words, the history of chemistry not only informs us about our great chemical heritage, but justifies the future of chemistry itself. Such a justification echoes the liberal and moving words of the first major historian of chemistry, Hermann Kopp[1]:

> The alchemists of past centuries tried hard to make the elixir of life ... These efforts were in vain; it is not in our power to obtain the experiences and views of the future by prolonging our lives forward in this direction. However, it is possible and in a certain way to prolong our lives backwards, by acquiring the experiences of those who existed before us and by learning to know their views as if we were their contemporaries. The means for doing this is also an elixir of life.

It is in this spirit that *The Norton History of Chemistry* has been written.

THE NORTON HISTORY OF
CHEMISTRY

On the Nature of the Universe
and the Hermetic Museum

Maistryefull merveylous and Archimastrye
Is the tincture of holy Alkimy;
A wonderful Science, secrete Philosophie,
A singular grace and gifte of th'Almightie:
Which never was found by labour of Mann,
But it by Teaching, or by Revalacion begann.
(THOMAS NORTON, *The Ordinall of Alchemy,*
c. 1477)

In 1477, having succeeded after years of study in preparing both the Great Red Elixir and the Elixir of Life, only to have them stolen from him, Thomas Norton of Bristol composed the lively early English poem, *The Ordinall of Alchemy.* Here he expounded in an orderly fashion the procedures to be adopted in the alchemical process, just as an Ordinal lists chronologically the order of the Church's liturgy for the year. Unfortunately, although the reader learns much of would-be alchemists' mistakes, and of the ingredients and apparatus, of the subtle and gross works, and of the financial backing, workers and astrological signs needed to conduct the 'Great Work' successfully, the secret of transmutation remains tantalisingly obscure.

The historian Herbert Butterfield once dismissed historians of alchemy as 'tinctured with the kind of lunacy they set out to describe'; for this reason, he thought, it was impossible to discover the actual state of things alchemical. Nineteenth-century chemists were less embarrassed by the subject. Justus von Liebig, for example, used the following notes to open his Giessen lecture course:

> Distinction between today's method of investigating nature from that in olden times. History of chemistry, especially alchemy . . .

Liebig's presumption, still widespread, was that alchemy was the precursor of chemistry and that modern chemistry arose from a rather dubious, if colourful, past[1]:

> The most lively imagination is not capable of devising a thought which could have acted more powerfully and constantly on the minds and faculties of men, than that very idea of the Philosopher's Stone. Without this idea, chemistry would not now stand in its present perfection . . . [for] in order to know that the Philosopher's Stone did not really exist, it was indispensable that every substance accessible . . . should be observed and examined.

To most nineteenth-century chemists, and historians and novelists, alchemy had been a human aberration, and the task of the historian seemed to be to sift the wheat from the chaff and to discuss only those alchemical views (chiefly practical) that had contributed positively to the development of scientific chemistry. As one historiographer of the subject has put it[2]:

> [the historian] merely split open the fruit to get the seeds, which were for him the only things of value. In the fruit as a whole, its shape, colour, and smell, he had no interest.

But what was alchemy? The familiar response is that it involved the pursuit of the transmutation of base metals such as lead into gold. In practice, the aims of the alchemist were often a good deal broader, and it is only because we take a false perspective in seeing chemistry as arising from alchemy that we normally narrowly focus on to alchemy's concern with the transformation of metals. However, as Carl Jung pointed out in his study *Psychology and Alchemy*, there are similarities between the emblems, symbols and drawings used in European alchemy and the dreams of ordinary twentieth-century people. One does not have to believe in psychoanalysis or Jungism to see that the most obvious explanation for this is that alchemical activities were often concerned with a spiritual quest by humankind to make sense of the universe. It follows that alchemy could have taken different forms in different cultures at different times.

At the beginning of the twentieth century, after the elderly French chemist, Marcellin Berthelot, had made available French translations of a number of Greek alchemical texts, an American chemist, Arthur J. Hopkins (1864–1939), showed how they could be interpreted as practical procedures involving dyeing and a series of colour changes. He was able to show how Greek alchemists, influenced by Greek philosophy and the practical knowledge of dyers, metallurgists and pharmacists, had followed out three distinctive transmutation procedures, which involved either tincturing metals or alloys with gold (as described in the Leiden and Stockholm papyri), or chemically manipulating a 'prime matter' mixture of lead, tin, copper and iron through a series of black, white, yellow and purple stages (which Hopkins was able to replicate in the laboratory), or, as in the surviving fragments of Mary the Jewess, using sublimating sulphur to colour lead and copper.

While Hopkins' explanation of alchemical procedures has formed the basis of all subsequent historical work on early alchemical texts, and while Jung's psychological interpretation has stimulated interest in alchemical language and symbolism, it was the work of the historian of religion, Mircea Eliade (1907–86), who, following studies of contemporary metallurgical practices of primitive peoples in the 1920s, firmly placed alchemy in the context of anthropology and myth in *Forgerons et Alchimistes* (1956).

These three twentieth-century interpretations of alchemy, dyeing, psychological individuation and anthropology, together with the historical investigation of Chinese alchemy being undertaken by Joseph Needham and Nathan Sivin in the 1960s, stimulated the late Harry Sheppard to devise a broad definition of the nature of alchemy[3]:

> Alchemy is a cosmic art by which parts of that cosmos − the mineral and animal parts − can be liberated from their temporal existence and attain states of perfection, *gold* in the case of minerals, and for humans, longevity, immortality, and finally redemption. Such transformations can be brought about on the one hand, by the use of a material substance such as 'the philosopher's stone' or elixir, or, on the other hand, by revelatory knowledge or psychological enlightenment.

The merit of such a general definition is not only that it makes it clear that there were two kinds of alchemical activity, the exoteric or material and the esoteric or spiritual, which could be pursued separately or together, but that *time* was a significant element in alchemy's practices and rituals. Both material and spiritual perfection take time to achieve or acquire, albeit the alchemist might discover methods whereby these temporal processes could be speeded up. As Ben Jonson's Subtle says in *The Alchemist*, 'The same we say of Lead and other Metals, which would be Gold, if they had the time.' And in a final sense, the definition implies that, for the alchemist, the attainment of the goals of material, and/or spiritual, perfection will mean a release from time itself: materially through riches and the attainment of independence from worldly economic cares, and spiritually by the achievement of immortality.

The definition also helps us to understand the relationship between the alchemies of different cultures. Although some historians have looked for a singular, unique origin for alchemy, which then diffused geographically into other cultures, most historians now accept that alchemy arose in various (perhaps all?) early cultures. For example, all cultures that developed a metallurgy, whether in Siberia, Indonesia or Africa, appear to have developed mythologies that explained the presence of metals within the earth in terms of their generation and growth. Like embryos, metals grew in the womb of mother Nature. The work of the early metallurgical artisan had an obstetrical character, being accompanied by rituals that may well have had their parallel in those that accompanied childbirth. Such a model of universal origin need not rule out later linkages and influences. The idea of the elixir of life, for example, which is found prominently in Indian and Chinese alchemy, but not in Greek alchemy, was probably diffused to fourteenth-century Europe through Arabic alchemy. The biochemist and Sinologist, Joseph Needham, has called the belief and practice of using botanical, zoological, mineralogical and chemical knowledge to prepare drugs or elixirs 'macrobiotics', and has found considerable evidence that the Chinese were able to extract steroid preparations from urine.

Alongside macrobiotics, Needham has identified two other operational concepts found in alchemical practice throughout the world, aurifiction and aurifaction. Aurifiction, or gold-faking, which is the imitation of gold or other precious materials – whether as deliberate deception or not depending upon the circumstances (compare modern synthetic products) – is associated with technicians and artisans. Aurifaction, or gold-making, is 'the belief that it is possible to make gold (or "a gold", or an artificial "gold") indistinguishable from or as good as (if not better than) natural gold, from other different substances'. This, Needham suggests, tended to be the conviction of natural philosophers rather than artisans. The former, coming from a different social class than the aurifictors, either knew nothing of the assaying tests for gold, or jewellery, or rejected their validity.

CHINESE ALCHEMY

Aurifactional alchemical ideas and practices were prevalent as early as the fourth century BC in China and were greatly influenced by the Taoist religion and philosophy devised by Lao Tzu (*c.* 600 BC) and embodied in his *Tao Te Ching* (*The Way of Life*). Like the later Stoics, Taoism conceived the universe in terms of opposites: the male, positive, hot and light principle, 'Yang'; and the female, negative, cool and dark principle, 'Yin'. The struggle between these two forces generated the five elements, water, fire, earth, wood and metal, from which all things were made:

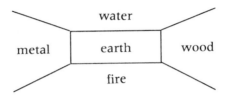

Unlike later Greco-Egyptian alchemy, however, the Chinese were far less concerned with preparing gold from inferior metals than in preparing 'elixirs' that would bring the human body into a state of perfection and harmony with the universe so that immortality was achieved. In Taoist theory this required the adjustment of the proportions of Yin and Yang in the body. This could be achieved practically by preparing elixirs from substances rich in Yang, such as red-blooded cinnabar (mercuric sulphide), gold and its salts, or jade. This doctrine led to careful empirical studies of chemical reactions, from which followed such useful discoveries as gunpowder – a reaction between Yin-rich saltpetre and Yang-rich sulphur – fermentation industries and medicines that, according to Needham, must have been rich in sexual hormones. As in western alchemy, Taoist alchemy soon became surrounded by ritual and was more of an esoteric discipline than a practical laboratory art.

Belief in the transformation of blood-like cinnabar into gold dates from 133 BC when Li Shao-chun appealed to the Emperor Wu Ti to support his investigations:

> Summon spirits and you will be able to change cinnabar powder into yellow gold. With this yellow gold you may make vessels to eat and drink out of. You will increase your span of life, you will be able to see the *hsien* of the P'eng-lai [home of the Immortals] that is in the midst of the sea. Then you may perform the sacrifices *fang* and *shang* and escape death.

From then on, many Chinese texts referred to the consumption of potable gold. This *wai tan* form of alchemy, which was systematized by Ko Hung in the fourth century AD, was not, however, the only form of Chinese alchemy.

The Chinese also developed *nai tan*, or physiological, alchemy, in which longevity and immortality were sought not from the drinking of an external elixir, but from an 'inner elixir' provided by the human body itself. In principle, this was obtained from the adept's own body by physiological techniques involving respiratory, gymnastic and sexual exercises. With the ever-increasing evidence of poisoning from *wai tan* alchemy, *nai tan* became popular from the sixth century AD, causing a diminution of laboratory practice. On the other hand, *nai tan* seems to have encouraged experimentation with body fluids such as urine, whose ritualistic use may have led to the Chinese isolation of sex hormones.

As Needham has observed, medicine and alchemy were always intimately connected in Chinese alchemy, a connection that is also found in Arabic alchemy. Since Greek alchemy laid far more stress on metallurgical practices – though the preparation of pharmaceutical remedies was also important – it seems highly probable that Arabic writers and experimentalists were 'deeply influenced by Chinese ideas and discoveries'.

There is some evidence that the Chinese knew how

to prepare dilute nitric acid. Whether this was prepared from saltpetre – a salt that is formed naturally in midden heaps – or whether saltpetre followed the discovery of nitric acid's ability to dissolve other substances, is not known. Scholars have speculated that gunpowder – a mixture of saltpetre, charcoal and sulphur – was first discovered during attempts to prepare an elixir of immortality. At first used in fireworks, gunpowder was adapted for military use in the tenth century. Its formula had spread to Islamic Asia by the thirteenth century and was to stun the Europeans the following century. Gunpowder and fireworks were probably the two most important chemical contributions of Chinese alchemy, and vividly display the power of chemistry to do harm and good.

As in the Latin west, most of later Chinese alchemy was little more than chicanery, and most of the stories of alchemists' misdeeds that are found in western literature have their literary parallels in China. Although the Jesuit missions, which arrived in China in 1582, brought with them information on western astronomy and natural philosophy, it was not until 1855 that western chemical ideas and practices were published in Chinese. A major change began in 1865 when the Kiangnan arsenal was established in Shanghai to manufacture western machinery. Within this arsenal a school of foreign languages was set up. Among the European translators was John Fryer (1839–1928), who devoted his life to translating English science texts into Chinese and to editing a popular science magazine, *Ko Chih Hui Phien* (*Chinese Scientific and Industrial Magazine*).

GREEK ALCHEMY

Although it is possible to argue that modern chemistry did not emerge until the eighteenth century, it has to be admitted that applied, or technical, chemistry is timeless and has prehistoric roots. There is conclusive evidence that copper was smelted in the Chalcolithic and early Bronze Ages (2200 to 700 BC) in Britain and Europe. Archaeologists recognize the existence of cultures that studied, and utilized and exploited, chemical phenomena. Once fire was controlled, there followed inevitably cookery (gastronomy, according to one writer, was the first science), the metallurgical arts, and the making of pottery, paints and perfumes. There is good evidence for the practice of these chemical arts in the writings of the Egyptian and Babylonian civilizations. The seven basic metals gave their names to the days of the week. Gold, silver, iron, mercury, tin, copper and lead were all well known to ancient peoples because they either occur naturally in the free state or can easily be isolated from minerals that contain them. For the same reason, sulphur (brimstone) and carbon (charcoal) were widely known and used, as were the pigments, orpiment and stibnite (sulphides of arsenic and antimony), salt and alum (potassium aluminium sulphate), which was used as a mordant for vegetable dyes and as an astringent.

The methods of these early technologists were, of course, handed down orally and by example. Our historical records begin only about 3000 BC. With the aid of techniques derived ultimately from the kitchen, these artisans extracted medicines, perfumes and metals from plants, animals and minerals. Their goldsmiths constructed wonderful pieces of jewellery and their metallurgists worked familiarly with the common metals and their alloys, associating them freely with the planets. Jewellers were particularly interested in the different coloured effects of the various alloys that metallurgists prepared and in the staining of metallic surfaces by salts and dyes, or the staining of stones and minerals that imitated the colours of precious minerals. In fact, throughout the east we find an emphasis upon colour, and the establishment of what Needham describes as the industry of aurifiction. Clearly there existed a professional class of artisans, metallurgists and jewellers who specifically designed and made imitation jewellery from mock silver, gold or artificial stones. The Syrians and Egyptians appear to have developed a particular talent for this work, and written examples of their formulae or recipes have survived in handbooks that were compiled centuries later in about 200 BC. For example, to prepare a cheaper form of 'asem', an alloy of gold and silver:

> Take soft tin in small pieces, purified four times; take four parts of it and three parts of pure white copper and one part of asem. Melt, and after casting, clean several times and make with it whatever you wish to. It will be asem of the first quality, which will deceive even the artisans.

Or, in the equivalent of nineteenth-century electroplating, to make a copper ring appear golden so that 'neither the feel nor rubbing it on the touchstone will discover it':

> Grind gold and lead to a dust as fine as flour; two parts of lead for one of gold, mix them and incorporate them with gum, coat the ring with this mixture and heat. This is repeated several times until the object has taken the colour. It is difficult to discover because the rubbing power gives the mark of an object of gold and the heat [test] consumes the lead and not the gold.

In one sense this aurifictional technology can be described as simple empiricism. To say that, however, does not mean that its practitioners were devoid of ideas about the processes they worked, or that they had no model to underpin their understanding of what was happening. Given that these technologies were evidently closely bound up with magic, ritual and trade secrecy, this was equivalent to a theoretical underpinning. Although these artisans may not have had any sophisticated chemical theory to explain or guide their practices, that experience was undoubtedly bound up with ritualistic beliefs concerning the objects that were handled. We need only notice the more than obvious connection of the names of metals with the planets, and

TABLE 1.1 *The ancient associations of metals and the heavens.*

Metal	Symbol	Planet	Day of week
Gold	☉	Sun	Sunday
Silver	☽	Moon	Monday
Iron	♂	Mars	Tuesday (Saxon, Tiw = Mars; French, mardi)
Mercury (quicksilver)	☿	Mercury	Wednesday (Saxon, Woden = Mercury; French, mercredi)
Tin	♃	Jupiter	Thursday (Saxon, Thor = Jupiter; French, jeudi)
Copper	♀	Venus	Friday (Saxon, Friff = Venus; French, vendredi)
Lead	♄	Saturn	Saturday

from them the names of the week (table 1.1), as well as beliefs that metals grew inside the earth, to conclude that myth and analogy played the equivalent role of chemical theory in these technologies. Moreover, it seems highly likely from later written records that metallurgists believed that, while metals grew normally at a slow pace within the earth, they could accelerate this process within the smithy, albeit an appropriate planetary god or goddess had to be propitiated by ritual purification for the rape of mother earth. It was this element of ritual, albeit in a Christianized form in the Latin west and a Taoist form in China, that was handed on to the science of alchemy.

For a science alchemy was. Theory controlled and exploited the empirical. Alchemy became a science when the masses of technical lore connected with dyeing and metallurgy became confronted by and amalgamated with Greek theories of matter and change. Greek philosophers with their strong sense of rationality and logic contributed a theory of matter that was able to order, classify and explain technological practice. The pre-Socratic philosophers of the sixth century BC had conjectured that the everyday substances of this material world were generated from some one primary matter. Both Plato (*c* 427–*c* 347 BC) and Aristotle (384–322 BC), teaching in the fourth century BC, had also written of this prime matter as a featureless, quality-less stuff, rather like potter's clay, onto which the various qualities and properties of hotness, coldness, dryness and moistness could be impressed to form the four elements that Empedocles (*d. c.* 430 BC) had postulated in the fifth century BC. This quartet of elementary substances, in their turn, mixed together in various proportions to generate perceptible substances. Conversely, material substances could, at least in principle and often in practice, be analysed into these four components:

WATER	has qualities moist and cold		
AIR	has qualities moist and hot		
FIRE	has qualities dry and hot		
EARTH	has qualities dry and cold		

Although Aristotle seems not to have articulated a theory of cohesion, we may assume that the four elements were 'bound together' by the moist quality. Expressed in rectangular diagrammatic form, which became the basis for later geometrical talismans and symbols, each adjacent element can be seen to possess a common quality; hence all four of the elements are, in principle, interconvertible. Thus, by changing the form or forms (transformation) of bodies, Nature transmutes the underlying basic, or primary, matter into different substances. Despite pertinent criticisms by Theophrastus (371–286 BC), Aristotle's pupil and successor at the Lyceum, that fire was different from other elements in being able to generate itself and in needing other matter to sustain it, the theory of the four elements was to remain the fundamental basis of theoretical chemistry until the eighteenth century.

For Aristotle there was a fundamental distinction between the physics of the heavens, which were eternal, perfect, unchanging and endowed with natural circular motion, and the sublunar sphere of the earth, which was subject to change and decay and where movement was either upwards or downwards from the centre of the universe. This sublunar region was composed from Empedocles' four elements. Aristotle had rejected the atomic theory introduced in the fifth century BC by Democritus. The claim that the apparent differences between substances arose from differences in the shapes and sizes of uncuttable, homogeneous particles, while ingenious, seemed to Aristotle pure invention, whereas the four elements lay close to human sensory experience of solids and liquids and of wind and fire, or of hot and cold, wet and dry objects. How could atomism account for the wide variety of shapes and forms found in minerals in the absence of a formal cause? Moreover, to Aristotle, the postulation of a void meant that there was no explanation for motion, and without motion there could be no change. Atomism also failed to distinguish between physical and mathematical division – a problem that was overcome after Aristotle's death by Epicurus (341–270 BC), who allowed that, although atoms were the unsplittable physical minima of matter, because an atom had definite size, it could be said to contain mathematically indivisible parts. Epicurus also explained the compounding of atoms together as they fell with equal speeds through the void as due to sudden 'swerves' or deviations. These unpredictable swerves are a reminder that atomism, as popularized in Epicurean philosophy, had more to do with the establishment of a moral and ethical philosophy than as an interpretation of the physics and chemistry of change.

Swerving atoms allowed for human free will. Atomism for the Epicureans, as well as for its great poetic expositor, the Roman Lucretius in *De rerum natura* (*c.* 55 BC), was a way of ensuring human happiness by the eradication of anxieties and fears engendered by religions, superstitions and ignorance. Ironically, in the sixteenth century, atomism began to be used as a way of eliminating the superstitions and ignorance of Aristotelianism.

The other great post-Aristotelian system of philosophy, Stoicism, because it adopted and adapted considerable parts of Aristotelianism, was more influential. Founded by the Athenian, Zeno (342–270 BC), during the fourth century BC and refined and developed up to the time of Seneca in the first century AD, Stoicism retained Aristotle's plenistic physics and argued for the indefinite divisibility of matter. Stoics laid stress on the analogy between macrocosm and microcosm, the heavens and the earth, and distinguished between inert matter and a more active form, the latter being called the *pneuma*, or vital spirit. Pneuma pervaded the whole cosmos and brought about generation as well as decay. Ordinary substances, as Empedocles and Aristotle had taught, were composed from the four elements, albeit hot and dry, fire and air were more active than passive wet and cold, water and earth. From this it was but a short step to interpreting air and fire as forms of pneuma, and pneuma as the glue or force that bound passive earth and water into cohesive substances. The concept was to have a profound effect on the interpretation of distillation.

Chemical compounds (an anachronism, of course) were mixtures of these four elements in varying proportions – albeit Aristotle's and the Stoics' views were rather more sophisticated than this bald statement suggests. The central theorem of alchemy, transmutation, could be seen in one of two ways, either as what we would call chemical change caused by the different proportions of elements and their rearrangement, or as a real transmutation in which the qualities of the elements are transformed. Alchemy allowed far more 'transmutations' than later chemistry was to allow, for it permitted the transmutation of lead or other common metals into gold or some other precious metal. A real transmutation of lead and gold was to be achieved by stripping lead of its qualities and replanting the basic matter that was left with the qualities and attributes of gold. Since lead was dense, soft and grey, while gold was dense, soft and yellow, only a change of colour seemed significant. However, although alchemy is usually taken to be the science of restricted metallic transmutations, it is worth emphasizing that it was really concerned with all chemical changes. In that very general sense, alchemy was the basis of chemistry.

One of the most important geographical areas for the creation of alchemy was Egypt during the Hellenistic period from about 300 BC to the first century AD. Egypt was then a melting pot for Greek philosophy, oriental and Christian religions, astrology, magic, Hermeticism and Gnosticism, as well as trade and technology. Hermeticism, which took its title from *Hermes*, the Greek form of the Egyptian deity, Thoth, the father of all book learning, was a blend of Egyptian religion, Babylonian astrology, Platonism and Stoicism. Its vast literature, the Hermetic books, supposedly written by Hermes Trismegistus, was probably compiled in Egypt during the second century BC. Gnosticism, on the other hand, was an ancient Babylonian religious movement, which stressed the dualism between light and darkness, good and evil. *Gnosis* was knowledge obtained only through inner illumination, and not through reason or faith. Humankind was assured of redemption only from this inner enlightenment. Gnosticism both competed with early Christianity and influenced the writing of the Gospels. As its texts show, however, Gnosticism was as much influenced by contemporary alchemy as it influenced alchemical language. For example, in the Gnostic creation story, chemical expressions referring to sublimation and distillation are found, as in the phrase 'the light and the heavy, those which rise to the top and those which sink to the bottom'. The most important of the Gnostics, Theodotos, who lived in the second century AD, used metaphors of refining, filtering, purifying and mixing, which some historians think he may have drawn from the alchemical school of Mary the Jewess. When Gnostic language is met in alchemical texts of the period, such as the *Dialogue of Kleopatra and the Philosophers*, however, it is difficult to know whether the author is referring to the death and revivification of metals or to the death and regeneration of the human soul. Exoteric alchemy had become inextricably bound with esoteric alchemy.

Most historians have seen three distinctive threads leading towards the development of Hellenistic alchemy: the empirical technology and Greek theories of matter already referred to, and mysticism – an unsatisfactory word that refers to a rag-bag of magical, religious and seemingly irrational and unscientific practices. Undoubtedly this third ingredient left its mark on the young science, and it in turn has left its mark on 'mysticism' right up until the twentieth century. In Hellenistic Egypt, as in Confucian China, there was a distinctive tendency to turn aside from observation and experiment and the things of this world to seek solace in mystical and religious revelations. It was the absorption of this element into alchemy that splintered its adherents into groups with different purposes and which later helped to designate alchemy as a pseudo-science.

Recent studies have shown the considerable extent of pharmacological knowledge within the Arabic tradition. This tradition was to furnish the Latin west with large numbers of chemical substances and apparatus. It was clearly already well established in Greek alchemy, and it is to medicine that the historian must also look for another of alchemy's foundation stones. For it was the Greek pharmacists who mixed, purified, heated and pulverized minerals and plants to make salves and tinctures. In Greek texts the word for a chemical reagent is, significantly, *pharmakon*.

The modern conspectus is, therefore, that practical alchemy was the bastard child of medicine and pharmacy, as well as of dyeing and metallurgy. By applying Aristotelian, Neoplatonic, Gnostic and Stoic ideas to the practices of doctors and artisans, Greek alchemists reinterpreted practice as transmutation. This point is especially clear in a seventh-century AD text by Stephanos of Alexandria, *'On the great and sacred art, or the making of gold'*, in which he attacked goldsmiths for practising aurifiction. If such craftsmen had been properly educated in philosophy, he commented, they would know that gold could be made by means of an actual transformation.

For one group of such-minded alchemical philosophers, astrology, magic and religious ritual grew at the expense of laboratory and workshop practice. Alchemical symbolism and allegory appealed strongly to the early Gnostics and Neoplatonists. The 'death' of metals, their 'resurrection' and 'perfection' as gold or purple dyes were symbolical of the death, resurrection and perfection of Christ and of what should, ideally, happen to the human soul. This esoteric alchemy is more the province of the psychologist and psychiatrist, as Jung claimed, or of the historian of religion and anthropology, than of the historian of chemistry. Nevertheless, as in the case of Isaac Newton, the historian of science must at all times be aware that, until the nineteenth century at least, most scientific activities were, fundamentally, religious ones. The historian of chemistry must not be surprised to find that even the most transparent of experimental texts may contain language that is allegorical and symbolical and which is capable of being read in a spiritual way.

Exoteric alchemists continued their experimental labours, discovered much that was useful then and later, and suffered the indignities of bad reputation stemming from less noble confidence tricksters. Another group became interested in theories of matter and promoted discussion of ideas of particles, atoms or *minima naturalis.* Finally, the artisans and technologists continued with their recipes, uninterested in theoretical abstractions.

The primitive notion that metals grew inside the earth had been supported by Aristotle in his treatise *Meteorologica* – the title referred to the physics of the earthly, as opposed to the celestial, sphere, and had nothing to do with weather forecasting. Less perfect metals, it was supposed, slowly grew to become more noble metals, like gold. Nature performed this cookery inside her womb over long periods of time – it was for this reason that, during the middle ages, mines were sometimes sealed so as to allow exhausted seams to recover, and for more metals to grow. If one interpreted the artisans' aurifictions as aurifactions, then it appeared that they had successfully succeeded in repeating Nature's process in the workshop in a short time. Perhaps further experimentation would bring to light other techniques for accelerating natural alchemical processes.

Although Aristotle had never meant by 'prime matter' a tangible stuff that could be separated from substances, this was certainly how later chemists came to think of it. Similarly the tactile qualities became substantialized (substantial forms) and frequently identified with the aerial or liquid products of distillation, or pneuma.

In gold-making, much use of analogy was made. Since there is a cycle of death and regrowth in Nature from the seed, its growth, decay and regeneration as seed once more, the alchemist can work by analogy. Lead is taken and 'killed' to remove its form and to produce the primary matter. The new substance is then grown on this compost. In the case of gold, its form is impressed by planting a seed of gold on the unformed matter. To grow this seed, warmth and moisture were requisite, and to perform the process, apparatus of various kinds – stills, furnaces, beakers and baths – was required, much of it already available from artisans or readily adapted from them.

A secret technical vocabulary was developed in order to maintain a closed shop and to conceal knowledge from the uninitiated, a language that through its long history became more and more picturesque and fanciful. In Michael Maier's *Atalanta fugiens* (1618), we read that 'The grey wolf devours the King, after which it is buried on a pyre, consuming the wolf and restoring the King to life.' All becomes clear when it is realized that this refers to an extraction of gold from its alloys by skimming off lesser metal sulphides formed from a reaction with antimony sulphide and the roasting of the resultant gold – antimony alloy until only gold remains. As Lawrence Principe has noted, this incomprehension on our part is surely little different from today's mystification when the preparative organic chemist issues the order, 'dehydrohalogenate vicinal dihalides with amide ion to provide alkynes'. In other words, although alchemists undeniably practised deliberate obfuscation, much of our incomprehension stems from its being in a foreign language, much of whose vocabulary has been lost. On the other hand, we must recognize that obscurity also suited the rulers and nobility of Europe, who patronized alchemists in the hope of solving their monetary problems.

ARABIC AND MEDIEVAL ALCHEMY

Greeks alchemy spread geographically with Christianity and so passed to the Arabs, who were also party to the ideas and practices of Indian and Chinese technologists and alchemists. The story that alchemical texts were burned and alchemists expelled from Egypt by the decree of the Emperor Diocletian in 292 AD appears to be legendary. Alchemy does not seem to have reached the Latin west until the eleventh century, when the first translations from the Arabic began to appear. In Arabic alchemy (the word itself is, of course, Arabic), we meet for the first time the notion of the philosopher's stone and potable gold or the elixir of life. Both these ideas are found in Chinese alchemy. Two alchemists who were much revered later in the Latin west were Jābir and Rhazes.

Over two thousand writings covering the fields of alchemy, astrology, numerology, medicine and mysticism were attributed to Jābir ibn Hayyān, a shadowy eighth-century figure. In 1942, the German scholar Paul Kraus showed that the entire Arabic Jābirian corpus was the compilation of a Muslim tenth-century religious sect, the Ism'iliya, or Brethren of Purity. No doubt, like Hippocrates, there was a historical Jābir, but the writings that survive and which formed the basis for the Latin writings attributed to Geber were written only in the tenth century. Until very recently, no Arabic originals for the Latin Geber were known and many historians suspected that they were western forgeries, or rather original compilations that exploited the name of the famous Arabic alchemist. William Newman has shown, however, that the Geberian *Summa Perfectionis*, arguably the most influential of Latin works on alchemy, was definitely based upon manuscripts of Jābirian translations already in circulation, and that it was the work of one Paulus de Tarento, of whom nothing is yet known.

The Jābirian corpus as well as the Latin *Summa* were important for introducing the sulphur–mercury theory of metallic composition. According to this idea, based upon Aristotle's explanation in *Meteorologica*, metals were generated inside the earth by the admixture of a fiery, smoky principle, sulphur, to a watery principle, mercury. This also seems to have been a conflation with Stoic alchemical ideas that metals were held together by a spirit (mercury) and a soul (sulphur). The theory was to lend itself beautifully to symbolic interpretation as a chemical wedding and to lead to vivid conjugal images in later alchemical texts and illustrations. As critics in the Latin west like Albertus Magnus were to point out later, this did not explain satisfactorily how the substantial forms of different metals and minerals were produced. What is most interesting, therefore, is that the *Summa* clearly speaks of a particulate or corpuscular theory based upon Aristotle's concession, despite his objection to atomism, that there were *minima naturalia*, or 'molecules' as we would say, which limit the analysis of all substances. The exhalation of the smaller particles of sulphur and mercury inside the earth led to a thickening and mixing together until a solid homogeneity resulted. Metals varied in weight (density or specific gravity) and form because of the differing degrees of packing of their constituent particles – implying that lighter metals had larger particles separated by larger spaces. Since the particles of noble metals such as gold were closely packed, the alchemists' task, according to the author of the *Summa*, was to reduce the constituent particles of lighter, baser metals in size and to pack them closer together. Hence the emphasis upon the sublimation of mercury and its fixation in the practical procedures described by Geber. As in the original Jābirian writings, such changes to the density, malleability and colour of metals were ascribed to mercurial agents that were referred to as 'medicines', 'elixirs' or 'tinctures'. Although these terms were also adopted in the west, it became even more common to refer to the agent as the 'philosopher's stone' (*lapidens philosophorum*). References to a stone as the key to transmutation in fact go back to Greek alchemy and have been found in a Cairo manuscript attributed to Agathodaimon, as well as in the earliest known alchemical encyclopedia, the *Cheirokmeta* attributed to Zosimos (*c.* 300 AD).

Apart from its influence on alchemical practice, the *Summa* also contained an important defence of alchemy and, with it, of all forms of technology. Alchemy had always been too practical an art to be included in the curriculum of the medieval university; moreover, it had seemed theologically suspect insofar as it offered sinful humankind the divine power of creation. The *Summa* author, however, argued that people had the ability to improve on Nature because that was part of their nature and cited, among other things, farmers' exploitation of grafting and alchemists' ability to replicate (synthesize) certain chemicals found naturally. As Newman has suggested[4]:

During this innovative period, alchemical writers and their allies produced a literary *corpus* which was among the earliest in Latin to actively promote the doctrine that art can equal or outdo the products of nature, and that man can even change the order of the natural world by altering the species of those products. This technological dream, however premature, was to have a lasting effect on the direction taken by Western culture.

Exoteric alchemy, committed as it was to laboratory manipulation, in this way bequeathed a commitment to empiricism in science and emphasized the centrality of experiment.

Al-Rāzī (850–c. 923), or Rhazes, was a Persian physician and alchemist who practised in Baghdad and who compiled the extremely practical text, *Secret of Secrets*, which, despite its esoteric title and hint of great promises, was a straightforward manual of chemical practice. Rhazes classified substances into metals, vitriols, boraxes, salts and stones on the grounds of solubilities and tastes, and added sal ammoniac (ammonium chloride), prepared by distilling hair with salt and urine, to the alchemists' repertory of substances. Sal ammoniac was soon found to be most useful in 'colouring' metals and in dissolving them.

A rationalist and systematist, Rhazes seems to have been among the first to have codified laboratory procedures into techniques of purification, separation, mixing and removal of water, or solidification. But although he and other Arabic authorities referred to 'sharp waters' obtained in the distillation of mixtures of vitriol, alum, salt, saltpetre and sal ammoniac, it is doubtful whether these were any more than acid salt solutions. On the other hand, it was undoubtedly by following the procedures laid down by Rhazes and by modifying still-heads that Europeans first prepared pure sulphuric, hydrochloric and nitric acids in the thirteenth century.

The *Secret of Secrets* was divided into sections on substances – a huge list and description of chemicals and minerals – apparatus and recipes. Among the apparatus described and used were beakers, flasks, phials, basins, crystallization dishes and glass vessels, jugs and casseroles, candle and naphtha lamps, braziers, furnaces (athanors), files, spatulas, hammers, ladles, shears, tongs, sand and water baths, hair and linen filters, alembics (stills), aludels, funnels, cucurbits (flasks), and pestles and mortars – indeed, the basic apparatus that was to be found in alchemical, pharmaceutical and metallurgical workshops until the end of the nineteenth century. Similarly, Rhazes' techniques of distillation, sublimation, calcination and solution were to be the basis for chemical manipulation and chemical engineering from then onwards. We must be careful, however, not to take later European artists' representations of alchemical workshops at face value.

A few of the techniques described by Rhazes deserve further comment. Calcination originally meant the reduction of any solid to the state of a fine powder, and often involved a change of composition brought about by means of strong heat from a furnace. Only later, say by the eighteenth century, did it come to mean specifically the reduction of a metal to its calx or oxide. There were many different kinds of furnace available and they varied in size according to the task in hand. Charcoal, wood and straw were used (coal was frowned upon because of the unpleasant fumes it produced). The temperature was raised blacksmith-fashion by means of bellows – hence the derogatory names of 'puffers' or 'workers by fire' that were applied to alchemists. Direct heat was often avoided in delicate reactions by the use of sand, dung or water baths, the latter (the *bain-marie*) being attributed to the third-century BC woman chemist known as Mary the Jewess. Needless to say, because heating was difficult to control, apparatus broke frequently. Even in the eighteenth century when Lavoisier found need to distil water continuously for a period of months, his tests were continually frustrated by breakages. By the same token, since temperature conditions would have been hard to control and replicate, the repetition of processes under identical conditions was difficult or impossible. However, whether alchemists were aware of this is doubtful.

Distillation, one of the most important procedures in practical chemistry, gave rise to a diversity of apparatus, all of which are the ancestors of today's oil refineries. Already in 3000 BC there is archaeological evidence of extraction pots being used in the Mesopotamian region. These pots were used by herbalists and perfume makers. A double-rim trough was percolated with holes, the trough itself being filled with perfume-making flowers and herbs in water. When fired, the steam condensed in the lid and percolated back onto the plants below. In a variation of this, no holes were drilled and the distillate was collected directly in the trough around the rim, from where it was probably removed from time to time by means of a dry cloth. In the Mongolian or Chinese still, the distillate fell from a concave roof into a central catch-bowl from which a side-tube led to the outside. Modern experiments, using working glass models of these stills, have shown that[5]:

> the preparation of strong spiritous liquor was, from a technological point of view, a rather simple matter and no civilisation had a distillation apparatus which gave it an advantage.

Even so, although the Chinese probably had distilled alcohol from wine by the fourth century AD, it was several centuries later before it was known in the west. Even earlier, in the second century of our era, the Chinese had discovered how to concentrate alcohol by a freezing process, whereby separation was achieved by freezing water and leaving concentrated alcohol behind.

The observation of distillation also provided a solution to the theoretical problem of what made solid materials cohere. The binding material could not be Aristotelian water since this patently could not be extracted from a heated stone. Distillation of other materials showed, however, that an 'oily' distillate commonly succeeded the 'aqueous' fraction that first boiled off at a lower temperature. It could be argued, therefore, that an 'unctuous', or fatty, moisture was the cohesive binder of solid bodies. This notion that 'earths' contained a fatty material was still to be found in Stahl's theory of phlogiston in the eighteenth century.

An improvement on distillation techniques was apparently first made by Alexandrian alchemists in the first century AD – though, in the absence of recorded evidence, it is just as likely that these alchemists were merely adopting techniques and apparatus from craftsmen and pharmacists. This is particularly evident in the 'kerotakis', which took its name from the palette used by painters and artists. This wedge-shaped palette was fitted into an *ambix* (still-head) as a shelf to contain a substance that was to be reacted with a boiling liquid, which would condense, drip or sublime onto it. These alchemists made air cooling in the distillation process more efficient by separating the distillate off by a continuous process and raising the ambix well above the *bikos* or cucurbit vessel embedded in the furnace or sand bath. (In 1937 the word *Ambix* was adopted by the Society for the History of Alchemy and Early Chemistry as the title of the journal that ever since has played an important role in the history of chemistry.) In the Latin west the word *alembic* (from the Arabic form of ambix, 'al-anbiq') came to denote the complete distillation apparatus. By its means, rose waters, other perfumes and, most importantly, mineral acids and alcohol began to be prepared and explored in the thirteenth century.

Continuous distillations were also made possible in the 'pelican', so-called because of its arms, which bore resemblance to that bird's wings. Such distillations were believed to be significant by alchemists, who were much influenced by Jābir's reputed success at 'projection' (the preparation of gold) after 700 distillations. The more efficient cooling of a distillate outside the still-head appears to have been a European contribution developed in the twelfth century. Alchemists and technologists referred to these as water-cooled stills or 'serpents'. This more efficient cooling of the distillate probably had something to do with the preparation of alcohol in the twelfth century, some centuries after the Chinese. This became an important solvent as well as beverage in pharmacy. By then chemical apparatus was becoming commonly made of glass. It should be noted that, although 'alcohol' is an Arabic word, it had first meant antimony sulphide, 'kohl'. In the Latin west, alcohol was initially called 'aqua vitae' or 'aqua ardens' (the water that burns), and only in the sixteenth century was it renamed alcohol. It had also been named the 'quintessence', or fifth essence, by the fourteenth-century Spanish Franciscan preacher, John of Rupescissa, in an influential tract, *De consideratione quintae essentiae*. According to John, alcohol, the product of the distillation of wines, possessed great healing powers from the fact that it was the essence of the heavens. An even more powerful medicine was obtained when the sun, gold, was dissolved in it to produce 'potable gold'. John's advocation of the quintessence was extremely important since it encouraged pharmacists to try and extract other quintessences from herbs and minerals, and thus to usher in the age of iatrochemistry in the sixteenth century. Here was the parting of the ways of alchemy and chemistry.

The sixteenth century saw great improvements in chemical technology and the appearance of several printed books dealing with the subject. Such treatises mentioned very little chemical theory. They aimed not to advance knowledge, but to record a technological complex that, in Multhauf's opinion, 'although sophisticated, had been virtually static throughout the Christian era'. Generally speaking they discussed only apparatus and reagents, and provided recipes that used distillation methods. Many recipes, especially those for artists' pigments and dyes, bear an astonishing resemblance to those found in the aurifictive papyri of the third century and therefore imply continuity in craftsmen's recipes for making imitation jewellery, textile dyeing, inks, paints and cheap, but impressive, chemical 'tricks'.

One such book was the *Pirotechnia* of Vannoccio Biringuccio (1480–1538), which was published in Italy in 1540. This gave a detailed survey of contemporary metallurgy, the manufacture of weapons and the use of water-power-driven machinery. For the first time there was an explicit stress upon the value of assaying as a guide to the scaling up of operations and the regular reporting of quantitative measurements in the various recipes. On alchemy, despite retaining the traditional view that metals grew inside the earth, Biringuccio provides a sceptical view based upon personal observation and experience[6]:

Now in having spoken and in speaking thus I have no thought of wishing to detract from or decrease the virtues of this art, if it has any, but I have only given my opinion, based on the facts of the matter. I could still discourse concerning the art of transmutation, or alchemy as it is called, yet neither through my own efforts nor those of others (although I have sought with great diligence) have I ever had the fortune to see anything worthy of being approved by good men, or that it was not necessary to abandon as imperfect for one cause or another even before it was half finished. For this reason I surely deserve to be excused, all the more because I know that I am drawn by more powerful reasons, or, perhaps by natural inclination, to follow the path of mining more willingly than alchemy, even though mining is a harder task, both physical and mental, is more expensive, and promises less at first sight and in words than does alchemy; and it has as its scope the observation of Nature's powers rather than those of art – or indeed of seeing what really exists rather than what one thinks exists.

That is succinctly put: by the sixteenth century, the natural ores of metals, and their separations and transformations by heat, acids and distillations, had become more interesting and financially fruitful than time spent fruitlessly on speculative transmutations.

Alchemy had been transmuted into chemistry, as the change of name reflected. Here a digression into the origins of the word 'chemistry' seems appropriate. There is, in fact, no scholarly consensus over the origins of the Greek word 'chemeia' or 'chymia'. One familiar suggestion has been a derivation of the Coptic word 'Khem', meaning the black land (Egypt), and etymological transfer to the blackening processes in dyeing, metallurgy and pharmacy. What is certain is that philosophers such as Plato and Aristotle had no word for chemistry, for the term 'chymia', meaning to fuse or cast a metal, dates only from about 300 AD. A Chinese origin from the word 'Kim-Iya', meaning 'gold-making juice', has not been authenticated, though Needham has plausibly suggested that the root 'chem' may be equivalent to the Chinese 'chin', as in the phrase for the art of transmutation, *lien chin shu*. The Cantonese pronunciation of this phrase would be, roughly, *lin kem shut*, i.e. with a hard 'k' sound. Needham concludes that we have the possibility that 'the name for the Chinese "gold art", crystallised in the syllable *chin* (kiem) spread over the length and breadth of the Old World, evoking first the Greek terms for chemistry and then, indirectly, the Arabic one'.

Whatever the etymology, the Latin and English words *alchemia*, alchemy and chemistry were derived from the Arabic name of the art, 'al Kimiya' or 'alkymia'. According to the *Oxford English Dictionary*, the Arabic definite article, 'al', was dropped in the sixteenth century when scholars began to grasp the etymology of the Latin 'alchimista', the chemist or practitioner; but it is far more likely to have followed Paracelsus' decision to refer to medical chemistry as 'chymia' or 'iatrochemia'. The word 'chymia' was also used extensively by the humanist physician, Georg Agricola (1494–1555), whose study of the German mining industry, *De re metallica*, was published in 1556. Although he used Latin coinages such as 'chymista' and 'chymicus', it is clear from their context that he was still referring, however, to alchemy, alchemical techniques and alchemists, and that he was, in the tradition of humanism, attempting to purify the spelling of a classical root that had been barbarized by Arabic contamination.

Agricola's simplifications were widely adopted, notably in the Latin dictionary compiled by the Swiss naturalist, Konrad Gesner (1516–65) in 1551, as well as in his *De remediis secretis: liber physicus, medicus et partim etiam chymicus* (Zurich, 1552). As Rocke has shown, the latter work on pharmaceutical chemistry was widely translated into English, French and Italian, and seems to have been the fountain for the words that became the basis of modern European vocabulary: *chimique, chimico, chymiste, chimist,* etc. Curiously, the German translation of Gesner continued to render 'chymistae' as 'Alchemisten'. German texts only moved towards the form *Chemie* and *Chemiker* in the early 1600s.

By then, influenced by the practical textbook tradition instituted by Libavius, as well as by the iatrochemistry of Paracelsus (chapter 2), 'alchymia' or 'alchemy' were increasingly terms confined to esoteric religious practices, while 'chymia' or 'chemistry' were used to label the long tradition of pharmaceutical and technological empiricism.

NEWTON'S ALCHEMY

When the economist, John Maynard Keynes, bought some of Newton's manuscripts in 1936 when Newton's papers were unfortunately dispersed, he drew attention to the non-mathematical, 'irrational' side of Newton. Here was a famous scientist who had spent an equal part of his time, if not the major part, on a chronology of the scriptures, alchemy, occult medicine and biblical prophecies. For Keynes, Newton had been the last of the magicians. Historians have tended to ignore Newton's alchemical and religious interests, or simply denied that they had anything to do with his work in mathematics, physics and astronomy. More recently, however, historians such as Robert Westfall and Betty Jo Dobbs, who have immersed themselves in the estimated one million words of Newton's surviving alchemical manuscripts, have seen his interest in alchemy as integral to his approach to the natural world. They view Newton as deeply influenced by the Neoplatonic and Hermetic movements of his day, which, for Newton, promised to open a window on the structure of matter and the hidden powers and energies of Nature that elsewhere he tried to express and explain in the language of corpuscles, attractions and repulsions.

For example, the German scholar, Karin Figula, has been able to demonstrate that Newton was steeped in the work of Michael Sendivogius (1556–1636?), a Polish alchemist who worked at the Court of Emperor Rudolph II at Prague, where he successfully demonstrated an apparent transmutation in 1604. In his several writings, which were translated and circulated in Britain, Sendivogius wrote of a 'secret food of life' that vivified all the creatures and minerals of the world[7]:

> Man, like all other animals, dies when deprived of air, and nothing will grow in the world without the force and virtue of the air, which penetrates, alters, and attracts to itself the multiplying nutriment.

As we shall see in the following chapter, this Stoic and Neoplatonic concept of a universal animating spirit, or pneuma, which bathed the cosmos, was to stimulate some interesting experimental work on combustion and respiration in the 1670s.

In a spurious work of Paracelsus, *Von den natürlichen Dingen*, it had been predicted that a new Elijah would appear in Europe some sixty years after the master's death. A new age would be ushered in, in which God would finally reveal the secrets of Nature. This prophecy may explain why, as William Newman has suggested, early seventeenth-century Europe was peopled by several adepts like Sendivogius who claimed unusual powers and insights. Another, this time fictitious, adept was 'Eirenaeus Philalethes', whose copious writings were closely read by Newton. It is possible that Newton developed his interest in alchemy while a student at Cambridge in the 1660s under the tutelage of Isaac Barrow, who had an alchemical library. But it is equally likely that it was Robert Boyle's interest in alchemy and in the origins of colours that stimulated Newton's interest, as well as making him a convinced mechanical philosopher. Like Boyle, Newton was interested in alchemical reports of transmutations as providing circumstantial evidence for the corpuscular nature of matter. In addition, however, Newton was undoubtedly interested in alchemists' Neoplatonic claims of secret (or hidden) virtues in the air and of attractions between heavenly and earthly matter, and in the possibility, claimed by many alchemical authorities, that metals grew in the earth by the same laws of growth as vegetables and animals. In April 1669 Newton bought a furnace as well as a copy of the compilation of alchemical tracts, *Theatrum Chemicum*. Among his many other book purchases was the *Secrets Reveal'd* of the mysterious Eirenaeus Philalethes, whom we now know to have been one of Boyle's New England acquaintances, George Starkey. The book, which Newton heavily annotated, aimed to show that alchemy mirrored God's labours during the creation and it referred to the operations of the Stoics' animating spirit in Nature.

Starkey laid stress upon the properties of antimony, whose ability to crystallize in the pattern of a star following the reduction of stibnite by iron had first been published by the fictitious monk, 'Basil Valentine' in 1604 in *The Triumphant Chariot of Antimony*, one of the most important alchemical treatises ever published. Valentine, who was supposed to have lived in the early fifteenth century, was the invention of Johann Tholde, a salt boiler from Thuringia. The *Triumphant Chariot* was concerned with the preparation of antimony elixirs to cure various ailments, including venereal disease. In *Secrets Reveal'd*, Starkey referred to crystalline antimony (child of Saturn from its resemblance to lead) as a magnet on account of its pattern of rays emanating from, or towards, the centre. Newton appears to have spent much of his time in the laboratory in the 1670s investigating the 'magnetic' properties of the star, or regulus, of antimony, probably in the shared belief with Philalethes that it was indeed a Royal Seal, that is, God's sign or signature of its unique ability to attract the world's celestial and vivifying spirit.

Very possibly it was Newton's interest in solving the impossibly difficult problem of how passive, inert corpuscles organized themselves into the living entities of the three kingdoms of Nature that drove him to explore the readily available printed texts and circulating manuscripts of alchemy, including, in particular, the works of Sendivogius and Starkey. As Professor Dobbs has expressed it[8]: 'it was the secret of [the] spirit of life that Newton hoped to learn from alchemy'. Newton's motive, which was probably shared by many other seventeenth-century figures, including Boyle, was quite respectable. Its purpose, ultimately, was theological. A deeper understanding of God could well come from an understanding of the 'spirit', be it light, warmth, or a universal ether, which animated all things.

THE DEMISE OF ALCHEMY AND ITS LITERARY TRADITION

Historians of science are the first to stress that any theory, however erroneous in later view, is better than none. Even so, many historians of science have expressed surprise that alchemy lasted so long, though we can easily underestimate the power of humankind's fear of death and desire for immortality – or of human cupidity. To the extent that it undoubtedly stimulated empirical research, alchemy can be said to have made a positive contribution to the development of chemistry and to the justification of applying scientific knowledge to the relief of humankind's estate. This is different, however, from saying that alchemy led to chemistry. The language of alchemy soon developed an arcane and secretive technical vocabulary designed to conceal information from the uninitiated. To a large degree this language is incomprehensible to us today, though it is apparent that the readers of Geoffrey Chaucer's 'Canon's Yeoman's Tale' or the audiences of Ben Jonson's *The Alchemist* were able to construe it sufficiently to laugh at it.

Warnings against alchemists' unscrupulousness, which

TABLE 1.2   *Chemicals listed in Chaucer's 'Canon's Yeoman's Tale.'*

Alkali	Litharge
Alum	Oil of Tartar
Argol	Prepared Salt
Armenian bole	Quicklime
Arsenic	Quicksilver
Ashes	Ratsbane
Borax	Sal ammoniac
Brimstone	Saltpetre
Bull's gall	Silver
Burnt bones	Urine
Chalk	Vitriol
Clay	Waters albificated
Dung	Waters rubificated
Egg White	Wort
Hair	Yeast
Iron scales	

Note that alcohol is not cited.
Adapted from W. A. Campbell, 'The Goldmakers',
Proceedings of the Royal Institution, **60** (1988)
163.

are found in William Langland's *Piers Plowman*, were developed amusingly by Chaucer in the *Chanouns Yemannes Tale* (*c.* 1387) in which he exposed some half-dozen 'tricks' used to delude the unwary. These included the use of crucibles containing gold in their base camouflaged by charcoal and wax; stirring a pot with a hollow charcoal rod containing a hidden gold charge; stacking the fire with a lump of charcoal containing a gold cavity sealed by wax; and palming a piece of gold concealed in a sleeve. Deception was made the more easy from the fact that only small quantities were needed to excite and delude an investor into parting with his or her money. These methods had hardly changed when Ben Jonson wrote his satirical masterpiece, *The Alchemist*, in 1610, except that by then the doctrine of multiplication – the claim that gold could be grown and expanded from a seed – had proved an extremely useful way of extracting gold coins from the avaricious.

As their expert use of alchemical language shows, both Chaucer and Jonson clearly knew a good deal about alchemy, as equally clearly did their readers and audiences (see Table 1.2). Chaucer had translated the thirteenth-century French allegorical romance, *Roman de la Rose*, which seems to have been influenced by alchemical doctrines, while Jonson based his character, Subtle, on the Elizabethan astrologer, Simon Forman, whose diary offers an extraordinary window into the mind of an early seventeenth-century occultist.

By Jonson's day, the adulteration and counterfeiting of metal had become illegal. As early as 1317, soon after Dante had placed all alchemists into the Inferno, the Avignon Pope John XXII had ordered alchemists to leave France for coining false money, and a few years later the Dominicans threatened excommunication to any member of the Church who was caught practising the art. Nor were the Jesuits friendly towards alchemy, though there is evidence that it was the spiritual esoteric alchemy that chiefly worried them. Athanasius Kircher

(1602–80), for example, defended alchemical experiments, published recipes for chemical medicines and upheld claims for palingenesis (the revival of plants from their ashes), as well as running a 'pharmaceutical' laboratory at the Jesuits' College in Rome. In 1403, the activities of 'gold-makers' had evidently become sufficiently serious in England for a statute to be passed forbidding the multiplication of metals. The penalty was death and the confiscation of property. Legislation must have encouraged scepticism and the portrayal of the poverty-striken alchemist as a self-deluded ass or as a knowing and crafty charlatan who eked out a desperate existence by duping the innocent.

Legislation did not, however, mean that royalty and exchequers disbelieved in aurifaction; rather, they sought to control it to their own ends. In 1456 for example, Henry VI of England set up a commission to investigate

FIGURE 1.1 The preparation of the philosopher's stone.
(After J. Read, *Prelude to Chemistry*; London: G. Bell, 1936, p. 132.)

the secret of the philosopher's stone, but learned nothing useful. In Europe, Emperors and Princes regularly offered their patronage – and prisons – to self-proclaimed successful projectionists. The most famous and colourful of these patrons, who included James IV of Scotland, was Rudolf II of Bohemia, who, in his castle in Prague, surrounded himself with a large circle of artists, alchemists and occultists. Among them were the Englishmen John Dee and Edmund Kelly and the Court Physician, Michael Maier (1568–1622), whose *Atalanta fugiens* (1618) is noted for its curious combination of allegorical woodcuts and musical settings of verses describing the alchemical process. It was Maier, too, who translated Thomas Norton's fascinating poem, *The Ordinall of Alchemy*, into Latin verse in 1618.

Such courts, like Alexandria in the second century BC, became melting pots for a growing gulf between exoteric and esoteric alchemy and the growing science of chemistry. Like Heinrich Khunrath (1560–1605), who 'beheld in his fantasy the whole cosmos as a work of Supernal Alchemy, performed in the crucible of God', the German shoemaker, Jacob Boehme (1575–1624), enshrined alchemical language and ideas into a theological system. By this time, too, alchemical symbolism had been further advanced by cults of the pansophists, that is by those groups who claimed that a complete understanding, or universal knowledge, could only be obtained through personal illumination. The Rosicrucian Order, founded in Germany at the beginning of the seventeenth century, soon encouraged the publication of a multitude of emblematic texts, all of which became grist to the mill of esoteric alchemy.

Given that by the sixteenth century, if not before, artisans and natural philosophers had sufficient technical knowledge to invalidate the claims of transmutationists, it may be wondered why belief survived. No doubt the divorce between the classes of educated natural philosophers and uneducated artisans (which Boyle tried to close) was partly responsible. There were also the accidents and uncertainties caused by the use of impure and heterogeneous materials that must have often seemingly 'augmented' working materials. As one historian has said, 'fraudulent dexterity, false philosophy, public credulity and Royal rapacity' all played a part. To these very human factors, however, must be added the fact that, for seventeenth-century natural philosophers, the corpuscular philosophy to which they were committed underwrote the concept of transmutation even more convincingly than the old four-element theory they rejected (chapter 2).

Nevertheless, despite the fact that the mechanical philosophy allowed, in principle, the transmutation of matter, by the mid eighteenth century it had become accepted by nearly all chemists and physicists that alchemy was a pseudo-science and that transmutation was technically impossible. Those few who claimed otherwise, such as James Price (1752–83), a Fellow of the Royal Society, who used his personal fortune in alchemical experiments, found themselves disgraced. Price committed suicide when challenged to repeat his transmutation claims before Sir Joseph Banks and other Fellows of the Society. By then, chemists had come to share Boerhaave's disbelief in alchemy as expressed in his *New Method of Chemistry* (1724). Alchemy had become history, and they happily accepted Boerhaave's allegory of the dying farmer who had told his sons that he had buried treasure in the fields surrounding their home. The sons worked so energetically that they achieved prosperity even though they failed totally to find what they had originally sought.

The absorption of the experimental findings of exoteric alchemy by chemistry left esoteric alchemy to those who continued to believe that there 'was more to Heaven and earth' than particles and forces. Incredible stories of transmutations continued to surface periodically during the eighteenth century. Indeed, legends concerning the 'immortal' adventurer, the Comte de Saint-Germain, continue into the twentieth century. In Germany, in particular, the Masonic order of *Gold- und Rosenkreuz*, which was patronized by King Frederick William II of Prussia, combined a mystical form of Christianity with practical work in alchemy based upon the study of collections of alchemical manuscripts. All of this increasingly ran against the rationalism and enlightenment of the age, and we know that at least one member, the naturalist, Georg Forster, left the movement a disillusioned man. Other alchemical echoes were to be heard in the speculative *Naturphilosophie* that swept through the German universities at the beginning of the nineteenth century and in the modified Paracelsianism of Samuel Hahnemann's homeopathic system, which he launched in 1810.

Modern alchemical esotericism dates from 1850 when Mary Ann South, whose father had encouraged her interest in the history of religions and in mysticism, published *A Suggestive Enquiry into the Hermetic Mystery*. This argued that alchemical literature provided the mystic religious contemplative with a direct link to the secret knowledge of ancient mystery religions. After selling only a hundred copies of the book, father and daughter burned the remaining copies. Later, after she had married the Rev. A. T. Atwood, she claimed that the bonfire had taken place to prevent the teachings from falling into the wrong hands. Whatever one makes of this curious affair, her insight that alchemists had been really searching for spiritual enlightenment and not a material stone, supported by the translation of various alchemical texts into English, proved influential on Carl Jung when, in old age, Mrs Atwood republished her study in 1920. It also inspired Eugène Canseliet in France to devote his career to the symbolic interpretation of the statuary and frescoes of Christian churches and chateaux, as a result of the publication in 1928 of *Le Mystère des Cathédrals* by the mysterious adept 'Fulcanelli'. The ability of the human mind to read anything into symbols has been mercilessly exposed by Umberto Eco in his novel, *Foucault's Pendulum* (1988). In counterbalance, Patrick Harpur's *Mercurius* (1990) paints a vividly sympathetic portrait of the esoteric mind.

Ironically, the growth of nineteenth-century chemistry encouraged a revival of alchemical speculation. Dalton's reintroduction of atomism, the scepticism expressed towards the growing number of chemical elements (chapter 4), the discoveries of spectroscopists and the regularities of the periodic table (chapter 9), all suggested the possibility of transmutation. Although the possibility was given respectability by Rutherford's and Soddy's work on radioactivity at the beginning of the twentieth century and physically realized on an atomic scale in the 1930s, it had earlier led in the 1860s to 'hyperchemistry'. We must not be surprised, therefore, to find gold transmutation stories occurring during even the most positivistic periods of Victorian science. During the 1860s, *Chemical News* (chapter 12) attributed the high price of bismuth on the metal market to a vogue for transmutation experiments. This was connected to a daring swindle perpetrated on the London stock-market by a Hungarian refugee, Nicholas Papaffy. Papaffy duped large numbers of investors into promoting a method for transforming bismuth and aluminium (then a new and expensive metal) into silver. This followed from a successful public demonstration at a bullion works in the classic tradition of Jonson's Subtle. Needless to say, after trading offices were opened in Leadenhall Street, Papaffy decamped with an advance of £40 000 from the company. Nor was the American government less gullible. In 1897 an Irish–American metallurgist, Stephen Emmens, sold gold ingots to the US Assay Office that he claimed to have made from silver by his 'Argentaurum Process'.

In France during the same period, hyperchemistry enjoyed the support of an Association Alchimique de France to which the Swedish playwright, August Strindberg, subscribed, and which influenced Madame Blavatsky's 'scientific' writings for the theosophists and inspired the

English composer, Cyril Scott (1879–1970), to compose the opera *The Alchemist* in 1925. The occult interest in alchemy has continued to the present day and has been given academic respectability since 1985 through the publication of the international scholarly review, *Aries*, a biannual devoted to the review of the history of esotericism, Hermeticism, theosophy, freemasonry, the Kabbalah and alchemy. Today, booksellers catalogue alchemy under 'Occultism' and not 'History of Science', while *Ambix*, the academic mouthpiece of the Society for the History of Alchemy and Chemistry (founded 1937) continues to receive occultist literature for review, as well as the occasional letter pressing its editor for 'the secret of secrets'.

In 1980, at the phenomenal cost of $10 000, a bismuth sample was transmuted into one-billionth of a cent's worth of gold by means of a particle accelerator at the Lawrence Laboratory of the University of California at Berkeley. The 'value' of the experiment is underlined in Frederick Soddy's ironic remark some sixty years before[9]:

> If man ever achieves this further control over Nature, it is quite certain that the last thing he would want to do would be to turn lead or mercury into gold – *for the sake of gold*. The energy that would be liberated, if the control of these sub-atomic processes were possible as in the control of ordinary chemical changes, such as combustion, would far exceed in importance and value the gold.

The Sceptical Chymist

> I see not why we must needs believe that there are
> any primogeneal and simple bodies, of which, as of
> pre-existent elements, nature is obliged to compound
> all others. Nor do I see why we may not conceive
> that she may produce the bodies accounted mixt out
> of one another by variously altering and contriving
> their minute parts, without resolving the matter into
> any such simple and homogeneous substances as are
> pretended.
>
> (ROBERT BOYLE, *The Sceptical Chymist*, 1661)

The phrase 'The Scientific Revolution' conjures up a rebellion
against Greek authority in astronomy and dynamics, and
physics in general. It reminds us of names like Copernicus,
Kepler, Galileo, Harvey, Descartes, Bacon and Newton.
Chemists' names are missing. Indeed, a sixteenth- and
seventeenth-century revolution in chemical understanding
does not readily spring to mind. What was there to rebel
against or to revolutionize? Was there a new *chemical* way
of looking at substances in the seventeenth century that in
any way paralleled the new *physical* way?

The historian's reply has usually been a negative one,
with the rider that chemistry developed much later than
either astronomy or physics or anatomy and physiology;
and that chemistry did not become a science until the
eighteenth century. Its revolution was carried out by
Lavoisier.

Whether or not this was the case, it can be agreed that
chemistry presented the early natural philosopher with

peculiarly difficult problems. The sheer complexity of most of the chemical materials with which chemists commonly worked can be seen, with hindsight, to have inevitably made generalizations extremely difficult. Chemists were considering with equal ardour the chemical components of the human and animal body, and of plants and minerals, the procedures of metallurgy, pottery, vinegar, acid and glass manufacture, as well as, in some quarters, abstractions like the philosopher's stone and the elixir of life. There was no universally agreed chemical language, no convenient compartmentalization of substances into organic and inorganic, into solids, liquids and gases, or into acids, bases and salts; and no concept of purity. For example, when Wilhelm Homberg (1652–1715) 'analysed' ordinary sulphur in 1703, he obtained an acid salt, an earth, some fatty matter and some copper metal.

But perhaps the greatest stumbling block to the further development of chemistry was a case of insufficient analysis – there was a complete absence of a knowledge or concept of the gaseous state of matter. Chemistry remained a two-dimensional science, which studied, and only had equipment and apparatus to handle, solids and liquids.

This does not mean that chemistry lacked organization, for there were any number of grand theories that brought order and classification to this complicated subject. The problem with these organizational theories was not only their mutual inconsistency, but the fact that by the 1660s they looked old-fashioned and part of the pre-revolutionary landscape that astronomers and physicists had moved away from. To many natural philosophers, therefore, chemistry seemed tainted; it was an occult or pseudo-science that was beyond the pale of rational discourse.

This was where Boyle came in, for he devoted his life to bringing chemistry to the attention of natural philosophers as a subject worthy of their closest and honest attention. His intention was to 'begat a good understanding betwixt the chymists and the mechanical philosophers'. In order to do this, he had to show, among other things, that the three or four traditional explanations of chemical phenomena lacked credibility and that a better explanation lay in the revived corpuscular philosophy.

PARACELSIANISM

Philippus Aureolus Theophrastus Bombast von Hohenheim (1493–1541), who rechristened himself Paracelsus in order to indicate his superiority to the second-century Roman medical writer, Celsus, was born near Zurich, then still nominally part of the Holy Roman empire and under Austrian domination. At the age of twenty-one, on the advice of his physician father, he visited the mines and metallurgical workshops in the Tyrol where he studied metallurgy and alchemy. After claiming a medical degree from Ferrara in Italy, Paracelsus became Medical Officer of Health at Basel, a position he was forced to leave in an undignified manner two years later after his abusive and bombastic manner had offended public opinion. Thereafter, he became a rolling stone, restlessly traversing the roads and countries of war-torn Europe, associating with physicians, alchemists, astrologers, apothecaries, miners, gypsies and the adepts of the occult.

It is easy to see why he offended. Not only did he lecture in German instead of Latin, an unorthodox behaviour for a physician, but he publicly burned the works of Galen and Avicenna to show his contempt for orthodox medical opinion – a ceremony that was to be repeated by Lavoisier and his wife 250 years later.

> If your physicians only knew that their prince Galen . . . was sticking in Hell, from whence he has sent letters to me, they would make the sign of the cross upon themselves with a fox's tail. In the same way your Avicenna sits in the vestibule of the infernal portal. Come then and listen, impostors who prevail only

by the authority of your high positions! After my death, my disciples will burst forth and drag you to the light, and shall expose your dirty drugs, wherewith up to this time you have compassed the death of princes. . . . Woe for your necks on the day of judgement! I know that the monarchy will be mine. Mine too will be the honour and the glory. Not that I praise myself: Nature praises me.

Is this rhetoric or the ravings of a lunatic?

Not surprisingly, contemporary estimates of Paracelsus varied tremendously. An opinion that 'he lived like a pig, looked like a drover, found his greatest enjoyment in the company of the most dissolute and lowest rabble, and throughout his glorious life he was generally drunk', may be contrasted with his pupils' expressions, 'the noble and beloved monarch', 'the German Hermes' and 'our dear Preceptor and King of Arts'. What did this contradictory, bewildering figure do for chemistry? What did he teach?

Most of his writings were only published posthumously and there has always been controversy between historians who accept only the 'rational' writings as genuine and those who view his eclectic mixture of rationalism, empiricism, Neoplatonic occultism and mysticism as the genuine Paracelsus. Although he definitely subscribed to alchemy, i.e. to the doctrine of transmutation, 'alchemy' had a wider meaning for Paracelsus. It entailed carrying 'to its end something that [had] not yet been completed'. It was any process in Nature in which substances worked or metamorphosed to a new end, and thus included cookery and the chemical arts as well as physiological processes such as digestion.

This widened sense of the word was to be reflected explicitly in what has been described as the first chemistry textbook, the *Alchemia* published by the Lutheran humanist, Andreas Libavius (1540–1616), in 1597, though, as we shall see, Libavius was contemptuous of Paracelsus. For

Paracelsus, chemistry was the key subject for unveiling the secrets of a universe that had been created by a chemist and operated by chemical laws. The views of Aristotle and Galen were those of heathens and heretics and had to be replaced by an empiricism that was controlled by Christian and Neoplatonic insights. Paracelsus and his followers, such as Ostwald Croll in his 'royal chemistry', the *Basilica Chymica* (1609), often made much of the story of creation in Genesis, which they interpreted as a chemical allegory. Paracelsianism thereby came to share many of the attributes of esoteric alchemy in which 'the art' was essentially a personal religious avocation.

On the other hand, Paracelsus saw himself essentially as a medical reformer, as someone destined to refute age-old teachings and to base medical practice on what he claimed were more effective mineral medicines. He taught that the principal aim of medicine should be the preparation of *arcana*, most of which turn out to be chemical, inorganic remedies as opposed to the herbal, organic medicines derived from Greco-Roman medicine. The arcana would destroy and eliminate poisons produced by disease, which itself was due to the putrefaction of the 'excrements' produced in any 'chemical' process. Diseases were therefore specific, as the new pandemic of syphilis then sweeping Europe suggested, and were to be cured by specific arcana.

Paracelsus taught that macrocosm (the heavens) and microcosm (the earth and all its creatures) were linked together. The heavens contained both visible and invisible stars (*astra*) that descended to impregnate the matter of the microcosm, conferring on each body the specific form and properties that directed its growth and development. Like acted upon like. The task of the chemist was, by experiment and knowledge of macrocosmic–microcosmic correspondences (the doctrine of signatures), to determine an astral essence or specific virtue capable of treating a disease. To isolate the remedy, the alchemist-physician had to separate the pure essence from the impure, by fire and distillation. Here, Paracelsus owed much to the medieval technology of distillers and to the writings of John of Rupescissa in the fourteenth century. The latter had identified Aristotle's fifth, heavenly element, the ether, as a quintessence that could be distilled from plants. Paracelsus and his followers were, however, rather more interested in the inorganic salts remaining after distillation than in the distillates themselves.

In this way Paracelsus initiated a new study he called 'iatrochemistry', which invoked chemistry to the aid of medicine. Whereas the Paracelsians were individualistic in their pantheistic interpretation of Nature, regarding chemical knowledge as incommunicable except between and through the inspiration proper to a magus, Libavius and the textbook writers who followed him argued that chemistry could be learned by all in the classroom, provided it was put into a methodical form. This construction of a pedagogical discipline involved the classification of laboratory techniques and operations and the establishment of a standardized language of chemical substances. Progress in chemistry, or in any science, would come only from a collective endeavour to combine the subjective, and possibly unreliable, contributions of individuals after subjecting them to peer review and measuring each one critically against past wisdom and experience.

Iatrochemical doctrines became extremely popular during the seventeenth century, and not unlinked with this was a rise in the social status of the apothecary. Both in Britain and on the Continent there was a compromise in which chemical remedies were adopted without commitment to the Paracelsian cosmology. Didactically acquired knowledge of iatrochemistry gave these medical practitioners (who in Britain were to become the general practitioners of the nineteenth and twentieth century) a base upon which they could branch out into their own medical practice and away from the control of university-educated physicians. The need for self-advertisement encouraged them to teach iatrochemical practice and to introduce inorganic remedies into the pharmacopoeia. They were therefore less secretive than the alchemists. Because they wanted to find and prepare useful medical remedies, they were keen to know how to recognize and prepare definite chemical substances with repeatable properties. In teaching their subject, what was wanted was a good textbook, which would provide clear and simple recipes for the preparation of their drugs, with clear unambiguous names for their substances and adequate instructions on the making and use of apparatus for the preparations. Theory could play second fiddle to practice.

Iatrochemistry became very much a French art and here the subject was helped in Paris by the existence of chemical instruction at the Jardin du Roi. Beginning with Jean Beguin's *Tyrocinium Chymicum* in 1610, which plagiarized a good deal from Libavius' *Alchemia*, each successive professor, Étienne de Clave, Christopher Glaser and Nicholas Lemery, composed a textbook for the instruction of the apothecary's apprentices who flocked to their annual lectures. Many of these texts went into other languages, including Latin and English. By 1675, when Lemery published his *Cours de Chimie*, a textbook tradition had been firmly established as part of didactic chemistry and which considerably aided the establishment of chemistry as a discipline. Some historians of chemistry believe that this formulation of chemistry as a scholarly, didactic discipline, which began with Libavius well before the establishment of the mechanical philosophy, was far more significant than the latter for the creation of modern chemistry.

In chemical theory, Paracelsus introduced the doctrine of the *tria prima*, or the three principles. Medical substances, he said, were ultimately composed from the four Aristotelian elements, which formed the receptacles or matrices for the universal qualities of a trinity of primary bodies he called salt (body), sulphur (soul) and mercury (spirit).

The world is as God created it. He founded this primordial body on the trinity of mercury, sulphur and salt and these are the three substances of which the complete body consists. For they form everything that lies in the four elements, they bear them all the forces and faculties of perishable things.

The doctrine of the *tria prima* was clearly an extension of the Arabic sulphur–mercury theory of metals applied to all materials whether metallic, non-metallic, animal or vegetable, and given body by the addition of a third principle, salt.

WATER	FIRE	EARTH
cold wet	dry hot	cold dry
|	|	|
MERCURY	SULPHUR	SALT

| Principle of: | fusibility volatility | inflammability | incombustibility non-volatility |

This theory of composition, which essentially explained gross properties by hypothetical property-bearing constituents, rapidly replaced the old sulphur–mercury theory, though not the Aristotelian four elements. Paracelsus was happy to use Aristotle's example of the analysis of wood by destructive distillation to justify the *tria prima* theory. Smoke was the volatile portion, mercury; the light and glow of the fire demonstrated the presence of sulphur; and the incombustible, non-volatile ash remaining was the salt. Water was included within the mercury principle, which explained the cohesion of bodies.

Van Helmont begged to differ and provided a simpler, and supposedly more empirical, alternative theory of composition.

HELMONTIANISM

Iatrochemistry came to fruition in the work of a Flemish nobleman, Joan-Baptista van Helmont (1577–1644). Present-day Belgium was then under Spanish control. In 1625, as a consequence of Helmont's controversial advocation of 'weapon salve' treatment in which a weapon, and not a wound, was treated, he was denounced as a heretic by the Spanish Inquisition and spent the remainder of his life, like Galileo, under house arrest. As with Paracelsus, it was van Helmont's posthumous writings that brought his name to fame and exerted a considerable influence upon seventeenth-century natural philosophers like Boyle and Newton. This influence was firmly established after 1648 with the posthumous publication of his *Ortus Medicinae*, which was issued in English in 1662 as *Oriatricke or Physick Refined*. Helmont, who claimed to have witnessed a successful transmutation of a base metal into gold, was a disciple of Paracelsus and an iatrochemist. However, like any good disciple, he modified, interpreted and disagreed with his master's doctrines considerably.

After studying several areas of natural philosophy, he chose medicine and chemistry for his career, calling himself a 'philosopher by fire'. He was strongly anti-Aristotelian, one facet of which was that he refused to accept the four-element theory. But neither was he able to accept Paracelsus' *tria prima*. To simplify a rather complex philosophy, we can say that according to van Helmont there were two first beginnings of bodies: water and an active, organizing principle, or 'ferment', which moulded the various forms and properties of substances. This return to a unitary theory of matter was influenced by his interpretation of Genesis, for water, together with the heavens and the earth, had been formed on the first day.

In more detail, he imagined that there were two ultimate elements, air and water. Air was, however, purely a physical medium, which did not participate in transmutations, whereas water could be moulded into the rich variety of substances found on the earth. Van Helmont did not consider fire to be a material element, but a transforming agent. As for earth, from his experimental observations, he believed that this was created by the action of ferments upon water.

> The first beginnings of bodies, and of corporeal causes, are two, and no more. They are surely the element water, from which bodies are fashioned, and the ferment.

As we have already seen in the introduction, the justification for this belief was an interesting, quantitative growth experiment with a young willow tree. Additional supporting evidence came from the fact that fish were nourished 'solely' by water, that seashells were found on dry land, and that solid bodies could be transformed into 'savoury waters', that is, into solution. In the latter case, Helmont took a weighed amount of sand, and fused it with excess alkali to form water-glass, which liquefied on standing in air. Here was a palpable demonstration of the reconversion of earth back into water. More remarkably, this 'water' could be reconverted back to 'earth' by treatment with acid, when the silica sand recovered was found to have the same weight as the starting material.

There are a number of interesting features about these experiments and Helmont's reasoning. Their most important feature is not that Helmont misinterpreted his observations because he ignored the role of air, but that they were quantitative. The experiments were also controlled. In the willow tree experiment, Helmont covered the vessel so as to prevent dust contamination, which might have affected the result. Similarly, he dried the earth beforehand and used only distilled water. He clearly had thought about the experiment and possible objections that might be raised against his conclusions because of the way the experiment had been designed. All this was the hallmark of the experimental method that was to lead to the transformation of chemistry. In addition, it is noticeable that he implicitly assumed that matter was conserved in any changes it underwent. When metals were dissolved in acids they were not destroyed, but were recoverable weight for weight. Helmont also postulated the existence of an *alcahest*, or universal solvent, which had the property of turning things back into water. Much time and effort was spent by contemporary chemists, including Robert Boyle, in trying to identify this mysterious solvent.

There is a further item of interest to be found in Helmont's writings. Since air could not be turned into water, he accepted it as a separate element. However, his keen interest was awakened by the 'air-like' substances that were frequently evolved during chemical reactions. Helmont identified these fuliginous effluvia as 'gases', from a Greek word for 'chaos' that Paracelsus had ascribed to air in another connection. Where did these uncontrollable, dangerous materials fit in Helmont's ontology?

Gases were simply water, not air, for any matter carried into the atmosphere was turned into *gas* by the cold and 'death' of its ferments. A gas was chaos because it bore no *form*. A gas might also condense to a vapour and fall as rain under the influence of *blas*, a term that did not stay in chemical language, and which Helmont coined to refer to a kind of 'gravitational', astral influence or power that caused motion and change throughout the universe.

In a typical gas experiment, Helmont heated 62 lb (28 kg) of charcoal in air and was left with 1 lb (2.2 kg) of ash, the rest having disappeared as 'spiritus sylvester' or wild spirit. When charcoal was heated in a sealed vessel, combustion would either not occur, or would occur with violence as the spirit escaped from the exploding vessel. This disruptive experience led to Helmont's definition of *gas*:

> This spirit, hitherto unknown, which can neither be retained in vessels nor reduced to a visible body . . . I call by the new name gas.

Although Helmont implied by this a distinction between gas and air, and even between different gases, these were features to which commentators paid scant attention. The reason for this is that, in the absence of any suitable apparatus to collect and study such aerial emissions, it was impossible to distinguish between them chemically. Helmont himself had to be content with classifying gases from their obvious physical properties: for example, the wild and unrestrainable gas (spiritus sylvester) obtained from charcoal; gases from fermentations; vegetable juices; from the action of vinegar on the shells of certain sea creatures; intestinal putrefactions; from mines, mineral waters and from certain caverns like the Grotto del Cane near Naples, which allowed men to breathe but extinguished the life of a dog.

In striking contrast to his French contemporary. René Descartes, who claimed that, apart from the existence of a human soul, life was a mechanistic process, Helmont refused to separate soul from matter itself. Matter became spiritualized and nature pantheistic. Such a spiritualization of matter proved especially attractive to various religious groups during the Puritan revolution in England. The writings of Paracelsus and Helmont circulated widely during the 1650s and 1660s, partly because they could be used as weapons in the power struggles between physicians and pharmacists, but also because religious ideology was in a state of flux. The Neoplatonic, unmechanical, vitalistic and almost anti-rational aspects of both Paracelsianism and Helmontianism appealed to many because they emphasized the significance of personal illumination against pure reason. This appealed to the Puritan conscience precisely because it could justify religious and political revolution for the sake of one's ideals.

But along with the ideology went the 'positive' science of Helmont: gases, quantification and measurement, and iatrochemistry. Once the Commonwealth was achieved, the concept of personal illumination had to be played down (as Libavius had foreseen) in order to prevent anarchy. In the 1660s, therefore, Helmontianism came under attack. Whereas in the 1640s it had been argued by some that Oxford and Cambridge Universities ought to be reformed under Paracelsian and Helmontian lines, by the mid 1660s this was out of the question and the mechanical philosophy of Descartes, Boyle and Newton was to be triumphantly advocated by the new Royal Society. Nevertheless, echoes of Helmontianism remained in the works of Boyle and Newton.

THE ACID-ALKALI THEORY

This dualistic theory, based upon the old Empedoclean idea of a war of opposites, also stemmed directly from Helmont's work. Helmont had explained digestion chemically as a fermentation process involving an acid under the control of a Paracelsian *archeus* or internal alchemist. At the same time, he was able to show that the human body secreted alkaline materials such as bile. One of his disciples, Franciscus Sylvius (1614–72), a Professor of Medicine at Leyden from 1658 until his death, and a leading exponent of iatrochemistry, extended Helmont's digestion theory by arguing that it involved the fermentation of food, saliva, bile and pancreatic juices. For Sylvius, this was a 'natural' chemical process and involved no archeus, supernatural or astral mechanism of transformation. The pancreatic juices were a recent discovery of physiologists. By taste they were acidic, as was saliva; but bile was alkaline. Since it was well known that effervescence was produced when an acid and alkali reacted together, as when vinegar was poured onto chalk, Sylvius believed that digestion was a warfare, followed by neutralization, between acids and alkalis.

He did not hesitate to extend this conception of neutralization between two chemical opposites to other physiological processes. For example, by suggesting that blood contained an oily, volatile salt of bile (alkali), which reacted in the heart with blood containing acidic vital spirits, he explained how the vital animal heat was produced by effervescence. From this normal state of metabolism, pathological symptoms could be explained. All disease could be reduced to cases of super-acidity or super-alkalinity – a theory that was quickly exploited commercially by apothecaries and druggists and which is not unfamiliar from twentieth-century advertisements.

Sylvius' theory was popularized by his Italian pupil, Otto Tachenius (1620–90), in the *Hippocrates Chemicus* (1666) – a title that advertised its iatrochemical approach explicitly. Amid its chemical explanations for human physiology lay a criticism that the greatest need in the 1660s was for a unifying theory of chemical classification and explanation to replace the tarnished hypotheses of the four elements and the three principles. Tachenius urged instead that physicians and chemists adopt a two-element theory that the properties and behaviour of substances lay in their acidity or alkalinity.

The fundamental problem with Tachenius' suggestion was that there was no satisfactory definition of an acid or an alkali beyond a circular one that an acid effervesced with an alkali and vice versa.

A SCEPTICAL CHEMIST

Robert Boyle (1627–91), who was born in Ireland as the seventh son of the Earl of Cork, was educated at Eton and by means of a long continental tour from which he returned to England in 1644. In the 1650s he became associated with Samuel Hartlib and his circle of acquaintances, who sometimes referred to themselves as the 'invisible college'. The Hartlibians were interested in exploiting chemistry both for its material usefulness in medicine and trade and for the better understanding of God and Nature. Since the group included the American alchemist George Starkey among its members, not surprisingly Boyle began to read extensively into the alchemical literature. Between 1655 and 1659 and from 1664 to 1668 Boyle lived in Oxford, where he became associated with the group of talented natural philosophers who were to form the Royal Society in 1661. Boyle was an extraordinarily devout man who, like Newton a generation later, wrote as much on theology as on natural philosophy. He paid for translations of the Bible into Malay, Turkish, Welsh and Irish, and left money in his will for the endowment of an annual series of sermons, to be preached in St Paul's Cathedral, that would reconcile and demonstrate how science supported religion.

The generation before Boyle had seen a revival in the fortunes of the atomic theory of matter. Throughout the middle ages, as the text of Geber's *Summa perfectionis* demonstrates, natural philosophers had been familiar with the Aristotelian doctrine of the *minima naturalis*, which they treated to all intents and purposes as 'least chemical particles'. Lucretius' poem, *On the Nature of Things*, had been rediscovered and printed in 1473. A century later, in 1575, Hero's *Pneumatica* was published and disseminated an alternative non-Epicurean atomic theory in which the properties of bulk matter were explained by the presence of small vacua that were interspersed between the particles of a body. This theory, which allowed heat to be explained in terms of the agitation of particles, was exploited by, among others, Galileo, Bacon and Helmont in their search for an alternative to Aristotelianism. A century later, in 1660, the French philospher, Pierre Gassendi (1592–1655), advocated the Epicurean philosophy of atoms to replace Aristotelian physics. His work, *Philosophiae Epicuri Syntagma*, was a rambling summary of atomism, but its assertion of the vacuum provided an alternative to Descartes' plenistic particle theory. Descartes' three grades of matter, i.e. large terrestrial matter, more subtle or celestial matter that filled the interstices of the former, and still subtler particles that filled the final spaces, bore more than a passing resemblance to the elements of earth, air and fire, let alone

Paracelsus' principles of salt, mercury and sulphur. To those who have studied the matter, it is clear that Boyle was much indebted both to Gassendi and to his English disciple, Walter Charleton, whose *Epicuro-Gassendo-Charletoniana* (1654) had not only presented a coherent mechanical philosophy in terms of atoms or corpuscles, but placed it in an acceptable Christian context.

In 1661 Boyle published *The Sceptical Chymist*, a critique of peripatetic (Aristotelian), spagyric (Paracelsian and Helmontian) chemistry and the substantiation of physical and chemical properties into pre-existent substantive forms and qualities. Although designed as an argument in dialogue form between four interlocutors, Carneades (a sceptic), Themistius (an Aristotelian), Philoponus (a Paracelsian) and Eleutherius (neutral), Boyle's rather verbose, digressive and rambling style makes it difficult for the modern reader to follow his argument. Much of the treatise becomes a monologue by Boyle's spokesman, Carneades. Fortunately, there exists in manuscript an earlier, more straightforward, less literary, and hence more convincing, version of the essay, 'Reflexions on the Experiments vulgarly alledged to evince the four Peripatetique Elements or the three Chymical Principles of Mixt Bodies'. Apart from one or two references to the later book, we shall follow the argument in this manuscript, which from internal evidence was written in 1658.

A typical defence of the four-element theory was to cite the familiar case of burning wood[1]:

> The experiment commonly alledged for the common opinion of the four elements, is, that if a green stick be burned in the naked fire, there will first fly away a smoake, which argued AIRE, then will boyle out at the ends a certain liquor, which is supposed WATER, the FIRE dissolves itself by its own light, and that incombustible part it leaves at last, is nothing but the element of EARTH.

Boyle, following Helmont quite closely, raised a number of objections to this interpretation. In the first place, although four 'elementary' products could be extracted from wood, from other substances it was possible to extract more or fewer.

> Out of some bodies, four elements cannot be extracted, as Gold, out of which not so much as any *one* of them hath been hitherto. The like may be said of Silver, calcined Talke, and divers other fixed bodies, which to reduce into four heterogeneal substances, is a taske that has hitherto proved too hard for Vulcan. Other bodies there be, that can be reduced into *more*, . . . as the Bloud of men and other animals, which yield, when analyzed, flegme, spirit, oile, salt and earth.

Here Boyle seems to have stumbled upon a distinction between mineral and organic substances, but he did not develop this point. Instead, he objected to the assumption that the four products of wood were truly *elements*. A little further chemical manipulation suggested, indeed, that the products were complex.

> As for the greene sticke, the fire dos not separate it into elements, but into mixed bodies, disguised into other shapes: the *Flame* seems to be but the sulphurous part of the body kindled; the *water* boyling out at the ends, is far from being elementary water, holding much of the salt and vertu of the concrete: and therefore the ebullient juice of several plants is by physitians found effectual against several distempers, in which simple water is altogether unavailable. The *smoake* is so far from being *aire*, that it is as yet a very mixt body, by distillation yielding an oile, which leaves an earthe behind it; that it abounds in salt, may appear by its aptness to fertilise land, and by its bitterness, and by its making the eyes water (which the smoake of common water will not doe)

and beyond all dispute, by the pure salt that may be easily extracted from it, of which I lately made some, exceeding white, volatile and penetrant.

This criticism clearly shows how carefully Boyle had studied the products of the destructive distillation of wood – an experiment that used to be one of the introductory lessons in British secondary school chemistry syllabuses in the twentieth century.

Finally, Boyle turned his penetrating criticism to the method of fire analysis itself. Why was it, he asked, that if the conditions of fire analysis were slightly altered or a different method of analysis was used, the products of analysis were different? Thus, if a Guajacum log was burned in an open grate, ashes and soot resulted; but if it was distilled in a retort, 'oile, spirit, vinegar, water and charcoale' resulted. And whereas *aqua fortis* (concentrated nitric acid) separated silver and gold by dissolving the silver, fire would, on the contrary, fuse the two metals together. Moreover, the degree of fire (the temperature) could make the results of analysis vary enormously.

Thus lead with one degree of fire, will be turned into minium [lead oxide], and with another be vitrified, and in neither of these will suffer any separation of elements. And if it be lawful for an Aristotelian, to make ashes (which he mistakes for Earthe) passe for an element, why may not a Chymist upon the same principle, argue that glas is one of the elements of many bodies, because by only a further degree of fire, their ashes may be vitrified?

Boyle concluded, therefore, that fire analysis was totally unsuited to demonstrating that substances are all composed of the same number of elements. To do this was like affirming 'that all words consist of the same letters'. Such a critique of the Aristotelian elements was by no means unique to Boyle. Indeed, there is considerable evidence that, apart from his own original experiments, he drew the main thrust of the critique from the writings of Gassendi, who had made similar points when reviving the atomic philosophy of Epicurus and Lucretius.

Once this is realized, the point of his objections to the three principles of Paracelsus becomes plain. Lying in the background to the 'Reflexions', and made explicit in *The Sceptical Chymist*, was a corpuscular philosophy. Boyle's argument was that, even if there were three principles or elements inside a material, it did not necessarily follow that an analysis into these three parts was possible, or that they were the ultimate parts. Oddly enough, nineteenth-century organic chemists were to be faced by exactly the same problem: what guarantee was there that the products of a reaction told one anything about the original substance?

> It is not altogether unquestionable that if three principles be separated from bodies, they were pre-existent in them; for, perhaps, when fire dos sever the parts of bodies, the igneous atoms doe variously associate themselves with the disjoined particles of the dissolved body, or else make severall combinations of the freed principles of the same body betwixt themselves, and by that union, or at least cohesion, there may result mixts of a new sort.

As Laurent discovered in the 1830s, such scepticism is valuable; but if taken too literally, it would prevent any use of reactions as evidence of composition.

Boyle therefore concluded of the Paracelsian principles that, until such time as someone analysed gold and similar substances into three consistent parts, 'I will not deny it to be possible absolutely . . . yet must I suspend my belief, till either experience or competent testimony hath convinced me of it'.

There was one further card up Boyle's sleeve; he was able to use the Helmontian theory of one element as an argument against the alternative three- and four-element theories. He appears at first to have had strong doubts concerning the truth of Helmont's water hypothesis; but after experiments of his own he had to admit that it seemed plausible. In both the 'Reflexions' and *The Sceptical Chymist*, Helmont's work appears in a favourable light. Nearly a third of the 'Reflexions' is devoted to a discussion of Helmont's work. Some of Boyle's own experiments seemed to support the water theory, though he remained agnostic on the question whether or not water was truly elementary. Indeed, in *The Sceptical Chymist* he argued that water itself was probably an agglomeration of particles.

Boyle's experiments were very similar to those of Helmont:

> I have not without some wonder in the analysis of bodies, marvelled how great a share of water goes to the making up of divers, whose disguise promises nothing neer so much. Some hard and solid woods yield more of water alone than all the other elements. The distillation of eels, though it yields some oile, and spirit, and volatile salt, besides the caput mortum, yet were all these so disproportionate to the water that came from them . . . that they seemed to have been nothing, but coagulated phlegme.

Boyle's own astute version of the willow tree experiment, after verification with a squash or marrow seed left to grow in a pot for five months, involved growing mint in water alone, for, as he reasoned, if the plant drew its substance entirely from water, the presence of earth in which to grow the seed or shoot was irrelevant.

Helmont's position, based upon a thorough experimental foundation, seemed on the face of things very attractive. But Boyle could find no evidence for the growth of metals or minerals from water; neither could he see how plant perfumes and nectars arose from water alone. There was no evidence that an alcahest existed and, in any case, the mechanical philosophy saw no ultimate physical difference between a solvent and a solute. Thus although Helmont's experiments were a useful stick with which to beat the Aristotelian and Paracelsian theories of elements, Boyle was no partisan of Helmont's alternative interpretation.

On the other hand, Helmont's theory appealed to Boyle's Biblical literalism, for the world, according to Genesis and Hebrew mythologies, had emerged 'by the operation of the Spirit of God, . . . moving Himself as hatching females do . . . upon the face of the water'. This original water could never have been elementary, but must have consisted 'of a great variety of seminal principles and rudiments, and of other corpuscles fit to be subdued and fashioned by them'. Possibly, then, common water had retained some of this original creative power.

Boyle's advice on the whole question of the evidence for the existence of elements was to keep an open mind and a sceptical front.

> The surest way is to learne by particular experiments what heterogeneous parts particular bodies do consist of, and by what wayes, either actual or potential fire, they may best and most conveniently be separated without fruitlessly contending to force bodies into more elements than Nature made them up of, or strip the severed principles so naked, as by making them exquisitely elementary, to make them laboriously uselesse.

There was irony in that final remark, for through his adherence to the corpuscular philosophy Boyle proceeded to make the concept of the element 'laboriously uselesse'. Before pursuing this point, however, what sceptical mischief did Boyle wreak on the acid–alkali theory?

This theory was not discussed in either *The Sceptical Chymist* or its manuscript draft version. Instead, Boyle criticized Sylvius' and Tachenius' views in 1675 in *Reflections upon the Hypothesis of Alcali and Acidium*. Ten years previously, in his *Experimental History of Colours* (see chapter 5), Boyle had made an important contribution to acid–base chemistry with the development of indicators. He had found that a blue vegetable substance, syrup of violets, turned red with acids and green with alkalis. The test was applicable to all the known acids and could be used confidently to give a working definition of an acid: namely, that an acid was a substance that turned syrup of violets red. The test was also quantitative in a rough-and-ready way, since neutral points could be determined.

When Boyle came to consider the Sylvius–Tachenius theory in 1675, he was able to object to the vagueness of the terms 'acid' and 'alkali' as commonly used in the theory. Effervescence, he pointed out, was not a good test of acidity, since it was also the test for alkalinity; it also created difficulties with the metals, which effervesced when added to acids. Were metals alkalis? If zinc was reacted with the alkali called soda (sodium carbonate), it was dissolved. Was zinc, therefore, an acid?

Whereas in *The Sceptical Chymist* Boyle had only played the critic and not put forward any concrete proposal to replace the Aristotelian and Paracelsian theories, in the case of his criticism of the acid–alkali theory, he was able to offer an alternative, experimentally based classification of acidic, alkaline and neutral solutions, which could be used helpfully in chemical analysis. By building on this experimental work, succeeding chemists were able to develop the theory of salts, which proved one of the starting points for Lavoisier's revision of chemical composition in the eighteenth century.

There was also a second important criticism of the acid–alkali theory. In its vague metaphorical talk of 'strife' between acidic and alkaline solutions, the theory possessed a decidedly unmechanical, indeed, anti-mechanical, air about it. To a corpuscular philosopher like Boyle, the theory was occult, in the seventeenth-century sense that it appealed to explanations that could not be reduced to the mechanical geometrical principles of size, shape and motion with which God had originally endowed them.

Even so, it is doubtful whether Boyle subscribed fully to the reduction of chemical properties to geometrical qualities, as early eighteenth-century philosophers were to do. The most Boyle was prepared to argue was that chemical properties depended on the way the particles that composed one body were disposed to react with those of others.

He was, no doubt, acutely aware of the fact that, by abolishing Aristotelian formal causes, an explanation of the distinction between chemical species was lost. Gassendi's solution, which Boyle followed, had been to introduce 'seminal virtues' or seeds, 'which fit the corpuscles together . . . into little masses [which] shapes them uniformly'. Boyle's experiments on variable crystalline shapes produced when the same acid was reacted with different metals enabled him to argue that each acid, alkali and metal had its own specific internal form or virtue, which could be modified in the presence of others. Here Boyle found the earlier idea of medieval *minima* and *mixtion* useful since, unlike physical atomism, it tried to explain combination by more than physical cohesion alone. As previously noted, another way forward, represented by Descartes, was to explain form geometrically by attributing chemical significance to the *shapes* of the ultimate physical particles. Descartes' three elements came in three shapes, irregular, massive and solid, and long and thin. Although there was an obvious analogy with Paracelsian sulphur, salt and mercury, Norma Emerton has also noted the parallel with contemporary Dutch land drainage schemes in which a framework of sticks interleaved with branches was covered with stones to form a *terra firma*. For Descartes, therefore, composition (mixtion) and the new form was caused by simple entanglement.

BOYLE'S PHYSICAL THEORY OF MATTER

Boyle used to be dismissed by historians of chemistry as only a critic, but this is certainly not the tenor of his work as a whole. He was an extremely prolix, rambling and, by today's standards, unmethodical writer who published some 42 volumes. He adopted a Baconian method towards his scientific activities, and this was often reflected in the apparently random method of composition, which never allowed him time to write a comprehensive treatise on chemistry. We know that his manuscripts were delivered to the printer in bits and pieces, always behind schedule, and full of addenda and 'lost experiments' from previous research projects. It is small wonder, then, that Peter Shaw, Boyle's eighteenth-century editor, found it necessary to apologize to readers for the lack of system in Boyle's collected works:

> But as Mr Boyle never design'd to write a body of philosophy, only to bestow occasional essays on those subjects whereto his genius or inclination led him; 'tis not to be expected that even the most exquisite arrangement should ever reduce them to a methodical and uniform system, though they afford abundant material for one.

Despite Shaw's defensive remark, there was in fact a system in Boyle's 'ramblings'. Elsewhere Shaw himself identified it when he referred to Boyle as 'the introducer, or at least, the great restorer, of the mechanical philosophy amongst us'. This claim that Boyle had restored the mechanical philosophy had first appeared in one of Richard Bentley's Boyle lectures, or sermons, several years earlier.

> The mechanical or corpuscular philosophy, though peradventure the oldest as well as the best in the World, had lain buried for many ages in contempt and oblivion, till it was happily restored and cultivated anew by some excellent wits of the present age. But it principally owes its re-establishment and lustre to Mr Boyle, that honourable person of ever blessed memory who hath not only shown its usefulness in

physiology (i.e. physics) above the vulgar doctrines of real qualities and substantial forms, but likewise its great serviceableness to religion itself.

By the mid seventeenth century there was no longer any conceptual difficulty involved in the acceptance of minute particles, whether atomic or (less controversially) corpuscular, which, though invisible and untouchable, could be imagined to unite together to form tangible solids. No doubt the contemporary development of the compound microscope by Robert Hooke and others helped considerably in stimulating the imagination to accept a world of the infinitely small, just as the telescope had banished certain conceptual difficulties concerning the possibility of change in the heavens. If only Democritus had a microscope, Bacon said, 'he would perhaps have leaped for joy, thinking a way was now discovered for discerning the atom'.

Boyle's corpuscles were neither the atoms of Epicurus and Gassendi, nor the particles of Descartes and the Cartesians. They were at once more useful and more sophisticated than either of them. Boyle's mechanical philosophy was built on the principles of matter and motion. The properties of bulk matter were explained by the size, shape and motion of corpuscles, and the interaction of chemical *minima naturalia* (molecules), the evidence for which lay in chemical phenomena. Like Bacon and his fellow members of the Royal Society, however, Boyle always claimed to dislike and distrust 'systems'.

It has long seemed to me none of the least impediments of true natural philosophy, that men have been so forward to write systems of it, and have thought themselves obliged either to be altogether silent, or not write less than an entire body of physiology.

Yet, while he disagreed with Cartesian physics, he seems

to have felt that Descartes' picture of the world as an integrated system, or whole, was a fruitful one. He agreed that there were no isolated pieces in Nature; that every piece of matter in the universe was continually acted upon by diverse forces or powers. The world was a machine, 'a self-moving engine', 'a great piece of clockwork' comparable to 'a rare clock such as may be seen at Strasbourg', then the engineering marvel of Europe. God was the clock-maker, the universe was the clock.

All this sounds like a 'system', as indeed it was. What Boyle meant by opposing systems, as such, was that they were usually based upon an *a priori*, experimentally indefensible set of hypotheses. They had usually been assembled from hypotheses that were not *verae causae* (true causes), as Newton was to call the kind of hypothesis that ought to be acceptable in natural philosophy.

We can see now why Boyle could accept a mechanical, corpuscular system of philosophy. The corpuscular philosophy was a *vera causa*, which could explain a tremendous range of diverse phenomena, and which could be experimentally defended. At the same time, it avoided and did away with 'inexplicable forms, real qualities, the four peripatetick elements . . and the three chymical principles'. Hotness, coldness, colour and the many secondary qualities and forms of Aristotelian physics were swept aside and explained solely in terms of the arrangements, agglomerations and behaviour of chemical particles as they interacted. Boyle's assertion of the corpuscular philosophy was like Galileo's claim that the book of Nature was written in mathematical terms. Boyle's book was 'a well-contrived romance' of which every part was 'written in the stenography of God's omnipotent hand', i.e. in corpuscular, rather than geometrical, characters. By revealing its design, like Gassendi and Charleton earlier, Boyle reconciled what had formerly been perceived as an atheistical system with religion and, indeed, with the tenets of the Anglican church that had become the re-established Church of England following the Civil War.

Boyle demonstrated the usefulness of chemistry not merely to medicine and technology (where it had long been accepted) but also to the natural philosopher, who had long despised it as the dubious activity of alchemists and workers by fire. Boyle aimed to show natural philosophers that it was essential that they took note of chemical phenomena, for the mechanical philosophy could not be properly understood otherwise. It was true, he admitted, that the theories of ordinary spagyrical chemists were false and useless; nevertheless, their experimental findings deserved attention, for if they could be disentangled from false interpretations, much would be found that would illustrate and support the corpuscular theory of matter.

In this way, Boyle strove to 'begat a good understanding betwixt the chymists and the mechanical philosophers'. Chemists recognized him as a fellow chemist, even though he was a natural philosopher; while the natural philosophers recognized him as a respectable chemist because he was also a member of their company. By advocating a mechanical philosophy, Boyle would raise the social and intellectual status of 'workers by fire', reduce their proneness to secrecy and mysterious language, and make them into natural philosophers. As he wrote in another essay of 1661[2]:

> I hope it may conduce to the advancement of natural philosophy, if, ... I be so happy, as, by any endeavours of mine, to possess both chymists and corpuscularians of the advantages, that may redound to each party by the confederacy I am mediating between them, and excite them both to enquire more into one another's philosophy, by manifesting, that as many chymical experiments may be happily explicated by corpuscularian notions, so many of the corpuscularian notions may be commodiously either illustrated or confirmed by chymical experiments.

Boyle may be said to have united the proto-disciplines of chemistry and physics. But the partnership proved premature, for Boyle succumbed to the danger of not replacing the elements and principles of the chemists with a mechanical philosophy that was useful to the working chemist. This criticism can be most clearly made when discussing Boyle's definition of the element in the sixth part of *The Sceptical Chymist*.

> I now mean by elements, as those chymists that speak plainest do by their principles, certain primitive and simple, or perfectly unmingled bodies; which not being made of any other bodies, or of one another, are the ingredients of which all those called perfectly mixt bodies are immediately compounded, and into which they are ultimately resolved.

Leaving aside the fact that Boyle made no claim to be defining an element for the first time (as so many modern chemistry textbooks claim), in his next sentence he went on to deny that the concept served any useful function:

> . . . now whether there be any one such body to be constantly met with in all, and each, of those that are said to be elemented bodies, is the thing I now question.

A modern analogy will make Boyle's scepticism clear. If matter is composed ultimately of protons, neutrons and electrons, or, more simply still, of quarks, this, according to Boyle, should be the level of analysis and explanation for the chemist, not the so-called 'elements' that are deduced from chemical reactivity. To Boyle, materials such as gold, iron and copper were not elements, but aggregates of a common matter differentiated by the number, size, shape and structural pattern of their agglomerations. Although he clearly accepted that such entities had an independent existence as *minima*, he was unable to foresee the benefit of defining them pragmatically as chemical elements. For

Boyle an 'element' had been irreversibly defined by the ancients and by his contemporaries as an omnipresent substance.

The seventeenth-century corpuscular, physical philosophy was all very well. It might explain chemical reactions, but it did not predict them, nor did it differentiate between simple and complex substances, the elementary and the compound. Nor, at this stage, did it align the supposed particles with weight and the chemical balance. Hence, although corpuscularianism was not overtly denied by later chemists, who were often content to accept it as an explanation of the *physical* character of matter, in chemical practice it was ignored. Chemists still needed the concept of an element and blithely returned to the four elements or to some other elementary concept. One thing had changed, however, as a result of Boyle's criticisms. It was no longer possible to argue seriously that *all* of the possible elements, however many a chemist might postulate, were ubiquitously present in a particular material. Boyle's scepticism suggested the possibility that some substances might contain less than the total number of elements; this made it possible for later chemists to be pragmatic about elements and to increase their number slowly and stealthily throughout the eighteenth century.

This more pragmatic view is seen clearly in Nicholas Lemery's *Cours de chymie* (1675; English trans. 1686)[3]:

The word *Principle* in Chymistry must not be understood in too nice a sense: for the substances which are so-called, are *Principles* in respect to us, and as we can advance no further in the division of bodies; but we well know that they may be still further divided in abundance of other parts which may more justly claim, in propriety of speech, the name of *Principles*: wherefore such substances are to be understood as *Chymical Principles*, as are separated and divided, so far as we are capable of doing it by our imperfect powers.

This comes pretty close to Lavoisier's operational definition of an element (Chapter 3).

It would be wrong to leave the impression that Boyle was a modern physical chemist, or, rather, chemical physicist. As a corpuscularian, Boyle had no difficulty in accepting the plausibility of transmutation of metals; indeed, a particle theory made 'the alchymists' hopes of turning other materials into gold less wild'. We know that Boyle took stories of magical events and of successful transmutations extremely seriously. In 1689 Boyle helped to secure the repeal of Henry IV's Act against the multiplication of silver and gold, on the grounds that it was inhibiting possibly useful metallurgical researches. Throughout his life he investigated alchemists' claims, albeit privately and cautiously and even secretly since, as recent research has shown, he clearly identified transmutation with the intervention of supernatural forces.

THE VACUUM BOYLIANUM AND ITS AFTERMATH

Boyle's other principal contribution to natural philosophy was his investigation of the air, made possible by the invention of the air pump. The vacuum pump was first developed in Germany by Otto von Guericke, who demonstrated at Magdeburg in the 1650s how air could be pumped laboriously out of a copper globe to leave a vacuum. He then found that the atmosphere exerted a tremendous compressing force upon the globe. This was demonstrated theatrically in the famous Magdeburg experiment, which involved sixteen horses in trying to tear two evacuated hemispheres apart. Details of Guericke's pumping system, which were published in 1657, rapidly awakened interest throughout Europe; for if a vacuum really was formed, this was *prima facie* evidence for the fallibility of Aristotelian physics and evidence in favour of the corpuscular philosophy.

Assisted by a young and talented laboratory assistant,

Robert Hooke, Boyle built his own air pump in 1658 and began to investigate the nature of combustion and respiration with its aid. Some forty-three of his experimental findings, most of which he had had carefully witnessed by reputable friends and colleagues, were published in 1660 in *New Experiments Physico-Mechanical touching the Spring of the Air and its Effects.* Boyle's law, linking pressure (the spring) and volume of the air, was developed from an experimental investigation provoked by a controversy after the book's publication. For many years subsequently the British referred to the vacuum affectionately as the 'vacuum Boylianum'.

Experiments with birds, mice and candles slowly led Boyle to conclude that air acted as a transporting agent to remove impurities from the lungs to the external air. (Incidentally, Boyle's observation that insects do not die in a vacuum was confirmed in the twentieth century by Willis Whitney at the General Electric Company.) Like Helmont, Boyle never conceived of the air as a chemical entity; rather, it was a peculiar elastic fluid in which floated various reactive particles responsible for the phenomena of respiration, the rusting of iron, deliquescence and the greening of copper. On the other hand, Boyle clearly perceived that something in the air was consumed or absorbed during respiration and combustion, but he remained suitably cautious about its identification. His followers, including Hooke, who, as Curator of Experiments for the Royal Society, soon carved out an independent career for himself, were more confident.

During the English Civil War, Oxford was a Royalist stronghold. King Charles' physician, William Harvey, who had demonstrated the circulation of the blood in 1628, was Warden of Wadham College, where he stimulated the development of co-operative investigations of physiology. The arrival of Boyle in Oxford in the 1650s further encouraged an interest in chemical questions among this community of undergraduates and Royalist exiles from

London, including Richard Lower, John Mayow, John Wallis, John Wilkins and Christopher Wren. In 1659 Boyle hired an Alsatian immigrant, Peter Stahl, to teach chemistry publicly in Oxford. Those who were particularly interested in solving some of Harvey's unanswered puzzles, including what happened to blood in the lungs or what was the origin of the blood's warmth, took Stahl's courses in the hope of finding chemical solutions. Among Boyle's assistants at this time were Hooke and Mayow.

In the *Micrographia* (1665), a pioneering treatise on microscopy and many other subjects, Hooke developed a theory of combustion that owed something to the two-element acid-alkali theory of Sylvius, and even more to a widely known contemporary meteorological theory that was based upon a gunpowder analogy. According to this 'nitro-aerial' theory, thunder and lightning were likened to the explosion and flashing of gunpowder, whose active ingredients were known to be sulphur and nitre. By analogy, therefore, a violent storm was explained as a reaction between sulphureous and nitrous particles in the air. Since it was also known that nitre lowered the temperature of water and fertilized crops, it could be argued that the nitrous particles of air were probably responsible for snow and hail and for the vitality of vegetables. Such ideas can be traced back to Paracelsus and to alchemical writers such as Michael Sendivogius.

Hooke laid out his version of this theory in the form of a dozen propositions. He assumed that air was a 'universal dissolvent' of sulphureous bodies because it contained a substance 'that is like, if not the very same, with that which is fixt in saltpetre'. During the solution process a great deal of warmth and fire was produced; at the same time, the dissolved sulphureous matter was 'turn'd into the air, and made to fly up and down with it'.

The nitro-aerial theory received its fullest development in the writings of the Cornish Cartesian physician, John Mayow (1641-79) in *Five Medico-Physical Treatises* published in 1674. How much of his work was mere summary of the ideas of Boyle, Hooke and the Oxford physician, Richard Lower, has been the subject of dispute. Even if his work was syncretic, it was of very considerable interest and influence. Mayow used the theory to explain a very wide range of phenomena, including respiration, the heat and flames of combustion, calcination, deliquescence, animal heat, the scarlet colour of arterial blood and, once more, meteorological events. He showed that, when a candle burned in an inverted cupping glass submerged in water, it consumed the nitrous part of the air, which thereupon lost its elasticity, causing the water to rise. The same thing happened when a mouse replaced the candle.

> Hence it is manifest that air is deprived of its elastic force by the breathing of animals very much in the same way as by the burning of flame.

Calcination involved the mechanical addition of nitro-aerial particles to a metal, which, as he knew from some of Boyle's findings, brought about an increase of weight – an explanation also propagated by Mayow's obscure French contemporary, Jean Rey. This explanation seemed confirmed by the fact that antimony produced the same calx when it was heated in air as when it was dissolved in nitric acid and heated.

Early historians of chemistry liked to find a close resemblance between Mayow's explanation and the later oxygen theory of calcination. But it is only the transference properties that are similar. Quite apart from different theoretical entities being used in the two theories, we must note that Mayow's theory was a mechanical, not chemical, theory of combustion. A more serious historiographical point is that Mayow's theory essentially marked a return to a dualistic world of principles and occult powers. Sulphur and nitre now replaced the *tria prima* of Paracelsus.

> Nitro-aerial spirit and sulphur are engaged in perpetual hostilities with each other, and indeed from

their mutual struggles they meet, and from their diverse states when they succomb by turns, all changes of things seem to arise.

Neither Boyle nor Hooke appears to have referred to Mayow's work in their writings. In any case, Boyle was sceptical of the 'plenty and quality of the nitre in the air'.

For I have not found that those that build so much upon this volatile nitre, have made out by any competent experiment, that there is such a volatile nitre abounding in the air. For having often dealt with saltpetre in the fire, I do not find it easy to be raised by a gentle heat; and when by a stronger fire we distil it in closed vessels, it is plain, that what the chemists call the spirit of nitre (nitric oxide), has quite differing properties from crude nitre, and from those that are ascribed to the volatile nitre of the air; these spirits being so far from being refreshing to the nature of animals that they are exceeding corrosive.

Despite the speculative character of the nitro-aerial theory, there is much to admire concerning Mayow's experimental ingenuity. Although he did not develop the pneumatic trough, he devised a method for capturing the 'wild spirits' that Helmont had found so elusive by arranging for pieces of iron to be lowered into nitric acid inside the inverted cupping glass. As we can see, however, the results were inevitably baffling to Mayow, for although the water level in the cup eventually rose (as the nitro-aerial theory predicted), it was initially depressed. (Insoluble hydrogen would have been the first product of this displacement reaction; secondary reactions would have then produced soluble nitrogen dioxide.)

NEWTON'S CHEMISTRY

Newton's interest in chemistry was life-long and reputedly aroused when, as a schoolboy at Grantham Grammar

School, he lodged with an apothecary. He wrote only one overtly chemical paper, but important and influential chemical statements are to be found in the *Principia Mathematica* (1687) and the *Opticks* (1704). As mentioned in Chapter 1, there also exist in manuscript thousands of pages of chemical and alchemical notes, much of them identifiable as transcriptions from contemporary printed or manuscript works. Newton seems to have been interested in both exoteric and esoteric alchemy, that is, his interest extended beyond the empirical and experimental information that might be gleaned from alchemical texts to the 'mysteries' and secrets that were imparted in metaphor and allegory.

Newton was principally influenced by Helmont and Boyle; he also found the nitro-aerial theory attractive as a sustaining principle reminiscent of Helmont's *blas*.

I suspect, moreover, that it is chiefly from the comets that spirit comes, which is indeed the smallest but the most subtle and useful part of the air, and so much required to sustain the life of all things with us.

And in the *Principia* Newton more than hinted that all matter took its origin in water.

The vapours which arise from the sun, the fixed stars, and the tails of comets, may meet at last with, and fall into, the atmospheres of the planets by their gravity, and there be condensed and turned into water and humid spirits; and from thence, by a slow heat, pass gradually into the form of salts, and sulphurs, and tinctures, and mud, and clay, and sand, and stones, and coral, and other terrestrial substances.

Nature was a perpetual worker; all things, he wrote in the *Opticks*, grow out of, and return by putrefaction into, water.

Nevertheless, Newton subscribed wholeheartedly to Boyle's corpuscular philosophy, to which he added the mechanisms of attraction and repulsion to explain not merely the gravitational phenomena of bulk planetary matter, but also the chemical likes (affinities) and dislikes (repulsions) that individual substances displayed towards one another. Such inherent powers of matter, which Newton attributed to a subtle ether that bathed the universe, replaced the astral influences of Paracelsus and the *blas* of Helmont as the causes of motion and change. Newton made this the subject of his only published chemical paper, 'De natura acidorium', written in 1692 but not published until 1710, as well as the 'Queries' 31 and 32 of the 1717 edition of the *Opticks*. In these writings Newton suggested that there were exceedingly strong attractive powers between the particles of bodies, which extended, however, only a short distance from them and varied in strength from one chemical species to another. This hypothesis of short-range force led him to speculate about what eighteenth-century chemists called 'elective affinities' and the reason why, for example, metals replaced one another in acid solutions. He gave the replacement order of six common metals in nitric acid.

The investigation of chemical affinity became one of the absorbing problems of chemistry. In 1718, Étienne Geoffroy (1672-1731) produced the first table of affinities, and more elaborate ones were produced by Torbern Bergman (1735–84) and others from the 1750s onwards. As the Newtonian world picture grew in prestige, chemists and natural philosophers also began to interpret these tables in terms of short-range attractions. In 1785 Buffon even identified the laws of affinity with gravitational attraction; but all attempts to satisfy what has been described as the 'Newtonian dream' to mathematize (i.e. quantify) affinity ended in failure. It was left to Claude Berthollet to point out in 1803 that other factors, such as mass (concentration), temperature and pressure, also decided whether or not a particular reaction was possible.

Newton's ether, the active principle of chemical change, was exploited by large numbers of eighteenth-century chemists, including the important Dutch teacher, Hermann Boerhaave (1668-1738). The latter's *Elementa Chemiae* (1732), which appeared in English in 1741, assimilated ether to fire. Fire, said Boerhaave, consisted of subtle, immutable bodies that were capable of insinuating themselves into the pores of bodies; it was 'the great changer of all things in the universe, while itself remaining unchanged'. Like his German contemporary Georg Stahl, whose work he ignored, Boerhaave treated fire, together with the other three Aristotelian elements, as one of the four 'physical instruments' available to chemists. Because of the connections that were established between the Scottish universities and the University of Leiden, where Boerhaave taught, Boerhaave came to have considerable influence on the teaching of chemistry to medical students in Scotland by William Cullen (1710–90) and his pupil, Joseph Black (1728–99).

Cullen, for example, explained chemical attraction as due to the self-repulsive character of the particles of etherial fire and to the relative densities of ether within two attracting bodies compared with the density of ether in the external environment. The solid and liquid states similarly depended upon the relative quantities of ether and ordinary matter within a substance – a model that was to have important consequences for the conceptualization of gases. This identification of ether and fire, or heat, stimulated Cullen's pupil, Joseph Black, to the study of calorimetry, the establishment of the concepts of specific heat capacity and latent heat, and the exploration of the qualitative difference between air and a 'fixed air' (carbon dioxide), whose presence in magnesia alba (basic magnesium carbonate) he had deduced in 1766.

Newton was also the inspiration behind the experimentally deft attempts made by Stephen Hales (1677-1761) to discover the mechanism of plant growth through an investigation of the movement of sap. It was while making these investigations in the 1720s that he discovered that plants and minerals contained, or held within their pores, large quantities of air. In his *Vegetable Staticks* published in 1727, Hales devoted over a third of the book to a demonstration of this finding, which he proved by heating solids and liquids in a gun barrel and collecting the ejected air over water in a vessel suspended from a beam. This discovery that air could be 'fixed' was the beginning of pneumatic chemistry, and a key factor in the eighteenth-century 'chemical revolution'.

THE PHLOGISTONISTS

By rejecting the claim that the ultimate elements could ever be identified by fire analysis alone, and by arguing that whatever was released by fire were not elements but classes of substances, Boyle failed to be helpful to the practical chemist. The result was that practical chemists went back to the elements. But with one difference. They now began to separate physical from chemical theories of matter and to accept that, to all intents and purposes, substances that could not be further refined by fire or some other method of analytical separation were effectively chemical elements. This did not preclude the possibility that these 'elements' were composed from smaller physical units of matter, but this was a possibility that the investigative chemists could ignore. Such a pragmatic attitude was to reach its final form in Lavoisier's definition of the element in 1789. We find a good example of this attitude in the theory of elements advocated by Georg Stahl (1660–1734), which is customarily referred to as the phlogiston theory. This in turn had been developed from the writings of Becher.

The severe economic problems of the several small and scattered states and principalities that made up the Holy Roman Empire had encouraged rulers to surround themselves with advisors and experts. As we have seen, this was one of the reasons why alchemists were often to be found at European courts, as were 'projectors' and inventors of various kinds. With the growth of government and civil service, the Germanies developed a tradition of cameralism (economics), which strove to make their countries self-sufficient through the strict control of the domestic economy and the efficient exploitation of raw materials and industry. It was the problems connected with mining and with glass, textile, ceramic, beer and wine manufacturing that encouraged the German states to take chemistry seriously. By the beginning of the eighteenth century, chemistry was to be found in many German universities in both the contexts of medicine and cameralism.

Johann Becher (1635-82?) was an early cameralist. With the backing of the Austrian emperor, Leopold I, he founded a technical school in Vienna in 1676 for the encouragement of trade and manufacture. Some years later he moved to the Netherlands to try to launch a scheme for recovering gold from silver by means of sea sand, and he is reputed to have died in London after investigating Cornish mining techniques. Becher wrote of himself in his most important book, *Physica Subterranea* (1667), that he was[4]:

> ... One to whom neither a gorgious home, nor security of occupation, nor fame, nor health appeals to me; for me rather my chemicals amid the smoke, soot and flame of coals blown by bellows. Stronger than Hercules, I work forever in an Augean stable, blind almost from the furnace glare, my breathing (sic) affected by the vapour of mercury. I am another Mithridates saturated with poison. Deprived of the esteem and company of others, a beggar in things material, in things of the mind I am Croesus. Yet among all these evils I seem to live so happily that I would die rather than change places with a Persian king.

Despite its title 'Subterranean physics', Becher's treatise was concerned with the age-old problem of the chemical growth of economically important minerals. A deeply religious work, it was vitalistic and Paracelsian in tone. For Becher, Nature, created by God the chemist, was a perpetual cycle of change and exchange, to which the mercantile economy was an analogy. He could not agree with Helmont's reduction of the elements to water, claiming that this was a misreading of Genesis; for the Bible had said nothing about the creation of minerals. Since these had clearly developed *after* the organic world, he supposed that they had been generated from earth and water. Although he rejected Paracelsus' *tria prima*, he argued that there were three forms of earth, which, for our convenience, can be symbolized as E1, E2 and E3:

> *terra fluida* (E1), or mercurious earth, which con-
> tributed fluidity, subtility, volatility and metallicity to
> substances;
> *terra pinguis* (E2), or fatty earth (the ancient
> unctuous moisture of the alchemists), which produced
> oily, sulphureous and combustible properties; and
> *terra lapidea* (E3) or vitreous earth, which was the
> principle of fusibility.

Air was not a part of mineral creation. Becher implied that the *terra pinguis* was an essential feature of combustibility, but, unlike Stahl later, he did not notice its participation in reversible reactions. He treated fire solely as an instrument, or agent, of change. Minerals grew from seeds of earth and water in varying proportions under the guidance of a formative principle. Because he had a unified view of Nature, he also referred at length to the more complex compositions of the vegetable and animal kingdoms, where both fire and air were incorporated. However, in re-editing the *Physica* in 1703, Stahl concentrated solely on the mineral theory.

Stahl, a Professor of Medicine at the newly opened University of Halle, was a Lutheran pietist and a vitalist who kept his chemistry separate from his medicine and vehemently denounced the claims of iatrochemistry. Like Becher, he worked in the cameralist tradition, his first publication, the *Zymotechnia Fundamentalis* (1697), being concerned with the preparation of fermented beers, wines and bread. It was to help improve the smelting of ores that he first turned to Becher's treatise.

Like Boyle and Newton, he believed that matter was composed of particles arranged hierarchically in groups or clumps to form 'mixts' or compounds. There were four basic types of corpuscle, Becher's three 'earths' and water. In 1718 Stahl redesignated Becher's *terra pinguis* (E2) as 'phlogiston'. If we symbolize water by W, then the four elements, whose existence we can only deduce from experiment, combine together by affinity or the cohesion of water to form secondary (chemical) principles. These substances, like gold and silver and many calces (earths) are extremely stable and cannot be simplified. They are in practice the simplest entities with which the chemist can work, and were to become the elements of modern chemistry. Further combinations among these secondary principles produced mixts such as the metals and salts:

E1 + E2 + E3 + W → secondary principles (e.g. gold) → mixts (e.g. metals) → higher mixts, etc. (e.g. salts)

Moreover, following Boyle, the ultimate four elements are not necessarily omnipresent; but for the secondary principles and mixts to be visible, the particles of the elements and secondary principles have to aggregate among themselves. Echoing Helmont, Stahl believed that 'gas' was a release of water vapour from a decomposing mixt.

Stahl, who appears to have had a good working knowledge of the practice of metallurgy, saw an analogy between organic combustion and the calcination of metals. Whereas contemporary metallurgists used charcoal in smelting to provide heat and to 'protect' the metal from burning, Stahl supposed that all flammable bodies contained the second earth, phlogiston, which was ejected and lost to the atmosphere during combustion:

$$(X + phlogiston) \rightarrow X + phlogiston \quad [oxidation]$$
metal calx

In the particular case of metals, X is the calx (oxide).

Stahl was astute enough to see that the reaction was reversed when a calx was heated with charcoal, and interpreted this as due to the transfer of fresh phlogiston from the charcoal:

$$X + phlogiston \rightarrow metal \quad [reduction]$$

Another brilliant explanation was the combustion of sulphur, and its recovery (synthesis) after treatment with salt of tartar (potassium carbonate):

burn
sulphur → universal acid + phlogiston
universal acid + salt of tartar → vitriolated tartar
vitriolated tartar + charcoal → sulphur

This cyclic transaction confirmed Stahl's belief that sulphur was a mixt containing phlogiston and the principle of acidity, which, following Becher, he called the 'universal acid' since he assumed that it was present in all acids. The universal acid itself was a mixt composed from the vitriolic earth and water.

Such transfers as occurred with metals, sulphur and acids were *not* possible with organic substances, that is, with materials extracted from animals and vegetables, and this made the study of mineral, or inorganic, chemistry all the more interesting. A metal could be made to undergo a series of chemical transformations and be restored completely weight for weight; but an organic material such as a potato would be totally destroyed by chemical manipulation and no amount of added charcoal would ever restore it. Stahl, still unaware of the significance of air in chemical change, had drawn a definite line between inorganic and organic chemistry. In the case of the latter, it appeared that an appeal to the supernumerary properties of a vital soul or organizing principle was still necessary. This was not needed in mineral chemistry, and Stahl rejected Becher's belief that minerals grew beneath the ground.

Stahl's phlogistic principle readily explained the known facts of combustion. Combustion obviously ceased because a limited amount of air could only absorb a limited amount of phlogiston. When the air became saturated, or 'phlogisticated air', combustion ceased. Equally, combustion might cease simply because substances only contained a limited amount of phlogiston. Obviously, however, phlogiston could not remain permanently in the atmosphere otherwise respiration and combustion would be impossible. Unlike Becher, Stahl assumed that phlogiston was absorbed by plants (as Helmont's willow tree experiment, and the properties of wood charcoal, demonstrated), which were then eaten by animals. There was a phlogiston cycle in Nature and phlogiston was the link between the three kingdoms of Nature. It was this cycle that was transformed into photosynthesis at the end of the eighteenth century.

To the modern mind the principal snag, indeed absurdity, of the phlogiston theory is that metals and other combustibles gain in weight when burned in air. But according to the phlogiston theory something is lost. Why, then, was there not a corresponding reduction in weight? Stahl himself noticed without comment that, in the reduction of lead oxide (i.e. during the addition of phlogiston), the lead formed weighed a sixth less than the original calx. Possibly this was an exception to the rule, for if Stahl's paradigm was organic distillation, organic substances do appear to lose weight when they are burned and if the gaseous products of combustion are ignored.

In any case, Stahl's phlogiston was a principle of far more than mere combustion; it did duty to explain acidity and alkalinity, the colours and odours of plants, and chemical reactivity and composition. Weight change was a physical phenomenon and, while it might be indicative of chemical change, it clearly did not assume a fundamental role in Stahl's conception of chemistry. Finally, we should note that eighteenth-century chemists were by no means unanimous that metals increased in weight during calcination. Improvements in heating technology had actually made it more difficult to demonstrate. Because experiments were frequently made with powerful burning lenses, which produced temperatures well in excess of the sublimation or vaporization points of oxides, we can well understand why chemists frequently reported losses in weight.

In reality, what seems to us today to be an acute problem with the credibility of the phlogiston theory only became problematical when the gaseous state of matter began to be explored in the 1760s. It was then that phlogiston began to take on bizarre and inconsistent guises: as an incorporeal, etherial fire; as a substance with negative weight; as the lightest known substance, which buoyed up heavier substances; or as one of the newly discovered factitious airs, inflammable air (hydrogen). Boyle's sceptical and investigative tradition then came into its own again when Lavoisier dismissed Stahl's theory of composition, and phlogiston in particular, as a 'veritable Proteus'.

CONCLUSION

It is clear that the kind of chemistry inherited from the seventeenth century was changed in at least six ways by the chemists of Lavoisier's generation: air had to be adopted as a chemically interactive species; the elemental status of air had to be abolished and exchanged for the concept of the gaseous state; the balance had to be used to take account of gases; the weight increases of substances burned in air had to be experimentally established; a working, practical definition of elements had to be established; and a revised theory of composition had to be adopted, together with a more satisfactory and less-confusing terminology and nomenclature that reflected compositional ideas. The thrust of these revisions was accomplished by Lavoisier and has usually been referred to as the chemical revolution. Does this mean, therefore, that we have to accept that there was no mood for change in the seventeenth century comparable to the revolutionary accomplishments of astronomers, physicists, anatomists and physiologists?

Seventeenth-century chemical practice encompassed four distinctive fields of endeavour. Alchemy, though intellectually moribund, still attracted attention both as a religious exercise and because, in principle, it would have given support to the new corpuscular philosophy. Practical alchemists even at this late stage of its development could still stumble upon important empirical discoveries. In 1675, for example, Hennig Brand, while exploring the golden colour of urine, caused excitement with his discovery of phosphorus. Among medically oriented chemists, iatrochemistry had received its impetus from the writings of Paracelsus, Helmont and the exponents of the acid-alkali theory. The iatrochemists were an important group because they considered their calling worth teaching. In France, in particular, chemistry came to acquire a public following that was reflected in the production of large numbers of textbooks and instruction manuals. The iatrochemists thereby helped to establish chemistry's respectability and ensured that it would become an important part of the medical and pharmaceutical curriculum. In effect, they began the first phase of the long chemical revolution. A third chemical constituency was that of the chemical technologists, who, in a small but significant way, continued to provide data from their observations and experiments, and who encouraged the cameralistic interest in chemistry.

Finally, there was the critical, but experimentally fruitful, work of Boyle, who did not hesitate to draw upon the work of the other three fields as evidence for the mechanical-corpuscular philosophy. In his hands chemistry became a respectable science. The 'occult' forms and qualities of Aristotle were replaced by geometrical arrangements and (in the hands of Newton) forces of attraction and repulsion; the secrecy of the alchemists and that of the technologists was abandoned, and an attempt was made to reform the chaotic and imprecise language of chemistry. While none of these reforms resulted in chemistry as we know it, it would be churlish to deny that chemistry changed during the seventeenth century and shared in the momentum of the general Scientific Revolution.

Nevertheless, the pragmatic element remained undefined and the subject remained the two-dimensional study of solids and liquids and ignored the gaseous state until the time of Hales. Until the role of gases was established and understood, there was a technical frontier that hindered further innovation. That was why late-eighteenth-century chemical progress has always seemed so much more impressive and why, fairly or unfairly, Lavoisier's synthesis of constitutional ideas and experiment appears as impressive as the work of Newton in physics the century before.

3

Elements of Chemistry

Doubtless a vigorous error vigorously pursued has
kept the embryos of truth a-breathing: the quest
for gold being at the same time a questioning of
substances, the body of chemistry is prepared for its
soul, and Lavoisier is born.

(GEORGE ELIOT, *Middlemarch*, 1872)

'Chemistry is a French science; it was founded by Lavoisier
of immortal fame.' So wrote Adolph Wurtz in the historical
'Discours préliminaire' of his *Dictionnaire de chimie pure et
appliquée* (1869). Needless to say, at a time of intense
European nationalism and rivalry, in science as much as
in politics, such a claim proved instantly controversial. In
fact, as early as 1794, Georg Lichtenberg (1742–99) had
argued that the anti-phlogistic chemistry was bringing
nothing new to Germany. 'France', he claimed, 'is not
the country from which we Germans are accustomed to
expect lasting scientific principles.' As far as Lichtenberg
was concerned, whatever might be of value in Lavoisier's
new system of chemistry was really of German origin.
Thorpe's riposte to Wurtz seventy years later was that
'chemistry is an English science, its founder was Cavendish
of immortal memory' – thus invoking an earlier controversy
over which European nation's chemists had first synthesized
water. Raoul Jagnaux's *Histoire de chimie* (1896) presented
the history of chemistry almost entirely as a French
affair, with Lavoisier, once again, as its founder. This
led twentieth-century German historians to write histories
that emphasized that the origins of modern chemistry lay

in the chemical contributions of Stahl and, before him, of Paracelsus.

Today we can smile at such nationalistic obsessions and agree that, even though Lavoisier could never have achieved what he did without the prior and contemporary investigations and interpretations of British, Scandinavian and German chemists and pharmacists, there is an essential grain of truth in Wurtz's statement. For Lavoisier restructured chemistry from fundamental principles, provided it with a new language and fresh goals. To put this another way, a modern chemist, on looking at a chemical treatise published before Lavoisier's time, would find it largely incomprehensible; but everything written by Lavoisier himself, or composed a few years after his death, would cause a modern reader little difficulty. Lavoisier modernized chemistry, and the benchmark of this was the publication of his *Traité élémentaire de chimie* in 1789. On the other hand, historians have come to recognize the continuities between Lavoisier's work and that of his predecessors. Lavoisier's deliberate decision to break with the past and to put chemistry on a new footing inevitably meant that he was cavalier with history and that he paid scant attention to his predecessors – thus indirectly providing a source of his own mythology as the father of chemistry.

A SCIENTIFIC CIVIL SERVANT

Antoine-Laurent Lavoisier was born in Paris on 27 August 1743, the son of a lawyer who held the important position of solicitor to the Parisian Parlement, the chief court of France. His wealthy mother, who also came from a legal family, died when Lavoisier was only five. Not surprisingly, therefore, Lavoisier's education was geared to his expected entry into the legal profession. This meant that he attended, as a day pupil, the best school in Paris, the Collège des Quatres Nations, which was known popularly as the Collège Mazarin. The building still survives and now houses the

Institut de France, of which the French Academy of Sciences is a part. The Collège Mazarin was renowned for the excellence of both its classical and scientific teaching. Lavoisier spent nine years at the Collège, graduating with a baccalaureate in law in 1763. This legal training was to help him greatly in the daily pursuit of his career and can be discerned in the precision of his scientific arguments; but his spare time was always to be devoted entirely to scientific pursuits.

One of the close friends of the Lavoisier family was a cantankerous bachelor geologist named Jean-Étienne Guettard (1715–86). Aware of young Lavoisier's scientific bent, Guettard advised him, while still at the Collège Mazarin, to join a popular chemistry course being given by Guillaume-François Rouelle (1703–70) in the lecture rooms of the Jardin du Roi. Rouelle was following in the tradition established in the seventeenth century of giving public lectures in chemistry aimed at students of pharmacy and medicine. Among his innovations was a new theory of salts, which abandoned both the Paracelsian view that they were variations of a salt principle, and Stahl's view that they were combinations of water and one or more earths. Instead, Rouelle classified salts according to their crystalline shapes and according to the acids and bases from which they were prepared. Rouelle was also responsible for propagating the phlogiston theory among French chemists by incorporating it into his broader view, adopted from Boerhaave and Stahl, that the four traditional elements could function both as chemical elements and as physical instruments. Thus, fire or phlogiston served a double function as a component of matter and as an instrument capable of altering the physical states of matter. This was different from Stahl, who allowed air and fire only instrumental functions. Air, water and earth could similarly serve as instruments of pressure and solution, and for the construction of vessels, as well as entering into the composition of substances. Rouelle, therefore, accepted Hales' proof that air could act chemically; like the other three elements, it could exist either 'fixed' or 'free'.

Rouelle's pupil, G. F. Venel, was one of the few French chemists to pursue Hales' work before the 1760s. He argued that natural mineral waters were chemical combinations of water and air, and that seltzer water could be reproduced by dissolving soda (sodium carbonate) and hydrochloric acid in water. He also advocated that the reactions of air had to be subsumed 'under the laws of affinity'. In this way, air came to occupy one of the columns of the many dozens of different affinity tables that were published during the middle of the eighteenth century.

Lavoisier's earliest knowledge of contemporary ideas concerning the elements, acidity, air and combustion was probably derived from Rouelle's lectures, which he attended in 1762, as well as from Macquer's *Élémens de chymie théorique* (1749) and Venel's article on 'chemistry' in the third volume of the great French *Encyclopédie* (1753). Between them, Rouelle, Macquer and Venel turned their backs on Boyle's seventeenth-century physical programme of attempting to reduce chemistry to 'local motion, rest, bigness, shape, order, situation and contexture of material substances'. Instead, inspired by Newton, they intended to fuse the corpuscular tradition with the more pragmatic chemical explanations of Stahl. They also introduced Lavoisier to the quantitative analysis of minerals.

During the 1750s and 1760s the French government became aware that industry was 'pushed much further in England than it is in France'. Wondering whether Britain's increasing wealth and prosperity from trade and manufacture came because 'the English are not hindered by regulations and inspections', the French commissioned a series of reports on their country's industries and natural resources. This interest had several effects: there was a sudden wave of translations of, chiefly, German and Scandinavian technical works on mining, metallurgy and mineral analysis; with these works, part and parcel, came an awareness of the phlogistic theory of chemical composition; moreover, chemists who had trained in pharmacy and medicine, like Macquer, began to find their services in demand for the solution of industrial problems. Guettard had long cherished an ambition to map the whole of France's mineral possessions and geological formations, and the government readily gave approval in 1763. Needing an assistant who could identify minerals, Guettard persuaded Lavoisier to join him on his geological survey, which lasted until 1766.

In their travels through the French countryside, Lavoisier paid particular attention to water supplies and to their chemical contents. One mineral that particularly interested him was gypsum, popularly known as 'plaster of Paris' because it was used for plastering the walls of Parisian houses. Why, Lavoisier wondered, did the gypsum have to be heated before it could be applied as a plaster? Since water could be driven from the plaster by further heating, it seemed that the water could be 'fixed' into the composition of this and other minerals – a phenomenon that Rouelle had already termed 'water of crystallization'. He then showed that it was the loss of some of the fixed water that explained the transformation of gypsum into plaster by heating. Lavoisier was to find the idea of 'fixation' significant.

Although Guettard's geological map of France was never published and Lavoisier's geological work remained largely unknown to his contemporaries, the work on gypsum was presented to the Academy of Sciences in February 1765, when Lavoisier was twenty-two. With a clear, ambitious eye on being elected to the Academy, the year before he had entered the Academy's competition for an economical way of lighting Parisian streets. (This was some forty years before coal gas began to be used for this purpose.) Although his involved, meticulous study of the illuminating powers of candles and oil and pieces of lighting apparatus did not win him first prize when the adjudication was made in 1766, his report was judged the best theoretical treatment. King Louis XV ordered that the young man should be given a special medal.

Thus by 1766, this ambitious man had succeeded in bringing his name before the small world of Parisian intellectuals. In the same year, two years before he reached his legal majority of 25, Lavoisier's father made a large inheritance over to him. To further his complete financial independence, in 1768 Lavoisier purchased a share in the Ferme Générale, a private finance company that the government employed to collect taxes on tobacco, salt and imported goods in exchange for paying the State a fixed sum of money each year. Members received a salary plus expenses, together with a ten per cent interest on the sum they had invested in the company. Such a tax system was clearly open to abuse; consequently, the *fermiers* were universally disliked and were to reap the dire consequences of their membership of the company during the French Revolution. All the evidence suggests that Lavoisier's motives in joining the company were purely financial and that, as political events moved later, he strove actively to rid the system of corruption and fraud. Unfortunately, Lavoisier's later suggestion that the *fermiers* should beat the smugglers by building a wall around Paris for customs surveillance was to lead to hostility towards him, as may be gathered from the punning aphorism 'Le mur murent Paris fait Paris murmurant' (The wall enclosing Paris made Paris mutter).

In 1771, at the age of twenty-eight, Lavoisier further cemented his membership of the Ferme Générale by marrying the fourteen-year-old daughter of a fellow member of the company, Marie-Anne Pierrette Paultze (1758–1836). Despite their difference of age and their childlessness, their marriage was an extremely happy one. Marie-Anne became her husband's secretary and personal assistant. She learned English (which Lavoisier never learned to read) and translated papers by Priestley and Cavendish for him, as well as an *Essay on Phlogiston* by the Irish chemist, Richard Kirwan. The latter was then subjected to a critical anti-phlogistic commentary by Lavoisier and his friends, which actually led to Kirwan's conversion. She also took lessons from the great artist, Louis David, in order to be able to engrave the extensive illustrations of chemical apparatus that appeared in Lavoisier's *Elements*. David, in turn, portrayed the Lavoisiers together.

Madame Lavoisier was also hostess at weekly gatherings of Lavoisier's scientific friends – a role she continued after his execution. It was through such continuing social activities in her widowhood that she met the American physicist, Benjamin Thompson (1753–1814), better known as Count Rumford, whose experiments on the heat produced during the boring of cannon had led him to question the validity of Lavoisier's caloric theory of heat. After rejecting the suits of Charles Blagden and Pierre du Pont (whose son, Irénée, was to found the huge American chemical company), widow Lavoisier married Rumford in 1805; but they soon proved incompatible and quickly separated. Madame Lavoisier is a good example of how, before the time when they enjoyed opportunities to engage in higher education and in independent scientific research, women played a discrete, but essential, role in the development of science. At a time when the well-off could afford domestic servants, wives and sisters had abundant leisure to help their scientifically inclined fathers, husbands and brothers in their researches.

As a rich and talented man, Lavoisier was an obvious candidate for election to the prestigious Academy of Sciences. Unlike the Royal Society, whose Fellows have always been non-salaried, the French Academy of Sciences was composed of eighteen working 'academicians' or *pensionnaires*. As civil servants, they were paid by the French government (until 1793, by the Crown) to advise the State and to report on any official questions put to them as a body. There were also a dozen honorary members drawn from the nobility and clergy, a dozen working, but unpaid, 'associates' (*associée*) and, to complete the pecking order, a further dozen unpaid assistants (*élèves* or *adjoints*). The Academy also made room for its retired pensioners and for foreign honorary associates.

Because of its tight restriction on the number of salaried members, and of members generally, election to the Academy was a prestigious event in the career of a French scientist. This accolade was in contrast to Britain's Royal Society, which allowed relatively easy access to its fellowship by those with wealth or social status as well as those with scientific talent; consequently, its fellowship lacked prestige. Indeed, until its election procedures were reformed in 1847, fellowship of the Royal Society was not necessarily the mark of scientific distinction that it is today.

The three working grades of the Académie, together with its aristocratic honorary membership, clearly reflected the rigid hierarchical structure of eighteenth-century French society. In practice, the pensioners were allocated between the six sciences of mathematics, astronomy, mechanics, chemistry, botany and anatomy (or medicine). Biology and physics were added under Lavoisier's directorship of the Académie in 1785. Like the Nobel prizes today, such a distribution frequently prevented the election of a deserving candidate because the most appropriate scientific section was full. There was also a tendency to elect or to promote on grounds of seniority rather than merit. Because membership was restricted, vacancies often led to intense lobbying for positions, factionalism, ill-feeling and sometimes (as with Lavoisier's election as an *associé* in 1772) to the bending of rules. The repeated failure of the revolutionary, Jean-Paul Marat, who fancied himself an expert chemist, to gain admission in the 1780s, led him and others to oppose the Academy. Its close association with Royal patronage and its reflection of the 'corrupt' hierarchical structure of the *ancien régime* in any case made it inevitable that it would be suppressed by the revolutionary government in August 1793.

Although, as was to be expected for one so brash and young, Lavoisier failed on his first attempt to join the Academy in 1766, by a modest bending of the rules to create an extra vacancy for him, he was successfully admitted to the lowest rank of assistant chemist in 1768. His chief sponsor described him as 'a young man of excellent repute, high intellect and clear mind whose considerable fortune permits him to devote himself wholly to science'. Any fears that his membership of the tax company would interfere with his role as academician were probably repressed by the thought that he would be able to entertain on a lavish scale!

Much of Lavoisier's fortune was probably spent on the best scientific apparatus that money could buy. Some of his apparatus was unique and so complex that his followers were forced to simplify his experimental procedures and demonstrations in order to verify their validity. It should not be thought from this that Lavoisier threw money away on instruments unnecessarily. For example, when measuring the quantity of oxygen liberated from lead calx in 1774, he found that traditional glass retorts were unusable because the lead attacked the glass; clay retorts gave similarly erroneous readings because of their porosity; hence for precise volumetric measurements Lavoisier was forced to design and have made an airtight iron retort. Expense was justified, then, because of the new standard of precision that Lavoisier demanded in chemistry. In the *Traité* he recognized that economies and simplifications would be possible, 'but this ought by no means to be attempted at the expense of application, or much less of accuracy'.

Lavoisier was to be a loyal servant of the Academy, by helping to prepare its official reports on a whole range of subjects including – to select from one biographer's page-long list – the water supply of Paris, prisons, hypnotism, food adulteration, the Montgolfier hydrogen balloon, bleaching, ceramics, the manufacture of gunpowder, the storage of fresh water on ships, dyeing, inks, the rusting of iron, the manufacture of glass and the respiration of insects. It has been pointed out that, without an ethic of service, such as was entailed in a centralized Royalist state, a privileged citizen such as Lavoisier would have had no incentive to involve himself in such a 'dirty' subject as chemistry.

THE CHEMISTRY OF AIR

The problem of the Parisian water supply came to Lavoisier's attention during the year of his election to the Academy when the purity of water brought to Paris by an open canal was questioned. The test for the potability of water involved evaporating it to dryness in order to determine its solid content. But the use of this technique reminded academicians, including Lavoisier, of the long tradition in the history of chemistry that water could be transmuted into earth. Obviously, if this were the case, the determination of the solid content 'dissolved' in water would reveal nothing about its purity.

As we have seen, the transmutation of water into earth had been a basic principle of Aristotle's theory of the four elements, and a crucial, experimental, factor in van Helmont's decision that water was the unique element and basis of all things. Although by the 1760s most chemists could no longer credit that such an apparently simple pure substance as water could be transmuted into an incredibly large number of complicated solid materials, it was seriously argued by a German chemist, Johann Eller, in 1746 that water could be changed into both earth and air by the action of fire or phlogiston. For Eller this was evidence that there were only two elements, fire and water. The active element of fire acted on passive water to produce all other substances.

It seems clear from the design of Lavoisier's experiment on the distillaton of water, which he began in October

1768, that he suspected that the earth described in Eller's experiment (which he probably read about in Venel's article on 'water' in the fifth volume of the *Encyclopédie* in 1755) was really derived from the glass of the apparatus by a leaching effect. By weighing the apparatus before and afterwards, and also weighing the water before and after heating continuously for three months, Lavoisier showed that the weight of 'earth' formed was more or less equal to the weight loss of the apparatus. Intriguingly, Lavoisier did not clinch his quantitative argument by analysing the materials in the sediment and showing that they were identical to those in glass. Moreover, since the correlation of weights was not exact, some room for doubt remained until two decades later when Lavoisier showed that water was composed of hydrogen and oxygen.

Enough had been done, however, to convince Lavoisier that Eller's contention that water could be transmuted into earth was nonsense. This was reported to the Academy in 1770. He also surmised, under the influence of Venel's views on the chemical dissolution of air in liquids and solids, that there was a more plausible explanation of water's apparent change into vapour or air when heated – namely, that heat, when combined with water and other fluids, might expand their parts into an aerial condition. Conversely, when air was stripped of its heat it lost its voluminous free aerial state and collapsed into, or was 'fixed' into, a solid or liquid condition, just as Stephen Hales had found in the 1720s when analysing the air content of minerals and vegetables.

Lavoisier recorded these ideas in an unpublished essay on the nature of air in 1772. Here was the basis for a theory of gases – though at this juncture Lavoisier knew nothing at all of the work of Priestley and others on pneumatic chemistry. He was also, not surprisingly, still interpreting his model of the gaseous state in terms of phlogiston. When air was fixed[1]:

... there had to be a simultaneous release of phlogiston or the matter of fire; likewise when we want to release fixed air, we can succeed only by providing the quantity of fire matter, of phlogiston, necessary for the existence of the gaseous state [*l'état de fluide en vapeurs*].

Lavoisier was now clear that there were three distinct states of matter[2]:

All bodies in nature present themselves to us in three different states. Some are solid like stones, earth, salts, and metals. Others are fluid like water, mercury, spirits of wine; and others finally are in a third state which I shall call the state of expansion or of vapours, such as water when one heats it above the boiling point. The same body can pass successively through each of these states, and in order to make this phenomenon occur it is necessary only to combine it with a greater or lesser quantity of the matter of fire.

Moreover, it followed from the fact that metals disengaged 'air' when they were calcined, that metals contained fixed air:

metal $\quad\quad$ + heat → calx + air

[calx + matter of air] $\quad$ [φ] $\quad\quad$ [matter of air + φ]

Apparatus for the preparation, collection and study of gases was a necessary factor in the chemical revolution. It was not until 1727 that Stephen Hales hit upon a way to isolate the 'air' produced from a heated solid. In order to estimate as accurately as possible the amount of 'air' produced and to remove any impurities from it, Hales 'washed' his airs by passing them through water before collecting them in a suspended vessel by the downward displacement of water.

Hales, like John Mayow in the seventeenth century, still thought in terms of a unique air element, but Joseph Black's demonstration that 'fixed air' (carbon dioxide) was different from ordinary air encouraged Henry Cavendish, Joseph Priestley and others to develop Hales' apparatus to study different varieties of air – or gases, as Lavoisier was to call them. An incentive here was the invention of soda water by Priestley, which encouraged interest in the potentially health-giving properties of artificial mineral waters generally. In 1765, while investigating spa waters, the English doctor, William Brownrigg, invented a simple shelf with a central hole to support a receiving flask or gas holder. This creation of the 'pneumatic trough' enabled gas samples to be transferred from one container to another and for gases to join solids and liquids on the chemical balance sheet.

Joseph Priestley (1733–1804) is surely one of the most engaging figures in the history of science. The son of a Yorkshire Congregational weaver and cloth-dresser, Priestley was trained for the Nonconformist ministry at a Dissenting academy in Daventry. Like most Nonconformist academies of the period, this taught a wider curriculum than the universities that included the sciences. After serving a string of ministries, where his theological views became increasingly Unitarian, and a teaching post at the famous Warrington Academy, in 1773 Priestley became the librarian and household tutor of William Petty, the second Earl of Shelburne who, while Secretary of State in Chatham's cabinet, had opposed George III's aggressive policy towards American colonists. Already the author of innumerable educational works, in 1767 Priestley had published a *History and Present State of Electricity*, which launched him upon a part-time career in science. While minister of a Presbyterian congregation at Leeds, and living next door to a brewery, Priestley had begun investigating the preparation and properties of airs. Under Shelburne's patronage, Priestley had the necessary leisure to prepare some five volumes containing detailed accounts of these experiments on airs, as well as a number of theological works. There was a connection here in that Priestley was attempting to explore the relationship between matter and spirit.

In 1780, retaining a life annuity from Shelburne, Priestley returned to the ministry at Birmingham's New Meeting. Here he found convivial philosophical and scientific company in the Lunar Society composed of rising industrialists and intellectuals such as Mathew Boulton, James Watt, Josiah Wedgwood and Erasmus Darwin. Although its members were united in their support for the American War of Independence and for the initial stages of the French Revolution, it was Priestley the preacher-orator who was publicly identified with radical criticism of English politics and the discrimination against Dissenters. In 1791 a 'Church and King' mob destroyed Priestley's home and chapel, forcing him to flee to London. Although he was eventually compensated for the loss of his property, in 1794 he decided to emigrate and to join two of his sons in America.

Here he was warmly welcomed in Philadelphia, where he was offered the Chair of Chemistry at the University of Pennsylvania. Instead, Priestley moved to Northumberland, in rural Pennsylvania, where he hoped to found an academy for the sons and daughters of political refugees who would join him there. It did not work out and Priestley spent his declining years cut off by distance from European, and even American, intelligence, and fighting a rearguard action against Lavoisier's chemistry in his fascinating *Considerations on the Doctrine of Phlogiston* (1796). Although outmanoeuvred by Lavoisier, Priestley lived on in two ways. His young executor, Thomas Cooper (1759–1839), a fellow refugee from English politics, acquired sufficient up-to-date knowledge of chemistry from studying in Priestley's library and laboratory to become one of America's leading chemical educators. A century after Priestley's discovery of oxygen, in August 1874, a national meeting of chemists, gathered at his home in Northumberland (now a Priestley Museum), decided to create the American Chemical Society.

It was Cavendish who began the collection of water-soluble gases over mercury, but Priestley who brought their study and manipulation to perfection. Curiously, believing that chemistry, like physics, required expensive and complicated instruments, Lavoisier only rarely used the pneumatic trough; instead, he developed an expensive and sophisticated gasometer. A good third of Lavoisier's *Elements of Chemistry* was devoted to chemical apparatus. Until the appearance of Michael Faraday's *Chemical Manipulation* in 1827, Lavoisier's descriptions remained the bible of instrumentation and chemical manipulative techniques.

In the spring of 1772, Lavoisier read an essay on phlogiston by a Dijon lawyer and part-time chemist, Louis-Bernard Guyton de Morveau (hereafter Guyton) (1737–1816). In a brilliantly designed experimental investigation, Guyton showed that all his tested metals *increased* in weight when they were roasted in air; and since he still believed that their combustibility was caused by a loss of phlogiston, he saved the phenomena by supposing that phlogiston was so light a substance that it 'buoyed' up the bodies that contained it. Its loss during decomposition therefore caused an increase of weight. Most academicians, including Lavoisier, thought Guyton's explanation absurd. Following his previous reflections on the role of air, Lavoisier speculated immediately that a more likely explanation was that, somehow, air was being 'fixed' during the combustion and that this air was the cause of the increase in weight. It followed that 'fixed air' should be released when calces were decomposed – just as Hales' earlier experiments in *Vegetable Staticks* had suggested.

One final *Encyclopédie* article seems to have influenced Lavoisier decisively at this juncture. This was an essay on 'expansibility' published in the sixth volume in 1756 by another pupil of Rouelle's, the philosopher and civil servant, Jacques Turgot. Like Lavoisier, Turgot combined a career of public service with spare-time research in chemistry. But he never published his reflections (or if he did so, he did it anonymously), and we only know of his interesting thoughts from his private correspondence. Turgot arrived independently at the same solution as Lavoisier, namely that Guyton's experiments could be explained as due to the fixing of air. He had actually learned of Guyton's work before Lavoisier in August 1771. In a private letter to Condorcet, Turgot noted[3]:

The air, a ponderable substance which constantly enters into the state of a vapour or expansive fluid according to the degree of heat contained, but which is also capable of uniting with all the other principles of bodies and forming in that state part of the constitution of different compounds ... this air combines or separates in different chemical reactions because of a greater or lesser affinity that it has for the principles to which it was attached or with those that one presents to it.

Given that Lavoisier was party to the same intellectual influences as Turgot, it was not surprising that they should have reached the same conclusions. Whether Lavoisier was aware or not of Turgot's thoughts, he took pains constantly to preserve priority of the idea that it was air that was fixed in calcination, rather than liberated, as he had first thought earlier in 1772. If air was an expanded fluid combined with phlogiston, as Turgot's *Encyclopédie* article had suggested, then the phlogiston released during combustion (the process of 'fixing air') would explain the heat and light generated during the reaction. It followed that heat and light came from the air, not the metal as the Stahlians had always maintained:

$$\text{metal} + \quad \text{air} \quad \rightarrow \quad \text{calx} \quad + \text{heat/light}$$
$$\text{[matter of air} + \phi] \quad \text{[metal} + \text{matter of air]} \quad [\phi]$$

Lavoisier was able to verify this in October 1772 by using a large burning lens belonging to the Academy. When litharge (an oxide of lead) was roasted with charcoal, an enormous volume of 'air' was, indeed, liberated. In order to investigate this phenomenon more closely, and in order to ensure priority after finding that sulphur and phosphorus also gained in weight when burned in air, Lavoisier deposited a sealed account of his findings in the archives of the Academy, which he allowed to be opened in May 1773[4]:

> What is observed in the combustion of sulphur and phosphorus, may take place also with all bodies which acquire weight by combustion and calcination, and I am persuaded that the augmentation of the metallic calces is owing to the same cause. Experiment has completely confirmed my conjectures: I have carried out a reduction of litharge in a closed vessel, with the apparatus of Hales, and I have observed that there is disengaged at the moment of passage from the calx to the metal, a considerable quantity of air, and that this air forms a volume a thousand times as great as the quantity of litharge employed. This discovery seems to me one of the most interesting that has been made since Stahl and as it is difficult in conversation with friends not to drop a hint of something that would set them on the right track, I thought I ought to make the present deposition into the hand of the Secretary of the Academy until I make my experiments public.

In committing himself to the hypothesis that ordinary air was responsible for combustion and for the increased weight of burning bodies, Lavoisier demonstrated that he was ignorant of most contemporary chemical work on the many different kinds of airs that can be produced in chemical reactions. In Scotland, a decade earlier in 1756, Joseph Black had succeeded in demonstrating that what we call 'carbonates' (e.g. magnesium carbonate) contained a fixed air (carbon dioxide) that was fundamentally different in its properties from ordinary atmospheric air. Unlike ordinary air, for example, it turned lime water milky and it would not support combustion. Black's work did not achieve much publicity or publication in France until March 1773. A few years later, Henry Cavendish studied the properties of a light inflammable air (hydrogen), which he prepared by adding dilute sulphuric acid to iron. These experiments were to stimulate the astonishing industry of Priestley who, between 1770 and 1800, prepared and differentiated some twenty new 'airs'. These included (in our terminology) the oxides of sulphur and nitrogen, carbon monoxide, hydrogen chloride and oxygen. The fact that most of these were 'acid' airs was to be, for Lavoisier, an intriguing phenomenon.

Hence, although largely unknown to Lavoisier in 1772, there was already considerable evidence that atmospheric air was a complex body and that it would be by no means sufficient to claim that air alone was responsible for combustion. Lavoisier seems to have been aware of his chemical ignorance. He wrote in his laboratory notebook on 20 February 1773:

> I have felt bound to look upon all that has been done before me as merely suggestive. I have proposed to repeat it all with new safeguards, in order to link our knowledge of the air that goes into combination or is liberated from substances, with other acquired knowledge, and to form a theory.

And, with the firm and confident intention of bringing about, in his own prescient words, 'a revolution of physics and chemistry', he spent the whole of 1773 studying the history of chemistry – reading everything that chemists had ever said about air or airs since the seventeenth century and repeating their experiments 'with new safeguards'. His results were summarized in *Opuscules physiques et chimiques* published in January 1774.

Ironically, far from clarifying his ideas, his new-found familiarity with the work of pneumatic chemists now led him to suppose that carbon dioxide, 'fixed air', in the atmosphere was responsible for the burning of metals and the increase of their weight. This was not unreasonable, and the explanation for Lavoisier's misconception will be clear. Most calces (that is, oxides) can only be reduced to the metal by burning them with the reducing agent, charcoal (C), when the gas carbon dioxide is produced:

calx + C → metal + fixed air

It was easy to suppose, therefore, that the same fixed air was responsible for combustion:

metal + fixed air → calx

As he noted plaintively in a notebook[5]:

> I have sometimes created an objection against my own system of metallic reduction which consists of the following: lime [CaO] according to me is a calcareous earth deprived of air; the metallic calces, on the contrary, are metals saturated with air. However, both produce a similar effect on alkalies, they render them caustic.

Obviously, Lavoisier needed to distinguish between air and fixed air, carbon dioxide. It should be noted how this reasoning was based upon the complementarity of analysis and synthesis. If two simple substances could be combined together to form a compound, then, in principle, it ought to be possible to decompose the compound back into the same components. Lavoisier was to find a perfect example of this in the red calx of mercury, a substance that caused him to revise his original hypothesis significantly.

Two things caused Lavoisier to change his mind. First, his attention was drawn by Pierre Bayen, a Parisian pharmacist, to the fact that, when heated, the calx of mercury (HgO), a remedy used in the treatment of venereal disease, decomposed directly into the metal mercury without the addition of charcoal. No fixed air was evolved. As Bayen pointed out, this observation made it difficult to see how the phlogiston theory could be right. Here was a calx regenerating the metal without the aid of phlogiston in the form of charcoal! Secondly, the mercury calx had also come to the attention of Priestley because of a contemporary uncertainty whether the red calx produced by heating nitrated mercury was the same as that produced when mercury was heated in air. In August 1774 he heated the calx in an enclosed vessel and collected a new 'dephlogisticated air', which he found, after some months of confusing it with nitrous oxide, supported combustion far better than ordinary air did. Unknown to Priestley the Swedish apothecary, Scheele, had already isolated what he called 'fire air' from a variety of oxides and carbonates in the years 1771–2. But Scheele, working in isolation even in Sweden, did not help to shape Lavoisier's views in the same way that Bayen and Priestley did. These experiments were reported directly to Lavoisier by Priestley when he was on a visit to Paris during October 1774, but he also published an account of the new air at the end of the same year.

Bayen's and Priestley's observations, together with his own experiments with mercuric oxide, caused Lavoisier to revise his hypothesis of 1774. In April 1775, Lavoisier read a paper to the Academy of Sciences 'on the principle which combines with metals during calcination and increases their weight' in which, still more confused, he identified the principle of combustion with 'pure air' and *not* any particular constituent of the air. This new hypothesis, which was published in May, was seen by Priestley. The latter, realizing that Lavoisier had not quite grasped that the 'dephlogisticated air' generated from the calx of mercury was a constituent part of ordinary air, gently put him right in another book he published at the end of 1775. This, together with further experiments of his own, finally led Lavoisier to the oxygen theory of combustion. In revising the so-called 'Easter Memoir' for publication in 1778, and in an essay published the year before, he wrote as follows:

> The principle which unites with metals during calcina- tion, which increases their weight and which is a

constituent part of the calx is: nothing else than the
healthiest and purest part of air, which after entering
into combination with a metal, [can be] set free again;
and emerge in an eminently respirable condition,
more suited than atmospheric air to support ignition
and combustion.

Because this 'eminently respirable air' burned carbon
to form the weak acid, carbon dioxide, while non-metals
generally formed acidic oxides, Lavoisier called the new
substance *oxygen*, meaning 'acid former'[6]:

... the purest air, eminently respirable air, is the
principle constituting acidity; this principle is common
to all acids.

The etymology, for those who no longer read Greek, is
still obvious in the German word for oxygen, *Sauerstoff*. By
this Lavoisier did not mean that all substances containing
oxygen were acids, otherwise he would have been hard
pressed to explain the basic reactions of metallic oxides.
Oxygen was only a potentially acidifying principle; for its
actualization, a non-metal had also to be present. Although
soon destined to be overthrown as a model of acidity,
this was the first chemical theory of acidity; it suggested
a general way of preparing acids (by the oxidation of
non-metals with nitric acid) and, in terms of 'degrees
of oxidation', it provided for the time a very reasonable
explanation of the different reactivities of acids.

By 1779 half of Lavoisier's revolution was over. Oxygen
gas was a ponderable element containing heat (or caloric,
as Lavoisier called it to avoid the word phlogiston), which
kept it in a gaseous state. On reacting with metals and
non-metals, the heat was released and the oxygen element
affixed to the substance, causing it to increase in weight.
Metals formed basic oxides, non-metals formed acids (acid
anhydrides). In respiration, oxygen burned the carbon in
foodstuffs to form the carbon dioxide exhaled in breath,

while the heat released was the source of an animal's internal warmth. (Lavoisier and the mathematician, Pierre Simon Laplace, demonstrated this quantitatively with a guinea pig in 1783 – the origin of the expression 'to be a guinea pig'.) Respiration was a slow form of combustion. The non-respirable part of air, mofette or azote, later called nitrogen, was exhaled unaltered.

At first glance, in this new theory, phlogiston seems to be transferred from a combustible, such as a metal, to oxygen gas. In reality, although Lavoisier waited some years before articulating the new theory in detail, there were major differences between caloric and phlogiston. Caloric was absorbed or emitted during most chemical reactions, not just those of oxidation and reduction; like Boerhaave's etherial 'fiery vigour', it was present in all substances, whereas phlogiston was usually supposed absent from incombustibles; when added to a substance, caloric caused expansion or a change of state from solid to liquid, or liquid to gas; above all, caloric could be measured thermometrically, whereas phlogiston could not.

Nevertheless, Lavoisier did not challenge the old theory until 1785.

The principal reason why Lavoisier was unable to suggest in 1777 that chemists would be better off by abandoning the theory of phlogiston was that only this theory could explain why an inflammable air (in fact hydrogen) was evolved when a metal was treated with an acid, but no air was evolved when the basic oxide of the same metal was used. If the metal contained phlogiston, the explanation, as Cavendish suggested, was simple:

$$
\begin{array}{ccccccc}
\text{metal} & + & \text{acid} & \rightarrow & \text{salt} & + & \text{inflammable air} \\
\text{[calx} + \phi] & & \text{solution} & & \text{solution} & & [\phi] \\
\text{calx} & + & \text{acid} & \rightarrow & \text{salt} & & \\
& & & & \text{solution} & &
\end{array}
$$

Lavoisier's gas theory gave no hint why these two reactions behaved differently. Similarly, his belief that all non-metals burned to form an acid oxide appeared to be weakened by the case of hydrogen, which seemed to produce no identifiable product. If this seems odd, it must be borne in mind that moisture is so ubiquitous in chemical reactions that it must have been easy to ignore and overlook its presence.

It was Priestley who first noticed the presence of water when air and 'inflammable air' (hydrogen) were sparked together by means of an electrostatic machine. He described this observation to Cavendish in 1781, who repeated the experiment and reported it to the Royal Society in 1784:

> By the experiments . . . it appeared that when inflam-mable air and common air are exploded in a proper proportion, almost all of the inflammable air, and near one-fifth of the common air, lose their elasticity and are condensed into dew. It appears that this dew is plain water.

Cavendish told Priestley verbally about his findings. Priestley then told his Birmingham friend James Watt, the instrument maker, who independently of Cavendish arrived at the conclusion that water must be a compound body of 'pure air and phlogiston'. Watt made no statement to this effect until after Lavoisier announced his own experiments and conclusions, which themselves were triggered by references to Cavendish's experiments that were made by Cavendish's secretary, Charles Blagden, during a visit to Paris in 1783. Watt then claimed priority, but found himself forestalled by the prior appearance of Cavendish's paper.

Much ink and rhetoric was to be spilled over rival claims – Cavendish or Watt in England, or Lavoisier in France. In fact, it was only Lavoisier who interpreted water as a compound of hydrogen and oxygen; Watt agreed, albeit within the conceptual framework of the phlogiston theory, while Cavendish instead viewed water as the product of the elimination of phlogiston from hydrogen and oxygen:

hydrogen   oxygen

[water + φ] + [water − φ] →   water

In other words, for Cavendish this was not a synthesis of water at all; instead, as a phlogistonist, he preferred to see inflammable air as water saturated with phlogiston and oxygen as water deprived of this substance. When placed together the product was water, which remained for him a simple substance. As we shall see, it was this same experiment of Cavendish's that led him to record that nitrous acid was also produced – owing to the combination of oxygen with nitrogen – but that a small bubble of uncondensed air remained (chapter 9).

For Lavoisier, however, Cavendish's work was evidence that water was not an element. Assisted by the mathematical physicist, Simon Laplace (1749–1827), he quickly showed that water could be synthesized by burning inflammable air and oxygen together in a closed vessel; and with the help of another assistant, Jean-Baptiste Meusnier, he showed that steam could be decomposed by passing it over red-hot iron. Priestley was never convinced by this analysis, arguing that the hydrogen could have come from the iron, not the water. The matter was settled (though never for Priestley) in 1789 when two Dutch chemists, Adriaan van Troostwijk (1752–1837) and Jan Deiman (1743–1808), synthesized water from its elements with an electric spark. The same electric machine could be used to decompose water into its constituents. Once current electricity became available with the voltaic cell in 1800, this same experiment was to usher in the age of electrochemistry. Given Lavoisier's commitment to oxygen as an acid former, it is not surprising that he should have been so quick off the mark if Cavendish's work provided him with an essential clue; in fact Lavoisier's notebooks show that after 1781 he had repeatedly burned hydrogen in search of an acidic product.

Whatever the merits of the claim that Lavoisier was the

first to grasp that water was a compound of hydrogen (meaning 'water producer') and oxygen, the important point was that he could now explain why metals dissolved in acids to produce hydrogen. This, he asserted, came not from the metal (as the phlogistonists claimed, some even identifying phlogiston with inflammable air), but from the water in which the acid oxide was dissolved:

metal + acid → metal oxide + hydrogen

[metal oxide] [acid oxide + water]   [acid oxide]

calx + acid →   salt solution

[metal oxide + acid oxide + water]

Although it was left to Davy and others to develop the point, the understanding of water also helped lead to a hydrogen theory of acidity.

THE CHEMICAL REVOLUTION

Lavoisier was now in a position to bring about a revolution in chemistry by ridding it of phlogiston and by introducing a new theory of composition. His first move in this direction was made in 1785 in an essay attacking the concept of phlogiston. Since all chemical phenomena were explicable without its aid, it seemed highly improbable that the substance existed. He concluded:

All these reflections confirm what I have advanced, what I set out to prove [in 1773] and what I am going to repeat again. Chemists have made phlogiston a vague principle, which is not strictly defined and which consequently fits all the explanations demanded of it. Sometimes it has weight, sometimes it has not; sometimes it is free fire, sometimes it is fire combined with an earth; sometimes it passes through the pores of vessels, sometimes they are impenetrable to it. It explains at once causticity and non-causticity, transparency and opacity, colour and the absence

112 · *Elements of Chemistry*

of colours. It is a veritable Proteus that changes its form every instant!

By collaborating with younger assistants, whom he gradually converted to his way of interpreting combustion, acidity, respiration and other chemical phenomena, and by twice-weekly soirées at his home for visiting scientists where demonstrations and discussions could be held, Lavoisier gradually won over a devoted group of anti-phlogistonists. Finding that editorial control of the monthly *Journal de physique* had been seized by a phlogistonist, Lavoisier and his young disciple, Pierre Adet (1763–1834), founded their own journal, the *Annales de Chimie* in April 1789. The editorial board soon included most converts to the new system: Guyton, Berthollet, Fourcroy, G. Monge, A. Seguin and N. L. Vauquelin. This is still a leading chemical periodical. While Director of the Academy of Sciences from 1785, Lavoisier was also able to alter its structure so that the chemistry section consisted only of anti-phlogistonists.

It is significant that Lavoisier's new theory was one of acidity as much as combustion. Stahlian chemists had not foreseen that there were many types of 'airs' or gases, but, as Priestley's career shows, they actually had little difficulty in conceptualizing them within a phlogistic framework. The appearance of gases also led to a modification in the phlogistic theory of acidity. According to Stahl, vitriolic acid (sulphuric acid) was the universal acid – 'universal' in the sense of being the acid principle present in all substances that displayed acidic properties. However, with the discovery of fixed air, several chemists, led by Bergman in Sweden, had decided that this, not vitriol, was the true universal acid. Such a view was argued vociferously by the Italian, Marsilio Landriani, during the 1770s and 1780s. Landriani claimed to have found evidence that fixed air was a component of all three mineral acids as well as the growing number of vegetable acids such as formic, acetic, tartaric and saccharic acids. It was really this theory of acidity that Lavoisier had to challenge in the 1780s.

Lavoisier's method was to challenge the theory as displayed in the French translation undertaken by his wife of Richard Kirwan's *Essay on Phlogiston and the Constitution of Acids.* He was able to convince Kirwan that the acidity of fixed air was sufficiently explained by the fact that it contained oxygen. The irony here was that Lavoisier's new theory retained in effect the Stahlian notion of a universal acid principle in the form of oxygen. In practice, the explanation of properties by principles was not to last much longer after the advent of Dalton's atomism and the evidence that not all acids contained oxygen.

The demonstration by Hales that fixed air formed part of the composition of many solids and liquids had also given rise to speculations that this air was vital to vegetable and animal metabolisms. For example, in 1764, an Irish physician, David Macbride, concluded that 'this air, extensively united with every part of our body', served to prevent putrefaction, a prime example of which was the disease called scurvy. The recognized value of fresh vegetables in inhibiting scurvy, he suggested, was due to their fermentative powers. The fixed air that they produced during digestion served to prevent putrefaction inside the body.

It was this suggestion that inspired Priestley to investigate the effects of airs on living organisms – a programme of research that was to form the basis of Davy's earliest research some time later. Initially, in 1772, Priestley concluded that fixed air was fatal to vegetable life, but this was probably due to the fact that he used impure carbon dioxide from a brewery, or that he was using it in excess. Others, including Priestley's Mancunian friend, Thomas Henry, found the opposite, that flowers thrived in fixed air. It was while repeating these findings that Priestley discovered that, in the presence of sunlight (but not otherwise), plants growing in water, such as sprigs of mint, gave off dephlogisticated air. This had already been anticipated in 1779 by Jan Ingenhousz (1730–99) who, together with Jean Senebier (1742–1809) in Geneva, laid the foundations of a theory of photosynthesis in plants.

Three particularly important converts to the new chemistry were Guyton (whose work had earlier catalysed Lavoisier's interest in combustion), Claude-Louis Berthollet (1748–1822) and Antoine Fourcroy (1755–1809). Berthollet's conversion to Lavoisier's views seems to have arisen because of his own perturbation at the weight changes involved in calcination, to which Guyton had drawn attention. In his *Observations sur l'air* (1776), Berthollet explained acidity and weight changes in combustion by means of fixed air, and otherwise incorporated Lavoisier's work on oxygen into the phlogiston framework. It was the analysis of water, together with increasing personal contact with Lavoisier in the Academy, where they found themselves drawing up joint referees' reports, that converted Berthollet to Lavoisier's position by 1785. In fact, Berthollet always had certain reservations. In particular, he never accepted the oxygen theory of acidity, and his investigation of chlorine (first prepared by Scheele in 1774 and assumed by Lavoisier to be oxygenated muriatic acid) seemed to confirm his doubts. In later life he also firmly rejected the notion that chemical properties could be explained in terms of property-bearing principles.

Fourcroy was Lavoisier's principal interpreter to the younger generation. His ten-volume *Système des connaissances chimiques* (1800) codified and organized chemistry for the next fifty years around the concepts of elements, acids, bases and salts. Fourcroy saw this structure not only as 'consolidating the pneumatic doctrine' but as affording 'incalculable advantage(s)' for learning and understanding chemistry (see Table 3.1).

While still a phlogistonist, Guyton was much exercised by the inconsistent nomenclature of chemists and pharmacists. Unlike botany and zoology, whose terminology had been revised and made more precise earlier in the century by the

TABLE 3.1 *The contents of Fourcroy's* Système des connaissances chimiques *(1800) arranged by classes of substances.*

Class	Volume
1. Undecomposed or simple bodies	1
2. Burned bodies; oxides or acids	2
3. Salifiable bases; earths and alkalis	2
4. Salts	3, 4
5. Metals and metal salts containing an excess of acid (although belonging to class 1, these were dealt with separately because of their number and importance)	5, 6
6. Minerals	6
7. Vegetable compounds	7, 8
8. Animal compounds	9, 10

Swede, Karl Linnaeus, chemical language remained crude and confusing. In 1782 Guyton made a series of proposals for the systematization of chemical language.

Alchemical and chemical texts written before the end of the eighteenth century can be difficult to read because of the absence of any common chemical language. Greek, Hebrew, Arabic and Latin words are found, there was widespread use of analogy in naming chemicals or in referring to chemical processes, and the same substance might receive a different name according to the place from which it was derived (for example, *Aquila coelestis* for ammonia; 'father and mother' for sulphur and mercury; 'gestation' as a metaphor for reaction; 'butter of antimony' for deliquescent antimony chloride; and 'Spanish green' for copper acetate). Names might also be based upon smell, taste, consistency, crystalline form, colour, properties or uses. Although several of these names have lingered on as 'trivial' names (which have even had to be reintroduced in organic chemistry in the twentieth century because systematic names are too long to speak), Lavoisier and his colleagues in 1797 decided to systematize nomenclature by basing it solely upon what was known of a substance's composition. Since the theory of composition chosen was the oxygen system, Lavoisier's suggestions were initially resisted by phlogistonists; adoption of the new nomenclature involved a commitment to the new chemistry.

Following the inspiration of Linnaeus, Guyton suggested in 1782 that chemical language should be based upon three principles: substances should have one fixed name; names ought to reflect composition when known (and if unknown, they should be non-committal); and names should generally be chosen from Greek and Latin roots and be euphonious with the French language. In 1787, Guyton, together with Lavoisier, Berthollet and Fourcroy, published the 300-page *Méthode de nomenclature chimique*, which appeared in English and German translations a year later. One-third of this book consisted of a dictionary, which enabled the reader to identify the new name of a substance from its older one. For example, 'oil of vitriol' became 'sulphuric acid' and its salts 'sulphates' instead of 'vitriols'; 'flowers of zinc' became 'zinc oxide'.

Perhaps the most significant assumption in the nomenclature was that substances that could not be decomposed were simple (i.e. elements), and that their names should form the basis of the entire nomenclature. Thus the elements oxygen and sulphur would combine to form either sulphurous or sulphuric acids depending on the quantity of oxygen combined. These acids when combined with metallic oxides would form the two groups of salts, sulphites and sulphates. In the case of what later became called hydrochloric acid, Lavoisier assumed that he was dealing with an oxide of an unknown element, murium. Because of some confusion over the differences between hypochlorous and hydrochloric acids, in Lavoisier's nomenclature hydrochloric acid became muriatic acid and the future chlorine was 'oxygenated muriatic acid'. The issue of whether the latter contained oxygen at all was to be the subject of fierce debate between Davy, Gay-Lussac and Berzelius during the three decades following Lavoisier's death.

The French system also included suggestions by Hassenfratz and Adet for ways in which chemicals could be symbolized by geometrical patterns: elements were straight lines at various inclinations, metals were circles, alkalis were triangles. However, such symbols were inconvenient for printers and never became widely established; a more convenient system was to be devised by Berzelius a quarter of a century later.

During the eighteenth century some chemists had turned their minds to quantification and the possible role of mathematics in chemistry. On the whole, most chemists agreed with Macquer that chemistry was insufficiently advanced to be treated mathematically. Although he believed, correctly as it turned out, that the weight of bodies bore some relationship to chemical properties and reactions, the emphasis on affinity suggested that the project was hopeless. Nevertheless, Lavoisier, inspired by the writings of the philosopher, Condillac, believed fervently that algebra was the language to which scientific statements should aspire[7]:

> We think only through the medium of words. Languages are true analytical methods. Algebra, which is adapted to its purpose in every species of expression, in the most simple, most exact, and best manner possible, is at the same time a language and an analytical method. The art of reasoning is nothing more than a language well arranged.

In a paper on the composition of water published in 1785, Lavoisier stressed that his work was based upon repeated measuring and weighing experiments 'without which neither physics nor chemistry can any longer admit anything whatever'. Again, in another essay analysing the way metals dissolve in acids, Lavoisier used the Hassenfratz–Adet symbols:

118 · *Elements of Chemistry*

In order to show at a glance the results of what happens in the solution of metals, I have constituted formulae of a kind that could at first be taken for algebraic formulae, but which do not have the same object and which do not derive from the same principles; we are still very far from being able to obtain mathematical precision in chemistry and therefore I beg you to consider the formulae that I am going to give you only as simple annotations, the object of which is to ease the workings of the mind.

The important point here was that Lavoisier used symbols to denote both constitution and quantity. Although he did not use an equals sign, he had effectively hit upon the idea of a chemical equation. As we shall see, once Berzelius' symbols became firmly established in the 1830s, chemists began almost immediately to use equations to represent chemical reactions.

While producing the *Méthode de nomenclature chimique* with Lavoisier and the others, Guyton was converted to the new chemistry. Because the new language was also the vehicle of anti-phlogiston chemistry, it aroused much opposition. Nevertheless, through translation, it rapidly became and still remains the international language of chemistry.

TABLE 3.2   *Lavoisier's 'elements' or 'simple substances'.*

Light	Sulphur	Antimony	Mercury	Lime
Caloric	Phosphorus	Arsenic	Molybdena	Magnesia
Oxygen	Charcoal	Bismuth	Nickel	Barytes
Azote	Muriatic radical	Cobalt	Platina	Argilla
Hydrogen	Fluoric radical	Copper	Silver	(alumina)
	Boracic radical	Gold	Tin	Silex
		Iron	Tungsten	(silica)
		Lead	Zinc	
		Manganese		

Lavoisier's final piece of propaganda for the new chemistry was a textbook published in 1789 called *Traité élémentaire de chimie (An Elementary Treatise on Chemistry).* Together with Fourcroy's larger text (published in 1801), this became a model for chemical instruction for several decades. In it Lavoisier defined the chemical element pragmatically and operationally as any substance that could not be analysed by chemical means. Such a definition was already a commonplace in mineralogical chemistry and metallurgy, where the analytical definition of simple substances had become the basis of mineralogical classification in the hands of J. H. Pott, A. F. Cronstedt and T. Bergman. It was for this reason that Lavoisier's list of 33 basic substances bore some resemblance to the headings of the columns in traditional affinity tables. Lavoisier's list included substances such as barytes, magnesia and silica, which later proved to be compound bodies.

After discussing the oxygen theory in part I of the *Traité*, he discussed their preparation and properties, their oxides and then their salts formed from acidic and basic oxides in part II. Caloric disengaged from oxygen explained the heat and light of combustion. It has been said that the elements formed the bricks while his new views on calcination and combustion formed the blueprint. The *Traité* itself formed a dualistic compositional edifice. Whenever an acidic earth and metal oxide (or earth) combined, they produced a salt, the oxygen they shared constituting a bond of union between them. As was appropriate for an elementary text, part III, a good third of the book, was devoted to chemical instrumentation and to the art of practical chemistry.

Lavoisier's table of elements did not include the alkalis, soda and potash, even though these had not been decomposed. Why were they excluded from his pragmatic definition of simple substances? Two reasons have been suggested. In the first place, he was prepared to violate his criterion because of the chemical analogy between these two alkalis and 'ammonia', which Berthollet had decomposed into azote (nitrogen) and hydrogen in 1785. Lavoisier was so confident that soda and potash would be similarly decomposed into nitrogen and other unknown principles, that he withheld them from the table of simple substances. On the other hand, although confident that muriatic acid was also compound, because the evidence was not so strong as for the alkalis, he included it in the list of elements. While we may admire Lavoisier's prescience – Davy was to decompose soda and potash in 1808 – this was a disturbing violation of his own pragmatism. What guarantee did the chemist have that any of Lavoisier's simple substances were really simple? As we shall see, Lavoisier's operational approach caused a century of uncertainty and helped to revive the fortunes of the ancient idea of primary matter.

A second explanation is more subtle. Lavoisier's simple substances were arranged into four groups (see table 3.2). Three of the groups contained the six non-metals and seventeen metals then known, both of which were readily oxidizable and acidifiable, together with the group of five simple 'earths'. The remaining group was light, caloric, oxygen, azote (nitrogen) and hydrogen. At first glance these elements appear to have nothing in common, but the heading Lavoisier gave them, 'simple substances belonging to all the kingdoms of nature, which may be considered the elements of bodies', provides the clue. Lavoisier probably saw these five elements as 'principles' that conveyed fundamental generic properties. Light was evidently a fundamental principle of vegetable chemistry; caloric was a principle of heat and expansibility; oxygen was the principle of acidity; hydrogen was the principle of water that played a fundamental role in all three kingdoms of Nature; and nitrogen was a principle of alkalinity. If the 1789 list of elements is compared with a preliminary list he published in 1787, it is found that azote was moved from its original position among the non-metals. It is not unlikely that this change was connected with the decomposition of ammonia and Lavoisier's decision that soda and potash were compounds of 'alcaligne', a nitrogenous principle of alkalinity.

If this interpretation is correct, it illustrates again the role of continuity in Lavoisier's revolutionary chemistry. Although we cannot now know if this was the position Lavoisier held – a position that was in any case subject to refutation and modification within a few years – it is intriguing to notice that organic chemists (beginning with Liebig) came to see certain elements, namely hydrogen, oxygen, carbon and nitrogen, as the 'universal' or 'typical' elements of mineral, animal and vegetable chemistry. It was on the basis of this that Gerhardt and Hofmann were to build a 'type theory' or organic classification and from which Mendeleev was to learn to classify a greatly extended list of elements in 1869.

By the mid 1790s the anti-phlogistonian camp had triumphed and only a few prominent chemists, such as Joseph Priestley, continued as significant critics. Unfortunately, by then the French Revolution had put paid to the possibility that Lavoisier would apply his insights to fresh fields of chemistry.

THE AFTERMATH

Although opposition to Lavoisier's chemistry remained strong in Germany for a decade or more, largely for patriotic reasons, and although Cavendish and Priestley never converted, the speed of its uptake is impressive. Much depended, of course, on key teachers. In Germany, Sigismund Hermstadt (1760–1832) translated the *Traité* in 1792, and in the same year Christoph Girtanner (1760–1800) published a survey of Lavoisier's chemistry. At Edinburgh the French-born Joseph Black, who had always taught that phlogiston was a principle of levity, lectured on the new chemistry while not necessarily committing himself to it until 1790. His successor, Thomas Charles

Hope (1766–1844), ensured that large audiences of medical students learned the new theory after 1787. Scottish opposition seems to have been largely confined to geology, where James Hutton found phlogiston more accommodating to his theory that it was solar light and his need for a plutonic ignitor in the absence of oxygen deep inside the earth; and animal physiology, where, despite Lavoisier's view of animal heat as the natural exothermic product of burning food inside the body, Adair Crawford developed a complex mechanism involving air, heat, blood, phlogiston and the specific heat capacity of blood.

Despite Lavoisier's continued research after 1789 – for example, he began some promising work on the analysis of organic substances – he found his official activities as an academician and *fermier* taking up more and more of his time as the Revolution, which broke out in that year, created more and more technical and administrative problems.

When Lavoisier was born, France was still a monarchy and power lay firmly in the hands of the Crown and aristocracy together with the Roman Catholic church. These two powerful and sometimes corrupt groups, or Estates, which were virtually exempt from taxation, were the landlords of the majority Third Estate of peasant farmers, merchants, teachers and bankers from whom France's wealth was derived. Agricultural depression, a rise in population and a succession of expensive wars (including France's intervention in the American War of Independence in 1778) led France towards bankruptcy in the 1780s. The only solution to this seemed to be to introduce a more equitable system of taxation, which, in turn, involved the reformation of political structure, including the reduction of King Louis XVI's despotic powers.

On 14 July 1789 revolution broke out with the storming of the Bastille prison in Paris. In fear of their lives, Crown and aristocracy renounced their privileges, while a National Assembly composed of the Third Estate drew up the Declaration of the Rights of Man. National unity was short-lived, however, as the more radical Jacobins manoeuvred for political power and the downfall of the monarchy. War with Austria and Prussia was to prove the excuse for the King's execution on 21 January 1793. In the period of terror and anarchy that followed, Lavoisier was to lose his life. For, despite his undoubted support for the initial phase of the Revolution and his hard work within the Academy in improving the quality of gunpowder or in devising the metric system in 1790, his services to France and his international reputation were, in the words of one historian, 'as dust in the balance when weighed against his profession as a Fermier-Géneral'. On 24 November 1793 Lavoisier and his fellow shareholders (including his father-in-law) were arrested and charged, ludicrously, with having mixed water and other 'harmful' ingredients in tobacco, charging excessive rates of interest and withholding money owed to the Treasury.

Although later investigations by historians have revealed the worthlessness of these charges, they were more than sufficient in the aptly named 'Age of Terror' to ensure the death penalty. Even so, there is some evidence that Lavoisier, alone of the *fermiers*, might have escaped but for the evidence that he corresponded with France's political enemies abroad. The fact that his correspondence was scientific did not, in the eyes of his enemies, rule out the possibility that Lavoisier was engaged in counter-revolutionary activities with overseas friends.

Lavoisier was guillotined on 8 May 1794. The mathematician Lagrange commented, 'It required only a moment to sever his head, and probably one hundred years will not suffice to produce another like it.' Following the centenary of the French Revolution in the 1890s, a public statue was erected to commemorate Lavoisier. Some years later it was discovered that the sculptor had copied the face of the philosopher, Condorcet, the Secretary of the Academy of Sciences during Lavoisier's last years. Lack of money prevented alterations being made and, in any case, the French argued pragmatically that all men in wigs looked alike anyway. The statue was melted down during the Second World War and has never been replaced. Lavoisier's real memorial is chemistry itself.

CONCLUSION

A rational reconstruction of what seem to have been the essential features of the 'chemical revolution' would draw attention to six necessary and sufficient conditions. First, it was necessary to accept that the element, air, did participate in chemical reactions. This was first firmly established by Hales in 1727 and accepted in France by Rouelle and Venel. Although Hales tried to explain the fixation of air by solids by appealing to the attractions and repulsions of Newtonian particle theory, there was no satisfactory explanation for its change of state. Secondly, it was necessary to abandon the belief that air was elementary. This was essentially the contribution of the British school of pneumatic chemists. Beginning in 1754 with Black, who showed that the 'fixed air' released from *magnesia alba* had different properties from ordinary air, and continuing through Rutherford, Cavendish and Priestley, it was found possible to prepare and study some twenty or more 'factitious airs' that were different from ordinary air in properties and density. Their preparation and study were made possible by the development of apparatus by Hales for washing air, the pneumatic trough, thus extending the traditional 'alchemical' apparatus of furnaces and still-heads that had hitherto largely sufficed in chemical investigations. Whether factitious airs were merely modifications of air depending upon the amounts of phlogiston they contained, or distinct chemical species in an aerial condition, or the expanded particles of solid and liquid substances, was decided by Lavoisier's development of a model of the gaseous state.

The concept of a gas was a necessary third condition for the reconstruction of chemistry. By imaging the aerial state as due to the expansion of solids and liquids by heat, or caloric, Lavoisier brought chemistry closer to physics and made possible the later adoption of the kinetic theory of heat and the development of chemical thermodynamics. The balance pan had always been the principal tool of assayers and pharmacists, while the conservation of mass and matter had always been implicit in chemists' rejection of alchemical transmutation and their commitment to chemistry as the art of analysis and synthesis. With the conceptualization of a whole new dimension of gaseous-state chemistry, however, it was necessary that chemical analysis and book-keeping should always account for the aerial state. Here was a fourth necessary condition that raised problems for phlogistonists when Guyton demonstrated conclusively in 1771 that metals increased in weight when they were calcined in air. Many historians, like Henry Guerlac, saw this as the 'crucial' condition for effecting a chemical revolution and the event that set Lavoisier on his path to glory.

Largely for pedagogic reasons, generations of historians, chemistry teachers and philosophers of science have interpreted the chemical revolution as hinging upon rival interpretations of combustion – phlogiston theory versus oxygen theory. More recently, those historians who have seen Lavoisier's chemistry as literally an anti-phlogistic chemistry have had a wider agenda than combustion in mind. In particular, it now seems clear that the interpretations of acidity was a major issue for Lavoisier and the phlogistonists. Indeed, it could be argued that, once Lavoisier had the concept of a gas, it was the issue of acidity, not combustion, that led him to oxygen – as its very name implies. The transformation of ideas of acidity, therefore, formed a fifth factor in the production of a new chemistry.

Finally, and not least, the sixth necessary condition was a new theory of chemical composition and organization of matter in which acids and bases were composed from oxygen and elements operationally defined as the substances that chemists had not succeeded in analysing into simpler bodies. Oxygen formed the glue or bond of dualistic union between acid and base to form salts, which then compounded in unknown ways to form minerals. To make this more articulate and to avoid confusion with the unnecessary thought patterns of phlogiston chemistry, a new language was required – one that reflected composition and instantly told a reader what a substance was compounded from. After 1787 chemists, in effect, spoke French, and this underlined the new chemistry as a French achievement.

Although he pretended at the beginning of the *Traité* that it had been his intent to reform the language of chemistry that had forced the reform of chemistry itself, it was clearly because he had done the latter that a new language of composition was needed. As historians have stressed, the new nomenclature was Lavoisier's theoretical system. He justified its adoption in terms of Condillac's empirical philosophy that a well constructed language based upon precise observation and rationally constructed in the algebraic way of equal balances of known and unknown would serve as a tool of analysis and synthesis.

Observation itself involved chemical apparatus – not merely the balance, but an array of eudiometers, gasometers, combustion globes and ice calorimeters, which would enable precise quantitative data to be assembled. In this way chemical science would approach the model of the experimental physicists that Lavoisier clearly admired and with whose advocates he frequently collaborated.

This last point has led some historians to question whether Lavoisier was a chemist at all and whether the chemical revolution was instead the result of a brief and useful invasion of chemistry by French physicists. Others, while admitting the influence of experimental physics on Lavoisier's approach, continue to stress Lavoisier's participation in a long French tradition of investigative analysis of acids and salts to which he added a gaseous dimension. Even Lavoisier's choice of apparatus, though imbued with a care and precision lacking in his predecessors' work, was hallmarked by the investigative procedures of a long line of analytical and pharmaceutical chemistry. All historians agree, however, that until about 1772, when events triggered a definite programme of pneumatic and acid research in his mind, Lavoisier's research was pretty random and dull, as if he were casting around for a subject ('une belle carrière d'expériences à faire') that would make him famous. Seizing the opportunity, the right moment, is often the mark of greatness in science. Priestley and Scheele believed that science progressed through the immediate communication of raw discoveries and 'ingenious simplicity'. Lavoisier's way, to Priestley's annoyance, was to work within a system and to theorize in a new language that legislated phlogiston out of existence.

Like Darwin's *Origin of Species*, Lavoisier's *Traité* was a hastily written abstract or prolegomena to a much larger work he intended to write that would have included a discussion of affinity, and animal and vegetable chemistry. Like Darwin's book, it was all the more readable and influential for being short and introductory. If more information was required, Fourcroy's encyclopedic text and its many English and German imitations soon provided reference and instruction. But this was not the end of the chemical revolution. To complete it, Lavoisier's elements had to be reunited with the older corpuscular traditions of Boyle and Newton. This was to be the contribution of John Dalton.

A New System of Chemical Philosophy

Atoms are round bits of wood invented by
Mr Dalton.
(H. E. Roscoe, 1887)

Before Dalton came on the scene, chemistry can hardly be described as an exact science. A wealth of empirical facts had been established and many theories had been erected that bound them together, not the least impressive of which were Lavoisier's new dualistic views of chemical composition and his explanations of combustion and acidity. Most of eighteenth-century chemical activity had been qualitative. Despite the Newtonian dream of quantifying the forces of attraction between chemical substances and the compilation of elaborate tables of chemical affinity, no powerful quantitative generalizations had emerged. Although these empirically derived affinity relations often allowed the course of a particular chemical reaction to be predicted, it was not possible to say, or to calculate, *how much* of each ingredient was needed to perform a reaction successfully and most economically. Dalton's chemical atomic theory, and the laws of chemical combination that were explained by it, were to make such calculations and estimates possible – to the benefit of efficient analysis, synthesis and chemical manufacture.

As a consequence of the power of the corpuscular philosophy, by the end of the seventeenth century it had become a regulative principle, or self-evident truth, that all matter was ultimately composed of microscopic 'solid, hard, impenetrable, moveable' particles. As we saw in the second chapter, however, such ultimate descriptions of Nature were of little use to practical chemists, who preferred to adopt a number of empirically derived elementary substances as the basic 'stuffs' of chemical investigation. Lavoisier's famous definition of the element in 1789 made it clear that speculations concerning the ultimate particles or atoms of matter were a waste of time; chemistry was to be based on experimental knowledge[1]:

> All that can be said upon the number and nature of elements [i.e. in an Aristotelian or Paracelsian sense] is, in my opinion, confined to discussions entirely of a metaphysical nature. It is an unsolvable problem capable of an infinity of solutions none of which probably accord with Nature. I shall be content, therefore, in saying that if by the term *elements* we mean to express those simple and indivisible atoms of which matter is composed, it seems extremely probable we know nothing at all about them; however, if instead we apply the term *elements* or *principles of bodies*, to express our idea of the last point which analysis is capable of reaching, we must admit as elements, all the substances into which we are capable, by any means, to reduce bodies during decomposition. Not that we can be certain that these substances we consider as simple may not be compounded of two, or even a greater number of principles; but, since these principles cannot be separated, or rather since we have not hitherto discovered the means of separating them, they act with regard to us as simple substances, and we ought never to suppose them compounded until experiment and observation has proved them to be so.

For the same reason, although Dalton believed in physical

atoms, most of his interpreters were content with a theory of *chemical* atoms – the 'minima' of the experimentally defined elements. Whether these chemical atoms were themselves composed from homogeneous or heterogeneous physical atoms was to go beyond the evidence of pure stoichiometry.

Stoichiometry was a subject invented by the German chemist Jeremias Richter (1762–1807), who had studied mathematics with the great philosopher, Immanuel Kant, at the University of Königsberg, and for whom he wrote a doctoral thesis on the use of mathematics in chemistry. This was, in practice, nothing grander than an account of the determination of specific gravities, from which Richter calculated the supposed weights of phlogiston in substances. Just as Kepler had searched for mathematical relations and harmony in astronomical data gathered by Tycho Brahe, so Richter spent his spare time as a chemical analyst in the Berlin porcelain works searching for arithmetical relations in chemistry. As Partington noted sardonically, Richter spent his entire life finding 'regularities among the combining proportions where nature had not provided any'.

The exception was his discovery in 1792, while investigating double decompositions, that, because neutral products were formed, the reactants must 'have amongst themselves a certain fixed ratio of mass'.

> If, e.g., the components of two neutral compounds are $A-a$, a and $B-b$, b, then the mass ratios of the new neutral compounds produced by double decomposition are unchangeably $A-a{:}b$ and $B-b{:}a$.

This law of neutrality was a special case of what came to be known as the law of reciprocal proportions. Richter referred to the study of these ratios as 'stoichiometry' and went on to examine how a fixed weight of an acid was neutralized by different weights of various bases. This investigation led him to claim, erroneously, that combining proportions formed arithmetical and geometrical series. It was Ernst Fischer, a Berlin physicist, who, when translating Berthollet's *Recherches sur la lois de l'affinité* into German in 1802, pointed out that Richter's results could be tabulated to show equivalent weights of a series of acids and bases. If 1000 parts of sulphuric acid was taken as a standard and the base equivalents needed for neutralization arranged in one column, and the amounts of other acids needed to neutralize these bases in another, then an analyst could gather at a glance how much of a particular base would neutralize a particular acid:

Bases		Acids	
Alumina	525	Fluoric	427
Magnesia	615	Carbonic	577
Ammonia	672	Muriatic	712

Thus, 672 equivalents of ammonia neutralized 427 of fluoric, 577 of carbonic and 712 of muriatic acids. Analysts now had a definite method of controlling the accuracy of their work and of calculating beforehand the composition of salts under investigation.

Dalton's atomic theory was to provide a rational explanation for these regularities. There has been some debate as to whether Dalton was directly influenced by Richter. He certainly knew of Richter's investigations, but probably not until after he had derived his own explanation from other sources.

DALTON'S 'NEW SYSTEM'

What was 'new' in John Dalton's *A New System of Chemical Philosophy*? The obvious reply seems to be the introduction of chemical atomism – the idea that each of Lavoisier's undecompounded bodies was composed from a myriad of homogeneous atoms, each element's atom differing slightly in mass. The surprising thing, however, is that only one chapter of barely five pages in the 916-page treatise was devoted to the epoch-making theme. These five pages, together with four explanatory plates, appeared at the end of the first part of the *New System*, which was published in Manchester in 1808 and dedicated to the professors and students of the Universities of Edinburgh and Glasgow, who had heard Dalton lecture on 'Heat and the Chemical Elements' in 1807, and to the members of Manchester's Literary and Philosophical Society, who had 'uniformly promoted' Dalton's researches. A second, continuously paginated, part of the *New System*, dedicated to Humphry Davy and William Henry, was published in 1810. Astonishingly, the third part, labelled as a second volume, did not appear until 1827. Even then the design was incomplete and a promised final part concerned with 'complex compounds' was never published.

Dalton's apparent dilatoriness is easily explained by the fact that he earned his living as a private elementary teacher, which left him little time for the exacting experimental work and evidence upon which he based the *New System*. For it was a 'new' approach that he was taking, familiar though his scheme has become. Dalton recognized his innovation as being a 'doctrine of heat and general principles of chemical synthesis'. A theory of mixed gases, which he developed in 1802, led him in 1803 to 'new views' on heat as a factor in the way elements (or, rather, atoms) combined together, a process he referred to as 'chemical synthesis'. The fact that chemical compounds, or compound atoms (molecules), might be binary, ternary, quaternary, and so on up to a maximum of twelve atoms, gave Dalton a structure for his text: a detailed experimental examination of heat and the gaseous state, a theory of atomism and combination, which included the measure of atomic mass as a relative atomic weight, followed by a detailed account of the properties of the known elements, their binary combinations, ternary combinations and so on. Thus, although the exegesis of the atomic theory was limited to five pages, the whole of the *New System* was, in fact, imbued with a new stoichiometric approach to chemistry – that elements compounded together in fixed proportions by weight because of attractions and repulsions between the tiny particles of heat and elementary forms that made up laboratory chemicals. Inevitably, because Dalton was a slow worker and unable to spare time from teaching for research and writing, it was left largely to others, notably Thomas Thomson and Jacob Berzelius, to exploit the full consequences of Dalton's insight.

DALTON'S LIFE

John Dalton (1766–1844) was born at Eaglesfield in Cumbria, the son of a weaver, and, like most contemporary members of the Society of Friends, was a man of some learning. The highly efficient Quaker network of schooling and informal education ensured that Dalton received a good schooling; he himself began to teach village schoolchildren when he reached the age of twelve. In his teens he mastered sufficient geometry to be able to study Newton's *Principia*. At the age of fifteen, Dalton and his brother moved to Kendall, in the English Lake District, where they acquired their own school, which offered Greek, Latin, French and mathematics. At Kendall, Dalton was befriended by the blind Quaker scholar, John Gough, who further encouraged Dalton's mathematical abilities and knowledge of Newtonian natural philosophy, including the work of Boyle and Boerhaave. The constant stimulation of rapidly changing weather conditions among the mountains and lakes of Westmorland and Cumberland (present-day Cumbria) interested him in meteorology. The records he kept over a five-year period were published in *Meteorological Essays* in 1793. In the same year, on Gough's recommendation, Dalton moved to Manchester as tutor in mathematics and natural philosophy at New College, a Dissenting academy that had begun its distinguished life elsewhere as the Warrington Academy. Here Priestley had taught between 1761 and 1767.

Although Manchester New College moved to York in 1803, Dalton, finding Manchester congenial, spent the remainder of his life there as a private teacher and industrial consultant. Not only was there an abundance of paid work in Manchester for private tutors because of a rising industrial middle class (Dalton's most famous pupil was a brewer's son, the physicist James Prescott Joule), but the presence of the Literary and Philosophical Society, whose Secretary Dalton became in 1800 and President from 1817 until his death, proved a congenial venue for the presentation and articulation of his scientific work. Dalton read his first scientific paper, on self-diagnosed colour blindness (long after known as Daltonism) to the Society in 1794. He went on reading papers and reports to the Society up to his death. From about 1815 onwards, however, Dalton failed more and more to keep pace with the chemical literature. In 1839 he suffered the ignominy of having a paper of his on phosphates and arsenates rejected by the Royal Society on the grounds that a superior account of these salts had already been published by Thomas Graham.

Despite such failings, Dalton retained the respect of the chemical and scientific communities. Together with two other Dissenters from Anglicanism, Michael Faraday and Robert Brown, the botanist, and despite the angry opposition of Oxford High Churchmen, Dalton was awarded an honorary degree by Oxford University in 1832. A year later the government awarded him a Civil List pension for life, and in 1834 Edinburgh University gave him another honorary degree. His final accolade was a public funeral in Manchester. Even if we grant that some of these honours served a secondary purpose of drawing attention to scientists and their contribution to culture in Victorian

Britain, we are bound to ask: What did Dalton do to merit such public honours?

THE ATOMIC THEORY

The straightforward answer is that Dalton rendered intelligible the many hundreds of quantitative analyses of substances that were recorded in the chemical literature and that he provided a model for the long-standing assumption made by chemists that compounds were formed from the combination of constant amounts of their constituents. He regarded chemical reactions as the reshuffling of atoms into new clusters (or molecules), these atoms and compound atoms being pictured in a homely way as little solid balls surrounded by a variable atmosphere of heat.

This statement, however, tells us little about Dalton's originality; after all, the atomic theory of matter had existed for a good two-thousand years before Dalton's birth. In Ireland, at the end of the eighteenth century, William Higgins (1762–1825) had used atomism in his *A Comparative View of the Phlogiston and Antiphlogiston Theories* (1789) to refute the phlogistic views of his countryman, Richard Kirwan. Higgins later claimed that Dalton had stolen his ideas – an inherently implausible notion that, nevertheless, has been supported by several historians in the past. In fact, Dalton's originality lay in solving the problem of what philosophers of science have called *transduction*; he derived a way of calculating the relative weights of the ultimate particles of matter from observations and measurements that were feasible in the laboratory. Although atomic particles could never be individually weighed or seen or touched, Dalton provided a 'calculus of chemical measurement' that for the first time in history married the theory of atoms with tangible reality. He had transduced what had hitherto been a theoretical entity by building a bridge between experimental data and hypothetical atoms.

Dalton's calculus involved four basic, but reasonable, assumptions. First, it was supposed that all matter was composed of solid and indivisible atoms. Unlike Newton's and Priestley's particles, Dalton's atoms contained no inner spaces. They were completely incompressible. On the other hand, recognizing the plausibility of Lavoisier's caloric model of changes of phase, Dalton supposed that atoms were surrounded by an atmosphere of heat, the quantity of which differed according to the solid, liquid or gaseous phase of the aggregate of atoms. A gas, for example, possessed a larger atmosphere of heat than the same matter in the solid state. Secondly, Dalton assumed, as generations of analysts before him had done,. that substances (and hence their atoms) were indestructible and preserved their identities in all chemical reactions. If this law of conservation of mass and of the elements was not assumed, of course, transmutation would be possible and chemists would return to the dark days of alchemy. Thirdly, in view of Lavoisier's operational definition of elements, Dalton assumed that there were as many different kinds of atoms as there were elements. Unlike Boyle and Newton, for Dalton there was not one primary, homogeneous 'stuff'; rather, particles of hydrogen differed from particles of oxygen and all the particles that had so far been defined as elementary.

In these three assumptions Dalton moved away completely from the tradition of eighteenth-century matter theory, which had emphasized the identity of matter and of all material substances. In so doing. Dalton intimately bound his kind of atomism to the question of how elements were to be defined. In a final assumption, he proposed to do something that neither Lavoisier nor Higgins had thought of doing, namely to rid metaphysical atomism of its intangibleness by fixing a determinable property to it, that of relative atomic weight. To perform this transductive trick, Dalton had to make a number of simple assumptions about how atoms would combine to form compound atoms, the process he termed chemical synthesis. In the simplest possible case, 'when only one combination of two bodies can be obtained, it must be presumed to be a *binary* one, unless some cause appear to the contrary'. In other words, although substances A and B might combine to form A_2B_2, it is simpler to assume that they will usually form just AB. Similarly, if 'two combinations are observed, they must be presumed to be a *binary* and a *ternary*':

$$A + 2B = AB_2 \qquad \text{or} \qquad 2A + B = A_2B$$

Dalton made similar rules for cases of three and four compounds of the same elements, and pointed out that the rules of synthesis also applied to the combination of compounds:

$$CD + DE = CD_2E \qquad \text{etc.}$$

These assumptions of simplicity of composition, which, as we shall see, had a theoretical justification, have long since been replaced by different criteria. Although they led to many erroneous results, the assumptions proved fruitful since they allowed relative atomic weights to be calculated. Two examples, both given by Dalton, will suffice.

Hydrogen and oxygen were known to form water. Before 1815, when hydrogen peroxide was discovered, this was the only known compound of these two gases. Dalton quite properly assumed, therefore, that they formed a binary compound; in present-day symbols:

$$H + O = HO$$

From Humboldt and Gay-Lussac's analyses of water, it was known that 87.4 parts by weight of oxygen combined with 12.6 parts of hydrogen to form water. This ratio, H : O :: 12.6 : 87.4, must also be the ratio of the individual weights of hydrogen and oxygen atoms that make up the binary atom of water. Since hydrogen is the lightest substance known, it made sense to adopt it as a standard and to compare all heavier chemical objects with it. If the hydrogen atom is defined as having a weight of 1, the relative atomic weight of an atom of oxygen will be roughly 7. (Dalton always rounded calculations up or down to the nearest whole number.) Similarly, Dalton assumed ammonia to be a binary compound of azote (nitrogen) and hydrogen. From Berthollet's analysis he calculated the relative atomic weight of nitrogen to be 5 or, after further experiments in 1810, 6.

TABLE 4.1   *Some of Dalton's relative weights.*

	1803	1808	1810
Hydrogen	1	1	1
Azote	4.2	5	5
Carbon	4.3	5	5.4
Oxygen	5.5	7	7
Phosphorus	7.2	9	9
Sulphur	14.4	13	13
Iron		38	50
Zinc		56	56
Copper		56	56
Lead		95	95

Dalton was well aware of the arbitrary nature of his rules of simplicity. In the second part of the *New System* in 1810 he allowed the possibility that water could be a ternary compound, in which case oxygen would be 14 times heavier than hydrogen; or, if two atoms of oxygen were combined with one of hydrogen, oxygen's atomic weight would be 3.5. This uncertainty was to plague chemists for another fifty years.

From the beginning, Dalton symbolized his atoms[2]:

   . . . by a small circle, with some distinctive mark; and the combinations consist in the juxta-position of two or more of these.

The synthesis of water and ammonia were represented as:

Such symbols referred to the *atom* and were therefore conceptually very different from alchemical symbols or those of Hassenfratz and Adet, which only had a hazy or qualitative meaning. Earlier symbols had been a shorthand; Dalton's circles conveyed a theoretical meaning as well as being a convenient abbreviation.

Dalton was never to become reconciled to the symbols introduced by Berzelius, even though he himself used alphabetical abbreviations within circles for elements such as iron, sulphur, copper and lead. In 1837, soon after the British Association for the Advancement of Science had persuaded British chemists to adopt Berzelius' symbols, Dalton wrote a testimonial for Thomas Graham's application for the Chair of Chemistry at University College London.

> Berzelius's symbols are horrifying: a young student in chemistry might as soon learn Hebrew as make himself acquainted with them. They appear like a chaos of atoms. Why not put them together in some sort of order? . . . [They] equally perplex the adepts of science, discourage the learner, as well as to cloud the beauty and simplicity of the Atomic Theory.

Clearly Dalton felt strongly about his innovation and was prepared to criticize a professorial candidate with one hand while supporting him with another. Indeed, Dalton suffered the first of his two strokes in April 1837 after angrily discussing symbols with a visitor.

Dalton's symbols did not survive, mainly one suspects because they were an additional printing expense, but both they, as well as Berzelius' simplification, encouraged people to acquire a faith in the reality of chemical atoms and enabled chemists to visualize relatively complex chemical reactions. As in mathematics, chemistry could advance only to a certain degree without an adequate symbolism for its deeper study. Between them, Lavoisier and Dalton completed a revolution in the language of chemistry.

Dalton's hieroglyphs also reveal that he had a three-dimensional geometrical model of combination in mind. When three or more particles combined, he conceived that like particles stationed themselves as far apart as possible. This conception offers not only an important clue concerning the origins of Dalton's atomic theory, but an explanation of his opposition to the notion derived from the *volumetric* combination of gases that equal volumes contained equal numbers of particles.

THE ORIGINS OF DALTON'S THEORY

How did Dalton come to think of weighing atoms? There have been many different attempts by chemists and historians to explain this. Dalton supplied three, mutually inconsistent, accounts of his voyage of discovery. Reconstruction has been made difficult by the fact that most of Dalton's surviving papers were destroyed during the Second World War, and, but for the fact that Henry Roscoe and Arthur Harden quoted from them in a historical study published in 1896, historians would have been hard-pressed for evidence. Although the debate over influences remains unresolved, all historians agree that Dalton must have come to his 'new views' through the study of the physical properties of gases, which in turn depended upon his youthful interest in meteorology. For, once air had been shown to be heterogeneous, and not a homogeneous element, the question arose whether oxygen, nitrogen, carbon dioxide and water vapour were chemically combined in air (perhaps a compound actually dissolved in the water vapour?) or merely mixed together. The fact that atmospheric air appeared to be homogeneous and that its gaseous components were not stratified according to their specific gravities (itself an indication that chemists like Priestley were prepared to think in terms of the specific weights of gas particles long before Dalton) made most late-eighteenth-century chemists believe that atmospheric gases were chemically combined.

Dalton thought differently. His long study of Newton's *Principia* had made him familiar with Newton's demonstration that Boyle's law relating pressure and volume could be derived from a model in which homogeneous air particles were self-repulsive with a power inversely proportional to the distance. As a result of his meteorological studies, Dalton had become convinced by 1793 that water vapour could not possibly be chemically combined in air; instead, it was diffused among the other aerial particles and so freely available for precipitation or condensation as rain or dew. But if water was not chemically combined, why should the other constituents of air be?

If Newton's model of the self-repulsion of air particles was translated into a model of self-repulsive constituents of air, what would be the consequences? Provided particles of one kind did not repel particles of a different gas, as Dalton showed, each gas or vapour would behave as if in a vacuum. The net effect would be a homogeneous mixture as the different gas particles repelled their own kinds. As to the cause of their self-repulsion, Lavoisier's model of a gas supplied a satisfactory candidate: caloric. By imagining that the particles of oxygen, nitrogen, carbon dioxide and water vapour were surrounded by atmospheres of heat, Dalton arrived at a theory of mixed gases and, incidentally, a law of partial pressures that proved essential in quantitative work in gas analysis and barometry.

Dalton's 'New theory of the constitution of mixed aeriform fluids and particularly of the atmosphere' was published in *Nicholson's Journal* in 1801. It proved controversial, but this was no bad thing for Dalton's British and European reputation. Most chemists who believed in the chemical theory of air wondered how it was that caloric

142 · *A New System of Chemical Philosophy*

atmospheres in different particles did not repel one another. Why suppose that there were 'as many distinct *kinds* of repulsive powers, as of gases ... and that heat was not the repulsive power in any one case'?

Dalton's ingenious reply to this difficulty was published in full in the second part of the *New System* and was premised on differences of *size* of gaseous particles, the size being a function of both the atom's volume and the radius of its atmosphere of heat. Using diagrams that look like the later magnetic force diagrams popularized by Faraday, Dalton showed visually that 'no equilibrium can be established by particles of different sizes pressing against each other'. It followed that different particles would 'ignore' one another even when surrounded by the repulsive imponderable of heat. Such a static model remained the only satisfactory explanation of gaseous diffusion, partial pressures and atmospheric homogeneity until it was replaced in the 1850s by the kinetic theory of gases.

As historians of chemistry have shown, this second model of mixed gases, which was dependent on the sizes of atoms, was first developed by Dalton in September 1804, a full year after he had developed the first list of particle weights. The question of *size* offers a clue to his thinking during the previous year.

One of Dalton's few supporters for the first theory of mixed gases was his Mancunian friend, William Henry (1774–1836), the owner of a chemical works for the manufacture of the pharmaceutical, milk of magnesia, used in the treatment of digestive complaints. Henry had at first opposed Dalton, only to be converted when he found that 'water takes up the same volume of condensed gas as of a gas under ordinary pressure'. Henry's law that the solubility of a gas at a given temperature depended upon pressure, which he discovered in 1803, was powerful evidence that solution was a purely mechanical effect. If chemical affinity was not involved, it seemed equally unlikely to be involved in the atmosphere. Moreover, as Henry found, a mixture of gases dissolved in water was 'retained in its place by an atmosphere of no other gas but its own kind'.

Henry's experiments were intriguing. Why, Dalton wondered, did different gases have different solubilities in water? Why were light and elementary gases such as hydrogen and oxygen least soluble, whereas heavier compound gases such as carbon dioxide were very soluble? If his first theory of mixed gases was correct, why should gases have different solubilities? Was solubility proportional to density and complexity? At this stage Dalton clearly thought solubilities were a function of the sizes of particles[3]:

> I am nearly persuaded that the circumstance depends upon the weight and number of the ultimate particles of the several gases: those whose particles are lightest and single being least absorbable, and others more according as they increase in weight and complexity.

One can see how this line of reasoning would lead automatically to 'an inquiry into the relative weights of the ultimate particles of bodies . . . a subject as far as I know, entirely new'. It is important to realize, however, that Dalton really needed to know the weights of particles only because he wanted an estimate of their sizes from the simple relationship, density = weight/volume.

As we have seen, at the end of 1803 Dalton estimated the weights of gas atoms using known chemical analyses and the rule of simplicity. From these he derived a number of atomic volumes and radii, but was unable to find any simple or regular correlation with solubility. Even so, as late as 1810 in the *New System* he continued to record atomic sizes alongside atomic weights.

It was evidently not until 1804 that Dalton realized that relative atomic weights were a useful explanation of the law of constant composition and that the simple rules of chemical synthesis from which he had derived them explained and predicted that, when elements combined to form more than one compound, the weights of one element that combined with a fixed weight of the other were bound to be small whole numbers. For example if

$$A + B = AB \qquad \text{and} \qquad 2A + B = A_2B$$

then the weights of A combined with weight B are in the simple ratio of 1 : 2. Dalton drew attention to the fact that this was the ratio of hydrogen to carbon in methane (CH_4) and ethane (C_2H_4), and that in the difficult and complicated cases of the oxides of nitrogen the ratio of oxygen to nitrogen was 1 : 2 and 1 : 3.

There were a large number of cases of this 'law of multiple proportions' that had been reported in the literature as a result of the dispute between Proust and Berthollet. When Berthollet accompanied Napoleon's expedition to Egypt in 1798, he was surprised to find huge deposits of soda by the shores of salt lakes. Mineralogical analysis showed that the soda arose from a reaction between salt and limestone in the lake bottom, in complete contradiction to the usual laboratory reaction in which soda [sodium carbonate] and calcium chloride reacted to form salt and limestone [calcium carbonate]. He concluded that the enormous concentration of salt in the lakes had forced the reversal of the usual reaction. In other words, the action of mass (concentration) could overcome the usual play of elective affinities between substances. In modern terms, Berthollet had stumbled upon an equilibrium reaction:

$$CaCl_2 + Na_2CO_3 \rightleftharpoons CaCO_3 + 2NaCl$$

It was this awareness of the role of mass in reactions that caused Berthollet during the next few years to challenge the usual implicit presumption of chemists that substances combined together in fixed proportions, or that *constant* saturation proportions always characterized chemical union. Instead, Berthollet proposed that compounds combined together in variable and indefinite proportions, and he pointed to solutions and alloys, and what would today be defined as mixtures, as empirical evidence for his claim.

This radical reconceptualization of composition was immediately challenged by a fellow Frenchman, Joseph-Louis Proust (1754–1826), who worked as an analyst in Spain. In a long series of meticulous analyses and friendly challenges to Berthollet, Proust argued that there was overwhelming evidence that regular compounds were formed from their constituents in fixed and definite proportions. There might well be more than one compound of the same two substances, but their proportions were regular.

Although neither contender gained a definite victory (for Berthollet was perfectly correct in his position over some of the difficult substances like glasses that he examined), by 1810, and in the light of Dalton's theory, it was seen that the laws of definite and multiple proportions offered a securer foundation for quantitative chemistry. For the time being Berthollet's views, which were eventually to illuminate physical chemistry and the theory of semiconductors, served only to confuse and handicap the development of analytical chemistry, which was so beguilingly explained by Dalton's theory.

In 1808 William Hyde Wollaston and Thomas Thomson provided further convincing experimental examples of multiple proportions when they showed that there was a $2 : 1$ ratio of CO_2 in the bicarbonate and carbonate of potassium (viz. $KHCO_3$ or $K_2O.2CO_2.H_2O$ and K_2CO_3 or $K_2O.CO_2$), and, for the same amount of acid in the normal and acid oxalates of potash and strontia, there was double the amount of base in the acid oxalates.

It was in the context of this experimental work with oxalates that Thomson recommended Dalton's chemical atomism, having already briefly referred to it in the third edition of his important textbook, *System of Chemistry*, in 1807. Thomson's initial account was based directly on conversations Thomson had had with Dalton in Manchester in 1804. Soon afterwards Dalton had read an account of his first list of atomic weights in a paper read to the Manchester Literary and Philosophical Society in October 1803 (published with differences in 1805). Thomson was also directly responsible for inviting Dalton to Scotland in 1807 to lecture on his views on air, heat and chemical synthesis to audiences at the Universities of Edinburgh and Glasgow. It was these lectures that led to the *New System*.

Although Dalton's brilliant insight was developed by others, it is worth emphasizing that he retained other imaginative insights that remained undeveloped for decades. In particular, it is clear from surviving remnants that Dalton built models of atoms and compounds in order to illustrate his theory. This model-building followed directly from his first thoughts on mixed gases in 1803[4]:

> When an element A has an affinity for another B, I see no mechanical reason why it should not take as many atoms of B as are presented to it, and can possibly come into contact with it (which may probably be 12 in general) *except so far as the repulsion of the atoms of B among themselves are more than a match for the attraction of an atom of A*. Now this repulsion begins with 2 atoms of B to 1 of A, in which case the 2 atoms of B are diametrically opposed; it increases with 3 atoms of B to 1 of A, in which case the atoms of B are only 120° asunder; with 4 atoms of B it is still greater as the distance is then only 90°; and so on in proportion to the number of atoms. It is evident then from these positions, that, as far as powers of attraction and repulsion are concerned (and we know of no other in chemistry) *binary* compounds must first be formed in the ordinary course of things, then *ternary*, and so on, till the repulsion of the atoms of B (or A, whichever happens to be on the surface of the other), refuse to admit any more.

This statement shows that Dalton's apparently intuitive appeal to a principle of simplicity in chemical synthesis was backed up by a geometrical force model – a model that, in a radically different setting, was to be used by ligand-field theorists a century and a half later. But it was entirely speculative, and, although it gave 'order' to Dalton's symbols, it was not a path that the empirically minded Berzelius was to follow in his own symbolic language.

ELECTRIFYING DALTON'S THEORY

Dalton presented his theory within the context of ideas concerning heat at a time when the chemical world had become excited by the news of galvanic or current electricity. In 1800 the Italian physicist, Alessandro Volta (1774–1827), described his 'voltaic pile' or battery in a paper published by the Royal Society. This simple machine made from a 'pile' or 'battery' of alternating zinc and silver discs gave chemists a powerful new analytical tool. As Davy said later, its use caused great excitement and it acted as 'an alarm-bell to experimenters in every part of Europe'. Almost immediately it was found that the battery would decompose water into its elements. While there was nothing extraordinary about this further confirmation of Lavoisier's chemistry, the puzzling fact was that hydrogen and oxygen were ejected from the water at different poles – the hydrogen at what Volta designated as the negative pole, and the oxygen at the positive pole. Two chemists who particularly concerned themselves with this galvanic phenomenon (the term 'electrolysis' was not coined by Faraday until 1832) were Davy and Berzelius.

Humphry Davy (1778–1829) was born at Penzance in Cornwall and educated locally. Intending to qualify as a doctor, he was apprenticed to a surgeon in 1795 and began to read Lavoisier's *Elements of Chemistry* in French in his spare time. Though ignorant and completely self-taught, like Priestley before him, Davy began to repeat, correct and devise new experiments. Apart from this growing interest in chemistry, he wrote poetry (for this was the era of Romanticism when young men poured forth their individual feelings in verse), he admired the rich Cornish scenery and he fished. Through a friendship with Gregory Watt, the tubercular son of James Watt, Davy came to the attention of Thomas Beddoes, a pupil of Joseph Black and a former lecturer in chemistry at the University of Oxford, who had resigned from 'that place' because of his support for the French Revolution and his suspiciously radical politics. In 1798 Beddoes, convinced that the many gases that Priestley had discovered might prove beneficial in the treatment of tuberculosis (TB) and other urban diseases, founded a subscription-based Pneumatic Institute in Bristol. He persuaded Davy, whom he recognized as a man of talent, to join him as a research assistant. Davy probably still expected to qualify as a doctor, perhaps by saving sufficient money to enter Edinburgh University as a result of this experience. In the event, he became a chemist.

Davy's risky and foolhardy experiments at Bristol, in which he narrowly escaped suffocation on several occasions, brought him fame and notoriety in 1800 when he published his results in *Researches, Chemical and Philosophical; Chiefly Concerning Nitrous Oxide . . . and its Respiration*. None of his inhalations demonstrated chemotherapeutic benefits — though his results with nitrous oxide (laughing gas) were to be the cause of regular student 'saturnalia' in chemical laboratories throughout the nineteenth century. Not until 1846 was the gas used as an anaesthetic. This inhalation research, and some further essays published in 1799, which included an attack on Lavoisier's notion of caloric and the substitution of light for caloric in gaseous oxygen (phosoxygen), brought Davy's name to the attention of another patron, Benjamin Thompson, who had also denied that heat was an imponderable fluid.

Count Rumford, as he is better known, had founded the Royal Institution in London in 1799 as a venue for publicizing ways in which science could help to improve the quality of life of the deserving poor and for the rising middle classes. By 1801 Rumford needed a new Professor of Chemistry. Davy's appointment coincided with the wave of contemporary interest in electrolytic phenomena and, although he lectured, dazzlingly, on many other subjects at the Royal Institution, it was his research on electrochemistry that captured the public's imagination and ensured the middle-class success of the Institution.

By building bigger and more powerful batteries, and by using fused electrolytes rather than electrolytes in solution, Davy confirmed Lavoisier's hunch that soda and potash were not elementary by isolating sodium and potassium in 1807. In the next few years he demonstrated that Lavoisier's alkaline earths were also compounds and prepared calcium, strontium and barium electrolytically. Later still, Davy argued convincingly against the view that muriatic acid contained oxygen, and for the opinion that oxymuriatic acid, which he renamed chlorine, was an undecompounded elementary body – a point supported by his isolation of its conjoiner, iodine, in 1813.

This succession of corrections to Lavoisier's chemistry has led some historians to feel that Davy set out systematically to destroy French chemistry. Indeed, by 1815 he had critically and effectively questioned most of the assumptions of the antiphlogistic chemistry – that acidity was due to oxygen, that properties were due to 'principles' rather than arrangement, that heat was an imponderable fluid rather than a motion of particles, and that Lavoisier's elements were truly elementary. Although Davy was often bold in his speculations and use of analogical reasoning, in stripping Lavoisier's system to its empirical essentials he did not replace it with any grand system of his own, except to suggest that chemical affinity was, in the final analysis, an electrical phenomenon.

In the early 1800s there were two different opinions on the cause of electrolysis. According to the 'contact theory' advocated by Volta, electricity arose from the mere contact of different metals; an imposed liquid merely acted as a conductor. Since this theory did not easily account for the fact that the conducting liquid was always decomposed, the alternative 'chemical theory' argued that it was the chemical decomposition that produced the electric current. Davy found fault with both theories and as so often in the history of science, he drew a compromise: the contact theory explained the 'power of action' of, say, zinc becoming positively charged when placed in contact with copper; this power then disturbed the chemical equilibrium of substances dissolved in water, leading to a 'permanent action' of the voltaic pile. As to the cause of the initial 'power of action', Davy was in no doubt that it was chemical affinity[5]:

> Is not what has been called chemical affinity merely the union or coalescence of particles in naturally opposite states. And are not chemical attractions of particles and electrical attractions of masses owing to one property and governed by one simple law?

If Davy was the first chemist to link chemical reactivity with electrolytic phenomena, it was the Swede, Berzelius, who created an electrical theory of chemistry. Davy had concluded from his long and accurate work on electrolysis that, in general, combustible bodies and bases tended to be released at the negative pole, while oxygen and oxidized bodies were evolved at the positive pole[6]:

> It will be a general expression of the facts in common philosophical language, to say, that hydrogen, the alkaline substances, the metals, and certain metallic oxides, are attracted by negatively metallic surfaces [i.e. electrodes]; and repelled by positively electrified metallic surfaces; and contrariwise, that oxygen and acid substances are attracted by positively electrified metallic surfaces, and repelled by negatively electrified metallic surfaces; and these attractive and repulsive forces are sufficiently energetic to destroy or suspend the usual operation of elective affinity.

Berzelius, with his patron-collaborator, William Hisinger, had reached the same conclusion independently in 1804, but only developed the important and influential electrochemical theory, which was to leave a permanent mark on chemistry, in 1810 after he had learned of Dalton's atomic theory. Jöns Jacob Berzelius (1779–1848), after being brought up by his stepfather, studied medicine at the University of Uppsala. Here he read Fourcroy's *Philosophie chimique* (1792) and became convinced of Lavoisier's new system. A competent reader and writer of English, French and German, and alert to the latest developments outside Sweden, his graduation thesis in 1802 was on the medical applications of galvanism. This brought him to the attention of Hisinger, a wealthy mine owner, who invited Berzelius to use the facilities of his home laboratory in Stockholm. Together they not only drew important conclusions about electrolysis, but discovered a new element, 'ceria', in 1803, which later turned out to be the parent of several 'rare-earth' elements (see chapter 9).

By 1807 Berzelius had become independent of Hisinger's patronage when he was elected to a Chair of Chemistry and Pharmacy at the Carolian Medico-Chirurgical Institute in Stockholm. His light lecturing duties allowed him plenty of time to research in the Institute's modest laboratory. Elected a member of the Swedish Academy of Sciences in 1808, in 1818 he became one of its joint secretaries. The appointment included a grace-and-favour house in which he built a simple laboratory adjacent to the kitchen. Here he took occasional pupils, such as Mitscherlich and Wöhler.

Berzelius first learned of Dalton when planning his own influential textbook, *Larbok i kemien*, the first volume of which was published in 1808. Somehow Berzelius had acquired a copy of Richter's writings on stoichiometry (he remarked on how unusual this was) and so learned of the law of reciprocal proportions and of the idea of equivalents. He saw immediately how useful these generalizations were for analytical chemistry. An avid follower of British chemical investigations, Berzelius learned of Dalton's theory when he read a reference to it in Wollaston's report on multiple proportions in *Nicholson's Journal*. Because of the European wars, which made scientific communication difficult, he was unable to obtain a copy of Dalton's *New System* (from Dalton himself) until 1812. Nevertheless, just from Wollaston's brief account he saw immediately that a corpuscular interpretation of these analytical regularities was 'the greatest step which chemistry had made towards its completion as a science'.

His own analytical results more than confirmed that, whenever substances combined together in different proportions, they were always, as Dalton had already concluded, in the proportions A + B, A + 2B, 2A + 3B, A + 4B, etc. Berzelius reconciled this regularity with Berthollet's views on the influence of mass in chemical reactions. He agreed that Berthollet was right in supposing that substances could combine together in varying proportions; but these proportions were never continuously variable, as Berthollet had argued against Proust, but fixed according to Dalton's corpuscular ratios.

Berzelius' teaching duties included the training of pharmacists. He was, therefore, conscious of the fact that the Swedish Pharmacopoeia had not been revised since the days of phlogiston chemistry and that by 1810 its language had become embarrassingly out of date. In 1811, in an attempt to persuade the government to make a sensible decision on its pharmaceutical nomenclature, Berzelius devised a new Latin classification of substances, which exploited the electrochemical phenomena that he and Davy had studied, and firmly founded the organization of ponderable matter on the dualistic system that lay at the basis of Lavoisier's antiphlogistic nomenclature.

Ponderable bodies were divided into two classes, 'electropositive' and 'electronegative' according to whether during electrolysis they were deposited or evolved around the positive or negative pole. Since these definitions reversed

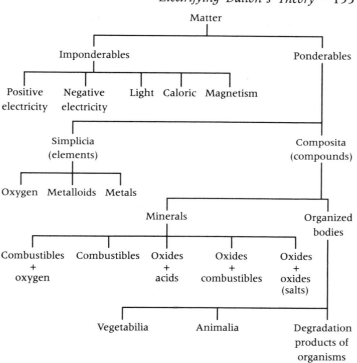

FIGURE 4.1   Berzelius' classification of substances. (Based on
C. A. Russell, *Annals of Science*, **19** (1963): 124.)

the convention that Davy had already introduced, Berzelius
was soon obliged to conform to the definition that electropositive substances were attracted to the negative pole. It
was because of the theoretical implications of galvanic
language that Faraday, in 1832, introduced the value-
neutral nomenclature of electrodes, cathodes, anodes and
so on. Berzelius' electropositive and electronegative substances then became anions and cations respectively.

Oxygen, according to Berzelius, was unique in its extreme
electronegativity. Other, less electronegative substances,
like sulphur, could be positive towards oxygen and negative
towards metals. On combination, a small residual contact

charge was left, which allowed further combination to occur to form salts and complex salts. Thus, electropositive metals might form electropositive (basic) oxides (as electrolysis demonstrated), which would combine with electronegative acidic oxides to form neutral salts. The latter, however, might still have a residual charge that allowed them to hydrate and to form complex salts:

$$M^+ + O^- = (MO)^+$$
$$X^+ + O^- = (XO)^-$$
$$(MO)^+ + (XO)^- = [(MO)\,(XO)]^+$$
$$[(MO)\,(XO)]^+ + (HO)^- = [MO.OX,\,HO]^+$$
$$[M_1O.OX_1,\,HO]^+ + [M_2O.OX_2,\,HO]^- = [M_1O.OX_1,\,HO][M_2,\,OX_2,\,HO]$$

The scheme allowed the elements to be arranged in an electrochemical series from oxygen to potassium, based upon the electrolytic behaviour of elements and their oxides. Because salts were defined as combinations of oxides, Berzelius had to insist for a long time that chlorine and iodine were oxides of unknown elements, and that ammonia was similarly an oxide of 'ammonia'. It was not until the 1820s that Berzelius finally capitulated and agreed that chlorine, iodine and bromine (which he placed in the special category of forming electronegative 'haloid' salts) were elements and that ammonia was a compound of nitrogen and hydrogen only.

It was this electrochemical system which was to have far-reaching analogical implications for the classification of organic substances. It also allowed Berzelius in 1813 to introduce a rational symbolism based upon the Latin names of the elements. Compounds were denoted by a plus sign between the constituents, as in copper oxide, $Cu + O$, the electropositive element being written first. Later, Berzelius dispensed with the plus sign and set the two elements side by side as in algebra. Different numbers of elements were then indicated by superscripts, e.g. S^2O^3, a molecule of 'hyposulphuric acid'. These joined symbols, which were criticized initially for being potentially confusing with algebraic symbolism, only began to be used in the 1830s. It was Liebig who, in 1834, introduced the subscript convention we still use today, though French chemists went on using superscripts well into the twentieth century. Because of the importance of oxygen in Berzelius' system, he abbreviated it to a dot over its electropositive congener, i.e. Ċu = Cu + O. In 1827 he extended this to sulphur, which was indicated by a comma, i.e. copper sulphide, Cu᾽.

In a further 'simplification', which in practice wrought havoc in the classification of organic compounds and in communication between chemists, Berzelius in 1827 introduced 'barred' or underlined symbols to indicate two atoms of an element. (Since the bar was one-third up the stem of the symbol it involved printers making a special type, thereby losing one advantage over Dalton's symbols; hence the use of underlined symbols in some texts.) The symbols for water and potash alum thus became, respectively:

$$\overline{H} \quad \text{or} \quad \underline{H} \quad \text{and}$$

$$\overset{.\ ...}{K\,S} \quad + \quad \overset{...\ .}{Al\,S} \quad + \quad 24\,\overset{.}{\overline{H}}$$

Although Berzelius introduced symbols as a memory aid to chemical proportions, they were initially adopted by few chemists. Berzelius himself virtually ignored his own suggestions until 1827, when he published the organic chemistry section of his textbook, which appeared in German and French translations soon afterwards. Indeed, the development of organic chemistry was undoubtedly the key factor into pushing chemists into symbolic representations. Following the determination of a group of younger British chemists to introduce Continental organic research into Britain, Edward Turner employed Berzelius' symbols in the fourth edition of his *Elements of Chemistry* in 1834. From then on, together with chemical equations, whose use in Britain was pioneered by Thomas Graham, symbols became an indispensable part of chemical communication.

TABLE **4.2** *The development of the chemical equation.*

1. Using alchemical symbols, in the mid-eighteenth century Torbern Bergman represented the exchanges of affinity in a double decomposition by a four-cornered diagrammatic scheme:

Bergman   Modern equivalent

This visual aid scheme was adopted by William Cullen and popularised in chemistry teaching in Scotland by Joseph Black:

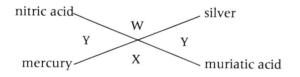

where letters or numbers indicated strengths of affinity, such that here $y > x$ and $z > w$ and $y + z > x + w$

2. After the introduction of Dalton's atomic weights and Berzelian symbols, Bergman's system was often transformed into the following:

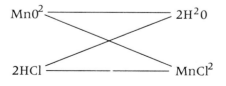

3. Faraday and others in lectures and textbooks often used diagrams:

$$
\text{1 chlorate of potash} = 124
\begin{cases}
\text{1 chloric acid} = 76 \\
\text{1 potash} = 48
\end{cases}
\begin{cases}
\text{5 oxygen} = 40 \\
\text{1 chlorine} = 36 \\
\text{1 oxygen} = 8 \\
\text{1 potassium} = 40
\end{cases}
\begin{aligned}
&\text{6 oxygen} = 48 \\
&\text{1 chloride of potassium} = 76
\end{aligned}
$$

4. A more mechanistic alternative also found in early-nineteenth-century texts is:

water = oxygen and hydrogen

iron ⎤ = oxide of iron

sulphuric acid ⎤ = salt of iron

5. In the 1840s, George Fownes wrote additive equations with equivalent weights:

alcohol $C_4H_6O_2$
+ 4 equiv. oxygen $\underline{O_4}$
                 $C_4H_6O_6$

acetic acid $C_4H_3O_3$
+ 3 equiv. water $\underline{H_3O_3}$
                 $C_4H_6O_6$

It was Thomas Graham who turned this into the more familiar balanced linear form during the same decade:

$$C_4H_6O_2 + 2O_2 = C_4H_3O_3 + 3HO$$

As we have seen, Dalton angrily rejected Berzelius' symbols mainly on the grounds that they did not indicate structure but were merely synoptic. Nor was he at all pleased with the way Berzelius had taken over his creation and transformed it electrochemically. On his part, Berzelius, after struggling for years to obtain a copy of Dalton's *New System*, expressed deep disappointment with the book when he eventually read it in 1812[7]:

> I have been able to skim through the book in haste, but I will not conceal that I was surprised to see how the author has disappointed my hopes. Incorrect even in the mathematical part (e.g. in determining the maximum density of water), in the chemical part he allows himself lapses from the truth at which we have the right to be astonished.

Berzelius' extensive account of his interpretation of Dalton's theory was published in English in Thomas Thomson's monthly *Annals of Philosophy* in 1813. These articles were criticized by Dalton on at least five grounds. Whereas Dalton could see no good reason geometrically why atoms had to be spherical or all the same size, these were cardinal assumptions of Berzelius, who put them to good use in 1819 when he explained the isomorphism of crystals that Mitscherlich had discovered when studying with him in Stockholm. (Isomorphism refers to the fact that a family of salts containing different metals tend to have similar or identical crystal shapes.) Again, unlike Dalton, Berzelius refused to allow combinations of the type 2A + 2B or 2A + 3B on the grounds that, logically, nothing would prevent such 'atoms' from being divided. Dalton disagreed, since self-repulsions could be appealed to. Only after a lifetime's analysis, in 1831, did Berzelius accept that occasionally two atoms of an element could combine with two or more other atoms. Before then this had led Berzelius to assume that all metallic oxides had the form MO. In the cases of the alkali metals and of silver, which are actually M_2O, this led to atomic weight values that were double those of today. Because organic acids were quantitatively determined from their silver salts, this had a serious knock-on effect on the molecular formulae of organic compounds (see chapter 6).

Dalton also objected to the imposition of electrochemical ideas on his atoms, as if nobody had the right to tamper with his original theory. But Berzelius pressed ahead, and in 1818 produced a masterly synthesis, which appeared in French the following year as *Essai sur la théorie des proportions chimiques et sur l'influence chimique de l'électricité*. This included not only a comprehensive listing of two thousand atomic and molecular weights based upon Berzelius' own determinations, but the comprehensive polar theory of chemical combination. That it was this electrochemical theory, rather than Dalton's simple corpuscular theory, that was adopted by chemists raises the question why it was found preferable. There were, in fact, a number of problems associated with Daltonian atomism. While these were not entirely resolved by Berzelius' interpretation, and indeed there remained persistent difficulties and reinterpretations of atomism for the remainder of the century, Berzelius' system seemed more securely founded on accurate experimental analysis.

Historians have identified four difficulties with Daltoninan atomism: his failure to explain chemical reactivity; his acceptance of as many varieties of atoms as there were elements; his failure to marry volumetric and gravimetric data; and his passive acceptance of the existence of unseen atoms in the first place. Each of these difficulties, or criticisms, led to a research programme in chemistry.

CHEMICAL REACTIVITY

The Newtonian dream in the eighteenth century had been to produce a quantitative or mathematical theory that would identify the attractive and repulsive powers, or forces, and explain why some substances reacted together while others did not. Dalton turned his back on this affinity tradition. He accepted the analytical results as they were found and then identified regularities of combination that could be explained as due to the fact that, for whatever reason, atoms chose to combine in fixed and multiple proportions. Although he explicitly acknowledged the existence of attractions between atoms and repulsions that he identified as caused by caloric, he did not develop any theory of chemical reactivity. Berzelius, on the other hand, exploited electricity and the idea of atomic polarities to explain reactivity and the heat and light involved in chemical reactions. Although not a quantitative theory it had the advantage over Dalton's model of broadening the base of atomism by including the phenomena of electrolysis.

PROUT'S HYPOTHESIS

Although based on simple assumptions, Dalton's theory was not simple. Insofar as he had decided that there were as many different chemical atoms as there were chemical elements, he was forced to postulate the existence of nearly fifty kinds of atom. By marrying his atomism to Lavoisier's elements, to many contemporaries it seemed atomism was a hostage to the fortune of the status of the chemical element. And because there were serious doubts as to what constituted an element, the status of Dalton's theory was compromised.

At the start of the nineteenth century several chemists, including Davy, found it impossible to believe that God would have wished to design a world from some fifty different building blocks. Their scepticism that Lavoisier had identified the truly elementary blocks was reinforced by Davy's experimental work in which he showed that several of Lavoisier's elements, including the alkaline earths, were not truly elementary. His own scepticism was underlined by his refusal to use the word 'element' in chemical discourse and his use of the circumlocution, 'undecompounded body'. On several occasions Davy went further and implied that undecompounded bodies probably contained hydrogen and that the true principles of chemistry would eventually be found to be few in number.

Davy's hints, which some saw as an attempt to revive a phlogiston theory, were a stimulus to the Edinburgh-trained physician, William Prout (1785–1850). At Edinburgh, Prout had steeped himself in classical reading and learned of the Aristotelian tradition that all substances were modifications of a primary matter. In London, where he settled in 1812, Prout thought about Dalton's atomic theory and noted that atomic weights were close to whole numbers – so much so, that Dalton himself had rounded them up or down to integers. Prout's innovation was to calculate the specific gravities of elements, using air as a standard, and then to compare the results with that of hydrogen taken as having a specific gravity of one. He thereby compared the weights of equal volumes.

In two papers published in *Annals of Philosophy* in 1815 and 1816, he drew attention to the fact that all of his calculations (some of which were very dodgy indeed) produced whole numbers, and, in a famous query, he wondered whether this indicated that hydrogen was the basis of all matter[8]:

> If the ideas we have ventured to advance be correct, we may almost consider the *proto hyle* of the ancients to be realised in hydrogen; an opinion, by the by, not absolutely new. If we actually consider this to be the case, and further consider the specific gravities of bodies in their gaseous state to represent the number of bodies condensed into one [volume]; or, in other words, the number of the absolute weight of a single volume of the first matter which they contain, which is extremely probable, multiples in weight must always

indicate multiples in volume, and *vice versa*; and the specific gravities, or absolute weights of all bodies in a gaseous state, must be multiples of the specific gravity or absolute weight of the first matter, because all bodies in the gaseous state which unite with one another unite with reference to this volume.

In other words, if the atomic weight of chlorine was 36, this indicated that 36 volumes of hydrogen had condensed to form this 'element'.

These two hypotheses, of integral atomic weights and of the unity of matter, became known ambiguously ever after by Berzelius' term, 'Prout's hypothesis'. As a tantalizing and attractive simplifying view of matter it proved to be a continuous source of inspiration to chemists and physicists until the work of Francis Aston on isotopes in the 1920s. On the one hand, for example. Prout's views received support from chemists such as Thomas Thomson, Jean-Baptiste Dumas, Jean Marignac and Lothar Meyer; on the other hand, Berzelius, Turner, Jean Servais Stas and Dmitri Mendeleev opposed him. Yet, whatever attitude individual experimentalists and theoreticians had towards the hypotheses, the work done in support or refutation proved incredibly fruitful. The hypotheses stimulated the improvement of analytical techniques; they enforced interest in the determination of atomic weights and hence in the atomic theory of matter; they gave impetus to the search for a system of classification of the elements, so many of whose properties seemed similar; and, when the periodic law was revealed in 1869, they encouraged speculation about the evolution of elements and structural theories of the atom.

VOLUMETRIC RELATIONS

As Prout noted in 1816, 'the advantage in considering the volume of hydrogen equal to the atom' was that the specific gravities of elements would either coincide with, or be a multiple of, their atomic weights. Prout undoubtedly drew this conclusion from the work of Gay-Lussac on the combining volumes of gases – research that Dalton rejected. In 1808, Joseph Louis Gay-Lussac (1778–1850) had drawn attention to the fact that 'gases combine amongst themselves in very simple proportions':

100 vols carbon monoxide + 50 vols oxygen = 100 vols carbon dioxide

100 vols nitrogen	+	300 vols hydrogen	=	200 vols ammonia
100 vols hydrogen	+	100 vols oxygenated muriatic acid [chlorine]	=	200 vols muriatic acid [hydrogen chloride]

Like Berzelius with gravimetric combining proportions, Gay-Lussac reconciled this finding with Berthollet's claim that the action of mass would bring about variable composition by arguing that where definite, simple ratios of components were present, these always separated out more easily.

It is easy to see why Dalton was forced to deny the experimental validity of Gay-Lussac's integral-volumes law. It implied that equal volumes of gases under the same conditions of temperature and pressure contained either the same number, or a simple multiple, of particles. This would imply, however, that gas particles (or atoms) would have to 'split'. For example, in the case of the synthesis of water, if n is the number of particles in a unit volume, the

2 vol hydrogen + 1 vol oxygen = 2 vols water
2nH nO   2nHO

particles of the oxygen would have to divide in order to produce two particles of water occupying two volumes.

Since by definition an atom could not be divided, Dalton was forced to deny Gay-Lussac's experimental results.

Berzelius, on the other hand, happily reconciled the gravimetric and volumetric data[9]:

> What in the one theory is called an *atom* is in the other theory a *volume*. In the present state of our knowledge the theory of volumes has the advantage of being founded upon a well-constituted fact, while the other has only a supposition for its foundation.

Since *two* volumes of hydrogen combined with one of oxygen to form water, Berzelius was prepared to go beyond Dalton's rule of binary simplicity and to assert that water's formula was H^2O. The use of the barred or underlined atom (or, rather, volume, since Berzelius' symbols really referred to volumes), however, made Berzelius' formula, $\underline{H}O$, look very similar to Dalton's formulation when written with Berzelius' symbols.

We must at all costs avoid concluding from this that Berzelius was prepared to believe that elementary gases like hydrogen and oxygen contained two or more atoms, or that their atoms split in half in redistributing their volumes. For Dalton, chemical particles could not contain two or more atoms because of their self-repulsion from heat; similarly for Berzelius, electrochemical theory postulated that like-charged particles would repel. He did not, therefore, apply the volume theory to compound gases (which for him still included chlorine and nitrogen) and he was able to save the phenomena of Gay-Lussac's law by supposing that compound gases 'diminish in volume at the moment of chemical combination, since the repulsive force of one or all the elements is diminished by the juxtaposition of an atom of another element'.

He ingeniously used the volume theory to deduce the atomic weights of non-gaseous elements. For example, since one volume of oxygen combined with one part of carbon to form *two* volumes of carbon monoxide, the formula of this oxide had to be either C + O (if no contraction of volume occurred and carbon occupied one volume) or 2C + O if contraction did occur. Because carbon monoxide reacted with half its volume of oxygen to form carbon dioxide, the latter had to be CO^2. From this line of reasoning it followed that the atomic weight of carbon was 75 (O = 100; or C = 12 when O = 16).

At this point most histories of chemistry point out that, despite Berzelius' impressive exploitation of his knowledge of chemical reactions, the answer to the determination of molecular formulae from which atomic weights could be easily calculated was a hypothesis proposed by Amedeo Avogadro (1776–1856) in 1811, that equal volumes of gases contained the same number of molecules, the latter being stable, multi-atomed particles. In point of fact Avogadro's hypothesis was without any impact or influence on the calculation of atomic weights at this time. Not until the explanatory power of electrochemical theory had temporarily waned in the 1850s under the weight of difficulties in organic chemistry, and chemists and physicists found it convenient to accept (without explanation) that dimers such as H_2 and O_2 could exist, was a complete reconciliation of gravimetric and volumetric data possible. Until then the dimerization of like-charged atoms remained impossible.

SCEPTICISM TOWARDS ATOMISM

Although Boyle largely overcame the religious objections towards material atomism in the seventeenth century, the philosophical difficulties remained. Atoms were theoretical, metaphysical entities, which could not be seen, touched or tasted. Despite Dalton's transductive scheme whereby atoms were assigned weights, he could provide no physical proof of their existence. Dalton's contemporaries, Davy, Wollaston and others, therefore made a careful distinction between belief in a metaphysical theory of atoms and the experimental evidence of combining proportions. When Davy, as President of the Royal Society, presented Dalton with a Royal Medal in 1826, he stressed that it was for the 'development of the theory of definite proportions, usually called the atomic theory of chemistry'. To mark this distinction the majority of Dalton's contemporaries and all textbook writers spoke and wrote of 'equivalent weights', 'combining weights' or 'proportional numbers' rather than atomic weights. Indeed, although Dalton continued to refer to atomic weights, his loose terminology of 'atom' and 'compound atom' shows that he, too, was prepared to distinguish between physical and chemical atoms.

While making no commitment to physical atoms, the practice of most chemists was to adopt an arbitrary or conventional system of elementary weights for each element and compound. Chemical atomism was therefore the conceptual basis for assigning these relative weights. Like Lavoisier's definition of the element, the chemist could have no opinion on whether chemical atoms were themselves composed from physical atoms.

From hindsight the claim that the determination of equivalent weights or proportional numbers was empirical and theory-free does not stand up to scrutiny, as Alan Rocke has forcefully shown. Moreover, the pretence of empiricism, that chemistry was founded on the Lavoisierian bedrock of laboratory experience, caused enormous confusion as different chemists made different assumptions concerning the calculation of combining weights. Such calculations were not helped by the proliferation of different and shifting standards for 'atomic weights'. These made international, and even national, communication difficult as the standard moved from H = 1 (Dalton), O = 1 (Thomson) or 10 (Wollaston) or 100 (Berzelius) or $\underline{H}$ = 1 (i.e. H = $^1/_2$; Berzelius from 1831). Confusion was compounded during the 1820s when Dumas determined vapour densities on the basis that 'molecules' of simple gases might divide during combination, so that water was defined as a compound containing one atom of hydrogen and half an atom of oxygen. His further determinations of the densities of mercury, phosphorus, iodine and sulphur (which are all actually polyatomic) brought even more confusion, so much so that by 1837 Dumas went on record that 'if I were master I would efface the word atom from science'.

Even as late as the 1860s, after Cannizzaro (chapter 11) had clarified the distinction between molecules and atoms and Clausius' equipartition of energy theorem had demanded polyatomic molecules, chemists were no nearer a commitment to physical atoms. It was during this decade that Sir Benjamin Collins Brodie (1817–80), a pupil of Liebig's and a Professor of Chemistry at Oxford, objected to atomism on the grounds of philosophy and simplicity. Like Lavoisier earlier, he proposed to put chemistry back onto its empirical feet by ridding it, not of phlogiston, but of atoms. Because Berzelius' symbols – by then the daily language of chemists – implicitly referred to atoms, he proposed the adoption of the Greek alphabet to symbolize all chemical events. Like the French nomenclaturists, he saw that a new chemistry had to have a new language. The result was 'the calculus of chemical operations', so-called because Brodie believed that chemists ought only to give operational descriptions of the weight and volume changes that occurred during chemical reactions. It was not legitimate to account for such changes in terms of atoms and molecules; to do so was metaphysics, not chemistry.

Unusually for a chemist of his generation, Brodie had trained as both a chemist and mathematician. As a mathematician and logician, Brodie had been particularly influenced by the new algebra devised by George Boole in 1847, an early form of set theory that included the relationship $x + y = xy$. Brodie's calculus, which was published in two parts in 1866 and 1877, was based upon a 1000 cm³ unit of space as his standard of measurement. On this unit *operations* were performed (i.e. chemical transformations) each of which was symbolized by a

Greek character. Like vectors, these symbols represented both a definite substance and a definite weight. An example of Brodie's method will make his procedure clearer.

If a compound weight such as water (= 9 units of combining weight) is made up of two substances A and B whose operations (or recipes for making them) are x and y, then a suitable symbol for the compound weight is xy, for this is the result of performing operation x, and then the operation y, upon a unit of space. From Boolean algebra, xy will also be the symbol of a single weight whose operation is $(x + y)$. To develop a symbol for oxygen, let ϕ = symbol for a unit of water, let ϕ_1 = symbol for a unit of hydrogen, and let ϕ_2 = symbol for a unit of oxygen. Let

$$\phi = \alpha^m \xi^{m}{}_1 \qquad \phi_1 = \alpha \qquad \phi_2 = \alpha^n \xi^n{}_1$$

From Gay-Lussac's empirical law of volumes (i.e. in modern symbols, $2H_2 + O_2 = 2H_2O$)

$$2\alpha + \alpha^n \xi^n{}_1 = 2\,\alpha^m \xi^m{}_1$$

but since $x + y = xy$

$$\alpha^2 \alpha^n \xi^n{}_1 = (\alpha^m \xi^m{}_1)^2$$

On collecting terms for α and ξ

$$2m = 2 + n \qquad \text{and} \qquad 2m_1 = n_1$$

The *simplest* integral solutions are

$$n = 0,\ m = 1 \qquad \text{and} \qquad n_1 = 2,\ m_1 = 1$$

Hence the operational symbol for water is $\alpha\xi$ and of oxygen is ξ^2. (Interestingly there was no justification given for taking only integral solutions, though this would follow if atoms were postulated as the explanation for operational regularities!) If hydrogen is chosen as the standard of comparison with weight 1, then the weight of $\xi^2 = 8$.

Contemporary chemists (and mathematicians) found Brodie's calculus extremely odd and difficult to follow.

What generally struck them, however, as it also struck Brodie, was that the calculus generated three different kinds of symbols:

1. Those like hydrogen, carbon and potassium, with only *one* operation, e.g. α.
2. Those like oxygen and sulphur, with *two identical* operations, e.g. ξ^2.
3. Those like chlorine, other halogens and arsenic, with *two different* operations, e.g. $\alpha\chi^2$.

The third class of symbols was fascinating since it was formally analogous to the class of compounds like hydrogen peroxide, $\alpha\xi^2$. Such analogies within the system inevitably led to the speculation, which an empiricist, anti-theoretical system had no business suggesting, whether the halogens, arsenic and other symbols from the third class of elements were really compounds of hydrogen with unknown elements. Did χ and χ^2 exist?

Such questions would have been dismissed as speculative nonsense in the 1820s, but in the 1860s they provided a possible solution to the problem of the sources of unknown lines in the spectra of stars and nebulae. Like the voltaic pile, the spectroscope, which had been developed by the chemist Robert Bunsen and the physicist G. R. Kirchhoff in 1859, had led rapidly to the identification of new elements such as rubidium and thallium. Collaborations between astronomers and chemists had then provided knowledge of the composition of the sun and other heavenly bodies, from which it seemed plausible to assume that lines that could not be identified with known elements were undiscovered elements. This had been the strategy of Norman Lockyer and Edward Frankland in 1868 when they identified some unknown solar lines as an element that seemed not to be present on earth and which Lockyer named helium. Brodie therefore had no hesitation in suggesting that 'ideal' elements such as χ were the causes of mysterious spectral lines.

The announcement by Darwin of the theory of evolution in 1859 had also awakened chemists to the possibility that the elements had 'evolved', a particularly attractive speculation to those who were committed to Prout's hypotheses. This speculation seemed to be given credence by Henri Sainte-Claire Deville's experiments on the dissociation of compounds under high temperatures. Brodie was able to speculate, therefore, that, in the intensely hot atmospheres of the stars and nebulae, entities such as χ and χ^2 existed in a free state. As conditions had cooled in other parts of the universe, including the earth, these ideal elements had combined with hydrogen to form elements of the third class.

It is ironic that a scheme devised as an antidote to metaphysical speculation ended up supporting Prout's hypothesis that elements were really compounds, a view that itself had been urged against Dalton's brand of chemical atomism.

In 1869 Brodie's views led to a large-scale debate at the British Chemical Society in which he, Williamson, Frankland, Tyndall, Maxwell and many others participated. The interesting thing about this discussion is that chemists agreed with Brodie that there was no evidence for physical atomism, even though they drew a line at adopting Brodie's calculus. Instead, they expressed their continuing content with the use of chemical atoms as a heuristic model. On the other hand, the physicists present were much more committed to physical atomism and urged the marriage of chemical and physical atoms through the kinetic theory of gases that Clausius had established in the mid 1850s. Not all physicists and physical chemists were to agree in the final quarter of a century. Ostwald, for example, resolutely believed that energy and thermodynamics formed a securer basis for scientific reasoning than material atoms.

As for Brodie's calculus, it failed like all positivistically devised systems to include room for new information. When in 1874 le Bel and van't Hoff showed that a satisfactory way of explaining certain puzzling cases of isomerism in organic chemistry was to assume that atoms arranged themselves tetrahedrally around a central carbon atom, Brodie was forced to rethink how his operational symbols could differentiate between stereoisomers. He died in 1880 with the problem unsolved. A logical symbolic system can be devised to include stereoisomers, as a twentieth-century Dutch logician has shown; but its fearsome complexity is a vivid demonstration of why chemists preferred, in the end, to adopt the atomic–molecular theory initiated by Dalton.

CONCLUSION

There were two types of atomism in the nineteenth century: a universally, if usually only implicitly, accepted chemical atomism, which formed the conceptual basis for assigning relative elementary weights and for assigning molecular formulae; and a highly controversial physical atomism, which made claims concerning the ultimate mechanical nature of all substances. Although the two types were intimately related and were both implicitly advocated by Dalton, chemists generally left physical atomism to physicists. By the 1870s, the identity of these two theories was becoming clearer and unification was finally achieved in the early years of the twentieth century – oddly, just at the time when the structure of atoms was beginning to be explored by chemists and physicists.

By then, as Liebig had noted to Henry's son as early as 1854:

All our ideas are so interwoven with the Daltonian theory, that we cannot transpose ourselves into the time, when it did not exist. . . . Chemistry received in the atomic theory, a fundamental view; which overruled and governed all other theoretical views. . . . In this lies the extraordinary service which this theory rendered to science, viz.: that it supplied a fertile soil for further advancements: a soil which was previously wanting.

Instructions for the Analysis of Organic Bodies

An diesen Apparat ist nichts neu als seine Einfachkeit und der vollkommene zu verlässigkeit, welche gewährst. [There's nothing new about this apparatus except its simplicity and thorough trustworthiness.]
(JUSTUS VON LIEBIG, 1831)

Because of the widespread use of analytical techniques in modern chemistry, biochemistry, pathology, industry and nuclear physics, the development of analysis forms one of the principal foundations of the history of chemistry. Chemistry is both a qualitative and a quantitative science, which is concerned with the analysis and synthesis of materials, their properties and their explanation. It is a common historical judgement that chemistry did not become a successful science on a par with astronomy and physics until the time of Lavoisier. As we have seen, to explain this lack of progress, appeal has been made to the complexity of the subject, the unsatisfactory *a priori* and competitive nature of the several theories that tried to account for the phenomena, the absence of knowledge concerning the gaseous state, and the fact that a concept of purity, and the means of analysis, were crude and ill-developed.

PURITY

Purity has been rightly described as the fundamental concept of chemistry. For without the concept of a homogeneous substance, a quantitative science based on the balance is useless, while qualitative analysis would be impossible. Insofar as assaying techniques are found in early metallurgy, some kind of purity concept must have been recognized, if only dimly, by early practical chemists. The noun 'test' and the verb 'to test' are constant reminders that early assayers used small cup-like pots (*cupule* or *testus*) to assess the quality of an ore or other material. The fusion of this practical kind of purity with the idealistic purity of the alchemists was insufficient, however; and the mature appreciation of purity presumably dates from the beginning of the nineteenth century. Purity requires the recognition that some substances are homogeneous because they have reproducible properties under identical conditions. Many everyday substances like wood, soil and urine appear to have a variety of properties. Others like silver, gold, distilled water and crystalline salt have constant reproducible properties. Over the centuries these differences of behaviour were implicitly interpreted into existential empirical laws – 'substance *x* has properties *y* to define it'. The eighteenth-century Swedish pharmacist, Carl Scheele, for example, constantly used crystal form, boiling point and solubility as qualitative guarantees for reproducible conditions.

Now it may well be that chemists possessed no perfect concept of purity until Lavoisier formally defined pragmatic elements, to which Dalton could apply a theory of homogeneous atoms. Yet clearly, long before then, chemists had accepted the existence of a large number of unique substances. Indeed, control of the purity of gold and silver, of salt and alum, and the prevention of counterfeiting and adulteration were always a primary concern of administrators of the very earliest civilized communities. Certainly by the end of the eighteenth century we find analysts like Klaproth, Macquer and Bergman emphasizing the need for reagent purity; and in his *Considérations générales sur l'analyse organique* (1824), Chevreul discussed ways of purifying organic compounds and invoked melting points as a means of identifying them. The process was completed' by Samuel P. Mulliken, an American pupil of Wislicenus at the Massachusetts Institute of Technology (MIT). His painstaking four-volume *Method for the Identification of Pure Organic Compounds* was published between 1899 and 1904.

Without a first-order hypothesis about homogeneous substances, chemists could not go on to generalize that their subject dealt only with the combination and decomposition of pure substances; that pure substances having undergone chemical change might be recovered qualitatively and quantitatively by other chemical changes; and, most important of all, that some pure substances which refused all attempts to change them into simpler pure substances were to be considered the elements from which other more complex or compound pure substances were composed. Then, to paraphrase Stahl in *Fundamenta chymiae* (1727), analysis could become the art whereby pure compound substances are resolved into their pure components. It was to avoid any alchemical implications that German chemists at the end of the seventeenth century began to replace the word 'Chemie' by 'Scheidkunst', or art of separation. Chemistry was the art of analysis.

Guaranteed pure reagents were first described and advertised by C. Krausch, an employee of the Darmstadt chemical and pharmaceutical firm of E. Merck in 1888. His *Die Prüfung des chemischen Reagentien auf Reinheit* was regularly reissued by Merck from then until 1912, when a second, larger edition was published. The Merck company, which had originated in a Darmstadt pharmacy founded in 1668, had expanded into the industrial manufacture of alkaloids during the 1820s through the encouragement Justus von Liebig gave to Emanuel Merck (1794–1855). The latter's grandson, George Merck, founded an independent branch of the firm in New Jersey in 1894. The American firm made possible the issue of an authorized English translation of the Merck purity standards by Henry Schenck, *Chemical*

Reagents. Their Purity and Tests (1914). This was reissued with improvements up to 1931. Meanwhile, the American Chemical Society (ACS) had held committee meetings on the purity of laboratory chemicals since the early 1900s. It seems to have hoped that the Washington Bureau of Standards would issue guidelines similar to those upheld by Merck and that these standards would be demanded of all chemical supply companies. Since this was not the case, from 1925 the ACS published the deliberations and recommendations of its own Committee on Analysed Reagents in *Industrial and Engineering Chemistry*. These were finally published in collected form as official ACS specifications in 1951 as *Reagent Chemicals*.

If American purity standards were largely dictated by committee, in Britain they were achieved through a manufacturers' voluntary code. The original Merck specifications of 1888 were first translated into English by J. A. Williams and A. Dupré in 1902 as *The Testing of Chemical Reagents for Purity*. During the First World War when, like America, British chemists found themselves cut off from the supply of pure chemicals from Germany, a joint committee of the Institute of Chemistry and the Society of Analytical Chemists drew up standards ('AR' for Analytical Reagent or, perhaps, 'all right'), which they urged British manufacturers to uphold, including the consortium, British Drug Houses (BDH). Many of these war-time specifications were taken from those issued in 1911 by the independent drug house of Hopkin & Williams, *Analytical Reagents, Standards and Tests*, which, in turn, had been influenced by Merck's standards. In 1926 BDH issued its own code of specifications, which, because they differed slightly from those of Hopkin & Williams, began to cause misunderstandings and research difficulties. Therefore, in 1934 an agreement was made to combine forces to make one authoritative British standard of purity for all common chemicals used in laboratories, the 'AnalaR' *Standards for Laboratory Chemicals. Qualitative and Quantitative Analysis.*

THE BASIS OF CHEMISTRY

The analysis of substances has been advanced by chemists at two levels: they have tried to resolve materials either into their 'proximate' or 'intermediate' principles (e.g. the resolution of carbonates into oxides and carbon dioxide), or into their ultimate elements (e.g. the analysis of lime into calcium, carbon and oxygen, or into some other 'elements'). Although both kinds of analysis may be pursued qualitatively or quantitatively, the analysis into proximate principles is usually relatively unsophisticated and associated with qualitative ends or the determination of structure, while elementary analysis (which usually succeeds proximate analysis) is more closely associated with quantitative procedures. The objectives of analysts have been identified as speed, selectivity and sensitivity; but special requirements have inevitably demanded the emphasis of one of these criteria to the neglect of others. Industrial chemists may be more interested in speed or selectivity than sensitivity, while a public health inspector may be more concerned with sensitivity. But, as Michael Faraday noted in *Chemical Manipulation* (1827), method is one thing; accuracy in applying a method 'depends entirely upon manipulation'. Experimental skill is always a requirement.

The qualitative constitution of materials cannot be determined *a priori*. The experimentalist must operate upon substances to see their responses, to determine the chemical nature of their components, and to discover their relative quantities by weight. Here lies the heart of chemistry[1]: for 'without analysis there would be no synthesis, without analytical chemistry there would be no chemistry'.

Although analytical techniques, such as cupellation and wet assay, can be traced back to antiquity, analysis as we know it began only during the late middle ages when mineral acids became available. Then salt solutions could be prepared from metals and used for specific tests. A guide here was the empirical lore of medieval dyers and painters, who had found that plants were a source of a wide palette of colours depending not only on the season of the year that they were collected, but also on how they were made into solution. The purple juice of the iris, for example, when combined with alum produced the 'iris green' used in manuscript illumination; the lichen *Rocella* was either used as a purple dye, or alkalinated with fermented urine to produce a red, or acidified to produce orchil blue.

These techniques were still known and widely practised by artisans when Boyle came to write his *Experimental History of Colours* in 1664. In this, Boyle reasoned that if dyers and artists could prepare widely different colours from a single plant extract merely by adding acid or alkali, it would also be possible to use such extracts as 'indicators' of acidity or alkalinity in unknown substances. It was from this deduction that the litmus test, using the natural dye from *Rocella*, was derived. Medieval painters are known to have soaked small pieces of linen cloth in the purple juice of the turnsole plant (*Crozophora tinctoria*). When the dried cloths, or folia, were soaked in water, a bright red solution was formed, which could be used as a water colour – especially if vinegar was added to strengthen the colour. If, instead, the folia were treated with lime water before soaking them in turnsole, the dried folia gave a violet paint, or if urine was used as the solvent, a blue paint was produced. Whether Boyle borrowed the idea of using small strips of paper saturated in litmus from the folium technique of medieval painters is not known, although it seems entirely plausible.

A theoretical prerequisite of qualitative analysis was the acceptance of a corpuscular philosophy: for if the theory of chemistry is epigenetic and permits real transformations of forms and qualities, then analysis is meaningless. The adoption of a preformationist corpuscular hypothesis implied that chemically invariant candidates were available for identification routines.

From the late fourteenth century onwards, continuous medical demands for the analysis of mineral waters and urine led to many advances in inorganic and organic chemistry. For example, the first chemically significant part of animal chemistry developed through uroscopy, the inspection of urine samples; and water analysis dominated British chemistry well into the nineteenth century, when attention shifted from its analysis for therapeutic purposes to its potability for town water supplies. During the iatrochemical period, clarification of chemical thought was a direct result of analytical improvement – largely the development of wet methods. Most of the chemical reactions on which the classical system of qualitative analysis was to be based were discovered during this period.

By the end of the seventeenth century the washing and drying of precipitates had become standard practice, and Boyle (if not Otto Tachenius and Friedrich Hoffmann) had appraised the sensitivity of several reagents. The pace of progress quickened during the phlogiston period, which also saw the beginning of industrialization in Europe. The metallurgically based industries, which had previously stimulated analysis through assay, now began to use qualitative and quantitative methods, including the blow-pipe, while the growing textile industries produced a new form of wet analysis, titrimetry. The analytical demands of mineralogy and of forensic medicine and the public health movement's concern with food and drug adulteration must also have been factors.

Andreas Marggraf's late-eighteenth-century methodical examination of the behaviour of metallic solutions when treated with alkalis shows a growing concern to miniaturize and reduce the quantities of materials used in tests. Marggraf used remarkably small quantities of materials compared with his contemporaries, and he provided such a wealth of new methods (including the flame test) that he brought qualitative analysis to the point where it demanded classification and systematization. The first systematist was Torbern Bergman, who actually gave analysis the status of a separate branch of chemistry. He defined reagents, their preparation, application and sensitivity; he gave precise directions for the analysis of mineral waters and minerals by both wet and dry methods, and of metals for their phlogiston content. Although Bergman occasionally used hydrogen sulphide, he failed to see its possibilities as a strategic analytical reagent.

Quantitative analytical chemistry did not spring unheralded from the mind of Lavoisier. As we have seen, stoichiometric laws evolved spontaneously from the activities of eighteenth-century analysts and were made explicit in the debates between Proust and Berthollet. The three stages in the development of quantitative analysis appear to have been the assayer's interest in a single component, which led to specific tests rather than to tests for whole compounds, and which led first to the formulation of percentage composition. In the eighteenth century this was followed by the tacit acceptance of constant and definite proportions; finally, at the beginning of the nineteenth century, Dalton, Wollaston and Thomson enunciated a doctrine of equivalent compositions, which was decided practically by the analyst's discovery of common components in different compounds. Such stoichiometric laws led, in turn, to improvements in analytical methods.

Analysts tended not to provide theoretical explanations for their work, while theoreticians often failed to assist the spread of their viewpoints because their experimental techniques were poor. Here was a role for chemists who were outstanding in both theory and practice: Berzelius and, to a lesser extent, Thomas Thomson. Once these two rivals had shown how accurate atomic or equivalent weights could be determined, Dalton's atomic theory and the laws of stoichiometry became an integral part of quantitative analysis.

Berzelius' work was much aided by the mushroom

growth of mineralogy during the period 1790–1810 through the hands of Richard Kirwan, Martin Klaproth and Nicolas Vauquelin. These three men combined rigour with considerable practical ability. Klaproth, for example, insisted that precipitates had to be dried to constant weight, while Vauquelin was esteemed for the purity of his reagents. Very few reagents and analytical equipment were available commercially on the Continent at this time, and the analyst had to prepare and to make his own. Bergman and Berzelius produced several schemes for the analysis of specific mixtures of metals, but neither elaborated any general scheme of qualitative analysis, viz. a strategic deductive succession of tests. Berzelius' dualism, however, reinforced the assayer's emphasis on tests for specific ions.

The first major analytical textbook was published in 1824 by C. H. Pfaff. He made extensive use of hydrogen sulphide, but its systematic deployment was the responsibility of Berzelius' German pupil, Heinrich Rose (1795–1864). The latter's *Handbuch der analytischen Chemie* (1829) described for the first time what became the classical scheme of group separation – though not in the order familiar in the twentieth century, which was refined as a result of Ostwald's physical chemistry. Rose's treatment was, however, so dull and over-comprehensive that Carl Remigius Fresenius (1818–97) was provoked to write the textbook of qualitative analysis that remained in use in Great Britain (at least) until it was replaced in the 1930s by the texts of Arthur I. Vogel (1905–66). Fresenius, as we shall see, also founded the *Zeitschrift für analytischen Chemie* in 1862, as well as establishing his own private school of analytical chemistry at Wiesbaden.

Perhaps the most spectacular use of hydrogen sulphide to settle a point of analysis occurred in 1845, when Lyon Playfair was asked to report on the sanitary conditions of Buckingham Palace. He quickly found that the plumbing was in an appalling state of neglect. 'A great main sewer ran through the courtyard, and the whole palace was in untrapped connection with it.' He illustrated this forcefully to the civil servants responsible for the Palace's upkeep by having a basement room painted with white lead, $Pb(CO_3).Pb(OH)_2$, and sealing it for a night. The room's walls were quite black by morning. Playfair's report was kept secret, though the Palace drains were immediately rectified. The affair led not only to Playfair's personal friendship with Prince Albert, but to his career as a scientific adviser to the government.

The habit of folding the paper of an exercise book, or ruling columns in such a book, probably arose during training of Liebig's students at the University of Giessen. Model tabulations were not used by either Rose or Fresenius in the early editions of their manuals, so it seems likely that the tradition of folding paper or ruling columns began at Giessen and was handed on to analysts like Fresenius, who, with Rose and Heinrich Will (1812–90), principally contributed to the teaching and development of group separation methods. Will's *Outlines of the Course of Qualitative Analysis followed in the Giessen Laboratory*, which had appeared in German in 1846, was translated by A. W. Hofmann in the same year for use in the Royal College of Chemistry in London. Neither Rose nor Fresenius offered any advice on the way to record results, which suggests that methods of tabulation, like so many of the tricks and dodges and tacit knowledge of practical chemistry, developed through an oral teaching tradition. The twentieth-century flow-chart method of recording analytical and other experimental results appears to have been imported from industrial practice.

Quantitative analysis was developed by Black, Bergman and the pneumatic chemists. In gravimetry, the systematicists were again Rose and Fresenius. Improvements in accuracy were sought and achieved throughout the nineteenth century: ash-free filter paper by 1883; the robust filter crucible of the American, Frank Gooch (1852–1929), in 1878; the introduction of microgravimetry by Karl

Haushofer and Theodor Behrens at the end of the century; and the ever-increasing use of organic precipitants in the twentieth century. Yet, like qualitative analysis, it developed as an empirical art until the theoretical factors that governed precipitation were examined by Ostwald in the 1880s. Important lessons were also learned during the long disputes over the status of Prout's hypothesis concerning the integral nature of atomic weights, and in the accurate determination of atomic weights by Morley, Richards, Scott and others.

Titrimetry, or volumetric analysis, did not come into widespread use until the 1860s. Unfamiliarity, suspicions of inaccuracy and contempt for its industrial connotations all helped to make volumetric analysis avoided by mineralogists and restricted to industrial chemists. Gay-Lussac had developed accurate methods of titrimetry from the work of predecessors like Henri Descroszilles (1751–1825), who made the first burettes and pipettes; but because his standard solutions were not based on stoichiometrically significant measures, they could only be used for analyses of specific weights or volumes of samples. By the late 1840s, however, standard solutions based upon atomic, molecular, or equivalent weights were used more frequently, with the advantage that, once such normal solutions had been made up, there was no further need for weighings; all measurements were truly volumetric. This practice had arisen in Great Britain where analysts, working with a non-metric system of weights and measures, found it difficult to devise standard solutions whose consumption by the sample would give the percentage of component directly. Such are the advantages of conservatism!

Alexander Ure's use of normal solutions was adopted by J. J. Griffin and by Carl Mohr (1806–79), whose *Lehrbuch der chemisch-analytischen Titrimethode* (1855) made methods of acidimetry, alkalimetry, permanganatometry and iodometry widely known. To a great extent, however, titrimetry failed to live up to Mohr's expectations of accuracy and range, largely because of the difficulty of finding suitable indicators that would define endpoints precisely. Many otherwise excellent volumetric methods, such as cerimetry, failed to achieve practical importance during the nineteenth century for this reason. It was only after organic chemists had produced synthetic indicators such as phenolphthalein and methyl orange, and the physical chemists had produced theoretical interpretations of their functions, and the theory of hydrogen ion concentration, that titrimetry came into its own.

It was Ostwald, the anti-atomist, who created modern analytical chemistry, which he defined as 'the art of testing substances and their constituents', and who insisted that it was an indispensable 'servant to other sciences'. He was nevertheless curiously blind to the need for determining the quantitative information demanded for mathematical analysis. He also more or less ignored the work on redox processes of his pupil Walther Nernst (1864–1941), who was an atomist. Redox methods were first used by biochemists and biophysicists, who in their turn gave analytical chemists the concept of pH and of buffer solutions. Subsequently, when these concepts were taken into the mainstream of chemistry during the 1920s, there developed new techniques of electrometric analysis, including potentiometric and conductimetric titrations and polarography.

Other instrumental methods also originated in nineteenth-century investigations. Electrogravimetry began with Liebig's American pupil, Oliver Wolcott Gibbs (1822–1908). Spectroscopy arose historically from flame photometry, but the ubiquitous sodium yellow was largely responsible for the failure of analysts to realize that flame colour was a characteristic of a substance, and not its temperature. Spectroscopy never proved particularly amenable to quantitative analysis; colorimetry, on the other hand, was immediately adapted for quantification. Instrumental methods, such as column and gas-phase chromatography, ion-exchange methods, and infrared and nuclear magnetic resonance spectroscopy have, since the 1960s, virtually replaced traditional wet and dry routines. The analyst is now dependent on electronic engineers for the design, construction and maintenance of his art.

THE SUPPLY OF APPARATUS AND CHEMICALS

Mid-nineteenth-century entrepreneurs like John Joseph Griffin (1802–77) were to make the task of chemists easier by supplying ready-made chemicals, reagents and apparatus. Griffin, born into a publishing and bookselling family, learned chemistry by attending classes at the Andersonian University in Glasgow. The Andersonian had been endowed in 1795 by Thomas Anderson with the intention that only mutual benefit could arise from the 'enlightenment' of working tradesmen in Glasgow. During his lifetime, as Professor of Natural Philosophy at the University of Glasgow, Anderson had offered popular, instructive courses illustrated by experiments. This tradition was continued by his successors at the Andersonian, George Birkbeck (who was to become associated with similar mechanics institutes in England), Thomas Garnett (who preceded Davy as lecturer at the Royal Institution) and Alexander Ure (1778–1857). When Griffin attended Ure's chemistry course in the early 1820s, there were over four-hundred attenders each year. This was the time when Thomas Thomson at the University of Glasgow was setting up a laboratory for practical instruction in chemistry. It seems very likely that this example rubbed off on the Andersonian, although the large audiences necessitated that such 'hands on' experience was performed at home. It was this need for home-based instruction that inspired Griffin to write *Chemical Recreations* in 1823.

Chemistry textbooks of the early nineteenth century fall into three categories: advanced, introductory or general. Thomas Thomson's *System of Chemistry* or William Brande's

Manual of Chemistry were rival advance texts suitable for students who were reading medicine. Pinnock's *Catechism of Chemistry* or Mrs Marcet's *Conversations on Chemistry*, on the other hand, were introductory and often gave insight to youths and amateurs meeting the subject for the first time. The 'general' category included course books of a broader nature, including compendia intended for those whose primary interests were in the arts and manufacturing. Typically, John Murray's *Elements of Chemistry* or Samuel Parkes' *Chemical Catechism* (which was not actually a catechism) are the kind of works with which Griffin's *Chemical Recreations* might be compared – though Griffin had something new and different to offer.

In a section entitled 'First Lines of Chemistry', Griffin set down a rationale for chemical study, which embraced five aims: cognitive understanding of natural phenomena; affective reasons, that is those to do with comfort, happiness and luxury; application of the arts; medical education; and the pursuit of truth, which 'confers dignity and superiority on those who successfully pursue it'. Any analysis of texts of the period will show the commonality of these aims; but Griffin capped them with something else, an urge to experiment. Pragmatically, he told his mechanics:

> The hearing of lectures, and the reading of books, will never benefit him who attends to nothing else; for Chemistry can only be studied to advantage practically. One experiment, well-conducted, and carefully observed by the student, from first to last, will afford more knowledge than the mere perusal of a whole volume. It may be added to this, that chemical operations are, in general, the most interesting that could possibly be devised – Reader! what more is requisite to induce you to MAKE EXPERIMENTS?

Indeed, if chemistry had so much to offer through its variety of aims, then, like some religion, it was necessary to practise it rather than to expect a knowledge of it *ex cathedra.* Griffin's self-chosen task, therefore, was 'to make experiments' possible for the masses.

Two decades earlier, William Henry of Manchester had followed up a lecture course with a slim tract under the title *An Epitome of Chemistry* (1801). This was a reformist start in which students were not only guided through the work of Lavoisier, Chaptal and Fourcroy and the English authorities Nicholson, Pearson and Parkinson, but most importantly they were given a number of simple experiments (mostly of a mineralogical nature) to try out for themselves. Its success led Henry to write a comprehensive two-volume compendium, *Elements of Chemistry* (1806), which through its several editions became a standard work. It was not the first text of its kind to exemplify chemical practice: this can be traced fruitfully from the time of William Lewis's *Elaboratory Laid Open* (1758) and a *Course of Practical Chemistry* (1746). It was, nevertheless, influential upon many authors, including Frederick Accum, the London analytical chemist. Accum, like Henry, boxed up chemicals for his readers and students; but this was not to be Griffin's first plan. His earthy approach was closer to the needs of Glaswegian mechanics than Accum's well-to-do fashion seekers.

When it came to giving advice on the conduct of experiments, it was Henry that Griffin followed as mentor, particularly when it came to 'method, order and cleanliness'. A further, and perhaps less expected, source of influence on Griffin came from Humphry Davy's *Elements of Chemistry* (1812). Griffin explained how it was essential that readers of *Chemical Recreations* should understand how powerful agents could be brought to bear on small quantities of matter. The electric machines, the galvanic battery and the blowpipe had each in turn brought new revelations, such as the discovery that diamond was carbon, or new metals. Furthermore, Griffin's mechanics were to be encouraged by Davy's observation that:

> The active intellectual powers of man in different times are not so much the cause of the different successes of their labours, as the peculiar nature of the means and artificial resources in their possessions.

Here was an invitation for the ordinary working man to take part in the culture of science, though, inevitably, this entailed a reinterpretation of the subject in terms of what appealed and what was possible both practically and cheaply.

In London both Accum and Davy had been good publicists for chemistry, though their audiences could do little about getting to grips with laboratory instruments other than by studying them from books. To appreciate this cutting edge of science it was necessary – at a very minimum – to know about, even if not acquiring the skills in using, thermometers, air pumps, calorimeters, pyrometers, saccharometers, balances and batteries. Thus, in order to gain maximum benefit from a public lecture, the form and function of individual pieces of apparatus had to be studied at home. This was the stated purpose behind an elaborate anonymous work by Accum, *An Explanatory Dictionary of the Apparatus and Instruments Employed in the various Operations of Philosophical and Experimental Chemistry* (1824). This remarkable and profusely illustrated treasure house of information may be viewed as 'the London solution' for assisting students with practical studies; it did not, however, bring them any closer to performing experiments themselves. A similar motive probably inspired a Weimar pharmacy to issue, by subscription, *Das Laboratorium* between 1825 and 1841. This profusely illustrated compendium was culled from plates in German, French, English and American periodicals.

Henry had been sympathetic to his students' needs when he described how they might 'avoid the encumbrance of various instruments, the value of which consists in show rather than in real utility' by providing helpful apparatus lists. Simple Florence flasks, common vials and wine glasses were easy recommendations to make, but the means of supplying heat other than by expensive furnaces was a different matter. Charles Aikin's *Chemical Dictionary* (1814), for designs of apparatus by W. H. Pepys or W. H. Wollaston, was hardly likely to be studied by Griffin's mechanics, who required plain instructions. A new approach was definitely needed.

The Glasgow solution when it appeared in *Chemical Recreations* was the simple but effective step of telling the student 'where he may obtain the different utensils and how much they will cost him'. The innovatory part of this lay in Griffin recommending alternative designs of apparatus that could be made up locally, thereby placing the material side of chemistry within easier reach. It was also necessary that he should explain precisely how the apparatus should be handled.

> In short, as we proceed with our instructions, we shall continually bear in mind, that the persons we are addressing both need and are inclined to receive information; that they have neither the time to be lost, nor money to be thrown away, – and thus understanding the situation of our readers, we shall model our discourse.

Griffin had in fact cracked the major obstacle that he and his fellows at the Andersonian must have felt while studying under Ure.

It is appropriate here to sympathize with the student starting out on his studies and setting up a minimal laboratory by avoiding the expense of an instrument-maker, or a school that decided to introduce chemistry lessons. The student or the school would require scales and weights, vessels of various kinds, some means of heating, and specimens of metals, chemicals and reagents. To boost their confidence for dealing with alternative sources for such supplies they would need some idea of the designs and dimensions of apparatus and, naturally, the cost likely to be incurred. All this is handled by Griffin: how to purchase scales at apothecaries; funnels and flasks from a glassworks and oil men; pestle and mortar and crucibles from a Wedgwood-ware shop; a chemical heating lamp from a tin-smith; and a wooden pneumatic trough from a carpenter.

The success of the first six editions of the *Recreations* is a testimony to Griffin's strength as a teacher; that is, his forte as a communicator through the written word. His mechanics must have appreciated the forthright approach and the style, which was in part journalistic. In 1827 he published a digest on the blowpipe, that essential tool for those wishing to practise chemical analysis. And in 1831 he published two translations from French and German on glass-blowing together with Rose's *Manual of Analytical Chemistry*. The *Lancet* review praised Griffin for his 'improvement and diffusion of chemical knowledge'.

No evidence of Griffin's trade in apparatus (if any) prior to the mid–1830s had come to light. The seventh edition of *Chemical Recreations* (1834) does suggest some link with Robert Best Ede in London for the supply of portable laboratories to accompany his text, replacing the advice on local tradesmen as suppliers. By the eighth edition (1838), following studies in Heidelberg and contacts with German and French suppliers, Griffin had begun to market his own goods following a personal project to supply cheap apparatus. The major boost in the sales of chemical goods came from a policy to supply sets of apparatus to accompany in-house published texts; this was very much the move behind the *Scientific Miscellany* series of books in 1839. Griffin's Glasgow 'Chemical Museum' offered accompanying apparatus for William Gregory's translation of Liebig's *Chemical Analysis of Organic Bodies* (1839), including the Kaliapparat to be discussed below, as well as Griffin's own *A System of Crystallography* (1841). Both of these works were designed to offer students a wider range of laboratory apparatus beyond the customary systematic inorganic analysis or the usual chemical manipulations. Simultaneously with these works was issued a *Descriptive Catalogue of Chemical Apparatus* (July 1841), which specifically detailed the apparatus intended for Liebig's text. The transition was appropriately marked by the *Lancet's* reference to Griffin as 'an enterprising bookseller of Glasgow who now devotes his time to the sale of apparatus and books connected with chemistry'.

By the mid 1840s, however, Glasgow was no longer an ideal centre for chemistry, and certainly an awkward place from which to import and distribute apparatus when the balance of trade leaned towards London. Not surprisingly, therefore, in 1848 Griffin moved to London, where he launched a monthly descriptive and illustrated catalogue of his wares under the title of *Scientific Circular*.

The Chemical Museum, just opened in London, is under the personal supervision of John J. Griffin, F.C.S., . . . who respectfully offers his services to Amateurs and Professional Chemists, especially to Colonial Chemists, to collect or prepare every description of Scientific Apparatus.

There was, indeed, a wide miscellany of apparatus to catch the attention of amateurs and professionals in Britain and her empire, although the principal objective was to supply researchers, travellers, explorers and industrialists with special equipment in response to the growing legislative, educational and emigrant needs. For the first time, chemical laboratories in portable cabinets were listed for voyagers, lecturers and school teachers. Vast ranges of test tubes (a device first developed by Michael Faraday to replace the larger wine glass test glass), alkalimeters, acidimeters, hydrometers, chlorimeters, eudiometers, gas tubes, liquid measures and Liebig's combustion apparatus fill Griffin's catalogues.

The rise to pre-eminence of John Joseph Griffin & Co. within only four years of setting up the London base can be partly explained by a decline in energy of some of the older and more traditional philosophical instrument-makers, who did not respond to the rising demands of the industrial and educational age for chemical apparatus and remained content with their sales of telescopes, microscopes and surveying instruments. Griffin, by contrast, met this challenge and was particularly fortunate in being able to respond to the mid-century interest in science teaching. Henry Moseley, science inspector to the Committee of Council on Education, when commissioned to look into the details of how practical science might be introduced into the elementary school curriculum, naturally turned to Griffin for advice. When he reported to the government, who were to offer grants-in-aid to schools, he recorded that 'no man has probably laboured more than that gentleman [Griffin] to simplify and economize the construction of such apparatus'. Similar tributes were forthcoming in Hofmann's Jury Reports of the 1862 London International Exhibition.

> It must be conceded that to the exertions of Mr Griffin, commenced twenty years ago, in rendering to the public efficient chemical apparatus at a moderate price combined with the production of elementary works on all branches of science, the present wide-spread development of a taste for the acquisition of chemical knowledge is in a great measure attributable.

Similar accounts of chemical suppliers in other countries await documentation by historians. In America, for example, until the 1850s, there was scarcely any domestic production of chemical apparatus or reagents, most of which were imported from Britain, France and Germany and sold through dealers in scientific instruments, opticians or pharmacies. Reminiscent of the situation in Griffin's Glasgow in the 1820s, American chemists bought their burners from plumbers, water baths from tin-smiths, and beakers from glass factories. In 1850, however, encouraged by meeting the American chemist, Eben Horsford, at Giessen, Liebig's assistant, Bernard G. Amend, set up a drug and laboratory supply store in New York. He was soon joined by a school friend, Carl Eimer. Together with the Fisher Scientific Co., founded at Pittsburgh in 1902, Eimer and Amend became America's chief laboratory suppliers.

A great stimulus to native entrepreneurial activity was the campaign waged by the Department of Agriculture for pure foods and drugs. This was premised upon accurate methods, chemical analysis and purity control. When, for example, at the University of Wisconsin in 1890, Stephen Babcock developed a simple apparatus for estimating the quantity of butter fat in milk, the consequences were not only a decline in the adulteration of milk by farmers and a fairer method of pricing by quality, but a sudden need and demand for the hand-operated centrifuge, graduated test bottles, pipettes and small graduated cylinders for the measurement of the sulphuric acid used in the test. All these items had to be manufactured at a price dairy farmers could afford. It was this need that gave F. Kraissl the opportunity to expand the Kimble Glass Company he had set up in New Jersey in 1887 and to issue the first American laboratory-wares catalogue in 1892. Kraissl also found that similar apparatus was needed in the burgeoning petroleum industry of Philadelphia, so that the oil refiner paid a fair price for the crude oil that was mixed with water, mud and sand. The final take-off of the American chemical apparatus industry occurred during the First World War when, like Britain, America was forced to become self-sufficient. Among the many useful innovations of this experience was chemical experimentation with borosilicate glasses by the Corning Glass Works in 1915, which led to the manufacture of 'Pyrex' glassware for use in both the home and the laboratory.

LIEBIG, ORGANIC ANALYSIS AND
THE RESEARCH SCHOOL

Nineteenth-century organic chemists faced tremendous technical difficulties. But the intellectual problems of organic chemistry would never have been promoted or solved without the analysts' dogged search for adequate foundations. Each practical chemist searched for the organic analysts' philosopher's stone – the perfect method. William Prout, for example, spent twelve years looking for an apparatus and a technique that would produce really accurate analyses of organic materials. The results were time-consuming. Although Alexander Ure could write optimistically that his own method allowed him to make six determinations in a single day, even Liebig (in recommending the time saved by his method) could only claim four-hundred analyses per year with an army of research assistants.

Since all methods for determining the carbon, hydrogen and oxygen content of organic substances were to depend on measurements of carbon dioxide and water, final accuracy was dependent not only on the accurate determination of their quantities, but also on accurate knowledge of their composition. Organic analysis, therefore, has always been a specialized branch of gasometry.

Most of Lavoisier's organic analyses remained unpublished at his death, and his use of oxidizing agents remained largely unknown. Although some success using his cumbersome, dangerous and rather inaccurate method of oxidation was employed by the Swiss chemist Saussure, most chemists continued to use methods of proximate analysis by destructive distillation. Organic substances had been analysed by distillation for centuries, and by the beginning of the nineteenth century the products were usually collected, and often weighed, as fractions of gas, oil, phlegma and residue. Such distillation techniques continued to be used in vegetable analysis long after Gay-Lussac and Thenard, frustrated by Berthollet-type distillations, revolutionized organic analysis in 1810 by adopting an oxidizing agent.

Not that their use of potassium chlorate was a satisfactory solution to the problem. It proved time-consuming, dangerous and very much dependent on the operator's skill for its accuracy. Certainly the two Frenchmen obtained important results; but it would not appear that other chemists adopted their apparatus.

Berzelius, whose untranslated Swedish textbook of animal chemistry appeared between 1806 and 1808, continued to rely mainly on proximate analysis until 1812, and seems to have been unaware of the French method until his return to Sweden from England that year. In the hands of Berzelius, the Frenchmen's cumbersome apparatus was transformed into a safer and simpler horizontal arrangement, and uncertain volumetric estimations were replaced by the direct weighing of carbon dioxide and water by absorption and condensation. The whole process took about two hours, though Berzelius' proper insistence on purification, and the drying of the substances over sulphuric acid, made the complete process much longer.

Berzelius' technique underwent modifications at the hands of various chemists, most of whom quickly adopted copper oxide as an oxidizing agent when it was introduced by Gay-Lussac in 1815. The final version of Berzelius' apparatus and method was that of Liebig in 1830, which used a coal fire instead of dusty charcoal, or cool spirit lamp. Water (the oxidation product of the substance's hydrogen content) was absorbed in a bulb of hygroscopic calcium chloride, which could be weighed directly. Carbon dioxide (the oxidized product of the substance's carbon content) was similarly weighed directly by absorption in a solution of potassium hydroxide in an ingeniously arranged array of glass bottles that became known as the Kaiapparat. Oxygen was determined by difference.

The full details of Liebig's method were published in 1839 in the student manual, *Instructions for the Analysis of Organic Bodies*. This, like most of Liebig's books, was simultaneously published in both German and English. The method proved so perfect that few changes had to be made when Liebig published a second edition in 1853, by which time his pupil and translator, A. W. Hofmann, had begun to experiment with gas heating to replace the spirit lamp. Apart from the adoption of the bunsen burner in the 1860s, Liebig's method remains in current use.

Some of the apparatus developed between 1814 and 1830 was extraordinarily elaborate and expensive; the one by Prout (1827), which used pure oxygen and with which he analysed milk into oleaginous substances (fats), albuminous substances (proteins) and sugars (carbohydrates), was particularly bizarre. Nevertheless, it would be a mistake to think that Prout's method was never used by other chemists, for the apparatus was frequently mentioned by English textbook writers and it seems to have been available on commission from instrument-makers. It produced excellent results for Prout and, as Dumas and Hess found, for very accurate work the use of oxygen with copper oxide was indispensable.

In fact, individual chemists who had not trained at Giessen personally only found the Liebig method easiest and best after much heart-searching. What was the best form of heating? How should substances be purified? Should the products of combustion be estimated volumetrically or gravimetrically? What could be done to diminish the hygroscopic nature of copper oxide, or its perverse habit of absorbing air when warmed? Should substances be triturated? Were rubber tubing or cork stoppers best for connecting the parts of apparatus, and which would alter least in weight during a combustion? How could nitrogen be accurately estimated? How were the determined elements arranged in the molecule?

No wonder Prout exclaimed, 'to conquer these, every means that could be thought of, as likely to succeed, were tried, but without effect, and I was obliged to relinquish the matter in despair'. The great advantage of Liebig's method, as he was the first to admit, was not that he introduced anything radically new over Berzelius, or that he offered new heights of accuracy, but that he refused to be trapped by such questions. As he said, defeatism merely means you do not do any research. Here, he suggested, was a simple, cheap and reliable method, which answered well enough for everyday determinations of carbon, hydrogen and oxygen. Nitrogen remained a separate issue, and was always to be the subject of separate elaborate determinations along with other more rare organic elements such as sulphur.

TABLE 5.1 *Example of an organic analysis: the composition of cholalic acid (cholic acid)*

Cholalic acid, today known as cholic acid, was first discovered in bile by Berzelius and investigated by Adolph Strecker (1822-71) in Liebig's Giessen laboratory in 1848. The procedure for determining its composition was described by Liebig in the second edition of his monograph on organic analysis.

Combine with barytes (barium oxide) and find the equivalent weight of cholalate of barytes.

(1) 0.5235 gms of cholalate of barytes gives with sulphuric acid 0.1270 gms of sulphate of barium;

(2) 0.5800 gms of cholalate of barytes gives with carbonic acid 0.1210 gms of carbonate of barium.

Since the equivalent weight of sulphate of barytes is 116.5, that of cholalate of barytes is, from (1)

$0.1270 : 116.5 = 0.5235 : x = 480.2$

And, since the equivalent weight of carbonate of barytes is 98.5, that of cholalate of barytes from (2) is

$0.1210 : 98.5 = 0.5800 : x = 472.1$

Taking the mean, we have 476.2

On combustion of barytes of cholalic acid with lead chromate

(1) 0.3361 gms of barytes of cholalic acid gives 0.7425 gms CO_2 corresponding to 220% or 60.24% of carbon

(2) 0.3410 gms of barytes of cholalic acid gives 0.7505 gms CO_2 corresponding to 220.1% or 60.02% of carbon. Taking the mean: 100 parts of barytes of cholalic acid = 220.5 parts CO_2, or 60.13 carbon.

Also 0.3361 gms of cholalic acid salt gives 0.2500 gms water and

$$\frac{0.3410 \text{ gms}}{0.6771} \dots\dots\dots\dots \frac{0.2530 \text{ gms water}}{0.5030}$$

Therefore 100 parts cholalate of barytes contains 8.25 parts hydrogen.

Calculate oxygen by difference:

C	=	60.13
H	=	8.25
BaO	=	16.07
O	=	15.55
		100.00

To determine the formula from barytes salt equivalent of 476.2

60.13 × 4.762 =	286.3	parts carbon
8.25 × 4.762 =	39.3	hydrogen
16.07 × 4.762 =	76.5	barytes
15.55 × 4.762 =	74.1	oxygen
	476.2	

Since one equivalent of cholalate of barytes contains 286.3 parts carbon, on dividing by the equivalent weight of carbon (6), and similarly for other constituents (0 = 8)

286.3 ÷ 6	= 48 carbon
39.3 ÷ 1	= 39 hydrogen
76.5 ÷ 76.5	= 1 barytes
74.1 ÷ 8	= 9 oxygen

So formula is $C_{48}H_{39}O_9$ BaO

Compare with theory:

			theory	found
48 equivalents	C =	288	60.57	60.13
39	H =	39	8.20	8.25
9	O =	72	15.14	15.55
1 .... BaO =		76.5	16.09	16.07
		475.5	100.00	100.00

In practice, the hydrogen was slightly underestimated by Strecker and this threw out his estimate of oxygen. The present-day formula is $C_{24}H_{40}O_5$, where C = 12 and O = 16.

When the twenty-one-year-old Justus von Liebig was appointed Assistant Professor of Chemistry at the small, sleepy University of Giessen some twenty miles to the north of Frankfurt in 1824, he hoped to make his name and his fortune through the establishment of a private pharmacy school rather than through the academic teaching of chemistry at the University. This had been done very successfully by J. B. Trommsdorff (1770–1837) at the University of Erfurt, where he also ran a private pharmacy school. In the event, although large numbers of Liebig's students were destined for Germany's apothecary shops, he and Giessen were to become chiefly renowned as a model institution for the teaching of practical chemistry. With his headquarters in an unheated and disused barracks, the Giessen laboratory, or laboratories as they had become by 1839, were the most famous in the world for practical instruction in chemical analysis and especially for a sure-fire method of organic analysis.

Liebig (1803–73) was one of eight children born to lower-middle-class parents at Darmstadt in the tiny state of Hessen-Darmstadt. His parents ran a *Drogerie*, which sold paints and varnishes, and other household wares such as boot polish, several of which were made up by Liebig's father in an adjacent workshop. Liebig's family was never well off. In 1817, during a period of severe agricultural and trade depression following the Napoleonic war, Liebig had to be withdrawn from the local Gymnasium and apprenticed to an apothecary at the neighbouring town of Heppenheim. Unfortunately, Liebig's father could not afford the full apprenticeship fee and his son's training was abruptly terminated after only six months. The successful adult Liebig obviously found his boyhood poverty embarrassing, and so he told stories of causing explosions in the pharmacy that had earned him dismissal as an unruly apprentice. Back in Darmstadt, Liebig worked in his father's workshop preparing varnishes and pigments, while reading chemistry books from the Ducal library, which, in an act of enlightenment, Duke Ludwig seems to have thrown open to worthy citizens. By the time Liebig was seventeen, trade had improved and Liebig had decided that he wanted to be a chemist and possibly a chemical industrialist.

Through the happy accident that his father supplied chemicals to Karl Wilhelm Kastner (1783–1857) at the University of Bonn and had also written a paper on liquid manure for Kastner's short-lived *Zeitschrift dem Gewerbsfreund,* Kastner agreed to take Liebig on as his personal assistant and to train him in chemistry. This opportunity meant that Liebig was able to attend Kastner's lectures even though he did not possess the Arbitur, or school-leaving, certificate necessary for matriculation at a German university. In later life Liebig was rude about Kastner's chemical competence and decidedly ungracious towards him; but without Kastner's support and patronage Liebig might well have remained a small-town hardware salesman. At Bonn and Erlangen (where Kastner took the Chair of Chemistry in 1821) Liebig plunged into the serious study of French, Latin and mathematics, botany and chemistry, as well as entering fully into the social life of student fraternities and their politics, and having a passionate, and possibly homosexual, friendship with the poet, August von Platin. To Kastner, too, Liebig owed a travel grant to study in Paris, which Kastner obtained for his protégé from the benevolent Grand-Duke Ludwig of Hessen-Darmstadt. Clearly, Liebig was perceived as an exceptionally promising young man, so much so that Kastner was even able to persuade the Erlangen faculty to award Liebig what was in effect an honorary degree *in absentia* in 1822. It is one of the ironies of Liebig's teaching career that he himself never presented a thesis for his doctorate.

In Paris Liebig attended the lectures of Gay-Lussac and Thenard, from whom he also learned how to analyse animal and vegetable (organic) materials. Using their technique, Liebig was able to analyse the explosive silver fulminate, which he had first prepared in Erlangen, and to show that it was a derivative of an unknown organic acid, fulminic acid. He published his analyses with Gay-Lussac in 1824, just when Friedrich Wöhler (1800–82) was analysing silver cyanate in Berzelius' home laboratory in Stockholm where he had gone to perfect his analytical technique. Wöhler showed that silver cyanate was a salt of another new acid, cyanic acid, identical in composition with Liebig's fulminic acid. Since fulminates and cyanates have very different properties, it was assumed by their contemporaries that one of the two young men was an incompetent analyst. Liebig was quick to make this charge against Wöhler; but after they had met in 1826 and had gone through their analyses together, each agreed that their original findings had been justified and Liebig graciously admitted that he had blundered in describing Wöhler's analyses as incorrect.

Not only did their little conflict lead to the greatest friendship and partnership in the history of chemistry (over a thousand letters exchanged between Liebig and Wöhler have survived), but it was one of the factors that led Berzelius to announce the doctrine of isomerism in 1831 – that two (or more) substances might have the same composition, yet different properties, because their atoms were differently arranged. By then, of course, Wöhler had made an even more sensational discovery. In 1828 he found that the urea extracted from a dog's urine had exactly the same composition as ammonium cyanate. Between them, Liebig and Wöhler had revealed the source of richness (and fascination) of organic chemistry, that the simple elements of carbon, oxygen, hydrogen and nitrogen could combine together in myriads of different ways to produce millions of different compounds.

Paris, as the centre of European scientific life, provided Liebig with invaluable social contacts, including that of Alexander von Humboldt, the traveller and geographer who was then Prussian Ambassador to France. It was after learning of Liebig's impressive and dangerous work on the analysis of silver fulminate, which Liebig had performed in Gay-Lussac's private laboratory, that Humboldt wrote to the Grand-Duke of Hessen-Darmstadt recommending Liebig for an academic position. This recommendation coincided with the Duke's and his advisers' enlightened view that chemistry had reached the stage of being of vital importance to the economic viability of a nation state. Chemistry was no longer a subject only of use to doctors, but knowledge that could improve agriculture, mining and manufacturing. This cameralistic viewpoint was not, however, being met by the existing Professor of Chemistry, Wilhelm Zimmermann (1780–1825).

It was Humboldt's powerful patronage, together with the Duke's edict that pharmacy students were to be transferred from the medical faculty to the philosophical faculty, where chemistry was taught, that brought Liebig to Giessen in 1824. Within a year, following the suicide of Zimmermann, Liebig was completely in a position to shape the fortunes of his laboratory and able to teach chemistry as well as bread-and-butter pharmacy.

Both because of his early interest in fulminates and cyanates, but mainly because of his commitment to the training of state pharmacists, Liebig's research during the 1820s was turned towards organic chemistry. He became a close friend of the Heidelberg pharmacist Phillipp Geiger (1785–1836), who interested him in the alkaloids that dozens of German pharmacists were busily analysing. It was Geiger who persuaded Liebig to co-edit a journal he had been editing since 1824 called the *Magazin für Pharmacie*. Geiger had been using this periodical to bolster the scientific foundations of pharmacy, which he did by experimentally checking authors' reports. Retitled the *Annalen der Pharmacie* in 1832, following Geiger's death, Liebig became its sole editor and was able to transform it into a journal of chemistry, as reflected in the transposed title, *Annalen der Chemie und Pharmacie*. Geiger had needed Liebig to check that authors' chemical statements were accurate – a task that Liebig accepted with relish. His bitter editorial denunciations of German and overseas colleagues soon made him enemies, while at the same time making the *Annalen* indispensable reading. Above all, it gave Liebig a stage for developing his talents as a publicist and writer. Liebig also became involved in Geiger's plans to edit a huge *Handbuch der Pharmacie*, which he generously saw through the press after Geiger's sudden death, in order to support his widow.

We are now in a position to explain how Liebig built up a great teaching and research school that became the model for others in Germany and overseas. In a seminal article, J. B. Morrell suggested that the necessary conditions for Liebig's success were intellectual, institutional, technical, psychological and financial. In the first place Liebig had a definite programme of research (the analysis of organic compounds) and of instruction (the practical teaching of qualitative and quantitative analysis). By 1831 he had more than adequately established a national and international reputation for the prosecution of these related programmes, while the *Annalen* was to become a mouthpiece for him and for his students. This reputation, together with the growing awareness that he had a skill and technique to impart whose study could be extremely useful in the prosecution of pharmacy and medicine, and by the 1840s, agriculture and chemistry teaching, ensured that another necessary condition of success – an adequate supply of students – was fully met.

As we have seen, this position was mainly advanced through Liebig's management of a private pharmaceutical institute separate from his state-supported teaching at the University, though there must have been some overlap of activities. Unfortunately, no details have survived concerning student numbers, or where this private operation was carried out and how financially successful it was. All that is known is that the institute did succeed in attracting students from other German states and, significantly, from overseas. In 1833, following some bargaining with the government, Liebig amalgamated his private school with his official university course, by which time we know he was teaching ten to fifteen pharmacy students and three to five chemistry students per annum. Over the next two decades the number of students reading chemistry was to exceed those in pharmacy:

	1830–5	1836–40	1841-5	1846–50	Totals
Chemistry	15	75	174	143	407
Pharmacy	53	63	74	62	252

From J. S. Fruton, *Contrasts in Scientific Style* . . . (Philadelphia: American Philosophical Society, 1990).

By 1852, when he left Giessen for the University of Munich, over 700 students of chemistry and pharmacy had passed through Liebig's hands.

Such large numbers could only be dealt with in a much bigger laboratory than the premises Liebig had in the 1820s. It was not, however, until 1839 that he, together with the architect Paul Hofmann (whose son was soon to become Liebig's favourite pupil), obtained funds from the government to enlarge the facilities. This included a lecture theatre and two separate laboratories for pharmacy and chemistry students. The latter's laboratory – familiar in the famous engraving by Trauschold – was fitted with glass-fronted cupboards in which the fumes from dangerous reactions could be vented directly into the outside air through a special chimney. Such 'fume cupboards', which hitherto had only been found in the private laboratories of Gay-Lussac in Paris and the pharmacist W. H. Pepys in London, soon became standard laboratory furniture in laboratories all over the world.

The enlargement of Liebig's laboratory also suggests another vital feature of his success, state patronage and its corollary, financial support. As Morrell has shown, all previous teaching laboratories had failed because of a 'Catch 22' situation: if a teacher charged a low fee in order to encourage large numbers of students, he was unable to meet the large expenses of running a laboratory of sufficient size; if, on the other hand, he charged realistic fees to cover laboratory expenses, few students (other than those motivated by a lucrative career as a German apothecary) were attracted. The result of this situation, especially in the Scottish universities, had been that university teachers were discouraged from running practical classes; they opted for low fees, very large classes and chemical entertainment by lecture demonstrations.

Liebig had the advantage that from the very beginning the state provided the University of Giessen with a modest annual subsidy for laboratory expenses over and above the Professor's salary and such fees as he was able to take from students. By being prepared to use some of his salary and student income to subsidize the laboratory costs for several years, Liebig was able to bargain his success in attracting students to the University of Giessen, as well as his own growing fame as a chemist, to obtain not only increases of salary, but increases in laboratory expenses. As he noted to the University Chancellor in 1833[2]:

The resources of the laboratory have been too small from the beginning. I was given four bare walls instead of a laboratory; despite my solicitations, nobody thought of a definite sum for its outfitting [and] for the purchase of supplies. I needed instruments and [chemical] preparations and was obliged to use 3–400 florins per year of my meagre salary for the purchase of preparations; I have needed in addition to the attendant paid by the state [since 1828], an assistant, who costs me 320 florins; if you subtract these two expenditures from my stipend [800 fl] not much remains to clothe my children.

These continual complaints, together with the real danger that Liebig would be poached by another university, to the great loss of Hessen-Darmstadt, persuaded the government to satisfy Liebig's demands, as table 5.2 shows.

TABLE 5.2 *A sample of Liebig's 'resources'.*

Year	Liebig's salary (florins)	Event	Laboratory expenses paid by the state (florins)
1824	300	Associate Professor	100
1825	500	April: raise	400
	800	July: full Professor	446
1833	880	Complains and threatens to resign	619
1835	1250	Invited to Antwerp; promised larger laboratory	714 plus Ettling's salary
1837	1650	Invited to St Petersburg	
1840	3200	Invited to Vienna	1500
1843			1900

In addition, the government provided generous funds for the enlargement of the laboratory between 1838 and 1839, so enabling Liebig to expand his student numbers still further. By then, students were being attracted from overseas – particularly from Britain. Such an arrangement and recognition by a government that it was unreasonable to expect a large science school to be financed entirely from a professor's own pocket soon became widely recognized by other German states. Liebig's Scottish pupil, William

Gregory (1803–58), regarded Liebig's arrangement at Giessen as a model for similar schools in the British Isles. But when the Royal College of Chemistry was finally opened in London in 1845, despite bearing most of the hallmarks of the Giessen laboratory, by being privately financed, it lacked the vital financial stability of its German model. Although amazingly successful because its Director fulfilled the Liebigian conditions intellectually, technically and psychologically, it was only after 1853, when the British government took over the management of the College, that the institutional and financial conditions of Liebig's success were fully met.

Finally, it is worth emphasizing that large numbers of students flocked to Giessen, particularly overseas students, because in the Kaliapparat Liebig had a wonderful technique for analysis. Triangular series of five glass bulbs filled with potassium hydroxide were first described in *Poggendorff's Annalen* at the end of 1830. Although Liebig had learned glass-blowing in Paris, the making of the bulbs demanded very considerable skill and it was probably his assistant, Carl Ettling (1806–56), who perfected the apparatus. It was the latter, on a visit to the British Association in 1840 at Glasgow, who showed a Scottish glass-blower the necessary technique. (It would be nice to find that he worked for Griffin, but there is no evidence for this.) As glass-blowers became more skilled, the inelegant prototypes became transfigured into objects of beauty, so much so that the bulbs, like Kekulé's benzene hexagon or the alchemist's uroboros [snake devouring its own tail], have become part of chemistry's heraldry. The bulbs, for example, appear on the shield of the American Chemical Society and on the badges of various American Greek chemical fraternities. A bust of Liebig himself adorns the staircase of the Royal Society of Chemistry's premises in London.

CONCLUSION

At the beginning of the nineteenth century organic chemistry had seemed a mysterious and unfathomable world: in Wöhler's memorable phrase, it was like a dark forest with few or no pathways. It is easy to blame the seeming lack of progress in organic chemistry on vitalism, but progress in animal and vegetable chemistry in the first part of the last century was held back less by a belief that vital forces overruled the forces of chemical affinity in organic compounds than the sheer difficulty of organic analysis. To take a later parallel, biochemistry has only been able to develop so rapidly in the twentieth century because of the introduction of microanalytical methods by Fritz Pregl in 1917, the building of the ultracentrifuge by The Svedberg (1884–1971) in 1925, the development of electrophoresis by Arne Tiselius (1902–71) in 1936, and the perfection of chromatography by John Martin and Richard Synge in the 1940s.

Too much attention has been paid in histories of chemistry to the conceptual confusions and difficulties over nomenclature and atomic weights, vitalism and organic models in the uneasy development of organic chemistry before the emergence of structural theory; not enough consideration has been paid to the tremendous difficulties caused by impurity, the supply of apparatus and reagents, and the technical difficulties of analysis. Liebig's speedy, reliable method of analysis altered this situation completely (see Table 5.2). Not only was this the secret of his own personal success as a teacher, but the method led to a burst of activity and an immense clarification of the chemical evidence: relationships between organic compounds could be seen for the first time and classifications of species became possible. Wöhler's forest turned out to be a well ordered arboretum.

By the middle of the century, as analytical chemistry became a commercial commodity and one in which chemical careers could be made, Fresenius realized that moral and ethical questions were also involved as well as knowledge and skills. His Hippocratic Oath for analysts is worth quoting by way of conclusion[3]:

> Knowledge and ability must be combined with ambition as well as with a sense of honesty and a severe conscience. Every analyst occasionally has doubts about the accuracy of his results, and also there are times when he knows his results to be incorrect. Sometimes a few drops of the solution were spilt, or some other slight mistake made. In those cases it requires a strong conscience to repeat the analysis and not to make a rough estimate of the loss or apply a correction. Anyone not having sufficient will-power to do this is unsuited to analysis no matter how great his technical ability or knowledge. A chemist who would not take an oath guaranteeing the authenticity, as well as the accuracy of his work, should never publish his results, for if he were to do so then the result would be detrimental, not only to himself, but to the whole of science.

6

Chemical Method

Fifty years ago the stream of chemical progress had divided into two branches. The one flowed, chiefly on French soil, through luxuriant flower-decked plains; and those who followed it, with Laurent and Dumas at their head, could reap, during the whole voyage, almost without effort, an abundant harvest. The other followed the course indicated by an old and approved guide-post set up by the great Swedish chemist, Berzelius; it led for the most part through broken boulders, and only later on did it again reach fertile country. At length, as the two branches had again approached much nearer to one another, they were separated by a thick growth of misunderstanding, so that those who were sailing along the one side neither saw those on the other, nor understood their speech.

(AUGUST KEKULÉ, 1890)

Metaphors were the order of the day in the speeches given in 1890 to mark the jubilee of Kekulé's hexagonal conceptualization of the structure of benzene in 1865. But they had been prevalent among the pioneers of organic chemistry too, as when Wöhler referred to the organic domain as a dark forest, and Liebig and Wöhler to their work on benzaldehyde as a light in 'the dark province of organic nature'. For Laurent, the sheer fecundity of organic chemistry produced a labyrinth[1]:

When we consider the great number of organic substances that have been discovered during the last dozen years, and the increasing rapidity with which chemistry daily discovers fresh ones; when we see, that from a simple hydrocarbon and chlorine, we may produce a hundred compounds, and that from them we may obtain a great number of others: lastly, when we reflect upon the absence of all system, all nomenclature, for the classification and denomination of this multitude of bodies, we demand with some anxiety, whether, in a few years' time, it will be possible for us to direct ourselves in the labyrinth of organic chemistry.

Organic compounds were initially defined simply according to their principal source, animal or vegetable, and according to their main chemical functions, acid, base, fat, dye and so on. By the 1820s and 1830s, however, a growing confidence in analysis (chapter 5) and knowledge of the interconnections (metamorphoses) between organic compounds suggested that it might be possible to clarify the proliferation of such compounds by using chemical criteria to group them. Later systematists, such as Leopold Gmelin, referred to this first taxonomic attempt as the radical theory.

CLASSIFICATION BY RADICALS

According to the electrochemical theory of Berzelius, 'organic bodies obey the same general laws as that regulating the formation of inorganic combinations', the sole difference being that, whereas the latter contained only binary combinations, organic compounds were frequently tertiary or even quaternary in composition. In the *Essai sur la théorie des proportions chimiques* (1819) Berzelius applied dualistic principles to organic compounds, arguing that they always consisted of oxygen combined with a compound radical. 'In the case of plant substances', he suggested, 'the radical generally consists of carbon and hydrogen, and in the case of animal substances of carbon, hydrogen and nitrogen'. In modern terminology, organic compounds had the general composition $(XYZ)^+O^-$, where X, Y, Z are C, H or N, and the task of the organic chemist was to seek out analogies with inorganic chemistry. For example, if sulphuric acid was $(SO^3 + H^2O)$, by analogy, acetic acid could be $[(C^4H^6)O^3 + H^2O]$, with the radical C^4H^6 playing the role of sulphur in the organic acid.

Ever since the era of Guyton de Morveau and Lavoisier, the term 'radical' had referred to a stable part of a substance that retained its identity through a series of reactions even though it was known to be a compound. This was the sense in which it was used by Gay-Lussac in 1815 when, in an investigation of prussic acid and its derivatives, the cyanides, he found that the radical CN behaved analogously to the elements chlorine and iodine in chlorides and iodides.

There followed a decade of uncertainty before there seemed to be sufficient evidence for Berzelius' proposal that radicals pre-existed in a series of compounds. During the 1820s Dumas and the pharmacist, Pierre Boullay senior, investigated the sweet-smelling salts of organic vegetable acids called esters and found a useful analogy between them and ammonium salts. In the case of the ester of ethyl alcohol, they suggested that it was a compound of the radical C_4H_8, analogous to the ammonia in ammonium chloride. Berzelius agreed enthusiastically, naming the C_4H_8 group 'etherin' in 1827. Ethyl chloride could then be formulated as $C_4H_8.HCl$ and its parent alcohol as $C_2H_4.H_2O$ on the analogy of

$$NH_3 + HCl = NH_3.HCl$$

Between 1832 and 1833, however, Robert Kane and Liebig pointed out that, on the basis of other reactions, ethyl chloride could just as equally be formulated around an 'ethyl' radical, C_4H_{10}:

$$C_4H_{10}Cl + H_2O = C_4H_{10}OH + HCl$$
$$2C_4H_{10}OH = (C_4H_{10})_2O + H_2O$$

At the same time, in a brilliantly executed series of chemical transformations, Liebig and Wöhler showed how the oil of bitter almonds (benzaldehyde) could be converted into a range of different compounds, each of which had in common a group $(C_{14}H_{10}O_2)$ that they named 'benzoyl'. Although Berzelius praised their experimental findings, because he disliked the idea of electronegative oxygen as part of the radical, he redefined benzoyl as the hydrocarbon radical Bz = $C_{14}H_{10}$, and BzO = benzoic acid, BzH_2 = benzaldehyde, Bz + NH_2 = benzamide.

By the mid 1830s, it seemed clear, therefore, that it was possible to classify organic compounds as the derivatives of an ever-growing number of electropositive radicals that could be identified by the metamorphosis of compounds and the careful quantitative analysis of reaction products using Liebig's improved method of combustion analysis (chapter 5). These radicals were a mixture of the hypothetical and of others that had an apparent independent existence in the laboratory. In its most triumphant year, 1837, Robert Bunsen expressed the results of his dangerous investigation of poisonous and explosive organo-arsenic compounds in terms of the most complex radical to date, *cacodyl* $(C_4H_{12}As_2)$. In the same year, fresh from his first successful tour of Great Britain, Liebig collaborated with his French arch rival, Dumas, on a joint paper that defined organic chemistry as the chemistry of compound radicals, The task of future chemists, they maintained, was to identify these radicals, to sort out their relationships, and to find useful analogies with inorganic chemistry as an aid to classification.

This was wishful thinking. By 1837 there were already a number of problems connected with the radical theory. The fact that Berzelius, Liebig and Dumas each used different atomic weights meant, for a start, that radicals tended to look different in different countries.

	H	C	O
Berzelius	1	12	16
Liebig	1	6	8
Dumas	1	6	16

The phenomenon of isomerism also raised the question of how to justify the assumption that radicals remained stable and did not undergo some kind of internal rearrangement during reactions. A similar point had been raised by Boyle nearly two centuries before when criticizing the pre-existence of 'elements' in compounds. In 1823, as a result of considering Liebig's and Wöhler's strange demonstration that silver cyanate and silver fulminate had identical compositions, Gay-Lussac and Chevreul argued categorically that future chemists would have to consider carefully the possibility that radicals might differ in internal arrangement. This point was underlined in 1828 when Wöhler found that ammonium cyanate had an identical composition with the urea extracted from a dog's urine.

It was Berzelius himself, however, who, after failing to detect any compositional difference between racemic and tartaric acids, named the phenomenon *isomerism* in 1830. This was to prove one of the fundamental ideas of organic chemistry, since it explained the superabundance of carbon compounds compared with the relative austerity of inorganic chemistry. Procedurally, it demonstrated that the chemical properties of organic compounds did depend on the constitution of organic compounds and that a knowledge of the ultimate constitution had to be the goal of future research. But, as Laurent was to underline formally in *Chemical Method*, if isomeric radicals have exactly the same composition, what are the guarantees that meaningful classifications are possible?

If every chemist follows his own particular course and changes his formulae as often as he obtains a new reaction, [then] we should arrive at results quite as satisfactory by putting the atomic letters of a formula into an urn and then taking them out, haphazard, to form the dualistic groups.

In other words, if one based composition on the evidence of reactions, one could postulate *different* radicals. If A + B → X and also C + D → X, which in turn could be decomposed in two ways into E + F or G + H, was X = A + B, or C + D, or E + F, or G + H? From its reactions alone, barium sulphate, for example, could be assumed to be (BaO + SO³) or (BaO² + SO²) or (BaS + 2O²). Moreover, if one religiously followed the electrochemical formulation of the radical theory, how were substitution reactions to be classified? The problem, which was already implicit in Liebig and Wöhler's demonstration that benzaldehyde, $(C_7H_5)H$ (C = 12), could be made to produce benzyl chloride, $(C_7H_5)Cl$, became critical as early as 1834.

The crisis began innocently enough with a Royal reception in Paris when the candles set on the tables burned with an acrid, smoky flame. France's leading chemist, Jean-Baptiste Dumas (1800–84) was consulted and asked to improve candle manufacture. He found that some of the chloride used to bleach wax during manufacture combined with the animal fats used in the process. It proved a simple matter to rectify (using sulphuric acid as a purification agent rather than chloride), but the spin-off was Dumas' investigation of how chlorine combined with fatty acids. Dumas found that, when the one atom of hydrogen in chloroform (first prepared by Liebig in 1831) was removed as hydrogen chloride, it could be replaced by exactly one atom of chlorine, bromine or iodine.

Although Dumas had been careful to call the reaction one of exchange ('metalepsy'), not substitution, his pupil, Laurent, had no hesitation in interpreting the reaction as a palpable substitution of electropositive hydrogen by electronegative chlorine. Since this was electrochemically 'impossible', Laurent concluded that the electrochemical dualism that was the method of classification by radicals needed modification. This inevitably outraged Berzelius, who, to Dumas' dismay, accused him of agreeing with Laurent. Dumas wrote to Berzelius ungenerously:

> You attribute to me an opinion precisely contrary to that which I have always maintained, viz. that chlorine in this case takes the place of the hydrogen . . . . The law of substitution is an empirical fact and nothing more; it expressed a relation between the hydrogen expelled and the chlorine retained. I am not responsible for the gross exaggeration with which Laurent has invested my theory; his analyses moreover do not merit any confidence.

Then, in 1838, Dumas found that trichloracetic acid could be prepared very simply by the action of chlorine on acetic acid, and that the properties of the two acids were virtually identical. Now the possibility of literal substitution already espoused by Laurent had to be taken seriously.

Here was the parting of the chemical streams described in Kekulé's later metaphor. There was no alternative; either one followed Berzelius in the ingenious adaptation of the radical theory of classification so that an electrochemical explanation of combination was preserved; or one ignored the question of what glued atoms together and looked instead at the unitary forms of molecules in their reactions. Given the facts, both approaches were entirely legitimate and logical attempts to deal with the problem.

Berzelius' solution, the theory of copulae or co-ordination, which he announced in 1840, modified his previous insistence that all organic compounds were derivatives of radicals. He now suggested not only that some radicals might co-ordinate with one another, but accepted that radicals might undergo alteration during a substitution reaction. If acetic acid was formulated as the oxide of a methyl radical, trichloracetic acid then became a carbon chloride radical or copula united with the anhydride of oxalic acid without an electrochemical mechanism:

acetic acid $C_4H_6^+ . O_3^- + H_2O$

trichloracetic acid $C_2Cl_6 \frown C_2O_3 + H_2O$

Since both oxalic acid and the perchloroethane (C_2Cl_6) actually existed, Berzelius' only hypothesis was that the latter's fastening, or attachment, to oxalic acid did not affect its acidic properties. This assumption could be supported by the abundant evidence that the saturation capacities of mineral acids were unaffected by combinations with organic groups.

Unfortunately for Berzelius, no sooner was the 're-arrangement of radicals' explanation of substitution in place than Dumas' pupil, Louis Melsens, showed in 1842 that trichloracetic acid could be simply reduced by hydrogen back to acetic acid! Since both acids were clearly analogous, or of the same 'type' as Dumas put it, Berzelius was forced to concede that substitution was a real phenomenon.

But out of defeat came the astonishingly creative and fruitful notion that most organic compounds were copulated, with all substitutions occurring within the non-electrochemical copulae attached to radicals. Acetic acid now became a methyl copula attached to oxalic acid, with an exact analogy with trichloracetic acid:

acetic acid $C_2H_6 \frown C_2O_3 + H_2O$

trichloracetic acid $C_2Cl_6 \frown C_2O_3 + H_2O$

To the eye of the modern reader such formulae look astonishingly like the structural formulae $CH_3.CO.OH$ and $CCl_3.CO.OH$, as well as an implicit differentiation between covalent and ionic bonding. But to become these, mid-nineteenth-century chemists needed to agree on atomic weight standards, and to merge Berzelius' copulae with the alternative stream of unitary types developed by Dumas, Laurent, Gerhardt and others.

Dumas' solution to substitution had been to classify organic molecules as 'chemical types' when, like chloracetic and acetic acids, they contained the same number of equivalents, united together in a similar manner and possessed the same fundamental properties and reactions. The analogy here was with isomorphism – a suggestion that he took from Laurent, as we shall see. On this basis, rather unwisely, he speculated that the law of substitution might apply to elements other than hydrogen, and even to carbon. This was a signal for Wöhler's famous spoof letter in *Annalen* in 1840 in which the author 'S. C. H. Windler' claimed to have completely chlorinated manganous acetate atom for atom in sunlight. It was found that the product, chlorine, had preserved the type! Despite Liebig's editorial support for this satire, it is clear that by 1840 he too acknowledged that strict electrochemical dualism had had its day, though, tired of theories, he remained agnostic.

Dumas' identification of 'fundamental chemical properties' shared by compounds of the same chemical type was potentially important, since it solved the problem of deciding between the relative significance of the various reactions undergone by compounds. As we have seen, radical theorists had no way of differentiating between possible constitutions based upon reactions. Oxidation of alcohol to acetic acid justified Liebig's acetyl radical, C_4H_3; its esterification also justified Liebig's ethyl radical; while its conversion to chloral justified Dumas' etherin. In practice, as Berzelius pointed out, Dumas had no absolute criteria for defining chemical types, and the idea proved sterile until transformed into the substitution types of Gerhardt.

Dumas had also defined 'mechanical types' (molecular

types) for substances in which hypothetical substitutions would produce similar formulae even though the actual substances had very different properties. For example:

Methane	$C_4H_2H_6$
Methyl ether	C_4OH_6
Formic acid	$C_4H_2O_3$
Chloroform	$C_4H_2Cl_3$

But for the fact that old atomic weights were used, mechanical types might have revealed the notion of valency, or combining powers; as it was, however, the classification was without influence until exploited by Kekulé. Until 1858 it was an extreme example of chemists' determination to explore every possible classificatory avenue.

Auguste Laurent (1808–53) was the second of four sons of a wine merchant. His early education, which was severely classical, was reflected in his later penchant for unusual neologisms. Not wanting to follow his father's business, he was advised by his teachers to adopt a scientific career and, in 1826, with financial support from a maternal uncle, he entered L'école de mines in Paris, where he became interested in crystallography and organic chemistry. After graduating in 1830 he became a research assistant to Dumas at L'école des arts et manufactures. From 1833 to 1835 he was chief analyst at the famous porcelain factory at Sèvres, but, finding that this interfered with his research on the relationships between the higher fatty acids, he became a private chemistry teacher. From 1838 until his formal resignation in 1848 he was Professor of Chemistry at the Science Faculty in Bordeaux, where he made a study of coal-tar derivatives, isolating phenol in 1841 and showing that it was identical to a previously isolated carbolic acid. During a brief visit to Liebig's laboratory at Giessen in 1843, Laurent was able to collaborate with A. W. Hofmann on the conversion of phenol into aniline. The nitration of phenol produced picric acid (trinitrophenol), which some earlier chemists had extracted from indigo.

Discontented with provincial life, and in failing health from the tuberculosis that was to lead to his early death, he returned to Paris in 1845, commuting to Bordeaux when necessary for teaching. Laurent's fiercely Republican politics were rewarded after the 1848 Revolution when he was given the assayership at the Paris Mint, which allowed him to equip a modest cellar-laboratory for his researches. In 1850 he competed unsuccessfully for the vacant Chair of Chemistry at the Collège de France; but the position went to the elderly A. J. Balard, who already had access to two good laboratories. Bitterly disappointed, Laurent's health declined further. In 1851, he and his Republican friend, Charles Gerhardt, opened a practical school of chemistry and Laurent began the composition of his magnum opus, *Méthode de chimie*, which was completed on his deathbed and published posthumously in 1854.

Charles Gerhardt (1816–56) was the son of a Swiss-Alsatian manufacturer of white lead, who expected him to enter the family business. To this end Gerhardt was sent to study science at the Karlsruhe Polytechnikum (1831–3) and the University of Leipzig (1833), where he studied chemistry with Otto Erdmann. Rebelling against his father's wishes, Gerhardt joined a regiment of lancers at Hagenau (which is perhaps the origin of the report that he looked and dressed like a brigand), from which career he was bought out by a friend for 2000 francs. Following a reconciliation with his father, in 1836 Gerhardt studied with Liebig at Giessen. It was Liebig who advised him to complete his chemical training in Paris with Dumas, to whom he provided an introduction. In 1838, after briefly working with Persoz at Strasbourg, Gerhardt became Dumas' lecture assistant, obtained research facilities in the laboratory of Chevreul, and supported himself by making translations of Liebig's books and papers, and other journalism. In 1841, after obtaining his doctorate, and through Dumas' influence, he was made provisional Professor of Chemistry at the Science Faculty in Montpellier. Because laboratory facilities were poor, Gerhardt rapidly became disenchanted, claiming that he was regarded with jealously and dislike by the other professors because he was the only one to do any research. His repeated absences in Paris, as well as his pronounced political views, did not help, and he was sacked in 1851.

Gerhardt's personality was complex, aggressive, impetuous and dogmatic to an extreme. He was convinced, perhaps rightly, of his own importance and accomplishment. On his deathbed in 1856, scarcely a year after he had been made Professor of Chemistry and Pharmacy at the Science Faculty in Strasbourg, he claimed to have advanced chemistry by fifty years. Like Laurent, his influence was certainly great: positively on British and German chemists like Williamson, Odling, Hofmann and Kekulé; more negatively, in his positivistic and sceptical attitude towards the existence of physical atoms and towards the possibility of deducing the deeper structures of molecules. The latter attitude, held by other French chemists, was to hold back the progress of theory in France.

Gerhardt raised the bile in most of his contemporaries because of the uninhibited style of his criticisms of their work and his apparent lack of respect for his seniors. In return he was slandered as a 'highwayman', 'a dog' and 'a shameless liar', but loyally defended from his foes by the equally maligned, and equally sharp-tongued, Laurent. Less aggressive and dictatorial, but more irritable and imaginative than his companion rebel, Gerhardt, whose 'misdeeds' reflected fairly or unfairly upon him, Laurent's continual lack of appreciation from senior French contemporaries made him bitter. When aroused, he was sharply critical and scornful of other chemists' attempts to retain what he considered to be outmoded ideas. He developed particularly aggressive feelings towards his former teacher, Dumas. Laurent was a romantic and an artist at heart. His letters are full of fun, and he once composed text and music of a comic opera. He was passionately devoted to pursuing his research, putting this above even his filial commitments. He refused secure positions in industry and preferred to starve with his independence in Paris rather than to be 'exiled' in the provinces with a regular salary.

Considering the poor laboratory facilities that were available to Laurent, his experimental output was phenomenal. Some of it proved incorrect, but (unlike Gerhardt) he was always willing to recognize his mistakes. Laurent's name is permanently linked with that of Gerhardt even though their collaboration lasted scarcely ten years; nevertheless, to contemporaries who ostracized them they were permanently identified as 'les deux' or 'les enfants terribles'.

Laurent was already a well known chemist before he first met Gerhardt in 1843, and there is little doubt that he was the driving force behind the way in which Gerhardt expressed his later ideas on atomic weights, notation and the classification of organic compounds between 1843 and his own death in 1856. Unlike Laurent, whose style was sometimes obscure and rendered impenetrable by an intensely logical, but extremely difficult, nomenclature of organic compounds, Gerhardt wrote elegantly and with clarity. It has been said, somewhat unfairly, that Gerhardt promoted Laurent's ideas as his own through motives of self-interest. Whatever their true relationship may have been, and despite their individually important contributions to chemistry, their combined and complementary geniuses were needed before chemists could confidently reject Berzelius' dualistic view of molecules for a unitary one, which eventually allowed chemical properties to be ascribed to the arrangements of atoms. During the 1850s, and through the influence of Laurent's *Method* and Gerhardt's *Traité de chimie*, came the idea of types, the revision of atomic weights, the idea of valency and the structural theory of organic molecules. All of these hinged on the solution to the problem of classifying organic substances.

From the 1770s onwards, French mineralogists had paid much attention to crystallography. In 1784, René-Just Haüy (1743–1822) laid the foundations for a mathematical theory of crystallography based upon the idea of 'molécules integrantes' – ultimate particles of the mineral species which aggregated together by definite rules of accretion to form the familiar external shapes of crystals.

Crystallography was important to Laurent for two reasons. First, the goniometer could be used like a reagent as an instrument of analysis to identify substances crystallographically by their chemical forms. In 1846, when working briefly in Balard's laboratory, he met Louis Pasteur, then a student, and suggested that he should investigate the relationship between optical activity and crystalline form. Laurent thus laid the foundation of Pasteur's career. Secondly, Laurent saw that the phenomenon of isomorphism, which had been discovered in inorganic crystals by Mitscherlich in 1818, offered useful organic analogies. The regularities of isomorphous crystalline forms suggested the persistence of a particular structure, or grouping of atoms. This notion also tied in initially with the etherin theory of Dumas. Laurent supposed that these hidden structures, so reminiscent of the integral molecules of Haüy, determined chemical reactivity, just as the phenomenon of allotropy also implied. Naturally, in the absence of the technique of X-ray analysis, which was not available for another seventy years, Laurent's inferences were often preposterous. The development of such views as a method of classifying organic substances brought Laurent up against the views of older-established chemists like Berzelius and Dumas.

When Laurent began to work with Dumas in 1831, he prepared pure naphthalene from coal tar and studied its halogen derivatives. By 1833 he had been forced to reappraise the contemporary opinion, first developed by Berzelius as a consequence of the electrochemical theory, that organic molecules were composed from two oppositely charged radicals when he found that two chlorides could be derived from naphthalene and that one of them was isomorphous with the hydrocarbon itself (a recognition of what in the twentieth century were called addition and substitution products). Inspired by the inorganic model of isomorphism, instead of regarding these as chlorides of radicals formed by the loss of hydrogen from naphthalene, he regarded them as new unitary types. Naphthalene, he suggested in 1835, was a 'fundamental radical' whose transformations gave rise to new 'derived radicals', which possessed their own corpus of reactivity. The term 'radical' was no longer to be used in a dualistic sense of a positively or negatively charged group of atoms, but more in the later sense of a hydrocarbon group or chain.

Laurent's nucleus theory, as he termed it in his doctoral thesis of 1837, involved a geometrical crystallographic model. Imagine a prism whose eight corners are occupied by carbon atoms, and whose twelve edges contain twelve atoms of hydrogen. This will be the fundamental nucleus of an unsaturated hydrocarbon, C_8H_{12}. By the addition of one volume of hydrogen, chlorine or oxygen to the face of the prism, pyramidal derivatives are obtained, e.g. $(C_8H_{12} + H_2)$, $(C_8H_{12} + O)$, etc. But if chlorine or oxygen is substituted for the edge hydrogens, the structure, or shape, or form, is maintained, and a new isomorphous derived nucleus is produced, e.g. $(C_8H_{11}Cl)$, which can then form its own addition compounds such as $(C_8H_{11}Cl + Cl_2)$.

It will be observed that in this mode of classification the nucleus (and in the later interpretation, the carbon chain) determined the group of compounds to which a molecule belonged and its resistance to modification. Such a model gave chemists a series of meaningful relationships for classifying organic compounds. When Leopold Gmelin compiled the fourth edition of his *Hand-Book of Chemistry* in 1847, to Laurent's delight, he used it as a basis for nomenclature and the systematization of organic chemistry. Gmelin's system, in its turn, formed the basis for Friedrich Beilstein's *Handbuch der organischen Chemie* (1880–2), which, in its current edition, remains to this day the principal reference work for checking whether a particular compound has been reported.

For Laurent, it was the position of an atom within a molecule that determined chemical behaviour, not the nature of the atom itself. Buried within a nucleus, chlorine was as electrically neutral as hydrogen. The point was underlined beautifully by Laurent's investigation of 'isomeromorphs' in the 1840s. Such substances, prepared by inverse polysubstitutions, were both isomeric and isomorphous. For example, when naphthalene was brominated, and then chlorinated, the product, though isomeric and isomorphous, differed very slightly from that produced by chlorination followed by bromination.

In the absence of a large number of known reversible reactions, Laurent's taxonomic principle had to be that 'if one or more compounds are converted to the same body without loss of carbon, then we can conclude with virtual certainty that all these bodies belong in a single series'. This taxonomic commitment ensured that later chemists based their classifications on the assumption that the carbon skeleton remained intact. Fortunately, the organic rearrangements that became one of the more fascinating areas of organic research only became problematical in the 1880s long after the firm establishment of the structural theory. It was safe, therefore, to assume a principle of minimum structural change. It is to Laurent that chemists owe the arrangement that all compounds are considered to be derived from hydrocarbons by substitutions and that the number of carbon atoms is the sole basis for classifications into series.

After Dumas had prepared trichloracetic acid (predicted by Laurent) by the chlorination of acetic acid in 1838, and found that the two acids were closely similar in properties, he joined both Laurent and Gerhardt in rejecting dualistic classification and announced his own unitary type theory. According to this mode of classification, organic types were conserved even if equal volumes of halogens were substituted for hydrogen in the hydrocarbon prototype. The obvious similarity between this model of classification and Laurent's nucleus theory inevitably led to a dispute between the two men. The polemic even reached the titles of papers (e.g. Laurent's 'Troisième mémoire sur la série du phenyle et la vingtième sur les types ou radicaux derivés (types que n'ont pas été decouverte par M. Dumas)'. Other French chemists joined in the controversy, which was largely conducted in a new journal, Dr Quesneville's *Revue scientifique*. But from 1846 to 1852, Laurent and Gerhardt edited their own radical and iconoclastic review, *Comptes rendus des travaux chimiques*, in which they reported their own ideas and experiments and critically reviewed the work of other chemists.

Although Laurent contributed much to the establishment of a unitary viewpoint, he was wary of throwing out the dualistic baby with the unitary bath water[2]:

> The validity of a theory is judged by the progress in science that it brings about. Now when we consider the immense advantages which the [dualistic] theory possess for nomenclature, for the learning of chemistry, and now its application to organic chemistry, we would still be constrained to use it, even if it should be demonstrated that it is false, and the [unitary] theory true.

Indeed, Berzelius' electrochemical theory was to continue to bear fruit.

Methodologically, Laurent was one of chemistry's greatest thinkers; for him, a theory or hypothesis was neither right nor wrong, but was to be measured by its fruitfulness in answering experimental puzzles and by its success in suggesting new investigative procedures.

Between 1839 and 1842, Gerhardt developed a theory of double decomposition that slowly involved him in the revision of atomic weights such that the formulae of both inorganic and organic compounds referred to comparable magnitudes, namely that of the two volumes occupied by two grams of hydrogen. As an explanation of elimination reactions, Gerhardt formulated a mechanism of 'residues'. When two molecules combined together, he suggested, the eliminated parts (which bore little or no relationship to the radicals of classical dualism) combined together to form simple inorganic molecules like water, while the 'residues of the organic molecules united, or copulated together' (*accouplement*). For example, in modern notation:

This theory aroused considerable antagonism in France, Sweden and Germany because Gerhardt would not admit that the residues were electrically charged and pre-existent radicals within the molecule, as the theory of electrochemical dualism demanded. Gerhardt's residues had no formal existence, and his formulae were merely classificatory symbols that summarized the observed course of a reaction. Unlike Laurent, Gerhardt always maintained that the ultimate nature of molecular groupings was unsolvable; all the chemist could ever know were the reactions typical of a particular group of substances. Hence structural concepts, the idea of modelling the actual arrangements of atoms within a molecule, must never be read into his formulae. With some ingenuity, the residue theory could also be used to classify substitution reactions, the principal concern of Laurent and Dumas, as the replacement of the eliminated element by an equivalent of the residue of the reactant. For example,

$$CH_3COOH + Cl.Cl = CH_2ClCOOH + HCl$$

acetic acid   chlorine   monochloroacetic acid

The principal significance of the system of residues,

however, was for the reconceptualization of atomic weights. Berzelius had based the formulae of organic acids on their silver salts; but since his atomic weight for silver was double the modern value (i.e. 2 × 108), the molecular weights of organic acids were also doubled. In 1843 Gerhardt pointed out that, when these organic acids were employed in his theory of residues, the inorganic products eliminated were double those normally employed in inorganic chemistry. In the jargon of the day they were four-volume formulae, based on H_4O_2, compared with two-volume formulae, based on H_2O.

Gerhardt proposed to achieve the necessary uniformity between the two branches of chemistry by either doubling the molecular weights of all simple inorganic compounds, or of uniformly halving those of organic compounds. In either case formulae were always to be consistently derived by comparing equal volumetric magnitudes. Although in one sense it was a matter of indifference to Gerhardt which standard was chosen, he pointed out that the advantage of a two-volume standard was both its simplicity and its agreement with the hitherto much-neglected Avogadro–Ampère hypothesis that equal volumes of gases at the same temperature and pressure contained the same number of molecules. If this were chosen, then the formula of acetic acid would be $C_2H_4O_2$, which had the advantage of simplicity, but the disadvantage that it could not possibly be construed in terms of accepted radicals. It would become a unitary molecule.

These alterations highlighted the contemporary confusion in chemists' minds between atomic, equivalent and molecular weights. Gerhardt himself was unclear, and even bewildered. From Liebig he had learned to use four-volume formulae; while the French tradition of Dumas had emphasized the value of the Avogadro–Ampère two-volume relationship in vapour density determinations; other chemists, particularly in Germany, still used 'equivalents' based upon HO as the formula of water. In despair, Gerhardt, like Liebig earlier, determined to go back to experimental 'facts' and to avoid hypothesis completely – in practice, an unattainable state. He therefore concluded wildly and indiscriminately in 1843 that 'atoms, volumes and equivalents are synonymous terms'.

Laurent, whose ideas on this subject were very clear, thereupon privately criticized Gerhardt and emphasized to him that, whereas atomic weights were fixed, equivalent weights were always variable. In 1846 Laurent published a fundamental set of distinctions between atomic, equivalent and molecular weights, and stressed the value of Gerhardt's revisions of atomic weights because they were based upon equal volumes and the Avogadro principle.

> Each molecule of an element is divisible at least into two parts which we will call *atoms* [this is not invariably the case, as Cannizzaro showed in 1858]; these molecules can be divided only in the case of combinations. The atom of Gerhardt represents the smallest quantity of a body which can exist in a compound. My molecule represents the smallest quantity of a body which must be used to effect a combination, a quantity which is divided into two by the act of combination. Thus Cl may enter into a combination, but to do this Cl_2 must be used. . . . The equivalent is the quantity of an element which must be used to replace another element so as to play its part, and is the same as, or a multiple of, the molecular weight.

More importantly, Laurent extended Gerhardt's use of two-volume formulae to the elements themselves and thereby recognized the diatomicity of common molecules like H_2, Cl_2, O_2, etc. As he wrote in *Chemical Method*:

> By following out the system of volumes, we obtain the formulae which afford the greatest degree of simplicity; which best recall the analogies of the bodies; which accord best with the boiling point and isomorphism; which allow the metamorphoses

to be explained in the most simple manner, &c, and in a word, satisfy completely the requirements of chemists.

It should be noticed that what has been called 'the quiet revolution' of atomic weights occurred several years before the Karlsruhe conference and the publication of Cannizzaro's argument that a two-volume standard should form the basis of teaching chemistry (chapter 11). These definitions were adopted by Laurent and Gerhardt and their English disciples, Brodie, Williamson, Odling and Hofmann, as well as by Cannizzaro in Italy, and led to the successful reform of chemical language and of molecular and atomic weights in the 1860s. Gerhardt was thereby enabled to explain several puzzling substitution reactions in terms of double decompositions and residues. For example,

$$HH \quad + \quad ClCl \quad = \quad HCl \quad + \quad HCl$$
$$C_2H_4 \quad + \quad ClCl \quad = \quad C_2H_3Cl \quad + \quad HCl$$

Despite this classification, Gerhardt remained wary of using the revised atomic weights and formulae in case his writings went unread. The first three volumes of his masterly summary of contemporary organic chemistry, the *Traité de chimie organique* (1853–5), which he was commissioned to write as an update of the French translation of Berzelius' *Traité*, used both one- and four-volume formulae; only in the final posthumous volume (1856) did he adopt, and argue for, two-volume standardization. This represented a partial, though not complete, return to Avogadro's and Ampère's hypotheses that equal volumes contained the same number of particles. The final revision of atomic weights was achieved between 1858 and 1860 by Stanislao Cannizzaro (1826–1910), who showed that, in enthusiastically formulating *all* metal oxides as M_2O, Gerhardt had been led to halve the atomic weights of several multivalent elements.

Laurent also adumbrated the notion of a 'water type' in

his paper of 1846 when he suggested that alcohol, ether and potassium hydroxide could be represented as analogues of water:

OHH	OEtH	OEtEt	OHK
water	alcohol	ether	potassium hydroxide

The experimental exploitation of these analogies, and the extension of the water type classification, was due to Williamson in 1850, while the use of four different types was codified by Gerhardt in 1853. Laurent never claimed that such formulae, which he called 'synoptic', were real. Nevertheless, since chemical properties depended on the internal arrangements of atoms, by classifying substances by their similar and dissimilar properties, one would, he believed, be led to formulae that said something meaningful about the internal arrangements of atoms. This conviction proved to be the basis for structural theories of chemistry.

As we have seen, the pressing problem of organic chemistry before the 1860s was classification. In his first book, *Précis de chimie organique* (1844–6), Gerhardt adopted a rather bizarre classification in which organic compounds were arranged in families containing the same number of carbon atoms. This effectively placed modern families, like esters and acids, in different groups. Laurent was very critical, and argued that such an artificial system hid important chemical interrelationships. Between 1842 and 1845 Gerhardt evolved a more useful classification, which involved what he called 'homologous series'. Such series of compounds differed in composition from each other by CH_2, while their melting and boiling points, as was shown conclusively by the German Hermann Kopp, showed constant differences. As Gerhardt pointed out, 'these substances undergo changes according to the same equations, and it is only necessary to know the reactions of one in order to predict those of the others'. The beauty of the idea for the chemical taxonomist was that, starting with a fundamental group, compounds differing by CH_2 could be arranged in one series. For example, primary alcohols could be expressed by the general formula $C^nH^{2n+2}O$ (i.e. $H(CH_2)_nOH$).

This finding, which he called 'a ladder of combustion', was a synthesis of earlier work by Laurent, Schiel and Dumas on particular series of compounds. Dumas' priority in the discovery of homology was certainly a factor in the feud that developed between Dumas and Gerhardt at the time, but it was exacerbated by Gerhardt's continual advertisement of his superiority towards established authorities like Dumas, his boorishness and his espousal of the unitary theory of Laurent, which Dumas opposed. (It is also interesting to note that Karl Marx, in the third edition of *Capital* (1887), used homologous series to illustrate how quantitative changes in money affected qualitative changes in capital.)

Gerhardt also defined 'isologous series' of compounds, which were related in chemical behaviour but were not homologous, for example ethyl alcohol and phenol; and 'heterologous series' in which compounds were not related by properties at all but were prepared from one another by simple reactions, for example ethyl alcohol and ethyl chloride. Both isologous and heterologous series, he pointed out, provided chemists with vertical and horizontal classifications of organic compounds. To Laurent, however, these were games, and the homologous series was little more than a dictionary. Not only did it fail to tackle isomerism (it could not predict secondary alcohols, for example) but it lacked any leading idea governing the relationships between series.

By using two-volume empirical formulae, Gerhardt was able to unify compounds that had hitherto been dichotomized by the imagination of the dualists; there would now be *one* chemistry of both inorganic and organic kingdoms, unified by basing formulae on the hydrogen molecule, $H_2 = 2$. This commitment, combined with the use of homology in the classification by homologous series, led to the emergence of the 'new type theory', which was codified by Gerhardt in 1853.

In the late 1840s, Dumas' pupil, Adolph Wurtz (1817–84), who was friendly with Gerhardt, tried to hydrolyse 'cyanic' esters in the way that had been achieved with the alkyl cyanides by Kolbe and Frankland. But instead of the expected acid salt and ammonia, Wurtz obtained a new substance, ethylamine, $C_2H_5.NH_2$. In 1850, Hofmann related this new class of amines to his own work on aniline, proposing that amines could be represented as substituted ammonia. Indeed, by treating ammonia with ethyl iodide, Hofmann succeeded in obtaining successively not merely mono-, di- and triethylated ammonia, but tetraethylammonium iodide, which corresponded to an ammonium salt.

As mentioned, in 1846 Laurent had adumbrated the idea of the 'water type', H_2O, in which substances like alcohol and potassium hydroxide could be represented, or classified, as substitution products of water. Experimental proof of this was given by Alexander Williamson in 1850 in his superb investigation of the relationship between alcohol and diethyl ether. Williamson (1824–1904) was educated in England, France and Germany before entering upon a medical course at Heidelberg in 1841, where he was inspired by Leopold Gmelin to become a chemist. From 1844 to 1845 he studied with Liebig at Giessen, and from 1846 to 1849 he studied mathematics and philosophy with Auguste Comte in Paris, where he also kept a private laboratory and met Laurent and Gerhardt. In 1849 he was elected Professor of Practical Chemistry at University College, London, where he remained until his retirement in 1887.

Williamson was a weak child and permanently blind in his right eye and paralysed in his left arm. These bodily disabilities, together with his philosophical upbringing (his parents were friends of the philosophers James and John Stuart Mill), inevitably tended to make him impatient of the minutiae of experimental research and moulded him into a speculative thinker. He was gifted with a logical mind and acute reasoning power, but often tended to be over-dogmatic, caustic and outspoken in discussions with other chemists. Although he made some important researches on Prussian blue and the bleaching action of chlorine, his reputation rests securely on the single, concise and epoch-making paper on etherification that he published in 1850.

Inspired directly by Gerhardt's classification of organic compounds into homologous series, Williamson intended to develop a method of synthesizing higher alcohols by substituting alkyl groups for one of the hydrogen atoms in ethyl alcohol. To his surprise, when he reacted alcohol (in the form of sodium ethylate) with ethyl iodide, he obtained ordinary ether (diethyl ether). His further examination of this reaction, thereafter known as 'Williamson's synthesis', threw new light on the molecular relationships between alcohols, ethers and water, and confirmed the opinions of Laurent and Gerhardt that, since equal molecular magnitudes were involved, the formulae of alcohol and ether had to be expressed in terms of the formula for water, H_2O instead of HO or H_4O_2:

$$\left.\begin{array}{c} C_2H_5 \\ \\ K \end{array}\right\}O \;+\; C_2H_5I \;\longrightarrow\; KI \;+\; \left.\begin{array}{c} C_2H_5 \\ \\ C_2H_5 \end{array}\right\}O$$

No other possible equivalent arrangement for ether was possible, since 'mixed' or asymmetric synthetic ethers could also be prepared:

$$\left.\begin{array}{c} C_2H_5 \\ \\ K \end{array}\right\}O \;+\; CH_3I \;\longrightarrow\; KI \;+\; \left.\begin{array}{c} C_2H_5 \\ \\ CH_3 \end{array}\right\}O$$

methyl iodide

Both alcohol and water, therefore, could be expressed as a molecule of water in which one or both atoms of hydrogen had been replaced by the ethyl radical, C_2H_5:

$$
\left.\begin{array}{c} H \\[20pt] H \end{array}\right\}O
\qquad
\left.\begin{array}{c} C_2H_5 \\[20pt] H \end{array}\right\}O
\qquad
\left.\begin{array}{c} C_2H_5 \\[20pt] C_2H_5 \end{array}\right\}O
$$

The method here employed of stating the rational constitution of bodies by comparison with water seems to me susceptible of great extension; and I have no hesitation in saying that its introduction will be of service in simplifying our ideas, by establishing a uniform standard by which we may judge of.

Following Laurent, Williamson called this method of classification the 'water type', and soon exploited it as the basic model for inorganic salts and acids, as well as organic substances:

$$
\left.\begin{array}{c} H \\[20pt] H \end{array}\right\}O
\quad
\left.\begin{array}{c} H \\[20pt] K \end{array}\right\}O
\quad
\left.\begin{array}{c} K \\[20pt] K \end{array}\right\}O
\quad
\left.\begin{array}{c} NO_2 \\[20pt] K \end{array}\right\}O
\quad
\left.\begin{array}{c} NO_2 \\[20pt] H \end{array}\right\}O
$$

Implicit within these formulations was the idea that oxygen linked, or co-ordinated, two different atoms or groups – a view that was made explicit, and extended to other elements, by Frankland, Odling and Kekulé.

It is worth noting at this juncture that Williamson's synthesis was also important for the future of physical chemistry and mechanistic studies in organic chemistry. The traditional method for preparing ordinary ether was to react alcohol with sulphuric acid. In this process, known as continuous etherification, the acid was recovered afterwards unaltered. The reaction had been explained either in terms of a mysterious catalytic force (to which the positivistic Williamson could not subscribe) or to the breakdown of an intermediately formed product, ethyl hydrogen sulphate. Williamson showed that the reaction proceeded in two stages, first with the formation of the postulated ethyl hydrogen sulphate from one molecule of the alcohol, and then the reaction of a second molecule of alcohol with the intermediate:

$$
\left.\begin{matrix} H \\ H \end{matrix}\right\} SO_4 \; + \; \left.\begin{matrix} C_2H_5 \\ H \end{matrix}\right\} O \; \longrightarrow \; \left.\begin{matrix} C_2H_5 \\ H \end{matrix}\right\} SO_4 \; + \; \left.\begin{matrix} H \\ H \end{matrix}\right\} O
$$

$$
\left.\begin{matrix} H \\ C_2H_5 \end{matrix}\right\} SO_4 \; + \; \left.\begin{matrix} C_2H_5 \\ H \end{matrix}\right\} O \; \longrightarrow \; \left.\begin{matrix} C_2H_5 \\ C_2H_5 \end{matrix}\right\} O \; \; \left.\begin{matrix} H \\ H \end{matrix}\right\} SO_4
$$

The net reaction was a molecular rearrangement with loss of water:

$$2C_2H_5OH \rightarrow (C_2H_5)_2O + H_2O$$

This was one of the first mechanistic studies in organic chemistry, and historically important because Williamson stressed that his mechanism was inconceivable unless a *dynamic* view of the atomic constituents of the molecules was taken. Atoms, he stressed, were not at rest but in a constant state of motion and in a state of dynamic equilibrium with one another.

Williamson's work suggested to him the possibility of synthesizing monobasic acid anhydrides, e.g.

$$\left.\begin{array}{l} CH_3CO \\ \\ CH_3CO \end{array}\right\} O$$

in contrast to the known anhydrides of dibasic acids like succinic acid. It fell to Gerhardt to verify experimentally the existence of acetic anhydride by the action of acetyl chloride on anhydrous sodium acetate. This was a triumphant vindication of the water type. It gained Gerhardt well deserved respect, and a Chair at Strasbourg.

But Gerhardt went further, and suggested that four inorganic types, water, ammonia, hydrogen and hydrogen chloride, would permit the classification of *all* organic compounds. Each type could be conceived as 'the unit of comparison for all bodies which, like [them], are susceptible of similar changes or result from similar changes' (1852). The water type embraced oxides, sulphides, tellurides, salts, alcohols and ethers; halides and cyanides belonged to the hydrogen chloride type; amines, nitrides, phosphides and arsenides belonged to the ammonia type; and paraffins, metals and metal hydrides to the hydrogen type.

It must be strongly emphasized that such formulae still carried no structural significance for Gerhardt; they were purely heuristic classificatory devices or recipes, which informed a chemist of the reactions a substance would probably undergo. Yet, in the hands of Williamson, Odling and Kekulé, together with the revised Berzelian radicalism of Frankland and Kolbe, and the inspiration of Laurent's posthumous *Method*, this new type theory metamorphosed into the structural theory of carbon compounds. For example, in 1853, William Odling, who translated Laurent's *Method* at Williamson's request, extended the water type to double and triple multiple types. He argued that all acids and salts could be classified with one or other of these types, and he used superscript vertical lines or primes to indicate the 'replaceable value' compared with hydrogen of the element or group within the type formula:

single water type

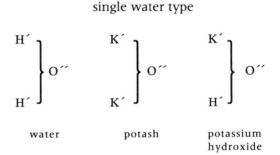

water   potash   potassium
                                     hydroxide

double water type

sulphuric acid

triple water type

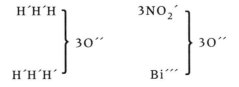

bismuth nitrate

This useful notation was quite widely adopted in British publications during the 1850s and undoubtedly helped to advance the concept of valency. If dibasic acids like sulphuric acid were written as simple water types

$$\left.\begin{array}{l} HSO_3 \\[40pt] H \end{array}\right\} O$$

it suggested a difference in function between the two hydrogens that was not observed; but if they were written as a double water molecule

$$\left.\begin{array}{l} SO_2 \\[40pt] H_2 \end{array}\right\} O_2$$

the two hydrogens were equivalent. This clearly suggested that SO_2 replaced two equivalents of hydrogen. Moreover, if the formula was written as a double type

then it could be seen that multiple types were 'held together' by atoms or radicals.

Gerhardt's type theory received its fullest exposition in

the influential 'Géneralités' in the fourth volume of his *Traité*. Four types were necessary, Gerhardt believed, because, in his maturity, and now socially secure, he was prepared to absorb certain meritorious features of electrochemical dualism into the unitary system. According to whether electropositive or electronegative elements, or radicals, were substituted in the types, acidic, neutral or basic properties resulted. In this way extremes of behaviour within a type were accommodated. Finally, Gerhardt brilliantly merged his old residue theory into the type theory, regarding monatomic acid radicals as the carbonyl radical conjugated with a hydrocarbon radical. For example, acetyl (C_2H_3O) could be resolved into $CH_3.CO$, and acetic acid rendered on the water type as

What he had referred to formerly as 'copulated residues' were now renamed 'conjugated radicals', although they still referred to the fact that certain groupings could transfer during double decomposition as a unit. Again, it has to be emphasized that these elongated type formulae had no structural significance.

Such conjugated types proved very popular in the chemical literature of the 1850s and 1860s. Their self-defeating drawback was that several formulae could be given for any one substance, and large numbers of conjugated atoms could be said to be 'equivalent' to hydrogen. Consequently, what one chemist classified as a water type another might illustrate as a hydrogen chloride molecule. Such confusing formulae were to be clarified by the concept of valency, a product of Kekulé's alternative waterway of Berzelian radicalism.

On the Constitution and Metamorphoses of Chemical Compounds

Suddenly a loud shout of triumph resounded from the host of the adherents of the type theory. The others also had arrived – Frankland at their head. Both sides saw that they had been striving toward the same goal, although by different routes. They exchanged experiences; each side profited by the conquests of the other; and with united force they sailed onward on a reunited stream. One or two held themselves apart and sulked; they thought they alone had held the true course – the right fairway – but they too followed the stream.

(AUGUST KEKULÉ, 1890)

THE ESTABLISHMENT OF QUANTIVALENCE

Berzelius' rigid adherence to radicals as realities forced him, in the face of Melsens' reduction of chloracetic acid to acetic acid in 1842, to adopt copulae as neutral parts of molecules that had no influence on an electrically active radical such as the anhydride of oxalic acid. In other words, chlorine occupied the same place in a molecule where hydrogen had been, and the common properties of the two acids arose from their common possession of the active C_2O_3 group and not, as Laurent believed, to an identity of atomic arrangement within the *whole* molecule. Both interpretations were logically and empirically impeccable. But, as Kekulé noted in his *Lehrbuch der Chemie* (1859), by multiplying copulae, appendages to the radicals, Berzelius undermined the radical theory's taxonomic usefulness. To Berzelius, who had always seen 'the discovery of rational constitution' as the chief issue in organic chemistry, classification had only ever been a means to such an end. This view was passionately shared by his German disciple, Hermann Kolbe, who, rather like Laurent, believed that obsession with classification was symptomatic of the lazy chemist; real chemists thought about constitution. It is one of the greatest ironies in the history of chemistry that a man so dedicated to the discovery of rational constitution should have bitterly opposed Kekulé's theory of structure.

Convinced that Berzelius' views on the constitution of acids were correct, in the mid 1840s Kolbe showed experimentally that they were useful and predictive. By demonstrating that the copula C_2Cl_6 of trichloracetic acid formed paired compounds with other acids (1844), by synthesizing acetic acid from carbon dioxide via oxalic acid (1844), by converting alkyl cyanides into fatty acids (1848), and by preparing 'hydrocarbon radicals' (actually paraffins) by the electrolysis of acids, Kolbe appeared to confirm triumphantly the constitutional intuition of the Swedish giant. These successes persuaded Kolbe to extend Berzelius' theory, not by multiplying copulae, but by substituting copulae within copulae or, in other words, exploring the inner constitution of copulae and radicals, just as Laurent had attempted within the different tradition of the nucleus theory, or Gerhardt did by placing radicals within his types. This was necessary, Kolbe observed, in order to preserve chemical analogies between different series of compounds. For example, work on 'acetyl' (C_4H_3) compounds convinced him that it consisted of 'ethyl' conjugated with two equivalents of carbon, which acted as 'the exclusive point of action for the powers of affinity of oxygen, chlorine, etc.':

$$C_4H_3 = (C_2H_3)C_2$$

Although Kolbe took a major step in breaking radicals and copulae down into their constituents, it remained for Kekulé to take the logical step of resolving them completely into their constituent atoms and to take carbon as the point of action and attachment. On the other hand, it was Kolbe's English friend, Edward Frankland, working within the same 'new radical theory' tradition, who was first inspired towards the notion of valency. Influenced by his youthful friendship with Kolbe and his training in Bunsen's laboratory, Frankland began his career as an organic chemist in the 1840s within Berzelius' radical school.

Berzelius' suggestion that acetic acid was probably a preformed electropositive methyl radical (C_2H_3, C = 6) conjugated with an electrochemical radical of oxalic acid (C_2O_3) inspired Kolbe and Frankland to conjecture that the homologues of this acid such as propionic acid were similarly constituted, with higher alkyl radicals replacing methyl. This idea received support from Fehling's demonstration in 1844 that carboxylic acids were produced by the hydrolysis of alkyl nitriles or cyanides. In 1847 Kolbe and Frankland succeeded in producing propionic acid from ethyl cyanide, confirming their hunch that propionic acid was an ethyl-conjugated oxalic acid.

From this point the two friends were independently inspired to vindicate their viewpoint through the actual isolation of the postulated alkyl radicals. In 1849 Frankland apparently succeeded by reacting zinc with alkyl iodides in sealed tubes:

$$C_4H_5I \quad + \quad Zn \quad \rightarrow \quad C_4H_5 \quad + \quad ZnI \quad (C = 6)$$
ethyl iodide   'ethyl'

However, after much argument, in which Hofmann played a leading role, he was forced to admit on the grounds of vapour density and boiling point determinations that the formulae of the 'radicals' he had prepared had to be doubled; they were not free radicals, but the inert paraffin hydrocarbons. In modern terms:

$$2C_2H_5I + Zn = \underset{\text{butane}}{C_4H_{10}} + ZnI_2 \quad (C = 12)$$

Ironically, Frankland's misconception led him not only to the unifying concept of valency, but to important experimental techniques of synthetic chemistry using organo-metallic compounds.

Among the many by-products of the reaction just discussed, Frankland isolated the highly reactive and explosive compound, zinc methyl – the first of the important class of organo-metallic compounds. He went on to prepare similar reactive compounds with tin and boron, but found to his surprise that such compounds (which at this stage he still regarded as free radicals) possessed different powers of combination to the free metal. This could hardly be the case, he reasoned, unless the conjugation of the alkyl group with a metal in some way affected the latter's power of combination. For example, he observed that tin diethyl (stanethylium) could only form *one* compound with oxygen, whereas tin itself was able to form at least two oxides.

This discrepancy led Frankland to an important empirical generalization. On 10 May 1852, in a paper to the Royal Society on organo-metallic compounds, he drew attention to the analogies between inorganic and organic chemistry, and observed that in both departments the elements possessed very definite powers of combination:

When the formulae of inorganic compounds are considered, even a superficial observer is impressed with the general symmetry of their construction. The compounds of nitrogen, phosphorus, antimony, and arsenic, especially, exhibit the tendency of these elements to form compounds containing 3 or 5 atoms of other elements; and it is in these proportions that their affinities are best satisfied: thus in the ternal group we have NO_3, NH_3, NI_3, NS_3, PO_3, PH_3, PCl_3, SbO_3, SbH_3, $SbCl_3$, AsO_3, AsH_3, $AsCl_3$, etc; and in the five-atom group, NO_5, NH_4O, NH_4I, PO_5, PH_4I, etc. Without offering any hypothesis regarding the cause of this symmetrical grouping of atoms [it is unclear whether Frankland had a three-dimensional geometrical image in view], it is sufficiently evident from the examples just given, that such a tendency or law prevails, and that, no matter what the character of the uniting atoms may be, the combining power of the attracting element, if I may be allowed the term, is always satisfied by the same number of atoms.

At this time, Frankland still used equivalent, or combining, weights ($C = 8$) rather than strict atomic weights. Consequently his concept of combining power dampened clarity with a confusion that Frankland exacerbated by using the misleading term *atomicity* for an element's power of combination. The term *valence* or *valency*, from *quantivalence* or equivalence, only began to be adopted by chemists after about 1865. In practice, the development of the valency as a structural concept for explaining the way atoms are linked together within a molecule owed more to the publications by Kekulé in the 1850s and 1860s than to Frankland. Kekulé, however, was working within the rival tradition of the type theory, and the precise influence that Frankland asserted on him (little or none if Kekulé himself is to be believed) is difficult to assess. On the other hand, as a teacher, Frankland played an important role in spreading the idea and use of valency among the younger generation of chemists (see chapter 11).

KEKULÉ AND THE THEORY OF CHEMICAL STRUCTURE

Friedrich August Kekulé (1829–96) spent a long apprenticeship in chemistry before becoming Professor of Chemistry at the Universities of Ghent in 1858 and Bonn in 1867.

His original plan to study architecture at the University of Giessen in 1847 was, to his parents' disapproval, thwarted by the magnetism of Liebig's lectures on chemistry. Liebig advised Kekulé (like Gerhardt previously) to undertake further chemical studies with Dumas in Paris, where, between 1851 and 1852, he became a close friend of Gerhardt's. He spent a year and a half working for a wealthy independent chemist in Switzerland, following which Liebig found him a post with his disabled former student, John Stenhouse, at St Bartholomew's Hospital in London. Here, between 1854 and 1855, Kekulé fell under the spell of Williamson and Odling. A further year as a Privatdocent at Heidelberg completed his graduate education.

Although his interest in architecture has usually been seen as a significant factor in Kekulé's creation of the carbon chain and of the benzene ring, N. W. Fisher has rightly drawn attention to Kekulé's interest in botany, butterflies and biological taxonomy when he spent part of 1850 with his parents in Darmstadt. Given that it was the problem of organic classification that the various radical and type theories had been designed to solve, it is hardly surprising that Kekulé's initial research was devoted to such issues. By the time he had completed his apprenticeship, however, in both the camps of typists and radicalists there had grown a division between those like Gerhardt who sought only synoptic formulae as an aid to classification, and those like Laurent, Williamson and Kolbe who sought formulae that exposed the actual constitutions of organic compounds. Kekulé was caught between these two approaches. Synoptic classification seems to have been his initial preoccupation; it was only later that the structural implications of his own work became clear to him. Rational reconstruction of the triumphs of his career in old age and the enormous strides that organic chemistry made once structural theory was adopted may well have led Kekulé to overlook the intellectual taxonomic roots and scaffolding that produced the insight.

Kekulé's first important contribution to chemical litera-
ture resulted from a dispute between Williamson and
Kolbe in 1854. According to Williamson's type theory, and
Gerhardt's successful preparation of acetic anhydride,

$$\left.\begin{array}{c} C_2H_3O \\ \\ C_2H_3O \end{array}\right\} O$$

acetic acid was best conceived as containing an oxygenated
'othyle' radical [acetyl], C_2H_3O (C = 12), viz.

$$\left.\begin{array}{c} C_2H_3O \\ \\ H \end{array}\right\} O$$

Kolbe, on the other hand, as we have seen, argued at
this time that it was a conjugated oxalic acid, $(C_2H_3)C_2O_3$
(C = 8). Both parties appeared to have facts on their side
because the presence of 'methyl' in acetic acid could easily
be demonstrated by electrolysis, and that of 'othyle' from
the existence of acetic anhydride. Kekulé's proof that
othyle chloride (i.e. acetyl chloride) was produced when
acetic acid was reacted with phosphorus pentachloride
gave support to Williamson's case. More significantly,
however, Kekulé found that treatment of acetic acid with
phosphorus pentasulphide brought about the replacement
of 'the oxygen of the [water] type by sulphur to form
thioacetic acid' – the first thio-acid to be prepared. Whereas
the pentachloride produced acetyl chloride *and* hydrogen
chloride, the pentasulphide produced only a single molecule
of thioacetic acid.

Kekulé spelled out this difference in the reactions: the

quantity of oxygen and sulphur equivalent to two atoms of chlorine was not divisible. Here was a clear recognition of Odling's idea that elements themselves could be dibasic. For Kekulé, in 1854, the most interesting feature of a dibasic atom was that it somehow bound together the atoms with which it combined. This was made even clearer in Kekulé's formulations of the reactions as both water, hydrogen sulphide and hydrogen chloride types ($O = 16$, $C = 12$):

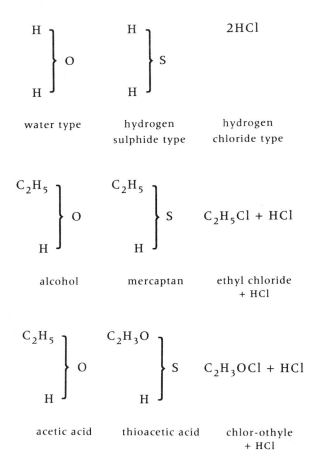

water type	hydrogen sulphide type	hydrogen chloride type
alcohol	mercaptan	ethyl chloride + HCl
acetic acid	thioacetic acid	chlor-othyle + HCl

How did Kekulé free himself from the Gerhardtian tradition of a key type atom to one in which no atom was more important than another within a constitutional formula? A key factor was probably a conversation with Odling, who, in 1856, added a 'marsh gas' (methane) type to Gerhardt's classification models. In his paper, Odling pointed out that, because all four hydrogens were equivalent in methane, no one particular representation ($CH_3.H$, $CH_2.H_2$, $CH.H_3$ or $C.H_4$) had any absolute validity.

This key feature of what was to become structure theory was adopted by Kekulé in a German paper on mercury fulminate in 1857. (Here, for the benefit of his German readers, he used $C = 6$, so that the hydrogens of the methane combined with double carbon atoms.)

					Gerhardt's type
C_2H	H	H	H	Marsh gas	CH_4
C_2H	H	H	Cl	Methyl chloride	HCl
C_2H	Cl	Cl	Cl	Chloroform	HCl
$C_2(NO_4)$	Hg	Hg	(C_2N)	Mercury fulminate	NH_3

Kekulé recognized that he was here reviving Dumas' idea of a mechanical type; but he also referred significantly to Williamson's idea of dynamic atoms[1]:

These bodies can all be classed together in a single series, a mechanical type. All contain the same number of atoms (if the nitro-group and the cyanide group are considered as radicals analogous to elements); but these bodies show great differences in their individual properties, which are occasioned by differences in the dynamic natures of the component elements.

Kekulé's method of classification now depended upon carbon's purely mechanical attribute of combining with four atoms or groups, just as oxygen and sulphur bound two atoms or groups together. It ignored the chemical behaviour of the component atoms in reactions that had been a feature of both the earlier radical and type taxonomies[2]:

> Carbon is, as may easily be shown and I shall explain in detail later, tetrabasic or tetratomic, that is, one atom of carbon = C = 12 is equivalent to 4 atoms of hydrogen.

In some lectures on the 'constitution and classification of organic compounds' given as a Privatdocent at the University of Heidelberg in 1857–8, Kekulé began to represent the marsh gas type by 'sausage formulae':

But in his publications, on Williamson's advice, he used barred symbols to represent the revised atomic weights of Gerhardt (C = 12). (Kekulé's well-intentioned use of barred symbols until about 1867 unfortunately exacerbated the confusion over atomic weights since for many other German chemists, including Kolbe, $\bar{\text{C}}$ meant C_2, where C = 6.)

A year later, without any reference to Frankland's prior insight, Kekulé referred to the atomicities or basicities of the elements themselves instead of radicals, and so arrived at the fundamental notion of catenation, or the linking of carbon atoms into a chain. His statement is worth quoting at some length since it represented a shift from a primary concern with classification to one of constitution and structure[3]:

> When the simplest compounds of [carbon] are considered (marsh gas, methyl chloride, chloride of carbon, chloroform, carbonic acid, phosgene, sulphide of carbon, hydrocyanic acid, etc.) it is seen that the

quantity of carbon which chemists have recognized as the smallest possible, that is to say, as an atom, always unites with 4 atoms of a monatomic or with 2 atoms of a diatomic element; that in general the sum of the chemical units of the elements united with one atom of carbon is 4. This leads us to the view that carbon is tetratomic or tetrabasic.

In the cases of substances which contain several atoms of carbon, it must be assumed that at least some of the atoms are in the same way held in the compound by the affinity of carbon, and that the carbon atoms attach themselves to one another, whereby a part of the affinity of the one is naturally engaged with an equal part of the affinity of the other. The simplest and therefore the most probable case of such an association of carbon atoms is that in which one affinity unit of one is bound by one of the other. Of the 2×4 affinity units of the two carbon atoms, two are used up in holding the atoms together, and six remain over, which can be bound by atoms of other elements. In other words, a group of two carbon atoms, C_2, will be sexatomic, and will form a compound with six atoms of monatomic elements, or generally with so many atoms that the sum of the chemical units of these is equal to six.

If Frankland was the first to recognize the saturation capacities of elementary atoms and the abilities of poly-valent atoms to couple in characteristic ways (an idea also developed by Kolbe), it was undoubtedly Kekulé who developed the full concept of valency through his treatment of carbon. It was one of the consequences of the 'two streams' of classification theories, however, that Kekulé treated Frankland's contribution cavalierly. Only towards the end of his life did he acknowledge the value of Frankland's insight. The two men also differed over the variability of valency. For Frankland, elements might display different saturation capacities, but for Kekulé, valency was fixed. In order to explain apparent cases of multiple valency, therefore, he had to introduce the idea of molecular compounds. For example, nitrogen was trivalent in ammonia, NH_3; its apparent pentavalency in ammonium iodide, NH_4I, was explained as being due to a molecular complex, $NH_3.HI$.

Kekulé's well known claim as an old man that the idea of the carbon chain had first occurred to him in the summer of 1854 when he was drowsing on top of a London omnibus, while psychologically plausible, does not seem to fit well with his public pronouncements at the time or the deep conceptual transformation from taxonomy to constitution that it involved. The matter remains controversial. What is clear, as Kekulé did fairly admit in 1858, was his indebtedness to Williamson, Odling and Gerhardt.

Nevertheless, for one considered the creator of structural theory, Kekulé remained strikingly cautious. For years afterwards, because of Williamson's dynamical ideas, he was to doubt that absolute constitutions of organic molecules could ever be given. If, in chemical reactions all was flux, how could the fixed, or static, configurations of atoms with respect to one another ever be discovered? Here was a fundamental philosophical conundrum, the principle of minimum structural change noticed by Laurent, which most chemists were to escape by simply ignoring it. But Kekulé could not, and therefore continued to use type formulae in his papers and his textbook, *Lehrbuch der Chemie* (1866–87), where he defined organic chemistry as 'the chemistry of carbon compounds'.

In 1864, an inmate of Hanwell (London's largest lunatic asylum) had sent an ironic letter to *Chemical News* pointing out the absurdity of chemists' disagreement over the formula of such a simple substance as water. Kekulé agreed, and in the *Lehrbuch* he went one better by printing twenty different formulae for acetic acid that had appeared in the chemical literature (see Table 7.1).

TABLE 7.1   *Kekulé's formulae for acetic acid.*

Formula	Theory
$C_4H_4O_4$	Empirical formula
$C_4H_3O_3 + HO$	Dualistic
$C_4H_3O_4 \cdot H$	Hydrogen acid theory
$C_4H_4 + O_4$	Nucleus theory
$C_4H_3O_2 + HO_2$	Longchamp
$C_4H + H_3O_4$	Graham
$C_4H_3O_2 \cdot O + HO$	Radical theory
$\left.\begin{array}{l} C_4H_3O_2 \\ H \end{array}\right\}O_2$	Gerhardt's type ($O = 8$)
$\left.\begin{array}{l} C_4H_3 \\ H \end{array}\right\}O_4$	Schischkoff's type
$C_2O_3 + C_2H_3 + HO$	Berzelius' copula
$HO \cdot (C_2H_3)C_2, \ O_3$	Kolbe
$HO \cdot (C_2H_3)C_2, \ O, \ O_2$	Kolbe
$\left.\begin{array}{l} C_2(C_2H_3)O_2 \\ H \end{array}\right\}O_2$	Wurtz
$\left.\begin{array}{l} C_2H_3(C_2O_2) \\ H \end{array}\right\}O_2$	Mendius
$\left.\begin{array}{l} C_2H_2 \cdot HO \\ HO \end{array}\right\}C_2O_2$	Geuther
$C_2\left[\begin{array}{l} C_2H_3 \\ O \\ O \end{array}\right\}O + HO$	Rochleder
$\left(\dfrac{H_3 + CO_2}{C_2CO}\right) + HO$	Persoz
$C_2\left[\begin{array}{l} C_2\left[\begin{array}{l} O_2 \\ H \end{array}\right. \\ H \\ \dfrac{H}{H} \end{array}\right\}O_2$	Buff

He then pointed out how structural ideas – principally the idea of the carbon chain – could form a much more effective taxonomic tool and reduce the acetic acid menu to a single choice. However, apart from the occasional use of sausage formulae, Kekulé did not express formulae graphically. It was left to others to assume that the rational formulae based upon carbon's tetravalency actually represented the real arrangements of a molecule's atoms. Only in the 1870s did Kekulé begin to agree.

The lead here had been taken in 1858 by a Scottish pupil of Adolph Wurtz, Archibald Scott Couper (1831–92), and his Russian friend, Aleksandr Butlerov. Early in that year, and independently of Kekulé, Couper derived the idea of carbon's tetravalency and of the carbon chain, which he represented graphically by dotted lines within type-looking formulae. These were not types, however, as the philosophically trained and constitutionally minded Couper made clear:

> To research the structure of words we must go back, seek out the decomposable elements, viz the letters, and study carefully their powers and bearing. Having ascertained these, the composition and structure of every possible word is revealed.

methyl alcohol   ethyl alcohol   acetic acid   glycol

In another paper of 1858 solid lines were used to indicate butyl alcohol:

(Note that some dotted lines represented more than one bond. C = 12, O = 8.)

Couper clearly appreciated the advantage of such formulae over types insofar as the drawing of atomic linkages avoided hypothetical cases of isomerism such as ethyl hydride and dimethyl represented by the hydrogen types:

$$\left\{ \begin{array}{l} C_2H_5 \\ \\ H \end{array} \right. \quad \text{and} \quad \left\{ \begin{array}{l} CH_3 \\ \\ CH_3 \end{array} \right.$$

Unfortunately for Couper, because Wurtz was not at this time a member of the French Academy of Sciences, the presentation of Couper's paper was delayed until after Kekulé's paper had appeared in the *Annalen* in May 1858. When Couper's paper was published, Kekulé, in typical nineteenth-century fashion, claimed priority, and Couper, after a row with Wurtz, accusing him of deliberate delaying tactics, was dismissed from the laboratory. Although he obtained a research post at Edinburgh with Lyon Playfair, by 1859 Couper had become so severely depressed that he gave up chemistry completely. It was only in this century that Couper was 'rediscovered' when Kekulé's pupil and biographer, Richard Anschütz, drew attention to his tragic genius.

Aleksandr Butlerov (1828–86), a Professor of Chemistry at the University of Kazan, spent a study leave at Heidelberg in 1857, where he met Kekulé, and in Wurtz's laboratory in Paris, where he befriended Couper. Despite publishing in French, German and Russian, Butlerov's innovations in structure theory tended to be overlooked as they were assimilated into textbooks and became the unquestioned assumptions of teaching and research. Subsequently, he spent much of his later career in polemics with iconoclastic German chemists seeking due acknowledgements for his insights – acknowledgements that only came to him outside the Soviet Union in the 1950s.

Although Couper had used the word 'structure' in a linguistic analogy to refer to the order and arrangement of atoms, it was Butlerov who popularized the phrase 'chemical structure' as a synonym for constitution and to mean that the particular arrangement of atoms within a molecule was the *cause* of its physical and chemical properties. He did this consistently from 1861:

> Only one rational formula is possible for each compound, and when the general laws governing the dependence of chemical properties on chemical structure have been derived, this formula will express all of these properties.

Butlerov's materialism, which stood nineteenth-century organic chemists in good stead, proved too sanguine, and in the 1920s chemists had to concede that the question of structure was more problematical (chapter 14).

Couper's graphic formulae, though clear enough when double oxygens are replaced by single ones, are nevertheless cumbersome. In his doctoral thesis of 1861, Alexander Crum Brown (1838–1922) extended their use, and popularized them three years later by enclosing the elementary symbols in circles (as Dalton had done):

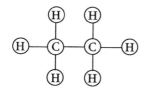

After further extensive airing by Hofmann and Frankland in Britain, and by Erlenmeyer in Germany (who dropped the circles in 1866), graphic formulae became an essential component of the language of the theory of chemical structure.

THE TRIUMPH OF STRUCTURAL THEORY

As we saw in chapter 4, Brodie's attempt to avoid the concept and language of atomism came unstuck over the issue of isomerism. The explanation of the latter, in all of its many forms, was a signal triumph for the structural theory, as was Kekulé's brilliant solution to the representation of benzene in the burgeoning branch of aromatic chemistry, and the hexagon's triumphal ability to suggest successful strategies for the synthesis of organic compounds (chapter 16).

The structural theory provided a simple and elegant explanation of the already large number of cases of isomerism that organic chemists had accumulated by 1860. It also allowed chemists to predict cases. For example, during the 1860s there was a spate of reports concerning the synthesis of primary, secondary and tertiary alcohols, e.g. $CH_3(CH_2)_3OH$, $CH_3CH(OH).CH_2CH_3$ and $(CH_3)_3.COH$. The historian of science must not press this success too far, however, since it was Kolbe, an arch-opponent of structural chemistry, who had first predicted such isomeric alcohols on the basis of the conjugated radical theory in 1854. The roots of Kolbe's opposition will become clear in the context of stereochemistry.

Although Dalton clearly thought geometrically when developing the atomic theory and made wooden models to illustrate atomic combinations, it was the crystallographic tradition that projected chemistry into space. As early as 1812 Wollaston, following Haüy's drawings, constructed models to show how piles of spherical particles could be arranged so as to produce the external forms of crystals. In 1815, the French physicist, J. B. Biot (1774–1862), found that many organic liquids were, like the Iceland spar crystals investigated by Huygens in the seventeenth century, capable of rotating the direction of polarization of a beam of polarized light that was shone through them. That is, the beam emerged polarized at an angle to the plane of vibration of the original polarized beam. Since these organic molecules were not crystalline, Biot concluded that their power to alter light must be inherent in the structure of their molecules – a view supported by the theory of short-range forces developed by Biot's patron, Laplace.

By the 1840s it was recognized that there were two different kinds of tartaric acid. One turned the plane of transmitted polarized light to the right, the other (racemic acid) produced no effect at all. Since their crystalline shapes and, by implication, their molecular forms, seemed to be identical, as were their chemical properties, it was a puzzle as to how their solutions could have such different effects on polarized light. This was the problem that Louis Pasteur, encouraged by Laurent, tackled successfully for his doctorate in 1847.

Pasteur noticed that the polarizing, or optically active, tartaric acid crystals possessed some distinctive facets, which seemed to be absent in the non-polarizing crystals. Detailed comparisons made with a magnifying glass showed that the inactive crystals were apparently symmetrical, whereas the active crystals were asymmetrical. The polarization effect seemed, therefore, to depend upon the existence of asymmetric crystals. Upon preparing much larger crystals of racemic acid, Pasteur noticed by eye that there were, in roughly equal proportions, two different kinds of crystals in the sample; both were asymmetric, but one lot were mirror images of the other. Pasteur then boldly concluded that, since the former rotated the plane of polarization to the right (*dextro* form), the latter ought to turn it to the left (*laevo* form). Because both groups of crystals were present in equal proportions in the racemate, the contrary polarization effects normally cancelled each other out.

Pasteur had prepared a new form of tartaric acid that did not occur naturally in grapes. In later life Pasteur made the famous anthologized statement that 'chance favours only the prepared mind'. Pasteur was, indeed, extremely fortunate in his choice of crystal, for fewer than a dozen crystalline racemates can be separated optically; moreover, tartaric acid racemate will only separate into the *dextro* (*d-*) and *laevo* (*l-*) forms below 27°C.

As classificatory systems, neither the radical nor the type theories encouraged model-building, though in his *Handbuch* Gmelin refers to the use of wax models to explain isomerism. Kekulé seems to have used wire models from about 1858 for the same purpose. Following Crum Brown's lead, in the 1860s Hofmann and Frankland used coloured wooden balls in their teaching, and it was the use of such croquet ball models (glyptic formulae) that so infuriated Brodie in 1867. All such models, however, arranged molecules linearly, that is, with atoms strictly at right angles to one another. This was despite speculations by Pasteur, Kekulé and Butlerov that molecular asymmetry either arose from atoms being arranged tetrahedrally, or that the tetravalency of carbon was best imagined as distributed tetrahedrally. In 1867 the Scottish chemist (and later physicist) James Dewar, when studying with Kekulé, actually designed wire models illustrating the geometrical shapes that might arise from tetrahedral carbon.

The idea of tetrahedrally directed carbon bonds was not, therefore, new when Jacobus van't Hoff (1852–1911) published a twelve-page pamphlet in Dutch, 'Proposal for the extension of the formulae now in use in chemistry into space, together with a related note on the relation between the optical rotating power and the chemical constitution of organic compounds', in September 1874. A year later van't Hoff published a more extensive monograph in French, *La chimie dans l'éspace*; the word 'stereochemistry' was only coined by Victor Meyer in 1890.

As van't Hoff admitted, the inspiration for his hypothesis had come from the argument made in 1869 by Johannes Wislicenus that cases of what he called 'geometrical isomerism', where isomers had different physical and chemical properties, but did not necessarily display optical activity, would have to be explained by the different arrangements of their atoms in space. In the case of the lactic acids, Wislicenus wrote:

> Here is given the first definitely-proved case in which the number of isomers exceeds the number of possible structures. Facts like these compel us to explain different isomeric molecules with the same structural formula by different positions of their atoms in space, and to seek for definite representations of these.

Van't Hoff's explanation, which was enthusiastically welcomed by Wislicenus, was simple. If the four valencies of carbon were assumed to be at right angles, then far more isomers were predicted than were found in methane derivatives of the type $CH_2(R_1)_2$; but if the valencies were directed towards the angles of a tetrahedron, with four different atoms or radicals, there would be a perfect match between predicted and experimentally prepared isomers. The reason was that two of the isomers would be mirror images of one another, as Pasteur had argued. In the case of Pasteur's tartaric acids, two of the four isomers arose from asymmetry (L and D), one from the fact that internal symmetry compensated for the presence of asymmetry (*meso*), while the fourth was simply Pasteur's racemic mixture.

L-form   **D**-form   **meso**-form

Van't Hoff showed that in all known cases of optical activity the substance possessed an asymmetric carbon atom. Double and triple bonds, which Kekulé and Erlenmeyer had introduced in the early 1860s to explain the constitution of unsaturated olefins, acetylenes and their derivatives, could be represented by the combination of tetrahedra along their edges or faces. (Erlenmeyer coined the term 'unsaturated' to signify that such compounds formed addition compounds, as opposed to saturated compounds that usually underwent substitutions.) Since such geometry would prohibit rotations, two non-superimposable forms would frequently be possible. In this way van't Hoff brilliantly explained the puzzling isomerism of maleic and fumaric acids:

cis-maleic acid   *trans*-fumaric acid

Here, the plane of symmetry was the double or triple bond itself. Because geometrical configuration, not an asymmetric carbon atom, was responsible for such enantiomorphs, van't Hoff recommended that Wislicenus' term 'geometrical isomerism' should be restricted to such instances. The *'cis–trans'* terminology was introduced by Adolf Baeyer in 1892 to replace the more cumbersome terms 'maleoid' and 'fumaroid' or 'axial' and 'central symmetric' that chemists had used initially.

Within a month of van't Hoff's first publication, Joseph le Bel (1847–1930), an assistant of Wurtz in Paris, deduced geometrically that any molecule with four different groups attached to a carbon atom would be optically active unless there was internal compensation (a plane of symmetry) within the molecule. Le Bel, whose inspiration was found in Pasteur's work, used no diagrams. Although clear, his more general and abstract approach made his presentation and its consequences less easily grasped than that of van't Hoff; nor did le Bel show the same originality as van't Hoff in deducing geometrical isomerism as a consequence of double and triple bonds.

In the second of his satirical Carlylean essays on 'Signs of the Times' in the *Journal für praktische Chemie* in 1877, Kolbe ridiculed van't Hoff, who was then unestablished and unknown, as an example of the slipshod education of chemists in the 1870s:

> A Dr J H. van't Hoff of the veterinary school at Utrecht, finds, as it seems, no taste for exact chemical investigation. He has thought it more convenient to mount Pegasus (obviously loaned at the veterinary school) and to proclaim in his *La chimie dans l'éspace* how during his bold flight to the top of the chemical Parnassus, the atoms appeared to him to have grouped themselves throughout universal space.

Doubtless, if van't Hoff had not reprinted Kolbe's attack in the second edition (1887) of his *Chemistry in Space*, Kolbe's scathing satire would have been quietly forgotten. In the event, it has tarred Kolbe with the historical reputation of being an obscurantist and a fool. He was neither of these things. To Kolbe, talk of directed valencies was pure fantasy, marking a return to the *a priori* speculations typical of German *Naturphilosophie* before Berzelius and Liebig had placed organic chemistry on to the firm empirical grounds of analysis. Quite unfairly, Kolbe held Kekulé personally responsible for what he perceived as a kind of chemical laziness that had been induced among younger chemists by the theory of structure:

> It is one of the signs of the times that modern chemists hold themselves bound to consider themselves in a position to give an explanation for everything, and, when their knowledge fails them, to make use of supernatural [*sic*] explanations.

There is no doubt that, if Kolbe had had any interest in optical activity, he might have been more circumspect.

Ironically, it was van't Hoff's strongest supporter, Wislicenus, who inherited Kolbe's chair at Leipzig in 1885. What Kolbe did not like was that structural theory *did* undoubtedly make organic chemistry easier: not only was the awfully puzzling classification of organic compounds solved for all time, but relationships that before had taken years of empirical exploration, and syntheses that hitherto had taken years of careful preparation, could now be plotted on paper, or predicted on the blackboard, and routinely verified in the laboratory. It was, indeed, a sign of the chemical times; but it did not necessarily mean that chemists no longer had to think, for structural chemistry soon produced new conundrums, such as internal rearrangements and tautomerism, to tantalize its best theoreticians and experimentalists. Not the least of these conundrums was benzene, whose structure Kekulé had determined in 1865.

It is one of the ironies of chemical history that benzene was first identified in compressed oil gas by Faraday in 1825, and not in the aromatic spices and resins that had formed part of the luxury end of commerce since time immemorial. Although benzoin, and benzoic acid, had been called 'aromatics' before the 1820s, it was Hofmann who, in the 1850s, identified benzene and its derivatives as belonging to a chemical family of aromatics. Only in the 1880s did Otto Wallach show that, although carbon-rich like benzene, most of the familiar olefactory aromatics of commerce (frankincense, camphor, turpentine, etc.) were derivatives of the ten-carbon compounds that Kekulé had named terpenes in 1864.

Kekulé's hexagonal model for benzene owed everything to his prior innovation of the carbon chain. By the mid 1860s, Kekulé had reached the stage of writing about aromatic compounds in his *Lehrbuch*. There were many experimental difficulties in the investigation of benzene derivatives, not the least of which was that the presence of slight impurities lowered melting points considerably, thus making their differentiation and identification difficult. Charles Mansfield's introduction of fractional distillation in 1849 and the take-off of the coal-tar and petroleum industries in the decade 1858–68 had made it easier for mid-century chemists to obtain the basic chemicals of benzene chemistry. Although the exploitation of benzene chemistry to industry lay in the future, it was undoubtedly the excitement of exploring the reactions of the mysterious substances that were being used in the coal-tar and petroleum industries that encouraged Kekulé and others to apply the new structural theory to them.

Given that the empirical formula of benzene, C_6H_6, and the rules of carbon bonding were known, if is scarcely surprising that structural formulae were proposed before Kekulé's solution in 1865. Between 1858 and 1861, for example, Couper and Josef Loschmidt proposed a diallene structure, $H_2C=C=CHHC=C=CH_2$; but neither man produced experimental support. Loschmidt's *Chemischen Studien* (1861), which contained pages of *a priori* chemical structures, including a circle for benzene to indicate that its structure was mysterious and indeterminate, were dismissed by Kekulé as 'Confusionsformeln'.

Even so, Kekulé was undoubtedly right to note deprecatingly that the hexagon was bound to have occurred to anyone who tinkered long enough with the structure theory. 'What else', he asked, could a chemist 'have done with the two valences' left over on benzene other than to form a ring with them? Whether this notion occurred to Kekulé in a dream before a Ghent fireside has been much debated in recent years. While historians of science are happy to concede that the well-springs of scientific innovation are often to be found outside the culture of science, and there is no particularly strong reason to doubt Kekulé's account of the hypothetico-deductive method in action, others have argued to the contrary that Kekulé invented the story to ensure his priority over other possible hexagon claimants. Whatever the truth of the matter, the consequences of any subconscious creation of the ring concept had to be honed and perfected at the laboratory bench. 'Let us learn to dream, gentlemen,' Kekulé said, 'but let us also beware of publishing our dreams until they have been examined by the wakened mind.'

Kekule's first paper, 'Sur les constitution des substances aromatiques' was presented to the recently founded Société Chimiques de Paris in January 1865. All aromatics, he suggested, contained a six-carbon nucleus – the terminology was, of course, Laurentian – represented by a closed chain of alternating single and double bonds. This was illustrated in the paper by linear sausage formulae:

open chain   closed chain

A *hexagonal* sausage was first used by Kekulé's pupils, Hermann Wichelhaus and Paul Havrez, in the same year, and reproduced in Kekulé's *Lehrbuch* in 1866:

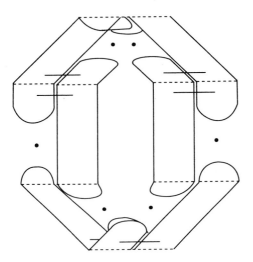

The bare, unadorned hexagon was probably introduced by a former student of Kolbe's, Adolph Claus (1840–1900), in his rare book, *Theoretische Betrachtungen und deren Anwendung zur Systematik der organischen Chemie* (Freiburg, 1866), though Claus is better remembered for suggesting the alternative diagonal or 'centric' forms in the same text:

Claus believed that one or more diagonal bonds explained positional isomerism within the nucleus more clearly than the simple hexagon. Finally, it was Hofmann, as founder editor of *Berichte*, who ensured that the hexagon became extensively used after 1868.

Kekulé's first paper had been content to show how the

closed chain nucleus explained the structural isomerism and homology of the better-known compounds of benzene, xylene, toluene and cresol. The new model soon proved 'an inexhaustible treasure trove', as he excitedly told Baeyer. In particular, it enabled Kekulé to tackle the problem of positional isomerism within the ring. If benzene were hexagonal, there could only be one isomer of a mono- or pentahalogenobenzene, but three isomers each of a di-, tri- and tetrahalogenobenzene. These, and other, predictions were rapidly confirmed by Kekulé's German student, Albert Ladenburg (1842–1911), and by his Italian co-worker, Wilhelm (Guglielmo) Körner (1839–1925).

In 1874, following his return to Italy, Körner brilliantly demonstrated the equivalence of benzene's six hydrogen atoms and formulated a definitive routine for establishing whether disubstituted isomers were *ortho, meta* or *para* with respect to one another.

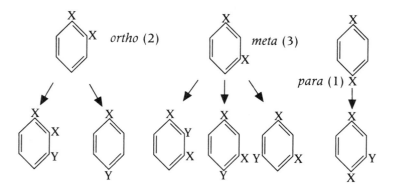

This was two years after Kekulé, again following Williamson's concern for the dynamic nature of chemical change, had explained the non-existence of isomers differentiated by the position of substituents with respect to single or double bonds by supposing that the two possible forms of the benzene hexagon were in dynamic equilibrium:

Although several alternative formulae for benzene (e.g. the centric and prism formulae) were explored by later chemists, they all shared the assumption that benzene contained a cyclic array of six tetravalent carbon atoms. They did not, therefore, challenge, but rather sought to extend, structural theory. By the late 1860s almost all of the prominent younger chemists who published in organic chemistry were structuralists. They included Armstrong, Baeyer, Butlerov, Crum Brown, Fittig, Graebe, Heintz, Körner, Ladenburg and Naquet. Moreover, the older generation of Dumas, Hofmann, Liebig, Williamson, Wurtz and Wöhler made no opposition – indeed, both Frankland and Hofmann began to use the theory with great success.

Only Kolbe stood out against the structural theory, though none of his pupils – notably Armstrong and Beckmann – followed him in his lonely campaign of denigration. To Kolbe, the idea of linking atoms together 'democratically' was philosophically absurd. As he interpreted the radical theory, atoms or radicals were arranged hierarchically within a molecule, with one atom, usually carbon or a hydrocarbon radical in organic chemistry, more important or central than its neighbours. In his own military metaphor, methyl was a 'commando' unit with a carbon 'corporal' who led three hydrogen 'privates'. Such a perspective had undoubtedly brought him great research successes in the 1860s, but proved impossibly difficulty to exploit among the aromatic compounds that were proving industrially important, or to account for the stereochemical phenomena readily explained by the approach of le Bel and van't Hoff. His hatred of Kekulé, whom he blamed for this state of affairs, knew no bounds; he literally despised him and ended his days in a state of paranoia concerning Prussian chemical and military conspiracies. With Kolbe's death in 1884, all criticism was silenced.

In his Kekulé Memorial Lecture to the London Chemical Society in 1898, Francis Japp concluded that Kekulé's benzene theory was the:

> most brilliant piece of scientific production to be found in the whole of organic chemistry . . . three-fourths of modern organic chemistry is directly or indirectly, the product of this theory.

Just as Picasso later transformed art by allowing the viewer to see within and behind things, so Kekulé had transformed chemistry. Chemical properties arose from the internal structures of molecules, which could now be 'seen' and 'read' through the experienced optic of the analytical and synthetic chemist. The future of chemistry, as well as industry, after 1865 was, indeed, to lie in structural chemistry at the sign of this hexagon. But it was also to lie in a closer familiarity with physics, for it was this that provided a closer understanding of the combining capacities of atoms.

Chemistry Applied
to Arts and Manufactures

The production of artificial soda is now one of the
most important branches of manufacturing chemistry,
although the art was, little more than half a century
ago, almost entirely unknown. It may indeed be
averred, without fear of contradiction, that since the
first application of chemical science to manufacturing
operations, few discoveries have been made having
such an important bearing, whether considered in
relation to social life, to commerce, or to the progress
and successful prosecution of useful arts, as that of the
production of carbonate of soda from common salt.
(J. S. MUSPRATT, 1854–60, vol. ii)

James Sheridan Muspratt's *Chemistry Theoretical, Practical and
Analytical* is chiefly remembered today for its thirty-one
introductory steel engravings of nineteenth-century chemists.
Generations of historians of chemistry and chemistry textbook
writers have reproduced these illustrations, which were
originally issued periodically with Muspratt's encyclopedia
as attractive bonuses to accompany its monthly parts. Many
were framed to hang in the corridors of school laboratories
and university chemistry departments, so that it is rare today
to find an ungrangerized copy of Muspratt's *Chemistry*.
  Muspratt's volumes were by no means comprehensive –
their two-thousand pages contain only about eighty entries.
Nor was the idea of a chemical dictionary original with
Muspratt. He was following a tradition first established

by 'philosophical chemists' in the mid eighteenth century. As we have seen, philosophical chemists tried to explain chemical phenomena in terms of particles and forces, of ether, phlogiston and elective affinities. They persevered despite a realization that their explanations were unsatisfactory. As Joseph Black noted[1]:

> Chemistry is not yet a science. We are very far from the knowledge of first principles. We should avoid every thing that has the pretensions of a full system. The whole of chemical science should, as yet, be analytical, like Newton's Optics, in the form of a general law, at the very end of our induction, as the reward of our labour.

Despite such uncertainties, chemistry was amazingly popular in the eighteenth century: students flocked to lectures at Glasgow, Edinburgh and Paris, the members of the Lunar Society made it their priority, itinerant lecturers like Peter Shaw made a successful career stalking the countryside in praise of chemistry, while in London, at the end of the century, the Royal Institution's first professorship was in chemistry. This popularity came from the fact that chemistry was clearly perceived as of potential benefit to medicine and technology. As William Cullen told his students at Edinburgh[2]:

> Chemistry is the art of separating mixt bodies into their constituent parts and of combining different bodies or the parts of bodies into new mixts for the purposes of philosophy and arts, that is, for the purposes of philosophy by explaining the composition of bodies, the nature of mixture and the properties of bodies thereon depending, and *for the purposes of arts by producing several artificial substances more suitable to the intention of various arts than any natural productions are* [my stress].

Such statements, as well as the actual practice of chemical

technology, give the lie to the traditional views of historians and economic historians that the industrial revolution had little or nothing to do with science – on the grounds that science was both too primitive and incorrect to be applied seriously to technological problems. On the contrary, to the eighteenth-century philosopher, it was possible to think of better technical methods and of different substances for producing useful materials. Before Lavoisier had placed chemical theory on a new basis, chemistry was undergoing a technical revolution. As the Clows showed, in 1952, in their study of this technical 'chemical revolution', the search for improvements to existing chemical technologies in agriculture, mining, bleaching, soda-making, dyeing and leather production all produced benefits. Britain, more commercially minded than other nations, was particularly aware of the need for chemicals to bolster its budding textiles industry.

One way that philosophical chemists believed that they could aid the improvement of chemical trades by artisans was through the compilation of natural histories of the properties of substances. These 'directories', it was believed, would lead eventually to economic improvements. The results were, in France, the enormous *Encyclopédie* of Denis Diderot and his collaborators (1751–65), which provided comprehensive accounts of provincial industries, and P. J. Macquer's *Dictionnaire de chimie*. These, and the monographs and papers that poured from the presses of enlightenment, contained hundreds of analyses of waters, airs, earths and minerals in the expectation that some, if not all, of the information would be useful in particular industries. Philosophical chemists, Cullen suggested, were 'assay masters' to the arts in general[3]:

> Does the mason want a cement? Does the dyer want the means of tinging a cloth of a particular colour? Or does the bleacher want the means of discharging all colours? It is the chemical philosopher who must

supply these . . . . Wherever any art requires a matter endued with any peculiar physical properties, it is the chemical philosophy which either informs us of the natural bodies possessed of these properties or induces such in bodies which had them not before, or lastly, produces new bodies endued with the necessary qualities.

It was the sheer quantity of information, as much as any belief in Newtonian powers of elective affinity, that prompted chemists such as Bergman to order information into affinity tables, or Macquer into dictionaries. Macquer's famous *Dictionnaire de chimie* (2 vols, 1766) was translated into English by the Midlands industrial chemist, James Keir, in 1771, and there were several German, Italian and Danish translations, which provided models for other national dictionaries and chemical encyclopedias. In Britain, Macquer and Keir inspired the journalist William Nicholson, who edited a monthly *Journal of Natural Philosophy, Chemistry and the Arts*, between 1798 and 1814, to produce a handsomely illustrated *Dictionary of Chemistry* in 1795; this was enlarged in 1808 as *A Dictionary of Practical and Theoretical Chemistry*, which drew heavily on the *Chimie appliquée aux arts* of the French industrial chemist, Jean-Antoine Chaptal (1756–1832), which Nicholson translated in four volumes in 1807. Chaptal similarly inspired the brothers A. and C. R. Aikin to publish *A Dictionary of Chemistry and Mineralogy, with an Account of the Processes employed in many . . . chemical manufactures* (3 vols, 1807–14).

Like successive editions of contemporary reference works such as the *Ullmann Encyklopädie der technischen Chemie* or the American *Kirk-Othmer Encyclopedia of Chemical Technology*, these early dictionaries had long lives of metamorphosis. Nicholson's *Dictionary* was revised by the Scot, Alexander Ure, in 1821. After three editions Ure recast it completely as the *Dictionary of Arts, Manufactures and Mines* in 1839. Six years before, Ure had compiled his famous *Philosophy of Manufactures* (1833), which clearly reveals the classificatory nature of such compilations. Ure divided industrial operations into those which used mineral, vegetable or animal raw materials. *Ure's Dictionary*, as his later compilation became known, was subsequently revised by many other chemists, and remained a standard reference work until the 1870s. By then it was rivalled by the British Chemical Society's comprehensive, and still useful, *Dictionary of Chemistry*, edited in three volumes by the Society's librarian, Henry Watts, between 1863 and 1875. Ironically, this was itself a revision of the fifth (1859) edition of *Ure's Dictionary*, which others independently revised on two further occasions. Although there were further revisions of *Watts' Dictionary* at the end of the century, its failure to embrace the development of chemical technology and chemical engineering stimulated Thomas E. Thorpe to the production of the magisterial *Dictionary of Applied Chemistry* in the 1890s. This spawned many twentieth-century revisions, the most recent being between 1937 and 1956.

Muspratt's own models were the Chaptal-inspired *Traité de chimie appliquée aux Arts*, which J. B. Dumas assembled and published in Paris in eight volumes between 1828 and 1846, and the remarkable survey of *The Industrial Resources of Ireland*, which Robert Kane, like Muspratt a pupil of Liebig, had compiled while Professor of Natural Philosophy at the Royal Dublin Society in 1844. Muspratt must also have been aware of Liebig's collaboration with Wöhler and Poggendorff on the large *Handwörterbuch der reinen und angewandten Chemie* (9 vols, 1836–62). This had inspired two more of Liebig's pupils with industrial connections on Tyneside, Edmund Ronalds (1819–89) and Thomas Richardson (1816–67), to compile a three-volume account, *Chemical Technology: or Chemistry in its Applications to the Arts and Manufactures* (1847).

With the exception of Kane's guide to Irish industrial

resources, the hallmark of these Continental and British reference guides to the state of pure and applied chemistry was that they were issued in parts, or fascicules. Muspratt's *Chemistry* was printed in Glasgow in sixty-six parts between 1854 and 1860 before being bound into two hefty quarto volumes. (There was a production hiatus in 1859 on the death of his wife, the American actress, Susan Cushman.) Each fascicule of thirty-two pages craftily ended in the middle of an entry, so that the subscriber had the incentive to purchase the next monthly part.

Muspratt's *Chemistry* was perhaps distinctive in its uncompromising emphasis on the practice of chemical technology from acetic acid, alcohol, alum and ammonia through to varnish, water, wine and zinc. Unlike Dumas', Liebig's and Ure's reference works, Muspratt largely ignored theoretical chemistry – though he used formulae and atomic weights – and got on with the job of describing and explaining industrial processes. His work, therefore, is a mirror of chemical industry and technology in the 1850s, while his own family history was a reflection of most of European chemical technology since the 1780s. Such was the pace of change, however, that when Muspratt's Glaswegian publisher wanted to revise the dictionary after Muspratt's death – it was reissued under the same title, with Muspratt's name suppressed, in eight handsomely bound volumes between 1875 and 1880 – it required some seventy experts to compose new entries. It is a mark of the usefulness of Muspratt's *Chemistry* that it was also translated into German by J. Stohmann. By its fourth German edition it had been transformed into twelve volumes and retitled an *Encyklopädisches Handbuch der technischen Chemie* (1888–1922). There was also a Russian translation, while the Americans, through Harvard University, awarded Muspratt an honorary doctorate for his achievement.

THE ALKALI INDUSTRY

Sheridan Muspratt (1821–71) was the oldest of the four Giessen-trained sons of the Irish industrial chemist, James Muspratt (1793–1886), who is often regarded as the founder of the British chemical industry. James Muspratt was born in Dublin of English parents, who apprenticed him to a druggist and wholesale chemist when he was fourteen. In 1811 he joined the army to fight in the Peninsular Wars in Spain, but, after catching fever and being left behind enemy lines, he quit the war and made his way back to Ireland as a midshipman. In Dublin he returned to his original training and began to manufacture yellow 'prussiate of potassium' (potassium ferrocyanide) by fusing animal horn and blood (which are rich in nitrogen) with potassium carbonate in iron vessels. The resulting ferrocyanide was then used to prepare the valuable pigment known since its discovery in 1710 as Prussian blue by precipitation with ferric chloride.

From the manufacture of pigment, it was a small step for Muspratt to produce alum salts as mordants, and chlorine and bleaching powder for the Irish linen industry. A similar progression is found in Muspratt's older rival, Josias Christopher Gamble (1776–1848) of Enniskillen. Gamble, who had been trained for the Presbyterian ministry at the University of Glasgow, where he learned his chemistry, abandoned his parish duties in 1815 to set up in Dublin as a manufacturer of bleaching powder and sulphuric acid. Following Berthollet's demonstration in 1785 that oxygenated muriatic acid (chlorine) could be used as a bleaching agent, the Glaswegian entrepreneur, Charles Tennant (1768–1838), began to use 'chloride of lime' in 1788 to bleach cotton fabrics.

Hitherto bleaching had involved repeated treatments of fabrics with alkali (ammonia from stale urine), dilute acid (sour milk or, after 1750, sulphuric acid) and grassing by exposing fabrics to sunlight in fields for several weeks. Chlorine bleaching released valuable agricultural land and speeded up textile processing a thousandfold. In 1798 Tennant patented a solid 'bleaching salt', or powder, which he prepared by passing chlorine over slaked lime, the chlorine being generated from the action of hydrochloric acid on manganese dioxide. The necessary hydrochloric acid was produced from salt and sulphuric acid; bleaching thereby became connected with the alkali industry.

Muspratt, Gamble and Tennant were well aware of Nicholas Leblanc's method for the preparation of 'artificial' soda. Traditionally, in the eotechnical stage of the 'chemical industry', soda ('alkali'), an essential raw material for the manufacture of soap, glass and paper and in bleaching and dyeing operations, had been extracted from the barilla plant, which grew around the Mediterranean sea, or from sea kelp, which was gathered around the northern coasts of Scotland. Chemical industry was a simple matter of the searching for and the gathering and burning of raw materials. With the rise of analytical knowledge in the eighteenth century, it became well known that common salt and soda shared the same base. Not surprisingly, therefore, it occurred to several eighteenth-century chemists in both Britain and France that it ought to be possible to convert sodium chloride into soda by treating it with sulphuric acid to form Glauber's salt, followed by various carbonation processes.

Such experiments proved particularly successful in England and Scotland, where James Keir, a member of the Lunar Society, and Alexander Fordyce developed satisfactory, albeit small-scale, soda plants to supply their soapworks. Many of these British processes were patented and there were also Parliamentary petitions to have the taxes on salt reduced. The 'chemical industry' thereby underwent a paleotechnical revolution whereby raw materials were manipulated with coal and chalk. Engineering skills, however, remained largely a matter of rule of thumb even when there was some understanding of the chemistry involved in the transformations.

The news of British success was an inspiration to similar

attempts at making artificial soda in France, a country that relied heavily on imports of natural soda from Spain and Sicily and potash from America, and which was therefore extremely vulnerable to British blockades of shipping during time of war. In 1777 the Benedictine chemist, l'abbé Malherbe (1733–1827), won a prize for a soda-making process in which sodium sulphate was heated with charcoal and scrap iron in the open atmosphere (to reduce NaOH to Na_2CO_3). Although this process worked (and even underwent a revival in the mid-nineteenth century in Germany) and was of government interest, Malherbe's process proved a costly failure. Given France's intervention in 1778 in America's War of Independence and the loss of her imported potash from America, this may seem surprising. The reason seems to have been that the sulphide impurities in Malherbe's soda, together with its higher cost, made it impossible to sell.

Meanwhile, Lavoisier's improvement of the traditional method for making gunpowder made potash a vital commodity. Because of the blockade on American supplies, and in order to conserve the trees used in native potash production, the government encouraged manufacturers to use soda instead of potash in glass and textile manufacture. With the prospect of a greater demand for soda, the Academy of Sciences offered a prize in 1781 for 'the simplest and most economical process for decomposing salt' and transforming it into alkali. The prize was never awarded (there were few entrants), since it conflicted with the fact that the government was already granting privileges to work various soda processes before the contest had been decided. The French Revolution saw the abolition of such local 'privileges' and their replacement by a national patent system in 1791, which made the capitalization of commercial schemes more attractive.

Nicholas Leblanc (1742–1806) was a surgeon by training and only began the study of chemistry in the 1780s. Stimulated by the Academy's prize competition, he began laboratory studies of the reactions of salt in 1784 and achieved a successful process in 1789. Like Malherbe, he began by converting salt into sulphate:

$$2NaCl + H_2SO_4 = Na_2SO_4 + 2HCl$$

In the second stage, he converted the sulphate to crude soda with charcoal and chalk (instead of the iron that Malherbe had used):

$$Na_2SO_4 + 2C + CaCO_3 = Na_2CO_3 + CaS + 2CO_2$$

How Leblanc arrived at this second stage is unclear, although a clue may have come from a review of industrial processes by Delamétherie, the pro-phlogiston editor of the *Journal de physique*, in which he drew attention to the possibility of fusing charcoal with Glauber's salt. He supposed that the sulphuric acid would evaporate off, leaving pure soda behind. Delamétherie's speculation may have been the result of some poorly understood industrial espionage he had indulged in during a visit to England. If Leblanc tried this approach, he would have found that only sodium sulphide was formed. However, knowing that sulphides were decomposed by acids, in the face of this difficulty, it has been suggested, he may have tried the effect of bubbling carbon dioxide through the sulphide solution. This proving successful, by further trial and error he could then have found that the greatest yield of soda came from heating solid carbonate (chalk) with charcoal and Glauber's salt.

Since Leblanc gave no explanation for the reactions used in his process, historians have commonly supposed that he founded a major chemical industry on empiricism alone. J. G. Smith has shown, however, that there were explanations of the Leblanc process available in the 1790s and that, by the 1820s, when the industry was well established in France, it was generally understood that sodium sulphate was first reduced to sulphide by the coal and then underwent simple double decomposition with the chalk:

$$Na_2SO_4 + 2C = Na_2S + 2CO_2$$
$$Na_2S + CaCO_3 = CaS + Na_2CO_3$$

In order to judge the 'quality' or purity of the manufactured soda, Descroizilles introduced an 'alkalimeter' to the industry in 1806. In this forerunner of the burette, the quality of alkali was estimated by titrating it against a standard solution of sulphuric acid. By the 1820s it had become usual in France to quote alkali strengths with prices.

In 1791, capitalized by his former medical employer and patron, the Duc d'Orléans, Leblanc set up a prototype works to the north of Paris and was granted a patent, which he was allowed to keep secret. The works were not a success, partly because of technical difficulties with furnaces and hydrogen chloride corrosion, but mainly because he was overtaken by political events. With sulphur commandeered for the manufacture of gunpowder after the outbreak of the Revolution, sulphuric acid proved unobtainable. With the execution of the Duc d'Orléans in 1793, the works passed to the state. Legal problems, as well as the unresolved problem of sulphuric acid supply, prevented Leblanc from regaining access to his factory until 1800. Under-capitalized, and unable to obtain legal redress from the government for his business losses, he committed suicide in 1806.

Despite this personal tragedy, the Napoleonic wars had proved a great stimulus to the creation of a thriving French chemical industry. French scientists had been encouraged to make the country self-sufficient in tobacco, dyestuffs, cotton and sugar (from sugar-beet) and prizes had been regularly awarded for scientific and industrial development. Scientific recruitment was also encouraged by the establishment, under Napoleon, of a system of school secondary education (the lycée system), which together with the École Polytechnique, whose students were given advanced courses in mathematics, engineering and chemistry, were to produce France's scientific workforce. By the eve of Waterloo, the French were producing some 15 000 tons [15 240 tonnes] of artificial soda and 20 000 tons [20 322 tonnes] of sulphuric acid a year. In Alsace, France also had a thriving natural dyes and calico printing industry, while chemists such as Berthollet and Chaptal pioneered the use of chlorine in artificial bleaching. Leblanc has usually been portrayed as a heroic figure whose noble research aspirations were thwarted and ended in penury and disaster[4]:

> He emerges the devoted inventor, betrayed by his scientific colleagues and ruined by competitors who took advantage of his patriotism and misfortunes to secure a commanding headstart in exploiting his own invention.

The reality is that there were some half-dozen proven laboratory methods of making sodium carbonate before Leblanc, and that some of these were working commercially in Britain. Initially, in both France and Britain, artificial soda proved to be more expensive and chemically inferior to natural soda. In Britain, it is usually claimed, the high tax on salt (fifteen shillings per bushel, or eight gallons capacity) inhibited the growth of the industry. Again the truth is that natural soda and potash were abundant, cheaper and superior in quality. In any case, the discovery by soap-makers at the end of the eighteenth century that Glauber's salt could be extracted from their spent lyes meant not only that salt tax could be evaded, but that they could, to some extent, be self-sufficient in soda. This explains how the Leblanc process came to be worked on Tyneside, far from salt fields, in 1819. It is true, of course, that Scotland paid lower duties on salt than England and that this was probably a factor in John Tennant's decision to work the Leblanc process at his St Rollox works, Glasgow, in 1818, following his success as a bleacher. Here he developed a vertically integrated industry by making and selling his own sulphuric acid, and manufacturing bleach and soda. Natural soda was also a factor in James Muspratt's success in Liverpool, where he began sulphuric acid manufacture in 1822, the year that import taxes on barilla were reduced. Since Liverpool soap-makers thereby lost the advantage of using the cheaper soda supplied by Scottish manufacturers whose costs were lower than those on Tyneside because Scotland paid less salt tax than England, Muspratt saw the opportunity for artificial soda sales if the product could be made cheaply. The reduction of salt tax in 1823 enabled him to give his first tonnages of soda away free as promotional gifts against permanent contracts for supplying soda; and his business was launched.

In their *History of the Modern Chemical Industry* (1966), Hardie and Pratt pointed out that 'during the first half of the nineteenth century, and even later, the alkali industry was *the* chemical industry'. Indeed, not much before the 1880s did British chemical manufactures widen in scope, largely under the influence of technical changes and market competition, which led to new production methods. The alkali industry also shaped the British and French landscapes in ways that are still evident, though the 'alkali town' as described by Partington in 1919 is mercifully no longer extant[5]:

> . . . rows of chimneys emitting black smoke from the unscientific combustion of coal, the enormous lead chamber towers, revolving furnaces, waste heaps with escaping steam, the noise and smell of acids, chlorine and sulphuretted hydrogen.

This was the sight that appalled Dickens, Disraeli, Mrs Gaskell and the social novelists of the 1840s and Zola in the 1880s. Working conditions were appalling. A report in 1846 noted that, when the men of St Helens:

> by any chance inhale more than the usual quantity of gas, vomiting and fainting are brought on and they are obliged to be carried out of the works for air.

A later report by Robert Blatchford described St Helens as[6]:

a sordid ugly town. The sky is a low-hanging roof of smeary smoke. The atmosphere is a blend of railway tunnel, hospital ward, gas works and open sewer. The features of the place are chimneys, furnaces, steam jets, smoke clouds and coal mines. The products are pills, coal, glass, chemicals, cripples, millionaires and paupers.

The industry was a wasteful consumer of materials and labour. In 1863 it was estimated that the alkali trade consumed 1.76 million tons of raw materials per annum, producing only 0.28 million tons of products such as soap and bleaching powder. The overwhelming waste products littered landscapes that had once been productive agriculturally and fouled the air with 1.48 million tons of dangerous hydrogen chloride gas and solid waste each year. Alkali manufacture was not an efficient science-based industry; and yet it was worth £2.5 millions per annum and gave employment in Britain to 40 000 people by 1880. Like the synthetic dye industry later, however, this urban employment had been achieved at the cost of destroying the livelihoods of those agricultural communities of Ireland, Scotland and the Mediterranean dependent upon collecting and burning plants for their barilla and potash.

The key chemical was sulphuric acid; as Liebig was to remark, sulphuric acid was the barometer of a nation's commercial prosperity (while soap was a measure of a nation's state of civilization). It proved an essential chemical for dyers, calico printers, bleachers and alkali manufacturers. Initially, in an eotechnical phase, sulphuric acid had been made on a small scale by distilling natural sulphates or 'vitriols'. In the mid eighteenth century there had been a scaling up of production when the 'bell chamber' method was introduced whereby sulphur was burned with nitre and the vapours dissolved in water. In 1746 John Roebuck of Birmingham engineered this into a large-scale process by replacing glass vessels by huge wooden boxes that were lined with lead.

It must be stressed that, like all paleotechnical technologies, this was not a continuous process; this lead chamber process wastefully emitted volumes of foul gases, as demonstrated by Clement and Desormes' explanation of the reaction in 1806:

$$SO_2 + NO_2 + H_2O = H_2SO_4 + NO$$
$$NO + \tfrac{1}{2}O_2 = NO_2$$

This process was greatly improved in the 1830s and 1860s after the addition of Gay-Lussac's and Glover's towers, which made it possible to recycle these waste gases and to reduce the amount of saltpetre used in catalysing the reaction.

Because sulphuric acid was a dangerous chemical to transport, alkali manufacturers tended to make their own, thus leading the industry into diversification and vertical integration. Sulphur for sulphuric acid was mined in Sicily, thus promoting Britain's strong interest in the island and its politics. It was in order to avoid the possibility of embargos on Mediterranean supplies of sulphur that British manufacturers began to use iron and copper pyrites after the 1840s. The sulphur dioxide these pyrites emitted on combustion were fed directly into the lead chambers. The waste products of copper and iron proved valuable economically. Nitre for the process was imported from Chile, leading again to British political interests in the South American continent.

Geographical factors, namely that manufacturers needed to be near large ports where coal, nitre, sulphur and possibly limestone could be brought in, encouraged the development of the Leblanc industry in the Cheshire–Liverpool region, where there were also abundant deposits of salt, Tyneside and Clydeside, and Philadelphia in America. In each of these regions there was also plenty of land for dumping waste materials. Britain's large-scale production of alkali meant that it could sell to Europe and America at prices lower than French, German or American manufacturers, who therefore tended to specialize in sulphuric acid production. The latter proved advantageous for the take-off into the superphosphate industry in the 1850s and for the introduction of the Solvay process in the 1870s.

Liebig's *Chemistry in its Applications to Agriculture and Physiology* appeared in 1840. His 'mineral theory' presented in this important book argued misleadingly that, whereas plants obtained their carbon and nitrogen directly from the atmosphere, inorganic nutrients were absorbed from the soil. Consequently the latter needed constant replenishment by artificial manures. Only in this way was a law of the minimum preserved. In 1845 Liebig devised and patented in Germany and Britain a mineral fertilizer that he got J. S. Muspratt to manufacture at his father's alkali works. The results were disastrous; as became clear later, Liebig had deliberately devised an insoluble feed formula in order to prevent the constituents soaking too rapidly into the soil before absorption. British and German farmers never forgave Liebig for his costly error. Liebig's sense of self-importance, his belief in the 'rightness' of his own approach and his touchiness in the face of opposition from any quarter only goaded his British and German critics to humiliate him for the mistakes he inevitably made.

It became clear in 1850 from the work of the agriculturalist, J. T. Way, that soils have remarkable properties of absorption and that a soluble fertilizer is best. Ironically, it was Liebig who had also drawn attention to the potential value of phosphates and potash in replenishing agricultural land. Animal (and human) bones had long been used by farmers, but the English aristocratic farmer, Sir John Lawes, was able to seize upon Liebig's suggestion that bone phosphorus would prove more soluble if treated with sulphuric acid. In 1843 Lawes patented a superphosphate process and set up manufacture at Deptford in London's East End. At the same time, together with Liebig's pupil, J. H. Gilbert, Lawes used his estates at Rothamsted in Hertfordshire to assess Liebig's theories of farming over a long time period, and to show, in particular, that nitrogenous fertilizers were needed.

By the 1850s there were a dozen or more superphosphate works in Britain and Germany, and by 1900 world production was over 4.5 million tons a year, with large quantities of sulphuric acid being used in processing. These phosphate fertilizers were supplemented by supplies of natural guano (sodium nitrate from bird droppings that are rich in nitrogen), fossil guano (coprolites), which was mined extensively in Cambridgeshire, ammonium sulphate, a waste product of the burgeoning gas lighting industry, and the potash salts that began to be worked extensively at Stassfurt in the tiny principality of Anhalt from 1861 onwards and which gave Germany an important monopoly.

Lacking wealthy land-owning experimentalists like Lawes in England and Boussingault in France, Liebig's American disciples had to solicit patronage from farmers and politicians, only to find that they could not always fulfil their patrons' immediate expectations. Subsequently, some (like Liebig's pupil, Eben N. Horsford) abandoned agricultural chemistry for more lucrative ventures in industrial chemistry (in Horsford's case, the baking powder empire of the Rumford Works). Not until the 1880s was agricultural research institutionalized in experimental stations.

Such stations were founded earlier in the Germanies. It was by drawing attention to the use of chemistry in agriculture that the Baden government, and other German states, hoped to dispel the revolutionary fervour of German farmers and peasants, as well as emulating Britain's state of industrialization and standard of living. These political decisions led to the further sponsorship of Giessen-type laboratories and to the diversification of existing pharmacy-based industries into fertilizers and coal-tar products, as the growing numbers of professionally trained chemists, finding few vacancies in agricultural industries or in academic positions, sought employment abroad or in new chemical industries of their own devising.

As the French quickly discovered, a major problem with the Leblanc process was the hydrogen chloride emitted in converting salt into sodium sulphate. The gas rained down as hydrochloric acid on to agricultural property, as well as being a health hazard. Private prosecutions in both France and Britain, some of which were malicious, frequently led to the relocation of alkali works; but eventually the problem was resolved by other methods. In Britain, in the 1860s, William Gossage developed a method for washing hydrochloric acid from the waste gases before they were vented from the tall chimneys that characterized the industry. This development conveniently coincided with the fact that two processes (by Walter Weldon in 1866 and Hugh Deacon in 1868) had been developed for turning hydrogen chloride into chlorine, which could then be used directly for preparing bleach. Manufacturers were stimulated towards the recycling of waste products not merely by economic factors such as the use of hydrochloric acid for bleaching and glue manufacture from bones, but by legislation. In France, planning by-laws concerning the location of the industry, and horizontal limestone absorption channels, prevented some of the damage, while in Britain in 1863 an Alkali Act compelled manufacturers to absorb ninety-five per cent of their hydrogen chloride output.

The other major waste product, calcium sulphide, had the dreadful property of producing hydrogen sulphide in rain and drizzle. Since it also locked up the sulphur that had been expensively imported to make sulphuric acid, many works chemists tried to find ways of using it. They had no success until Alexander Chance, in 1882, developed a furnace process for its oxidation:

$$CaS + H_2O + CO_2 \quad \xrightarrow{\text{burn}} \quad H_2S \quad \rightarrow \quad S + H_2O$$

In this way, by the 1880s, the Leblanc alkali process had reached a modicum of efficiency as a self-contained series of interlocking processes. But it has been estimated that from a total of 9000 units of raw materials, only 3000 units of saleable commodities resulted.

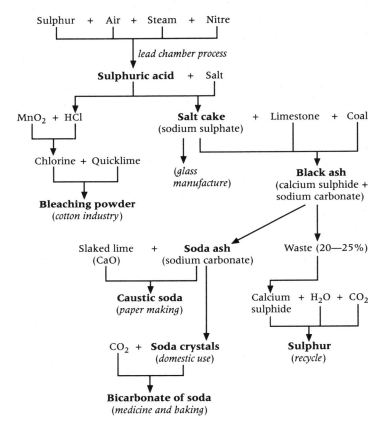

FIGURE 8.1 The Leblanc alkali process. (Based on K. Warren, *Chemical Foundations. The Alkali Industry in Britain to 1926* (Oxford: Clarendon, 1980), p. 29.)

It was because the Leblanc process was so wasteful and unpleasant to work that attempts to find a cleaner, more efficient, way of using salt were tried throughout the nineteenth century. As early as 1810, A. J. Fresnel in France showed that ammonium salts could be used to generate soda:

$$NaCl + NH_3 + CO_2 + H_2O \rightarrow NH_4Cl + NaHCO_3$$
$$\text{(insoluble)}$$

$$2NaHCO_3 \rightarrow Na_2CO_3 + CO_2 + H_2O$$

$$\overset{\text{heat}}{2NH_4Cl + CaO \rightarrow CaCl_2 + 2NH_3 + H_2O}$$
$$\text{(waste)} \quad \text{(re-use)}$$

On paper the process looked very attractive, but it was extremely difficult to work efficiently, mainly because of the loss of ammonia. There were many English patents and attempts to manufacture soda by this 'ammonia–soda' method. James Muspratt, for example, sank £8000 into the venture in 1838, but abandoned the method after only a few years.

The complex engineering problems associated with the process were not resolved until 1861 when the Belgian chemist, Ernst Solvay (1838–1922), designed a carbonating tower (the Solvay tower) in which a rain of ammoniated salt was met by an up-current of carbon dioxide. Solvay formed a company in Belgium to work the process in 1863, though he made no money from the enterprise until two years later. The process had the enormous advantages that it avoided pollution, and that the raw materials of brine and ammonia (from gasworks) were readily available. Less fuel was used than in the Leblanc process, and no sulphur or nitre was involved. On the other hand, the capital costs of erecting a tower that worked were much higher. Its one economic weakness was that the chlorine used in the salt remained locked up in the single waste product, calcium chloride, which had to be dumped.

Although this problem was solved by Ludwig Mond in the 1890s, so that the chlorine could be used to make bleach and so compete with the Leblanc process, in practice the industry was moving into its final neotechnical phase, and it had become cheaper to make chlorine and bleach by electrolysis. Even so, despite this one spot of inefficiency, by the 1880s it is estimated that Leblanc soda was costing manufacturers seventy per cent more than that prepared by the Solvay process.

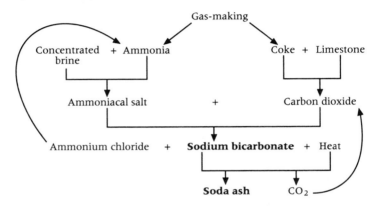

FIGURE 8.2   The Solvay ammonia–soda process. (Based on K. Warren, *Chemical Foundations. The Alkali Industry in Britain to 1926* (Oxford: Clarendon, 1980), p. 29.)

Ludwig Mond (1839–1909) was a German pupil of Robert Bunsen, who worked initially in the German Leblanc soda industry. Appalled by its wastefulness, he came to England in 1862 to see if the British made soda any more efficiently. In Manchester he developed a method for recovering sulphur from calcium sulphide by combustion in the presence of a nickel catalyst; however, this failed to interest English manufacturers. The English experience, however, led to a friendship with the accountant, John Brunner (1843–1919), and together they formed a partnership to work the Solvay process in Britain. A licence being obtained from Solvay, who took a liking to Mond, the latter built a works at Northwich in Cheshire in 1872. By the 1890s, the Brunner–Mond Company had stolen the edge over the Leblanc process in both output and profitability. In response, in the biggest shake-up of chemical industry ever known, the Leblanc manufacturers combined forces in 1890 to form the United Alkali Company and began to modernize and to sell off obsolescent plant.

One sign of the times was that the new company built a Central Research Laboratory at Widnes in 1891, with a German chemist, Ferdinand Hurter, in charge of a research programme to improve the efficiency of the Leblanc process. Although a competent analyst and an efficient research worker, Hurter was a conservative thinker. By warning the company off the newly developed, largely American, electrolytic processes, the Leblanc alkali works missed the opportunity of dominating the market in chlorine, bleach and caustic soda production. Instead, by diversifying its products as much as possible, and by dominating the production of sulphuric acid, United Alkali remained viable and increasingly efficient as its constituents gradually moved over to the Solvay process. In 1920 the last of the Leblanc works in England was closed. In 1926, Brunner–Mond and United Alkali, together with many other smaller chemical firms, joined forces to form Imperial Chemical Industries (ICI). This merger was necessary in the face of increasing overseas competition. James Muspratt's grandson, Sir Max Muspratt (1872–1934), was one of ICI's chief managers.

Until the advent of electrolytic methods, Leblanc soda manufacturers had used a process for causticizing soda that had been developed by William Gossage:

$$Na_2CO_3 + Ca(OH)_2 = 2NaOH + CaCO_3$$

Faraday had investigated the electrolysis of salt as early as 1834 and, although an industrial process was patented in Britain in 1852, there were too many engineering problems (such as the chlorine and sodium reacting at the anode and cathode) to be overcome at this date. The Austrian engineer, Carl Kellner, developed a mercury cathode system that had been first devised by the American, H. Y. Castner, in 1892, and put it successfully into operation at Weston in 1897. This was the first of the large, clean, smokeless chemical works in the world. This works was bought out by Brunner–Mond in 1920 and so became part of ICI in 1926.

The years between 1860 and 1880 have been called the golden years of the Leblanc soda industry. It had no competition, it was technically efficient, albeit relying on a large workforce for its batch processing (wives and children were also involved), and it was slowly overcoming the problems of waste and pollution. But in the 1880s it experienced severe competition from the Solvay process in Britain and on the Continent, and profits fell dramatically. The industry fought back by reducing its output of soda and maximizing its output of sulphuric acid, bleach and caustic soda, only to be caught out again by the introduction of the cheaper electrolytic process for making caustic soda. Possibly, the industry's lack of technically trained managers, who listened too keenly to Hurter's advice, was a factor in the disintegration of the industry. More aware of continental developments in the industry, Brunner–Mond took steps to ensure that it had a technically qualified staff. On the other hand, the Leblanc alkali owners often played an important role in local community education and politics. They may have been inefficient scientifically, but their money and patronage were often wisely used to provide and to improve the housing, schools, libraries and recreational facilities of their local communities.

The problems faced by the alkali industry, whether Leblanc or Solvay processes, were essentially those of engineering rather than chemistry. Leblanc's initial design problem in transferring a laboratory method to a large-scale factory was the construction of suitable furnaces, and many of the subsequent improvements to the final purity of soda had to do with small changes in furnace design that led to greater and more economic heat efficiency. The problems of hydrogen chloride disposal and its recovery for bleaching powder production did not involve any deep chemical insights, but rather the ability to design and build tall chimneys, or absorption conduits or towers. Roebuck's skill in transferring sulphuric acid manufacture from glass bottles to wooden sheds lined with lead was that of the builder and engineer rather than the chemist. Similarly, all the tricks of recycling wastes that eventually made the Leblanc process economically efficient were essentially the products of engineering skills. Solvay's and Mond's struggles to make the ammonia–soda process work were the struggles of engineers, for the chemistry was known to work. Indeed, apart from the need for chemical skills in the monitoring by volumetric analysis of the quality of products at various stages of production, it was the engineer who was the essential creative force in the growth of the chemical industry. It was the engineer who was needed to maintain furnaces, trace leaks, replace equipment and design ways of leading gases from one part of a plant to another without leakages, Muspratt's statistics of alkali production for 1852 clearly show that UK manufacturers spent enormous sums (£832 000 in 1852) on equipment and repairs (see Table 8.1).

Engineering skills were equally germane in what is always regarded as the most scientifically advanced of the chemical industries, that of dyestuffs and calico printing.

DYESTUFFS AND COLOURING

August Wilhelm Hofmann's influence as a teacher and experimentalist on British and German chemistry was profound. He was responsible for continuing the method of teaching by laboratory instruction that had been established and popularized by Liebig at Giessen and for transferring it to London in 1845 and to Berlin in 1865. (Sheridan Muspratt also opened a Royal College of Chemistry in

TABLE 8.1 *The British alkali trade in 1852.*

	Tyneside	Lancashire	Clydeside	Rest	Total
Raw materials consumed (tons)					
Sulphur	7 580	none	3 000	940	11 520
Pyrites	33 750	40 220	9 000	17 292	100 262
Salt	57 905	40,152	19 120	20 370	137 547
Coal	232 020	136 400	80 000	71 000	519 420
Production (tons)					
Alkali (NaOH)	23 100	26 743	12 000	9 750	71 593
Soda	42 794	3 500	6 000	8 750	61 044
Bicarbonate	4 046	1 200	none	516	5 762
Bleaching powder	5 000	1 250	5 000	1 850	13 100
No. of men employed	3 067	1 519	900	840	6 326
Expenditure on equipment (£s)	344 000	172 000	100 000	86 000	702 000
Expediture on repairs (£s)	69 500	23 000	20 000	17 200	129 700
Tonnage of shipping used	189 100	72 200	70 000	43 000	374 300

Values	
71 493 tons alkali at £10	£711 930
61 044 tons soda at £5	305 220
5 762 tons bicarbonate at £15	86 220
13 100 tons bleach	131 000
	£1234 580

Cost of imports	
11 520 tons sulphur at £6	£69 120
4 800 tons sodium nitrate at £15	72 000
12 000 tons manganese at £2.10.0	30 000
	£171 120

Net contribution of alkali trade to annual UK income = £1066 460

Note: 1 British ton = 1.0161 metric tonnes.
From J. S. Muspratt, *Chemistry Theoretical, Practical and Analytical* (Glasgow, 1854–60), vol. ii, p. 938.

Liverpool in 1848 in emulation of the Giessen–London model.) Hofmann created, like Liebig, a distinctive school of chemists who were interested primarily in experimental organic chemistry – in investigating the natural history of organic compounds – and in the industrial applications of their findings. Among his distinguished British pupils were F. A. Abel, who joined the War Department as an explosives expert, William Crookes, the founder of *Chemical News*, Charles B. Mansfield, who made benzene chemistry possible, and William H. Perkin and E. C. Nicholson, who launched the British synthetic dyestuffs industry; and the Germans, Peter Griess, C. A. Martius and J. Volhard, who all distinguished themselves as dyestuffs chemists.

Hofmann (1818–92) was the son of the architect who enlarged Liebig's Giessen laboratories in 1839. He matriculated at Giessen in 1836 intending to study law and languages (at which he proved very adept), but gradually he became attracted by Liebig's chemistry classes. He was awarded a doctorate in 1841 for his investigation of the chemistry of coal tar. In the autumn of 1845, through Liebig's influence, he agreed to direct the privately funded Royal College of Chemistry in London. Here the theme and variations of his many publications were coal tar and its derivatives. In his first publication in Germany in 1843, he showed that many of the supposedly different substances extracted from coal tar naphtha were a nitrogenous base, aniline, hitherto only known as an extraction product of the natural dye, indigo. During the 1840s Hofmann, as well as Laurent in France, traced the relationship between aniline and phenol. A decade later he classified such bases on the analogy of ammonia, while encouraging his eccentric student, Charles Mansfield (1819–55), to develop methods of fractional distillation and fractional freezing that enabled Hofmann and his pupils to separate some twenty different substances from coal tar, including pure benzene, xylene and toluene. Mansfield's patent of 1848 was, effectively, the beginning of the neotechnical phase of the chemical industry.

The rapid growth of the gas lighting industry in the 1830s had produced large quantities of its waste products in the form of an unpleasant treacly tar whose only use seemed to be in the preservation of the railway sleepers that were needed by the millions during the railway-building mania of the 1840s. Mansfield's fractionation technique meant, however, that coal tar could be worked and investigated, and possible beneficial uses found for its constituents. The emergence of a public health movement in the same decade, with its stress on urban and personal cleanliness and hygiene, provided a ready market for disinfectants. It was the discovery of the disinfectant properties of phenol, for example, that led to its use not only in certain hygienic soaps but also in attempts to destroy the stench of sewage. It was the coupling in Joseph Lister's mind of phenol's employment as a sewage disinfectant with Pasteur's demonstration that aerial germs were a factor in the spread of disease that first led him to employ phenol (or carbolic acid) on the operating table in 1867. Benzene and its congeners were also rapidly exploited for their solvent properties, from which a dry-cleaning industry emerged, as well as new varnishes and finishes.

On the pharmaceutical side, large amounts of opium, morphine, cocaine and quinine were being used in the treatment of real and imaginary medical conditions. These were expensive drugs to import and process. Many pharmacists and chemists must have wondered whether a cheaper synthesis of these expensive natural commodities might be possible. Nothing was known, of course, of the structures of such complicated organic molecules in the 1850s; nevertheless, this could not prevent chemists from reasoning by analogy and rationally attempting to put two and two together to see whether something similar to a natural product would not materialize. Hofmann himself had speculated in 1849 that the drug, quinine, might be prepared if an amine group could be added to naphthalene. As is well known, in 1856, while working at home during a break from his course at the Royal College of Chemistry, William Henry Perkin (1838–1907), who had been attracted to chemistry by photography, attempted to synthesize quinine ($C_{20}H_{24}N_2O_2$) by mixing together impure allyl toluidine ($C_{10}H_{13}N$) with potassium dichromate on the assumption that quinine differed from the double molecule by only two equivalents of water:

$$C_3H_5Cl + C_7H_9N \rightarrow C_3H_5C_7H_8N + HCl$$

allyl chloride   toluidine [$C_{10}H_{13}N$]

$$2C_{10}H_{13}N \rightarrow C_{20}H_{24}N_2O_2$$

quinine

Instead, Perkin prepared a brownish mess, which, he thought, could be a general test of aromatic bases. On carrying out the same reaction with impure aniline sulphate, he obtained a black precipitate, which stained purple a cloth he used for mopping up spills on the bench. The substance also dyed silk a beautiful mauve.

By the 1850s the natural dyestuffs industry was a large and profitable business. The entry on dyes in Muspratt's *Chemistry*, which would have been written about the time of Perkin's discovery, is the longest in the treatise with 316 pages, or nearly five times the space devoted to the alkali trade. In 1856 some 75 000 tons [76 207 tonnes] of natural dye materials worth over two million pounds were imported into Britain (see Table 8.2). With the rise to dominance of a middle-class consumerist society in nineteenth-century Europe, colour was beginning to be important in the decoration of homes and women's dress. There was therefore a very strong market for new colours and fashionable annual variations.

Perkin had the sense therefore to ask the Scottish firm of Pullars whether his purple 'mess' had any potential as a colouring matter. Pullars reported favourably that Perkin's product could be successfully mordanted to silks and that it showed reasonable colour-fastness to sunlight. The result of this report was that, although only eighteen,

TABLE 8.2   *Natural dyes in production c.1850.*

Name	Plant	Colour
Anchusin	*Anchusa tinctoria*	Dark-red
Aloetin	Aloes	Brown
Annotta	*Bixa orellana*	Orange-red
Archil/litmus	Lichens	Violet
Berberin	Barberry root	Brown
Barwood	Barwood	Red
Brazilin	Brazil wood	Red
Catechu	Khair tree	Rust brown
Chica	*Bignonia chica*	Red
Cochineal	Insects	Red
Fustin	Fustet	Yellow
Gallic acid	Galls	Black
Indigo	Indigofera	Blue
Kermes	Insects	Red
Logwood	Logwood	Violet blue
Madder	Madder	Yellow
Morindin	Sooranjee	Yellow
Uercitrin	*Quercus nigra*	Yellow
Rhamnin	Berries	Yellow
Safflower	*Carthamus tinctorius*	Yellow
Woad	*Isatis sativa*	Red

The coloured salts of arsenic, chromium, copper, iron, manganese and tin were also used.
Based on J. S. Muspratt, *Chemistry Theoretical, Practical and Analytical* (Glasgow, 1854–60), vol. ii. entry for 'dyestuffs'.

Perkin, his brother Thomas and their father (who supplied the necessary capital) built a factory at Greenford Green, near Harrow, to synthesize and market 'aniline purple' or 'mauve' – the name being chosen because of the dye's close resemblance to a commercially successful purple (*poupre Français*) being marketed by French colourists. The Harrow site, abutting the Grand Union Canal and close to a sulphuric acid factory, was chosen so as to avoid new nuisance regulations in the metropolis!

Contrary to many accounts, Perkin's mauve was not the first artificial dye. Dyemakers in France and Manchester had for years exploited the murexide reaction between uric acid (prepared from bird dung) and nitric acid. The French purple against which Perkin's mauve competed was, in fact, a murexide derivative. Perkin's success soon stimulated new synthetic dyehouses, such as Read Holliday of Huddersfield (1860), who had been distilling coal tar for naphtha lamps and timber treatment since the 1840s, Roberts, Dale & Co. of Manchester (1860), Ivan Levinstein of Manchester (1864), Renard Frères at Lyon (1859) and the Badische Anilin Co. (BASF) at Elberfeld (1863). In his report on the dye industry for the industrial exhibition held in London in 1862, Hofmann graciously predicted that Britain would become the chief exporter to the world. This proved wishful thinking.

As is well known, Hofmann was strongly opposed to Perkin's entry into commerce. That this opposition had nothing to do with industry *per se* is clear from Hofmann's encouragement of other pupils and his later very cordial, consultancy relationship with the dyestuffs industry in Germany. No doubt he thought Perkin too young and inexperienced to enter industry and he was also still distraught over Mansfield's appalling death the year before after a benzene fire. More significantly, he would have been aware that it would lead to Perkin's loss to laboratory investigation, for Hofmann must have realized that the problems Perkin would encounter in manufacturing mauve would be engineering, not chemical, ones.

As Tony Travis has demonstrated, Perkin's chief achievement in manufacturing mauve successfully was in scaling up a laboratory procedure and in making the dangerous procedures involving benzene and the manufacture of his own fuming sulphuric acid (oleum) safe for his small workforce. Put beside these acute problems, capitalization, the ability to find reliable suppliers of his raw materials, and the trial-and-error search for the best mordant (tannin) were fairly trivial.

It is easy to overstate the significance of Perkin's synthesis, as self-interested partisans of the British dye industry did at the end of the century. It never proved as colour-fast as natural dyes; it was expensive to manufacture; and, thwarted by the rosaniline patents of Simpson, Maule and Nicholson, Perkin was unable to produce useful derivatives of the dye, which, in any case, after a wave of popularity as a mourning colour, was superseded by others like the pink, safranine. Economic historians rightly stress that what was far more significant for the growth of a neotechnical science-based chemical industry was the synthesis of an artificial dye − the equivalent for this industry of the replacement of barilla and kelp by artificial soda and potash. Such a synthesis, based now on the knowledge of structural organic chemistry suggested by Kekulé rather than on the empirical exploitation of known organic reactions, was first achieved in the laboratory for the alizarin extracted from the madder plant in 1869.

The synthetic route in which anthracene was first oxidized to anthraquinone and then hydrolysed with sulphuric acid and alkali fusion was significantly established simultaneously by both Perkin and Heinrich Caro (1834–1910), a German calico printer colourist who had worked in the Manchester trade for many years before returning to Germany and joining BASF as a research chemist. Their independent processes, which only differed in small details, were patented within twenty-four hours of each other in Britain, Caro's on the 25 June and Perkin's on the 26 June 1869. This meant that a profitable German market was lost to Perkin, who could only make alizarin under German licence, or find an alternative synthesis. The breakthrough here had come from Adolf Baeyer's demonstration in 1868 that complicated organic mo ecules could be broken into simpler, and known, compounds by heating with zinc. His two research assistants, Carl Graebe and Carl Liebermann, had then, at Baeyer's suggestion, applied the procedure to alizarin. The main product of the reduction was anthracene. By reversing their procedure they reobtained alizarin. It was this laboratory procedure, which was commercially impracticable, that had stimulated Caro and Perkin.

Synthetic alizarin had a much greater economic impact than mauve. It quickly replaced the madder industry, which proved a major disaster for French farmers. This agricultural upheaval was to be repeated, more slowly, after Baeyer showed in 1880 that indigo, a product of the woad plant farmed in India, could be synthesized from dinitrodiphenylacetylene, *o*-nitrocinnamic acid or *o*-nitrobenzaldehyde. Baeyer sold the commercial rights of the process to BASF, but it proved unworkable technically. In 1890 Carl Heumann (1850–93), at Zürich Polytechnic, developed a simpler synthesis from anthranilic acid, which, as BASF's technical chemist, E. Sapper, showed, could be cheaply made from naphthalene using a mercury salt as catalyst. The latter was discovered serendipitously when a mercury thermometer broke inside a reaction vessel.

Following enormous development costs, synthetic indigo began to replace the natural dye from about 1900, and within a few years British farmers in India began to migrate back to England to their cheap seaside bungalows. After about 1908, indigo began to be made in the UK, albeit by a German, not British, company. The success of synthetic alizarin and indigo showed how a knowledge of chemical theory and of the detailed structures of organic substances could pay commercially. This knowledge encouraged large and even small chemical firms to introduce research laboratories and to diversify into pharmaceutical manufacturing – processes particularly associated with German industry.

One of Hofmann's first pupils in 1845 had been an eighteen-year-old druggist's apprentice, Edward Chambers

Nicholson. He had come to London to work with the druggist and chemical supplier, John Lloyd Bullock, one of the main protagonists in the creation of the Royal College of Chemistry (RCC) in 1845 and a personal friend of Liebig and Hofmann. By 1848, when another Lancastrian, George Maule, entered the College, Nicholson was one of Hofmann's personal assistants and was about to publish important research on the constitution of aniline, cumene, cumidine, caffeine and strychnine.

Nicholson's demonstration that mesitylene (the 1,3,5-trimethylbenzene first isolated by Robert Kane in 1838) was isomeric with cumene (isopropylbenzene) prompted Hofmann to suggest to Maule that he should prepare further mesitylene derivatives to establish isomeric compounds through analogous reactions. Since Nicholson had earlier converted cumene into nitrocumene and into the new base, cumidine, and Cahours had converted cumene into another unknown base, nitrocumidine, Maule decided to nitrate mesitylene and to reduce the nitrated product to form nitromesidine. His one published paper of 1849 described the preparation of bright yellow crystals of this substance.

Apart from also forming salts with hydrochloric acid, platinum dichloride, etc., Maule made no further contributions to the published literature, confirming Frankland's later comment that, 'although I induced him to engage in chemical research, he had no real interest in science'. This makes it somewhat puzzling that Nicholson and George Simpson (a London paint-maker and oil man), who had also attended Hofmann's classes in 1845 with Nicholson, should have chosen to go into partnership with Maule.

In 1853 the firm of Simpson, Nicholson and Maule was established in its factory at Locksfields at Walworth, south London, for the manufacture of the fine chemicals used in early photography, such as pyrogallol, ether and collodion cotton for pharmaceutical use. It is not known what Maule did between leaving the RCC in 1849 and

1853. It is possible that he joined Simpson's paintworks in the Walworth area; alternatively, he may have inherited a small sum of money, which helped to capitalize the firm. Whatever the reason, it is clear that Simpson and Nicholson were the real brains behind the operation. In 1859, for example, Nicholson, together with David Price, another RCC graduate, discovered a method of oxidizing aniline to form the red dye, fuchsine, which they marketed as magenta (naming it after Garibaldi's victory in north Italy in 1859). This was a superior process to one developed by Verguin in France and marketed by Renard Frères at Lyon.

Unfortunately, a similar method of making magenta using arsenic acid as an oxidizing agent was discovered simultaneously by another of Hofmann's pupils, Henry Medlock, who (unlike Nicholson) patented the process. Medlock's patent rapidly became notorious for the litigation it caused, though the legal wrangles produced handsome fees for the many chemical witnesses called by litigants and defenders. The patent was declared invalid in 1866, driving down the price of fuchsine from £6 per gallon [4^1/$_2$ litres] in 1860 to seven shillings per gallon a decade later.

Nicholson also developed 'aniline blue' and its salts. Frederick Field's comic song for the Chemical Society's B-Club, 'The Feast of the Blues', contains the lines:

> Mr Maule . . . thinking but little of blue, but more of yesterday's hunting – or of tomorrow's meeting of the 'Surrey'.

This strongly suggests that Maule was the firm's sleeping-partner. As Frankland said later, 'he had no real interest in science, and after his great pecuniary success [with the firm] he abandoned it altogether, and devoted his life to hunting and other sports'.

This pecuniary success no doubt came about after 1856 when the firm began to make nitrobenzene for William Perkin and for Hofmann's researches. In 1859, Simpson,

Nicholson and Maule began to make roseine (magenta or rosaniline), and their entry into synthetic dyestuffs necessitated a move into larger premises, the Atlas Works at Hackney Wick. Hofmann was retained as a consultant (in Berlin he was to be the consultant for AGFA, the firm founded by his German pupil, Carl Martius (1838–1920)). Further success came in 1863 when the firm introduced the first yellow azo dye, amidoazobenzene, or aniline yellow.

The rest of the story is quickly told. In 1868, both aged forty-one, Nicholson and Maule retired and sold their interests to Edward Brooke, a Lancashire tar distiller, and William Spiller, Nicholson's assistant. As Brooke, Simpson and Spiller, the firm bought Perkin's alizarin knowhow and factory at Greenford in 1874 when Perkin too decided to retire in order to devote himself to chemical research and the Anglican ministry. Two years later, however, the firm was bought by the tar distillers Burt, Boulton and Hayward who, because of growing pollution problems at Harrow, moved the operations to Silvertown in London's East End. They, in turn, became part of the empire of British Alizarine Company in 1882, which was absorbed by ICI in 1926.

Why did Nicholson and Maule opt out of the industry at the early age of 41? Both men lived on until 1890, so ill-health was an unlikely factor (though Nicholson's death from cancer of the throat might be significant). In Maule's case, gentrification, leisure and pleasure are sufficient answers. Having a genuine love for neither science nor business, and having made his fortune (he left £43 000), he abandoned industry for the life of a gentleman, retaining only the ownership of a distillery in Regent's Park. As for Nicholson, did he abandon industry because he was dismayed by the Medlock patent affair? Haber speculates that his retirement may have been connected with Hofmann's decision to return to Germany in 1865 (there remaining a chance until 1868 that he might have resettled in London); but this explanation does little credit to Nicholson's own chemical prowess, for much of Hofmann's early work on rosaniline owed more to Nicholson than Hofmann gave him credit for, and in any case there were plenty of other chemical consultants, such as Price and Field, or even Frankland, that the firm could have employed.

More plausibly, Alec Campbell has suggested that, with the expiry of their own patents, like Perkin, Nicholson and Maule were simply not interested in the 'world of expanding business'. Neither man could have foreseen the dramatic change the dyes industry would undergo after 1869 when alizarin was synthesized. Perhaps historians have asked a meaningless question when asking why the pioneers of the British dye industry retired in 1868 at the very moment it was poised to take a major change in direction. For the implication behind the question is to find a scapegoat or cause for Britain's supposed industrial decline. Because of Hofmann's later close connection with the rise of the German dyestuffs (and hence pharmaceutical) industry, it has been easy to claim, as the Victorians and Edwardians did, that Nicholson, Maule, Perkin and for that matter Greville Williams, Arthur Green or even Hofmann himself were somehow to blame for Britain's loss of industrial leadership to the Germans. The tax on alcohol, free trade and the absence of import tariffs, and the British patent laws that did not insist on patents being worked in Britain until 1907 were also blamed.

In 1868, fresh from Britain's relatively poor showing at the Paris Exhibition the previous year (where Liebig and Hofmann were jurists), Frankland drew attention to the large number of original chemical papers from German chemists compared with those read to the Chemical Society. Three years later in *Nature* he added:

Not only are we behind in the aggregate of activity in discovery, but our individual productiveness is also markedly below that of Germany and

France .... It is highly remarkable that a country which, perhaps more than any other, owes its greatness to the discoveries of experimental science, should be distinguished for its neglect of experimental research.

Frankland's complaint was to lead the British Association for the Advancement of Science to attempt a register of research; but the response was so apathetic that the scheme never got off the ground. But the attempt is indicative of a fear and tension in the minds of some members of the British chemical community in the 1870s concerning their role in society. This was the decade that saw the foundation of the Institute of Chemistry in 1877 and of the Royal Commission on Scientific Instruction and the Advancement of Science.

'Declinism' was not unique to Britain and is found repeatedly voiced by the scientific communities of France and Germany. It has been a pretty universal response by the scientific community to certain historical situations from 1800 onwards. One of the public voices, or rhetorical devices of science, is evidently to threaten dire consequences if certain courses of action are not taken. Such actions are not disinterested since, if executed, they would tend to benefit men or women of science either individually or as a group.

It is, of course, easy to find defects and absurdities in the declinist argument. Was the yardstick absolute decline or decline relative to other nations in chemistry? But the point about dyestuffs was that a spokesman such as Perkin himself, Levinstein, Meldola, Roscoe and Armstrong could and did all claim that Britain's loss of the hegemony in dyes to Germany was a powerful illustration of a more general decline, and that, unless the state was willing to patronize teaching, research and education more lavishly, the situation would only become worse. It must be reiterated that similar statements were being made in France and, ironically, even in Germany.

As Ernst Homberg has stressed, however, the real history of the dyestuffs industry concerns a long and well established natural dyeing and textile printing industry in which professional colourists, as opposed to academic chemists, played key roles. In other words, the industrial reality was different from the rhetoric of Hofmann, Perkin, Armstrong and Levinstein, who, in Homberg's view, were really struggling to legitimate the academic discipline of organic chemistry.

The pronouncements of Perkin, Armstrong, Roscoe and others, or the subtle propaganda in chemists' obituaries (such as Nicholson's), which bewailed Britain's loss of dyestuffs hegemony to Germany, all carry a strong emphasis on the expansion of the institutions of academic chemistry. We have to be cautious in reading this rhetoric back to 1868. By all accounts, then, the situation was pretty healthy and businesses were responding intelligently to short-term considerations as to the economists' 'costs, markets and other conditions'. For, given that the economic value of British dye production was scarcely one per cent of the textiles to which they were applied, it can hardly have seemed to make much sense to invest scientifically trained workers and research in it when the proven paleotechnical technologies of alkali and textiles were more profitable.

By 1880, of course, despite the continued expansion of Britain's chemical industry, with the exception of dyes, the British share of the world's trade market was declining. But the reason for this failure to expand dyestuff production, if indeed it is fair to describe it as a failure and not just business sense, has little or nothing to do with Hofmann's decision to return to Germany, or Nicholson's, Maule's and Perkin's decisions to retire from the industry. Given the strength of German industry, it made far more sense for Britain, with its vast reserves of coal, to export coal-tar raw materials to the Germans and to import their finished dyes from them, only to re-export them as dyed and printed fabrics and textiles. By 1913 Britain imported about £1.8

millions of dyes, but the export of inorganic chemicals and fertilizers brought in £14.3 millions.

Thus it was that in 1914 the British government found itself importing German khaki dye through neutral Switzerland for army uniforms. Through its huge empire, Britain also possessed favoured markets that reduced the need to compete with Europeans. The problem came in the 1890s when Germany's huge steel industry began to produce sufficient tar from its coking plants not to need British tar supplies. The lack of vertical integration in dye companies, as opposed to alkali, then proved a devastating handicap, and it made sense to integrate with ICI in the 1920s and to develop a native synthetic pharmaceuticals industry.

Unlike their British competitors, Hofmann's German pupils, especially Martius, grasped the idea that, once the theory of structure had been laid down by Kekulé, the secret of commercial success lay in continuous chemical research. They also perceived that dyes led to pharmaceuticals. There were a number of factors that favoured the German take-over of the French and British dye industries. In France, because patent law was interpreted in 1864 as covering a product however it was made, the fuchsine patent belonging to Renard Frères of Lyon remained unchallengeable. Consequently, competitors either abandoned manufacture of dyes or set up in Switzerland the businesses that became Geigy, Ciba and Durand-Huguein. Nor did France's geography help. Although France had salt in the east and south-west, coal had to be imported, and it proved difficult to expand into synthetic dyestuffs. Like Britain, therefore, France's early lead in dyestuffs was passed to Germany and Switzerland.

The argument whether chemistry should be based upon theory or practice was a crucial factor in its slow recognition as a respectable university subject on the Continent. The resolution of this debate at the end of the eighteenth century involved a new distinction between pure and applied chemistry – a distinction that stressed chemistry's usefulness and successfully ensured its popularity. And yet, by the 1870s, this most practical of the sciences prospered in Britain almost entirely as an academic discipline. In London, at the beginning of the nineteenth century, a broad social divide separated members of the chemical community, who comprised gentlemen chemical philosophers of independent means, industrial entrepreneurs and the professional chemists whose hitherto uncertain social standing began to be strengthened and institutionalized by changes in medical education.

Meanwhile, in Scotland, the social divide was bridged by professional teachers such as William Cullen, Thomas Thomson and Thomas Graham and their students, who enjoyed good relations with local industries and who cleverly used the British Association for the Advancement of Science, the Chemical Society they fostered in 1841 and the privately financed Royal College of Chemistry established in 1845 to move to the centre of the chemical stage. Receptive to Berzelian and Daltonian atomism, symbolism and continental development in organic chemistry, this group succeeded in uniting the chemical constituency by appealing to the pure–applied dichotomy. Their success was undoubtedly helped by contemporary debates over liberal education in the heavy quarterly reviews: an education in pure chemistry (preferably with research training attached) would fit a student for any practical chemical vocation.

Chemical manufacturers agreed: the practice of chemistry was better learned on the job than in the classroom. In any case, teaching applied chemistry might give away too many commercial secrets. By concentrating on teaching the principles of pure chemistry, not only might existing technologies be improved but new ones might be developed from the abundant unexploited raw materials in the environment. In any case, as we have seen, the real problems of chemical industry in the 1860s were largely to do with engineering, and in the absence of a deeper understanding of chemical processes that physical chemistry was to provide in the twentieth century, an academic training that stressed analytical skills was precisely what industrialists wanted and expected from graduates.

The chemistry course at the Royal College of Chemistry (despite the fact that few students followed it in its entirety) rapidly became the model for scientific courses generally — including the B.Sc. degree course of the University of London. In this way, academic chemistry became divorced from practice and it became generally assumed that 'applied science' was merely the routine application of pure science to industrial situations. This was the viewpoint that prevailed during the period of inquiries into scientific and technical education from the Samuelson Select Committee of 1867–8 to the Devonshire Commission of 1870–5, and which was to justify and create the academic industries of teacher training and examinations.

Behind such rhetoric lay the irony that it was engineers rather than chemists that the chemical industry really required. It is notable that, in the patent infringement cases of the 1860s in Britain, academic chemists supported the various defendants. But after Perkin's, Maule's and Simpson's withdrawal in 1868, a divide opened between academic and industrial chemists that was only healed by the creation of the Institute of Chemistry in 1877 and the Society of Chemical Industry in 1881. The Chemical Society thereby became free to pursue academic chemistry, but at some loss.

Principles of Chemistry

There must be some bond of union between mass and the chemical elements; and as the mass of a substance is ultimately expressed . . . in the atom, a functional dependence should exist and be discoverable between the individual properties of the elements and their atomic weights. But nothing, from mushrooms to a scientific law, can be discovered without looking and trying. So I began to look about and write down the elements with their atomic weights and typical properties, analogous elements and like atomic weights on separate cards, and this soon convinced me that the properties of elements are in periodic dependence upon their atomic weights.

(MENDELEEV, *Principles of Chemistry*, 1905, vol. ii)

Of all the faces in the history of chemistry, that of Dmitri Mendeleev (1834–1907) is the most hypnotic. Notorious even among hirsute Victorians for only having his hair cut and beard trimmed once a year, he stares out from photographs like an image of Du Maurier's Svengali. In the west he is remembered and honoured for two things: for the announcement of the periodic classification of the elements in 1869; and for a huge and fascinating textbook, *Principles of Chemistry*, which first appeared in the same year. The latter went through eight editions during Mendeleev's lifetime and was translated into English in 1891. In Russia, however, Mendeleev is also remembered for his creation of the modern petroleum industry in the Black Sea area.

Mothers usually get short shrift in the history of science,

but Mendeleev's mother, Maria Kornileva, as he recognized, was an extraordinary Siberian woman. After the birth of Mendeleev, the last of her fourteen children, her husband, the headmaster of the Gymnasium in Tobolsk [now Tyumen Oblast], Siberia, where Mendeleev received his education, went blind. Retired, with an inadequate pension for so large a family, Mendeleev's mother became the family's breadwinner. She added to the family's income by taking over and running a glass factory and, at the same time, supervising the education of her employees' children. When the glass factory was destroyed by fire in 1848, at the age of 57 she and Mendeleev hitch-hiked 14 000 miles to Moscow to complete his education. As a Siberian, however, Mendeleev was barred from matriculating at the University of Moscow. Mother and son therefore tramped a further 400 miles to St Petersburg (Leningrad) where, in 1850, he obtained a government grant to train as a secondary school teacher at the Institute of Pedagogy. Of his mother, who died from exhaustion the same year, Mendeleev said later when dedicating a book to her memory:

> She instructed by example, corrected with love, and in order to devote him to science, left Siberia with him, spending her last resources and strength.

At the St Petersburg Institute, Mendeleev was fortunate to be taught by one of Liebig's Russian pupils, Alexander Woskressensky (1809–80), a pioneer of naphthalene chemistry, the discoverer of the alkaloid, theobromine, in cocoa and the first person to prepare quinone. By the 1850s, Woskressensky had become more interested in inorganic chemistry and was particularly fascinated by the metals tungsten, osmium, vanadium and iridium. The fact that these are transition elements with similar properties cannot but have alerted Mendeleev to the many puzzling similarities and differences between the physical and chemical properties of the elements. He also attended lectures in zoology, where his surviving notes show that he took a particular interest in classification; and in geology and mineralogy. The latter subjects stimulated his interest in isomorphism, which formed the subject of his graduation thesis.

For a few years Mendeleev was a school science teacher at Odessa in the Crimea. When he had saved enough money, he returned to St Petersburg in order to obtain a higher degree in chemistry. This was sufficient to gain him a lectureship to teach physics and chemistry at the University of St Petersburg and to begin research on the physical properties of liquids, a subject that always fascinated him. In 1859 the Russian government, mindful of the need to modernize its educational system and to keep up with western developments in science and technology, paid for Mendeleev to undertake two years of further chemical training in Europe. On the advice of his friend Alexander Borodin, the chemist and composer, he studied in Paris and then joined the small Russian colony of students in Heidelberg. The proximity to Karlsruhe meant that he was able to attend the famous chemical congress arranged by Weltzien in 1860. Mendeleev had already used Gerhardt's textbook, *Traité de chimie organique*, in his teaching in Russia and so was already an exponent of 'two-volume' unitary formulae, and an opponent of electrochemical explanations.

Although already converted, the conference does appear to have stimulated his thoughts on classification and how 'real' atomic weights – not conventional ones – could afford a basis for generalization. Gerhardt had written a decent textbook of organic chemistry because he had been able to classify carbon compounds around the concept of 'types' or typical forms. Inorganic chemistry, by contrast, lacked such a cohesive and pedagogically useful device. Russian teachers, Mendeleev believed, badly needed a comprehensive, well arranged, textbook of general chemistry that would present the chemical and physical properties of the elements in a lucid way. How could some seventy diverse elements, their compounds and salts be brought to order and 'typed' in the way that organic chemists had successfully done?

SORTING THE ELEMENTS

This was one of the main problems that Mendeleev thought about on his return to St Petersburg in 1861 as Professor of Technical Chemistry at a Technological Institute and (from 1866) Professor of General (Inorganic) Chemistry at the University, where his organic colleague was Butlerov. As we have seen in earlier chapters, classification had been a perennial problem in organic chemistry. There had also been earlier discussions, inspired by Linnaeus' eighteenth-century success in ordering plants, animals and minerals, as to how elements could be classified. Ampère, for example, had proposed a natural system of classification in 1816 that deduced order and analogies from 'the *ensemble* of the bodies which we propose to classify'. This was to be essentially Mendeleev's approach; but the problem was what feature or features of the 'ensemble' to choose? Ampère himself criticized Aristotelian bifurcations such as metal/non-metal, combustibles/supporters of combustion as far too simplistic because they led chemists to neglect or overlook important analogies. His own solution was, however, curiously unpromising. He proposed to divide elements into gazolytes (like oxygen and nitrogen), which formed permanent gases with one another; leucolytes, or fusible metals, which formed colourless solutions; and chroicolites, which only fused at high temperatures and which formed coloured solutions. Mercifully, this chemically unperceptive scheme never caught on.

Because of the widespread disagreement over atomic weights and their confusion with equivalent and combining weights, the quantitative criterion of relative atomic weights as a determinant of properties was by no means an obvious one before the 1860s. Even so, Goethe's friend, Johann

Döbereiner (1780–1849), a Professor at Jena, spotted the existence of triads among the oxides of Davy's recently discovered alkaline earths as early as 1817. On Wollaston's oxygen scale of 10,

$$\text{strontia [SrO]} = \frac{1}{2} \{\text{lime [CaO]} + \text{barytes [BaO]}\}$$
$$= \frac{1}{2} (59 + 155)$$
$$= 107$$

A decade later, a year after the discovery of bromine by A. J. Balard (of whom Liebig wickedly said that 'bromine discovered Balard'), Döbereiner noticed the elementary halogen triad:

$$Br = \frac{1}{2}(Cl + I) = \frac{1}{2}(35.470 + 126.470) = 80.970$$

which was close to Berzelius' value of 78.383 for the atomic weight of the marine element.

Many other similar triads were reported by Leopold Gmelin in the several editions of the great *Handbuch der Chemie*, beginning in the fourth edition in 1843. Gmelin noted in particular that elements formed sporadic arithmetic series if the lowest common denominator was taken. For example,

$$Al : Gl : Yt : Ce = 1 : 2 : 3\frac{1}{2} : 5$$

(where Gl = glucinium, later beryllium; and Yt = yttrium, later symbol Y). He was convinced that such relations were a reflection of the 'inner nature of substances'. Inspired by this, Liebig's friend, the apothecary and sanitarian, Max von Pettenkofer, reported in 1850 that there were often constant differences of weight between chemically similar elements, or what he called 'a natural group of elements'. To Pettenkofer, as to so many other numerologically minded chemists, these mathematical relationships were hints that Prout had always been right to suspect that the so-called elements were really compound bodies.

It was about this time that, inspired by Prout's hypothesis,

Dumas arranged the elements into three series according to whether their atomic weights were integers or multiples of halves or quarters, and uncovered complicated arithmetical series such as:

a	$a + d$	$a + 2d + d'$	$a + 2d + 2d' + d''$
F	Cl	Br	I
19	19 + 16.5	19 + 33 + 28	19 + 33 + 56 + 19
[19]	[35.5]	[80]	[127]

As we now know, such mathematical series do not exist. Aware that this neo-Pythagoreanism could be made to work whether or not the elements had similar properties, William Odling in 1857 insisted that such musings were only valid if the elements appeared to be naturally related. On the basis of comparisons between an ensemble of properties such as atomic heats, atomic volumes, isomorphism and basicity of acids, Odling obtained thirteen natural groups (table 9.1).

TABLE 9.1 *Odling's groups.*

Group	Elements within group
1	F, Cl, Br, I
2	O, S, Se, Te
3	N, P, As, Sb, Bi
4	B, Si, Ti, Sn
5	Li, Na, K
6	Ca, Sr, Ba
7	Mg, Zn, Cd
8	Gl*, Yt*, Th
9	Al, Zr, Ce, U
10	Cr, Mn, Co, Fe, Ni, Cu
11	Mo, V, W, Ta
12	Hg, Pb, Ag
13	Pd, Pt, Au

*See text.

These groups were achieved without direct use of atomic weights – though, of course, they were built into his values of the atomic heats and volumes.

This urge to find a natural system of elements was also the inspiration for the French geologist and mineralogist, Alexandre de Chancourtois (1820–86). In 1862, with the intention of bringing order to mineralogy, and support for Prout's hypothesis, he devised a three-dimensional array of the elements that he called a *vis tellurique* from the fact that tellurium occupied the midpoint position in the helical graph. In this graph, which was unforgivably left out of the original paper published in *Comptes Rendus*, similar elements fell into vertical groups, with corresponding points differing by 16, the new atomic weight for oxygen. From the hindsight of Mendeleev's periodic table, Chancourtois' three-dimensional curve makes sense, but with its inclusion of compounds and alloys, and without the drawing (which he published later) it was, not surprisingly, ignored by chemists.

John Newlands (1837–98), a London sugar refiner who had studied with Hofmann at the Royal College of Chemistry and fought with Garibaldi in Italy, was not ignored. Newlands' original concern had been with the classification of organic compounds, and this undoubtedly triggered an interest in arranging the elements themselves. Between 1863 and 1864, at first using equivalent weights, and then two-volume atomic weights, he published a series of brief papers in *Chemical News* drawing attention to the fact that, when ordered by increasing weight, every eighth element was related, or analogous, to the first element in the group; elements were multiples of eight, like the eighth note of a musical octave. Describing this as a 'law of octaves', he also designated the serial order of atomic weights starting with hydrogen (H = 1). Like Mendeleev later, he had the courage of his chemical convictions to invert the order of a few elements where chemical analogies seemed to demand it; but his predictions concerning gaps in his table were unsuccessful – unlike Mendeleev's – being based upon false premises and false analogies.

In March 1866 Newlands described a more complete scheme to a meeting of the Chemical Society, which by then, in contrast to Crookes' policy for *Chemical News*, had a rule of not publishing papers of a speculative nature – especially ones that evoked extravagant analogies with the musical scale. George Carey Foster, a chemist turned physicist, made the half-sarcastic, half-humorous jibe that Newlands might just as well have arranged the elements alphabetically, making the serious point that such a table (or tables, because Newlands kept altering his arrangements) can easily result from coincidence. As we have seen, Newlands' table was but one of many projected during the 1860s. His contemporaries cannot be blamed for failing to see that his scheme, based firmly upon atomic weights as the operative criterion, was better than others. In 1884, following Newlands' chagrin at seeing Mendeleev awarded the Davy Medal of the Royal Society, he republished all of his papers in book form. Hindsight then showed that Newlands had, indeed, possessed a fundamental insight, and that like Mendeleev he had been struggling to evolve and perfect it. In reparation the Royal Society (of which he was never a Fellow) awarded him the Davy Medal in 1887.

Little or none of the work of these precursors was known to Mendeleev until the 1870s. His derivation of the periodic law was undoubtedly independent and original. It occurred as follows. In 1861, after only seven months' hectic writing, he published a massive textbook on organic chemistry. He was forcibly struck while writing this (as Kopp and Newlands had been) that there was a relationship between the molecular weights and the physical properties of members of a homologous series. Might there be an analogous relationship between atomic weights and the properties of elements?

In 1867 Mendeleev began to write *Osovy Khimi*, or *Principles of Chemistry*, as a text that could be used by students attending his university lectures. Gerhardt had based organic chemistry around three typical molecules, H_2, H_2O and NH_3, to which Kekulé and Hofmann had added CH_4. In the hands of Williamson, Odling, Frankland and Hofmann, these molecules had become seen to exhibit a scale of quantivalence from one to four, as in H^IH, $O^{II}H_2$, $N^{III}H_3$ and $C^{IV}H_4$. The elements hydrogen, oxygen, nitrogen and carbon might, therefore, be called 'typical' elements. Their valencies suggested a natural order of presentation in a textbook. Because Gerhardt had also included HCl as a typical molecule, and because this acid and the halide acids generally readily formed salts with the alkali metals, Mendeleev decided that the first volume of the *Principles* would treat H, O, N and C, together with the four known halogens and alkali metals. These were, he noticed, all elements with low atomic weights and were widely distributed in Nature. Many twentieth-century chemical students have been puzzled as to why these elements were labelled 'typical elements' in Mendeleev's periodic tables, not knowing that it referred to the concept of organic 'types' and was not an assertion that they were representative of all the elements. In the event, the alkali metals had to be held over to a second volume. As to the ordering of the halogens and the alkali metals, it took only a moment's thought to decide upon a quantitative variable such as density or mass or, in other words, their atomic weights. Thus, by 1868 Mendeleev had ordered a dozen elements by valency and atomic weight.

What elements should be treated in the *Principles* after the alkali metals? Three criteria suggested themselves. First, since Mendeleev rejected Prout's hypothesis, he would not base a classification upon triads of 'primary matter'. Secondly, because he intended to take pains to contrast the properties of the halogens and the alkali metals, which commonly formed salts of the type Na^ICl, his attention was drawn to the fact that metals like copper and silver displayed divalency with halogens, as well as univalency

TABLE 9.2 *A partial sequence following the* Principles.

		Ca = 40	Sr = 87.6	Ba = 137
Li = 7	Na = 23	K = 39	Rb = 85.4	Cs = 133
	F = 19	Cl = 35.5	Br = 80	Te = 127
	O = 16	S = 32	Se = 79	
	N = 14	P = 31	As = 75	
	C = 12	Si = 28		
	B = 11	Al = 27		U? = 116
	Be = 9	Mg= 24	Zn = 65	Cd = 112
H = 1			Cu = 63	Ag = 108

(e.g. Cu^ICl, $Cu^{II}Cl_2$ and Ag^ICl, $Ag^{II}_2Cl_2$). Such metals seemed to form a 'transition' group following the alkali metals. Thirdly, since valencies greater than the tetravalency of carbon were found among the elements, this would be a way of highlighting other 'typical' elements, e.g. V^VO_5, Cr^VIO_3, $Mn^{VII}O_7$ and $Fe^{VIII}O_4$. If atomic weights were then used as an ordering principle, a (partial) sequence like that in table 9.2 was obtained. The vertical columns (later termed periods) showed a rough-and-ready progression in the differences between atomic weights. By writing out the names and properties of elements on cards, and playing Patience or 'chemical solitaire' with them on long railway journeys, Mendeleev gradually filled in the gaps, while all the time guided by atomic weights, the display of valency and that important guide to similarities, isomorphism. By 17 February 1869 he had arrived at the law that 'elements placed according to the value of their atomic weights present a clear periodicity of properties'. Mendeleev stressed, however, that he referred to post-Karlsruhe atomic weights; on the C = 8 scale, the alkaline earths bore no relationship whatever.

In practice, there were serious problems with the scheme. The resemblances between transition elements, which Mendeleev was forced to lump together in an eighth group, together with the perplexing enigma of the rare-earth elements remained thorns in the flesh of classifiers for many more years. Nor was atomic weight always a clear-cut criterion of periodicity. For example, if the atomic weight 14 was adopted for beryllium, it fell into a group with nitrogen and phosphorus with which it bore little relation. If, however, one supposed its oxide to be BeO (on the analogy of MgO, which it resembled closely) and not Be_2O_3, then a revised weight of 9.4 brought it into the magnesium family. Mendeleev took the bull by the horns and bravely made such changes on the basis of his chemical knowledge and intuition. More sensationally, he not merely drew attention to possible gaps, or missing unknown elements, but dared to forecast the likely properties of an 'eka-aluminium', 'eka-silicon' and 'eka-zirconium'. ('Eka' is Sanskrit for numeral one. Chemists were not to borrow from the Sanskrit again until Woodward and Hoffmann, running out of Greek and Latin spatial terms, coined the word *antarafacial* in 1970).

The discovery had come too late for the printing of the first volume of *Principles*, but was included in the second volume published in 1871. In March 1869 Mendeleev announced the classification system at a meeting of the Russian Chemical Society, which he had helped to found in St Petersburg in 1868. Not until 1871 did he actually refer to the law as 'periodic', all his earlier references being to a 'natural system of the elements'. It has been said that 'periodic system' is a regrettable term in English; grammatically we should refer to a 'system of periods' or 'period system'. But the phrase has been immortalized in the textbooks. Mendeleev's first paper – he was to write dozens more on the subject – was abstracted in German in the *Zeitschrift für Chemie* in 1869, but it attracted little attention until Lothar Meyer (1830–95), who had arrived at the same relationship independently in the same year, published his own account in 1870.

Meyer had originally trained to be a doctor, but was persuaded by Bunsen to take up chemistry as a career.

Because of his background, Meyer's teaching career in various institutions was usually directed at medical students until, in 1876, he became Professor of Chemistry at Tübingen. Like Mendeleev, because of this teaching commitment, Meyer had felt the need to write a fresh and clear textbook. His *Die Modernen Theorien der Chemie*, which first appeared in 1864, achieved this aim, being the first German text to use the revised atomic weights consistently. Like Mendeleev, Meyer had been present at the Karlsruhe meeting and had become convinced by Cannizzaro's arguments. In the first edition of his textbook, Meyer had achieved some kind of order among the elements by arranging them according to their displays of valency. He did not use atomic weights as a criterion at all.

By 1868, while revising the text for a second edition, Meyer had come across the notions of Gmelin, Pettenkofer and Dumas. Armed with the new atomic weights he was able to devise a sixteen-columned table that brought analogous elements into periodic groups. Unfortunately, a change of job led to delay in publication of the new edition until 1872, by which time Mendeleev's principle was familiar. Ironically, Meyer's publication of a short sketch of the idea he was to include in the textbook, which he published in the *Annalen* in 1870, not only acknowledged Mendeleev's precedence but brought it more prominently into notice. By plotting the atomic volumes of solid elements against atomic weights in 1870, Meyer vividly conveyed the essence of Mendeleev's periodic law.

Besides revising the atomic weight and periodic table position of beryllium, Mendeleev was also forced to deviate from the strict order of atomic weights in several places in order to preserve chemical analogies. The two cases (a third was found when the rare gases were isolated) were cobalt (58.95) and nickel (58.69), and iodine (126.8) and tellurium (127.6). In the latter case, iodine was very obviously a member of the halogen family; so much so, that Mendeleev suspected that the atomic weight of tellurium had been incorrectly reported and that it ought to be about 125. When Mendeleev's Czech supporter, Bohuslav Brauner (1855–1935), after the most careful redeterminations in 1883, found that Te = 127.6, he concluded still that, despite precautions, he must have worked with impure tellurium. Such was the power of theory over experimental observation that Brauner spent many fruitless years searching for an unknown element in tellurium ores.

TABLE 9.3 *Mendeleev's predictions.*

	Predicted	Found experimentally
	Eka-aluminum (1871)	Gallium (1875)
At.wt	68	69.9
Sp.gr.	6.0	5.96
At.vol.	11.5	11.7
	Eka-boron (1871)	Scandium (1879)
At.wt	44	43.79
Oxide	Eb_2O_3; sp.gr. 3.5	Sc_2O_3; sp.gr. 3.86
Sulphate	$Eb_2(SO_4)_3$	$Sc_2(SO_4)_3$
	Eka-silicon (1871)	Germanium (1886)
At.wt	72	72.3
Sp.gr.	5.5	5.47
Oxide	EsO_2	GeO_2
Chloride	$EsCl_4$; b.p. <100°C density 1.9	GCl_4; b.p. 86°C density 1.89

Cobalt and nickel, with their tiny 'difference' in atomic weights, proved less of an experimental puzzle. Inorganic chemists, like Werner, who worked with the complex salts of cobalt and nickel, naturally assumed that, because cobalt salts were isomorphous with those of rhenium and iridium, cobalt had to come before nickel in the periodic table.

Mendeleev had little to say about such inversions, or what Henry Roscoe charmingly called 'the restorations of waifs to the family from which they had been separated by an unkind fate'. He was far more concerned with the filling in of gaps and the prediction of the properties of unknown elements from *a priori* reasoning by analogy (see Table 9.3). Prediction can be a hazardous business, as the development of science fiction attests. Mendeleev's astonishingly accurate forecast of the properties of gallium (eka-aluminium), discovered by Emil le Coq de Boisbaudron (1838–1912) in 1875; of scandium (eka-boron), discovered by Lars Nilson (1840–99) in 1879; and of germanium (eka-silicon), discovered by Clemens Winkler (1838–1904) in 1886, even more than Mendeleev's original announcement of the periodic law, set the chemical world ablaze with excitement. Incidentally, it is a reflection of the growth of European nationalism in the 1880s that these elements should have been named by their discoverers in honour of their countries.

Perhaps the most extraordinary aspect of these predictions was Lecoq's reaction. A French chemist who was using spectroscopy to investigate the complex sequence of rare earths, Lecoq was initially unaware of the periodic law when he identified the spectrum of gallium and separated the element in sufficient quantities to determine its atomic weight (69.9) and to give its density as 4.7. When Mendeleev claimed that gallium was the predicted eka-aluminium (68), Lecoq, assuming that Mendeleev was claiming priority and being dishonourable to France, argued that his element was significantly different. However, a second determination of its specific gravity confirmed that Mendeleev's forecast of 5.94 had been accurate to within one per cent. As Kedrov has commented, 'the scientific world was astounded to note that Mendeleev, the theorist, had seen the properties of a new element more clearly than the chemist who had discovered it'.

Not all of Mendeleev's predictions had such a happy

outcome; like astrologers' failures, they are commonly forgotten. The very great difficulty of sorting out the rare earths inevitably led Mendeleev into a minefield. A predicted homologue of cerium of atomic weight 54, between calcium and hafnium, never materialized; nor did eka-niobium (146) and eka-caesium (175); while

TABLE 9.4 *Mendeleev's later predictions.*

Mendeleev's name	Predicted at.wt	Density	Name	Atomic wt	Density
Eka-manganese (1871)	100	+ 11	Technetium (1939)	99 (isotope)	—
Eka-niobium (1871)	146				
Eka-caesium (1871)	175				
Tri-manganese (1871)	190	—	Rhenium (1925)	186	20.5
Dvi-tellurium (1889)	212	+ 9.3	Polonium (1898)	210	9.4
Dvi-caesium (1871)	220		Francium (1939)	223	
Eka-tantalum (1871)	235		Protactinium	231	15.4
Coronium (1902) (newtonium)	0.4		Ionized iron		
Ether (1902)	0.17				

his predictions of eka-manganese (technetium, 1939), tri-manganese (rhenium, 1923), dvi-tellurium (polonium, 1898), dvi-caesium (francium, 1939) and eka-tantalum (protactinium, 1918) were fortuitous guesses rather than predictions based upon a firm and accurate placing of their homologues in the table.

The discovery by Lockyer of helium in the solar spectrum in 1868 inevitably led other astronomers and chemists to assume that mysterious lines in the solar and stellar spectra might be due to other non-terrestrial elements. There was much talk of coronium (which proved eventually to be the spectrum of highly ionized iron). Mendeleev and others were inclined to speculate that there might be lighter elements between hydrogen and lithium, or elements still lighter than hydrogen. In 1902, having previously rejected the existence of the electron and of radioactivity as incompatible with a periodic law based upon the fixity of elements and the indestructibility of atoms, Mendeleev published *An Attempt at a Chemical Conception of the Universal Ether*. Convinced as he was all his life that mass was the fundamental concept in science, Mendeleev had an unbounded admiration for Newton. Just at the moment that Einstein was poised to overturn Newtonian physics and to argue that a universal ether was an unnecessary physical assumption, Mendeleev argued that both ether and coronium (which he renamed newtonium) were extremely light rare gases whose atomic weights could be extrapolated (rather obscurely) from the atomic weights of Ramsay's inert gases. This gave newtonium an atomic weight of 0.4 and ether one of 0.17. And because there were only four halogens, but five alkali metals (astatine was not known until 1940), he surmised that there ought to be a lighter analogue of fluorine of mass 3 (see Table 9.4).

Historians have usually seen the non-empirical Pythagoreanism of Mendeleev's last years as a sign of senility; but these speculations were only more extreme examples of his lifelong use of analogy prompted by the increasing mysteriousness of spectroscopy and the phenomenon of radioactivity. By explaining radioactivity in terms of a universal ether, Mendeleev hoped to preserve chemistry from the horrors of transmutation and chemical evolution, both of which undermined the sanctity of Newtonian mass as the arbiter of physical and chemical properties.

THE RARE EARTHS

The rare-earth elements had begun to be uncovered in 1794 when John Gadolin (1760–1852) showed that a black mineral mined at the village of Ytterby, near Stockholm, contained an unknown earth (oxide). This was duly labelled yttria by A. G. Ekeberg (the discoverer of tantalum) in 1797. Six years later, Klaproth identified another earth that he called ceria. Yttria and ceria were to be the starting points for over a century of difficult and puzzling analytical chemistry. Berzelius, who subjected both earths to intense investigation, was convinced that they were mixtures of several rare earths, or rare elements. By the 1840s he had persuaded Carl Mosander (1797–1858), his successor at the Carolinian Medico-Chirurgical Institute in Stockholm, to try to separate distinct substances.

Mosander succeeded brilliantly in identifying lanthanum, cerium, 'didymium', terbium, yttrium and erbium as forming part of the ceria earth. Because of their close similarities in properties, physical separation of these elements was fiendishly difficult; consequently the chemical literature was filled with reports, claims and counter-claims concerning supposed new elements. Most of these proved spurious. For example, Mosander's didymium was separated by Auer von Welsbach (1858–1929) in 1885 into praseodymium and neodymium. Auer, a pupil of Bunsen, showed that the rare-earth elements could be financially rewarding. In Bunsen's laboratory he had noted the brilliant light that many rare-earth oxides displayed in the bunsen burner's flame. Given that gas lighting was the predominant form of domestic illumination in the 1880s, he wondered whether the earths could be used to increase the illuminating power of town gas. The result was a 'lace' gas mantle consisting of thorium oxide mixed with small quantities of cerium oxide. Such gas mantles were the salvation of the coal-gas industry faced by competition from electricity. They remained in use well into the 1940s. It was

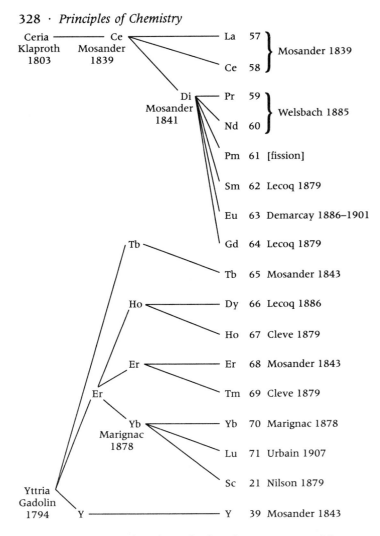

FIGURE 9.1 Lanthanides and other elements extracted from rare-earth sources.

for such services – he also replaced tungsten filaments in light bulbs by osmium in 1898 – that Auer was ennobled in 1901, becoming Carl von Welsbach. A year later, at the same time as Urbain, he independently revealed the heaviest natural rare-earth element, lutetium.

Many chemists came to specialize in rare-earth chemistry because of its challenges. In Switzerland, when not involved in atomic weight determinations, Jean de Marignac (1817–94) reinvestigated yttria and identified ytterbium in 1878 and gadolinium in 1880. In Sweden, Per Cleve separated holmium and thulium in 1879, while Nilson identified scandium (not a rare earth) in the same ores in 1879. And in France, using spectroscopy to great advantage, Lecoq identified samarium (1879) and dysprosium (1886).

All these discoveries were embarrassing and bewildering to Mendeleev. Because of the very close proximity of their atomic weights, the very great difficulty of accurately determining them, and the almost identical properties of these elements, the rare-earth elements seemed to break the periodic law. Indeed, just as it has been said of Kepler that he was lucky not to have had too accurate measurements of planetary positions, otherwise he would never have deduced the elliptical law of planetary motions, so Mendeleev was fortunate in 1869 that only six rare earths (including 'didymium') had been identified. It was only because most of the family was missing that Mendeleev could see a simple pattern.

By assuming that the six elements were trivalent, rather than bivalent, Mendeleev calculated atomic weights that enabled him to squeeze the six elements into groups III, IV and V of his original table. Meyer left the rare earths out altogether, which was a strategy many chemists were inclined to adopt after 1886, by which time a further six rare earths had been distinguished. Undaunted, Mendeleev continued to classify all of them as homologues of known elements, despite that fact that this created gaps for yet more unknown elements (see Table 9.5).

Brauner in 1902, perhaps with a view to incorporating yet more unknown elements, suggested that the rare earths should be placed collectively in one space of the periodic

TABLE 9.5 *Mendeleev's arrangement, 1881.*

				Group III			
Nb	94	Zr	90	Y	89
Di	146	Ce	142	La	138
Ta	182		?	Yb	173
	?	Th	231		?

table in group IV between lanthanum and tantalum. But Mendeleev, in his last pronouncement on the subject in the same year, reiterated the need to base their classification on homologies, even though this then produced seventeen gaps[1]:

> A whole large period is wanting between Ce = 140 and Ta = 183, but the series of rare earth elements (they have not been fully investigated) – e.g. Pr = 140.5 ... Yb = 173 &c – have, as far as is now known, atomic weights which exactly fill this interval, and therefore this portion of the periodic system is, in a way, broken and requires fresh researches.

Mendeleev thereby made it clear that he believed future research would reveal sufficient numbers of different properties among these elements to confirm that they really did obey the periodic law. For that reason they had to be incorporated in the table rather than boxed into one group (as Brauner proposed) or classified separately from the main table, as became the rule after 1913.

Until Moseley's key work in 1913, when it was finally confirmed that there were exactly fourteen rare-earth elements and that all other claims were spurious, the position of these elements remained confusing. But with the introduction of atomic numbers and Bohr's model of electronic shells, it became clear, as R. J. Meyer noted, that the rare-earth group formed 'a miniature periodic system in which the relationships of the main system are reflected.'

THE INERT GASES

In his investigation into the nature of phlogisticated air (nitrogen) in 1783, Henry Cavendish had used frictional electricity to spark together mixtures of this air with Priestley's dephlogisticated air (oxygen). He then found that 'when five parts of pure dephlogisticated air were mixed with three parts of common air, almost the whole of the air was made to disappear'. Nitrous acid (oxides of nitrogen) was formed. After some weeks of refining these experiments, Cavendish concluded that:

> ... if there is any part of the dephlogisticated air of our atmosphere which differs from the rest and cannot be reduced to nitrous acid, we may safely conclude that it is not more than 1/120 part of the whole.

This 'bubble' of unreactive air was not examined further by Cavendish. Although his accuracy and experimental dexterity astonished later admirers of his work like Clerk Maxwell, Cavendish no doubt put the bubble down to inevitable experimental error; this would certainly have been the impression of his contemporaries. Nineteenth-century experimentalists were far more concerned to show that the ratio of nitrogen to oxygen in the atmosphere was virtually constant throughout the world, whatever the weather conditions, than to bother with Cavendish's unsparkable nitrogen.

The observation might have been forgotten altogether but for a mid-century nationalistic controversy over whether the British or the French had discovered the compound nature of water. Convinced that Cavendish deserved the credit over Lavoisier, or other contenders, George Wilson, a Professor of Chemical Technology at the University of Edinburgh, undertook Cavendish's biography, and in reviewing Cavendish's work he quoted the above passage concerning the bubble of unreactive nitrogen. As a student, William Ramsay (1852–1916) bought a second-hand copy of Wilson's book and he was to recall the passage in the 1890s.

Convinced that the close proximity of atomic weights to whole numbers could not be entirely random, as Prout had argued, and that chemists had not paid sufficient attention to careful physical measurements such as densities, Lord Rayleigh, Professor of Cambridge University's Cavendish Laboratory and one of Britain's last aristocratic scientists, decided in 1888 to redetermine the densities of oxygen and nitrogen. From these, their atomic weights could be found by simple calculation.

Rayleigh's value for the density of atmospheric nitrogen, determined to an accuracy of one part in ten thousand, was in general agreement with previous determinations. The problem came when Rayleigh, like any good analyst, examined other samples of nitrogen, namely those obtained from chemical reactions such as the reduction of ammonia over red-hot copper. 'Chemical' nitrogen turned out to be one-thousandth part lighter than atmospheric nitrogen. Following a meticulous re-examination of the conditions of his experiments to rule out possible contamination, Rayleigh published a letter in *Nature* in September 1892 in which he asked for suggestions for ways of solving the puzzle.

A month later there was a reply from William Ramsay, Professor of Chemistry at University College, London, confessing himself equally 'stumped' by the discrepancy. Rayleigh, who received various suggestions, none of which he felt penetrated to 'the root of the matter', then wrote up his results for the Royal Society, warning that:

> Until the questions arising out of these observations are thoroughly cleared up, the above number [density] for nitrogen must be received with a certain reserve.

From perusal of Rayleigh's notebooks and correspondence with William Crookes, it is clear that he already suspected that there could be an inert contaminant in his nitrogen samples from the atmosphere rather than an impurity in his chemically prepared nitrogen. The same thought had occurred to Ramsay, who, with Rayleigh's permission, in April 1893 began to heat magnesium in air to form the nitride with the intention of seeing if anything was left over after oxygen, water vapour and carbon dioxide had also been removed. He also mentioned to Rayleigh Wilson's account of Cavendish's experiment, which both men repeated with admiration for their predecessor's accuracy. While Professor of Chemistry at University College, Bristol, between 1880 and 1887, Ramsay had worked on the dissociation of gases and the determination of vapour densities. This had led him to develop new methods for manipulating gases that proved extremely useful at University College, London.

By the summer of 1894 both Rayleigh and Ramsay had become convinced that they had identified an unknown, inert constituent of the atmosphere and agreed, courteously, upon a partnership: Rayleigh would investigate its physical properties, while Ramsay would identify its chemical behaviour. When the preliminary announcement was made at the British Association meeting in Oxford in August 1894, they were faced by some hostile criticism. A new gas was unlikely; it was far more probable that the new gas was a product of their preparative techniques. For example, since oxygen when sparked produced ozone, O_3, was it not entirely possible that nitrogen did something similar and produced an 'ozone-nitrogen', N_3? James Dewar at the Royal Institution, where he was investigating the liquefaction of hydrogen, had often noticed a white solid in liquid air, and thought that this was probably an allotrope of nitrogen similar to the one Rayleigh and Ramsay were detecting. Other critics pointed out that, if the unknown gas had chemical properties, it was highly unlikely to have escaped previous detection in minerals.

All these were points that Ramsay and Rayleigh had considered, tested and rejected. Spectroscopic evidence, which they used extensively as a tool of identification, showed 'certain groups of red and green lines which do not appear to belong to the spectrum of any known gas'. Despite extensive experiments, Ramsay failed in all of his attempts to make the gas combine with other materials, including hydrogen, sodium, fused red-hot caustic soda and platinum black. It was the consistency of these results that led them to call the gas argon, from the Greek word for 'idle':

> The gas deserves the name 'argon', for it is a most astonishingly indifferent body in as much as it is unattacked by elements of very opposite character varying from sodium and magnesium on the one hand, oxygen, chlorine and sulphur on the other. It will be interesting to see if fluorine also is without action, but for the present that experiment must be postponed on account of difficulties of manipulation.

In May 1894 Ramsay wrote to Rayleigh:

> Has it occurred to you that there is room for gaseous elements at the end of the first column of the periodic table? Thus Li Be B C N O F X, X, X, etc. Such elements should have the density 20 or thereabouts, and 0.8 pc (1/120th about) of the nitrogen of the air could so raise the density of nitrogen that it would stand to pure [chemical] nitrogen in the ratio 230 : 231.

Ramsay was obviously excited by the prospect of there being more than one unknown gas, and, like Mendeleev, he was able to use the periodic law to predict density.

It is intriguing to note that publication of their results was deliberately delayed because Ramsay had entered their account for the Smithsonian Institution's Hodgkin's Prize for the most important discovery to do with atmospheric air. Needless to say, they won this prize, at which point, in the summer of 1895, papers were published in the *Philosophical Transactions* of the Royal Society. Despite this commercial delay, the conditions for the prize had not prevented oral presentation of the work earlier to the Royal Society on 31 January 1895. Only Dewar was notably absent.

By then Rayleigh and Ramsay were able to adduce physical evidence for the existence of argon and for the determination of its atomic weight, which could not, of course, be determined chemically. During the late 1820s, Thomas Graham (1805–69) had shown that the rate of diffusion of a gas through a porous earthenware vessel was inversely proportional to the square root of its density. This gave Rayleigh not only a way of separating nitrogen and argon, but an independent measure of the latter's density. It was in fact 19.7 (H_2 = 1), close to Ramsay's prediction. William Crookes and Arthur Schuster were invited to help with spectroscopic determinations, and argued that the absence of the characteristic yellow line of nitrogen from the argon samples confirmed that a new gas was being identified. Finally, and most significantly, the specific heats of argon at constant pressure and volume were determined since, by the kinetic theory of gases established mathematically by Rudolf Clausius in 1857, their ratio would reveal its state of atomicity. The surprising result was that, unlike other atmospheric gases, which are diatomic, argon proved monatomic. Because argon was twenty times heavier than hydrogen (H_2), it followed that the atomic weight of argon was 40.

Such a value was extremely awkward. Not only had Mendeleev failed to predict argon's existence, but the atomic weights of potassium and calcium were 39.1 and 40 respectively. Should argon come before or after calcium? Henry Armstrong, who had done much to establish the credentials of the periodic law in his excellent 1876 *Encyclopaedia Britannica* article on chemistry, urged that this was a good enough reason to reject the 'wildly speculative' idea of argon's monatomicity. By making argon Ar_2 the general diatomicity of gases would be preserved and argon's atomic weight of 20 would allow its incorporation into the periodic table without compromise. But the physicists held their ground; the dynamic reasoning was absolutely sound and, if anything had to bend, it must be the empirically based, non-mathematical law of periodicity.

This thought weighed heavily on Mendeleev's devoted Czech disciple, Brauner, in Prague. He reiterated the idea in *Chemical News* that argon simply had to be an allotropic modification of nitrogen whose atoms were so closely packed together that a 'monatomic' reading was given for the ratio of specific heats. Mendeleev agreed, adding that it was 'condensed nitrogen'. Only in 1900, following the discovery of neon, krypton and xenon, did Mendeleev and the several chemists who distrusted the use of physical evidence in chemistry accept the existence of a zero-valency group of elements.

Fed up with such constant criticism from chemists, Rayleigh returned to his beloved physics where, he stated sharply, 'the second rate men seem to know their place'! Clarification dawned later in 1895 when Ramsay isolated helium from a mineral called cleveite, which its discoverer had reported as emanating nitrogen. Spectroscopic examination of the gas evolved from the mineral showed it to be the element that the astronomer Norman Lockyer had identified in the sun in 1868. Helium had now been found on the earth. Density measurements showed that it had an atomic weight of 4 and that, like argon, it was also monatomic. There were two odd zero-valent elements to place in the periodic table and the suspicion voiced by Ramsay to Rayleigh a year earlier, that there might be a whole missing group of gases, now seemed worth pursuing.

The search was now entirely in Ramsay's hands. Since large quantities of air were required to separate minute amounts of these 'rare' gases, the easiest method was to use the new technology of liquid air that Dewar had perfected at the Royal Institution. Unfortunately, Dewar and Ramsay detested and mistrusted one another. In the absence of the possibility of collaboration, Ramsay exploited the liquefaction process that had been developed independently by William Hampson (who actually claimed that Dewar had stolen the idea from him). Hampson's process was developed by the Brin Company, which later became the giant firm of British Oxygen.

By 1898, after a long series of arduous and difficult separations, Ramsay and his experimentally gifted assistant, Morris Travers (1872–1961), succeeded in identifying three more rare gases. These were named neon, krypton and xenon. All of them were chemically inert. The periodic group was finally completed by Ramsay in 1903 when Rutherford's co-worker, Frederick Soddy, identified a gaseous emanation from radium, radon. A year later Ramsay became the first British chemist to be awarded the Nobel prize. From fixed air to radon, the atmospheric gases had been isolated and identified by British chemists. As Travers said of his final work with Ramsay, *finis coronat opus*.

Fluorine, the most reactive element known, had resisted all of Davy's, Gay-Lussac's and Faraday's attempts to isolate it during the first decades of the nineteenth century. Its extreme toxicity had even led to the deaths of at least two chemists. Undaunted, in 1886, Henri Moissan (1852–1907) had ingeniously isolated it electrolytically. When Ramsay sent him a small sample of argon in 1894, however, attempts to spark the two gases into combination proved unsuccessful. Despite this rather impressive demonstration of inertness in the face of what the alchemists would have taken as the alcahest, France's elder statesman of chemistry, Marcellin Berthelot, claimed to have formed an argon compound by sparking it with benzene vapour. Ramsay always expressed scepticism and suspected that argon had merely dissolved in the benzene or been trapped in the resinous mass left in the reaction vessel. The matter intrigued H. G. Wells, who, in the *War of the Worlds* (1898), had the Martians attack London with a toxic brown argon

TABLE 9.6   *Atomic structure of noble gases according to Bohr.*

Quantum group	1	2	3	4	5	6
He 2	2					
Ne 10	2	8				
Ar 18	2	8	8			
Kr 36	2	8	18	8		
Em* 86	2	8	18	32	18	8

*Em = emanation, the old name for radon, Rn.

compound, only to be defeated themselves by the common cold. The so-called 'clathrate' compounds, in which a gas is trapped inside a crystal, produced several examples with the rare gases; but chemical combination is not involved. In 1912, Rayleigh's son and biographer, Robert Strutt, Professor of Physics at Imperial College, London, repeated Berthelot's experiments and showed categorically that combination had not occurred.

The theoretical developments over the next decade, which led to a deeper understanding of the electronic configurations of the elements (see table 9.6) showed that the 'inert' gases had completed shells of electrons and therefore zero valency. This seemed more than a sufficient reason to explain their lack of chemical properties; indeed, according to the octet rule propagated by Lewis and Langmuir (chapter 13), elements combined in an attempt to complete their outer-shell configurations and so assume the state of an inert gas. In 1924, the German expert on isotopes, Friedrich Paneth, reported categorically that[2]:

the unreactivity of the noble gas elements belongs to the surest of experimental results.

Warned, perhaps, by those who had dismissed Prout's hypothesis as unbridled speculation, or because he knew that it was impossible to prove a negative proposition,

Ramsay had been more circumspect. At the conclusion of his own account of his researches, he wrote[3]:

> It cannot, of course, be stated with absolute certainty that no elements can combine with argon; but it appears at least improbable that any compounds will be formed.

Yet that is precisely what did happen in 1962. This dénouement belongs properly to chapter 15, since it involved co-ordination chemistry; but it will be told here in order to complete the story logically.

In the autumn of 1961, while teaching in Canada, the co-ordination chemist, Neil Bartlett (*b*. 1932), succeeded in preparing an unusual salt of oxygen and platinum hexafluoride in which oxygen played the role of a positive cation, $[O_2]^+[PtF_6]^-$. It dawned on Bartlett while preparing an undergraduate lecture at the University of British Columbia that, since the energies required to remove one electron (first ionization potential) from oxygen and xenon were extremely close (12.2 eV and 12.13 eV, respectively), it ought to be possible to prepare an analogous xenon salt because PtF_6 was 'a better oxidizer than anyone had believed could exist'. It is worth emphasizing that Bartlett worked entirely by analogical reasoning. It was pure opportunism; no theoretical knowledge was used beyond that of ionization potentials, which were extracted directly from a textbook.

The result, a yellow-orange solid that was stable at room temperature and had the formula $XePtF_6$, was isolated on 23 March 1962. Bartlett intended to announce his discovery in *Nature*, but frustrated by its editor's use of surface, rather than air, mail and the consequent delay in publication of such sensational news, he arranged for fast publication in the *Proceedings of the Chemical Society* in June 1962. Within a few months, another group of chemists, who had first prepared PtF_6 in 1957 but failed to notice its oxidizing powers, had succeeded in preparing xenon fluoride, XeF_4.

Within a decade, a complete volume of Gmelin's *Handbook* was being devoted to noble-gas compounds.

In retrospect it is easy to see why Moissan's experiments with argon and fluorine failed – the ionization potential of argon was too great. Ironically, had Ramsay been able to send Moissan samples of xenon, he might have been successful. With the development of Sidgwick's covalent link as the explanation for co-ordination compounds (chapter 15), it ought to have been possible to conceive of heavier rare gases as potential electron donors in certain situations. Pauling had in fact predicted the existence of rare-gas compounds on crystallographic grounds in 1933, but even his reputation had been insufficient to crack the 'closed shell–closed mind' attitude engendered by the superb coherence of the electronic model of atomic structure. The quantum chemist, Charles Coulson, in reviewing the nature of bonding in xenon compounds noted:

> It is surely not without interest that no essentially new type of bonding needs to be postulated, and that conventional theories are able to account in a semi-quantitative way for almost all known experimental facts in this interesting series of molecules. It is no exaggeration to say that in principle almost everything described in this survey could have been said thirty years ago.

The moral, of course, was that chemists should never take their models seriously.

MANUFACTURING ELEMENTS

The deeper meaning of Mendeleev's periodic law was revealed only six years after his death when, in 1913, Henry Moseley, working in Rutherford's laboratory in Manchester, found a constant relationship between the frequency of the shortest wavelength X-ray line of an element and what he, following A. van den Broek, called its atomic number[4]:

It is at once evident that Q [a spectroscopic function of frequency] increases by a constant amount as we pass from one element to the next using the chemical order of the elements in the periodic system. . . . While, however, Q increases uniformly the atomic weights vary in an apparently arbitrary manner, so that an exception in their order does not come as a surprise. We have here a proof that there is in the atom a fundamental quantity, which increases by regular steps as we pass from one element to the next. This quantity can only be the charge on the central positive nucleus, of the existence of which we already have definite proof [from Rutherford's work].

The arbitrary nature of atomic weights was explained about the same time by Soddy's and Fajans' assumption of isotopy.

Although he owed his skills as an experimentalist to chemical training. Moseley proved a better physicist than chemist. Overly impetuous, the potential clarifications of his X-ray measurements were initially clouded by miscalculations and overconfident assertions. Nevertheless, Moseley's clarification gave chemists for the first time a clear principle for deciding how many elements there really were, where they should be placed in the periodic table, and where they should be looked for in the mineral kingdom. The 'terrible confusion' of the rare earths was no more. Gaps were no longer speculations, they could be precisely identified. For example, Moseley himself searched for element 72 in rare-earth samples in 1914. A prior claim to have isolated 'cerium' from concentrations of lutetium made by Urbain in 1911 turned out to be unacceptable. By the end of the First World War in 1918, it was clear that only six elements remained to be discovered – assuming, of course, that uranium was the last. These were 43 (between molybdenum and ruthenium), 61 (between neodymium and samarium), 72 (between lutetium and tantalum), 75 (between tungsten and ruthenium), 85 (between polonium and radon) and 87 (between radon and radium). Moseley did not live to see these discovered (he was drafted and killed in action at Gallipoli in 1915), nor to receive the Nobel prize for physics, which went to the Swede, Karl Siegbahn (1886–1978) in 1924 for the confirmation of his work and its extension to the rare earths.

A further clue to where to search for these elements came from Bohr's detailed portrait of the distribution of electronic shells in 1921. His conclusion that the four-quantum shell was completed at lutetium (71) meant that 72 was not a rare earth (as Urbain and Moseley had thought) but a homologue of zirconium. A spectroscopic search of zirconium minerals made by Dirk Coster and Georg von Hevesy (1885–1966) in 1923 led to the identification of hafnium, named after Copenhagen (Hafnia), the city where they were working. After some dispute with Urbain, who claimed prior identification in 'cerium', the matter was resolved when it was shown that the latter was simply impure lutetium.

Similarly guided were the Berlin husband-and-wife team of Walter Noddack and Ida Tacke, who searched for eka-manganese (43) and element 75 in platinum and Colombian ores in 1925. They again used Moseley's X-ray spectroscopy to identify and to measure lines, and identified what they named rhenium (75) after Tacke's birthplace on the Rhine, and 'masurium' after Noddack's homeland in East Prussia. Whereas rhenium was readily accepted and discovered independently by others in the same year, masurium proved more controversial. The Noddacks were able to concentrate milligram samples of rhenium from hundreds of kilograms of ores, but were unable to do this for masurium. By the 1930s, despite entries for masurium in textbooks and lists of elements, it was generally considered that the X-ray data were insufficient to justify claims for the element's existence. The Noddacks, it was supposed, had rushed to judgement. Ironically, as is now known, element 43 (technetium) is a fission product of uranium, and it has been shown that the ores used by the Noddacks would have contained sufficient uranium to account for the presence of masurium-technetium in their X-ray photographs.

In 1934, Enrico Fermi (1901–54) bombarded uranium nuclei with neutrons, interpreting the results as evidence for the synthesis of 'transuranic elements'. Ida Noddack challenged this interpretation, arguing on chemical grounds that fragments of elements lighter than uranium should be looked for first:

> With the irradiation of heavier nuclei with neutrons these nuclei decay into several larger fragments; these fragments turn out to be isotopes of known elements, but not neighbours of the irradiated element.

In other words, Ida Noddack was proposing what Otto Hahn and Fritz Strassmann were to call 'fission' in 1939. Her suggestion was totally ignored, even though, in reinterpreting his results, Fermi used the chemical enhancement technique that Noddack used to reach her conclusion. Several reasons have been adduced as to why she was ignored, but the most likely explanation is that it was felt that her expertise was in doubt after the identification of masurium. By the same token, when, in 1937, Carlo Perrier and Emilio Segrè (1905–89) analysed the radioactivity produced when molybdenum was irradiated with deuterium in a cyclotron, they concluded that it was due to an isotope of the still-missing element 43. Assuming that the element could not exist naturally, they had the privilege of naming it. Because it had been produced artificially, rather than by standard chemical manipulations, they called it technetium. There is little doubt, however, that technetium was the Noddacks' masurium.

Element 91 (protactinium) had been fairly easily identified by Soddy and Cranston, and independently by Hahn and Meitner, in the radioactive decay of uranium in 1917. Elements 61, 85 and 87 (eka-caesium) were now the only missing pieces in the elementary jigsaw puzzle. In 1913, Soddy's assistant, John Cranston, had noted that mesothorium 2 (one of the many products of thorium radioactive decay) emitted both α- and β-particles. According to Soddy's group displacement law, such dual disintegration would produce element 87 during the α-decay.

In the 1920s, Hahn and Hevesy searched radioactive ores for 87 without success − not surprisingly, since $^{224}87$ has a half-life of only two minutes. In 1939, however, Marguerite Perey (1909–75), working as a technician in Madame Curie's Institut du Radium in Paris, found that actinium, which is isotopic with mesothorium 2, also exhibited dual disintegration.

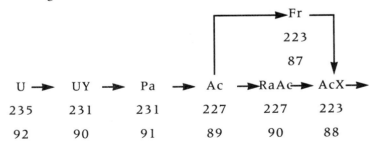

Because the istotope $^{223}87$ had a half-life of over twenty minutes, she was able to experiment with it and confirm that it behaved like a group I alkali metal. Since it was the most electropositive of all elements (how Berzelius would have loved that), Perey first thought of naming it 'catium'. Even in French this sounded more like 'cat' than 'cation' and she was persuaded to name it francium instead. With this discovery, apart from the unstable elements, promethium (61) and astatine (85), which were prepared artificially during the 1940s by C. D. Coryell and E. Segrè, Mendeleev's classical periodic table was complete with 92 elements.

Although Fermi had been premature in assuming that his neutron bombardment experiments produced transuranic elements, the atom bomb project soon confirmed that such elements were possible. The confirmation of atomic fission by Hahn, Meitner and Strassmann in 1939 very quickly led to the identification of neptunium as a daughter element of ^{239}U by Ernest McMillan (1907–91):

$$^{238}_{92}U + {}^{2}_{1}H \rightarrow {}^{238}_{93}Np + 2n \quad (n = neutron)$$
$$^{238}_{93}Np \rightarrow {}^{238}_{94}Pu$$

A new sixty-inch cyclotron at the University of California at Berkeley then enabled plutonium to be prepared from neptunium in 1940.

Because of the Manhattan Project's need for secrecy, information about these elements, as well as their successors, americium and curium, prepared in 1944, was kept secret until 1946. Bohr's suggestion in 1921 that a group of elements similar to the rare earths, in which 5f orbitals were used in preference to the 6d shell, had already familiarized chemists with the idea of an inner transition 'neptunian group'. Not all chemists agreed and many periodic tables published in the 1930s implied that, if transuranic elements existed, they would simply follow uranium in the periodic table. In either case, the Manhattan Project team chemists, McMillan and Glenn Seaborg (*b.* 1912), and electrical engineer, Albert Ghiorso (*b.* 1915), had a guide to the probable physical and chemical properties of such elements. The initial failure to synthesize americium and curium because Seaborg had assumed analogies with plutonium, had convinced him by 1944 that the transuranium elements formed another rare-earth group that began, not with uranium, but with actinium. He therefore called them 'actinides' and depicted them separately on the periodic table. By 1959, eleven transuranic elements filled the fourteen-member actinide series.

It followed that, with their 5f shells complete, elements beginning with 104 would return to the main table after actinium. Element 104 would be an analogue of titanium, zirconium and hafnium, while 118 would be another noble gas. At element 122, a super-actinide series would begin with the filling of 5g or 6f shells. Such Mendeleevian predictions could be confidently made whether or not anyone felt it worth expending energy on

TABLE 9.7 *Partial periodic table showing Seaborg's positioning*

Cs	Ba	La	Hf	Ta	W	Re	Os	Ir
55	56	57	72	73	74	75	76	77
Fr	Ra	Ac	Rf	Nb				
87	88	89	104	105	106	107	108	109
119	120	121						

Lanthanide series

Ce	Pr	Nd	Pm	Sm	Eu	Gd	Tb	Dy
58	59	60	61	62	63	64	65	66

Actinide series

Th	Pa	U	Np	Pu	Am	Cm	Bk	Cf
90	91	92	93	94	95	96	97	98

Super-actinide series

122	123	124	...

making such elements. The 'periodic snail', an ingenious spiral periodic table that was developed by O. T. Benfey in 1975, summarizes these developments.

Given that at least three of the elements, einsteinium, fermium and mendeleevium, had been identified in the debris from thermonuclear weapons testing explosions, it is hardly surprising that nationalistic–political controversy came to surround their investigations. This rose to prominence over rival American–Swedish–Russian claims to have identified nobelium (102) and lawrencium (103). The manufacture of nobelium was formally announced by Ghiorso and Seaborg in 1958, but later work at Dubno, in the Soviet Union, by Georgii Flerov and E. D. Donets and others, cast doubts on the accuracy of the American claims. The name nobelium (rather than joliotium) was nevertheless kept.

Similar Soviet doubts were raised by the same American

of the lanthanides and actinides and predicted artificial elements.

Pr	Au	Hg	Tl	Pb	Bi	Po	At	
78	79	80	81	82	83	84	85	86
110	111	112	113	114	115	116	117	118

Ho	Er	Tm	Yb	Lu
67	68	69	70	71

Es	Fm	Md	No	Lw
99	100	101	102	103

team's announcement of lawrencium in 1961, but again the name prevailed. Between 1964 and 1966, Flerov and his colleagues prepared element 104 and named it kurchatovium in honour of the famous Russian nuclear physicist, but the American team claimed that the Soviet group had misinterpreted their delicate experiments. In 1969, Ghiorso, who had succeeded Seaborg as leader of the Berkeley group when Seaborg became Chairman of the Atomic Energy Commission, announced the firm identification of what he called rutherfordium, the name that prevailed. A similar wrangle developed over the naming of 105 as nielsbohrium (Soviet) and hahnium (USA) between 1967 and 1970.

In order to prevent such unseemly political wrangles in the future, the International Union of Pure and Applied Chemistry (IUPAC) decreed that elements after lawrencium should not be named after people, places or astronomical bodies. Instead, a numerical code, nil = 0, un = 1, bi = 2, etc., plus a suffix 'ium' was to be used. Thus element 104 became 'unnilquadium'. In practice, the IUPAC agreed that a discoverer would still have the right to coin a trivial name for an element once the discovery had been internationally recognized. In 1989, German physicists announced the manufacture of single-atom quantities of elements 108 and 109.

MENDELEEV'S PRINCIPLES

In a whimsical simile inspired by Francis Galton's publications on heredity, Henry Roscoe imagined a series of human families represented by Dumas of France, Newlands of England, Meyer of Germany and Mendeleev of Russia. Under each name was written the name of their father, followed by grandfather, greatgrandfather, and so on, together in each case with the number of years that had elapsed since their births[5]:

We must then find that these numbers regularly increase by a definite amount, *i.e.* by the average age of a generation, which will be approximately the same in all the four families. Comparing the ages of the chemists themselves, we shall observe certain differences, but these are small in comparison with the period which has elapsed since the birth of their ancestors. Now each individual in this series of family trees represents a chemical element; and just as each family is distinguished by certain idiosyncrasies, so each group of the elementary bodies thus arranged shows distinct signs of cosanguinity.

The vividness of this 'family' metaphor makes it all the more important to underline the fact that Mendeleev himself was totally opposed to the idea that the elements were generated from primeval matter. As far as he was concerned, atomic weights were not whole numbers and Stas in the early 1860s had scotched Prout's hypothesis once and for all[6]:

I shall not form any hypothesis, either here nor further on to explain the nature of the periodic law. For first of all, the law itself is too simple; and secondly, this new subject has been too little studied yet, in its diverse parts for us to form any hypothesis.

There are several ironies here. In the first place, the periodic law, coming only ten years after Darwin's announcement of evolution, only strengthened chemists' feelings that elements had evolved. Crookes and Berthelot were quick to point this out, and, of course, it was Rayleigh's belief that there was something in Prout's hypothesis that led to the discovery of a new group of noble gases. A second irony is that it was precisely because Mendeleev had rejected Prout's hypothesis that he avoided previous chemists' obsession with triads and hidden arithmetical series. By committing himself to the belief that unchanging mass (or its measure, atomic weight) was the ultimate cause of the similarities and differences between elements and their component atoms, he was enabled to reach a unifying generalization. This was a necessary condition for his success. The fact that he was trying to organize a textbook was also, for him, a necessary condition, but not a sufficient one, since both William Odling and Lothar Meyer thought about classification while they wrote their textbooks.

Mendeleev had many interests besides the periodic law. In chemistry, his other chief passion was the nature of solutions, where he developed a controversial theory that discontinuities existed between solutes and solvents. For Mendeleev this was evidence of chemical combination. This chemical, or hydrate, theory of solution was announced in 1887, the same year that Arrhenius proposed the very different theory of electrolytic dissociation. Much of the later editions of the *Principles* was concerned with the physical properties of gases and liquids.

Mendeleev was also deeply interested in technological questions, and, as Russia's chief scientific adviser, he strove continuously to modernize its agriculture and industry following the abolition of serfdom in 1861. He argued vehemently that Russia's future economic prosperity lay in national investment in science. In Pennsylvania, the opening of Drake oil well in August 1859 had led to a repetition of the Gold Rush of 1849, as prospectors rushed to stake claims. By 1863, when Russia began slowly to develop her own industry at Baku on the Caspian Sea, American oil products were being distributed all over the world, including Russia. Mendeleev was highly critical of the slow development of Baku, and the government restrictions that limited its production to a yellow kerosene oil that could be used as an illuminating agent. Large-scale expansion began in 1873, when Alfred Nobel, and other foreign nationals, were, on Mendeleev's urging, allowed to exploit the Baku site. In 1876, as a consultant for Russian oil producers, Mendeleev toured the Pennsylvanian oil fields.

Like Charles Dickens earlier, he viewed America with some dismay[7]:

> Why do [the Americans] quarrel, why do they hate Negroes, Indians, even Germans? Why do they not have science and poetry commensurate with themselves? Why are there so many frauds and so much nonsense? . . . It was clear that in the United States there was a development not of the best, but of the middle and worst sides of European civilization. . . . A new dawn is not to be seen on this side of the Atlantic.

Mendeleev's democratic leanings led to his resignation from his university post in 1890 after he had openly supported student claims for reform. Even so, he kept in favour with the Tsar. A blind eye was turned on his private life. His first marriage in 1862 had been one of convenience, his sisters having considered that he needed looking after. Constant quarrels led to the couple's separation. When a divorce was granted in 1882, Mendeleev found that legally he could not remarry for seven years. In desperation Mendeleev paid for an Orthodox priest, who was subsequently defrocked, to grant him dispensation. When a courtier complained that Mendeleev had left his family and bigamously married a young artist, the Tsar is reputed to have said: 'I admit Mendeleev has two wives, but I have only one Mendeleev.' In truth, this instantly recognizable nineteenth-century Einstein, with his unruly hair, grey beard and enormous head, was a law unto himself. For the last decade of his life he was Director of the government's Bureau of Weights and Measures. Students bore huge periodic tables above the funeral procession in 1907.

By calling his text *Principles of Chemistry* (an alternative translation would be *Fundamentals of Chemistry*), Mendeleev drew attention both to the fact that he was concerned with the ultimate principles of matter (elements) that had always been chemists' theoretical concern, and to the fact that chemistry was now finally based upon experimentally derived principles or laws, including the idea of atomic weight as the primary definition of an element. Beginning with the typical elements, the periodic law was not derived until the fifteenth and final chapter of the first volume. Mendeleev never altered this 'inductive' method of presentation, and it was left to later textbook writers to begin with the periodic law itself and then proceed to individual elements via families. The *Principles* is an extraordinary and diverting text whose clarifying, but discursive, footnotes became longer and longer with each edition. By the eighth edition in 1906 they had grown so unwieldly that they had to be collected together at the end of the volumes as appendices. Their encyclopedic range was evidently a reflection of his lecturing style. One student recalled[8]:

> Mendeleev made of his course as it were an encyclopaedia of natural science, connected by the basic thread of inorganic chemistry. Excursions in the fields of mechanics, physics, astronomy, astrophysics, cosmogeny, meteorology, geology, physiology, both plant and animal, agriculture, and even side branches of aeronautics and artillery were included as part of his lectures.

Well could Mendeleev declare that the *Principles* was his favourite child, his 'likeness, experience as a teacher and most sincere scientific ideals'.

CONCLUSION

Following Lavoisier's definition of the chemical element, chemists concluded that the world was made up from large numbers of these different substances. The question naturally arose: Were these elements related? And if so, how? Of the two possibilities, that elements were genealogically related, or fixed and discontinuous, Mendeleev decided upon the latter. He was guided here both by being convinced that Prout's hypothesis, which asserted that elements were agglomerates of a primary matter, had been disproved by the researches of Stas, and his conviction that mass ought to be a chemist's fundamental principle. Guided by the availability of an internationally agreed system of atomic weights following the Karlsruhe conference of 1860, and by the analogy of carbon chemistry, where physical properties were a function of molecular weights, Mendeleev was led to the periodic law in 1869.

For most of the nineteenth century, inorganic textbooks had been descriptive. By the late 1860s they clearly lacked the organizing principles of classification that organic chemists had developed arduously during the previous thirty years. Mendeleev's *Principles* was the first book to change this by using the periodic law as an organizing principle – albeit he preferred to present it inductively rather than to announce it *ab initio*, as was done subsequently by twentieth-century textbook writers.

Mendeleev's system, in which atomic weight became the fundamental feature, or chemical standard, for identifying and defining elements, was sufficiently elastic to allow the prediction of missing elements, or the inclusion of whole new groups such as the noble gases and the actinides. The law also laid down new paths for chemical research. The discovery of the rare gases, although unpredicted by Mendeleev, proved more important than any prior discoveries of new elements. Their atomic weights, and position in the periodic table, had to be decided by the application of the physicists' kinetic theory, rather than by the application of traditional chemical methods. Their identification confirmed the power and use of spectroscopy in deciding chemical issues – a power that, in X-ray spectroscopy, showed how the explanation of the law lay in a theory of atomic structure. Following Moseley's concept of atomic number, and its correlation with Rutherford's idea of nuclear charge, it became possible to place a finite figure on the number of possible elements, and to redefine atomic weights as an averaging out of isotopic masses. These new models and concepts clarified the problem that the rare-earth elements had always posed, and helped in the identification of the remaining missing elements, or their artificial creation using the methods of nuclear chemistry that were developed from 1939 onwards. Most artificially prepared elements were destined to remain chemical curiosities; some, like plutonium and technetium, were found destructive or creative uses in thermonuclear weapons or in the treatment of cancer. The marriage between Mendeleev's periodic law and the electronic theory of valency that had been stimulated by the discoveries of atomic physics produced its own dogmatic rationale as to why the rare, or noble, gases discovered by Ramsay and Rayleigh were chemically inert. This dogma was broken only in 1962 by Bartlett, whose preparation of xenon fluoride compounds shows how much chemistry owed to experimental opportunism rather than to experiment guided by theoretical understanding.

The periodic classification of the elements is one of the greatest and most valuable generalizations in science. Important in its late-nineteenth-century construction for the clarification it brought, and the guidance it gave to chemical research, it was able to adapt to the deeper analysis of the structure of matter revealed by nuclear physics in this century. In turn, since the 1960s, it has provided a stimulation and invaluable precedent for physicists' attempts to classify subatomic particles. The 'eightfold way' of Murray Gell-Mann owes much to Mendeleev and to what Rutherford described as a philosophical mind that elevated him above the ranks of the empirical enquiries of his contemporaries.

On the Dissociation of Substances Dissolved in Water

It is now generally known that within the last 15 years
a new branch of science has come into existence. This
branch, occupying a position between physics and
chemistry, is known as physical chemistry . . . .. The
new physical chemistry really begins with the chapter
on solutions.

(HARRY CLARY JONES, *The Elements of
Physical Chemistry*, 1902)

In a reminiscent mood, Arrhenius once told of how as a
young man he had gone excitedly to see Per Cleve, one
of his former teachers whom he greatly admired, and
said: 'I have a new theory of electrical conductivity as
a cause of chemical reactions.' But Cleve's only reaction
was to express polite interest and bid him goodbye. As
is well known, when Arrhenius presented his doctoral
thesis in May 1884, it was granted only fourth-class
approval, and since a higher classification was needed to
achieve an academic appointment in Sweden, Arrhenius
was bitterly disappointed. As the account is traditionally
rendered, the failure of Arrhenius' examiners to spot
the originality of his idea that solutions dissociate is
damned and the University of Uppsala is made to seem
the home of backwoodsmen. In fact, the experimental
part of Arrhenius' thesis (which would have counted
a good deal towards testing a candidate's competence
and originality), although it contained new data, lacked
originality. From the examiners' point of view it must have

seemed merely to extend the techniques well established by Hittorf, Kohlrausch and Arrhenius' teacher, Edlund. Equally seriously, Arrhenius' argument for partial dissociation was again not an original idea; indeed, Arrhenius sought support for dissociation historically from the work of Williamson and Clausius. The argument was, in any case, based upon data limited to rather dilute solutions, and he did not seriously consider alternative explanations, while overall the thesis seemed more intuitive than firmly rooted upon experimental foundations. There were, moreover, some false claims, such as that the resistance of a solution rose with a solvent's molecular weight. And, in any case, how did Arrhenius propose to explain the stable existence in solution of oppositely charged particles when the solution was not undergoing electrolysis?

As John Servos has observed, Arrhenius' thesis was what a modern examiner would describe as 'undisciplined' and no doubt today, at least in a British University, Arrhenius would have been referred and encouraged to resubmit a better thesis. Even so, it seems curious that Arrhenius' examiners allowed him to get away with a theory of rather partial applicability and one that ignored the role of the solvent at a time when chemical theories of solution were very popular. When coupled in 1887 with van't Hoff's treatment of osmotic pressure as an extension of the gas laws and with Ostwald's dilution law, Arrhenius' approach had the effect of confining the theory of solution in a strait jacket. Only in the 1920s was the ionic theory to break free. As several historians have commented, the ionic theory is a good example of how scientists hold fast to an unsatisfactory theory. For, when read by Wilhelm Ostwald, and placed within the context of other contemporary work on solutions that was being conducted by van't Hoff, Arrhenius' thesis came to seem the lynchpin of physical chemistry, and something worth defending against unbelievers. This new 'general chemistry', as Ostwald was to call it, was slowly to transform the face of chemistry

– a process that organic chemists only seriously confronted in the 1920s and 1930s, the inorganic chemists in the 1940s and 1950s – and was to be completed with the reforms of secondary and high-school chemistry in the 1960s.

PROTO-PHYSICAL CHEMISTRY

Although a self-consciously articulated discipline 'physical chemistry' only arose in the 1880s, many chemists had long taken interest in the physical properties of substances; indeed, well into the twentieth century teachers of elementary chemistry insisted that various 'physical properties' had to be learned alongside a substance's chemical preparation and reactions. In 1855 the London chemist, William Allen Miller, published a text, *Elements of Chemistry*, whose first volume was subtitled *Chemical Physics*. This included accounts of investigations of boiling and melting points, specific heats, atomic and molecular volumes, refractivity and behaviour with polarized light, as well as much on electricity, magnetism and heat. Such investigations of the former 'imponderables' of Lavoisier were not necessarily purely empirical in aim. Most investigators hoped to find qualitative, if not quantitative, relationships between physical and chemical properties. There were modest successes in this endeavour. Dulong and Petit's generalization concerning the specific heats of elements had assisted the determination of atomic weights during the 1820s, but Dumas' examination of vapour densities in the 1830s threw him into confusion and a state of scepticism concerning the value of the atomic concept.

In 1857 Henri Étienne Sainte-Claire Deville (1818–81), who was the first chemist to develop an industrial process for the production of aluminium, made a full investigation of the relative densities of substances vaporized at high temperatures. Most of the anomalies he found he was able to attribute to polymerization or to thermal dissociation (a word he coined). He found that, when the majority of apparently stable substances were heated to a sufficiently high temperature, they partly dissociated or disintegrated, so that the substance was in equilibrium with its decomposition products. He demonstrated this convincingly by suddenly cooling the products of dissociation. Although Deville disliked some of the theoretical interpretations that were made of his experimental work, it proved to Cannizzaro of great significance in the support of Avogadro's hypothesis, and hence in the determination of molecular weights. It also proved significant, however, for the study of chemical kinetics and, in the hands of Crookes and Lockyer in Britain, for fuelling astrophysical and chemical speculations concerning the structure of elements and atoms. Arguably, Lockyer's easily disproven speculations, and claimed experimental proof, for the dissociation of the elements in the sun and stars in his own Kensington laboratory, may well have made several British chemists wary of Arrhenius' claims for dissociation in solution. Physicists, on the other hand, who were beginning to work on the phenomena of cathode rays at low pressures in which gas molecules appeared to dissociate into positive and negative ions, were to be more receptive.

Prior to about 1884 physical chemistry was the study of the physical properties of chemical substances. Studies, such as those of Biot and Pasteur, often revealed important phenomena, like the discovery that isomers had different physical and chemical properties and that molecular arrangement alone could not explain all such cases, especially the tartaric acids, where chemical properties were identical and the only physical difference was in the way that isomers rotated the plane of polarized light. In this respect it is interesting to note that van't Hoff's first piece of original research in 1875 was in this area of optical activity. Here 'physical chemistry' was to lay the foundations for significant twentieth-century research in inorganic and organic stereochemistry. Polarization studies also proved fruitful in industry when the polarimeter was adopted by the brewing industry to help in monitoring the fermentation of sugar to form alcohol.

Between 1842 and 1855 at the University of Giessen, the historian of chemistry, Hermann Kopp, made elaborate investigations of the boiling points of large numbers of organic compounds. This led him to the conclusion that 'equal differences in the chemical composition of organic compounds correspond to equal differences in the boiling points' (table 10.1). Both Kopp and subsequent workers realized that the CH_2-increment relationship was only approximate and that boiling points depended upon the arrangement of atoms within a molecule (most isomers, for instance, were found to have different boiling points). The research programme eventually turned out to be far more significant as an accurate means for the identification and characterization of pure compounds in the way that

TABLE 10.1 *Kopp's investigation of the alcohol homologous series.*

Alcohol	Formula	Boiling point	Difference
Methyl	CH_4O	65°	
			$D = 13°$
Ethyl	C_2H_6O	78°	
			$D = 18°$
Propyl	C_3H_8O	96°	
			$D = 13°$
Butyl	$C_4H_{10}O$	109°	
			$D = 23°$
Amyl	$C_5H_{12}O$	132°	

Chevreul had suggested back in 1815. In any case, later determinations clearly showed that the boiling points of substances within homologous series decreased as compounds became more complex.

Dulong and Petit's work on the specific heats of elements also inspired searches for a similar law for compounds; but although regularities were found, no useful insights were gained. Other, rather sterile, generalizations and investigations were made with atomic and molecular volumes (the ratio of atomic or molecular weight divided by a substance's specific gravity) – though specific gravity [relative density] determinations *per se* found some uses in chemical industry as a simple monitoring technique and by governments interested in the taxation of alcohol.

Chemists also tried to discover relationships between physical properties – for example between the viscosity of liquids and the boiling points, and between refraction of light (refractivity) and density. Work on the latter, pioneered by John Hall Gladstone in England in the 1850s and developed by J. W. Brühl in the 1880s, did lead to relationships that proved promising and useful in determining the states of bonding and constitutions of carbon compounds. Eventually this research was to form a solid basis for twentieth-century instrumental devices. Brühl, for example, was able to support Kekulé's alternating single–double bonded hexagonal formula for benzene on the basis of its refractivity. However, the state of the art was insufficient for this to stand as definitive proof, and, in any case, using thermochemical evidence to identify types of bond, Jørgen Thomsen was able to claim that benzene's heats of combustion supported Ladenburg's alternative prism formula.

In the 1840s, the Swiss-Russian Germain H. Hess (1802–50), inspired by Dalton's and Berzelius' work to try to understand the nature of chemical affinity, investigated the heats of reactions. He noted that the amount of heat liberated in the neutralization of acids by bases was always

升 煉 水 銀

Condensing device

B

A

1a Chinese retort still for the
preparation of mercury, 1637

1b A conjectural diagram by
Joseph Needham to illustrate
the evolution of the still

1c Greek alchemical
apparatus, 3rd century AD

C

2a Vessels used in the Great Work, with symbols of the Four Evangelists, 17th century

2b Symbols of the four elements in *Musaeum Hermeticum*, 1678

Quæ funt in fuperis, hæc inferioribus infunt:
Quod monftrat cœlum, id terra frequenter habet.
Ignis, Aqua et fluitans duo funt contraria: felix,
Talia fi jungis: fit tibi fcire fatis!

D.M.a C.B.P.L.C.

3a J.L. David's portrait of Lavoisier and his wife, 1788

3b A plate of apparatus from Lavoisier's *Traité*, drawn by his wife

TRAITÉ ÉLÉMENTAIRE DE CHIMIE

4a Affinity table from C.E. Gellert, *Metallurgic Chemistry*, 1776

4b A spiral periodic chart designed by O.T. Benfey in 1970

5a John Dalton

5b August Kekulé

5c James Sheridan Muspratt

5d Dmitri Mendeleev

6a A typical university or industrial laboratory bench of the 1870s to 1950s

6b Painting of Wyggeston Boys' School, Leicester Chemistry laboratory, 1895

7a William Crookes

7b Svante Arrhenius

7c Wilhelm Ostwald

7d Linus Pauling

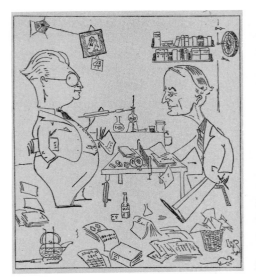

8a Cartoon by J.D.H. Mackie
of Christopher Ingold and
Edward D. Hughes, 1948

8b Ronald Nyholm

8d Wallace Carothers at work
on nylon in the 1930s

8c Fritz Haber

the same, no matter how many reaction pathways were used. Thus, if in the reaction A + B = C, *h* is the amount of heat involved (the units are immaterial), then if A and B are first prepared separately with amounts of heat *a* and *b* involved, then algebraically *a* + *b* = *h*. The law stimulated a great deal of calorimetric work, principally by Marcellin Berthelot (1827–1907) in France and Julius Thomsen (1826–1908) in Denmark. Hess also noted that usually little or no heat was detectable when solutions of neutral salts were mixed together, and he attributed this to a neutralization effect. The bases of both 'laws' were to be found in the later dissociation theory.

The proto-physical chemistry we have briefly reviewed clearly revealed large numbers of relations between physical properties, composition and constitution. But it was difficult to discriminate between truly significant relations and accidental oddities. As Harry Jones, the American disciple of Ostwald, commented in 1900, apart from certain investigations into thermochemistry, electrochemistry and chemical affinity concerning whose significance all were agreed, on the whole:

> We are impressed by the fact that the relations are only approximations; they are not sharply defined and rigorous. A relation was often discovered which, at first, seemed to be fairly exact, but as the experimental work became more refined, a larger number of exceptions appeared. Thus, in many cases, what seemed to be a quantitative relation was merely a qualitative one ... There is a lack of any definite mathematical conception, in terms of which the earlier work can be interpreted.

To the frequent disgust and unease of chemists reared in the laboratory tradition of emprical investigation, the new physical chemistry would demand mathematical sophistication and theory modelling. Ironically, with its interest in the 'directing power of groups', twentieth-century organic chemists were to find the measurements of physical properties such as acid strengths and dipole moments of great significance.

RAOULT AND VAN'T HOFF

The new physical chemistry was, nonetheless, much indebted to the data accumulated by the chemists (and physicists) who had worked in the older empirical tradition; none more so than to François Marie Raoult (1830–1901), whose elaborate and precise research on the effects of solutes on the lowering of the freezing points of different solvents revealed an interesting correlation with, and therefore an independent way of checking, molecular weights. He and others also uncovered a similar effect on the lowering of vapour pressure – a phenomenon that Ernst Beckmann (1853–1923) exploited in 1888 in a convenient apparatus for the determination of molecular weights that remained a standard technique until the introduction of the mass spectrometer after the Second World War.

Raoult's experimental achievements give the lie to the assumption that all important French work was done in Paris. Admittedly he was more revered abroad than in his own country and only rose to fame and fortune in the 1880s when he was already in his sixties. He was one of only three French chemists (the others being Berthelot and Le Chatelier) who were asked by Ostwald to sit on the editorial board of the *Zeitschrift für physikalische Chemie* in 1887. Following a Paris doctorate on electrolysis over which he struggled part-time for many years, Raoult had spent fourteen humdrum years as a lycée teacher before moving to Grenoble in 1867 – one of the ten provincial Science Faculties established by Napoleon. Facilities for research were decidedly poor[1]:

Each professor had his own little table; this room which was laboratory during the daytime served simultaneously as the living quarters for the concierge.

Here the physics professor arranged the instruments; the zoology professor dissected his rabbits and fed his pigeons; the geology professor broke his rocks and laid out his fossils; and the chemistry professor carried out all his operations.

But as so often in the history of science or in industrial research, such crowded uncongenial conditions were counterbalanced by enforced interdisciplinary camaraderie. Because Raoult's colleagues were interested in molecular processes such as surface tension and specific heats, and his own toxicological lectures at the local medical school involved adsorption phenomena, Raoult decided to complement their work with a study of the solution of gases and solids in water.

It had long been known – witness Fahrenheit's choice of 32° as the freezing point of water – that freezing points were depressed when substances were dissolved in water or other solvents. In 1788, Cavendish's secretary, Charles Blagden, had shown that the depression was proportional to the amount of substance (solute) in a given volume of solvent, and Raoult was made aware of Blagden's law from an investigation made by a Swiss chemist, Louis De Coppett, in 1871 in which 'atomic' depressions were calculated. By multiplying the depression for one gram in one-hundred grams of solvent by the 'atomic' weight, De Coppett had shown that nitrates, sulphates, carbonates, etc. produced very similar depressions.

Raoult's own studies showed that, ideally, one molecule of any substance dissolved in a hundred molecules of solvent lowered the freezing point by a nearly constant amount. Like De Coppett and Berthelot (whose lectures Raoult had attended in Paris), Raoult at first attributed freezing point depressions to a chemical theory of solution; namely, it was an effect due to the affinity of salts for water. He emphasized the value of the measurements for determining the analytical purity of the depressants. But further work with organic solvents in 1882 convinced him differently and shifted his attention to the determination of molecular weights from the data. With Berthelot in Paris as Minister of Education in 1886 decreeing that the atomic theory was a hypothesis that should not be taught in schools, Raoult was moving into a controversial area, since his results supported the Avogadro–Cannizzaro distinction between atoms and molecules and the 'new' atomic weight $O = 16$ rather than $O = 8$ advocated by Berthelot.

The investigation of sixty compounds dissolved in acetic acid gave molecular depressions of 39 for organic solutes and 18 (approximately $\frac{1}{2} \times 39$) for inorganic materials like hydrochloric acid. Similar results, with different constants, were found with other solvents. Clearly what mattered was the number of molecules dissolved and the identity of the solvent, not the number and arrangement of the atoms that composed the dissolved molecules. A purely physical theory of solution was possible. As Raoult reported in 1882[2]:

> The simplest manner of explaining the observed facts consists in allowing that in a constant weight of a determined solvent, all *physical* molecules produce the same molecular lowering of the freezing point. According to this hypothesis, if the *chemical* molecules of the dissolved body are completely separated from each other [cf. later electrolytes], the molecular lowering is a maximum and the same for all. If, in constrast, the chemical molecules are joined together [cf. later non-electrolytes] in more or less substantial numbers, molecular lowering is more or less inferior to the maximum. It is half when the chemical molecules are joined in pairs, and, in general, the abnormal lowerings correspond to this condition.

If depressions were classified by valency and ionic state, Raoult found:

Univalent negative	Cl, Br, OH, NO$_3$	19
Bivalent negative	SO$_4$, CrO$_4$, CO$_3$	9
Univalent positive	H, K, Na, NH$_4$	16
bi– (and poly–) valent	Be, Mg, Al	8

Hence the formula for aluminium chloride had to be Al$_2$Cl$_6$, giving $2 \times 8 + 6 \times 19 = 130$, the observed depression, rather than AlCl$_3$. This, in turn, supported an atomic weight Al $= 27$, rather than the combining weight Al $= 13.5$ advocated by Berthelot.

It is important to remember that Raoult's aim in 'cryoscopy' was to help to settle the French debate over atomic weights. Nevertheless, he must have been enormously pleased when, two years later, his data (including that on vapour pressure lowerings and boiling point elevations) were shown by Arrhenius to have wider implications, which he enthusiastically supported. It is worth noting, however, that Raoult did go on record that solvents must have some sort of role in the behaviour of strong electrolytes.

If Raoult's advantage was that he could straddle disciplines because there were no strongly established separate Chairs of physics and chemistry at Grenoble, van't Hoff also benefited from an interdisciplinary atmosphere at Amsterdam.

A quiet, dreamy, romantic man – his inaugural lecture at Amsterdam in 1887 was on the role of the imagination in science – Jacobus Henricus van't Hoff (1852–1911) was already a competent mathematician when he decided to study chemistry at the University of Leyden in 1871. After *Wanderjahre* spent at Bonn with Kekulé (whom he disliked) and with Wurtz in Paris (where he met le Bel), he presented a safe organic chemistry thesis for his Utrecht doctorate in 1874 – a month after announcing the daring principle of the tetrahedral carbon atom (see chapter 7). Although mocked by Kolbe for teaching in a Veterinary Academy at Utrecht, the position gave van't Hoff space and time for research. By 1878 he was Professor of Chemistry at Amsterdam and from 1891, less happily, at the prestigious University of Berlin, where, in 1901, he received the very first Nobel prize in chemistry for his contributions to physical chemistry.

How and why did van't Hoff shift his interests from organic to physical chemistry? As he himself explained in an autobiographical lecture, it was because the chemical constitution of stereoisomers depended upon a physical property, optical activity, that he turned to the examination of the relationships between physical properties and organic constitution. The result was a large text, *Ansichten über die organische Chemie* (2 vols, 1878–81), which an English obituarist unkindly described as unreadable. The mathematical approach and atomic modelling (which is reminiscent of later crystal-field theory) would undoubtedly have repelled most contemporary organic chemists, who, in any case, were not prepared to treat their discipline as a branch of mathematical physics for another fifty years.

One of van't Hoff's primary interests in the *Ansichten* (could there have been a passing reference to Alexander von Humboldt's *Ansichten der Natur* in this choice of title?) was, given that most organic compounds were thoroughly inert, why and how did reactions occur? Why, for example, is the oxidation of methane, CH_4, much more difficult than that of methyl alcohol, CH_3OH? Such questions forced van't Hoff to the study of thermodynamics and chemical kinetics. His very considerable innovations in these fields were published in Amsterdam in French, in 1884, as *Études de dynamique chimique*[3]:

> Reaction velocity was at first [my] chief aim, but chemical equilibrium was closely associated with it. Equilibrium resting, on the one hand, on the equality of two opposite reactions, and procuring a firm support on the other, through its connection with thermodynamics, you see how, to obtain my

object [reaction velocity], I was ever led further from it, which often occurs.

It was these studies that led van't Hoff to lay the foundations of chemical kinetics – the division of reactions into unimolecular and bimolecular (the order of reaction terminology was Ostwald's clarification in 1887), and ideas concerning equilibria and mass action. To understand reversible reactions (symbolically ⇌ instead of =), van't Hoff had to wrestle with the age-old unsolved problem of chemical affinity. The simplest, and therefore apparently most promising, case of this was the water of crystallization. Van't Hoff knew that Mitscherlich, in 1844, had determined the magnitude of the attractive force holding water in sodium sulphate (Glauber's salt) by exposing it in a mercury barometer. On the liberation of its water as a vapour, the barometer had fallen 5.45 mm, whereas water alone caused a depression of 8.72 mm. From this Mitscherlich had reasoned that the 'affinity' of sodium sulphate for water was equivalent to 3.27 mm, or 1/32 kg per square inch (0.0048 kg/cm^2). Van't Hoff thought this force much too small and wondered whether it could be measured more directly using water and a salt in solution rather than water in a compound state.

Thomas Graham and Justus von Liebig had been excited by the phenomenon of osmosis (the ability of water or other solvents to pass through animal or other membranes, the osmotic pressure being the pressure that must be applied to the solution to prevent the solvent diffusing through the membrane). However, this subject, which seemed to them to lie at the centre of any definition of 'life', had not advanced for want of convenient instrumentation. At Amsterdam, one of van't Hoff's colleagues was the plant physiologist, Hugo de Vries, who was then investigating the osmotic pressures of cells with a view to understanding plant nutrition. Casual conversations with de Vries led to van't Hoff's awareness of the tremendous technical advance that had been made in the determination of osmotic pressure by the German apothecary turned botanist, Friedrich Pfeiffer, and published in his *Osmotische Untersuchungen* in 1877. Pfeiffer had hit upon the trick of supporting semi-permeable membranes within the walls of gardeners' porous clay pots. He had also introduced the complex salt, copper ferrocyanide, as an artificial membrane that was able to withstand very high pressures, thus allowing the investigator to explore the pressures over a large range (see Table 10.2).

This proved a most convenient apparatus for van't Hoff's reanalysis of Mitscherlich's data concerning the affinity of salt for water. On placing a one per cent solution of cane sugar in a Pfeiffer cell surrounded by water, van't Hoff obtained an osmotic pressure of two-thirds of an atmosphere [67 550 Pa), over 130 times greater than Mitscherlich's reading for sodium sulphate's attraction for water. Moreover, examination of Pfeiffer's and de Vries' osmotic pressure readings suggested an analogy with the gas laws (see Table 10.3).

The great advantage of the gas-solution analogy was that the second law of thermodynamics, which applied to reversible reactions, could be applied to solutions. Thermodynamic analysis showed van't Hoff that both vapour pressure and osmotic pressure were connected and that they could be related to chemical affinity if the latter was assumed to be the work done in a reversible chemical process, including electrolytic processes. This led to a stream of important equations, including the reaction isochor,

$$\mathrm{d}(\ln K)/\mathrm{d}t = Q/RT^2$$

where K is the equilibrium constant derived from a reworking of Guldberg and Waage's account of mass action, Q the heat of reaction at constant volume, T the temperature and R a constant; and the equation linking an equilibrium constant with the work of affinity, A, where

$$-A = RT \ln K$$

Van't Hoff's starting point thermodynamically was the equation derived by Bunsen's pupil, August Horstmann, in 1873 for the equilibrium condition of dissociation of gases:

$$Q/T + R \ln(p_1/p_2) + C = 0$$

where p_1 and p_2 are the pressures of dissociated molecules, Q the heat of dissociation, T the absolute temperature and C a constant. Insofar as the equation helped to explain why the density of a dissociating gas was not constant, it gave support to the validity of Avogadro's hypothesis in dissociating systems and, as Horstmann noted, insofar as the equation had been derived from one concerning the vaporization of liquids, it implied that an analogy existed between gases and dilute solutions.

TABLE 10.2   *Pfeiffer's measurements of P/C for cane sugar at 14.6°C [76 mm = 1 pascal].*

Concentration, C (%)	Pressure, P (mm)	P/C
1	535	535
2	1016	508
4	2082	521
6	3075	513

Van't Hoff's studies of osmotic pressure suggested that the analogy between gases and solutions was complete. Support for this was already to be found in Pfeiffer's observations (see table 10.2) that osmotic pressure was proportional to concentration (in other words, inversely proportional to the volume), as well as proportional to the absolute temperature. Osmotic pressure followed the gas law

$$PV = kT$$

Van't Hoff was easily able to show that k was equal to the usual gas constant R, so that a given osmotic pressure was the same as the pressure that would be exerted by an ideal gas at the same temperature in the volume occupied by the solution (table 10.3):

TABLE 10.3   *Van't Hoff's results.*

Temperature	Osmotic pressure*	Equivalent gas pressure
6.8	0.64	0.665
13.7	0.691	0.681
14.2	0.671	0.682
15	0.684	0.686
32.0	0.716	0.725

*All pressures in mmHg, where 76 mm = 101 325 Pa.

At equal osmotic pressure and temperature, equal volumes of solutions contain an equal number of molecules . . . [indeed], the same number which, at the same temperature and pressure, is contained in an equal volume of gas.

This was no fanciful analogy for van't Hoff, since he explained the osmotic pressure by Clausius' kinetic gas model. The analogy held, van't Hoff argued, providing that the dilution was 'sufficiently great to allow one to disregard the reciprocal action of, and the space taken by, the dissolved particles'. Unfortunately, even with this condition, he found that, whereas most organic solutions like cane sugar obeyed the gas laws, the majority of inorganic acids, bases and salts did not. Just as Raoult had found that they gave much lower freezing points, they gave much higher osmotic pressure readings than theory predicted.

Van't Hoff's solution was to recall that the gas laws were 'ideal' laws – Boyle's law, for example, is only true over a limited range of pressures and volumes for different gases. If an empirical correction factor, i, was introduced into the gas law equation

$$PV = iRT$$

where i was always greater than 1, the relationship was restored to health. For example, for HCl i had to be 1.98, and for Na_2NO_3 *i* was 1.82. No comment was made on the fact that *i* seemed to be close to 2. These results were presented, in French, to the Royal Swedish Academy on 14 October 1885 and published the following year in both Swedish and Dutch journals. By then van't Hoff had become friendly with Ostwald and, through him, with Ostwald's protégé, Arrhenius. When the latter received offprints of van't Hoff's papers in February 1887 he quickly saw that a connection could be made between the empirical factor *i* and the work that he had done for his doctoral dissertation on electrical conductivity in 1884. Arrhenius replied to van't Hoff by letter on 30 March 1887 suggesting that *i* was nothing other than a measure of the dissociation of electrolytes. A week later van't Hoff indicated enthusiastic approval for the suggestion and in a paper published in the first volume of the new *Zeitschrift für physikalische Chemie* later in 1887 he reinterpreted his work in terms of ionization. 'It may have appeared daring', he wrote in 1887, 'to give Avogadro's law for solutions such a prominent place, and I should not have done so had not Arrhenius pointed out to me, by letter, the probability that salts and analogous substances, when in solution, break down into ions.'

ELECTROCHEMISTRY FROM FARADAY TO ARRHENIUS

Volta's battery had, as Davy said in 1810, sounded an alarm bell throughout Europe. It seemed that every scientist in every European city had a theory of electrolysis until the subject was placed on a sounder footing by both Davy and Berzelius during the first decade of the century. During the 1830s Davy's heir at the Royal Institution, Michael Faraday, had subjected electrolysis to the first quantitative examination and established that the amount of a chemical compound decomposed was proportional to the quantity of electricity used. Although Faraday, with the help of William Whewell, devised the terminology of ions for the parts of a compound discharged at the electrodes (another of their neologisms), it is important to note that Faraday's ions were not the same as those in Arrhenius' later theory. In the case of sodium sulphate, for example, Faraday's two ions were those posited by Berzelius' dualistic theory, namely NaO^+ and SO^-, not $2Na^+$ and SO_4^{2-}.

The stage for the later ionic forms was set by Faraday's friend and admirer, John Frederick Daniell (1790–1848), in 1839. How could the fact that hydrogen and oxygen were also liberated during electrolysis alongside the equivalents of the salt being electrolysed be reconciled with Faraday's quantitative law? Daniell's answer was that their discharge emanated from secondary reactions not promoted by the electric current. To explain this he adopted Davy's view announced in 1815 that acids (and hence their salts) derived their acidity by the arrangement of their parts and not from the presence of oxygen or hydrogen; in Daniell's words, 'a radical forms an acid with hydrogen, and a salt with sodium or any other metal'. Thus, if the ions of sodium sulphate were Na and (S + 4O), the appearance of hydrogen and oxygen at the cathode and anode could be explained as side reactions:

$$(S + 4O) + HO = [(S + 4O) + (H)] + O \uparrow \text{ (anode)}$$
$$\text{sulphuric acid}$$
$$Na + HO = (Na + O) + H \uparrow \quad \text{(cathode)}$$
$$\text{soda}$$

Electrolytic formulae might then be distinguished from

TABLE 10.4 *Distinction between formulae.*

	Chemical formulae	Electrolytic formulae
Sulphate of soda	(S + 3O) + (Na + O)	(S + 4O) + Na
Sulphate of potash	(S + 3O) + (P + O)	(S + 4O) + P
Phosphate of soda	(P + 2$\frac{1}{2}$ O) + (Na + O)	(P + 3$\frac{1}{2}$ O) + Na

Berzelius' chemical formulae (table 10.4). Fortunately, a terminology Daniell introduced for his electrolytic forms, 'oxysulphion of hydrogen', 'oxynitrion of potassium', etc., never caught on.

In 1841, Daniell was joined at King's College by William Allen Miller, who was later (1855) to write one of the standard mid-Victorian textbooks of chemistry. Together Daniell and Miller explored further electrolytic problems. The German, Theodor Grotthuss (1785–1822), had, as early as 1805, devised an influential model to explain how the products of electrolysis appeared only at the electrodes. Comparing electrodes to magnets, he supposed that chains of alternating positive and negative particles were set up in the solution. Horizontal filaments of metals deposited on a cathode certainly made it appear likely that the metallic part of salts followed the path of a horizontally driven current. In the case of water, when the negative oxygen nearest the anode was discharged, the freed positive hydrogen combined with a contiguous oxygen in the chain, and inverted itself, whereupon oxygen was again available for discharge. A similar process occurred with hydrogen at the cathode.

| − | + | − | + | − | + | − | + |
| o | h | o | h | o | h | o | h |

Grotthuss' model implied that ions moved with equal speeds in different directions. However, when in 1844 Daniell and Miller used a divided cell (a cell divided by porous diaphragms into three compartments of anode, cathode and central), they found that the changing concentrations of solutions around the electrodes implied that ions did not move equally rapidly and that, if anything, more cations travelled to the cathode in equal times than anions to the anode. No quantitative conclusions could be drawn because their instrumentation and technology were too crude.

Ten years later, however, Wilhelm Hittorf (1824–1914) in Germany, using diagrams (here simplified after Ostwald), deduced, and then confirmed experimentally, that ions migrated at different rates. If anions and cations moved equally fast, then the concentrations around the cathode and anode would be reduced equally from 3 to 2. And if the

before   +   +   +   +   +   +

             —   —   —   —   —   —

             _____

after   +   +   +   +   +   +

             —   —   —   —   —   —

cations moved twice as fast as the anions, after three cations and three anions are discharged the concentrations would be reduced from 3 to 2 around the cathode, and from 3 to 1 around the anode.

before   +   +   +   +   +   +

                    —   —   —   —   —   —

             _____

after   +   +   +   +   +   +   +

                    —   —   —   —   —   —   —

In Hittorf's words:

> ... if one ion moves $1/n$ of the way and the other $(n - 1)/n$, then in that part of the liquid in which the

first ion appears there will be $1/n$ equivalent more of it and $(n - 1)/n$ equivalent less of the other. The opposite relation will apply to the other side of the electrolyte.

In meticulous experiments using very weak currents he determined n and $(n - 1)$, what he called 'transport numbers', for a large number of electrolytes, showing that such numbers were independent of the current strength but varied with the starting concentrations of the solutions. He displayed the same experimental flair twenty years later when he investigated cathode rays.

By the 1840s both chemists and physicists were becoming more conscious of energy. Hittorf's work raised, not for the first time, the thorny question of how ions were teased apart from the full molecule in the first place. Given that Hittorf had used very weak currents and that Faraday had shown that even the smallest electromotive force produced a current, it seemed that ionization occurred without the expenditure of electrical energy. In an influential paper of 1857, one of the German pioneers of thermodynamics and kinetic theory, Rudolf Clausius, took the bull by the horns and posited that some of the molecules in solution had to be ionized before the current was applied. He was able to assert this confidently because he had already developed a dynamical view of heat. Consequently, he was prepared to think of molecules in both the gaseous and liquid states as constantly bombarding one another and exchanging positions. He also drew confidence from the fact that the chemist, Alexander Williamson, had already, in 1851, written of radicals changing positions in double decomposition. Indeed, Williamson had generalized that in any 'aggregate of the molecules of every compound, a constant interchange between the elements contained in them is taking place'. Although Clausius thought Williamson's dissociation model too speculative, it did give chemical credence to his model of the partial dissociation of electrolytes.

Hittorf embraced this Clausius–Williamson hypothesis enthusiastically, thus ensuring that, fifteen years later when reading the literature on electrolysis, Arrhenius would become well aware of it. Hittorf was also struck by the emerging analogy between the behaviour of solutions and Clausius' kinetic theory of gases. 'The analogies between substances in solution and gaseous substances', he wrote, 'force themselves on the attention of every one who is concerned with the exact study of the phenomena of solutions.' This was also to strike van't Hoff.

Hittorf's transport numbers only gave a measure of the relative velocities with which ions moved. With the adoption by physicists of Ohm's law relating current, voltage and resistance in the 1830s and the development of the Wheatstone bridge circuit in electric telegraphy in the same decade, it became feasible to determine the absolute speeds of ions through the measurement of the conductivities of solutions. (Conductivity is merely the reciprocal of the resistivity.) Early attempts to do this, however, met with the severe problem of polarization – that is, secondary gassing reactions at the electrodes caused extra resistance and interfered with the precise measurements. A satisfactory solution to this problem was found only in 1868 when the great German practical physicist, Friedrich Kohlrausch (1820–1910), eliminated polarization by using alternating currents generated by an induction coil. His results were calculated as 'molecular conductivities', λ; that is, concentrations were expressed as the molecular weight (in fact, initially, as equivalent weights) in grams per litre, $\lambda = k/m$, where k is the measured specific conductivity.

By studying molecular conductivity at constant temperatures for different concentrations, he found that λ increased with dilutions up to a limiting maximum λ_∞. He offered no explanation for this interesting increase. More intriguingly still, in 1875, Kohlrausch was able to show that λ_∞ was the sum of two constants, u and v, contributed by the cation and the anion respectively. He obtained this surprising result by comparing the conductivities of two electrolytes possessing common anions or cations, e.g.

KCl,	$\lambda_\infty = 140$	KNO_3,	$\lambda_\infty = 126$
NaCl,	$\lambda_\infty = 120$	$NaNO_3$,	$\lambda_\infty = 105$

The ions moved independently with their own definite velocities. This 'law of independent migration of ions' was another inexplicable empirical finding unless interpreted as a further example of the Clausius–Williamson effect, or as somehow due to the association of molecules of the solute and solvent.

THE IONIC THEORY

The former, and ultimately simpler, explanation was Arrhenius' interpretation in the thesis he presented at the University of Uppsala in 1884. The precocious and rather plump son of an estate manager, Svante Arrhenius (1859–1927) learned his chemistry at Uppsala from Per Cleve, a Swedish chemist interested in the rare earths. (He was to isolate holmium and thulium in 1879.) It had stuck in Arrhenius' mind that Cleve had stated in lectures that Raoult's methods did not allow the determination of the molecular weights of substances like cane sugar. (Nor could they be determined by vapour densities since they would not volatilize without decomposition.) In 1881, when Arrhenius began doctoral studies involving electrochemistry with the physicist Eric Edlund, he decided to see whether molecular weights of non-electrolytes like cane sugar could be determined from their lowering of molecular conductivities when mixed with a salt of known conductivity. Although, as so often in the history of science, he was unable to solve his starting problem, his experimental investigations revealed that molecular conductivities increased with dilution.

From an experimental point of view, although Arrhenius' thesis considerably extended Kohlrausch's measurements for dilute solutions and ranged over some forty-seven different electrolytes, it did little beyond confirming Kohlrausch's suggestion that dilution tended to increase the conductivities of electrolytes. However, in the second, more theoretical, part of his thesis, 'Théorie chimique des electrolytes', Arrhenius argued that his and Kohlrausch's measurements were only explicable if, following Clausius–Williamson, a salt solution was assumed to be a mixture of 'active' (electrolytes) and 'inactive' (non-electrolytes) parts. On dilution, the numbers of active parts were increased; in other words, electrolytic dissociation increased with dilution.

> All salts exist in solution as complex molecules, which
> in part decompose on dilution. With the help of this
> representation the properties of salts at all dilutions
> are explained, also the properties of all electrolytes at
> sufficiently high concentrations.

It is important to notice the reference to 'complex molecules', not ions, since it shows that at this stage (1884) Arrhenius probably thought that solutions involved the formation of chemical hydrates between solute and solvent (water), a theory that Mendeleev was then actively pursuing. As Mendeleev's and Raoult's work suggests, *a priori* there was no essential reason why solution phenomena had to be explained in terms of dissociation.

Born in German-speaking Riga, Latvia, which was then part of Russia, Ostwald (1853–1932) obtained his doctorate in chemistry at the University of Dorpat (now in Estonia). Many historians have commented on the similarities in background between Arrhenius, van't Hoff and Ostwald. Each was educated in the 'Scandinavian' margins of European science, the advantage of which was that they were less indoctrinated by central European scientific tradition. As Ostwald once commented, had he been born in Germany he would undoubtedly have become an organic chemist (and by implication, a dull one) and never have founded the *Zeitschrift für physikalische Chemie* in 1887. University studies on the perimeter also had the advantage, it would seem, of including physics, or natural philosophy, on the syllabus for chemists. It is one of the ironies of the history of chemistry, therefore, that the ionic theory was to find its ultimate justification in the atomic theory of matter that Ostwald strongly opposed until his capitulation in 1909. Like van't Hoff, Ostwald had been determined to solve the problem of chemical affinity. In making this the subject of his doctoral thesis in 1877, Ostwald had stumbled across the virtually unknown work of the Norwegian brothers-in-law, Cato Guldberg (1836–1902) and Peter Waage (1833–1900), the former a mathematician, the latter a chemist. It was through Ostwald's reference to their work that van't Hoff had been enabled to reinterpret the Norwegians' work thermodynamically.

As was the tradition then and now, Arrhenius sent copies of his thesis to Europe's leading electrochemists, including Ostwald at Riga, van't Hoff in Amsterdam and Oliver Lodge in Britain. Ostwald was excited since it offered an explanation of research he was completing on the neutralization of acids and bases, and sufficiently impressed to visit Arrhenius and to offer him a teaching position (Privatdocent-ship) at Riga for the sessions 1884 to 1886; while Lodge, though critical, made an English abstract for publication in the *Reports of the British Association for the Advancement of Science*. Since Ostwald was already well known as a rising chemist, his offer to Arrhenius proved embarrassing to his former examiners. They reasoned, perhaps, that it might prove even more embarrassing one day if Arrhenius disciplined himself and became famous. Face was to be saved by awarding Arrhenius a generous five-year travelling scholarship, which enabled him to spend time with Ostwald at Riga (where he consolidated his academic respectability by publishing and extending parts of his thesis). From there, between 1886 and 1891, he worked with Kohlrausch at Wurzburg and van't Hoff in Amsterdam before rejoining Ostwald in Leipzig. His growing friendship with van't Hoff led to the exchange of offprints and letters and, hence, to Arrhenius' famous commentary on van't Hoff's papers of 1886 in March 1887.

It was only in this letter to van't Hoff that Arrhenius articulated the full theory of ionic dissociation that he presented in the paper 'On the dissociation of substances dissolved in water'. In this he suggested that, just as a gas deviates from ideal laws when assumed to be undergoing dissociation by heat, 'the same expedient' could be used to explain van't Hoff's abnormal results for vapour and osmotic determinations of electrolytes.

> An assumption of the dissociation of certain substances dissolved in water, is strongly supported by the conclusions drawn from the electrical properties of the same substances.

If the number of dissociated ions could be calculated, it would be possible to calculate the osmotic pressure. Since maximum conductivity occurred at infinite dilution (when complete dissociation into ions could be assumed), the activity coefficient, α (or ratio of active to inactive molecules), could be taken as unity at that limit. For more concentrated solutions, α was less than unity. Van't Hoff's correction factor, i, could then be interpreted as the ratio between the observed osmotic pressure and the pressure the substance would exert if it consisted only of undissociated molecules. The same argument applied to Raoult's freezing point values. If m represented the undissociated molecules, n the dissociated ones and k the number of ions (viz. $k = 2$ for KCl, $k = 3$ for K_2SO_4), then

$$i = (m + kn)/m + n$$

This equation could be immediately linked with Arrhenius' measurable activity coefficients, since

$$\alpha = n/m + n \qquad \text{and} \qquad i = 1 + \alpha(k - 1)$$

Comparisons of the values of i derived from conductivities, osmotic pressures and freezing point lowerings agreed with one another within the limits of experimental error (e.g. temperatures were different) and providing a dilute enough solution was chosen (table 10.5). On this evidence Arrhenius drew the conclusion that his thesis concerning ionization was proven. The sole difference between this and gaseous dissociation was that, in a solution, active molecules (ions) were charged particles.

TABLE 10.5   *Comparison of* i *values made by Arrhenius.*

		i (freezing)	$i = (k - 1)\,\alpha$
Bases (15)			
Barium Hydroxide	$Ba\,(OH)_2$	2.69	2.67
Sodium hydroxide	$NaOH$	1.96	1.88
Ammonia	NH_3	1.03	1.01
Methylamine	CH_3NH_2	1.00	1.03
Acids (23)			
Hydrochloric	HCl	1.98	1.90
Nitric	HNO_3	1.94	1.92
Sulphuric	H_2SO_4	2.06	2.19
Acetic	CH_3COOH	1.03	1.01
Salts (40)			
Potassium chloride	KCl	1.82	1.86
Sodium chloride	$NaCl$	1.90	1.82
Potassium cyanide	KCN	1.74	1.88
Ammonium sulphate	$(NH_4)_2SO_4$	2.00	2.17
Organic compounds (12)			
Methyl alcohol	CH_3OH	0.94	1.00
Ethyl alcohol	C_2H_5OH	0.94	1.00
Acetone	C_2H_5CHO	0.92	1.00

(Ionic potassium in potassium chloride was, therefore, different from atomic potassium, and would not attack the water solvent in the usual spectacular way!) For this reason the theory came to be known as the theory of ionic dissociation.

All this was summed up in a German paper of 1887, 'On the dissociation of substances dissolved in water'. As Root-Bernstein has argued, in this paper, as well as in the writings of Ostwald, Arrhenius gave the impression that he had already articulated a theory of ionic dissociation in his thesis three years earlier, whereas he had gone little further than Raoult with his 'chemically-separated molecules'. There seems little doubt that Arrhenius was anxious to protect his priority against the physicist, Max Planck, who had independently arrived at the necessity of dissociation in dilute solutions from thermodynamic reasoning. Ostwald naturally sided with Arrhenius because both his and van't Hoff's work were dependent on its firm establishment. The new theory gave an elegant and simple explanation of Hittorf's and Kohlrausch's results, for 'the properties of a salt are the sum of the properties of the ions'. Such a slogan, together with the sense that the ionists were part of a historical tradition going back to Faraday and Volta, proved a powerful argument in favour of ionization as a mechanism. Chemists were easily able to verify from the literature and from new experiments on properties such as specific gravity, the alteration in volume when acids were neutralized by bases, the specific refractive power of salt solutions and the absorptive power of solutions that such powers were, indeed, additive.

From 1887 until his appointment as a teacher in the Technical High School in Stockholm in 1891, Arrhenius made several other valuable contributions to, and applications of, his theory and its defence. But with increasing age, rotundity and academic stature, he found wider fields to conquer that allowed him to indulge his strong speculative streak. Following his appointment in 1905 as

Director of the Physical Chemistry Department of the newly created Nobel Institute in Stockholm – he had been awarded the Nobel prize for chemistry in 1903 – he increasingly turned to the writing of popular accounts of science and to the applications of chemistry to geology, astronomy and biology. Many of his ideas here are still stimulating to read.

He did, however, make one further crucial contribution to theoretical chemistry in 1889. In a study of the inversion of cane sugar by weak acids, Arrhenius used van't Hoff's derivation for the rate constant

$$k = Ae^{-E/RT}$$

which is now known rather unfairly as 'Arrhenius' equation'. Arrhenius realized that only a deeper study of the effects of temperature on reaction velocities would lead to a complete understanding of reaction mechanisms. Although he did not need to introduce ionic mechanisms, it is interesting to see that he once again appealed to the idea of 'active molecules' – meaning now molecules with extra energy – to promote a chemical reaction. This concept of activated molecules and of an 'activated state' was to play á decisive role in the understanding of reaction mechanisms a few years after his death in 1927.

Meanwhile, at Leipzig, where Ostwald had become Director of a Physical Chemical Institute in 1887, and to which large numbers of British and American students flocked to study, the great entrepreneur of physical chemistry applied the electrolytic theory to the study of acids. He confirmed Arrhenius' finding that at infinite dilution the molecular conductivities of all acids were the same. He then reasoned that, since the dissociation theory explained the variations from the ideal gas laws that electrolytes displayed, it ought to be possible to apply the thermodynamic equation for a partly dissociated gas to a partly ionized solution. We need not follow the mathematical reasoning involved, but from it Ostwald deduced in 1887 the famous 'dilution law'

$$\alpha^2/(1 - \alpha)v = k \qquad \text{(a constant)}$$

where α was Arrhenius' degree of ionization (the formerly named activity coefficient) and v the volume of solution in litres containing a gram molecule [mole] of the electrolyte. Experimental tests confirmed the relationship for some 250 organic acids; e.g. see table 10.6.

TABLE 10.6   Ostwald's values for acetic acid.

v	α	k
8	1.193	0.00180
16	1.673	0.00179
32	2.38	0.00182
1024	12.66	0.00177
	average	0.00179

Ostwald's dilution law was to have wide application, particularly after he realized the following year that the constant, k, was the equilibrium constant, which could therefore be used as a measure of the relative strengths of acids and bases. A good deal of analytical chemistry relied upon volumetric titrations of acids and bases. Here the essential ionic exchange was assumed to be

$$H_2O \leftrightharpoons H^+ + OH^- \rightleftharpoons$$

Because the measured molecular conductivity of water was extremely low (about 10^{-5}) and its degree of dissociation about 10^{-8}, Ostwald's dilution law could be simplified to

$$k = \alpha^2/v$$

This allowed the equilibrium dissociation formula

$$k = [H^+][OH^-]/[H_2O]$$

to be reduced to

$$k = [H^+][OH^-]$$

because [H_2O] was constant. The 'ionic product' for water was therefore constant at particular temperatures. In practice, this was determined as 10^{-14} mol$^2/\ell^2$, so giving a hydrogen ion concentration of [H^+] = 10^{-7}.

Although various investigators had suggested that hydrogen ion concentrations could be used as indicators of the strengths of acids and bases, and the hydrogen electrode had become the standard for the measurement of electrode potentials by the early 1900s, it was not until 1909 that the Danish biochemist, Soren Sørensen (1868–1939), suggested the removal of the awkward negative index by taking the negative logarithm of [H^+] to form a scale. The *power* could then be represented by a 'pH' scale in which 7 was neutral, and 1 and 14 were the extremes of acidity and alkalinity, respectively.

The pH scale proved immediately acceptable and useful within the biochemical research community, which was fascinated by the ability of living tissues to 'buffer' against excessive acidity or alkalinity. It was not, however, until the German medical chemist, Leonor Michaelis (1875–1949), published a book on hydrogen ion concentration in 1914 that the scale became familiar to chemists. Michaelis' emigration to the United States in 1926 helped in this assimilation, as did the development by Arnold Beckman (*b.* 1900) in 1935 of a simple portable direct-reading pH meter.

THE RECEPTION OF THE IONIC THEORY

As Ostwald's first British pupil and disciple the Scot, James Walker (1863–1935), had the unenviable responsibility of being the chief English-speaking protagonist of the new physical chemistry. He proved an able propagandist, chiefly through his translation in 1890 of Ostwald's textbook, *Outlines of General Chemistry,* and most noticeably through his own readable text, *Introduction to Physical Chemistry* (1899), which went through ten editions and became a set book in most British university chemistry courses until the 1930s. By 1902, nine English-language textbooks had been published and Ostwald's 'chemistry of the future' seemed well established. William Ramsay's research school at University College, London, also gave houseroom to many of Ostwald's British doctoral students before they moved into regular academic positions.

One of the problems with the ionic theory was thrown into sharp relief by the dilution law: strong electrolytes simply did not obey the law, and therefore the law of mass action. How was this possible for electrolytes, which by definition strongly conducted electricity?

In retrospect it is possible to see that the ionic theory developed back to front. Today, when the electrolytic theory of solutions is taught, the student is first introduced to strong electrolytes – that is, to substances with stable ionic bonds with ions already present in the solid crystalline state – and told that they are completely ionized in solution. The complications of solvent interaction are not minimized and the fairly complicated equations of Debye and Hückel and Onsager are derived. Then, and only then, does the student learn about the simplifying cases of dilute solutions and the partial ionization that occurs with weak electrolytes. Today, Arrhenius' ionic theory is seen as only a small part of the chemistry of solutions. Given this broader picture, it is little wonder that the original ionic theory, and by implication the whole programme of physical chemistry, met with considerable opposition.

This opposition took both scientific and social forms. In Germany, the hostility had rather less to do with theory than with the fact that Ostwald's claims for the primary status of physical chemistry seemed to pose a threat to the comfortable lives of organic chemists. In France, because of the political hostility towards German culture after their defeat in the Franco-Prussian war, the ionic theory met with indifference. An interesting indicator here is that, although van't Hoff published the first edition of his chemical dynamics in French in 1884, possibly supposing that German chemists were too engrossed in organic synthesis to be interested, the second edition published in 1896 appeared in German. (An English translation also appeared the same year.) In Russia, Mendeleev, by then the most powerful and respected chemist in the country, had, since 1865, been developing his own hydrate theory to explain the properties of solutions. In this theory, the anomalies of freezing points and other colligative properties were attributed to the formation of different hydrate compounds at different temperatures. Meanwhile, in Britain, the ionic theory underwent intense scrutiny at debates held by the British Association for the Advancement of Science and in the pages of *Nature*. Much of the criticism of physicists such as George Fitzgerald centred on 'the dynamically-impossible idea that the ions are free'; but on the whole physicists were sympathetic.

Both Spencer Pickering and Henry Armstrong rejected ionization and replaced it with models that involved association between the molecules of the solute and the water solvent through a mechanism of residual affinity. Pickering argued that the lowering of vapour pressures or freezing points could be explained just as satisfactorily by a chemical theory that avoided invoking the gas-solution analogy of van't Hoff. If molecules of the solute formed non-volatile hydrates with a proportion of solvent molecules, it was, he pointed out, possible to derive van't Hoff's equation

$$\delta p/p = n/N$$

where δp was the lowering of pressure (or freezing point) for pressure p, and n and N the numbers of molecules of solute and solvent. But it was another twenty years before physical chemists came to understand that the analogy really depended upon how far molecules and ions came within each others' spheres of action.

For his part, Armstrong explained the abnormal osmotic

pressure of electrolytes as due to the formation of 'hydrone', a loose, polymerized form of water. However, neither he nor Pickering was able or willing to develop their models quantitatively to produce the match between theory and experiment achieved by the physical-chemical school for dilute solutions. Armstrong was pretty explicit that he disliked the new approach for philosophical and social reasons, as well as scientific ones. He spent the remainder of his long life attacking the 'ionists' at every opportunity. As he wrote in 1936, only a year before his death[4]:

> The fact is, there has been a split of chemistry into two schools since the intrusion of the Arrhenic faith, rather it should be said, the addition of a new class of worker into our profession – people without knowledge of the laboratory arts and with sufficient mathematics at their command to be led astray by curvilinear agreements; without the ability to criticise, still less of giving any chemical interpretation. The fact is, the physical chemists never use their eyes and are most lamentably lacking in chemical culture. It is essential to cast out from our midst, root and branch, this physical element and return to our laboratories.

In calling for such a witch hunt, Armstrong was no more happy in 1936 that the *scientific* problems of strong electrolytes had been resolved. To him, physical chemistry, with its mathematical symbolism, extrapolations and speculative theories, had caused chemistry to lose its tactile, sensuous base in the laboratory. This was the voice of the organic chemist; but as we shall see, even organic chemistry had been affected by physical chemistry when this remark was made. In general, the ionists' strategy, at least in their textbooks, was to present their arguments without reference to possible alternative explanations, like the association and hydration theories advanced by British critics. Only occasionally, as the New Zealander, J. W. Mellor, did in his outstanding *Chemical Statics and Dynamics*

(1902), was the reader referred to a different point of view – in this case, that of Kahlenberg.

The American, Louis Kahlenberg (1870–1941), of the University of Wisconsin, was fated to live out much of his career as an iconoclast. Ironically, Kahlenberg, the son of German immigrants to the United States, had received his doctoral training in Ostwald's Leipzig laboratory in 1894–5. He had returned, like all of Ostwald's students, a convinced ionist; he was the only one to oppose it with all the energy and bitterness of a man who had lost his faith in the one true church.

As John Servos has shown, America took to physical chemistry like a duck to water, not because college Presidents and Deans believed it to be the chemistry of the future (as Ostwald had claimed) or because America's then still primitive chemical industry was demanding its insights, but simply because American universities were in a phase of amazing expansion. With college enrolments increasing beyond anything known before, there were plenty of jobs for academically qualified chemists. More often than not, therefore, American chemists returning with their Leipzig doctorates began their careers teaching basic chemical analysis and inorganic chemistry. But they were able to use this as a basis later for introducing independent physical chemistry courses or, by underwriting qualitative analysis with explanations in terms of ions, equilibria and solubility products (as Ostwald had done in *Die wissenschaftlichen Grundlagen der analytischen Chemie* in 1894) in order to draw students' interests into thermodynamics and kinetics. Not without reasons did Armstrong come to view American developments with deep suspicion.

When Kahlenberg began to attract research students of his own at the University of Wisconsin, he rapidly became disillusioned by Arrhenius' theory. In his electrical researches, Michael Faraday had referred to the 'specific inductive capacity' of media such as glass or air. This constant factor, k, reduced the Coulomb force of attraction or repulsion between electrical charges separated by the medium, or dielectric, according to

$$f = i_1 i_2 / k r^2$$

In liquid media, this factor had come to be called the dielectric constant. In 1893, one of Ostwald's most enthusiastic disciples, Hermann Walther Nernst (1864–1941), an Associate Professor of Physics (and from 1894, Professor of Physical Chemistry) at the University of Göttingen, measured the dielectric constants of various liquids. Nernst found, as did J. J. Thomson in England at the same time, that solvents with high dielectric constants encouraged the ionization of solutes. This seemed to make good sense, for a high dielectric constant would reduce the forces of attraction between ions and allow them to separate more readily.

In 1901, in heroically dangerous work, Kahlenberg and his students measured the dielectric constant of liquid hydrogen cyanide during a frozen Madison winter. It proved to be higher (92) than that of water (80), but *not* as good as water in causing dissociation. In fact, Ostwald had already forestalled this difficulty in his *Grundriss der allgemeinen Chemie* (1899) by declaring categorically that the ionic theory applied only to aqueous solutions. The fact remained, though, that non-aqueous solvents did conduct electricity. And so Kahlenberg began a long-term research programme in which he acquired experimental results so markedly different from those of aqueous solutions that by 1901 he had concluded that the ionic theory itself was defective. An intense redetermination of conductivities and freezing point values for dilute solutions confirmed Kahlenberg's suspicions that, while dilution tended to increase conductivity, over a large range of conductivities all sorts of startling anomalies could be discovered. Although the figures for the degree of dissociation of a strong electrolyte, as calculated from the lowering of freezing points, roughly agreed with those obtained from conductivity measurements, the variation with concentration did not agree with the law of mass action at all. In 1901 he announced categorically that the ionic theory was insufficient to explain all experimental measurements and attacked van't Hoff for having seriously misled investigators with the gas-solution analogy. A satisfactory solution would have to include a role for the solvent.

For a few years Kahlenberg, a belligerent man who loved a good fight, found a platform among the more empirically minded industrial members of the Electrochemical Society of America that had been founded in 1902. He was also allowed to express his dissenting views freely in the *Journal of Physical Chemistry*, which another American Ostwald pupil, Wilder Bancroft, had founded in 1896. Bancroft was often criticized by colleagues such as Arthur Noyes of the Massachusetts Institutue of Technology (MIT) and Harry Jones of Johns Hopkins University for allowing Kahlenberg's critical opinions to be voiced for all to see. Bancroft's stoic refusal to capitulate to his fellow-ionists' pressure eventually led the ionists to move their papers to the *American Chemical Journal* or the *Journal of the American Chemical Society*. (The two journals merged in 1912.) Lack of broad support for Bancroft's journal brought financial difficulties, and although during the 1920s Bancroft was able to gather some formal (though not financial) international support, in 1932 he was forced to sell the *Journal of Physical Chemistry* to the American Chemical Society. The Society then immediately found its accession facing very stiff competition from the *Journal of Chemical Physics*, whose first volume in 1933 contained three of Linus Pauling's papers on the nature of the chemical bond.

By then Kahlenberg had been ignored and ostracized by the second generation of American physical chemists who had emerged around Noyes and G. N. Lewis at MIT and, later, the University of California. These chemists decided that, whatever its flaws, the ionic theory was extremely useful. As Lewis said in 1906[5]:

> Perfection is rare in the science of chemistry. Our scientific theories do not spring full-armed from the brow of the creator. They are subject to slow and gradual growth, and we must candidly admit that the ionic theory in its growth has reached the 'awkward age'. Instead, however, of judging it according to the standard of perfection, let us simply ask what it has accomplished, and what it may accomplish in scientific service.

The historian could hardly wish for a better statement of the fact that scientific theories are only displaced when there is consensus that an alternative viewpoint will be more useful.

One ionist for whom this pragmatism was unsatisfactory was Harry Jones, to whom chemistry was 'essentially a science of the ion'. A work fanatic, Jones published streams of textbooks and research papers on the theory of solutions. Despite his ardent advocacy of the theory, even he came to recognize that some better explanation of the behaviour of strong electrolytes was necessary. From 1900 onwards he developed a 'new hydrate theory' according to which, at high concentrations, electrolytes formed hydrates, which, therefore, effectively reduced the amount of solvent and proportionally lowered the freezing point or vapour pressure and increased the conductivity. Critics from his own camp quickly pointed out that Jones did not understand the law of mass action, for surely the greatest degree of hydration would be at infinite dilution? Hostile reviews, not merely from Kahlenberg, drove Jones into dark depression and he committed suicide in 1916. The case of Jones suggests that not all of the new physical chemists understood what they were dealing with. One is reminded of the story told by William Ramsay's pupil and biographer, Morris Travers, that for a whole year

Ramsay was unaware of the difference between molecules and ions.

Kahlenberg had, of course, been quite right in his assessment. In fact, serious anomalies in Ostwald's dilution law were already being quietly treated through the use of empirical 'quick-fit' formulae such as that devised by M. Rudolphi in 1895. As a young student in 1910 in Nernst's laboratory, the future historian, J. R. Partington, was also to invent such formulae for the anomalous behaviour of strong electrolytes. The physical meaning of the correction factors applied remained a mystery until two new insights became available. In 1909 the Dane, Niels Bjerrum (1879–1958), whose son, Jannik, became a distinguished co-ordination chemist, reported an investigation of the absorption spectra of chromium salts in different aqueous solution concentrations. Since the light absorbed remained constant, he argued that these salts (all strong electrolytes) must already be completely dissociated. If so, the variations in conductivities and freezing point depressions that Kahlenberg and others had reported had to be explained by inter-ionic forces. Arrhenius, who was present when Bjerrum read the paper in London, is said to have taken it as a personal affront on his work. In fact, the effects of inter-ionic forces had already been explored in some curiously incomprehensible papers in the *Philosophical Magazine* by an Australian physicist, William Sutherland, in 1902.

Bjerrum's suggestion received more positive support with the advent of X-ray crystallography by the Braggs in 1912. X-ray photographs revealed the ionic nature of many crystalline solids. It was then apparent that the so-called strong electrolytes were already completely dissociated; hence the difficulty of applying the mass law to their behaviour. This confirmation enabled S. R. Milner at the University of Sheffield to develop a mathematical model of inter-ionic action between solute ions and the solvent between 1912 and 1919. Although Bjerrum interpreted

Milner's work for chemists in 1918, he published in Danish and therefore made little impact. However, in a Faraday Society discussion of the status of the ionic theory in 1919, Arrhenius made it clear that he dismissed inter-ionic effects as unimportant. He rested his case upon his original explanation still giving an adequate explanation of experimental results over good ranges of concentrations. This was patently not the experience of other investigators by this time.

At this stage a young Indian chemist at the University of Calcutta, J. Chandra Ghosh (*d.* 1959), published four papers in the *Journal of the Chemical Society*. In these he assumed that the solid crystalline lattice of strong electrolytes was effectively preserved in solution. This assumption simplified the calculation of inter-ionic forces between solvent and solute and led to the Ghosh equation for the conductance ratio of a binary electrolyte. Ghosh's model and equation were taken up enthusiastically by textbook writers, but within a few years it was shown that there were not only errors in Ghosh's mathematics but that he had misquoted others' experimental data. The whole episode was an embarrassing mistake; Ghosh's equation quickly vanished from textbooks and from history. It is ignored by Partington, even though he was personally involved in such research. Ghosh himself went on to have a distinguished career as a scientific administrator in India.

Mistakes in the history of science can, however, be influential. It was Ghosh's equation that caught the attention of the Dutch physical chemist, Peter Debye (1884–1966). Together with Erich Hückel (who was later to develop molecular orbital theory for chemists), Debye re-examined and simplified Milner's model and developed a new function based upon the statistical interference of neighbouring ions on ionic mobilities. Although this model and its equations had to be further refined for non-aqueous solvents by Lars Onsager in 1927, to all intents and purposes the theory of solutions was complete by 1923, four years before Arrhenius' death in 1927. Ironically, neither Kahlenberg, who remained teaching at Wisconsin until 1940, nor Armstrong ever admitted the solution had been found.

How to Teach Chemistry

> Why only last term we sent a man who had never
> been in a laboratory in his life as senior science master
> at one of our leading public schools. He came [to this
> Scholastic Agency] wanting to do private coaching in
> music. He's doing very well I believe.
>
> (EVELYN WAUGH, *Decline and Fall*, 1928)

Evelyn Waugh might well have had John Christie in mind
when he satirized English public school teaching in his
novel, for Christie, albeit a Cambridge science graduate, had
taught science inexpertly at Eton College for many years
before founding the famous opera house at his country
seat at Glyndebourne. As the careers of Sedgwick, Buckland
and Murchison in geology, and Benjamin Silliman and
Amos Eaton in chemistry, attest, it can sometimes be
advantageous not to know anything about a subject in
order to teach it well; but this aside, by the 1930s there
was no excuse for teaching chemistry or any of the sciences
inefficiently or from ignorance, or for schools, colleges and
universities to appoint unqualified people.

Internationally speaking, the most significant contribution to the teaching of chemistry had come from
Cannizzaro, whose course at the University of Genoa
based upon a standard two-volume molecule derived from
Avogadro's hypothesis, that equal volumes of gases at the
same temperature and pressure contained the same number
of molecules, was publicized at the Karlsruhe chemical
congress in 1860. By adopting Avogadro's hypothesis and
Cannizzaro's distinction between atoms and molecules as
the underlying thread of their courses, the chemists of

the 1860s were able to unify and consolidate chemical formulae, to develop and build upon the concept of valency, to facilitate their understanding of the structures of organic molecules, and to reorganize inorganic chemistry on the basis of the periodic law. In his lectures at the Royal College of Chemistry, for example, A. W. Hofmann reformed the teaching of elementary teaching by relating all gas volumes to a new measure he called the *crith* (a barley corn), the weight of one litre of hydrogen (0.896 grams), and showing how it facilitated chemical calculations derived from chemical equations.

In Britain, besides Hofmann, who was to return to Germany in 1865, the two path-breakers in the teaching of chemistry were Edward Frankland and Henry Edward Armstrong, both of whom built upon the German experience and precedent of Liebig's great teaching laboratory at Giessen. This chapter therefore focuses on the development of chemistry teaching in the nineteenth and early twentieth centuries, the growth of laboratories, and the internationalization of approaches to chemistry teaching in the 1960s.

FRANKLAND'S STATE-SPONSORED CHEMISTRY

'I have not yet completely shaken off the effects' of lecturing at the Royal Institution, wrote Edward Frankland to his London friend, John Tyndall, in 1855, two years after first lecturing in London. 'For a whole year', he continued, 'I suffered severely from indigestion brought on by the continuing stress and anxiety attending these lectures.' Frankland had given these lectures while he was a Professor of Chemistry at Owen's College, Manchester, and ten years before he was made a Professor at the Royal Institution in 1863. Frankland's comment reveals something of the 'aweful' reputation that the 'semi-circular fountain of eloquence', the Royal Institution, had become under Michael Faraday's inspiring regime. A man of science needed (and still needs) endurance, courage and mettle to perform before this critical London audience.

Frankland's remarks perhaps suggest that he was a nervous and poor lecturer. Indeed, although he claimed later in life to enjoy lecturing above peripatetic laboratory teaching (which he seems to have left to assistants whenever possible), he undoubtedly never shone as a lecturer. He was certainly outshone in his own day by his X-Club friends, John Tyndall and Thomas Henry Huxley. For the same reason, perhaps, although Frankland became associated with the Royal Institution for six years, he is not one of the 'household names' like Davy, Faraday, Tyndall or James Dewar that are automatically associated with it by historians. Instead, we place Frankland alongside figures like William Odling, John Hall Gladstone, or even Huxley, who only spent brief parts of their careers at the Royal Institution. In actual fact, Frankland described his years in Albemarle Street as 'the happiest in my life', while the scientific work he did there on organic synthesis was, in chemical terms, as important as Faraday's on electromagnetism.

Frankland had three overlapping and interpenetrating careers: first, as a research chemist in organo-metallic, synthetic organic chemistry and valency theory; secondly, as a water analyst and official government adviser on river pollution; and thirdly, as a teacher of chemistry. How does history rate him as a teacher and communicator? We all know from personal experience that poor lecturers are not necessarily poor teachers; indeed, like Frankland, they are often good teachers because they find ways of compensating for their inadequacies as theatrical performers.

Frankland was born in Lancashire in 1825. His illegitimacy and his mother's straitened circumstances inevitably led to a disjointed education until, after being advised by one friendly schoolmaster to advance himself by becoming a doctor, Frankland's stepfather apprenticed him to a Lancaster druggist in 1840. Frankland later claimed to have learned little during his apprenticeship. But as C. A. Russell has argued, this has to be taken with a pinch of salt, for he attended classes at the local Mechanics Institute and he undoubtedly benefited (as Armstrong suspected) from the manual work and dexterity involved in the preparation of drugs.

In the event, Frankland qualified in neither pharmacy nor medicine, for in 1845 the local medical grapevine found him employment in Lyon Playfair's tiny laboratory at the Government Museum of Economic Geology in London. Here he received his first sophisticated training in chemical manipulation and he had the good fortune to meet the young German chemist, Hermann Kolbe, who had been sent to England by Robert Bunsen in order to assist the British government's enquiries into the nature of coal-mine gas explosions. Kolbe taught Frankland how to analyse gases, began his agnostic education (completed later by Tyndall) and took him for a vacation to Marburg to meet Bunsen in the summer of 1847.

From 1847 to 1848 Frankland was a schoolmaster at the enterprising Quaker school in Hampshire known as Queenwood College, which, if not the first school in Britain to teach science through practical laboratory and workshop practice, was undoubtedly the first to do so on such an extensive scale. During its lifetime the College gave employment to a number of young scientists, several of whom became Fellows of the Royal Society (like Bunsen's pupil Heinrich Debus) and distinguished for research as well as teaching. One of Frankland's fellow teachers was the physicist, John Tyndall, with whom he made a mutual improvement pact and life-long friendship. In 1848 they both abandoned school teaching to take doctorates at Bunsen's university at Marburg.

In 1851, following a brief period at a private engineering college, Frankland was appointed first Professor of Chemistry at Owen's College, Manchester, from where, in 1852, he published his important paper on the combining powers of atoms. Manchester gave Frankland the opportunity for further research in organic chemistry, the opportunity to interest himself in technical chemistry, and the chance to earn a reputation, albeit a slightly infamous one locally, as a scientific witness in the law courts.

The career of expert witness, or consultant chemist, became an important one in the nineteenth century; but it carried with it the danger that, becoming used to being given problems *ad hoc,* it could become difficult (as Lyon Playfair found at the University of Edinburgh after 1853) to give other people problems, and therefore to direct a research programme. Fortunately, despite the heavy calls upon his time, by 1855 Frankland had developed a small research school working on gas analysis and organo-metallic chemistry. Such activity was financed by the Royal Society's new Parliamentary Grant, which, in Frankland's words, enabled him to 'pitch commerce to the devil as much as I can afford'.

However, all was not well, for there was still the bugbear of elementary teaching:

> . . . to be eternally dragging mere children through the five Groups [of qualitative analysis] and no further is mere mechanical work, scarcely superior to breaking stones, and I feel it to be for me a waste of time.

No doubt Frankland felt himself cut off from the mainstream of scientific life in London. Russell has argued that Frankland's ideas on valency lacked impact in the 1850s because of his absence from London during the crucial period of Kekulé's residence there between 1853 and 1855. But Frankland was no Liebig and could not give up elementary teaching for several further years.

In 1857 he abandoned Manchester to seek his fortune in the capital – a wrench that did not please Owen's College at all (though Manchester manufacturers who had suffered prosecutions for air pollution at his hands were glad to see the back of him). The paralysis of John Stenhouse (Kekulé's former employer at St Bartholomew's Hospital) had forced Stenhouse to resign; and, through Tyndall, Frankland took up the hospital lectureship in chemistry. There were three lectures a week and no practical teaching. The salary proving insufficient, Frankland added the teaching of chemistry and physics to military cadets at Addiscombe College in Croydon. Neither of these two lectureships carried any kudos. However, the London venture paid off in May 1863 when he was made Professor of Chemistry at the Royal Institution. This 'accomplished chemical pluralist' (as *The Lancet* dubbed him) now had three jobs. 'I recall', said Frankland:

> becoming quite at home in this triple duty, and rather wishing that it could be made quadruple, by interpolating another lecture between St. Bartholomew's (or Addiscombe 10.00 a.m.) and the Royal Institution (3.00 p.m.), as it was quite impossible to settle down to research during this interval.

In 1864 Addiscombe was closed down, while the exciting pace of research at the Royal Institution forced him to resign some of his duties at St Bartholomew's to William Odling. Thus by 1864, Frankland's income was reduced to £200 p.a., forcing him to return to consulting work – jobs he called 'India rubbers' following a lucrative patent trial in Scotland concerning the vulcanization of India rubber. Undoubtedly it was his precarious financial position that made him think seriously about what was described in the 1870s as 'the endowment of research' question and also to prick up his ears when he heard of Hofmann's plans to return to Germany. In 1865 he succeeded Hofmann as Professor of Chemistry at the government-financed Royal College of Chemistry in Oxford Street, a post he held through the College's many transformations until his retirement in 1885. Despite occupying what was perhaps the most prestigious Chair of Chemistry in Great Britain, the taste for pluralism never left Frankland. He stayed on at the Royal Institution until 1869, having the year before joined an important Royal Commission on Rivers

Pollution. It was probably for his 'India rubber' work as a public water analyst, rather than as an organic chemist, that he was knighted in Queen Victoria's Diamond Jubilee Birthday Honours list in 1897. Frankland died in Norway in 1899 while dictating his memoirs to his mistress.

Like most of his colleagues in the X-Club, a small dining club founded in 1864, Frankland saw science education as a key factor in the future professionalization of science. 'Scientific education', wrote the young assayer and future economist, William Stanley Jevons:

> is one of the best things possible for any man, and worth any amount of Latin and Greek. It tends to give your opinions and thoughts a sort of certainty, force and clearness which forms an excellent foundation for other sorts of knowledge less precisely determined and established.

When Jevons made this comment, Britain, as a consequence of the Great Exhibition of 1851, had developed a centralized form of scientific and artistic education controlled by the Department of Science and Art (DSA). Whatever its faults, this machine or engine of education, which was a *de facto* system of secondary education, played a significant role in rendering the Victorians scientific. Many educationists have argued that its dismantlement by the 1902 Education Act was a serious policy error. During its lifetime the DSA was a force for educational change and, through Frankland, it particularly affected the way chemistry was taught.

There are two aspects of Frankland's activities as an educationist to consider. First, he was innovative as a teacher of the 'facts' of chemistry and their organization. This is clearly seen in his textbook, *Lecture Notes for Chemical Students*. Secondly, he had a quite extraordinary influence upon the teaching of practical chemistry through examinations and through another text, *How to Teach Chemistry*. These two activities were linked by both his long experience as a teacher dating back to 1847 and his position at the Royal College of Chemistry, where he found that he had inherited Hofmann's examining duties in chemistry for the DSA. They are also connected, however, with his membership of the X-Club and its commitment to a liberal education system whose theoretical justification lay in faculty psychology and which laid down that science was essential for the complete training of the minds of British citizens of all classes.

Lecture Notes for Chemical Students was first published in 1866. A second edition in two volumes appeared in 1870–2, with a third revised edition of the second volume on organic chemistry appearing in 1881. The *Notes* are a transcript of his Royal College of Chemistry lectures, with the omission of all descriptions and properties of elements and compounds. His aim was solely 'to classify and systematise' and 'to furnish the student with a kind of skeleton of the science'. The text, which only a first-class science printing house like Taylor and Francis could have handled in the 1860s, is a typographical phantasmagoria of bold and Roman typefaces, of dashes indicative of valency, of pages of equations and of Alexander Crum Brown's new graphic formulae shorn of their cumbersome circles. Frankland's purpose was thoroughly pedagogic[1]:

> I have often noticed with regret the great amount of labour which an earnest student expends in noting down the reactions and the names and formulae of substances which are presented to his notice in the lecture-theatre. He is thus greatly interrupted in following the arguments and explanations of the speaker, and he often loses more important generalisations in securing a record of details. One of my chief objects in the preparation of this book has been to relieve him from such distractions.

It was through this text that the new chemical ideas of valency and organic structure pioneered by Frankland and Kekulé were propagated in Great Britain. The *Lecture*

Notes ensured that the next generation of chemists would communicate by means of graphic or structural formulae. Frankland achieved this success because, as the DSA's chief examiner, he was directly responsible for laying down the syllabus, as well as setting the examinations for thousands of students and young adults who were studying chemistry at evening classes or in higher-grade elementary schools from 1865 onwards. In dramatic contrast to the French situation, where Marcellin Berthelot used his educational position within the government to prevent atomism and modern atomic weights from being taught in French schools, Frankland used his position to enhance and promote the atomic-structural approach to chemical understanding. The high sales of the *Lecture Notes* are indicative that the book was widely studied by examinees.

Frankland's DSA examination reports during the 1860s show his increasing exasperation at the way examinees revealed their ignorance of *practical* chemistry. School and college laboratories are so ubiquitous today in Europe and America that it seems curious to us that in the 1860s little or no attempt was being made to train young people practically, or to assess their practical knowledge. More curiously still, it was obviously believed that practical ability could be assessed from written work. (Chemistry was not the only example of this assumption; school cookery lessons for girls were entirely theoretical.) The consequences were, in Frankland's eyes, disastrous:

> The answers to the questions involving some knowledge of analytical chemistry show that very few of the candidates have had the advantage of laboratory manipulation, and they have consequently fallen helplessly into the error (unfortunately fostered by some of our textbooks) of giving special tests for individual elements regardless of the admixture, and consequent interference, of other substances.

This remark, incidentally, is a good example of the kind

of clarification of understanding that Ostwald, Noyes and other prosecutors of physical chemistry believed would follow its introduction into analysis.

Frankland's initial reaction was to set more questions, for example, on qualitative analysis, which involved practical experience, in the hope of stimulating practical work in DSA classes. However,. far from encouraging such work, examinees authoritatively described experiments that they had obviously never seen, or ones that could not possibly work.

Frankland's exasperation and growing anger at the futility of existing didactic teaching had three effects. First, in 1869 he estimated roughly how much it would cost to equip and run a minimal school laboratory course in chemistry; he arrived at a figure of £2 per pupil per annum. Two years later, he successfully persuaded the DSA to provide grants towards the endowment of laboratory facilities in *bona fide* science classes.

Secondly, to assist matters along, he used the examination syllabus, over which he had complete control, to begin to insist that teachers had to show a number of experiments directly to pupils. This is the origin of the strong tradition of science teacher demonstrations that remains in British practice. Frankland's list soon grew to precisely 109 experiments. Of course, the catch was that in order to conduct these demonstrations a chemistry class required a range of apparatus and chemicals; a minimum kit required 143 pieces of apparatus, which could be bought from the firm of J. J. Griffin. Although quite severe restrictions and conditions were imposed by the Treasury, by 1871 many non-endowed schools in Britain had taken advantage of the system, which also allowed the hire of more complicated apparatus for advanced organic preparations. It is no exaggeration to see this effort of Frankland's, upon which Armstrong was to build, as a major reason for the proliferation of school laboratories in the 1870s and 1880s.

TABLE 11.1   *Frankland's demonstration apparatus* *

1. Apparatus to decompose steam by stream of electric sparks
2. Apparatus for gas analysis
3. Apparatus for the determination of vapour densitites by Gay-Lussac's process and by Dumas' process
4. Apparatus for showing that hydrogen and chlorine do not contract in uniting to form hydrochloric acid
5. Apparatus for the decomposition of ammonia by spark current, and for the subsequent combustion of the liberated hydrogen by cupric oxide
6. Apparatus for the decomposition of marsh gas
7. Apparatus for showing that by the combustion of carbon and sulphur in oxygen no alteration in volume takes place
8. Siemens' ozone apparatus
9. Galvanometer
10. Thermopile
11. Daniell's hygrometer
12. Eudiometer to estimate oxygen in air
13. Diffusion tube
14. Oxyhydrogen blowpipe and gas-bags
15. Cavendish's eudiometer
16. Apparatus to prepare acetylene from hydrogen and carbon
17. Twenty cells of Grove's battery
18. Apparatus for preparing acetylene from coal gas
19. Model apparatus for coal gas
20. Apparatus for exposing equal volumes of hydrogen and marsh gas to various temperatures and pressures

*This set of apparatus could be hired by science schools from the Department of Science and Art. A set was also displayed in the Education Section of the South Kensington Museum.

Thirdly, and finally, Frankland realized that it was useless to equip science classes with laboratories, or to set practically based examination questions (and eventually practical examinations), unless the science teachers themselves were proficient at practical chemistry. Huxley had reached the same conclusion about biology teaching. The issue was related to the question of the qualifications of anyone who called themselves a 'chemist', and led to the establishment of the Institute of Chemistry in 1877. And so, in July 1870 Frankland invited sixty-five teachers who taught in DSA classes around the country to a summer school in his cramped Oxford Street laboratory. He worked them hard, German fashion, with an hour's lecture demonstration each morning – the teachers' notes were marked and assessed at the end of the week by his assistants because Frankland wanted teachers to improve the powers of expression of pupils – and there were seven hours of practical work in qualitative analysis and some organic preparations for the six days of the programme. The course was repeated over three weeks and was to become an annual event, being copied for biology and physics, and eventually mathematics, by other professors at the Royal College of Science.

So successful was Frankland's course, and so great the demand for information about it from teachers who could not attend (and whose livelihoods depended upon the fees earned by pupils' passes in the DSA examinations), that Frankland's six morning lectures were published, with his permission, in 1875. They were edited by George Challoner, one of the chemistry teachers who had attended a course in 1872. This is the origin of the small, but influential, booklet, *How to Teach Chemistry,* which was republished in Philadelphia in 1875 for the enlightenment of American high school teachers. In it Frankland described the 109 experiments that he believed all pupils should be shown by their instructors. Many of these were experimental demonstrations that Hofmann had developed at the Royal College of Chemistry and in his Berlin lectures following his return to Germany and propagated in his *Introduction to Modern Chemistry, Experimental and Theoretic* (1866). Between them, therefore, Hofmann and Frankland ensured that generations of schoolchildren would 'see' the preparation of elementary gases, the synthesis of water and experiments to confirm the volumetric composition of gases based upon Avogadro's hypothesis. Frankland's argument, like Hofmann's, was to demonstrate different types of reaction – union, displacement, exchange, rearrangement and decomposition – and simple types of molecules such as hydrogen, water and ammonia.

Significantly, these experiments became part of the syllabus laid down in the government's *Science Directory* each year (see Table 11.1). Although Frankland obviously believed from his own experience in the value of practical work by the pupils themselves, in his course for teachers he laid stress upon the more economical method of lecture-demonstrations. It was to be his pupil, Armstrong, with a slightly different vision of how and why chemistry should be taught, who successfully battled for 'hands-on' experience.

ARMSTRONG'S HEURISTIC METHOD

If the Royal Chemical Society were to name its Eduction Section after a distinguished educationist in line with its Dalton, Perkin and Faraday Sections, the most serious contender would be Henry Edward Armstrong (1848–1937). Although he made no outstanding chemical discovery, and often appears in the rearguard of significant advances like the discovery of the rare gases and the acceptance of the ionic theory, Armstrong's contributions to the elucidation of benzene derivatives and the structures of terpenes were significant, and, as historians of science are beginning to realize, he and his students and colleagues, Pope, Lapworth and Lowry, constituted a socially significant school of British chemists. It is his contributions to science education, however, that have had the most long-term effect.

In June 1884 an International Conference on Education was held at South Kensington in the newly opened City and Guilds of London Institute. Here, on 5 August, Armstrong, the Institute's new Professor of Chemistry, first began to make public a critical, but constructive, view of scientific education. During the remainder of his long life he was continually critical of didactic teacher-centred methods of learning, and he became the principal exponent of *heurism* – the child-centred method of learning through experience and experiment. How and why did an organic chemist become critical of his contemporaries' teaching?

In the eighteenth century, following the expansion of Newtonian thought, there were several methods by which the literate could obtain scientific instruction – through itinerant lecturers, the provincial philosophical societies, a plethora of periodicals, textbooks and encyclopedias, and the exciting Universities of Leyden, Edinburgh and Glasgow. However, little science reached the working classes except by way of their own honest individual effort. Industrialization and the opening and growth of mechanics institutes and mutual improvement societies in the early nineteenth century altered this slightly, as did the transplantation of the ideals of the democratic Scottish Enlightenment to London in the shape of the secular University of London in the 1820s.

On the other hand, the teaching of natural science in the endowed schools, and in the Universities of Oxford and Cambridge, hardly existed and, where it did, made little impression. That a definite movement, or campaign, for more science teaching occurred in the generation before Armstrong owed much to Liebig's example and to his array of British students, who returned to the United Kingdom to assume places of responsibility during the 1840s. Two of Liebig's pupils founded and directed the private Royal College of Chemistry in 1845, while another, Lyon Playfair, helped to establish the DSA and its effective, but destructive, method of payment by examination results as well as the Great Exhibition, whose profits were to create an educational city at South Kensington in the 1870s.

In the national schools there was little attempt to introduce the rudiments of science except through natural theology and object lessons. Isolated exceptions, such as the work of Frankland's older friend, the Rev. Richard Dawes, at King's Somborne in Hampshire, were nevertheless very influential. Dawes' secular work on the science of common things excited the government schools' inspector, Henry Moseley (a grandfather of Harold Moseley), and helped lead to the introduction of scientific instruction in teacher training colleges. Unfortunately, or so it seems in retrospect, the natural development of science teaching in elementary schools was stymied by bickering and demarcational jealousies between the Department of Science and Art and the Board of Education. In 1861 Robert Lowe's 'Revised Code' for state-supported elementary schools confined payment for the three 'R's alone, and placed responsibility for science teaching entirely on the shoulders of the DSA. Consequently, until 1990, when a National Curriculum introduced science to British junior (elementary) schools, little or no science was taught before the age of eleven in British schools.

It was in this context that the Glaswegian, John Joseph Griffin (chapter 5), wrote *Chemical Recreations* in 1823 as a guide to self-study and experiment using chemicals and oddments of rough-and-ready apparatus that could be bought cheaply from hardware stores or apothecaries. A later edition of 1834 recommended the purchase of a portable laboratory – a device that had long been popular with mineralogists and chemically minded physicians. Then, following a continental tour, in which he made business deals with some of the leading French and German philosophical instrument dealers, Griffin set himself up in London as a supplier of chemicals and apparatus in the same decade in which the Chemical Society and the Royal College of Chemistry were established and the government was giving its first thoughts to the introduction of science into the school curriculum. After Griffin had won several prizes at the 1851 Great Exhibition, a juror reported[2]:

It must be conceded that to the exertions of Mr Griffin commenced twenty years ago, in rendering to the public efficient chemical apparatus at a moderate price, combined with the production of elementary works on all branches of science, the present widespread development of a taste for the acquisition of chemical knowledge is in a great measure attributable.

In the 1860s, following the deeper understanding of physics, chemistry and biology developed through the concepts of energy, atomism, valency and evolution, the emerging scientific community began to form a powerful pressure group for urging on the wider public a fuller appreciation of, and a more systematic teaching of, their interests. Although there followed much debate over the relative merits of classics, mathematics and science as formative elements in 'liberal education', by the 1870s there was little doubt that science had grown strong roots into the British educational system.

Yet, when Henry Armstrong began teaching chemistry in 1870 it seemed to him that his students had been completely dulled from being subjected to the authoritarianism of didactic teachers and textbooks whose words related little to the practical things of life. His students were unable to think for themselves and were prepared only to memorize facts and formulae for examination questions. His predecessors had successfully brought some chemistry into schools, colleges and evening classes, but had stifled students in the process because no one had paused to ask how science ought to be taught, or how the science curriculum should be sequentially arranged. Armstrong's solution, developed over the next decade, was the heuristic method.

Armstrong had received a very practical education at the Royal College of Chemistry and had performed his first research, an improved method of water analysis, under Frankland. The latter had encouraged him to take a doctorate at Leipzig, which was by then the largest teaching and research laboratory in Germany. Here he was plunged into the excitement of aromatic chemistry and was forced to think out solutions to experimental problems under the benevolent, but scathingly critical, eye of Hermann Kolbe. Both Frankland and Kolbe can be seen to have encouraged Armstrong to believe in the value of self-education through laboratory research − a philosophy that had affinities with (and possibly its roots in) the child-centred pedagogical innovations of Pestalozzi in Switzerland.

On returning to England in 1870, Armstrong had been appointed to Frankland's old job of teaching medical students at St Bartholomew's Hospital. He coached students here for London University 'First M.B. Examinations' for twelve years 'with no little gain in experience' of students and of the influence of examinations. At the end of 1870 he was also appointed to succeed Frankland's great rival in water analysis, Alfred Wanklyn, at the London Institution − the City of London's answer to the Royal Institution in the West End. His duties were fairly nominal: the delivery of evening lectures to artisans on analytical chemistry and the methods of original investigation.

The students at the London Institution were very different from the medical students of St Bartholomew's. At the London Institution he was not tied by an examination syllabus, but was free to devise methods of teaching that would develop the fundamentals of chemistry in a relevant way for the practical trades followed by members of his class. Gradually he found ways of interesting his audiences by encouraging them to tackle problems experimentally in the confined and dusty Institution laboratory.

It was during Armstrong's period at the London Institution that Huxley published several essays on education, and began to criticize the wealthy City guilds for the neglect of their historical role as technical educators. In 1878 a Committee of the Livery Companies reported on technical education and recommended a plan for the creation of a central London institution that would serve as a model trade school. Eleven companies together financed this scheme, which became known as the City and Guilds of London Institute. Anxious to make an immediate start, the Institute created two lectureships in applied chemistry and physics. In October 1879 Armstrong was appointed to the former on the basis of his experience at the London Institution, and he began teaching in temporary premises.

It was at about this time that Armstrong appeared as a scientific witness in a patent trial. The experience of the court atmosphere, the dialectic, the way plaintiff and defendant marshalled their respective cases, and the clear and incisive manner in which judgement was delivered, was, Armstrong felt, the coping-stone on his own education. Scientific training had taught him to examine evidence and to ask questions; reading R. C. Trench's *Study of Words* (1851) had made him 'critical and anxious to get behind meanings'; the patent action made him alive to the 'need of searching cross-examination and judicial consideration of every item for and against a proposition'. Was this what made Armstrong such a formidable foe of Arrhenius' ionic theory?

Armstrong was to label this 'methodological use of knowledge' *scientific method.* He was convinced that it was best learned in a laboratory or workshop atmosphere by an autodidactic process he called *heurism.* (The word comes from the Greek meaning 'I have found out', as in Archimedes' reputed exclamation, 'Eureka!')

'Heuristic methods', said Armstrong, 'are methods which involve our placing students as far as possible in the attitude of the discoverer.' What students found out for themselves was best remembered because then they truly understood. Moreover, because a student-investigator is genuinely interested and involved in finding a solution to a problem, they would learn about it more efficiently than if they were given the solution didactically.

It seems clear that Armstrong developed these conclusions largely by intuition and from his experiences as a research chemist. Similarly, it seemed intuitively obvious to him that children would grasp certain ideas better at different ages, and that science syllabuses should be age-graded accordingly. The more thorough twentieth-century investigations that Piaget and other psychologists have made of children's cognitive development have confirmed Armstrong's hunches, though any too literal application of heurism would prove painfully slow, and potentially confusing, to both pupil and teacher.

These ideas led Armstrong to plan a new kind of chemistry course beginning, not like the syllabus of the DSA with the preparation and properties of metals and salts and what he angrily rejected as 'test-tube chemistry', but with elementary principles and the observation of familiar phenomena such as combustion, proceeding to pure and applied inorganic and organic chemistry, and concluding with a thorough outline of industrial chemistry. This was the programme that he and his Welsh demonstrator, John Castell-Evans, developed at the Finsbury Technical College, which the City and Guilds opened to students in February 1883. First-year subjects (mathematics, engineering drawing and elementary workshop practice, chemistry and physics) were common to all students; specialization was deferred to the second year. There was an entrance examination, but no externally controlled examinations. Armstrong and his colleagues in other sciences and engineering had a free hand to develop their own kind of teaching.

The way to learn chemistry, Armstrong believed, was to proceed 'systematically from the known to the unknown' by asking questions. Thus, if we begin with the observation of the action of burning a substance such as phosphorus and enquire into the process of chemical change in combustion, air and the phosphorus will have to be rigidly confined; but confined behind glass so that the investigator can see what happens; a fuel will also have to be chosen that can be ignited after the system is closed or confined. Hence the choice of a stoppered glass flask. Furthermore, in order to ensure a non-ambiguous answer to the student's enquiry (i.e. no hidden variables), both flask and phosphorus have to be as clean and dry as possible.

The student received printed instructions to ignite the phosphorus and to describe what happened ('a great change . . . with the evolution of heat and light') and also what happened when the flask was opened with its mouth under water ('the air has diminished in volume' *either* 'by mere condensation' *or* 'by the actual loss of some part'). The student then learned to quantify what had happened by roughly calibrating the volume of the flask into five equal parts and repeating the experiment – to find, of course, that roughly a fifth of the air had disappeared and that the four-fifths remaining would not burn more phosphorus.

Only at this point was the student told to call the four-fifths portion 'nitrogen', for it was Armstrong's general principle:

> not to employ any chemical *name* or *term* until [a student] has discovered by himself the *thing* or *process* represented by it.

In subsequent experiments a student sought to discover whether the reaction of phosphorus with air was unique and led to discover, by systematic testing, that other substances, such as iron and copper, would also reduce air by one-fifth of its volume. By the eighth experiment the student was ready to isolate this one-fifth portion, to call it 'oxygen', and to move on from air to water, 'and discover a new fuel' called 'hydrogen'. At this point the student was introduced more rapidly to carbon, the distinction between compounds and elements, and the laws of chemical combination. But only by experiment 91 was the student ready for equivalent weights, the notion of the atom, the determination of molecular and atomic weights and chemical formulae.

Once that stage was reached, the Finsbury course became more conventionally systematic, for the new pedagogic aid of the natural classification of the elements, or periodic law, could be used to treat elements in families or groups; at the same time the practical work on the artificial classification of elements by the experimentally determined groupings and separations of qualitative analysis could be investigated. However, in the spirit of 'prove all things', this was not mere test-tubing since the group tables had to be deduced from chemical reactions and not absorbed or copied from such well known aids as Fresenius' *Introduction to Qualitative Analysis*.

All this practical work was accompanied by parallel lectures on what might be called the 'physics of chemistry' – weights and measures, calorimetry, the gas laws, stoichiometric calculations, as well as regular tutorial problem classes. Here, then, was an innovatory course of chemical instruction emphasizing the practical and the quantitative; here was the course upon which Armstrong drew for his remarks to the International Conference on Education 'On the Teaching of Natural Science as Part of the Ordinary School Course' in 1884, which launched the heuristic movement that, in turn, triggered the school laboratory movement.

Armstrong left Finsbury College in 1884, but the method and curriculum for first-year teaching was continued by his successor, the dyes chemist, Raphael Meldola. The College itself fell upon increasingly hard times after the First World War in competition with new municipal technical colleges, for whom it had been the model. Finsbury Technical College closed its doors in 1926.

Until his death in 1937, Armstrong tirelessly committed himself to promulgating the notion that understanding came through doing. Precisely what was learned (information) was less important, at least in the earliest stages, than the method (process) involved in learning, thinking, or finding out about something. He believed, as the history of science suggested, that once a person had learned the techniques of experimentation, they could tirelessly acquire through their own efforts the mass of information which other teacher-oriented systems of education forced into children by rote, demonstrations and the penalty of examinations.

Hindsight suggests that Armstrong did not sufficiently distinguish between the 'discovery of understanding' – the 'I get it feeling' – that the tyro makes in a school or university laboratory, and the original discovery or innovation that a research chemist may make. That this point caused confusion and led to objections to heuristic methods is understandable. Nevertheless, until the First World War, heurism was probably the chief catalyst in transforming school science teaching in Great Britain, Armstrong himself being energetic in its promotion. Mainly using the British Association for the Advancement of Science as his platform, he developed a series of helpful suggestions for a chemistry course based upon pupil experimentation. Like the Finsbury programme upon which it drew, Armstrong abolished the traditional catalogue approach of 'elements, oxides and salts', which dated back to Lavoisier's time, and substituted real problems, such as 'why does iron rust?'

This syllabus attracted widespread attention and, following its approval by several teaching organizations, it also began to receive favourable attention in Germany and Japan. Further opportunities to promote heurism came through Armstrong's contacts with particular schools, like Christ's Hospital and St Dunstan's College, through the practical workshops that he held for London science teachers in 1896, and through a long essay he contributed to the Board of Education's widely read *Special Reports on Educational Subjects* (1898). He also practised what he preached with his own children. He sent three of his boys to St Dunstan's College and held weekend experimental sessions with his three youngest children on questions suggested by their story books.

By 1902, when Armstrong reviewed the situation before the education section of the British Association (which he had promoted in 1900), he quite properly associated the increase in number of school laboratories in Great Britain, from probably fewer than one hundred and fifty in the 1870s to over a thousand, as due in large measure to his heuristic campaign.

That the enthusiasm for the method did not maintain its momentum during the 1920s and 1930s was due to a variety of factors, notably the difficulty of using it with less-able children. Yet, even Armstrong's critics agreed that a laboratory orientation to chemistry teaching was essential. While scoffing at the use of terms such as research, discovery and proof in connection with experimental work, Ida Freund, a pioneer of women's science teaching at Newnham College, Cambridge, did much to reinforce the significance of illustrative experiments in teaching the fundamental laws of chemistry in her posthumous *Experimental Basis of Chemistry* (1920).

TWENTIETH-CENTURY DEVELOPMENTS IN TEACHING

Meanwhile, similar pupil-centred 'learning by doing' curricula had developed independently in America, associated with the names of Colonel F. W. Parker (1837–1902) and John Dewey (1859–1952). In 1895, at an American Chemical Society (ACS) meeting on teaching, A. F. Nightingale stressed the importance of high schools having a laboratory and the fact that teachers should be qualified chemists. By the 1920s, when the ACS formed its Division of Chemical Education (launching the *Journal of Chemical Education* in 1925), American high schools had organized syllabuses around the familiar triad of inorganic, organic and physical chemistry, with attention being paid to analysis in the laboratory. In the 1930s the ACS laid down minimum standards of chemical knowledge to which schools should aspire and began its still existing accreditation system in

1939. Both these plans, together with its annual production of objective examination test questions, did a great deal to ensure uniformity of standards across the vast American continent. The correlation of mathematics and science, however, remained a particularly American problem.

Apart from exceptional chemists like B. C. Brodie and A. C. Brown, who were trained in both mathematics and chemistry, nineteenth-century chemists managed without a knowledge of advanced mathematics. If mathematics was needed, then, like astronomers, who found that they wanted chemists' help in understanding stellar spectra in the 1860s, chemists turned to mathematician collaborators – as in the kinetic partnerships of Guldberg and Waage, and Harcourt and Esson. However, by the twentieth century the simple arithmetic demanded by elementary stoichiometry was no longer enough. Thermodynamics and the study of reaction rates, which demanded the calculus, came to play a fairly central role in chemistry and chemical engineering; crystallography demanded a knowledge of trigonometric functions and statistics; while quantum mechanics, more seriously, demanded acquaintance with partial differentiation, some advanced integrals and algebraic operators. Continental chemists could take these developments in their stride since both the German Gymnasia and the French lycées had sound traditions of mathematics teaching; but this was not the case either in Britain or least of all in America.

In John Slater's ideal world of an *Introduction to Chemical Physics* (1939), the gap between chemists and physicists was the fault of their respective training, not of the subject matter[3]:

> Physicists and chemists are given quite different courses of instruction; the result is that almost no one is really competent in all the branches of chemical physics. If the coming generation of chemists or physicists could receive training, in the first place,

in empirical chemistry, in physical chemistry, in metallurgy, and in crystal structure, and in the second place, in theoretical physics, including mechanics and electromagnetic theory, and in particular in quantum theory, wave mechanics, and the structure of atoms and molecules, and finally in thermodynamics, statistical mechanics, and what we have called chemical physics, they would be far better scientists than those receiving the present training in either chemistry or physics alone.

Slater's agenda reminds one of George Sarton's preposterous list of qualifications for historians of science, though, with the exception of metallurgy, Slater's criteria, all of which depended upon a knowledge of advanced mathematics, have been largely met in post Second World War revisions of the curriculum.

In Britain the standards of mathematical education in the school curriculum were considerably raised by improved secondary education after 1902, while the enterprising campaign of Armstrong's Finsbury colleague, the engineer, John Perry, to make mathematics more utilitarian, enabled trigonometry and the calculus to enter the school curriculum. On both sides of the Atlantic an education in mining or chemical engineering often proved a good basis for research in chemistry with a mathematical basis, as the careers of Noyes, Mulliken and Pauling attest.

In 1902, while holding an 1851 Exhibition Scholarship at the University of Manchester, the New Zealand chemist, Joseph William Mellor (1869–1938), composed an influential *Higher Mathematics for Students of Chemistry and Physics*. This became a standard advanced text for graduate students in both Britain and America. It was used, for example, by Farrington Daniels (1889–1972) in the physical chemistry course he introduced at the University of Wisconsin in 1920. Interestingly, Daniels had obtained his own Ph.D. in physical chemistry without knowing any calculus, which he only acquired as a result of teaching physical chemistry. He soon found Mellor's book too expensive and intimidating for his students and developed his own text, *Mathematical Preparation for Physical Chemistry,* in 1928.

In the same year, through an ACS symposium, he launched a national campaign for the improvement of mathematics teaching to science students. For Daniels, 'inadequate experience in mathematics is the greatest single handicap in the progress of chemistry in America'; indeed, it may well have been a factor that encouraged physical chemists like Richards, Noyes and Bancroft to make their mark in experimental and observational fields rather than mathematical ones. Daniels' campaign evidently paid off, for his department was able to dispense with a remedial 'maths for chemists' course in 1938 and rule that matriculated students must have the calculus. Yet, as high school curriculum reformers found in the 1960s, the correlation of science and mathematics remained a stumbling block in the American system.

As Mary Waring and others have suggested, the Nuffield Foundation Teaching Project, announced by the Minister of Education in April 1962, was 'a major landmark in English education practice'. It was the first attempt on such a large scale to obtain widespread reform of both content and teaching of science and mathematics by encouraging teachers to develop an 'articulated and comprehensive set of tested teaching materials'. These were to be resource materials, it was emphasized, not pre-packaged courses; resources from which classroom teachers in both grammar and secondary modern schools, as well as a growing number of co-educational comprehensive schools, could draw relevant and up-to-date materials in order to develop 'some insight into scientific thought and method' for both future science specialists and non-scientifically minded early school leavers.

The two most remarkable features of the Nuffield Ordinary Level (16+) examination syllabuses for chemistry were their emphasis upon theoretical models and learning by experimental discovery. The syllabus, devised between 1962 and 1967 by Frank Halliwell (a pupil of Percy Nunn's) with advice from the inorganic chemist, Ronald Nyholm, the chemistry textbook writer and examiner, E. H. Coulson, and Armstrong's Christ's Hospital School disciple, Gordon van Praagh, interpreted chemistry as 'process and product'. Pupils' powers of imagination, detective work and hunch-making were to be stimulated and encouraged by heuristic open-ended experimental work, which was to be explained through the use of the concepts of energy and the gram-atom (the mole). Complementing this process of investigation and explanation were the inculcation of the necessary degree of mathematical competence and the introduction of any relevant history of chemistry, together with relations with industry and the social welfare and improvement of humankind. Although some of the roots of the Nuffield revolution can be traced back to Armstrong's *virus heuristicum* (and even to Hofmann–Frankland explanatory analogues of the mole, like the crith), it also clearly borrowed freely from the post-*Sputnik* curriculum innovations of American chemistry teachers. These, likewise, were influenced by the British team.

Unlike Britain, America had two rival and rather different curriculum projects competing for the attention of high school teachers in the 1960s. The reform movement began at Earlham College, a small Quaker liberal arts college at Richmond in Indiana in 1957. Here Laurence Strong, a physical chemist, and O. Theodore Benfey, a student of Ingold's, decided that the four-year undergraduate curriculum was out of date: the syllabus was too large and cluttered with *ad hoc* accretions, it was too factual as were the textbooks prescribed for students, and the College's laboratory work was, in the final analysis, merely demonstrating what was taught by lecture. In their reform plan, each of the four undergraduate years was redesigned to allow the exploration of a particular chemical concept, rather than using the traditional divisions of analytical, inorganic, organic and physical chemistry.

In the freshman year the students would concentrate on interpreting different chemical substances structurally through the electronic theory; sophomores would be led to interpret chemical reactions through the consideration of structure and energy; juniors would learn how the direction and extent of chemical changes depended on changes of energy and entropy; and in the graduating year, seniors would study the rates and mechanisms of chemical change with the concept of the activation state. This radical programme attracted a good deal of attention (and caused some accreditation difficulties for the College with the ACS). It made good sense, therefore, for high school teachers, who, like their British cousins, were unhappy with existing curricula for the same reasons identified by Strong, Benfey and other critics, to ask the Richmond academics for advice.

The successful launch of *Sputnik* by the Soviet Union in 1957 had also galvanized public and government opinion in the United States that American science and technology were lagging and that the initiating fault lay in the schools. The result was the creation of the 'Chemical Bond' high school project, which was launched in 1959 and masterminded by Strong. After much testing in the classroom and refinements, the team produced an unusual textbook, *Chemical Systems*, in 1964, together with an equally original series of laboratory manuals, *Investigating Chemical Systems* by Anthony Neiding. *Chemical Systems*, which was almost a scaled-down version of the Earlham College programme (thereby raising questions of the intellectual demands being made of secondary school students), took the approach that chemistry is about systems of chemicals that change from an initial to a final state. It demanded attention to thermodynamics, including enthalpy diagrams, equilibria and kinetics. In retrospect, however, its most innovatory feature was its dismissal of 'right answers' and its use of two alternative theoretical models, or approaches, to the chemical bond: the electrostatic charge cloud model, which allowed the spatial geometry of molecules to be deduced, and atomic orbital theory, which explained spectra, but only allowed the geometry of molecules to be deduced by the assumption of resonance and hybridization. Most strikingly, all information on the preparation and properties of elements and compounds, and even the periodic table, was swept away, permitting emphasis upon: the nature of chemical systems; how they are recognized and interpreted; how a chemical change alters the surroundings of a system; why some compounds are formed and not others; what the conditions were that allowed reactions to reach completion; and why changes take time to occur.

Although not radical in a political sense – though there was at least one British Marxist critic in the 1960s who saw chemical syllabuses and textbooks as tools of industrial capitalism – the Chemical Bond Approach (CBA) was too much for the American Chemical Society. To their embarrassment, the Society had not been consulted by high school teachers, who had obtained their own funding for the project directly from the National Science Foundation. Not to be outdone, also in 1959, the ACS sponsored an alternative high school course to be called 'CHEM Study' (from 'The Chemical Education Material Study'). Thus a west-coast and more establishment-blessed project, which was also funded by the NSF, began operations at about the same time as the east-coast Chemical Bond project.

CHEM Study was headed by the Nobel laureate, Glenn Seaborg, who appointed J. Arthur Campbell of Harvey Mudd College, at Claremont, California, to direct the project and his Berkeley colleague, George C. Pimental, to edit a text, *Chemistry, An Experimental Course* (1963). Both programmes pioneered the use of programmed instructions – CHEM Study in order to remedy the continuing lack of correlation in schools between scientific knowledge and mathematical attainment, and CBA in order to reinforce the understanding of electrostatics and other abstract ideas used in the course. Such programmes were to be easily translated into computer programmes in the 1980s when cheap equipment became widely available for school and college use.

CHEM Study was much less theoretically demanding than CBA. Although not advised by educationists and psychologists, its syllabus was selected pragmatically by deciding whether an item was important in modern chemistry and whether it could be developed in an unfudged, but comprehensible, way from experiment and observation. Unlike CBA, it was prepared to simplify or to ignore material in the interests of understanding. Hence, though modern in outlook, CHEM Study retained a good deal of descriptive chemistry and therefore seemed to many teachers more reassuring and less unfamiliar than the very demanding syllabus of CBA. Although, unlike CBA, all historical material was removed as 'dead wood', CHEM Study's starting point was very Armstrongish, namely the study of the candle flame first popularized by Faraday in children's Christmas lectures at the Royal Institution a century before!

Both courses had considerable impact overseas. CBA was translated into Spanish, Japanese and, for Brazil, Portuguese. Even more successfully, CHEM Study appeared in Chinese, French, Gujarati, Hebrew, Hindi, Italian, Japanese, Korean, Portuguese, Spanish, Thai, Turkish and, in 1968, in an unauthorized Russian version. Both course teams also interacted with the Nuffield team in Britain, whose course was marketed successfully by the British Council to schools in the British Commonwealth. The OEEC (later OECD) also held an international meeting on chemical education in Ireland in 1960; by the time the third such meeting was held in Washington in 1967, CBA, CHEM Study and Nuffield had all come to fruition. It would seem that, by then, apart from the Australians, who had developed their own integrated school science course under the auspices of the inorganic chemist,

D. P. Mellor, the whole world had been touched by at least one of the three major curriculum designs. This 1960s attitude towards chemistry teaching can be summed up as follows: when teaching the chemistry of the atmosphere, it is no longer necessary to show students how to prepare oxygen and nitrogen; instead, take them straight from gas cylinders just like any other chemical.

Ironically, these exciting new curricula did not lead to greater enrolments in college and university chemistry courses, though they undoubtedly improved the quality of school chemistry lessons. In practice, it was found on both sides of the Atlantic that much of the new syllabuses only worked with brighter pupils (and, indeed, the more alert of teachers). As van Praagh remarked after advising the Tanzanian government on what kind of chemistry to teach children, the majority of whom would be farmers, 'the periodic table has nothing to say to the children of Tanzania'. This no doubt helps to explain why, unlike CHEM Study, *Chemical Systems* was not reprinted after its first edition was exhausted. Whether rivalry and animosity on the part of advocates of CHEM Study played a part in this is unclear. As for learning by discovery, among the majority of pupils, apart from the perennial problem of discipline in a large class, pupils either got the 'wrong' results or wormed the 'right' answer by deft questioning of the teacher. Closer scrutiny of the classroom situation by educational researchers in the 1970s revealed that children brought their own 'world view' preconceptions and intellectual baggage into the laboratory. It was less the case of discovering and learning something new than of unlearning a prior view and perceiving it anew. Two other factors undermined reliance on discovery methods in the late 1970s: new ideas on the psychology of learning, and a more critical philosophy and sociology of science. Both had the effect of aiding the reconstruction of syllabuses and classroom/laboratory practice, which would attempt to create a 'science for all' rather than a 'science for the few'.

THE LABORATORY

Frankland's and Armstrong's exertions in the nineteenth century and the curriculum reforms a century later all demanded adequate laboratory space, while, at the level of research, laboratories had been the *sine qua non* of a research programme since the time of Liebig.

As Partington noted succinctly: 'the size and arrangement of a laboratory depend on the kind of apparatus it contains and the nature of the work done in it'. When the apparatus was simple, consisting of flasks and alembics, and when manipulations were confined largely to chemical, pharmaceutical and metallurgical operations involving heating, a small room with windows and a chimney for ventilation was quite adequate. Even when large buildings were erected for scientific societies in the early 1800s, they were still likely to contain only these small, traditional room-laboratories, together with a larger lecture theatre embedded in the building.

Following his move to Munich in 1852, Liebig had had the opportunity to design a chemical institute from scratch. But, his research days over, he paid far more attention to the design of an ornate lecture theatre than to a laboratory. Consequently, when Baeyer succeeded him in 1873 he had to redesign the teaching and research space. By 1878 Baeyer's new institute had rooms and laboratories to accommodate over a hundred workers in both inorganic and organic chemistry.

More important as models for the expansion phase of laboratory building in the 1870s were those designed by Hofmann for the Prussian government at Bonn and Berlin in 1864. After some indecision, Hofmann took the Chair of Chemistry at Berlin in 1865, moving into a palatially decorated new building he had designed to house about seventy students in 1868. A few years later, when the Saxon government gave Kolbe the opportunity to build an even larger chemical institute at Leipzig, he modelled it on

Hofmann's Berlin design. Yet such was the pace of chemical advance, that when Fischer succeeded Hofmann in 1892 he found the Berlin accommodation totally inadequate and out of date. After lobbying industry for funds, Fischer designed a new institute large enough for 250 people. When this opened in 1900, it was the largest chemical laboratory suite in the world. This tendency to 'throw out the old; bring in the new' is one of chemistry's expensive luxuries. Because only rarely do the research interests of a successor to a professorial chair ever coincide with his or her predecessor's, it has become an inevitable expense in universities or organizations like the Royal Institution to refurbish laboratories for a new incumbent's research interests.

Clearly, with the development of science teaching in the nineteenth century, the emergence of research in unexploited areas such as physical chemistry and spectroscopy, the advent of basic engineering services such as running water, gas and electricity brought about a revolution in the design and complexity of laboratories. The main problems and needs were always clear. Chemists produce obnoxious and sometimes dangerous fumes and liquids; so the laboratory atmosphere needed artificial ventilation beyond the capability of a single window or open door, which might suffice for the single experimentalist, but not for fifty. (The term 'stinks' for school chemistry is no doubt attributable to the fact that early school laboratories were not ventilated.) Chemists need gas, water and strong drains to deal with the dangerously corrosive liquids that they discard – or used to, because there are now strict rules in most countries concerning waste disposal. As the architect A. E. Munby once commented:

> . . . laboratory drains always present problems and often troubles. Those accustomed to deal with ordinary domestic drains have to revise their ideas considerably when this special service is in question.

If nineteenth-century experience had shown the importance of collaboration between scientist and architect (as those of Armstrong with E. R. Robins or Roscoe with Waterhouse), the twentieth century produced new problems for designers and colleges. These were occasioned by the further expansion of teaching and research, together with the rising expense and complexity of equipment used by chemists and their students as the glass-blower technician gave way to the electronics expert.

Although historically serviceable laboratories have been converted from existing buildings – one immediately thinks of Liebig's barracks at Giessen, Bunsen's and Werner's cellars at Heidelberg and Zürich, or Hinshelwood's converted lavatory at Trinity College, Cambridge – sooner or later their users have found them inconvenient for teaching or research and have eventually persuaded their institutions to provide purpose-built accommodation. Chemistry and physics laboratories for teaching and research in Britain have been converted from a disused Bankruptcy Court (Leeds 1874), hotels (Aberystwyth 1872, Bangor 1884) and hospitals (Cardiff 1883, Edinburgh 1884, Reading 1902 and Leicester 1925), but in every case specially designed accommodation has followed as soon as private endowments or government aid has permitted. Chemists at Leeds moved into new laboratories in 1907, Aberystwyth in 1907, Bangor in 1926, Edinburgh in 1922, Cardiff in 1928, Reading in 1905 and Leicester in 1960.

In America, of the nine colleges in existence on Independence Day in 1776, only Philadelphia (*f.* 1740), King's (*f.* 1754; but renamed Columbia University) and William and Mary (*f.* 1693) at Williamsburg taught chemistry as a separate subject. The instructors were invariably either clergymen or, like Benjamin Rush (1745–1831) of Philadelphia, medical men, and their colleges possessed only small preparation laboratories unsuited to teaching or research. The first secular and non-medical chemist in America was Benjamin Silliman (1779–1864), a Yale law graduate who retrained as a chemist at Philadelphia and Edinburgh in order to be able to accept an offer of the Chemistry Chair at Yale. Silliman's interests were primarily mineralogical, but the *American Journal of Science,* which he founded in 1818, provided a valuable publishing forum for the tiny east-coast American chemical community and helped to ensure that Europeans were aware of American analytical work.

Silliman's greatest discovery was his pupil, Amos Eaton (1776–1842), another lawyer, who had been framed by clients and sent to prison for forgery in 1811. Following his pardon, at the age of forty, he took Silliman's course at Yale and then earned his living as an itinerant chemical lecturer and geological surveyor. The publication of his *Chemical Instructor* (1822) led to friendship with the rich and powerful land-owner, Stephen van Rensselaer. Eaton persuaded the latter to found the Rensselaer Polytechnic Institution at Troy, New York, to train analytical chemists and mining engineers, who could exploit America's rich mineral deposits. It is intriguing that, in the same year that Liebig began his teaching programme at Giessen, Eaton began his at Troy, using a strikingly similar approach. James Hall, Eaton's successor, wrote[4]:

Each student of the class was required to do laboratory work, and to prepare himself, his materials and apparatus to give each day, during his course, an extemporaneous lecture, illustrated by experiments, and full explanation of the phenomena and the laws concerning them. Every student was well grounded in the principles and elements of the science and by a method of teaching never surpassed, if ever equalled by any other.

One of Eaton's pupils, E. N. Horsford (1818–93), who studied with Liebig before founding the Rumford Chemical Works on Rhode Island, was disappointed to find Giessen so little different from Troy. Where Eaton acquired his teaching style is not known, but his success with laboratory-based teaching, like Liebig's, led others to copy.

At Yale in 1846, when Benjamin Silliman Jr (1816–85) succeeded his father, he and the European-educated Professor of Agricultural Chemistry, John Pitkin Norton (1822–52), built the analytical laboratory that later, following endowments, became the foundation of Yale's 'Sheffield Scientific School'. Yale became, in turn, the model for the development of the Lawrence Scientific School at Harvard (1847) and for similar developments at Amherst College, Massachusetts, and Union College, in the 1850s. The major expansion of America's science laboratories came after the passage of the Morrill Land Act of 1862. This donated federal lands for the creation of private or state engineering and agricultural colleges that enabled, among others, the Universities of Wisconsin, Illinois, Michigan and Cornell to become important centres of science teaching and research. The Morrill Act, together with the career opportunities that were opening up for chemists on state Boards of Health and agricultural research stations, gave incentives for many Americans to obtain more specialized training in Germany. At Göttingen, the aging but tireless Wöhler was to train over twenty American students, most of whom became college teachers in the 1880s.

The most important of these was Ira Remsen (1846–1927), whose vision of a great Germanic research university was realized in the founding of Johns Hopkins University at Baltimore in 1876, and shared by its first President, Daniel Gilman. Indeed, for Gilman, because 'the inhabited world is a great laboratory in which human society is busy experimenting', it was necessary for a university to function literally and figuratively as a laboratory and seminar. Unfortunately, Remsen's laboratory at Baltimore was a modest affair since Hopkins (a rich Baltimore merchant) had dictated that none of the capital of his endowment should be used for building purposes. For Remsen, who was more interested in science as a form of higher culture, what mattered was the moulding of his students in the laboratory, not the physical conditions of the laboratory. Despite the fact that Johns Hopkins helped to make the Ph.D. the *sine qua non* of American higher education (the Ph.D. was foreign to Britain until the 1920s), Remsen, whose own research was unadventurous, failed to create a great school of organic chemistry. He proved much more successful as an excellent teacher, textbook writer, editor of the *American Chemical Journal* (1879–1912) and, from 1901 to 1912, President of Johns Hopkins University. Only in 1925, two years before his death, did Hopkins acquire a purpose-built laboratory building.

That the costs of endowing laboratories were to rise during the twentieth century was due less to actual building costs than to the introduction of new equipment, though until the Second World War this was rather more true of physics than chemistry. But once the heavy equipment of mass spectrometry and chromatography became *de rigueur*, and because the subject remained fairly traditional in its teaching programmes up until then, research schools of chemistry of international eminence could exist on shoe-string budgets. At Bedford College, London, during the 1930s, the organic chemist, E. E. Turner, made the department's reputation while insisting that 'almost all their products [were prepared] from cheap starting materials'. At the University College of Leicester, Louis Hunter, despite a heavy teaching load, single-handedly became the leading British expert on the hydrogen bond.

In the late 1930s, however, the crystallographer, J. D. Bernal, attacked the uncritical British admiration for the 'sealing wax and string school of experimental work' familiar in the work of Thomson, Rutherford and Aston:

> One should not conclude that the material difficulties of earlier scientists were the cause of their greatness or that the creation of difficulties will automatically reproduce it. As science advances, the delicacy of

phenomena it observes continually increases, and this puts a premium on the use of more and more elaborate apparatus.

For Bernal, 'scientific puritanism' was self-defeating while, in any case, since the numbers of scientific workers was increasing and the level of intellectual ability inevitably declining, scientists would have to have apparatus that suited their level of ability. Not that Bernal was at all complacent concerning the marketing of scientific instruments and apparatus. As he noticed disapprovingly, by the 1920s, whereas instrument companies had previously mainly depended upon science laboratories for their survival, their new ability to sell devices (like wireless and later television) to a mass consumer market had reversed the relationship – with a consequent rise of prices to science departments!

A second wave of laboratory extensions and new building occurred between the wars. Many chemistry departments were in the position of Sheffield in the 1920s:

> There were far more students in the Department than there were benches, more even than there were cupboards to accommodate their apparatus, and the corridor was stacked with small padlocked boxes, each containing a set of apparatus. Each student who had no cupboard had one of these boxes, which he took to his bench on arriving and took back again on leaving.

Or, again, one reads of research students having to pack up their equipment to make way for an undergraduate class! New buildings were, however, forthcoming at Cambridge (1920), Edinburgh (1922), St Andrews (1923), Swansea (1923), Durham (1924), Bangor (1926), Bristol (1927), Cardiff (1928), Bedford College (1931), Leeds (1933), King's College, London (1933) and Birmingham (1937). During the Second World War many laboratories were requisitioned for military use, while the London science departments were evacuated to the Welsh colleges or to Cambridge and other cities – a process that often led to fruitful collaboration with the local chemists.

The post-war decision to expand British universities and to create new universities and polytechnics gave many architects the opportunity to rethink the design of scientific accommodation and to experiment with new materials. The Royal Institute of British Architects sponsored a symposium on teaching laboratories in 1958, while the Nuffield Foundation's Division for Architectural Studies carried out an elaborate investigation of the design of industrial research laboratories, which usually reflected university experience and design, at about the same date. Aware of the changing student numbers and scientific curriculum, architects began to pay more attention to flexibility in design and to the special environments needed for post-war equipment – air conditioning for mass spectrometry and spectroscopy, constant temperatures for chromatography, special facilities and shielding for the storage of radioactive materials and hazardous chemicals.

Chemistry designers, for the sake of convenience of servicing, moved away from the familiar nineteenth-century island bench to longer peninsular surfaces, and they took great pains to redesign that essential piece of equipment, the fume cupboard:

> In every way the fume cupboard seems to be the most awkward thing to deal with in laboratory planning, costly in itself, it can have expensive repercussions on the heating and ventilating of the laboratory, it consumes an inordinate amount of air, occupies valuable wall space or obstructs light, and the ducts from it have possibly to be taken through the floor above.

It was clear by the early 1960s that the expectation that a chemistry student would spend all the time not allocated for lectures in the laboratory (certainly the presumption, if not the obligation, in university departments earlier) was undergoing a dramatic change. With the diminishing importance of qualitative analysis in the training of chemists as it was replaced by micro-analysis and instrumental analysis, undergraduate students no longer needed to spend up to twenty-five hours a week in the laboratory.

The indications during the last thirty years are that designers, influenced by the special precautions needed for safe research, the availability of highly efficient ventilation systems, and the fact that laboratories in most countries fall within the orbit of much health and safety legislation, foresee a situation in which all actual experiments will be performed in centrally placed fume cupboards or shielded glove-boxes, leaving 'the open benches as places for assembling equipment and placing reagent bottles, spare glassware, notebooks, etc.'

The Chemical News

> The *Chemical News* (with its predecessor) has been increasing in circulation and wide distribution for nearly a generation. In its youth many of the leading Continental Professors were at school or college. It has grown up side by side with them; it has been their companion in their early days of laboratory work; it has now become an indispensable addition to their scientific libraries, and an oft-quoted record of the progress of chemical research.
>
> (F. D'ALBE, *The Life of Sir William Crookes*, 1924)

The development of the teaching of chemistry and the growth of laboratories are but two indicators of how chemistry has expanded since the 1840s. Two further indicators to be considered before looking at the nature of twentieth-century chemistry are societies and their publications. Although these two features of scientific growth are intimately connected, independent commercial publications have played an equal, if not decisive, role since the 'chemical revolution'. Chemical periodicals are particularly important; from the late eighteenth century they came to replace the monograph for conveying new chemical knowledge and for settling controversial issues. As Liebig wrote in 1834[1]:

> Chemical literature is not to be found in books; it is contained in journals. In books the individual author's opinion dominates and his judgment is without appeal. However, in journals there is defence, there is justification, and because of the necessity of

a mutual neutralization of opinions, we approach the common goal of science.

'The Chemical News and Journal of Physical Science (with which is incorporated the *Chemical Gazette*). A Journal of Practical Chemistry in all its Applications to Pharmacy, Arts and Manufactures' was first published on Saturday 10 December 1859, price 3d. What was distinctly new about the periodical was its weekly character and, as such, together with the weekly general organ *Scientific Opinion* (founded November 1868, collapsed 1870), it paved the way for Norman Lockyer's *Nature*, which began in November 1869, exactly ten years later. The last issue of *Chemical News*, the 3781st issue, appeared in October 1932, thus completing almost seventy years of continuous service to the chemical community.

As the subtitle 'with which is incorporated the *Chemical Gazette*' implies, *Chemical News* was not the first commercial chemical journal in English. Commercial journals, published for the profit of editors and proprietors, are to be distinguished from the publications of chemical societies like the Chemical Society of London, which had issued irregular *Memoirs* and *Proceedings* between 1841 and 1848, and which since 1848 had issued a regular Quarterly Journal printed by London's leading science printer, Richard Taylor.

Apart from an ephemeral artisan's journal, *The Chemist* (2 vols, 1824–5, edited by Thomas Hodgkin), unlike the French and Germans with their eighteenth-century periodical, *Crell's Chemisches Journal* (f. 1778), and Lavoisier's *Annales de chimie* (f. 1789), Britain had no special chemical journal until the mysterious Charles and James Watt launched the monthly medically and pharmaceutically oriented *Chemist; or Reporter of Chemical Discoveries and Improvements* in January 1840. With some tantalizing breaks in continuity, this journal lasted until 1858. Until the 1840s, therefore, both British and Continental chemical news was published in general commercial journals such as *Nicholson's Journal* (founded 1797, collapsed 1814) and Thomson's *Annals of Philosophy* (founded 1813, collapsed 1826) and in the long-surviving *Philosophical Magazine* (*f.* 1788), which since 1822 had been owned, published, printed and edited by Richard Taylor. In difficult circumstances, these journals and their continental models had played an enormously important role in conveying chemical information across national boundaries and linguistic frontiers. Perhaps as much as a half of the contents of these commercial chemical and general scientific periodicals were made up of translations from foreign competitors. Such translations served the chemical community well and were undoubtedly profitable for editors, who were not required to pay the original author. Indeed, linguistically able chemists like Berzelius began the habit of providing foreign editors with their own translations in order to ensure the rapid and accurate dissemination of their views. Later in the century, after schools of chemistry on the Liebig–Giessen model had emerged, trans-national teacher–pupil relationships enabled senior chemists to have pupils translate their work. As the huge Royal Society *Catalogue of Scientific Papers* (1867–1925) reveals, multiple publication of the same paper in different languages was a ubiquitous phenomenon of nineteenth-century science, and of chemistry in particular.

It also meant that information could be transferred with a speed and efficiency that astonishes the twentieth-century reader. A good example is Döbereiner's discovery in 1823 of what Berzelius was to call 'catalysis'. On 27 July 1823 Döbereiner found that hydrogen burned extremely rapidly in the presence of platinum. During that week he reported the phenomenon personally to five journal editors, as well as to his friend Goethe. His account was supplemented on 3 August by the invention of the Döbereiner lighter – the observation that, in the presence of spongy platinum, hydrogen ignited spontaneously. A month later his accounts were published in the *Journal für Chemie und Physik* (as the *Allgemeines Journal der Chemie* had become), *Annalen der*

Physik, Neues Journal der Pharmacie, Isis and the Genevan *Bibliothèque Universelle*. In August, too, Kastner of Erlangen wrote to Liebig, who was in Paris, about the discovery. At Humboldt's suggestion, Liebig told Thenard, who reported it to the Académie des Sciences on 26 August. Further experiments by Thenard and Dulong, reported to the Académie on 15 September, prompted Hatchette to write to Faraday in London. Faraday began some experiments of his own, and reported them in the Royal Institution's *Journal of Science and Arts* in October, the month that Döbereiner published a monograph on the subject. In the same month *Philosophical Magazine* published translations of the papers of Döbereiner, Thenard and Dulong. Thus, within the space of three months the discovery had been reported by monograph and in some dozen European science journals.

The Watts' *Chemist*, which seems to have been aimed at a readership of pharmacists, chemical analysts, chemical manufacturers and inventors, was almost immediately challenged by *The Annals of Chemistry and Pharmacy* (1842–3), but, unable to compete with Watts, this closed in February 1843. A greater challenge was Jacob Bell's *Pharmaceutical Journal* (f. 1841), which quickly became the house organ of the Pharmaceutical Society. Both these journals were opposed in their turn from 1846 by an offshoot of the *Medical Times* (1839–85) called the *Pharmaceutical Times,* which was edited by the genial Bohemian journalist, Gustav Strauss. The *Medical Times* itself had been founded by T. P. Healey to criticize Thomas Wakley's *Lancet*. Not surprisingly, therefore, like so many Victorian commercial medical journals, *The Chemist, Pharmaceutical Journal* and *Pharmaceutical Times* were extremely quarrelsome organs and served more as factional weapons of propaganda than as journals containing serious chemical, medical and pharmaceutical information. They make entertaining reading and are important sources for the social historian of science; but for serious chemistry the historian, like the nineteenth-century chemist, must look to Taylor's

Philosophical Magazine and its sister publication, the *Chemical Gazette*.

With the exciting expansion of organic chemistry in the 1830s, and with William Francis, Taylor's illegitimate son, who was educated at Berlin and with Liebig at Giessen, producing large numbers of translated chemistry papers, the *Philosophical Magazine* simply could not cope. In 1842, to alleviate the pressure on his father's journal, Francis, together with Henry Croft (who soon migrated to Toronto to be its university's first Professor of Chemistry), founded the serious and important bi-monthly, *Chemical Gazette*. This was published and printed by Taylor.

The *Chemical Gazette, or Journal of Practical Chemistry in all its Applications to Pharmacy* was very much the twenty-five-year-old Francis' pride and joy. Unfortunately, on his father's death in December 1858, Francis found, on inheriting the printing house, that he simply could not cope with editing three high-quality science journals like the *Chemical Gazette,* the *Philosophical Magazine* and the equally important *Annals of Natural History,* as well as running a firm that printed ninety per cent of the transactions of London's learned societies together with the examination papers of the University of London and the textbooks of many large London publishing houses. And so it came about that in November 1859 Francis sold the copyright of the *Chemical Gazette* to the twenty-seven-year-old William Crookes, whom he would have known through their mutual interest in photography and their joint membership of the convivial 'B Club', composed largely of Liebig's and Hofmann's former British pupils.

FORMING CHEMICAL SOCIETIES

In 1972, the British Chemical Society, the Royal Institute of Chemistry, the Society for Analytical Chemistry and the Faraday Society completed arrangements for amalgamation to form one large chemical society. From 1980, when a revised charter was awarded, this became the Royal Society of Chemistry (RSC). The original Chemical Society had formed in London in 1841 as one of the last in the group of specialist societies that had set themselves apart from the Royal Society. This process of specialization had begun with the Linnean Society (for botany and natural history) in 1788, continued with the Geological Society in 1807, the Royal Astronomical Society in 1820, and a host of specialized, but more popular, cultural societies such as the Horticultural, Zoological and Geographical Societies.

Given this degree of specialization before the 1830s, one might well ask why a national chemical society was not formed before 1841? One answer is undoubtedly that these early specialized societies were founded to accomplish specific collaborative projects. The Linnean Society was founded to catalogue and curate Linnaeus' specimens; the Geological Society intended to map the rocks and minerals of the British Isles; and the Astronomical Society was to catalogue stars and nebulae. Until Liebig revealed the possibility that organic analysis might, as a long-term project, lead to the improvement of agriculture, an understanding of disease and, possibly, an understanding of the nature of life, there appeared to be no co-operative chemical projects. Moreover, the chemical interests of the small and scattered chemical community were probably satisfactorily catered for within existing organizations: the Royal Society itself (there was an Animal Chemistry Club between 1808 and 1820 composed of Fellows interested in biochemistry), the Society of Arts (*f.* 1754) and the Royal Institution. Within these organizations, London chemists like Humphry Davy found a ready outlet for their work. However, such groups inevitably tended to be elitist and reserved for 'gentlemen'.

A second reason for the late emergence of a chemical society is connected with the way different classes of chemical practitioners had developed since the mid eighteenth century. The argument whether chemistry should be based upon theory or practice was a crucial factor in its slow recognition as a respectable university subject on the Continent. The resolution of this debate at the end of the eighteenth century involved the distinction between pure and applied chemistry – a distinction that stressed chemistry's usefulness and successfully ensured its popularity. In Britain, this most practical of the sciences tended to prosper almost entirely as an academic discipline. A broad social divide especially separated members of the London chemical community as the Industrial Revolution reinforced the dichotomy between chemical philosophers, or gentlemen interested in the nature of chemical phenomena, and the practical chemists. By the 1820s, practical chemists had also bifurcated into chemists and druggists and industrial chemists. Changes in the structure of the medical profession in the eighteenth century, in which apothecaries successfully strove to become general medical practitioners, allowed those who had earlier merely traded in drugs and chemicals to raise their social status by separating pharmaceutical chemistry, or pharmacy, from the commerce of drugs and chemicals. In the same year that the Chemical Society was formed, in 1841, Jacob Bell created the Pharmaceutical Society of Great Britain. Those left as druggists frequently moved into small-scale manufacture and by degrees became manufacturing chemists.

Other practical chemists, who were uninterested in drugs and pharmaceuticals, found roles as analysts and advisors in the burgeoning industries of alkali manufacture, gasmaking, calico printing and colouring, and brewing. Both practical and philosophical chemists were also discovering opportunities for the teaching of chemistry. These teaching opportunities arose partly from the changes in medical education that took place following the Apothecaries Act of 1815. Increasingly, from then on, medical education came to demand knowledge and experience of chemistry. Consequently, there were many chemical teaching positions in London hospitals and, increasingly, in provincial medical centres. Chemical lecturing, however, also satisfied a public demand among fashionable audiences at the Royal Institution, the Society of Arts and the provincial Literary and Philosophical Societies that had been founded all over the United Kingdom since the 1790s. Finally, some chemists were beginning to find opportunities to use their knowledge and skills, and to make a favourable impression on society, as consultants in legal cases and patent work, by advising industrialists and, last but by no means least, by advising government and local authorities on chemical issues related to public health, such as the potability of water.

By the 1830s, several types of chemical practitioner could be identified according to how chemistry afforded them a way of living. However, the effect was competitive rather than collaborative, and discouraging therefore of co-operation within a specialized society. As Bud and Roberts have argued, however, the social divide was bridged in Scotland by professional teachers such as Thomas Thomson, Thomas Graham and their students, who enjoyed good relations with local industries and who cleverly used the British Association for the Advancement of Science (BAAS) to move to the centre of the chemical stage. Receptive to Berzelian atomism and symbolism and to continental developments in organic chemistry (unlike the previous generation of metropolitan chemists), this group succeeded in uniting the chemical constituency by appealing to the pure–applied dichotomy. Their success was undoubtedly helped by the contemporary debates over liberal education in the heavy quarterly reviews: an education in pure chemistry (preferably with some research training attached) would fit a student for any practical chemical vocation.

Thomson, as we have seen, was a vocal supporter of Daltonian atomism and Prout's hypothesis, which on the whole London chemists were not. Moreover, at a time when there was much debate concerning the 'decline' of British science following the deaths of Wollaston and Davy in the period 1828–30, Thomson and his pupils looked to learn from European chemistry. In Thomson's own case, following his brutal treatment by Berzelius in a review of his analytical competence, the mantle of authority was passed to one of his Scottish pupils, Thomas Graham (1805–69), who moved to London in 1837 as Professor of Chemistry at University College in succession to Edward Turner. The latter, despite opposition from Dalton, had been one of the few London chemists to have encouraged British chemists to adopt Berzelius' nomenclature and formulae by working through the co-operative procedures that the BAAS, founded in 1831, had made possible. Graham now began to use BAAS as a forum for the promulgation of Continental chemical work among English chemists, and, above all, in emphasizing the significance of organic chemistry, as opposed to inorganic and mineral chemistry. Liebig's tours of Britain in 1837 and 1844, and his dedication of *Agricultural Chemistry* and *Animal Chemistry* of 1840 and 1842 to the BAAS, were not merely grist to Liebig's own mill of being recognized as Europe's greatest chemist, but convenient to Graham's involvement in the modernization of British chemistry.

The London Chemical Society was first mooted in the spring of 1841 by a group of seven academic chemists (including Graham and four of Thomson's former pupils), thirteen practising analytical chemists whose work had been radically transformed by the new techniques of Liebig, Rose and others on the Continent, five industrial chemists who were concerned with processes such as brewing and calico printing, and five people loosely describable as 'gentlemen chemists' or chemical philosophers. Invited by Robert Warington, a London brewery chemist and later the chief analyst at Apothecaries Hall, to develop an agenda for action, the heterogeneous group resolved 'to break down party spirit and petty jealousies . . . to bring science and practice together . . . to bring the experience of many to bear on the same subject' and to meet together to discuss original papers. In this way, under the Presidency of Graham, the

Chemical Society of London founded in May 1841 became a model for national chemical societies all over the world.

Its future was not all sweetness and light since, following the only model known, that of gentlemen's clubs, election to the Fellowship of the Society was the straightforward one of knowing the right people. The possibility of 'blackballing' a candidate was, therefore, a very real one and one that became increasingly used as competence at analysis became more and more the principal desideratum in appointments in industry and public health. As Russell has pointed out, competent analysts were needed not only for quality control in the alkali industry and gasworks, but also in the huge railway industry and in agriculture and to conform to the increasing government legislation concerning air pollution, and food and drug adulteration. A solution to these issues was found only in 1877, when, to prevent serious rupture within the Chemical Society, a separate Institute of Chemistry was founded. Its primary purpose was, like the earlier Pharmaceutical Society, to act as a qualifying association. By setting stiff examinations (the pass rate was rarely more than 50 per cent) the Institute ensured that local government and industrialists would only appoint proficient chemists to positions. This did not solve the problem of the large numbers of chemical technologists who worked in chemical industry. These formed their own Society of Chemical Industry in 1881, adding an important American branch in 1894, and issuing its own *Journal* from 1882. In this instance, German chemical industry followed, rather than led, the British: the Verein Deutscher Chemiker was formed only in 1887, its important *Zeitschrift für angewandte Chemie* (now *Angewandte Chemie*) starting the same year.

Earlier, because of public health legislation concerning food adulteration, a Society of Public Analysts was formed in London in 1874. This issued its own journal and abstracts, *The Analyst,* from 1877. Another specialist subcommunity, the dyestuffs chemists, formed a Society of Dyers and Colourists in 1884, while those interested in electrochemistry and the new physical chemistry formed the Faraday Society in 1903. This society became internationally renowned in the 1920s for its excellent interdisciplinary discussions of topics at the forefront of research.

It was precisely to prevent the hiving off of specialist interests that led American chemists to form divisions. However, as we have seen, it was not until the 1970s that discussions took place in Britain over how economies of publication and subscription rates could be achieved through amalgamation, while still retaining separate identities in the Analytical, Dalton (inorganic), Perkin (organic), Faraday (physical), Industrial and Education Divisions. Even then, largely because of Britain's peculiar class system in which managers and men are not expected to mix, the Society of Chemical Industry opted to remain independent of the RSC, with its own house journal, *Chemistry and Industry*.

THE CHEMICAL PERIODICAL

After some publication difficulties during the Revolution, the *Annales de chimie* established itself as the primary journal of French chemistry. It had been founded in 1789 by Lavoisier, de Morveau, Berthollet and Fourcroy as a monthly vehicle for their new chemistry, exception having been taken to the policy of the existing monthly, *Journal de physique, de chimie et d'histoire naturelle* (f. 1771) because of its pro-phlogiston stance, and following a failed attempt by Pierre Adet to issue a French translation of *Crell's Chemische Annalen*. The *Annales de chimie* adopted the policy of the contemporary German journals of supplying readers with translations from, in their case, German and English papers, as did the Italian *Annali di chimica* edited by Ludovico Brugnatelli from 1790. Despite the issue of a *Bulletin* by the Société Chimique in 1858, three years after the French chemical society's foundation in Paris, the *Annales* has remained France's most prestigious and long-running chemical periodical. In this respect, it remained little affected by the establishment of more specialized journals such as the *Journal de Pharmacie* in 1815 and *Journal de chimie physique* in 1903.

The home of specialized journals was Germany, where there was a flourishing book trade and many distinguished publishing houses. Here Lorenz Crell founded the first-ever chemical periodical, *Chemisches Journal,* in April 1778. Its formula of providing fresh chemical intelligence to middle-class doctors, apothecaries and chemical manufacturers who had little access to the proceedings of learned societies and academies proved financially viable and became a model for other enterprises in both Germany and abroad. After several changes of title, this *Chemische Annalen,* as it became, ceased publication in 1804 when its espousal of phlogistic chemistry had become anachronistic. Meanwhile, a German equivalent of the *Annales,* the voice of Lavoisier's chemistry, had been founded by Nikolaus Scherer of Jena in 1798. This *Allgemeines Journal für Chemie* soon supplanted Crell's journal and, under a succession of editors, A. F. Gehlen and J. S. C. Schweigger, and further changes of title, survived until 1834. It was then taken over by Otto Erdmann and renamed the *Journal für praktische Chemie.* Under Erdmann and his successor, the pugnacious Kolbe, the journal became the organ of the Leipzig research school, not only specializing in organic chemistry, but opening its pages to some of Ostwald's earliest work on physical chemistry before he founded the *Zeitschrift für physikalische Chemie* in 1877.

The tendency of the various schools of German chemistry to have their own journal had been first established when Liebig acquired the *Annalen der Pharmacie* in 1832. Following its founder's death, in 1840 Liebig changed the emphasis towards organic chemistry, as reflected by the new main title, *Annalen der Chemie.* Together with his co-editor Wöhler, and later under Hermann Kopp, the *Annalen* became the most important journal of chemical communication in the world, though for a time it was often rivalled by the Berlin-based *Annalen der Physik und Chemie* edited by J. C. Poggendorff. Similarly, at Göttingen, despite Wöhler's presence as a co-editor of *Annalen,* the young Privatdocenten, Beilstein, Fittig and Hübner, produced their own *Zeitschrift für Chemie* until 1871. This had been started by Kekulé in 1858 as a critical review of chemical progress and was continued by Erlenmeyer until it became the organ of the Göttingen school. Meanwhile, the commercially minded Fresenius, who had opened his own school of analytical chemistry at Wiesbaden, began a *Zeitschrift für analytischen Chemie* in 1862. Bunsen's pupil, Gerhard Krüss (1859–95), who was probably the first German to undertake postgraduate studies in America, launched the *Zeitschrift für anorganische Chemie* at Hamburg in 1892 specifically to counteract the predominance of organic chemistry in German research, teaching and industry. Like Ostwald, Krüss assembled an international advisory board.

Hofmann's return to Berlin in 1865 was to lead to the formation of the Deutsche Chemische Gesellschaft in 1867 on the British model. The almost exclusively organic *Berichte* of the society were begun later the same year. The German society was, in turn, the inspiration for the Russian Chemical Society and its *Zhurnal* in 1869. Through their journals and transactions, national chemical societies gave chemical communications a far more insular, even nationalistic, appearance than they had had in the earlier more urbane and trans-national commercial periodicals. For example, Russian chemists, who had hitherto published in German, turned exclusively to the Russian language. Consequently, as the practice of offering complete translations disappeared in the commercial journals and abstraction by societies took its place, nationalism proved particularly disadvantageous to chemists in Russia and Scandinavia.

By 1900, Germany led the world with a string of important chemical periodicals. It may well be asked, was this proliferation necessary? The answer is, of course, that editors did not lack copy. Major research chemists like

Kolbe, Baeyer and Fischer were frequently composing twenty to thirty papers a year of their own, which, together with a large output from research students, could easily justify and make up an annual volume of forty or fifty papers. Moreover, until American chemists had established their independent journals and *bona fides*, they usually also published their work in German periodicals. The German Chemical Society also took on the enormous responsibility of updating 'Beilstein' in 1896 – an essential multi-volume guide to whether or not an organic compound had been synthesized or prepared, which Friedrich Beilstein (1838–1906) had first produced single-handedly between 1880 and 1882.

Neither Britain, France nor America matched the variety of German literature until after the First World war, which also caused overseas readers considerable difficulty because of shipping embargoes and censorship. Not surprisingly, given the large numbers of Americans who had studied in Germany, personalized journals were an attraction to Uesanians, as Henry Armstrong called the Americans. In 1896 the wealthy Wilder Bancroft underwrote and edited the *Journal for Physical Chemistry* as the voice of the American ionists and, increasingly, as a specialist journal concerned with the colloidal state. As Servos has made clear, however, Wilder's periodical was never a success, and was even ostracized by Noyes and Lewis. Bancroft finally sold it to the American Chemical Society (ACS) in 1934. Earlier, in 1879, recalling the Göttingen model, Remsen gave prestige to Johns Hopkins by editing his own *American Journal of Chemistry*. For many years this was more important than the *Journal of the American Chemical Society*, which absorbed it in 1912.

Short-lived chemical societies were often formed in university cities like Edinburgh and Philadelphia towards the end of the eighteenth century. One such group, formed in Philadelphia in 1813, published a single volume of *Transactions* in 1813. This was not only the first American chemical journal, but also the first periodical issued by a chemical society anywhere in the world. But like all such early societies, which depended upon the presence of one dominant and enthusiastic figure, the Philadelphian society had petered out by 1814.

The idea of an American Chemical Society was first mooted in 1874 when H. Carrington Bolton of the Columbia School of Mines in New York, a pupil of Wöhler and a chemist sensitive to historical matters, suggested that the centenary of Priestley's isolation of dephlogisticated air in August 1774 should be celebrated by a gathering of chemists at Priestley's home at Northumberland, Pennsylvania. At this grand celebration, which seventy-five chemists from fifteen different states attended, Charles F. Chandler of New York moved that a national society should be formed on the British model. A number of chemists opposed this suggestion on the perfectly valid grounds, in the days before aeroplanes, that America was too vast, that the chemical community was too small and too dispersed, and that, in any case, the chemical section of the American Association for the Advancement of Science (AAAS), founded in 1848 on the model of the BAAS, provided American chemists with an adequate annual forum for debate, socializing and to review progress. (It was for many of these reasons that Canadian chemists never formed a society; their qualifying association, the Chemical Institute of Canada, was formed only in 1942.) It was agreed, therefore, that Bolton should explore ways of strengthening the chemical section of AAAS.

Although this would have been an entirely feasible option for American chemists, it was pre-empted when the New York chemists, led by Chandler, decided to form a New York Chemical Society in 1876. On discovering that this potential society could attract members from surrounding states in New England and the Delaware valley, Chandler decided unilaterally in April 1876 to declare that an American, not local, Chemical Society had been formed, with the spectroscopist, John W. Draper (1811–82), as its first President. As predicted, distance inevitably led New York chemists to predominate at meetings and as Council representatives. These features particularly upset Washington-based chemists such as F. W. Clarke and H. W. Wiley. Disgruntled, in 1884 they formed a separate Washington Chemical Society, to be followed by other local societies. Local tensions were only resolved in 1890 when, through Chandler's timely action, the ACS adopted a new constitution that specifically encouraged the formation of local sections of the mother society at New York, Washington and elsewhere, thus fending off a proposal of Frank Clarke's that American chemists should start from scratch a new national 'Continental Chemical Society'. Nevertheless, New York and its environs remained the largest concentration of chemists in America, enabling them to form, in 1898, a fine Chemists' Club where members and visitors could stay, read, dine and socialize.

At the national level probably the greatest step towards solidarity was achieved in 1893 when the *Journal of the American Chemical Society* (*JACS*) gave up its New York publishing base and moved its headquarters to Easton, Pennsylvania. The journal's new editor was Edward Hart, an analytical and industrial chemist who had run his own, highly successful, *Journal of Analytical and Applied Chemistry* since 1887. Hart's agreement to amalgamate his periodical with the *JACS* ensured the health of the ACS by bringing it many new members. By 1908, when specialist Divisions for Industrial Chemists and Chemical Engineers, Agriculture and Food Chemistry, Fertilizer Chemistry, Organic, Inorganic and Physical Chemistry were created, the ACS had some 3400 members. It already outnumbered the membership of the German Chemical Society whose hegemony as centre of world chemistry was to be challenged by America after 1919. A marker of this challenge was the spawning of divisional specialist periodicals such as *Journal of Industrial and Engineering Chemistry* (1909) and *Journal of Organic Chemistry* (1936).

Given the proliferation of chemical literature and the inability of commercial editors in practice to make their journals complete registers of the world's chemical papers, indexing and abstraction assumed importance from an early date. In Britain, from 1814, Thomas Thomson in the *Annals of Philosophy* hit upon the device of publishing an annual retrospective report on Continental chemistry in the January issue. Similarly, but largely because of Sweden's isolation, Berzelius single-handedly presented superbly executed reports on chemistry to the Stockholm Academy between 1822 and 1848. These had proved useful internationally after Wöhler, at considerable sacrifice of his time, made annual translations into German. Following Berzelius' death the system of annually reviewing the progress of chemistry was continued by Liebig and a team of successive editors until 1912. It was soon rivalled by *Chemisches Central-Blatt*, which began in 1856 after a previous incarnation as a pharmaceutical abstract.

Like Remsen at Johns Hopkins, determined to put the Massachusetts Institute of Technology (MIT) and his research school on the map, Arthur Noyes began a 'Review of American Chemistry' section in the college's *Technological Quarterly* in 1895. Noyes soon found this time-consuming and announced his intention of abandoning the service in 1902, the year that his distant cousin, William A. Noyes, became editor of the *JACS*. Rather than see what had become a useful service disappear, W. A. Noyes began to include the review, which had in practice become an abstracting service, in the *JACS*. By 1907 the section had become so large that the ACS decided to hive it off as a separate publication called *Chemical Abstracts*. Until the 1960s, these abstracts were prepared entirely by volunteers who agreed to survey particular subjects and journals.

The Chemical Society of London, at the urging of Armstrong and Williamson, had issued abstracts of foreign articles in its *Journal* since 1871, and, at the prompting of W. A. Tilden, begun an extremely useful series of *Annual*

Reports in 1905. But attempts to amalgamate, or at least to co-ordinate, the German, French, British and American abstracting services never proved feasible. In retirement after 1905, Ostwald campaigned idealistically to get chemists to abandon periodicals completely and to publish their papers on standardized loose leaves (Sammelschrift), which could then be filed. Chemists would subscribe only to 'papers' in their current field of interest. Moreover, if these papers were published in 'Ido', a derivative of Esperanto suited to chemical terminology, all problems of language and translation could be abolished. Although language can still be a problem, the computer database and the advent after 1967 of 'electronic' and dual-base journals have realized something of Ostwald's idealism.

Britain finally abandoned its abstracting service in 1954, substituting *Current Chemical Papers*, a simple listing of the contents of the world's major journals, in its place. The commercial American *Current Contents*, devised by the Philadelphian chemist, Eugene Garfield, followed two years later. Backed up by a library loans system and the growing availability of photocopying, this proved an effective means of rapid communication. By the 1970s, the success of on-line computing systems that produced the contents of *Chemical Abstracts* at the touch of a button had made a simple method for indexing chemical formulae imperative. The problem here was that the mere listing of a molecular formula was ambiguous since it referred to a large number of possible structures. From the 1950s many academic and industrial chemists developed notations that would represent structures uniquely by an unambiguous sequence of letters and numbers. In the late 1960s, *Chemical Abstracts* adopted an alphabetic–punctuation code that had been developed and refined since 1954 by the industrial chemist, William J. Wiswesser (1914–89). Another refinement to chemical literature searching made possible by the computer was the *Science Citation Index* developed by Garfield in 1961.

TABLE 12.1   *The Wiswesser line formula chemical notation (1954).*

The symbols of the elements are the same as Berzelius' except that:

1. Only the first letter is used; potential confusion between carbon and chlorine, and boron and bromine is resolved by giving chlorine the symbol G, and bromine that of E.

2. K, U, V, W, Y are used for different purposes. E.g., K stands for a nitrogen atom attached to more than three other atoms, while W indicates a non-linear (branching) dioxo group such as NO_2 or SO_2.

The molecule $HO–CH_2CH_2$ becomes Z2Q, where Z = $–NH_2$ group, the 2 showing the number of unbranched alkyl chains, and Q = a hydroxyl group.

Bromochloroaniline becomes ZRGE, where R is the benzene ring.

Complex ring structures can be accommodated by using symbols L and V together with the ampersand, hyphen, slash, asterisk and numerals which precede or follow symbols.

Although national chemical societies and their publications have been a visible barometer of the health of chemistry since the 1840s, we should recognize that commercial journals, like the defunct *Chemical News*, and those familiar today such as *Angewandte Chemie* (English version *f.* 1962) and *Tetrahedron* (*f.* 1957), have always played a vital role in chemical communications. Given the prominence of *Chemical News* in Victorian and Edwardian chemical communications, why is it no longer published?

WILLIAM CROOKES, CHEMICAL EDITOR

Crookes (1832–1919) was, like Norman Lockyer, the founder-editor of *Nature*, both a scientist of considerable originality and a journalist with sound commercial sense. Like Lockyer, he never held an academic appointment (his one attempt to exploit his editorship of *Chemical News* to obtain a Chair at the Royal Veterinary College in 1860 was unsuccessful), so his journalism, analytical consultancy work and many commercial ventures were his only means of support.

During the mid 1850s, when the technical development of photography was almost entirely in the hands of chemists, Crookes had served as editor of a number of photographic journals in Liverpool and London. Indeed, an agreement with the new weekly *Photographic News* in 1858 to give them first refusal of any articles he wrote on photography for two years meant that Crookes was initially prevented from covering photography personally in *Chemical News*. Otherwise, his target audience, including the medical profession, was pretty universal[2]:

> While Chemistry, in all its various branches, Scientific and Analytical, Technical, or in its relations to Agriculture, will . . . form the principal subject treated of, the Medical Profession will not fail to find recorded in its pages, every new discovery relating to Toxicology, Materia Medica and Pharmacy.

Bar the failed mechanics' *Chemist* of 1824–5, all previous chemical journals had been monthlies. Could Crookes find enough chemical news to sustain twenty-four columns of small type per week (i.e. twelve pages of double columns)? He evidently had little difficulty and, in fact, one of the characteristics of *Chemical News* was its trick of serialization, which was necessary both for variety of coverage and to sustain interest from week to week. We may read Faraday, Frankland, Hofmann, Odling, Pasteur, Wurtz and, of course, Crookes himself, in parts like a Dickens novel. To these serials Crookes added the customary reports of scientific meetings at the Chemical Society, Pharmaceutical Society and other societies, frequently giving information of discussions, which are not available elsewhere, from his own shorthand notes. There were also abstracts of articles from foreign journals, the coverage of French literature being particularly strong because of Crookes' friendship with L'abbé Moigno, editor of *Cosmos*. Although Crookes tried to remain neutral editorially, correspondence columns were often lively and fuelled by fractional differences over, for example, membership of the Chemical Society or, in the 1890s, the issue of whether Dewar or Ramsay should become President of the Society. The journal also noticed books and listed chemical patents.

Once this balance had been found, Crookes made little adjustment to the weekly formula. *Chemical News* shows virtually no change until 1920. In particular, he continued the *Chemical Gazette's* practice of including reports on toxicology, materia medica and pharmacy, saying that these features were specifically aimed at the medical reader. Following an initial period of financial difficulty at the beginning of the 1860s, and despite some electrifying competition from John Cargill Brough's *Laboratory* in 1867, which forced Crookes to improve the quality of his paper and type, and the pirating of copy by an American *Chemical News* issued in New York (1867–70), he was eventually able to make a financial success of it. Indeed, by 1900, according to D'Albe, Crookes was making an income of £400 p.a., and already by 1869 Crookes spoke of a sales run of 10 000 copies per week, including America. Proudly issuing its six-monthly index, Crookes called his journal the '*Jahresberichte* of Chemistry'.

The New York edition of *Chemical News* is interesting since it led to the establishment of America's first independent chemical journal. The unauthorized reprint had included a small supplementary insert entitled 'The American Chemist'. Crookes refused to do a deal with its publishers, Charles F. and William H. Chandler, and insisted that their re-publication should cease. He then made his own arrangements to have *Chemical News* distributed throughout the American continent. Not put out, the Chandlers launched the *American Chemist* as an independent monthly publication. As we have seen, Charles Chandler was an important figure in the foundation of the ACS in 1876. Given his publishing activities, it was natural that the new Society's early transactions and proceedings should appear in *American Chemist,* which, however, Chandler abandoned in 1877 when the ACS began its own *Proceedings* (from 1879, *Journal*).

Like the important weekly *English Mechanic,* which had begun in 1865, Crookes found a market among the intelligent artisan movement for whom the Department of Science and Art were providing classes and an examination system, and, of course, their teachers. Since this audience was interested in textbooks, they were regularly reviewed, often very critically. For example, the text of John Buckminster, who worked tirelessly for the Department of Science and Art, was dismissed as full of 'bad grammar, confused statements, bad chemistry and false chemistry'. Texts by Frankland, Hofmann and Williamson, on the other hand, received high praise. Given this new student audience, it can be no accident that the discussions of 'quantivalence', that is valency, found in the *English Mechanic* in the mid 1860s are also found in *Chemical News,* where 'valence' and 'valency' are first used from 1866. The importance of education is perhaps best seen in the 'student issues' that Crookes began annually from 1863 (an idea that he took from *The Lancet*). This is a most useful source of historical information concerning the way chemistry teaching slowly transformed from private to institutional teaching and for its demonstration of the continuing importance of hospital posts for chemists.

In sum, Crookes brilliantly overcame the 'difficulty of catering at once for the purely scientific reader, the practical chemist, and a still larger class of reader who, with but imperfect knowledge of the science, [sought] only for information which may be turned to account commercially'.

A monographic treatment of *Chemical News* would have

to discuss other changes of tone and the changing focus of interest in food adulteration, water analysis, chemical professionalization and debates over the endowment of research. What though, briefly, of its scientific content? There was, of course, fairly full coverage of the developments in chemistry: the historian can watch the way in which bracket type formulae continued in use until the 1870s – the first graphic or structural formula did not appear until 1871 and the benzene hexagon not until 1879 – and the way in which Crookes aided the standardization of nomenclature by adopting the Chemical Society's recommendations from 1880 onwards.

However, given that the journal was edited by William Crookes, the journal was an important vehicle for what may be termed 'metachemistry' (see chapter 1). There was a strong interest in the nature of the elements and their periodicity. Historians of chemistry recall that Newlands' speculative papers on 'the law of octaves' first appeared in *Chemical News*, as did many other speculative papers on the evolution of elements and on Prout's hypothesis. And when Crookes' interests shifted to radioactivity, the journal provided an important vehicle for research on radiochemistry. Much speculative nonsense was published by Crookes on these subjects, but his aim was obviously a good one – to encourage ideas about the ultimate nature of matter. This tradition continued after his death in 1919 with contributions during the 1920s from the schoolteacher, F. H. Loring.

If metachemistry was the journal's most obvious feature as far as pure science was concerned, the journal is also interesting and significant as a source for the social history of chemistry. A few random examples may be chosen. The absence of a pension system or benevolent fund for destitute chemists led to frequent appeals to readers to help the widows and children of minor chemical figures; for example, for the Chemical Society's librarian and editor, Henry Watts, who had heroically translated

Gmelin's *Handbook of Chemistry* and compiled a huge *Dictionary of Chemistry;* and for the former editor of *The Chemist and Druggist* and *Laboratory,* John Cargill Brough. Correspondence in the 1860s often drew attention to the scandal of purchased degrees from German universities. Similarly, readers were warned of chemical confidence tricksters who pretended to be the pupils or friends of eminent German teachers and who, by this means, borrowed or stole money from their English pupils. The journal reveals the extent to which A. W. Hofmann was revered in Britain, following his return to Berlin in 1865. In 1870 considerable publicity was given to Hofmann's appeal to British chemists for supplies of disinfectants to help in the Franco-Prussian war. It is a measure of the importance of analytical chemistry to Victorian chemists that advertisements for training courses at the Wiesbaden school of analytical chemistry run by Fresenius and his sons appeared regularly in the journal. Finally, more bizarrely, *Chemical News* also reveals the continuing survival of alchemical speculations and aspirations. In 1865 there were rises in the price of bismuth, which were attributed to a revival of alchemical experimentation. Although Crookes himself dismissed the possibility of alchemical transmutation, as befitted a metachemist, he was obviously interested in Emmens' pressure process for the transmutation of Mexican silver coins into gold, which received great publicity in 1897 (chapter 1). Emmens was even allowed to advertise in the journal.

What caused this once thriving journal to collapse in 1932?

By 1902 Crookes was seventy, and, although he oversaw the journal until the day he died in 1919, from about 1906 onwards the effective editor was Crookes' private laboratory assistant, J. H. Gardiner, who had become his research assistant when Charles Gimingham left in 1882. Gardiner became full editor on Crookes' death until 1924, when he was succeeded by John F. G. Druce (1894–1950), chemistry master at Battersea Grammar School, and one of the last schoolteachers to do original chemistry research. Druce was also a pioneer historian of science and narrowly missed the discovery of rhenium in 1925.

Druce was probably sole editor from 1924 until 1930. During this period *Chemical News* became much more of a secondary channel of chemical communication than a primary research journal. Although Gardiner had already changed the subtitle to reflect the fact that the journal no longer spoke for pharmacy and was more a 'journal of theoretical and practical chemistry and physics in their application to engineering and manufactures', the competition from the monthly *Chemical Age* (*f.* 1919) and the Society of Chemical Industry's weekly *Chemistry and Industry Journal* from 1923 effectively hived off the receipt of primary industrial articles as well as articles from the scintillating pen of the prolific Henry Edward Armstrong.

Nevertheless, the journal might still have survived as a general weekly review of science (along the lines of the monthly *Discovery* founded in 1920) but for the disastrous appointment of a new editor in 1930. This was the splendidly named and honoured[3]:

> H. C. Blood Ryan, M.A., D.Sc., LL.D., Vice President and Hon. Foreign Secretary of the European Branch of the Muslim Association for the Advancement of Science, Patron and Fellow of the British Radio Institution, Chairman of the National Institute of Criminology, Director of Research of the College of Pestology, etc.

He was also founder of the misleadingly titled Faculty of International Science in Gordon Square in the heart of the University of London.

Who exactly Ryan was is difficult to discover, though he is known to students of Nazi Germany as a 'fellow traveller of the right' who translated Göring's speeches and who blamed Hitler's rise to power on Franz von Papen. He was a journalist in the 1930s and early 1940s. His degrees were clearly phoney and he was exposed in *Nature* during the week that the final unusual thirty-two-page issue (instead of sixteen pages) of *Chemical News*, dated October 1932, appeared. This October issue carried no printed message of demise and no reference to the scandal surrounding its editor. However, a typed message tipped between the pages (a rare example is preserved in the Royal Institution's copy) announced:

> This is the only issue which will appear monthly. Publication as a weekly will resume on 25 November No. 3782. The strong Editorial Board of this journal will continue to function as hitherto.

It was not to be. On 25 October 1932 Chemical News Ltd was wound up. Dr Blood Ryan had led the company into bankruptcy. In this ignoble manner ended one of the great international organs of chemical communication.

The Nature of the Chemical Bond

> The energy of a covalent bond is largely the energy of resonance between the two atoms. The examination of the forms of the resonance integral shows that the resonance energy increases in magnitude with increase in the *overlapping* of the two atomic orbitals involved in the formation of the bond, the word 'overlapping' signifying the extent to which the regions in space in which the two orbital wave functions have large values coincide .... Consequently, it is expected that of the two orbitals in an atom the one which can overlap more with an orbital of another atom will form the stronger bond with that atom, and, moreover, the bond formed by a given orbital will tend to lie in that direction in which the orbital is concentrated.
>
> (LINUS PAULING, *The Nature of the Chemical Bond*, 1939)

Is Linus Pauling this century's greatest chemist? Like his nineteenth-century predecessors, Berzelius and Liebig, Pauling's long career has been punctuated by controversy – in Pauling's case, not merely within chemistry, but also in medicine and politics. Pauling has always craved the limelight and has used the media, the law courts and journalism with telling effect. At the Seattle, Washington, meeting of the American History of Science Society in October 1990, the eighty-nine-year-old Pauling was one of four speakers in a symposium on American science in the 1950s, when nuclear secrecy and the Cold War between western and eastern blocs had led to the witch hunting of liberal writers, Hollywood movie stars and scientists. A large crowd of historians had gathered to hear Pauling speak and became increasingly restless and disengaged from the interesting, but lengthy, papers of the other speakers. We had come to hear him, not them. At last the great man was allowed to speak and amusingly, but sardonically, he recalled how the US government had withdrawn his passport in 1952 because of his active involvement in the post-war campaign against the testing of nuclear weapons, for which he received the Nobel peace prize in 1962. In the discussion period a young woman asked how this disgraceful episode in American politics had interfered with his scientific research – meaning, did Pauling believe that he had missed solving the structure of deoxyribonucleic acid and the chance of a third Nobel prize because of the time he had been forced to waste in protecting his personal liberty. 'Probably not', was his candid answer, but when Watson, Crick and Wilkins were awarded the Nobel prize in 1962 for their 1953 double helix solution of DNA's structure, Pauling's wife had said to him: 'Linus, if this structure is so important, how come you didn't solve it?'

For, indeed, Watson, Crick and Wilkins had solved the problem by using the model-building techniques, based upon an accurate study of the lengths and angles of chemical bonds, that Pauling had used to solve the α-helix structure of proteins in 1948. That work, in its turn, had been made possible by Pauling's research on the nature of the chemical bond during the 1930s and on his introduction of the 'new' quantum mechanics into chemical thinking. His work had finally solved the problem left unresolved at the time of Cannizzaro's establishment of molecular weights in 1858, namely how two or more identical atoms (O_2, O_3, Cl_2, etc.) could combine to form a stable molecule. He had also provided an explanation of chemical affinity: why do elements combine together to form certain stable substances and not others? All of this had gained him the Nobel chemistry prize in 1954.

In 1931, at the age of thirty, Linus Pauling published the first of a series of seven papers entitled 'The nature of the chemical bond' in the *Journal of the American Chemical Society* (*JACS*) and the new *Journal of Chemical Physics*. Eight years later, in 1939, and following his tenure of the prestigious George Fisher Baker Non-resident Lectureship in Chemistry at the University of Cornell in the autumn of 1937, Pauling collected the papers together to form a book of the same title. This text was to transform the teaching of chemistry and to remain influential until the 1950s. One of the undoubted reasons for the book's success was that Pauling went out of his way to appease chemists' fears that quantum mechanics was too difficult for them by emphasizing the book's solid grounding in empirical data[1]:

> The advances which have been made have been in the main the result of essentially chemical arguments – the assumption of a simple postulate, which is then tested by empirical comparison with available chemical information, and used in the prediction of new phenomena .... The principal contribution of quantum mechanics to chemistry has been the suggestion of new ideas, such as the resonance of molecules among several electronic structures with an accompanying increase in stability.

Since its endowment by the New York banker, G. F. Baker, in 1928, Cornell University has assembled a cast list of almost all the world's leading chemists this century to deliver the Baker Lectures. Because publication is obligatory, like the Nobel Lectures, the resultant monographs form a synopsis of chemistry this century. Under the terms of publication, Pauling received no royalties for *The Nature of the Chemical Bond*, whose first edition was exhausted by 1940, but he was allowed royalties on any revised editions. Not surprisingly, then, such was the immediate demand for the book, the second edition of 1940 differed in only the most minor detail from the original. Later, in 1947, Pauling published a very successful undergraduate textbook, *College Chemistry,* which started the American trend, soon copied by foreign publishers, for opening with theory and liberally illustrating a text with striking photographs and line drawings.

Dedicated to G. N. Lewis, *The Nature of the Chemical Bond,* acknowledged its indebtedness to the influence of Lewis, Irving Langmuir, Arthur Noyes, Arthur Lapworth, Robert Robinson and Christopher Ingold. Since Pauling never had much interest in or time for organic chemistry, the fact that he mentions three British organic chemists, whose work will be discussed in the next chapter, illustrates how physical chemistry and its methods had become the general backbone of inorganic and organic chemistry during the 1920s and 1930s. In this respect, it is somewhat artificial for the historian to separate chemistry into its traditional compartments when dealing with twentieth-century history. Indeed, although this chapter will focus primarily upon the chemical bond, it will be necessary to refer to developments that were taking place concurrently in the ways by which inorganic, and especially organic, chemists were envisioning their compounds and reactions. As G. N. Lewis, with whom we begin, remarked in 1922[2]:

> The fact is that physical chemistry no longer exists. The men who have been called physical chemists have developed a large number of useful methods by which the concrete problems of inorganic chemistry, organic chemistry, biochemistry, and technical chemistry may be attacked, and as the applications of these methods grow more numerous, it becomes increasingly difficult to adhere to our older classification.

THE LEWIS ATOM

The son of a Boston lawyer, Gilbert N. Lewis (1875–1946) was brought up on a farm in the midwestern state of

Nebraska. He completed the chemical studies he began at the university there at Harvard under Theodore Richards, who had himself studied with Ostwald in 1895 and brought the new physical chemistry to Cambridge. After a year with Ostwald at Leipzig and with Nernst at Göttingen, Lewis returned to Harvard as an instructor; but disliking the Germanic authoritarianism of Richards' treatment of his assistants and his extremely empirical approach towards chemistry, Lewis left Cambridge to spend a year as an Inspector of Weights and Measures at Manila. This year in the Philippines (then an American possession) gave Lewis time to think about the role of theory in chemistry.

Although he was the first American to earn the Nobel prize in 1914, for his meticulously accurate determinations of atomic weights, in his lectures, like Ostwald, Richards always treated the atomic theory with scepticism. In introducing the word *bond* for an atom's combining power, or valency, in 1866, Frankland had cautioned that[3]:

> I do not intend to convey the idea of any material connection between the elements of a compound, the bonds actually holding the atoms of a chemical compound being, as regards their nature, much more like those which connect the members of our solar system.

The implication was not a model of rigid brackets, or hooks and eyes, but some force like gravitation. But to Richards this was metaphysical 'twaddle'[4]:

> A very crude method of representing certain known facts about chemical reactions. A mode of represent[ation] not an explanation.

Lewis did not agree and found Richards' attitude, as typified in the following letter to Julius Stieglitz, against the spirit of true research[5]:

> In my experience assistants who are not carefully superintended may be worse than none, for one

has to discover in their work not only the laws of nature, but also the assistant's insidious if not well meant mistakes. The less brilliant ones often fail to understand the force of one's suggestions, and the more brilliant ones often strike out on blind paths of their own if not carefully watched.

In a famous Faraday Lecture in London in 1881, Helmholtz had drawn out the conclusion from Faraday's electrolytic work that atoms (or ions) must have a constant charge, in which case whatever chemical affinity (the chemical bond) was, it had to be electrical in nature. But if Davy and Berzelius had been right all along that affinity was electrochemical, this did not help explain the existence of stable dimers like O_2 and Cl_2, which chemists and physicists had accepted since the 1860s. Everything that was known about electrical and magnetic forces told the investigator that such molecules had no right to exist. Arrhenius' postulation of free ions in dilute solutions existing independently of an electric current only increased chemists' bewilderment.

Clarification came from physicists' experiments on the conduction of electricity through gases at low pressures. In 1897, at the Cavendish Laboratory at Cambridge in England, J. J. Thomson identified a negatively charged corpuscle considerably lighter than the lightest known atom, hydrogen. Had the so-called atom been disintegrated? The sceptic's objection that the electron (as Stoney named it) might have emanated from the electric current used in forming cathode rays was scotched by Ernest Rutherford in 1902 when his researches on radioactivity identified the electron with α-radiation. By the beginning of the twentieth century, therefore, to progressive minds at least, there could be little doubt that the nature of chemical bonding was electrical and that it had something to do with the electron. Any satisfactory explanation would, however, depend in future upon a satisfactory model of the atom being developed. Thomson, not surprisingly, was quick to develop what critics were to dub the 'plum-pudding' model in which electrons were embedded like plums in circular arrays within a spherical pudding of positive charge. Chemical bonds were conceived as electrostatic effects caused by the transfer of electrons from one of the outer circles to an adjacent atom.

In the early 1900s, Lewis read Werner's *Neuere Anschauungen* (see chapter 15). Surviving notes, together with the fact that Lewis went out of his way in his *Valence* (1923) to admit his 'personal indebtedness' to Werner's revolutionary teachings, suggest that Werner was a spur to Lewis' thoughts on chemical bonding. While Werner's notion of the 'co-ordination' of atoms around a different central atom to form a positive or negative ion or neutral molecule seemed to Lewis a valuable way of dealing with inorganic complexes, he was less than happy with Werner's 'confusion between the concepts of affinity and valence' and his 'failure to give full recognition of the polar character of valence'. Werner had, of course, ignored the electron in his model of inorganic complexes; but, by 1902, this was something Lewis could not. Indeed, by 1904, Thomson had developed the first electronic theory of valency. According to this, a revival of Berzelius' electrochemical scheme mixed with Maxwell's electromagnetic theory, the chemical bond was nothing more or less than simple electrostatic attraction. A bond was formed when two atoms exchanged, or transferred, one or more electrons, the donor thereby becoming positively charged and the receiver, negatively charged. While Werner could be criticized for ignoring the polar nature of many bonds, the exciting thing, as far as Lewis was concerned, was that Werner had shown that there were other non-polar possibilities.

This notion was to be developed by Lewis as early as 1902 on the back of an envelope upon which he doodled a series of 'cubic atoms' in which contiguous cubes *shared*, rather than *exchanged*, outer electrons along a common edge. The cubic model was probably inspired less by crystallographic considerations than by the fact that Lewis, like many European chemists, had noticed that the stability of the rare gases (including helium, as was then thought) appeared to stem from their possession of eight electrons in the outermost sphere of the Thomson 'plum-pudding' model of the atom. In 1904 a 'rule of eight' was formally described by R. Abegg. He pointed to a feature of the periodic table, namely that the variable valencies (or 'principal' and 'contra-valencies') of the individual atoms in a compound seemed always to add up to eight, if electropositivity or electronegativity was ignored. Thus, in NaCl, the valency of Cl is -1, but in $HClO_3$ (if $O = -2$), Cl is $+7$:

Group	1	2	3	4	5	6	7
Primary valency	$+1$	$+2$	$+3$	$+4$	-3	-2	-1
Contra-valency	-7	-6	-5	-4	$+5$	$+6$	$+7$
	8	8	8	8	8	8	8

Might not the same stability be conferred on compounds if eight outer electrons were shared? This would explain the existence of binary gases such as O_2 and Cl_2. Unfortunately, Abegg, an electrochemist in Nernst's laboratory in Berlin, was killed in a ballooning accident in 1911 and was, therefore, unable to contribute further to valency theory.

Lewis, who may have continued to use the cubic atom as a heuristic teaching aid, did not publish these speculations. Instead, in 1904, after his return from Manila, he had joined the exciting atmosphere of the chemistry department at the Massachusetts Institute of Technology (MIT), where another Ostwald pupil, Arthur Noyes (1866–1936), was struggling to solve the problem of strong electrolytes. In this stimulating atmosphere, given the van't Hoff gas-solution analogy, it was natural that Thomson's work on the conductivity of gases and his ideas on the structure of atoms (the plum-pudding model in which spheres of electrons surrounded a central positive nucleus), which he had published in *The Corpuscular Theory of Matter* (1907), should attract close attention at MIT. As Servos has emphasized, it was the continuing problem of Arrhenius' theory of ionization that encouraged the MIT physical chemists to develop a theory of bonding. Despite his immersion in thermodynamics (a field for which he was to become renowned among students for his textbook with Merle Randall, *Thermodynamics and the Free Energy of Chemical Substances*, 1923), this subject deeply interested Lewis. Any bonding theory would have to explain why some substances ionized in solution and obeyed the law of mass action, while others did not.

The same thought occurred to William Ramsay in England in 1908 when he pictured electrons as 'amoeba-like' structures that surrounded atoms like the rind of an orange. On combination, the rind separated to form a layer or cushion between atoms, but in solution it rinded itself to one atom and not the other.

In 1910 one of Lewis's colleagues, K. George Falk, collaborated with John M. Nelson of Columbia University on a paper entitled 'The electron conception of valence'. This enthusiastically endorsed Thomson's notion that bonds were formed by the transfer of outer electrons such that one part was left positive, the other negative. They reintroduced the arrows on bonds that Thomson had suggested in his *Corpuscular Theory* to indicate the direction of electron transfer. For example:

It seemed to follow, they deduced, that, where double bonds occurred, electronic isomers ('electromers') might exist:

$$\overset{+}{CR_2} \longrightarrow \overset{-}{CR_2} \quad \text{and} \quad \overset{-}{CR_2} \longleftarrow \overset{+}{CR_2}$$

Although their polarity theory did not explain the bonding of non-ionizing molecules, much solid-phase chemistry seemed to support it. In the same year, an organic chemist at the University of Cincinnati, Harold S. Fry (1878–1949), explored how Thomson's model might aid the understanding of organic reaction mechanisms. His papers became notorious among compositors for demanding structural formulae liberally sprinkled with pluses and minuses, e.g.

In Russia, A. M. Berkenheim, who also adopted the polar theory, used dots and apostrophes instead, but this cannot have helped printers very much. Further essays on the possible existence of electronic isomers, such as $N^+ Cl_3{}^-$, from the hands of Noyes and Julius Stieglitz at the University of Chicago, firmly established a polar theory of chemical bonding within the cutting edge of American chemical research.

In 1912 Lewis moved from MIT to the University of California at Berkeley, where he established a research school that was to dominate American chemistry until his death in 1946. The school became renowned for its weekly workshops in which new ideas and experimental work were freely discussed and criticized. 'The members of the department became like the Athenians', J. H. Hildebrand recalled[6]:

> Anyone who thought he had a bright idea rushed to try it out on a colleague. Groups of two or more could be seen every day in offices, before blackboards or even in the corridors arguing vehemently about these 'brainstorms'. It is doubtful whether any paper ever emerged for publication that had not run the gauntlet of such criticism. The whole department thus became far greater than the sum of its individual members.

In this atmosphere doubts concerning the exclusive nature of the polar bonding model began to be raised. These were first articulated in print in 1913, not by Lewis, whose reservations clearly went back to 1902, but by two colleagues, William C. Bray (whom Lewis had brought from MIT) and an English chemist from Liverpool, Gerard E. K. Branch (1886–1954). While accepting that most inorganic chemistry depended upon the polar bond, they rejected it for organic chemistry. Much of their argument hinged on the phenomenon of tautomerism, the low dielectric constants and the poor conductivities of organic compounds. They proposed instead that a non-polar bond should be distinguished from the polar bond by a Wernerian-like notion of 'total valence' or 'polar number' (later termed the 'oxidation number' by Wendell Latimer) – that is, the total number of polar and non-polar bonds in the graphic formula of the substance.

This paper gave Lewis his first excuse to comment publicly on valency. While he endorsed Bray's and Branch's differentiation he pointed to a further distinction. Whereas non-polar bonds were clearly fixed in space, as classical structural chemistry demanded, because electrostatic forces were radially symmetric, the polar bond was not. Thomson's image of a vector bond, and Fry's, and Bray and Branch's, attempts to notate the exchange of electrons by adding a directional arrow to the bond line (e.g. Na→Cl), was misleading. How could one tell from which atom electrons came in two contrasting compounds like HCl and CCl_4? As Lewis commented[7]:

> Since all electrons are alike, and presumably leave no trail behind them, we cannot say that atom A loses an electron to atom B and atom C to atom D, but only that atoms A and C have each lost an electron and atoms B and D have each gained one.

This was to become a key point in the new quantum mechanics.

Developments now came thick and fast. In England, Thomson was forced to abandon the plum-pudding model by Rutherford's convincing evidence for a planetary–nuclear model of the atom. His own research with Francis Aston on positive ray analysis not only led to the discovery of isotopes, but also forced Thomson to revise his views that all bonds were essentially polar. For example, in the positive ray apparatus it was clear that CO_2 could form species in which both carbon and oxygen were positively charged. In 1914, therefore, independently of the Americans, Thomson came to the conclusion that there were two types of bond, polar and non-polar. Mathematical analysis enabled Thomson to picture Faraday 'tubes of force' anchoring electrons both to the nucleus and to an adjacent atom. This was the non-polar bond. In order to achieve electrical neutrality, however, Thomson had to assume that:

> for each tube of force which passes out of the atom, another must come in; and thus each atom containing n corpuscles must be the origin of n tubes going into other atoms and also the termination of n tubes coming from each atom.

The curious consequence of Thomson's mathematics was, therefore, that *two* tubes of force, or *two electrons*, one from each atom, participated in the bonding. In principle, he suggested, structural formulae ought to be drawn with two vector bonds instead of one whenever non-ionic bonds were represented: for example, Na—Cl; but a carbon–carbon single bond C=C and double bond C≡C, etc. In a further elaboration of this model, which will be ignored, Thomson deduced that there were two possible types of non-polar bond depending upon the number of electrons in the outer orbit.

In the same year, 1914, one of Lewis' British graduate students, Alfred Parson (1889–?), who was much taken by the magnetic research of the French physicist, Paul Langevin, suggested that bonding could be magnetic, not electrical, in origin. In his 'magneton' theory the electron became, in effect, an electromagnet. In the model, a variation of Thomson's plum-pudding atom, the magnetons were arranged not in spheres, but at the corners of cubes surrounding a central positive charge. The electromagnetic field generated by their motions constituted chemical affinity. Parson was actually able to build a working model and to show that stable configurations would be produced.

No doubt because Parson's model was pre-Rutherfordian and involved a horrendously complex notation, it was rejected by the *JACS*; however, William Albert Noyes, its editor and a cousin of Arthur Noyes, recognizing its theoretical interest, did arrange for publication elsewhere as a monograph. Like Thomson, Parson had to assume that, to complete octets, two types of magneton bonding were possible – 'negative action' in which nearly filled octets were completed by the transfer of magnetons (corresponding to a polar bond), and 'positive action' in which very incomplete octets avoided the large electrostatic charge that would accompany the transfer of magnetons by pairing (or sharing) magnetons instead.

By the time the monograph appeared in 1915, Parson was a shell-shocked volunteer on the fields of Flanders. He never returned to his promising scientific career. As Robert Kohler has suggested, it was probably the shy, eccentric Parson's reference to a cubic atom (chosen solely to fit the eight outer electron rule) that caused Lewis to 'exhume his eleven year old notes', and to re-examine them in the light of the speculations of Thomson, Parson and others. There was one new factor; unlike Parson, who disbelieved it, Lewis was persuaded that Moseley's X-ray spectral evidence of 1914 demonstrated that helium possessed only one pair of electrons.

Kohler, who has studied the matter very closely, is convinced that Lewis hit upon the shared electron pair while attempting to reconcile Thomson's and Parson's model with his cubic doodlings of 1902. For, if the edges of two cubes were aligned then, at one stroke, Lewis could eliminate the need for electron vectors, two tubes of force, and Thomson's two types of non-polar bonding, and produce a much more concrete, less abstract portrait of Parson's negative action.

Moreover, although in 1913 he had supported Bray and Branch's dualistic views – that there were two different bonding mechanisms – by 1916 he found the division 'repugnant'. Retrospectively, he wrote[8]:

> It seemed rather that the union of sodium and chlorine and the union of hydrogen and carbon must represent extreme types of a method of combination which ultimately would be found to be common to all kinds of compounds.

In other words, where electrons were equally shared, the molecule exhibited no polar properties, but if one atom took an unfair share, then the charge being unequally distributed, polarity would be produced. At one bound this explained the Noyes' research school's perennial problem: the difference between strong and weak electrolytes. In the former, the electron pair was closer to one atomic kernel than to the other and so easily fractured in a solvent with a high dielectric constant; alternatively, shared electrons were slightly displaced towards groups that were eager to attract electrons (what Ingold was to call electrophilic groups). A polar medium like water would encourage such molecules to ionize. Finally, non-electrolytes were molecules in which there was no displacement of the covalent bond. Such an explanation did not, of course, explain the anomalous conductance properties of strong electrolytes, which only began to be solved by Debye and Hückel in 1923.

Lewis' account of his chemical cubes was published as 'The atom and the molecule' in the *JACS* in 1916. Here he introduced a notation that, since the positive 'kernel' of an atom, corresponding to its atomic number, remains unaltered during reactions, the ordinary chemical symbol could be used to represent the kernel, viz. Li stands for Li^+, Be for Be^{2+}, etc. Then, following an earlier suggestion of William Ramsay in 1908 that the electron be treated like an additional element, the number of outer bonding electrons, E, could be indicated numerically, e.g. lithium fluoride $LiFE_8$, and lithium sulphate $Li_2SO_4E_{32}$. This symbolism never became generally used; much more influential was the suggestion in the same paper that paired electrons should be represented by a colon. This simple piece of typography was destined to replace the cubic atom itself.

The paper recognized that 'the atomic shells were mutually interpenetrable' so that an electron 'may form part of the shell of two different atoms, and cannot be said to belong to either one exclusively'. This assumption, which was to be a cardinal principle of the new quantum mechanics, illustrates the ease with which Lewis' concept could be translated into that new language at the appropriate time. This did not prevent the assumption becoming the butt of a well known objection voiced in the lectures of Kasimir Fajans:

Saying that each of two atoms can attain closed electron shells by sharing a pair of electrons is equivalent to saying that husband and wife, by having a total of two dollars in a joint account and each having six dollars in individual bank accounts, have got eight dollars apiece.

Similarly, given that Picasso and Braque had reached their cubic phase at about the same time, it was easy to ridicule Lewis' proposals. In a Faraday lecture, R. A. Mullikan derided what he called the 'loafer electron' theory in which American chemists had:

imagined the electrons sitting around on dry goods boxes at every corner, ready to shake hands with, or hold on to similar loafer electrons in other atoms.

Although Lewis suggested that double bonds might be represented by the joining of the faces of cubes, the paper was actually extremely spare in its use of cubic drawings. He clearly perceived the model's limitations: triple bonds could not be portrayed, and although one could suppose that the kernels might repel each other and produce strains in the geometry, the model did not encompass the facts of stereochemistry. Aboved all, compared with the contemporaneous Bohr–Sommerfeld model of the circulating and radiating electron, it said nothing about spectra. Given these problems, and the cynicism mentioned, not surprisingly Lewis never used the cubic atom after 1916. What survived though was the shared electron pair as the key feature of the chemical bond.

Just as Thomas Thomson had propagated Dalton's theory at the beginning of the nineteenth century, so Irving Langmuir (1881–1957) was to act as publicist for the shared pair immediately after the First World War. Lewis was a great teacher, but he lacked the dash and charisma of Langmuir, a metallurgy graduate from Columbia University and a pupil of Nernst, who had joined the General Electric

Company (GEC) as an industrial scientist in 1909. Under the direction of Noyes' former student, Willis R. Whitney, GEC became, in Kohler's words, 'one of the liveliest, most forward-looking and productive centers of chemical and physical research in America'. Langmuir was given a completely free hand and by 1919 he was celebrated internationally for his brilliant work on surface absorption and chemical kinetics and their industrial applications.

Langmuir's effective popularization of the shared pair, which soon became known as the 'Lewis–Langmuir' theory, put Lewis in an awkward position; on the one hand, he appreciated the publicity, but on the other hand, he resented the implication that the theory had needed improvement or correction, or that they had collaborated. Langmuir always acknowledged Lewis' priority, but Lewis' growing frostiness probably prompted Langmuir to abandon the field of bonding in 1921; the competition also prompted Lewis to compose his definitive and influential *Valence and the Structure of the Atom* (1923). It must have been galling to play second fiddle to the younger man, who, unlike Lewis, was to win the Nobel prize for chemistry in 1932. To be fair to Langmuir, he did make several significant contributions to the theory, not the least of which was to rename the non-polar bond the 'covalent bond' (he seems to have derived the term from Abegg's 'contra-valency'), and to reconcile Lewis' static electrons with the dynamic electrons of Bohr's theory.

Under Whitney's stimulating influence, research at GEC was conducted as freely and openly as it was with Noyes at MIT and Lewis at Berkeley. Langmuir's early work on the improvement of the tungsten filament of light bulbs had led him to the study of the effects of high temperatures on gases in which such filaments might be placed. In this way he had stumbled on the dissociation of hydrogen, the kinetics of which he studied, and the fact that oxygen formed a monomolecular layer on a tungsten surface. Research on the latter phenomenon had drawn Langmuir into theories of the mechanism of absorption of gases by solids, and hence into theories of bonding. Langmuir read widely before coming up with his own eclectic synthesis of the ideas of Thomson, Bohr, Parson, Lewis and another polar theory that had been developed in Germany in 1916 by Walther Kossel. Langmuir's innovation, in 1919, when he began a stream of 'somewhat cabalistic' papers and talks on the subject, was to arrange all the electrons in the elements of the periodic table into 'shells' using the *aufbau* (building) principle first developed by Bohr. (Langmuir's assumptions concerning the sequence of electronic shells were incorrect and were soon altered by Bury and Bohr.) Chemical properties were then explained by Lewis' concept of the pairing and sharing of electrons in a stable octet in the final shell. He was to make a great deal of an 'octet rule' that the number of shared pair bonds, p, was determined by the number of valence electrons, e, and the number of octets, n, by the rule $e = 8n - p$. For example, in NH_4Cl, $e = 16$, $n = 2$, so that p is zero. The bond between nitrogen and chlorine is, therefore, ionic, not covalent. The rule's misleading nature was to be responsible for chemists' failure to perceive that, under certain conditions, the rare gases might form compounds (chapter 9).

For a time the theory was called 'the octet theory of valency'; but the more abstract, mathematical tone of Langmuir's presentations was in the end its undoing, as was his over-enthusiastic use of cubic atoms, which Lewis had meanwhile dropped. But Langmuir did succeed brilliantly in giving Lewis' ideas some much needed post-war publicity within the chemical community, as can be gathered from the uplifting tone of a popular lecture of 1921[9]:

These things mark the beginning, I believe, of a new chemistry, a deductive chemistry, one in which we can reason out chemical relationships without falling back on chemical intuition. . . . I think that within a few years we will be able to deduce 90 per cent of everything that is in every textbook on chemistry, deduce it as you need it, from simple ordinary principles, knowing definite facts in regard to the structure of the atoms.

The chemical community was therefore openly receptive when Lewis published his masterpiece, *Valence and the Structure of Atoms and Molecules,* in 1923.

One of the pleasures of *Valence* is Lewis' awareness that writing a scientific monograph is like writing a newspaper article; it belongs to the 'ephemeral literature of science', he remarked. Nevertheless, it is remarkable how much of Lewis' essay still forms the backbone of chemical theory and structural chemistry, despite the fact that it pre-dated quantum-mechanical conceptions. The first part of *Valence* was a historical review of bonding theories since the time of Berzelius. This included a reproduction of the page from his notebook of 1902, as well as an account of the development of ideas of atomic structure and spectra. He then turned to the problem of how the essentially static, unchanging atom portrayed by the chemist and deduced from the periodic law and the chemical behaviour of elements and compounds could be reconciled with the image of moving electrons and electrical Coulomb forces of attraction and repulsion portrayed by physicists[10]:

Isomers maintain their identity for years, often without the slightest appreciable transformations. An organic molecule treated with powerful reagents often suffers radical change in one part of the molecule while the remainder appears to suffer no change. It appears inconceivable that these permanent though essentially unstable configurations could result from the simple law of force embodied in Coulomb's law.

An answer to this fundamental paradox had, he argued, been found in Bury and Bohr's recent extension of Bohr's original model. Electrons were now placed in shells protecting a nucleus. In this new model the important thing was the orbit 'as a whole', not the exact position of an electron within the orbit. Lewis then pointed out that this picture was essentially the same as the kernel model that he had published in 1916 and adumbrated in 1902. The pairing of electrons in outer shells (with some adjustment of the kernel structures of the transition elements) could then account for the reactivity of elements and compounds, without the need to assume the transfer of electrons[11]:

> The new theory, *which includes the possibility of complete ionization as a special case,* may be given definite expression as follows: Two atoms may conform to the rule of eight, or the octet rule, not only by the transfer of electrons from one atom to another, but also by sharing one or more pairs of electrons. The electrons which are held in common by two atoms may be considered to belong to the outer shell of both atoms [his stress].

Valency could then be redefined as 'the number of electron pairs which an atom shares with another atom', and expressed graphically, as with hydrogen and chlorine as H:H and Ċl:Ċl and hydrogen chloride as H:Ċl.

The polarity theory, which was dominating the thoughts of American chemists, could then be accommodated as displacements indicated by printers' white space, i.e.

$$H{:}H, \quad Na\ {:}H, \quad H\ {:}Cl{:} \quad or \quad [H]^+ \quad [{:}Cl{:}]^-$$

Such a displacement effect was to be taken up by organic chemists and renamed the 'inductive effect'. Double and triple bonds could also be rendered by double and triple colons, i.e.

oxygen $: O : : O :$

ethylene $H : C : : C : H$
                   H H

acetylene $H : C : : : C : H$

The special reactivity of unsaturated molecules like ethylene, acetylene and its congeners could also be easily understood if they were written as

$$H : \overset{\cdot}{\underset{\cdot}{C}} : \overset{\cdot}{\underset{\cdot}{C}} : H \qquad \text{and} \qquad H : \overset{\cdot\cdot}{C} : \overset{\cdot\cdot}{C} : H$$
$$\quad\ \ H\ \ H$$

Organic chemists were, again, to find this of value in understanding reaction mechanisms. The new dotted formulae were immediately adopted by Lewis' colleague, Joel Hildebrand (1881–1983), for a college text, *Principles of Chemistry* (1919).

Valence concluded with reference to two other important ideas. The first, Lewis' own, had originated in thoughts about the long debates over strong and weak electrolytes. Experimentally, the debate had shown that substances that behaved as strong acids in water might well behave only as weak acids, or even act as bases, in different solvents. Lewis, therefore, reached for a more general definition of acids as a class of substances. They were, he suggested, molecules able to accept a pair of electrons, while bases were potential donors. Since this definition included not only conventional acids like sulphuric acid, but strange new ones like boron and aluminium chlorides, the suggestion was to open up a whole new area of physical inorganic chemistry.

The second idea, which received Lewis' 'enthusiastic

support', had been conceived in his department by an undergraduate student, Maurice L. Huggins, in 1920. In a term essay, Huggins had struggled to explain the keto–enol tautomerism of acetoacetic acid by postulating a transition state in which a hydrogen kernel was simultaneously bound to a carbon and oxygen atom. Although Huggins was encouraged to write this up, publishing the idea in 1922, the notion was put to immediate use to explain the anomalous properties of water by two of Lewis' colleagues, Wendell Latimer and Worth Rodebush, in 1920. In *Valence,* Lewis referred to such hydrogen co-ordination as the 'hydrogen bond', adding that he considered it 'a most important addition to my theory'. In fact, although destined to be a vital component of Pauling's visualization of protein structure in the 1930s, hydrogen bonds were not immediately adopted by other chemists. Henry Armstrong, whose 'hydrone', or association theory of water, was threatened by the new bond, made wonderfully sarcastic remarks about it in *Nature* in 1926:

> I note that in a lecture . . . [Lowry] brought forward certain freak formulae for tartaric acid, in which hydrogen figures as a bigamist. I may say he but follows the loose example set by certain Uesanians, especially one E.[*sic*] N. Lewis a Californian thermo-dynamiter, who has chosen to disregard the fundamental canons of chemistry – for no obvious reason other than that of indulging in premature speculation upon electrons as the cause of valency.

One can almost hear Kolbe cheering Armstrong on from Elysium.

SPREADING THE ELECTRONIC THEORY

Apart from 'Henry the Prophet', as he once appropriately designated himself, who provided stimulatingly eccentric copy for editors in the 1920s and 1930s, British chemists adopted Lewis' views on valency with enthusiasm. In July 1923, just before the book was published, Lewis had been the first speaker at a Faraday Society discussion on 'The electronic theory of valency' organized by T. M. Lowry, with J. J. Thomson, the Master of Trinity College, in the chair. The details of this important discussion between chemists and physicists will be deferred until the following two chapters. Suffice it to say here that the mood was enthusiastic, though tempered by a realization that chemistry was at a 'transition stage' in understanding, comparable, as Sir Robert Robertson (1869–1949) put it, 'with that which obtained in the forties and fifties of last century when Gerhardt and Laurent and Williamson were formulating the facts of organic chemistry according to their partial hypotheses'.

Although Thomson's curiously old-fashioned *The Electron in Chemistry* (1923) could ignore Lewis and Langmuir (and for that matter Bohr as well), as Kohler has shown in his detailed analysis of the Lewis–Langmuir atom, there were, in practice, different rates of uptake of the electronic theory of valency by chemists in different countries. If the British, on the whole, found the transition easy because the theory was readily accommodated into a speculative–experimental tradition of organic chemistry that reached its peak in the 1920s, and into Sidgwick's important reworking of Werner's ideas in inorganic chemistry, matters were different in America, France and Germany. Lewis himself had very little interest in organic chemistry, but it was precisely here that the theory was most helpful theoretically. And outside Berkeley the commonest view of the structure of inorganic and organic compounds remained the electropolar models of Thomson, Noyes, Stieglitz, Fry and Falk. Indeed, in 1920 and 1921, Falk and Fry independently summarized their extreme versions of the Thomsonian polarity theory in their *Chemical Reactions. Their Theory and Mechanisms* and *The Electronic Conception of Valence and the Constitution of Benzene*. This was just when what Fry described as the 'Lewis–Langmuir bandwagon' was rolling. The consequence was that the fusion of physical and organic chemistry first took place in Britain rather than the USA and had to be imported into the States in the early 1930s.

The same seems to be true of Germany, despite the fact that physical chemistry had been created there by Ostwald. Part of Germany's problem was its great success in synthetic organic chemistry which, until the First World War, dominated its research activities. This powerful tradition of structural organic chemistry tended to be accompanied by antipathy towards theory – an antipathy that its masters, Bunsen, Kolbe, Baeyer and Fischer, had done much to establish. The quite proper educational decision of the German universities to insist that at least two years were spent on doctoral studies had also effectively discouraged British and American students from doing postgraduate (though not postdoctoral) work in Germany. As early as 1902, H. C. Jones had commented:

All in all, Germany has lost much of her prestige in chemistry. In physics the loss is greater. I am fully convinced that there is more good work being done in America in physics, physical chemistry, and inorganic chemistry than in Germany.

War, the terrible inflation of the 1920s, which inhibited travel to and from Germany, and the prevention of Germans from subscribing to foreign chemical journals, also took their toll on Germany's once powerful chemical reputation. In their isolation German chemists found it difficult to learn about the Lewis–Langmuir atom and turned back instead to pre-war theorists of their own, including Johannes Stark, a physics Nobel prizewinner who was later to be notorious for his support of the Third Reich. Stark's *Prinzipien der Atomdynamik* (1915) is filled with strange pictures of positive atoms connected to one or more electrons by tortuous Faraday tubes of force; like Parson's magneton theory it was pre-Rutherfordian in its premises and out of date before it was published. Another physicist, Walther Kossel, had also developed an electrostatic theory of bonding in 1916 in which a non-polar bond was mentioned; this was not the same as Lewis' idea, since for Kossel it was merely an incomplete transfer of an electron pair, not a sharing.

Indeed, apart from a school of physical chemists in Munich who, significantly, had spent some time abroad completing and broadening their chemical education, German chemists were slow to adopt the Lewis–Langmuir theory. Even then, the country's chemists tended to take a maverick road in bonding theory. In Breslau, and later Istanbul, where he fled from Nazi persecution in 1933, Fritz Arndt (1885–?) developed a theory of 'intermediate stages' (*Zwischenstafen*), which proved useful in his studies of organic reactions in the 1930s. However, Arndt found it extremely difficult to get theoretical work published in Germany and was able to express his views only in vague terms. In 1938, his writings banned in Germany, Arndt secretly encouraged his former pupil B. Eistert to publish *Tautomerie und Mesomerie*. Apart from W. Hückel's *Grundlagen der organischen Chemie* (1931), this was the first German monograph to identify the importance of electronic theory in organic chemistry. H. Hellman's quantum chemistry had to be published in Austria in 1937, just prior to the Nazi *Anschluss*, and several years after he had escaped to Moscow from Nazi persecution. His fate in the Soviet Union is still unknown. During the 1920s in Munich there was an awareness of Lewis' approach. Here, while he was an instructor in physical chemistry, the Pole, Kasimir Fajans (1887–1975), devised an essentially electrostatic theory of electron deformation whereby electrons might be torn loose from their outer orbits to form a new 'molecular orbit' that constituted the covalent bond. Fajans never came to terms with quantum mechanics, and after he had emigrated to the United States in 1936, he developed the model further, calling it the 'quanticule theory'.

In France the pervasive influences of Marcellin Berthelot

and Le Chatelier (1850–1936) tended to focus physical chemists' attention on thermodynamics and the study of equilibria. Moreover, since both chemists were opposed to atomism, despite the crucial evidence for the existence of atoms provided by Jean Perrin (1870–1942) in 1908, French research remained largely indifferent to the question of how bonds were broken and made. As in Germany, the First World War also had a devastating effect on scientific communications. Some of this was self-inflicted; at Lyon, for example, the University refused to subscribe to German science periodicals until 1923. Despite the stimulation that de Broglie's work gave to wave mechanics in the 1920s, the French did not participate in the creation of the quantum theory of the chemical bond. Only after he had won the Nobel prize for chemistry in 1926 was Perrin in a position to establish a large physical chemistry laboratory in Paris, but this tended to be eclectic in its research interests and, again, no particular line of research stood out. France's severe naturalization rules were also to inhibit Jewish refugee scientists from Germany and Austria from settling there and hence, unlike Britain and America, French chemistry did not benefit from an infusion of theoretical talent during the 1930s. It was not until the 1940s, in fact, that serious research on quantum chemistry began with Raymond Daudel (*b.* 1920) whose group helped considerably in making molecular orbital calculations useful to organic chemists.

Germany's reputation in mathematical physics was otherwise. In November 1895, while experimenting with a Crookes' cathode ray tube, Wilhelm Röntgen (1845–1923) discovered the penetrating radiation he called X-rays. Subsequent work by physicists in both Germany and Britain showed that, when elements were bombarded with X-rays, harder and softer reflections, labelled by C. G. Barkla rather arbitrarily as K, L and M, were obtained. In 1912 the German optical physicist, Max von Laue (with the help of Sommerfeld's graduate student, Paul Ewald), concluded that if X-rays were short-wave radiation then, assuming that crystals arose from a periodic array of atoms comparable in dimensions to the wavelength of the X-radiation, the waves ought to be diffracted. Such diffraction effects were immediately confirmed by Laue's assistants, Walter Friedrich and Paul Knipping. Soon after the first photographs were released, the two Braggs, the father William Henry Bragg (1862–1942), and his son William Lawrence Bragg (1890–1971), transformed what had been an experiment to clarify the nature of X-rays into a new science of crystal structure determination. From the diffraction equation,

$$n \lambda = 2d \sin \theta$$

where $n = 1, 2, 3, \ldots$ and λ is the wavelength, the distance d, between crystal planes could be determined and from this, after laborious calculation, the arrangement of atoms in the crystal deduced.

Laue's experiment also encouraged Harold Gwyn Moseley (1887–1915) to reshape Barkla's work into the science of X-ray spectroscopy. By measuring the wavelengths of Barkla's characteristic K, L and M reflections for each element, Moseley found a characteristic and unique 'atomic number'. By 1914 he had realized that when arranged *seriatim* the atomic number was, with a few significant exceptions, the same as the order of the elements given by atomic weights. Because it was equal to the positive nuclear charge, the physicist now knew how many neutralizing electrons surrounded the nucleus. Röntgen's discovery, therefore, not only revolutionized orthopedic surgery, but helped to transform chemists' ideas of the structure of materials and stimulated the physicists' interpretation of the nature of the atom.

By the end of the nineteenth century the fields of interest of chemists and physicists had become fairly distinct. Chemists dealt with a world consisting of some ninety-odd material elements, while physicists handled a more nebulous mathematical world of energy and electromagnetic waves that were perceived in light, radiant heat, electricity and magnetism and, by the 1890s, radio waves and X-rays. The chemists' matter was discrete and discontinuous, the physicists' energy continuous. To be sure, the new physical school of chemists, like Ostwald, tried to interpret chemistry solely in terms of energy, and there had been some success in applying physical methods to chemistry.

In the early 1900s Max Planck's thermodynamic investigations had led him to conclude that, at the atomic level, energy could not be emitted or absorbed continuously, but only in small discrete steps he called 'quanta'. In this quantum theory, energy radiated from a lamp or heat source only appeared to radiate continuously because it was a smoothed or averaged effect of large numbers of quanta or what, in the case of light, Einstein in 1905 called photons. In developing his planetary model of the atom in 1913, Niels Bohr (1885–1962) avoided the paradox of classical physics that revolving electrons would lose energy continuously and therefore slowly collapse into the nucleus, by adopting Planck's quantum theory. Accordingly, in the Bohr atom, electrons moved in circular orbits around the nucleus without radiating continuously. When an atom absorbed or emitted a photon, an electron jumped from one orbit to another, the light energy emitted or absorbed being perceived as a line in the substance's spectrum. Bohr had been able to obtain impressive agreement between his theory, which gave a value for the radiation frequency, and the frequency predicted empirically by Johannes Rydberg (1854–1919) in 1890 for the lines in the so-called Balmer series of the visible hydrogen spectrum. But atoms with more than one electron proved more recalcitrant.

Nevertheless, in the hands of Bohr in Copenhagen and Arnold Sommerfeld in Munich, the 'old quantum mechanics' (as historians like to call it), by adding various quantum numbers, *n*, *k* (later *l*), *m* and *s* to help to define the elliptical orbits and the magnetic and spin properties of electrons, proved successful in correlating theory with spectroscopic data. In so doing, C. R. Bury and Bohr had by 1923 mapped out in detail the electronic structure of elements within the periodic table. Electrons were distributed in shells corresponding to the values of the principal quantum number, n, the maximum number of electrons possible in successive shells moving out from the nucleus being 2, 8, 8, 18, 18, 32, with subshells being postulated when necessary to explain the properties of the transition and rare-earth elements.

In a thesis published in 1924, Louis de Broglie (1892–1987) argued that, if one took Einstein's photoelectric effect of 1905 to its logical conclusion that light possessed a dual nature, then perhaps electrons could also be considered to have both corpuscular and wave-like properties. This startling suggestion was not confirmed experimentally until 1927 when C. J. Davisson and L. H. Germer in America using a nickel crystal, and George P. Thomson in England using thin metal films, showed that, like X-rays, electrons could be diffracted by matter. Even in the absence of experimental evidence, however, de Broglie's suggestion had been sufficient to encourage Erwin Schrödinger (1887–1961), a theoretical physicist at the University of Zürich, to develop the hypothesis mathematically. In 1926 Schrödinger published his now famous partial differential equation:

$$\partial^2\psi/\partial x^2 + \partial^2\psi/\partial y^2 + \partial^2\psi/\partial z^2 + [8\pi^2 m/h^2]\,(E - V)\,\psi = 0$$

where ψ is the wave function and E and V the total and potential energies of the system. (It is to be underlined that this equation was for just one particle; for a system of electrons the equation took on what would have been for chemists in the 1920s a terrifying appearance.) In Schrödinger's interpretation, the square of the wave function, ψ^2, was a measure of the density of electron charge at each point on the three-dimensional co-ordinate system. Others pointed out that this was equivalent to a probability statement: ψ^2 would be a measure of the probability of the electron (*qua* particle) being found at a particular point in the wave cloud. More importantly, Pauling was to see that the distribution of the cloud was also an indicator of where bonds were most likely to be formed.

Meanwhile, in the same year, 1926, Werner Heisenberg (1901–76), who had been working with Bohr in Copenhagen, redeveloped Planck's treatment of discontinuous phenomena by using abstract matrix algebra. This 'new quantum mechanics' fitted the known spectral phenomena even better than Bohr's and Sommerfeld's treatment, and was soon found to be equivalent formally to the 'wave mechanics' treatment of Schrödinger. It was to discover first hand about these exciting developments in physics that Pauling visited Europe in 1926.

THE PAULING BOND

Linus Pauling was born in 1901 at Portland in Oregon into a lower-middle-class family. The early death of his father, an impoverished drugs salesman, left the family in poor circumstances, so that Pauling's education was frequently interrupted by or combined with humdrum physical jobs. As a boy he took an interest in minerals and thereby in chemistry. Naively believing that chemical engineering was what chemists did for a living, at the age of sixteen he enrolled at the Oregon State Agricultural and Engineering College (later Oregon State University). Halfway through his four-year course he had to work for a year to support his mother, and was made a teaching assistant in the qualitative analysis teaching laboratory. It says a lot for his teachers' belief in his talent that an undergraduate should be employed to help instruct his peers. Because his office was adjacent to the chemistry library, Pauling began to read original literature and so came across Lewis' and Langmuir's treatment of the electron pair, which he adopted immediately. The reading gave him 'a strong desire to understand the physical and chemical properties of substances in relation to the structure of the atoms and molecules of which they are composed'[12].

This desire became realizable in 1922 when, following his graduation as a chemical engineer, Pauling won a scholarship to the California Institute of Technology at Pasadena, where he was to spend the greater part of his life. 'CalTech', as it is usually called, had been founded in 1891 as the Throop Technical Institute. In the early 1900s it had been fortunate enough to secure the services of the astronomer, George Ellery Hale, who was then building the Palomar Observatory on top of neighbouring Mount Wilson. Hale, in whose interest it was to have a strong group of physical scientists to tackle astrophysical problems suggested by the telescope's observations, persuaded Arthur Noyes of MIT and the physicist Robert A. Millikan of the University of Chicago to spend three months every year at Pasadena. Post-war problems at MIT brought Noyes permanently to California where, in 1919, he was faced with the exciting task of building up a research school 'to train scientific leaders, rather than to afford mass education'. Given a magnificent new laboratory building by the philanthropists C. W. and P. G. Gates, CalTech (as it became in 1920 under Millikan's Presidency) was in Noyes' hands to become one of America's leading research laboratories in physical chemistry.

When Pauling arrived at CalTech in 1922 (having turned down a prestigious Rhodes scholarship to Oxford), one of its best developed areas of research was crystallography, a subject that Noyes had early recognized as significant for the future development of chemistry. In 1917 he had sent one of his MIT graduates, Roscoe Dickinson, to study the techniques of X-ray crystallography with the Braggs in England. Dickinson was appointed to the CalTech staff, along with a theoretical chemist who was yet another former Noyes student, Richard Tolman. Both became Pauling's mentors. From Dickinson, Pauling acquired his deep and confident knowledge of crystals and their structures; from Tolman, an understanding of thermodynamics and an introduction to the exciting new world of relativity and quantum mechanics – so much so that there was a real chance that Pauling might have turned physicist. Through Noyes, who immediately got him to correct the proofs of, and check the problems in, his and Miles Sherrill's revolutionary text, *An Advanced Course of Instruction in Chemical Principles,* he widened his knowledge of physical chemistry, and was persuaded not to leave chemistry for physics.

The attractions of physics were considerable. CalTech's physicists and astronomers, unlike the chemists, were able to attract world-renowned figures like Ehrenfest, Sommerfeld and Langevin to their seminars. It would also seem that the graduate courses that Pauling audited were, apart from Noyes' thermodynamics, entirely in physics. However, in the laboratory, after a number of abortive starts on structure determinations that proved too difficult for the state of the art, Dickinson put Pauling on to the mineral molybdenite, molybdenum disulphide, MoS_2. This gave Pauling his first publication in 1923. His surprising conclusion was that the molybdenum metal was surrounded by six sulphur atoms, not eight, and that it had a trigonal prism, not octahedral, structure. This was the first known example of trigonal co-ordination. More importantly for Pauling's subsequent studies was his discovery of the fact that estimates of the atomic radii of molybdenum and sulphur disagreed completely with those previously estimated by W. L. Bragg in 1920. Bragg's estimates had been based upon the structural analysis of metallic molybdenum and of pyrites, iron disulphide. According to Bragg, the molybdenite ought to be the sum of the radii of molybdenum and sulphur. Indeed, an additive law of inter-ionic data had been used by

Bragg to simplify the interpretation of X-ray photographs. But Pauling found that the sulphur–sulphur distance in molybdenite was over twice the Bragg radius for sulphur. To explain the discrepancy, Pauling made a special study of inter-ionic distances, concluding in his doctoral thesis of 1925 ('The Determination with X-Rays of the Structure of Crystals') that the effective radii of atoms were squashed in the direction in which they formed covalent bonds, i.e. shared electrons. Pauling's investigation of some sixty minerals, and the complete structural determination of some thirty of them during the following ten years, was to vindicate this early finding and to prove the usefulness of the determination of atomic/ionic radii in deciding the nature of the bonding between atoms.

The award of a prestigious Guggenheim scholarship in 1926 allowed Pauling the opportunity to visit Europe and spend some time with Bohr at Copenhagen, Sommerfeld at Munich and Schrödinger in Zürich. It was in Switzerland that he met Fritz London (1900–54), a young philosopher whose interest in quantum mechanics had led him to postdoctoral studies with Sommerfeld. He also met and discussed quantum mechanics at length with Sommerfeld's graduate student, Walter Heitler (1904–81). It therefore came as something of a surprise to Pauling the following year when Heitler and London produced the first ever quantum-mechanical treatment of a chemical system. Pauling, who had been kept completely in the dark, was to describe this event some years later as 'the greatest single contribution to the chemist's conception of valence' since Lewis' introduction of the shared pair in 1916.

Heitler and London's problem was to calculate the energy of the hydrogen molecule in which two electrons are held jointly by two protons. If the two nuclei were far apart the energy of the system was essentially that of two separate hydrogen atoms, and one only had to consider the force between an electron and a proton. But when the two nuclei were close together, four interactive forces were involved. By using mathematical theorems that Lord Rayleigh had devised to estimate the minimum energy of vibration of a bell, they were able to ignore the messy problem of the actual distribution of the electrons. Heisenberg's demonstration that electrons are indistinguishable ('resonance') also allowed them to make further simplifications. This gave them a fairly simple expression for the hydrogen wave function that could be fitted into the Schrödinger equation, the solution to which gave a binding energy impressively close to that obtained from spectroscopic studies. The snag was that the work was published in a German physics journal and was far too mathematical for chemists.

On Pauling's return to CalTech in 1928, Noyes asked him to teach a course in quantum mechanics. His analysis of the Heitler–London treatment (which they had extended to the hydrogen ion, $H_2{}^+$) led Pauling to develop what became known as the 'valence bond' approach to chemical bonding. His intention in doing this was, as J. H. Sturdivant has remarked, 'to make the results of quantum mechanics accessible and familiar to chemists untrained in the new theoretical physics, and to fuse the results into the foundations of chemical theory'. His technique, which he later called 'stochastic', was to try to link together quantitative measurements and theory and to use the links to suggest new experimental tests[13]:

> Whereas some scientists ask 'What do such and such experimental observations force us to believe about the nature of the world' I prefer to ask 'What is the most simple, general, and intellectually satisfying picture of the world that encompasses these observations and is not incompatible with them?'

By 1928 quantum physicists had shown that, in terms of polar co-ordinates, the solution of the Schrödinger equation for one outer electron produced a symmetrical spherical orbital. For reasons connected with the history of spectroscopy, quantum numbers and the way Bohr had notated the filling of electronic shells, such orbitals were known as s orbitals. Correspondingly, the next three electron energy shells, known as the p orbitals, were geometrically deformed into dumb-bell shapes along the three co-ordinate axes. Combination or chemical bonding was easily explained qualitatively (and potentially quantitatively by the Heitler–London method) as overlapping orbitals, providing that, as Pauling had insisted, the shared electrons had different spins. In 1925 the German physicist Friedrich Hund had also established 'a rule of maximum multiplicity', which recognized that successive electrons always preferred to occupy as many different orbits as possible singularly before pairing in one orbit with opposite spins. Whenever electrons were within a shared overlapping space, they were attracted by both nuclei, which gave the complete system a lowered energy and hence a preferred stability over existing in a higher energy state as two separate atoms. According to this view, therefore, the chemical bond was basically an electrostatic attraction between oppositely charged particles just as Berzelius had thought.

In the case of water, Pauling argued, oxygen's four p electrons will form three dumb-bell orbits along the x, y and z axes; two of these orbits will contain single electrons, and one (by Hund's rule) two electrons with opposed spins. The two unpaired electrons along, say, the p_x and p_y axes will readily overlap the s shells of two hydrogen atoms, thus giving two O–H bonds at right angles to one another. The fact that this angle, when measured spectroscopically, is slightly greater than 90°, could be explained as due to the neglect of repulsive forces between electrons.

Unfortunately, these visualizations and calculations would not account for the known stereochemistry of the carbon atom, for which it had long been agreed that carbon's four bonds were tetrahedrally disposed, and not at right angles. Moreover, since carbon has only two p electrons, its tetravalency appeared puzzling. Knowing the result required (tetrahedrally disposed tetravalency), in 1928 Pauling argued as follows. Since there are two inner 2s electrons, we may suppose that one of these is promoted to a 2p orbital, thus giving carbon three p electrons and altogether four unpaired electrons, 2s + 2p. By calculating the wave functions, Pauling was able to show that the energy required to promote one 2s electron to 2p was more than compensated for by its allowing carbon to form four instead of two bonds. Promotion reduced the overall energy of the system and made it more stable. Moreover, as a bonus, in gaining this energy efficiency when forming a compound, the four electron pairs formed would be perturbed or repelled by each other and so take up a tetrahedral orientation. Pauling called this kind of bond formation by the 'quantization of electrons' sp^3 hybridization, and published his account, after a couple of years of mathematical wrestling with the material, in the April 1931 issue of *JACS*.

Pauling also suggested other forms of hybridization whose resultant configurations linked beautifully with his crystallographic studies (table 13.1). The validity of Pauling's treatment was reinforced independently in the

TABLE 13.1 *Forms of hybridization suggested by Pauling.*

Wave function	Bonding	Configuration
s + p	sp	Linear
s + two p	sp^2	Trigonal
All s+ p	sp^3	Tetrahedral
All s + p + one d	sp^2d	Square
All s + p + two (or more) d	sp^3d^2	Octahedral
All s + p + three (or more) d	sp^3d^3	Tetrahedral

same year in a more rigorously mathematical way by John Slater. For this reason, during the 1930s the approach was often cumbersomely called 'the Heitler–London–Slater–Pauling' method.

This was not the only innovation in Pauling's treatment. In a chapter of *The Nature of the Chemical Bond* on the partial ionic character of the covalent bond, he triumphantly brought order and system to inorganic thermochemistry by determining the 'electronegativities' of compounds as the difference between their energies if all the bonds were covalent, and all were ionic. The results gave conclusive support to the suggestions of Lowry and Sidgwick in the 1920s that the double bond could be treated as partly ionic. Pauling also showed that the diamagnetism of most molecules was due to the opposed spins of electrons in the paired bond, whereas substances with unpaired electrons were paramagnetic. The other chapters, of a more crystallographic nature, were addressed to the determination of bond lengths, the sizes of ions and the thermodynamic determination of the energy of crystals, which had earlier enabled him to simplify the task of the crystallographer in choosing between alternative interpretations of X-ray data. For good measure the book also included an exciting chapter on the problem of interpreting the structure of benzene and its reactions, and ended with the prediction that, among other things, the approach he had outlined would find application in biochemistry.

In 1934, after having had a grant application for research in crystallography and mineralogy turned down by a financial board at CalTech, Pauling approached the Rockefeller Foundation in New York. The Foundation was just then beginning to fund biological, biochemical and medical research on a handsome scale. Pauling's work on the chemical bond had, as we have seen, embraced the magnetism of compounds. Since iron, the most paramagnetic of all the elements, was known to play the central role in the structure of haemoglobin, Pauling proposed a programme of study of how the structure changed during respiration. The application to Rockefeller was successful, and because he had so many good projects for which finance was easily obtained from the Foundation, Pauling's interests turned more and more to biochemistry in the 1930s.

Together with a postdoctoral student, Charles D. Coryell (1912–71), who was to help separate the element promethium in 1945, Pauling was able to show that oxygen was held to haemoglobin by a strong covalent bond, which gave arterial blood diamagnetic properties in contrast to the paramagnetism of venous blood. A generation later, between 1946 and 1949, Pauling returned to the study of haemoglobin after he learned of the genetic disease, sickle cell anaemia, from a physician friend. His demonstration that this anaemia was the consequence of a different form of haemoglobin in the victim's bloodstream made Pauling into an advocate of the study of macromedicine and, ultimately in some quarters, into a figure of fun because of his belief in the need for large vitamin C supplementation in the human diet.

The Rockefeller largesse also brought about Pauling's interest in the study of proteins. In 1936 he and Alfred E. Mirsky (who was also to become a victim of Senator McCarthy's thought police in the 1950s) developed a theory that proteins are coiled chains of polypeptide units linked together by hydrogen bonds. Breakage of these weak bonds by, for example, heat leads to a random configuration described macroscopically as denaturization. This proposal led Pauling into an ungainly quarrel with the British mathematician, Dorothy Wrinch (1894–1976), who, as a woman scientist in a largely male preserve, was fearsomely protective of her own cyclol theory of protein structure in which proteins were gathered in hexagonal rings. To Pauling, the X-ray work of William T. Astbury at Leeds on silk, wool and hair fibres seemed necessarily to imply that polypeptide chains were strung in coils; but when he and a postdoctoral CalTech Fellow, Robert B. Corey, attempted to make models of such a molecular system in 1937, they would not work. It was to be a decade later before the question was resolved.

In 1948, on a lecture tour of England, Pauling was briefly hospitalized in Oxford. There, in bed, by drawing extended structural formulae of peptides to scale on pieces of paper that he then rolled up askew into tubes, Pauling found that when the edges of the paper were drawn together it was obvious that a protein's stability was explicable if it was a helical structure with a non-integral repeat pattern of 3.7 residues. The stability would arise, he argued, because hydrogen bonding occurred between amide groups along the α-helix. He also gave an alternative γ-helix structure. Although these coiled structures had to be confirmed by more orthodox methods of crystallography, the dramatic unveiling of the α-helix at the 1951 International Union of Crystallography in Stockholm was to be the inspiration for James Watson and Francis Crick in their successful attempt to find a structure of DNA in 1953. The same thought, of applying the insights of protein structural analysis to nucleic acids, had of course occurred to Pauling; but for once in his life, when early in 1953 he and Corey published a three-strand DNA model based upon pre-war DNA photographs, he found that his intuition had led him badly astray.

By then the valence bond (VB) approach to chemical bonding was being seriously challenged. An alternative treatment of combining wave functions together, the 'molecular orbital' (MO) approach, had been developed by the spectroscopists Hund and, in America, Robert S. Mulliken (1896–1986). Mulliken's father, Samuel Mulliken, was an organic chemist at MIT, where he had compiled one of the first comprehensive handbooks for the identification of pure organic compounds from their physical properties. Inevitably, young Mulliken trained as a chemist, or rather as a chemical engineer, in Noyes' department. He then went on to the University of Chicago to work with William

D. Harkins, a pioneer of American studies of isotopes. Although Mulliken developed a successful technique for separating the isotopes of mercury, he rapidly decided that he was ham-fisted and that his bent was theoretical. On receiving a Fellowship in 1921, he therefore turned to spectroscopy to see whether an isotope effect was detectable in spectral lines. This was to prove a fruitful line of investigation for others, but for Mulliken it was merely the pathway that led him to his lifelong passion, the interpretation of molecular spectra. During a European tour in 1925, at Göttingen, Mulliken met Hund, who was then a Privatdocent at the University. They immediately began a powerful friendship, with Hund making Mulliken aware for the first time that quantum mechanics was a valuable interpretive tool for the spectroscopist. Together, with the aid of the new mechanics that became available in 1926, they re-established spectroscopy on a sounder theoretical footing, in the process transforming its notation. Whether their wholesale revision of nomenclature was a good thing for chemistry is debatable; one of the chief barriers between the layperson and post-1930 chemistry has surely been the awesome notation of capital and lower-case Greek letters with sub- and superscripts that has percolated from atomic and molecular spectroscopy into general chemistry.

The 'Hund–Mulliken' interpretation, which the two friends published in 1927–8, explained satisfactorily the more complex spectra of molecules by identifying, in the case of diatomic molecules like hydrogen, the vibrations due to the rotation of nuclei about one another, the oscillation in lengths of bonds between nuclei and the rotations and vibrations of the attached electrons. The trick was to treat the electronic contribution not as if the molecule was composed from two atoms, but to consider hydrogen as if it were derived from helium. If helium was imagined to fission into two hydrogen nuclei, its two 1s electrons could be supposed to deform into a 'molecular orbital' symmetrical about the H–H axis. In this treatment, by formal analogy the symmetrical s bond became a sigma (σ) bond, and the dumb-bell-shaped p bond became a pi (π) bond.

The model had at least three consequences. First, it codified and clarified spectroscopy for the first time and therefore attracted new research workers. Before he turned to novel writing in 1933, for example, C. P. Snow began his career as a spectroscopist at Cambridge using the insights provided by Mulliken. Secondly, energy considerations led Hund and Mulliken to the concept of 'electron promotion' and to the idea of correlating the orbitals of diatomic molecules with those of a 'united atom' and those of separated atoms. From the 1930s onwards, 'correlation diagrams' began to play a role not only in spectroscopy, but also in mechanistic studies, where the concept of 'excited states' had become important for the interpretation of the kinetics of reactions.

Finally, the molecular orbital method proved to be a powerful alternative, and unfriendly rival, to the valence bond treatment pioneered by Pauling. Mulliken himself had not been impressed by the Heitler–London treatment of hydrogen. Unlike Pauling, however, he was not a good communicator; his writing was cumbersome and littered with long footnotes, while the mental effort needed to master his notation must have seemed a waste of the ordinary chemist's time when Pauling's *The Nature of the Chemical Bond* explained everything that the chemist needed to know with painless mathematics. As Mulliken ruthfully reported in an interview with Thomas Kuhn in 1964[14]:

> Pauling made a special point of making everything sound as simple as possible and in that way making it very popular with chemists but delaying their understanding of the true [complexity of electronic structure].

Initially, as the Cambridge theoretical chemist John Leonard Jones found in 1929, there was little to choose between the two methods, since both gave roughly the same answers and needed the same number of, though different, assumptions to be made to reach a conclusion. It was not until the 1940s and 1950s that Charles Coulson (1910–74) and Christopher Longuet-Higgins (*b.* 1923), building on the approach of Erich Hückel (1896–1980), were able to persuade a new generation of chemists of the superiority of MO methods in dealing with polyatomic molecules. By then, as we shall see, both inorganic and organic chemists, who had a far better grounding in mathematics in their education, had become interested in molecular systems with which the VB method could not reasonably cope, and they turned to the MO treatment. And by the 1960s, even the value of the VB approach in elementary teaching was questioned as curriculum innovators explored other models that were closer in spirit to MO than VB.

One of the undoubted reasons for the decline of the VB method was the problem of resonance. In classical physics resonance refers to the ability of separated bodies to interact when they possess the same fundamental frequency. The phenomenon was familiar from music and from the study of pendula. If one moving pendulum is hung from the same suspension as another stationary one of the same frequency, it will be set in motion. In his fundamental paper on quantum mechanics in 1926, Heisenberg had made use of resonance as an analogy to make more concrete his abstract simplification that, since electrons could not be told apart (later formally rendered as the uncertainty principle), they could be interchanged without affecting the system. This was like, he suggested, a resonating system in mechanics.

This analogy proved unfortunate since for some it seemed to imply that an electron fluctuated between two positions. As we shall see later, since the 1890s, organic chemists had been investigating the phenomenon of tautomerism, while Kekulé had explained the absence of benzene isomers by invoking an oscillation formula for it in 1872. By the 1920s a number of British organic chemists were also referring to 'mesomerism', meaning an 'in-between' condition. Thus, when Pauling spoke of resonance in the 1930s, it was quite easy to think he meant that molecules in two or more different states in oscillating equilibrium were *actually* present in the system. Although it seems clear that Pauling did not intend this interpretation, he himself may have encouraged it in the 1931 paper and, above all, in his book, by picturing the VB treatment as equivalent to saying that mathematically the bonds of, say, AB, have to be built up from the polar and covalent forms A:–B, A–:–B and A–:B.

This was certainly the interpretation of Soviet Marxist critics who, in the late 1940s, began to assail Pauling for his mystifications and scandalous contempt for Butlerov's principles of chemical structure. This was the era when Lysenko was attacking western genetics as decadent bourgeois science. The Soviet fear seems to have been that Pauling was deploying 'fictional' molecules; to this Pauling replied that his approach was an honest extension of structural theory in which, in any case, all formulae were idealizations. Ironically, when this critique became known in the west, Pauling was under investigation in America for being a communist sympathizer.

If the Soviet attack on resonance was ideological, MO theorists, like the radical Oxford pupil of Sir Robert Robinson, Michael J. S. Dewar (*b*. 1918), objected to it on purely pragmatic grounds in his innovatory *Electron Theory of Organic Chemistry* (1949). It was absurdly difficult and unnecessarily complicated to have to mix five 'canonical forms' of benzene and perhaps as many as four dozen for naphthalene when the MO method handled such molecules much more simply. Walter Hückel (the brother of Erich), in the English translation of his outstandingly rigorous and thoughtfully historical *Structural Chemistry of Organic Compounds* (1950), said much the same, while in America, the kineticist, Henry Eyring (1901–82), attacked the mixing of widely different energy states in the VB method as ridiculous. Needless to say, Pauling rebutted these criticisms energetically – notably in his Nobel prize address at Stockholm in 1954 – and unapologetically continued to subscribe to resonance theory in the third and final edition of *The Nature of the Chemical Bond* in 1960. A measure of the text's continuing significance is a *Science Citation Index* analysis, which showed that between 1955 and 1983 there were over 16 000 references to Pauling's masterpiece.

In the final edition of this classic work, Pauling had no qualms about discussing the 'sandwich compound', ferrocene, as a resonance hybrid of 560 different structures, mentioning only in a footnote that the MO method had produced much simpler calculations for compounds of this kind! Only in 1967, in his *The Chemical Bond. A Brief Introduction to Modern Structural Chemistry*, did Pauling bow to the wind and include a substantial discussion of the MO method, while insisting that, for introductory teaching and for the treatment of the ground states of molecules, the VB method was still the best. Paradowski goes to the heart of the matter in his comment on the rivalry between VB and MO[15]:

> In physics it is possible to develop a simple and detailed model to explain certain classes of phenomena, but chemistry is too complex to be fully explained by such simple theories. To explain chemical phenomena at the present time [1972], one needs several good models. But these 'good' models are more flagrantly models, i.e. they explain only a selection of data, and hence the need for several models. Depending upon the symbolic apparatus used, different truths emerge.

Twenty years on, this assessment remains true. Theoretical chemistry is still a quirky empirical science based upon a Schrödinger equation that can hardly ever be solved.

Structure and Mechanism in Organic Chemistry

> It may sound like a lot of work to keep up with
> organic chemistry, and it is; however, those who
> haven't the time to do it become subject to decay
> in the ability to teach and contribute to the Science
> – a sort of first-order process the half-life of which
> can't be much more than a year or so.
>
> (WILLIAM J. LE NOBLE, *Highlights of
> Organic Chemistry*, 1974)

In a rare personal statement made in the year before his death, Christopher Kelk Ingold (1893–1970) noted that in 55 years of experimental and theoretical activity he had only ever had three periods of quiet contemplation when he had been able 'to help the pulling together of organic chemistry'. The first had been in 1932 when, as a visiting professor at Stanford University, he had written a seminal review paper, 'Principles of an electronic theory of organic reactions' for *Chemical Reviews* (1934). The second had not come until 1950 when, like Pauling before him, he was George Baker Non-Resident Lecturer in Chemistry at Cornell University and had been able to expand and transform the earlier review into a text for the mid century, the magisterial *Structure and Mechanism in Organic Chemistry* (1953). The third was in 1964, following his retirement as Professor of Chemistry at University College, London (UCL), when he was a National Science Foundation Fellow at Vanderbilt University. On this last occasion, the third example of American hospitality, perhaps unwisely and unnecessarily, he expanded and updated *Structure and Mechanism* into a second edition (1969).

The phrase 'structure and mechanism' referred not only back to the classical chemical theory that the properties of organic compounds could be explained solely in terms of the behaviour of tetravalent carbon atoms, but to the integration of the whole of organic chemistry in terms of the physical understanding of the causes, mechanisms and effects of basic reaction types such as additions, eliminations and rearrangements. Emphasis was to be placed upon the class of reactions rather than on the reactions of individual compounds.

Ingold was the great systematizer of twentieth-century organic chemistry and the chemist who firmly established the importance of physical chemistry in understanding the subject. He was trained as a conventional, classical structural chemist. A Londoner by birth, he spent his childhood on the Isle of Wight before rejoining the mainland as a science student at the then Hartley University College of Southampton. Although, like Pauling, he did far better in physics, he was attracted to the unfinished, muddled and unsystematic character of chemistry as portrayed by the Hartley Professor, David R. Boyd (1872–1955). Boyd single-handedly lectured on the whole of chemistry and did not hesitate to introduce matter directly from the latest issue of *Berichte*. Since he had also trained as a lawyer, he was able to weigh evidence in the presentation of his lectures. His courtly, old-world manner was also a role model for the young Ingold[1]:

By example [Boyd] taught us the arts of judgment, of scientific appraisal, of assessing possible significance of scientific insight; and he showed us how continually one has to exercise these mature qualities of thought in a 'living' science. . . . I did not get such good examination results in chemistry [he obtained second class honours]. But what did that matter? I did receive the spirit of science, and so, for that much better reason, I elected to specialize in chemistry.

Therefore, following graduation in 1913, Ingold became a postgraduate student with Armstrong's successor at Imperial College, London, Jocelyn Field Thorpe (1872–1940). Thorpe plunged Ingold into the intricacies of tautomerism and the structure of heterocyclic *spiro* compounds. Although clearly marked out for an academic career, Thorpe, who had briefly worked for the Bayer Company in Ludwigshafen in 1897, believed that a taste of industrial experience was invaluable to a chemist. So in 1918 Ingold was sent to Glasgow as a research chemist with the Cassel Cyanide Company. Collaboration with Thorpe was undiminished by their separation and in 1923 they jointly published *Synthetic Colouring Matters; Vat Colours,* Ingold's only contribution to applied chemistry. In 1920 Ingold returned to Imperial College as a lecturer and in 1923 he married his postdoctoral research assistant, Edith Hilda Usherwood. The latter was making an independent name for herself for the determination of the specific heats of organic compounds (which brought her into controversy with Partington in 1926) and for research on tautometric change.

It was not until 1924, however – an *annus mirabilis* for Ingold, in which he was made a Fellow of the Royal Society and elected to a Chair of Chemistry at the University of Leeds – that he became engrossed in the mechanisms of organic reactions. In retrospect, he was notably absent from the important Faraday Society discussion on the electronic theory of valency that Lowry organized at Cambridge in 1923. What, then, turned this thirty-year-old, classically trained organic chemist towards theoretical studies? The answer, not surprisingly, was the continuing conundrum of benzene.

In 1930, despite some opposition from Robinson, who had the post before taking the more prestigious Waynflete

Chair at Oxford, Ingold was given the second Chair of Chemistry at UCL. At the same time, the head of the department, the physical chemist, F. G. Donnan, appointed the Welshman, Edward David Hughes (1906–63), as a lecturer, thus making possible one of the great twentieth-century chemical partnerships, that of Ingold and Hughes. In 1937 Ingold succeeded Donnan as head of the department, which he saw through the disruptive war years and ran successfully until his retirement in 1961, to be succeeded by Hughes.

Ingold was to make many enemies. His foremost opponent in the development of the electronic theory of organic chemistry was the older Robert Robinson (1886–1975). The deadly rivalry and hostility that developed between them in the 1920s did not cease with Ingold's death in 1970. Robinson's posthumous autobiography, literally dictated in a blind rage when he thought of Ingold, explicitly accused him of plagiarism. The son of a Derbyshire surgical dressings manufacturer, Robinson had a varied and restless academic career. Much more worldly than Ingold, who seems to have had few interests outside chemistry until he was sixty, Robinson was passionately devoted to music, chess, mountaineering and the cultivation of friendships in high places. His training in chemistry at the University of Manchester under J. F. Thorpe (who only moved to Imperial College in 1913) and W. H. Perkin Jr (1860–1929) was inspired by his father's wish that he should contribute to the family business in a practical way. As a pupil of Baeyer and Wislicenus, Perkin's great interest was in synthesis and not in theoretical matters – he once said that 'physical chemistry is all very well, but it does not apply to organic compounds'. Robinson was to be different.

Following graduation in 1905, Robinson worked with Perkin on the structure of the dyewood colouring matter, brazilin, a research topic that must have been responsible for his lifelong interest in the chemistry of natural dyes, and also on the alkaloids. Like Ingold later, he by-passed the Ph.D., which was not fashionable in Britain until the 1920s, and proceeded directly to a D.Sc. on the basis of publications. In 1909 he was made a lecturer in Perkin's department and became friendly with Arthur Lapworth (1872–1941), a pupil of Armstrong, who had just arrived in Manchester as a Senior Lecturer in Inorganic and Physical Chemistry. It is interesting to note that Partington was Lapworth's first research student in Manchester. Lapworth was to stimulate Robinson's interest in the mechanism of reactions by a theory of 'alternative polarity' that he had first articulated in 1905.

For the three years 1912–15, Robinson held the Chair of Pure and Applied Organic Chemistry at the University of Sydney. Like other British chemists who briefly sojourned in Australia, the experience of the strange and exotic flora there made a lasting impression and increased Robinson's interest in the extraction, analysis and synthesis of natural products. It was for this that he was to be renowned long after his contretemps with Ingold. Back in England again in 1915, Robinson established an alkaloid research programme at the University of Liverpool, but war work on dyestuffs led him to accept the Directorship of the nationalized British Dyestuffs Corporation in 1919. Quickly finding this uncongenial, he moved to St Andrews University in Scotland in 1920, where he began serious use of Lapworth's theoretical ideas in his undergraduate lectures, only to leave in 1922 for the Chair of Organic Chemistry at his *alma mater*, the University of Manchester. Restlessly, and for no apparent good reason, he migrated to a Chair at University College, London, in 1928, and finally came to rest at Oxford when he succeeded Perkin in 1930. He retired in 1955, having been awarded a Nobel prize in 1947 for 'his investigations on plant products of biological importance, especially the alkaloids'. Although Ingold, like Robinson, was knighted for his services to chemistry, and recommended for a Nobel prize in the 1930s, that accolade was denied to him.

THE LAPWORTH–THIELE–ROBINSON TRADITION

In 1887 Henry Armstrong tried to explain the mechanism of substitution reactions generally and noted the mechanism that Williamson, using the water type classification, had employed to explain etherification. For Williamson, it will be recalled, the first step had consisted in action between dissociated portions of the interacting compounds – what Kekulé in his *Lehrbuch der Chemie* (1867) had called the formation of an 'association compound'. Armstrong had supported such a mechanism for many other reactions. During the same decade the concept that a substance had one unique formula was undermined when clear evidence emerged from their reactions that certain compounds, like acetoacetic ester, must exist in two different forms even though it was impossible to separate the isomers. Peter Laar (1853–1929) christened this phenomenon 'tautomerism' in 1885, and supposed that in such cases a hydrogen atom might oscillate backwards and forwards between two positions in the molecule. Two years later, P. Jacobson used the word 'desmotropism' for those cases where two isomers in dynamic equilibrium with each other could be isolated.

This was Lapworth's starting point. In 1898 he attempted to demonstrate[2]:

> that it is possible to refer the majority of reactions and changes in organic chemistry to necessary variations of one, or at most two, simple laws, which laws find their most general forms in the relationship between, for example, the two forms of 'tautomeric' and 'desmotropic' substances.

With this statement, Lapworth set in motion the twentieth-century movement to classify and interpret the mechanisms of reactions in terms of the structures of molecules.

In tautomeric reactions, he suggested that a univalent atom or group, M, was mobile:

(The colon referred, of course, to a double bond and had no electronic connotation.)

In desmotropic reactions, two labile atoms or groups (R_α, R_β, etc.) exchanged positions through a Williamson–Kekulé intermediate:

$$R_\alpha M_1 . R_\beta : R_\gamma M_2 \rightarrow R_\alpha : R_\beta . R_\gamma M_1 M_2 \rightarrow R_\alpha M_2 . R_\beta : R_\gamma M_1$$

Lapworth, inspired by Armstrong's doctrine of residual affinity (see chapter 15), did not suppose that the labile group was ever really free, as he made clear geometrically. Using tetrahedral diagrams he showed how rearrangement might occur through an intramolecular rotation through 180°. This is worth reproducing because it involved the use of curved arrows and because the imagined process bears a formal resemblance to the shift of electrons:

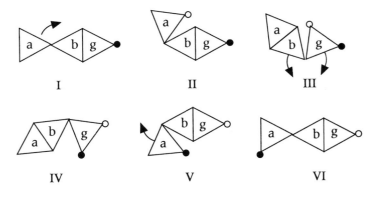

In later papers Lapworth called the reactive labile group 'the key atom' because of its ability to move along a chain of alternating single and double bonds as these bonds changed places in its path. As to the cause of a key atom's reactivity, despite Armstrong's aversion to ions, Lapworth was in no doubt that electrolytic dissociation was involved. In other words, key atoms possessed electropositive or electronegative polar qualities. On this assumption, in 1903, while teaching at Goldsmith's College in London, Lapworth interpreted the formation of cyanohydrins through the addition of a reactive —CN group to a ketone carbonyl group. If the cyanide radical was assumed to be negatively charged and carbonyl polarized by what Armstrong had called residual affinity, then the first stage of the reaction could be represented as:

$$C^+=O^- \quad + \quad CN^- \quad \rightleftharpoons \quad$$

(1)

By studying the kinetics of the reaction (in itself an innovation in mechanistic studies), Lapworth was able to deduce that this step was followed by the rapid uptake of hydrogen from the acid medium of the reaction:

(2)

cyanohydrin

The final proof was the isolation of salts of the product of reaction (1) by reacting the carbonyl group with an excess of sodium cyanide to give

He then extended the study to aldehydes and αβ-unsaturated ketones, as well as to the benzoin condensation, all the time building up evidence that ions played a crucial role in reaction mechanisms.

In Manchester Lapworth rationalized the scheme further into a general theory of 'alternative polarities' by extending the notion of latent polarities to all the atoms in a molecule and supposing the latency to be activated at the moment of chemical change by a reactant key atom. Acetaldehyde might then, for example, be written

which enabled one to understand why the hydrogen on the α-carbon atom could be easily removed by a base; alternating polarity would then explain why hydrogen bound to every second carbon atom removed from a ketone group was easily lost. There was action at a distance in chemistry: reactivity at one site influenced or induced action at another.

Although this theory of an inductive effect was only fully enunciated by Lapworth in 1920, Robinson, who shared bench space with Lapworth between 1909 and 1912 and again from 1922, has emphasized how stimulating he found these ideas. One of their contemporaries noted of their partnership in the 1920s[3]:

Arthur Lapworth and Robert Robinson not only discussed structure and reactivity and mechanism of reactions in the department, but often after lunch they could be seen in a corner of the staff common room covering old envelopes with + and − signs, partial valencies, equations, diagrams and arrows of many shapes indicating electron drifts and availabilities.

Robinson, however, also adopted a second theoretical principle, the influential residual valency theory of Johannes Thiele (1865–1927), which the latter developed when Professor of Chemistry at the University of Strasbourg. In 1899, noticing that in many cases when hydrogen or halogens were added to unsaturated systems the double bonds shifted position,

$$-CH=CH-CH=CH- \longrightarrow -CH_2-CH=CH-CH_2-$$
$$[H_2]$$

Thiele suggested that this could be explained by residual valencies, as if not all the combining power of the carbon atoms at double bonds had been used:

$$-CH=CH--CH=CH- \longrightarrow -CH_2-CH=CH-CH_2-$$
$$[H_2]$$

where the central brace indicated two partial valencies that saturated one another. (It should be noted that Thiele's model of residual affinity had been stimulated by Werner's views on the structure of inorganic complexes to be considered in the next chapter.) Thiele applied the idea to many other double bond, or conjugate, systems, including benzene, which he represented as with the implication that all six carbon positions were equivalent – an idea that Robinson was to portray in the 1920s.

Whereas Thiele saw unsaturated atoms as possessing residual combining powers *in addition* to their normal bonding powers or valency value, Robinson preferred to think of the normal bond as splitting into two (or even fractional) partial valencies. These were notated by both Thiele's dots and by Lapworth's polarities. Thus Thiele's butadiene reaction became:

$$\overset{+}{C}H \cdots \overset{-}{C}H$$
$$CH_2 \qquad \overset{}{C}H_2 \longrightarrow Br\,CH_2 - CH = CH - CH_2Br$$
$$\overset{+}{Br} \cdots \overset{-}{Br}$$

And, in a joint paper with his wife, Gertrude, in 1917, the action of methyl iodide on ethyl-α-aminocrotonate was represented as:

'The logical applications of schemes of partial dissociation', the Robinsons wrote[4]:

> single and conjugated, or addition and decomposition by making and breaking of partial valencies, and of redistribution of affinity, demands the consideration of these questions of polarity and leads to a system of mechanism of reactions which appears to be capable of including the representation of chemical changes of the most varied type, and the present authors are not acquainted with examples of reactions the course of which cannot be illustrated in the manner implied.

In other words, if Lapworth's key atom was considered to induce or relay the potential partial valencies of a system, the mechanism of any reaction (including complicated rearrangements) could be understood and put to service in the interest of chemical synthesis.

Despite the speculative and even intuitive nature of this position, the intriguing thing is how easily it was to be reinterpreted electronically. But before pursuing this transformation, we should pause – as Robinson was interrupted by the First World War – to consider briefly another rival theoretical tradition that was to influence the position adopted by Ingold.

THE MICHAEL–FLÜRSCHEIM–VORLÄNDER TRADITION

Thiele's views concerning residual valency met with particular criticism from chemists who were rediscovering the benefits of Berzelius' electrochemical insights for explaining the orientation effects of benzene substitution. As we saw in the chapter on Pauling, this school of thought was to be powerfully stimulated by the discovery of the electron and to lead to the exploration of ideas about electronic bonding, particularly in America. One of Thiele's principal critics was the rich and maverick American, Arthur Michael (1853–1942). A self-taught chemist from New

York, Michael had studied with Bunsen at Heidelberg and with Hofmann in Berlin before becoming Professor of Chemistry at Tufts College in Boston. There, in 1887, he discovered the important 'Michael condensation' reaction for transforming an unsaturated compound into a saturated compound with an additional carbon atom. Thereafter he applied himself wholeheartedly to the application of thermodynamics to an understanding of organic reactions. Something of a scientific hermit – he opted out of academe during 1891–4 in order to conduct research privately with his wife on the Isle of Wight – he preferred a polar explanation of reaction mechanisms, on the grounds that this satisfied Ostwald's rule that 'every system tends towards the state whereby the maximum entropy is reached'.

The Russian, Vladimir Markovnikov (1838–1904), had generalized in 1868 that, in the hydrohalogenation of unsymmetrical unsaturated compounds, addition of the hydrogen took place on the carbon with the most attached hydrogen, while the halide added to the carbon with the least number of hydrogen atoms. In the simplest case of propylene, $CH_3.CH:CH_2$, Michael explained this as due to the positive character of the methyl group. This made the adjacent $—CH$ more positive than the terminal $=CH_2$. Consequently, if approached by hydrogen iodide, H^+I^-, or iodine chloride, I^+Cl^-, $CH_3.CHI.CH_3$ or $CH_3.CHCl.CH_2I$ would be formed through the saturation of unlike charges. However, because there was little difference in positive charge in a halogen like BrCl, both $CH_3.CHBr.CH_2Cl$ and $CH_3.CHCl.CH_2Br$ would be formed. In secondary and tertiary olefins, spatial factors probably interfered with the polarity effect. It should be noted that Lapworth explained the same additions as due to the polar inductive effect of the key atom halogen.

Michael, who published most of his work in German, not American, journals, influenced Bernard Flürscheim (1874–1955), a pupil of both Werner and Thiele, who emigrated to England in 1905 and made a fortune from the invention of tetranitroaniline (TNA) in 1910. In 1902, in a synthesis of the ideas of Thiele and Michael, as well as Werner's notion of an affinity over and above the normal valency value, he pointed out that in any carbon chain strong and weak links would arise. If the two primary groups in a molecule had a strong affinity for one another, any addenda would be weakly bonded. He represented this state of affairs by bold (strong) and ordinary (weak) bonds:

X■A—B■C—D   o r   Y—A■B—C■D

Such alterations of affinity intensity, transmitted along a chain, seemed to explain benzene substitutions as the transmission of what he called 'affinity demand' and symbolized by bold arrowed bonds:

The similarities with the theory of alternative polarities are striking, and there is little doubt that Lapworth was influenced by Flürscheim's papers.

Another similar polar theory, which used the +/– notation developed independently by Fry in America, was produced by Daniel Vorländer (1867–1941) in 1919. Like Lapworth and Flürscheim, Vorländer was beginning to be conscious that the different rates of organic reactions might be explicable as electrical contrasts between positive hydrogens and the negative nuclear atoms of the carbon chain. He tried to symbolize this in structural formulae: long bonds indicated 'greater intramolecular tension', opposed to short bonds (coupled with a long bond), which indicated small electrical contrast. In chlorobenzene, he suggested, substitution could occur at the *ortho–para* positions because a negative contrast is induced at these positions; contrariwise, nitrobenzene induces *meta* substitution:

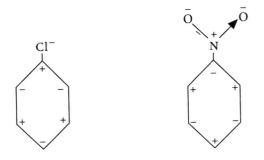

The rate of substitution was dependent, he argued, on the relative electrochemical contrast between the incoming substituent and the carbon at the *ortho, meta* or *para* positions. Thus, in chlorobenzene, H^+ substituted far more readily at the 2, 4 and 6 positions, while in nitrobenzene, Cl^- readily entered at 3 and 5.

The similarities between all of these theories of residual affinity, alternative polarities, alterations of affinity intensity and electrical contrasts are striking. Unfortunately, although they easily 'explained' a good deal of organic reactivity, there were problems. For example, some halogen additions in butadiene derivatives took place in the 1,2, not 1,4 positions demanded by Thiele's model, while Flürscheim (though not Vorländer) had difficulty in explaining *meta* substitution in benzene derivatives, or why methyl (which he treated as positive) directed benzene substituents to the *ortho* position. Nor could Vorländer explain why a nitro group in the side chain of phenylnitromethane increased *meta* substitution, in contradiction to the formula prediction:

By 1920, therefore, organic chemists had a number of competing explanations for the mechanisms of reactions. Each was *ad hoc* and ultimately dependent upon there being a satisfactory explanation for the induction, or cause, of a polar, or stronger or weaker affinity. Lapworth's explanation in terms of a key atom was neat, but untestable, since only the dipole moment of a complete molecule could, in principle, be determined, not the dipoles of individual bonds. On the other hand, Michael's, Flürscheim's and Vorländer's models appealed to an innate, almost Berzelian internal polarity of molecules that could be tested by the measurement of dipole moments. Although Debye had developed a theory of electric moments involving the dielectric constant in 1912, the necessary experimental techniques for their determination were not in place until the mid 1920s. By then the indeterminacy of these models had been resolved through their integration with G. N. Lewis' theory of the chemical bond as an electron pair.

THE ELECTRONIC THEORY OF ORGANIC REACTIONS

As we have seen, Langmuir was very much Lewis' publicity agent in putting across the idea that the covalent bond – the predominant form of bonding in organic molecules – was due to the sharing of electrons. In September 1921 he was a guest speaker on this subject at the British Association meeting in Edinburgh, which Robinson attended. Robinson quickly understood that the partial valencies he and Lapworth had been using could be easily translated into two valency electrons constituting the shared pair. The key intermediary was Julius B. Cohen (1859–1935). Born and bred in Manchester, Cohen took his doctorate with Baeyer at Munich before becoming head of the University of Leeds chemistry department in 1904. As a chemist he made a few contributions to organic synthesis and perpetuated Angus Smith's interest in environmental chemistry in a monograph, *Smoke, a Study of Town Air*. But it was as the writer of textbooks of organic chemistry that he deservedly won respect. Determinedly interested in theory, he prided himself in keeping these texts up to date. Not surprisingly, therefore, he seems to have been well aware of the possible significance of the Lewis–Langmuir shared pair. In October 1921 he wrote to Lapworth[5]:

> Why do you split up your bond into three partial valencies rather than two? If you took two it would fit in with the Lewis–Langmuir atom, and your partial valency might represent one electron.

Lapworth took the hint and may well also have alerted Robinson, who seems, however, to have arrived at the same solution independently after hearing Langmuir lecture. Robinson wrote to Lapworth in December 1921 from St Andrews that a saturated valency was a shared electron pair, a latent valency a free pair, and a virtual valency an incomplete octet. The two men agreed to publish independent papers during 1922.

Robinson's 'An explanation of the property of induced polarity of atoms and an interpretation of the theory of partial valencies on an electronic basis' was written in collaboration with William O. Kermack (1898–1970), whom he had met through British Dyestuffs. Kermack, who was blinded in a laboratory accident in 1924, went on to have a distinguished career in biochemistry. The key feature of this landmark discussion was the idea of the facile displacement of electrons in unsaturated systems[6]:

> Experience has shown that the alternating effect is transmitted but feebly by saturated atoms, whereas it may be discerned at the end of long chains wholly comprised of unsaturated atoms. This is easy to understand in view of the fact that unsaturated atoms share more electrons in common than saturated atoms. There will be a greater mobility of electrons, and the octet, when formed, will have some units at least which are not subject to restraint, a condition which tends to stability.

To represent this lability of electrons, Kermack and Robinson introduced curved arrows, as in the butadiene chain:

$$^+CH_2 \quad \colon \quad CH \quad : \quad CH_2 \quad \colon \quad CH \quad : \quad CH \quad \colon \quad CH_2^-$$

And the methylation of a crotonic ester, whose mechanism the Robinsons had explored in 1917 (see earlier in this chapter) became:

As we have seen, curved arrows had been used a quarter of a century before by Lapworth to represent a mechanism for rearrangement. Werner had also used 'squared arrows' in his *New Ideas on Inorganic Chemistry* (1905) to explain the mechanism whereby a double-bonded oxygen is replaced by hydroxyl:

In a series of papers on the causes of colour in dyestuffs in 1915, Edwin R. Watson (1880–1926), who spent most of his teaching career in India, had argued that colour arose from the fact that most dyes could assume tautometric quinonoid forms, which involved long alternating chains of single and double bonds. Colour was, then, a tautomeric vibration transmitted along the chain like the 'pulse of a shunting goods train'. He represented the effect by squared dotted arrows (presumably to suit the printer's convenience). Later, in his valuable book, *Colour in Relation to Chemical Constitution* (1918), written when he was on furlough with the British Dyestuffs Corporation during the First World War, Watson used curved arrows in many similar representations of tautomeric systems:

Of course, Watson's arrows did not represent electronic shifts, but given Robinson's interest in dyes and their joint connection with the British Dyestuffs Corporation during and after the war, as well as their, and Lapworth's, interest in tautomerism, it seems plausible to speculate that the curved arrow – the most important symbol in twentieth-century organic chemistry – was transmitted in this way.

Robinson and Kermack's paper, together with that of Lapworth in the same issue of the *Journal of the Chemical Society* (*JCS*), stimulated a good deal of discussion at the Chemical Society and in the correspondence columns of *Chemistry and Industry* and *Chemical News*. Further rather more polemical exchanges were stimulated by the Faraday Society discussion at Cambridge in July 1923. The chief correspondents were, inevitably, Robinson, Lapworth, Lowry (the organizer of the Cambridge meeting), Ingold and Flürscheim, with Henry Armstrong adding pungent and entertaining criticisms of the current 'madness', which revolved essentially around the mechanism of substitutions in benzene and on the nature of tautomerism. Each disputant advocated his own particular viewpoint: Lowry argued that organic chemistry could only progress if the electron was introduced and if partial ionic bonds replaced the double bond in unsaturated systems; Lapworth pressed an electronic interpretation of his alternating polarities; Robinson appeared to support and extend Lapworth's views; Flürscheim rejected electrons as explanatory tools altogether (a position he never abandoned) and emphasized the simplicity of his method of alternating affinities and how the approach differed from that of Lapworth; while Ingold (together with his mentor, Thorpe) seemed to share Armstrong's view that there had been no advance in theory of organic chemistry since the introduction of the tetrahedral atom by van't Hoff. Clearly, Ingold came to the electron and to understand the Lewis–Langmuir electron pair well after Robinson.

If, as John Shorter has suggested, Ingold showed little

sign of interest in physical issues in 1923, as the controversy with Lapworth and Robinson continued through 1924 and 1925, he came increasingly to support Flürscheim's position. Ingold was then in one of his most productive phases at the work bench, presenting some fourteen long experimental papers to the Chemical Society in eighteen months. Each time, he found himself criticized and baited by either Robinson or Lapworth, or by both men, either orally or by written comments when the papers were first read at the Chemical Society.

At the end of 1924, no doubt with the view to scotching the alternating polarities interpretation once and for all, Ingold began a series of papers on 'The nature of the alternating effect in carbon chains'. In the first paper, concerned with the directing effect of a nitroso group (—N=O) in benzene substitution, he proposed a crucial test between the Robinson–Lapworth and Flürscheim explanations: the latter's theory predicted that —N=O was *ortho–para* directing, whereas on the Robinson–Lapworth model it would be *meta* directing. Ingold's experimental results found for the former. But, as so often in the history of science, Robinson and Lapworth found no difficulty in finding reasons why, in the circumstances, their theory would also predict *meta* substitution.

Lapworth and Robinson

Flürscheim

Robinson's explanation of December 1924: conjugation of nitrogen with the ring leads to *meta* substitution

Ingold then made an embarrassing blunder. He asserted that addition reactions between nitrosobenzene and unsaturated compounds that he had been recently studying could only be explained by a reaction mechanism that contradicted that of Lapworth and Robinson. Unfortunately for Ingold, Lapworth quickly demonstrated that the products of Ingold's addition reaction had been completely misidentified; Ingold's critique was therefore irrelevant. There was worse to come.

Together with his wife, Ingold tried to counter with a benzene system in which no oxygen was attached to the ring. Choosing α-methoxyvinylbenzene, C_2H_5—C (OMe)=CH_2, he again asserted confidently that Robinson's mechanism would predict *ortho–para* substitution, whereas Flürscheim's predicted *meta*. Once again, Lapworth and Robinson revealed how their model was able to save the phenomena; such responses seemed to Ingold, and perhaps to other observers, at first glance *ad hoc* and *post hoc*.

Ingold's final challenge was made on 21 May 1925 when he predicted from Flürscheim's theory that, in a tertiary benzylamine salt, nitration would proceed at the *ortho* and *para* positions, whereas the free amine would undergo *meta* nitration. Experiments, claimed Ingold, confirmed this completely. This time Robinson admitted defeat and that the results were not explicable on his and Lapworth's model. Intrigued by this breakdown, Robinson had Ingold's work carefully repeated and, in January 1926, announced triumphantly that Ingold's experimental work was not only false, but completely the opposite of the truth; free benzylamines nitrated at *ortho–para*, whereas the tertiary salts went *meta!* This debacle must have been extremely embarrassing to Ingold coming so soon after his election to the Royal Society; possibly this public humiliation (analogous to the plot of C. P. Snow's novel, *The Search*, published in 1932) made him all the more determined to outsmart Robinson.

If neither man came out of this affray morally clean,

like most controversies in science there was significant shifting of ground by the protagonists. On the one hand, Robinson was forced to clarify his concepts; what appeared at first *ad hoc* saving of the phenomena turned out to be the weighing up of different electronic effects on a molecule's susceptibility to substitution. On the other hand, Ingold, more slowly perhaps, realized that the electronic interpretation of reaction mechanisms had a power of adaptability altogether lacking in Flürscheim's rigid scheme of things.

Clarification of Robinson's position came orally on 18 June 1925 when, together with a group of Manchester colleagues and students, J. Allan, A. E. Oxford and J. C. Smith (who were to be rarely heard of again), Robinson presented a coherent account of his electronic theory to the Chemical Society. He now suggested that there were two *different* electronic mechanisms at work in aromatic and conjugative systems: changes in the 'covalency functioning of electrons' (the transfer of electron pairs), which he and Kermack had earlier represented by curved arrows, and another effect (which went some way towards a compromise with Flürscheim and Ingold) 'due to electrostatic induction, the general effect requiring no changes in covalency'. In the case of Ingold's benzylamines[7]:

> a sufficiently positively-charged ammonium group might so strongly attract electrons as to produce the effect of meta substitution when separated from the nucleus by a methylene group. A relatively greater proportion of the meta-isomeride is therefore expected in the case of the benzylamine salts, the more powerful the base. In $CH_2Ph.NH.COMe$ and $CH_2Ph.NEtPh$ the nitrogen will acquire a positive charge owing to its conjugation with the CO and Ph, respectively, and should therefore produce meta substitution.

Unaware, at this stage, that Robinson was repeating his experimental work, Ingold actually congratulated Robinson in discussion on the plausibility of this reasoning.

The historian must rely on hearsay for the next stage for only the testimony of Robinson is available. Towards the end of 1925, or at the beginning of 1926 (the timing is vague), Robinson sent Ingold the written-up version of this June 1925 paper, which was eventually published during the spring of 1926. In his autobiography, Robinson quotes from an appreciative letter that Ingold wrote on 17 February 1926 when he returned the manuscript to Robinson. The explanations in the paper were, Ingold acknowledged[8]:

> a very fine effort, especially on the theoretical side, and the theory is certainly one of Organic Chemistry and not of Aromatic substitution only. . . . I find it easier to follow and I can now see in retrospect that its germination goes a long way back and is especially clear in your paper with Mrs Robinson in 1917. . . . I shall also publish again on the subject but am not ready just yet [*sic*]. When I do I shall turn right round. I do not care two straws what the public in general . . .

Unfortunately, the remainder of this potentially incriminating letter is lost. A week earlier, Ingold had submitted a new paper on the nature of the alternating effect to the Chemical Society. When this was read formally on 6 May 1926, Ingold, despite the hint of procrastination in his letter to Robinson, was seen to be wholeheartedly adopting electronic explanations. To his dying day Robinson believed that Ingold had appropriated the electrostatic and covalency shift mechanisms from having had preprint sight of the June 1925 paper. For his part, then and thereafter, Ingold always implied that he had developed the ideas independently and even that his paper preceded Robinson's. (For the record, Robinson's paper was submitted on 19 December 1925 and Ingold's on 10 February 1926.) Ingold's view of such an accusation of plagiarism or piracy was never committed to paper. It is clear from his 1926 paper, however, that, just as Robinson's theory was an electronic reworking of Lapworth's prior model, Ingold saw himself as making an electronic interpretation of Flürscheim's scheme[9]:

> It will be obvious [*sic*] that the distribution of forces here involved is qualitatively the same as in Flürscheim's theory, the completed charge corresponding with his figure for *o,p*-substitution

> In applying these suggestive ideas ... we would regard the above formulae as expressing only the direction of imaginary gross changes which actually do not at any time proceed to more than a limited (in some cases exceedingly small) extent.

And, in explaining 'the activating effect' of a methyl group, the Ingolds adopted Robinson's curved arrows, introducing calculus deltas to indicate the resulting polarity.

If Robinson might have been flattered in 1926 to find Ingold adopting his ideas (especially in view of thrashing him experimentally over benzylamines), he was to become increasingly irritated by Ingold's ability to organize these ideas into a comprehensive theory of organic chemistry whose validity was to be tested by the techniques and assumptions of physical chemistry. Robinson's main interest having always been synthetic organic chemistry, the theoretical insights we have discussed were, in fact, buried in a morass of experimental detail. In 1932 he tried desperately to regain his priority and the respect of the chemical community for his theoretical powers by composing the monograph *Outline of an Electrochemical (Electronic) Theory of the Course of Organic Reactions,* which was issued by the Institute of Chemistry, together with a more popular article in the highly specialized and professional *Journal of the Society of Dyers and Colourists.* Neither publication reached the wide audience that Ingold had already reached through the *Journal of the Chemical Society* and the Dutch *Recueil des traveux chimiques* and was to reach with his theoretical synthesis in *Chemical Reviews* in 1934. As the long-winded title of Robinson's monograph makes clear, and its curious reference to 'electrochemistry' and deliberate failure to use the vocabulary and insights that Ingold had introduced, it bore an old-fashioned look.

These publications, despite some influence on Oxford chemists like Alexander Todd and M. J. S. Dewar, who in the 1950s reinterpreted Robinson's views as forecasts of molecular orbital theory, did nothing to reduce the forceful clarity of Ingold's interpretation. In a belligerent Presidential address to the Chemical Society in 1941 and in an embarrassing Faraday Lecture in 1947, Robinson again attempted to reintroduce his outmoded interpretations, original notation and vocabulary. Ingold and Hughes were in the audience in 1947 and it is said they exchanged indulgent bemused glances. For although the documentary evidence is lacking, Ingold and Hughes had seriously believed in the 1930s that Robinson, as Britain's most senior and most respected chemist, lay behind the opposition that their views provoked.

ORGANIZING THE STRUCTURE OF ORGANIC CHEMISTRY

The *Annual Reports* that the Chemical Society began in 1905 varied enormously in the skill and application with which divers writers approached the task of reviewing the previous year's literature in different fields of chemistry. Many were purely bibliographical lists, lumping literature references together in an intimidating, unappetizing and unreadable form; others, like those of Frederick Soddy on radiochemistry or Ingold's on organic chemistry, were works of synthesis, masterly essays in which connections were made, and fresh insights revealed. Ingold's essays, which were written with his wife – though, typically of the time, this was not acknowledged on the title page – appeared between 1924 and 1928.

These reports gave him the opportunity to strengthen the vocabulary of the new electronic theory of organic chemistry. In 1926 he renamed Robinson and Lapworth's conjugative effect (or arrowed electronic shift) the 'tautomeric effect' on the grounds that it bore a resemblance to what organic chemists, including Thiele and Ingold himself in work with Thorpe, had adumbrated in the concept of tautomerism. In 1923, Lowry had suggested that in all double bonds a complete polarization took place whenever a molecule was activated. When this occurred, one of its shared electron pairs was transferred to the octet of another atom. Lowry had referred to this state of affairs, to Lewis' disgust, as a semipolar bond, as in

$$\overset{+}{C}-\overset{-}{C}-\overset{+}{C}-\overset{-}{O}$$

In Lowry's striking metaphor, such a theory and formulae showed 'the dog standing up and barking' as opposed to its different attitude 'when curled up and at rest'. The Ingolds proposed to call this transient polarizability the 'electromeric effect', as opposed to the more permanent tautomeric effect.

The polarizing effect in a carbon chain, to which Michael, Lewis and Robinson had drawn attention, had been elegantly substantiated by Howard Lucas in 1924. The Ingolds called this the 'inductive effect', or, more generally, a 'field effect', if the influence was transmitted through space rather than along a chain. This effect, they noted, was often supportive of the tautomeric effect, but where antagonistic, it could be used as a test of the validity of the theory.

In the case of dimethylaniline, the different electronegativities of carbon and nitrogen must produce an inductive effect favouring the appended methyl group; but any transient electromeric effect would work in the opposite direction and be likely to outweigh, or at least reduce, the former effect:

Since dipole measurements were possible by 1926, the determination of any permanent polarization would be revealed by the sign of the moment. The dipole moment of dimethylaniline, for example, would reveal 'whether tautomeric, like inductive, effects are associated with a permanent displacement of the electrons'.

This appeal to physical measurements – dipoles, parachors, heats of formation, polarizability as revealed by refraction, and degrees of molecular symmetry as shown by spectroscopy – was to be the hallmark of Ingold's style after 1926. Dipole determinations by H. Hogendahl and Leslie Sutton in 1927 and 1928 did, indeed, confirm the existence of permanent tautomeric effects, as opposed to transient electromeric effects that could be supposed to occur at the moment of chemical change. This conformation led the Ingolds between 1929 and 1933 (when it was fully articulated) to their final major generalization, namely that the tautomeric effect represented the chemists' best attempt to represent, or to capture on paper, the elusive structure of a compound, just as Heitler and London had tried to represent the bond between two hydrogen atoms by the quantum exchange of energy. For this reason, in 1933, Ingold renamed the tautomeric effect the 'mesomeric effect' or mesomerism ('in between') in recognition of the limitations of classical structural chemistry. He had clearly perceived what Pauling had arrived at independently and called 'resonance'. Flürscheim's permanently redistributed valencies, Ingold thought, had borne a close analogy to mesomerism.

Ingold, unlike Robinson, quickly saw the relevance of Pauling's work for a deeper understanding of reaction mechanisms. This, again, heightened the differences between Ingold and Robinson while enhancing the relevance of Ingold's work for the next generation of chemists. Less successfully, since chemical literature to this day remains completely confused by it, he represented these effects by the symbols T and I, together with plus or minus signs to indicate whether the effect would favour or inhibit reaction with a positively charged reagent. The key atoms, or reagents, which Lapworth had since 1925 referred to as 'anionoid' and 'cationoid' according to whether they had a positive or negative effect, and whose vocabulary Robinson always retained, were renamed 'nucleophilic' (electron pair donor) and 'electrophilic' (electron pair acceptor) in 1928. This made a generalized theory of aromatic substitution possible. A nucleophilic (electron-releasing) group like alkyl reduced positive polarization in an aromatic molecule and encouraged electrophilic substituents into the *ortho* and *para* positions because of alternating polarity in the ring. Conversely, an electrophilic group, with electron-withdrawing tendencies, like CCl_3, strongly retarded *ortho–para* substitution, but permitted *meta*. As the Robinson–Ingold controversy had shown, of course, there were many exceptions to this generalization. In those cases, both electromeric effects and inductive effects had to be considered.

Codification of reaction states was completed in the succinct fifty-page 1934 *Chemical Review* article where a fourfold classification of electron shifts included the differentiation of a permanent 'inductive effect' from a more transient inductomeric polarizability brought about in the transition state between reactants and products. A similar distinction needed to be drawn for conjugative electron displacements of mesomerism and the electromeric shifts of the transition state:

Electronic mechanism	Polarization	Polarizability
General inductive ($\rightarrow$) (I)	Inductive	Inductomeric
Tautomeric ($\curvearrowright$) (T)	Mesomeric (M)	Electromeric (E)

In his *Structure and Mechanism* (1953), in a possible concession to Robinson, the tautomeric effect was renamed the 'conjugative effect'.

With these principles, which Ingold suggested had emerged piecemeal historically, chemists now had a connected and coherent explanation of many chemical reactions in organic chemistry, with the possible exception of free radicals and certain rearrangements. During the next fifty years chemists would build on this foundation by exploring other mechanistic principles such as steric effects, guest–host complexions, non-classical ion intermediates, and the Woodward–Hoffmann rules for electrocyclic stereochemical effects.

That a few chemists were thinking along similar lines is

clear from the paper that Frank Whitmore (1887–1947) of Pennsylvania State University published in 1932. All reactions, he suggested, proceed through an electron-deficient intermediate (the later carbonium ion):

$$H : \ddot{A} : \ddot{B} : \ddot{X} : \longrightarrow H : \ddot{A} : \ddot{B}^+ \quad + \quad : \ddot{X} :^-$$

This intermediate was stabilized in one of three ways. In the first, it picked up a nucleophile from the solvent:

$$H : \ddot{A} : \ddot{B} :^+ \quad + \quad : \ddot{Y} :^- \longrightarrow H A B Y$$

In the second, it lost a proton, or other electrophilic group, to form an unsaturated compound:

$$H : \ddot{A} : \ddot{B}^+ \longrightarrow H^+ \quad + \quad : \ddot{A} :: \ddot{B} :$$

Finally, and this was Whitmore's most significant insight, if B had a greater electrophilic power for electrons than A, then the latter could cause an attached group to migrate with its electrons to form a new positive ion, which then stabilized by the first or second mechanisms. The total effect would be an intramolecular rearrangement:

$$\overset{H}{: \ddot{R} : \ddot{A} : \ddot{B}^+} \longrightarrow \overset{H}{\ddot{A} : \ddot{B} : \ddot{R} :^+} \longrightarrow either \quad : \ddot{A} :: \ddot{B} : \ddot{R} :$$

$$\longrightarrow or \ Y A B R$$

By identifying the products these theoretical mechanisms might be differentiated experimentally.

Apart from asserting that electron-withdrawing groups

would slow down aromatic substitution, Ingold's classification, as well as Whitmore's electronic concepts, did not help to explain chemical equilibria or the velocity of organic reactions – in other words the thermodynamic, kinetic and energetic properties of reactions. In fact, quite the opposite, it was the emergence of kinetic studies that was to complement, sustain and expand Ingold's classificatory insights. There are few signs that Ingold had thought seriously about kinetics before 1930 when, his wife having left chemistry to raise a family, Ingold's life was transformed by a new partner, Ted Hughes.

THE KINETICS OF MECHANISMS

Hughes was a working-class Welshman from Criccieth in Caernarvonshire. Born in 1906, he read chemistry at the small University College of North Wales at Bangor where Kennedy J. P. Orton (1872–1930) was pioneering research on the kinetics of organic reactions. Orton had started with the intention of studying medicine, but then switched to the Natural Science Tripos at Cambridge before taking his chemistry doctorate with Karl Auwers (1863–1937) in Heidelberg. He then taught chemistry to medical students for several years at St Bartholomew's Hospital in London before, in 1903, becoming the professor at Bangor. Like Boyd at Southampton, Orton had to teach chemistry single-handedly for many years while, somehow, finding time to watch birds and to continue research that he had begun in London on the halogenation of anilides. By the 1920s when Hughes was an undergraduate, however, Orton had assembled a small, but highly talented, research group that included H. B. Watson (1894–1975). The group was particularly concerned with unravelling the intramolecular rearrangements of aromatic nitrogen compounds by using kinetic studies to determine reaction pathways. These were the techniques that Hughes absorbed as a doctoral student with Orton and Watson. When Ingold organized an important Faraday Society discussion on mechanism and kinetics in 1941, he noted movingly:

> that more than half the reading matter we are to consider has come from the pens of five distinguished pupils of the late Professor Kennedy Orton . . . . A great leader and a pioneer of the movement we are to further, it is appropriate to notice the large part which, through the first generation of his successors, he has taken in our proceedings.

In 1930, having abandoned the idea of school teaching, Hughes joined Ingold at University College, London, as a postdoctoral fellow. They struck up an instant rapport, Hughes supplying the skills and knowledge of kinetic techniques, while Ingold (who had begun to realize from his Leeds colleague, H. M. Dawson, that kinetics could supply insights into mechanisms) supplied a wide knowledge and familiarity with chemistry and its theories. The partnership, which firmly established the role that physical chemistry was to play in future organic chemistry, was not broken by Hughes' brief return to Bangor as head of its chemistry department between 1943 and 1948 when Ingold persuaded University College to appoint Hughes to a second Chair of Chemistry. A stout, slow-moving, kindly figure with a high, fluty Welsh voice and very dry sense of humour, Hughes became famous for writing out his elegantly phrased lectures from memory in copperplate hand on the blackboard. There was always one memorable moment in his lecture course each year when he paused to fish out a card from his breast pocket that bore some quantitative data. He then said, with a twinkle, 'Ladies and Gentlemen. Even I do not expect you to remember this in an examination.' Hughes kept his Welsh roots and had an extensive life outside chemistry as a breeder and racer of greyhounds.

Although the basic theory of reaction kinetics was established by van't Hoff in the *Études de dynamique* in

1884 (see chapter 10), he had been able to exploit the data and insights of earlier workers. In 1850, for example, Ferdinand Wilhelmy (1812–64) in Germany had studied the rate of inversion of sucrose at various concentrations. He had concluded that the rate at which sugar concentration fell was directly proportional to its concentration at any given moment. Because he had the necessary mathematical knowledge, he was able to express this result as a differential equation. Wilhelmy's work, which was largely ignored until Ostwald drew attention to it in 1884, did prompt Berthelot and Leon Saint-Gilles (1832–63) to investigate the reaction between ethyl alcohol and acetic acid in 1862. They found that, after a certain time had elapsed, a chemical equilibrium was reached:

$$C_2H_5OH + CH_3.COOH \rightleftharpoons CH_3CO_2.C_2H_5 + H_2O$$

but until then, the rate of combination was proportional to the concentrations of both reactants.

This study, in turn, stimulated the Norwegian chemist, Peter Waage (1833–1900), and his brother-in-law mathematician, Cato Guldberg (1836–1902), to revive Berthollet's law of mass action in 1864. Their work was to remain peripheral until the 1870s when they began to publish more centrally in French and German, thereby drawing van't Hoff's attention. A similar collaboration between a chemist and mathematician occurred in the 1860s at the University of Oxford between August Vernon Harcourt (1834–1919) and William Esson (1838–1916). Harcourt made several meticulous studies of the reactions between hydrogen peroxide and hydrogen iodide, and between potassium permanganate and oxalic acid. Under Esson's mathematical scrutiny they were able to show how reaction rates depended upon concentrations and to differentiate between what Ostwald was to call 'first-' and 'second-order' reactions.

In the *Études*, van't Hoff classified reactions as unimolecular if their rate was proportional to the first power

540 · *Structure and Mechanism in Organic Chemistry*

of a reactant's concentration, $v = kc$; bimolecular if the rate was proportional to the square of the concentrations of one or the product of two reactants, $v = kc^2$ or $v = kc_1c_2$; and trimolecular if three concentration factors were involved. He was well aware that this indexing by molecularity was different from the numbers of molecules that were actually involved in a reaction — a point made clearer by Ostwald's distinction between the stoichiometric molecularity of a reaction, and its 'order', unimolecular, bimolecular, etc. For example, in the decomposition of arsine,

$$2AsH_3 = 2As + 3H_2$$

although two molecules of arsine are involved stoichiometrically, the rate is unimolecular, $v = k[AsH_3]$, where square brackets refer to concentration. The distinction was to be important in understanding Hughes and Ingold's studies, because they rather more logically applied the terms unimolecular, bimolecular, etc., to the molecularity, not the order. In his doctoral studies with Watson, Hughes had shown, for example, that the rate of halogenation of organic acids and ketones was independent of the concentrations of halogen present. The unimolecular rate determinant was the concentration of the organic acid or ketone. It is also worth noting that Hughes and Ingold used van't Hoff's 'differential method' to determine rate order. In this procedure, the rates are measured for various concentrations and plotted on a graph. Providing the relationship is of the form $v = kc^n$, then n (molecularity) can be easily found by plotting $\log v$ against $\log c$ (since $\log v = n \log c$).

Prior to leaving Leeds, Ingold had begun to study the mechanism of olefin formation and the decomposition of the quaternary ammonium salts ($R_4N^+X^-$) first prepared by Hofmann. As Hofmann had shown in the 1850s, when these ammonium salts were heated, a mixture of alcohols and olefins was produced, with the latter predominating. In

1928 Ingold recognized that there were competing processes of substitution and elimination at work:

substitution

$$HO:^- \ + \ [CH_3{-}N{-}CH_2.CH_2.CH_3]^+ {\longrightarrow} HOCH_3 \cdot \ +` \ :N{-}CH_2.CH_2.CH_3$$

with CH$_3$ groups above and below the N atoms.

elimination

$$[CH_3.CH_2.CH_2.NCH_3]^+ \ X^- \ \longrightarrow \ CH_3CH{=}CH_2 \ + \ NCH_3 \ + \ HX$$

At Leeds, however, Ingold was unable to decide whether substitution was a synchronous process (with 'the introduction of the replacing group and the expulsion of the replaced group occurring simultaneously'):

$$Y \ + \ R{-}X \ \longrightarrow \ Y{-}R \ + \ X^-$$

or whether dissociation into a reactive carbonium ion first occurred:

$$HCR_2.CR_2{-}X \ \longrightarrow \ HCR_2.CR_2^+ \ + \ X^-$$

$$[Y]^-$$

$$HCR.CR_2.Y$$

If the first mechanism took place, then two molecules were involved; if the second, then only one molecule was involved; but in 1928 Ingold had no method to differentiate these bimolecular and unimolecular mechanisms. This was still Whitmore's position in 1932. On the other hand, Ingold perceived that these eliminations were probably bimolecular, proceeding via the synchronous extraction 'of the protonic part of a combined hydrogen atom, while an electron-attracting group X simultaneously separates in possession of its previously shared electrons':

$$Y \ + \ H-CR_2-CR_2-X \longrightarrow YH \ + \ CR_2{=}CR_2 \ + \ X^-$$

In 1933, in one of their earliest, and certainly most important, theoretical papers, Hughes and Ingold distinguished these three possible mechanisms by the symbolism S_N2, S_N1 and E2, where S_N involves a substitution reaction and E an elimination mechanism, and the figure refers to the number of molecules involved in the slow (i.e. rate-determining) step (not the order of the reaction). Naturally, considerations of symmetry drove them to consider that an E1 mechanism should also be possible, and this was duly found by Hughes in olefin elimination reactions in 1935:

$$HCR_2.CR_2-X \ \longrightarrow \ HCR_2.CR_2^+ \ + \ X$$
$$CR_2{=}CR_2 \ + \ H^+$$

One of their more startling and controversial conclusions was that most, if not all, reactions could proceed in one or more ways according to the conditions of the reactions:

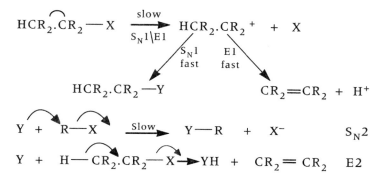

Thus, by the mid 1930s the Ingold school, as it was becoming known, had codified a good deal of organic chemistry. In all substitutions and eliminations a study of the kinetics of reactions promised to reveal whether the rate-determining step was uni- or bimolecular. Once this was known, it could be combined with Ingold's electronic insights into molecular structure, together with chemical experience and wisdom, to suggest a plausible reaction mechanism. Additional physical tools, such as measurements of dipole moments, dissociation constants, or Hughes' use of the isotope of hydrogen, deuterium, to label alkyl groups to confirm a mechanism, or thermodynamic variables to understand the activated transition state, all became grist to the mill of the British school.

In a thirty-year partnership, combining forces with several generations of students, who took their techniques and insights to other universities, schools and industrial workplaces, Ingold and Hughes explored the polarity effects of different solvents, and the rate–mechanism effects of catalysts, added salts and stereochemistry (where they were able to generalize that S_N2 always caused inversion, whereas racemization extensively occurred with S_N1), and the effects of steric hindrance, which was found to have less effect in S_N1 than in S_N2. They showed how these conditions affected and altered mechanisms and how, thereby, many well known reactions, such as the puzzling Walden inversion, might be explained (see Table 14.1).

TABLE 14.1   *The Walden inversion.*

The Walden inversion is like turning an umbrella inside out. In 1896, Paul Walden found that if *laevo*-malic acid was converted into *dextro*-chlorosuccinic acid, hydrolysis back to malic acid produced the *dextro* not *laevo* form. The latter could, however, be regenerated if the procedure was repeated with the *dextro* acid:

An inversion of configuration occurred during substitution; the problem was knowing at which stage this inversion occurred. In brilliant experimental work, which profoundly affected Ingold and Hughes, Kenyon and Phillips employed a series of chemical transformations between 1923 and 1935. These fixed some configurations with certainty and enabled Hughes in 1935 to use radioactive halogen isotopes to study inversion processes. In 1937, Ingold and Hughes concluded that bimolecular mechanisms were involved whenever inversion occurred during reactions:

When unimolecular mechanisms took place, racemization was the result. Their explanation was that, in S_N2 or E2 mechanisms, the attacking reagent approached an asymmetric carbon to the rear of the group to be replaced, whereas in S_N1 or E1 the carbonium ion formed was flat and could be attacked simultaneously from both sides. This allowed the production of equal quantities of *laevo* and *dextro* forms:

This combination of kinetic and stereochemical argument was to be the hallmark of mechanistic studies from 1940 onwards.

None of this was achieved without considerable opposition from classically trained and empirically minded organic chemists who objected to the need for physical chemistry, or who hated the Ingold school's expanding jargon of electromeric, mesomeric, duality of mechanisms, and S_N1, S_N2 symbolism. Armstrong, although no longer an active chemist, was inevitably pungent and must have spoken for many of the older and uncomprehending generation when he wrote in 'The coming of jargonthropos, the chemistry of the future'[10]:

'Influences of poles and polar linkings on tautomerism in the simple three carbon system. Part I. Experiments illustrating prototropy and anionotropy in trialkyl-propenylammonium derivatives'. Every word in this strange cacophanous medley needs explanation .... The theme is trivial – merely the production from the compound $CH_2Cl.CH.CH_2Cl$ of the two simple chlorallylammonium derivatives and the action of sodium ethoxide thereon. The behaviour brought out – the shift of the ethenoid junction – is that well known to be characteristic of such compounds and is in no way peculiar or momentous. The work at most adds a bare item or two to Beilstein. The discussion is superficial – a wordy paraphrase of the few simple statements which would have been held to be significant in the '70s and '80s.

Ingold and Hughes were also challenged on experimental grounds, the plausibility of their mechanisms ridiculed, and their kinetic evidence rejected. As might have been expected from the way Ingold had responded to Robinson in the 1920s, he did not take opposition lying down. Outwardly, and in oral discussion, Ingold was the most courteous, polite and gentlemanly of men, but he wrote with a rapier. When combined with Hughes' uncompromising non-conformist temper and conspiratorial belief that many Englishmen were villains, the joint effect could be explosive. No evidence actually survives to support their conviction that the chemical establishment, led by Robinson, was deliberately orchestrating a campaign of work that denigrated their findings; but that is undoubtedly how the two of them saw the situation during the 1930s. The reaction of Ingold and Hughes has been happily described as 'the invective effect': by choice sarcasm worthy of Liebig or Kolbe, coupled with clever experimental work, they slowly and devastatingly demolished the opposition. By the 1950s it had become a tradition at University College for professors to induct undergraduates into the heroic struggles of Ingold and Hughes who, unlike Laurent and Gerhardt, had lived to triumph over their enemies. Even so, in high schools, elderly chemistry teachers still frequently referred to reaction mechanisms as 'the Ingoldsby legends'.

One example of opposition must suffice. In the mid 1930s William Taylor, a research chemist at the Regent Street Polytechnic in London, argued on theoretical grounds, without doing all the necessary experiments, that in the alcoholysis of tertiary butyl chloride an S_N2 mechanism was involved. This was in contradiction to Hughes' prior demonstration of an S_N1 mechanism. Taylor had gone on to argue that probably all of the mechanisms labelled S_N1 by Ingold and Hughes were really bimolecular. In a massive overkill of sixteen papers occupying 110 pages and virtually a complete issue of *Journal of the Chemical Society* in 1940, Ingold, Hughes and various student collaborators showed that all of Taylor's work was riddled with experimental inexactitudes and that editors had no business accepting his papers. Whether because of the war, or because fairly or unfairly he did not dare take up a test-tube again, Taylor disappeared from chemistry. Like the rows of 1925–6, however, the controversy undoubtedly did some good, for it caused Ingold and Hughes to strengthen diagnostic tests for unimolecular reactions. Also, to avoid the implications of ionization, the breaking of a covalent bond so that both electrons were retained by only one of the separating atoms was renamed heterolysis:

$$H:H \rightarrow H^+ + \cdot H:^-$$

Conversely, in a decomposition where an electron was retained by each atom after bond breaking (free radicals), the reaction was called homolysis. The latter was most common in the gas phase, the former in solution. Further afield, in America, where their work was becoming influential by 1940, the controversies inspired new work on solvolysis, i.e. the exploration of reaction mechanisms in different solvents.

It fell to Ingold to write Hughes' obituary for the Royal Society following his early death in 1963, the same year that Ingold's student, Victor Gold (1922–85), began the annual review *Advances in Physical Organic Chemistry*. Their collaboration, Ingold wrote[11]:

> made it inescapably clear that the old order in organic chemistry was changing, the art of the

subject diminishing, its science increasing: no longer could one just mix things: sophistication in physical chemistry was the basis from which all chemists, including the organic chemist, must start.

Organic chemistry had come of age. But how had these insights spread and broken through the sustained opposition of the 1930s?

THE SPREAD OF PHYSICAL ORGANIC CHEMISTRY

The term 'physical organic chemistry' was first used in a textbook title by the American chemist, Louis P. Hammett (1894–1987), in 1940. At Columbia University during the 1930s, Hammett analysed organic molecules thermodynamically, demonstrating that the law of mass action and the kinetics of reactions were definitive guides to understanding reaction mechanisms. He was convinced that alterations of structure affected reactivity, as the Ingold school maintained, and that it ought to be possible to quantify such changes in terms of the free energies of molecules. During the mid 1930s, Hammett derived a large number of logarithmic relationships between the rate of a reaction and the equilibrium constant of a different, though related, reaction. In the case of benzene derivatives, in 1935, he was able to derive the 'Hammett equation'. Despite its empirical character, Hammett took great delight in pointing out that the equation required only two factors[12]:

to describe the interaction between a substituent and a reaction zone, not the four kinds of effect proposed in Ingold's publications.

A more rigorously defined 'Hammett acidity function', which he announced in 1934, proved of considerable use in studying the mechanisms of organic acid and ester formation in which a carboxylate is involved.

In the Preface to his *Physical Organic Chemistry. Reaction*

Rates, Equilibria and Mechanisms, Hammett noted how it had been almost a point of honour with both physical and organic chemists to profess ignorance of the other's field. In practice, this was far more true of America than of the Continent and Britain. In Europe, Arthur Hantzsch (1857–1935) trained many organic chemists in physical methods at Leipzig, including P. W. Robertson, who took the physical approach to New Zealand. Physical methods and theories of organic chemistry were also rigorously and critically expounded by Walter Hückel in his huge *Theoretische Grundlungen der organischen Chemie* (1931), which appeared in English only in 1958. In Britain, Lapworth at Manchester, Lowry at Cambridge, Orton at Bangor and Dawson and Ingold at Leeds had been using kinetic methods in the 1920s. As Saltzman has shown, however, interest in physical methods was a fragile thing. On Orton's death in 1930 he was replaced at Bangor by the terpene chemist, John L. Simonsen (1884–1957), who immediately discontinued research on physical organic chemistry. Much the same happened at Cambridge after Lowry's death in 1936.

The younger generation ensured, however, both continuity of research and that the physical approach to organic chemistry was taught to undergraduates. At Cardiff Technical College, where he moved from Bangor, Watson maintained a close connection with Hughes and Ingold, publishing a number of excellent reviews of mechanistic organic chemistry in the *Annual Reports* that were strongly supportive of the London duo. Watson's monograph, *Modern Theories of Organic Chemistry* (1937, 2nd edn 1941), offered chemists a helpful updating of progress since Ingold's 1934 review. In the absence of suitable teaching texts, another valuable British monograph was William A. Waters, *Physical Aspects of Organic Chemistry* (1935, 1937, 1942, 1950). Waters (1903–85), a lecturer at Durham University who was interested in the chemistry of free radicals, had begun this book with Lowry as a historical treatment of the subject, with mathematical contributions by C. P. Snow. But Lowry's illness and death allowed Waters to transform it into what he aptly described as 'a co-ordinate system' to the incoherent map of experimental observations with which students were usually confronted. These monographs, together with the marketing of Hammett's text in Great Britain, ensured that the physical approach to organic chemistry was firmly rooted in British universities by the early 1940s. Even so, as an undergraduate at Imperial College, London, during this decade, Derek Barton learned nothing of the work of Ingold and Hughes.

Despite physical chemistry's early entrenchment in American education, American response to the 'English heresy' was rather slower than the British. Lack of mathematical expertise was, as we have already seen, a perennial problem; but a more commercial attitude towards the function of organic chemistry may also have been a factor. Although some American organic chemists were happily using physical techniques such as polarimetry and electrolysis in the 1920s, there was a general scorning of thermodynamics, kinetics and the new quantum mechanics within the organic chemistry community. No doubt there was a kernel of truth in the reputed physical chemists' view of organic chemists as 'grubby artisans engaged in an unsystematic search for new compounds'. This was to change dramatically during the late 1930s as Ingold's mechanistic viewpoint infiltrated textbooks and research programmes. Ultimately the synthesis of organic compounds would benefit and the 'grubby search' would be transformed.

Even in Henry Gilman's massive *Organic Chemistry. An Advanced Treatise* (New York, 1938), Louis Fieser (1899–1977), a pupil of J. B. Conant (1893–1978) at Harvard, in his essay on aromatic chemistry, could dismiss Ingold's 'elaborate theory' on the grounds that he was not attracted by it. Another essay, by John R. Johnson of Cornell University, was explicitly concerned with Ingold's electronic theory. Nevertheless, Johnson felt obliged to note that:

> The molecular model which serves as a basis for the modern electrochemical (electronic) theories of reactions is one that visualizes a space distribution of atomic nuclei and electrons (as point charges) maintained by elastic forces about fixed relative positions. This simple picture has been elaborated, to the dismay and confusion of many organic chemists, by the introduction of wave mechanical ideas of a continuous statistical distribution of electron density, of quantized states, and of resonance (degeneracy). However, the more complicated picture has served, on the whole, merely [sic] to correlate and place upon a more definite physical basis a variety of phenomena that were long recognized by organic chemists.

Gilman's two volumes were a recognition that the American postgraduate student lacked suitably advanced reading. Until their appearance, Ingold's 1934 review had been obligatory reading in such circles. Hammett's excellent work appeared in 1940, closely followed by *The Theory of Organic Chemistry* (1941) co-authored by Gerard Branch and Melvin Calvin of the University of California at Berkeley. Branch (1886–1954) was an English emigrant who became a close friend of Ingold's following the latter's visit to Stanford University in 1932. Branch always called on Ingold to talk about theoretical organic chemistry whenever he was on vacation in London.

Significant pockets of research on physical organic chemistry were established by E. P. Kohler (1865–1938) at Harvard, where James B. Conant was groomed as his successor. Like Remsen, however, Conant was drawn into administration, becoming Harvard's President in 1933, and he never succeeded in building up a school comparable to that of Ingold and Hughes in Britain. Among Conant's pupils were Fieser, who disdained theory for adventures in synthesis and textbook compilation, Paul D. Bartlett (*b*. 1908), who was to make Harvard into the American centre of physical organic chemistry in the 1940s, and George W. Wheland (*b*. 1907). The latter, following postdoctoral studies with both Pauling and Ingold, devoted himself to quantum mechanics. His book, *The Theory of Resonance in Organic Chemistry* (1944), did much to ease chemists' struggles with the principles of resonance and mesomerism and to introduce valence bond ideas to organic chemists. Many chemists also found his *Advanced Organic Chemistry* (1949) exciting because of his exposure of fundamental philosophical problems in chemistry.

Another significant American teacher was Pauling's colleague at CalTech, Howard Lucas (1885–1963), who learned his physical chemistry at the University of Chicago with John Nef and Julius Stieglitz. Unable to take a Ph.D. because of financial problems, he seems to have been looked down upon by his CalTech colleagues. But Ingold was greatly impressed by his work on the inductive effect during the 1920s, while Lucas' textbook, *Organic Chemistry* (1935), was the first American undergraduate text to introduce reaction mechanisms. (Unfortunately, it treated resonance as an oscillation between two extremes.) He was also a great teacher. Among his pupils were William C. Young (1902–81) and the Canadian, Saul Winstein (1912–69) who, at the University of Los Angeles, extended structural and mechanistic principles by means of molecular orbital theory.

One final American group worth noting was that of Morris Kharasch (1895–1957) at the University of Chicago. As a consequence of studying the mechanism of the reaction between hydrogen bromide and hydrogenated alkenes in 1932, he stumbled upon examples of anti-Markovnikov addition. For example, propylene reacted with HBr to give n-propyl bromide instead of the expected i-propyl bromide. To explain this he was led to posit the intermediate production of free bromine radicals from the adventitious presence of oxygen or peroxides:

$$O_2 \rightarrow \dot{O} + \dot{O}$$
$$\dot{O} + H{:}Br \rightarrow O{:}H + \dot{B}r$$
$$\dot{B}r + CH_2{=}CHR \rightarrow BrCH_2{-}\dot{C}HR$$
$$BrCH_2\dot{C}HR + H{:}Br \rightarrow BrCH_2CH_2R + \dot{B}r$$

Such a 'peroxide effect' led him on to the study of free radicals generally and their role in reaction mechanisms – apart from Waters, an area left largely unexplored by the Ingold school. This subject, which had important industrial implications for the study of polymer chemistry, was to become a distinctive speciality of American organic chemists in the 1950s.

As Saltzman and Gortler have noted, the development of physical organic chemistry in America was initially limited geographically to just three centres on the Californian west coast, the California Institute of Technology (CalTech) and the University of California at Los Angeles (UCLA) and at Berkeley; to Chicago in the mid-west; and to Columbia and Harvard in the east. Each centre had only a small programme, but it sufficed to provide[13]:

a stream of graduates who in the post-1945 period would extend the study of physical organic chemistry to other parts of the U.S. and lead to the eventual domination by Americans of the subject after 1945.

Ingold's magnum opus, *Structure and Mechanism in Organic Chemistry*, hit the crest of this wave; but the wave soon passed. Donald Cram and George Hammond's *Organic Chemistry* (1959), which became a standard American undergraduate text in the 1960s, classified all reactions 'according to their mechanisms, rather than according to the structures of their starting materials or products'. When in 1972 American chemists launched the annual review volume *Progress in Physical Organic Chemistry*, it was Saul Winstein, not Ingold, whom the editor saw as his subject's founder.

AROMATICITY

From the time of Kekulé there were a large number of attempts by chemists to formulate some simple rule for the prediction (and explanation) of the orientation of substituents in benzene and its derivatives. These empirical rules appealed among other things to the periodic table, theories of alternative polarity and affinity, and later to the electronic configurations, dipole moments and dissociation constants of the reactants. The most notorious of these rules – distinguished as much for its failures as its successes – was the 'Crum Brown–Gibson rule', which Alexander Crum Brown and his Edinburgh student, John Gibson, articulated in 1892. It depended on the curious correlation that, if, for a substituent X, HX can be converted to HOX by direct oxidation (e.g. NO_2: $HNO_2 \rightarrow HNO_3$), then it substituted *meta;* but if HX was not directly oxidizable in one step to HOX (e.g. Cl_2: $HCl \rightarrow HOCl$), then *ortho* and *para* derivatives were formed. There were exceptions. In 1892 it was not possible to oxidize methane directly to methyl alcohol and therefore the *ortho–para* directing power of a methyl substituent seemed assured. However, when soon afterwards direct oxidation proved possible after all, application of the *meta* rule contradicted the facts. The advent of electronic theories, of course, allowed Robinson, Ingold and others to explain the rule and its defects in terms of the inductive and electromeric effects and, more fundamentally, aromaticity itself as a reflection of mesomerism.

As early as 1922 Robinson had explained the strange properties of the benzene ring as due to pairs of adjacent atoms sharing three electrons:

The properties of naphthalene, anthracene and the nitrogen aromatics, pyridine and pyrrole, were accommodated in a similar fashion. In 1925, however, he returned to, or rather modified, Thiele's partial affinity notation for benzene:

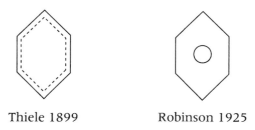

Thiele 1899   Robinson 1925

Robinson now ascribed the uniquely 'aromatic' properties of benzene and its analogues to the six 'extra' electrons that produced the 'stable association which is responsible for the *aromatic* character'. Although the term he used to describe this, the 'aromatic sextet', was later dismissed by him as 'a phantasy', and the Kekulé formula judged entirely satisfactory, the term, as well as Robinson's centric formula, became well established in the literature.

This was especially so after 1931 when Erich Hückel (1896–1980), as a consequence of quantum-mechanical calculations, showed that benzene's stability arose from six sigma (σ) bonds in the plane of the ring and six pi (π) electrons in orbits at right angles above and below the plane. These π orbitals, which explained benzene's diamagnetism, were considered to move above and below the main hexagonal frame and to provide the mesomeric, or resonance, energy that gave the molecule its extra stability by not confining its electrons to simple alternating single and double bonds (as in a Kekulé structure). By 1935, Kathleen Lonsdale (1903–74), extending previous work on hexamethylbenzene, had confirmed by X-ray analysis that benzene did have a planar and perfectly hexagonal structure. The first woman to be elected to the Royal Society in 1945, together with the microbiologist, Margaret Stephenson, in the same year Lonsdale joined the team of Ingold and Hughes at University College.

Despite these developments, as Ingold argued, Kekulé's hexagon remained useful for the interpretation of the transformation of the aromatic nucleus[14]:

> We attach the curved-arrow signs to Kekulé formulae, even though such formulae could not by themselves account for the stability of the nucleus, [because] it is convenient, for the purposes of following the reaction mechanism, to think of these electron pairs as having immediately come from localised positions.

As early as 1922, in closing the ring of a cyclobutanone ester to form orcinol,

Dewar intermediate

orcinol

Ingold had assumed a mechanism that involved a '*para*-bridged' intermediate with a Dewar benzene structure. In the same paper he suggested that benzene ought, therefore, to be considered a dynamic equilibrium of five hexagonal forms of benzene, the two postulated by Kekulé in 1872, together with the three possible Dewar forms:

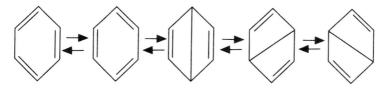

(A stable Dewar benzene was actually synthesized by E. E. Van Tamelen in 1963.) From this it would seem that the roots of Ingold's introduction of mesomerism between 1929 and 1933 lay in chemical structural theory. This is why the valence bond treatment of benzene as a 'mixture' of five or more 'canonical forms' appealed to him.

Hückel had also treated the benzene system by molecular orbital methods and generalized from this that, in any *n*-sided carbon polygon, the mesomeric energy could be expressed in terms of the energy of a π bond in ethylene and a quantum number. When simplified, this Hückel rule stated that aromatic properties would be shown whenever the number of π electrons in a closed ring could be expressed as $4n + 2$. This works for $n = 1$, 2 and 3 where rings (annulenes) of six, ten and fourteen members (benzene, naphthalene and anthracene) are clearly aromatic, and explained why the annulenes with four, eight and twelve members with alternating single and double bonds, such as cyclo-octatetraene, are not:

or

Much effort and synthetic ingenuity went into testing Hückel's rule during the 1960s. For $n = O$, aromaticity was predicted. This was confirmed by Breslow in 1962 for the cyclopropenyl cation. This is a three-membered ring with a double bond and a positive charge on the third atom:

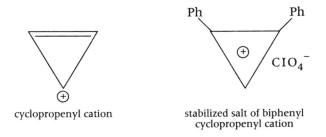

cyclopropenyl cation

stabilized salt of biphenyl cyclopropenyl cation

As knowledge of quantum mechanics spread among organic chemists, it became clear that the molecular orbital approach, with its ready correlation with the excited states of spectroscopy and visions of π orbitals and π bonding, offered many advantages over the valence bond approach popularized by Pauling. The crunch came in the 1950s when the availability of electronic computers began to replace tedious calculations on hand calculators and slide rules. By 1950, aromaticity was understood as a property of any 'cyclic compound with a large resonance energy where all its annular atoms take part in a single conjugated system'[15]. The MO method was to lead to the longest dispute in the history of organic chemistry, over non-classical ions, while at the same time, through the Woodward–Hoffmann rules (chapter 16), it placed synthetic organic chemistry on a sounder theoretical footing for the first time.

THE NON-CLASSICAL ION DEBATE

A passionate early spokesman for the MO treatment of organic chemistry was Robinson's outspoken Oxford pupil,

Michael J. S. Dewar (*b.* 1918), who viewed resonance (and with it, Ingold's mesomerism) as 'unfortunate anachronisms'. (Similar criticisms by Charles C. Price (*b.* 1913) of the University of Illinois at about the same time caused friction with Saul Winstein.) Following research at Courtauld's, Dewar succeeded Partington at the run-down Queen Mary College in the bomb-cratered East End of London. In 1959, exhausted by efforts to rehabilitate Queen Mary College, he emigrated to America where he eventually founded a school of theoretical organic chemistry at the University of Texas at Austin. To Dewar, MO theory, as visually interpreted, represented a return to the views of Thiele, whose partial valency theory (as Robinson had in Dewar's view perceptively realized) was a foreshadowing of the coupling of π electron orbitals.

Robinson, who was delighted with Dewar's brilliance, obviously saw him as vindicating his views over those of Ingold's. Together, in 1946, they planned a book that would quantify Robinson's electronic theory by translating it into the language of quantum mechanics and MO theory. Unfortunately, Robinson never had the time to sit down seriously with Dewar, who went ahead by himself to publish *The Electronic Theory of Organic Chemistry* in 1949. This did, however, contain a long Foreword by Robinson in which his theory, by then looking curiously obscure and out of date, was given in detail. This essay was essentially the paper that the Chemical Society had rejected in 1938 when Ingold demanded a right of reply.

In 1941, in a frigid exchange of papers, Robinson and Ingold had explained the benzidine rearrangement, in which a hydrazine unfolds itself into benzidine, by a complicated appeal to inductive and electromeric effects, or, in Ingold's case, to 'an exceptional resonance' or mesomeric argument. These mechanisms were challenged by Dewar in 1946 when he argued that the benzidine and other rearrangements could be more simply explained on the assumption that the π bonds of the two phenyl groups formed 'dative bonds' around which the rings underwent relative rotation following the cleavage of the N—H bond until they were 'anchored' by the formation of a new C—C bond. Such a mechanism, which appealed to the formation of what he called a 'π complex' intermediate, avoided 'the very long bonds and considerable distortions of bond angles' required when the electronic mechanisms of Robinson and Ingold were applied. Above all, π electron mechanisms would be advantageous in explaining the complicated stereochemistry of many rearrangements. In the first edition of *Structure and Mechanism*, Ingold dismissed this explanation in a curt footnote, but by the second edition in 1964, he gave it equal treatment. By then Saul Winstein (1912–69) at the University of California at Los Angeles had become a brighter star than Ingold in the firmament of organic mechanistic studies, while Dewar in *The Molecular Orbital Theory of Organic Chemistry* (1969) could say that any organic chemist who did not understand MO theory would be left 'high and dry'.

By the 1960s it had become possible to interpret the inductive effect as due to the formation of polar σ bonds between the carbon atoms of a chain and various substituents. The formation of a positive carbonium ion, or a negative carbanion, brought about the further polarization of π orbitals, which interacted in turn with the π electron orbitals of substituents to produce what Ingold had called the electromeric effect. For this reason, Dewar preferred to call the resulting intermediate structure a π complex. The justification for the existence of transient covalent σ bonds, which involved the sharing of a single pair of electrons between three nuclei, had been provided by the quantum-mechanical calculations at Oxford of Charles Coulson and Christopher Longuet-Higgins. Such intermediates had already been found necessary in inorganic chemistry to explain the reactions of 'electron-deficient' boron compounds. If mesomerism was really a process of π bond delocalization (resonance), then, by analogy, there ought to be a similar process of σ bond delocalization.

In 1937, in the last of a series of papers on the Walden inversion, Ingold and Hughes had speculated that a substituent might enter a carboxylate in such a way that the latter retained its stereochemical form by forming an internal electrostatic attachment:

This was an early example of what Winstein was to call 'neighbouring group participation'. Two years later, Ingold's former Leeds pupil and University College, London (UCL), colleague, Christopher Wilson (who was to emigrate to the University of Notre Dame), appealed to a bridged ion intermediate in order to explain the rearrangement of camphene hydrochloride. The isotopic studies that Hughes had made on the Walden inversion had used a Geiger counter and other equipment belonging to Brian Topley. The latter had never got on with Hughes and, when he left for a post in industry in 1938, he left the equipment to Wilson, who, in order not to upset Hughes further, began mechanistic studies of alicyclic compounds, including the camphors.

At first Hughes was sceptical of Wilson's bridged ion mechanism, though Ingold in 1940 was more supportive.

(There is some evidence that, but for the war, Ingold and Wilson (1909–85) planned to write what became Ingold's *Structure and Mechanism.*) By 1951, both Ingold and Hughes found such electrostatic stabilization of intermediates useful in explaining the kinetic timing of saturated rearrangements (e.g. the Wagner–Meerwein rearrangement) of terpenes such as bornyl chloride and its stereoisomer, isobornyl chloride. Ingold, borrowing a term from literary analysis referring to the smoothness of a poetic metre, called the acceleration of the rate produced by this unusual valency co-ordination 'synartesis' or 'synartetic acceleration', and the intermediate a 'synartetic ion'.

Independently, at about the same time, Winstein referred to such intermediates as 'bridged ions' and the 'kinetic lift' that they sponsored 'anchimeric assistance' (from the Greek for neighbouring parts); but the name that stuck, 'non-classical carbonium ions' (or simply 'non-classical ions'), was coined by John D. Roberts (*b.* 1918) in 1949 to apply to both σ and π bond complexes. In 1951, in one of the most cited papers of the twentieth century, Roberts, together with a student, Robert H. Mazur, investigated the intermediate formation of carbocations (carbonium ions) in the reactions of cyclopropylmethane. They explained the increasing thermodynamic stability of products bearing different side groups as due to an intermediate tricyclobutonium cation:

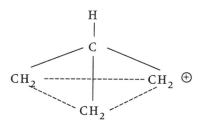

A chance meeting with Dewar confirmed that MO theory would justify the existence of such a structure, as well as an aromatic intermediate, benzyne:

(Ingold was so excited by the latter when Roberts lectured on the molecule at UCL in 1951 that he leaped across the bench to the blackboard to explain his thoughts.)

Such molecules seemed to Roberts so bizarre that, recognizing Ingold's, Wilson's and Winstein's priority, he labelled them 'non-classical', and the name stuck. Isotopic tagging of norbornyl compounds appeared to confirm the existence of such entities. Dewar felt that such terms as non-classical, bridges or synartetic ions, were confusing and that:

> most of the confusion in the literature can be cleared up immediately by translating the authors' statements and formulae into π-complex terminology and symbolism.

In practice, however, a different term was desirable since σ not π bonding was plausibly involved in many cases.

Winstein was as adept as Ingold in devising new vocabulary: neighbouring group participation, solvent participation, internal return, anchimeric acceleration (which soon replaced Ingold's synartesis), bridged ions, homoaromaticity and (with Doering and Woodward in 1951) the systematized terminology of carbanions, carbonium ions and carbenes for negative, positive and divalent neutral carbon systems. He had first developed the idea of neighbouring group π electron interaction while an undergraduate at UCLA in 1934 and refined it while he was a postgraduate at CalTech in 1938. Following work on the positive bromine (bromonium) ion, which complemented similar kinetic work that Hughes had done on the analogous chlorine structure, and in order to explain *trans* addition reactions, Winstein postulated a structure such as

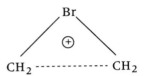

rather than simply $CH_2.CH_2.Br^+$ (see Table 14.2). Later, he was able to suggest that σ and π electron orbitals might interact to produce pseudo-aromatic properties in benzene wherein carbon had been replaced by cyclopropane

TABLE 14.2 Trans *addition.*

If addition of a halogen to a double bond proceeds by heterolysis, we would expect *cis* addition:

$$CH_2 {=}\, CH_2 \ + \ X \rightarrow \overset{+}{C}H_2 - \overset{-}{C}H_2 \xrightarrow{X} \underset{\qquad cis}{\overset{X\qquad\quad X}{\underset{|\qquad\quad |}{CH_2 - CH_2}}}$$

$$\rightarrow \overset{-}{C}H_2 - \overset{+}{C}H_2 \xrightarrow{X}$$

But *tra* compounds are formed:

$$\overset{X}{\underset{CH_2 - \underset{X}{\overset{|}{CH_2}}}{\overset{|}{|}}}$$

This was explained by Winstein as a two-step reaction:

The only way to explain the stereospecificity is to postulate a cyclic intermediate 'bromonium' or 'chloronium' ion:

rings. Such compounds, he speculated, might form a 'homoaromatic' series.

In 1959 he postulated the existence of the *tris*-homocyclopropenyl cation later prepared by Breslow:

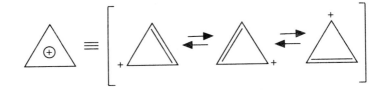

This was analogous to the bridged ions he had already deduced as producing the 'driving force' in many abnormally fast terpene reactions:

i.e. a bridged ion formed by migrating σ electrons of two neighbouring groups.

Such non-classical ions were angrily rejected by Herbert C. Brown (*b.* 1912), another English immigrant to America. Ironically, Brown, a student of Stieglitz at Chicago, obtained the Nobel prize in chemistry in 1979 for his exploration of boron–carbon compound chemistry – the very field to which many organic chemists had appealed in support of bridged ion intermediates. One of the reactions Brown had investigated was the hydroboration of the terpene, norbornene, to form *exo*-norborneol. (Confusingly, the *bor* of norbornene has nothing to do with boron; the parent terpene is norbornane, *bicyclo*[2.2.1]heptane; *nor* means without a substituent such as methyl.)

or in three dimensions

norbornane

(i) HB

(ii) [o]

exo-borneol

OH

H

Winstein explained the production of *exo*- as opposed to *endo*- norborneol

H

OH

as due to a non-classical intermediate,

but Brown, beginning in 1961, objected strongly to such inventions, arguing that the stereochemistry of the reaction could be explained as a classic piece of tautomeric isomerism:

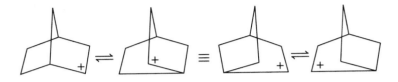

and that the anchimeric acceleration could be explained classically as due to the removal of steric hindrance.

The resulting debate[16]:

> ranks among the classics of chemical disagreements. It was fought out nationally and internationally . . . through seminars, meetings, referees reports, papers, books and private communications.

During the mid 1960s, George Olah used 'magic acid' (an intensely strong 'Lewis acid' consisting of antimony pentafluoride dissolved in excess fluorosulphuric acid) to prepare concentrated solutions of carbocations. Nuclear magnetic resonance spectra of the cold solutions, while throwing some doubt on the structures postulated by molecular orbital calculations, clearly indicated the presence of non-classical carbocations. In the face of this battery of physical evidence from chromatography, infrared and nuclear magnetic resonance spectroscopy of magic acid solutions, the controversy became increasingly one-sided, with only Brown defending the classical position – like 'Horatio at the bridge' – against Ingold, Winstein, Roberts, Bartlett and, latterly, Olah.

Oddly, because of the complexity of the issue, the debate passed by historians and philosophers of science, while, within chemistry itself, it was confined to organic chemists. It forms a good example of how appeals to the simplest hypothesis in science (essentially Brown's position) may break down under the combined attack of experimental and theoretical evidence. Not only has the debate led to the extension of valency theory, it has revolutionized stereochemical procedures in synthesis, while at the same time providing new insights into the mechanism of solvolysis.

CONCLUSION

Wöhler, in a famous metaphor, had compared organic chemistry in the 1830s to a dark jungle. Nineteenth-century structural chemists revealed the nature of the trees and leaves of this forest and pointed to common patterns of growth as well as methods for getting quickly from A to B. But their maps of this jungle were presented to the tyro as a catalogue of preparations and reactions. The Ingold revolution was to look for patterns in reactivity and to explain why reactions occurred in the way they did by relating reactivity to molecular structure. This mechanistic approach, like the periodic table in inorganic chemistry, simplified the task of the learner – but at the cost of demanding much more competence in mathematics than was had by Victorian chemists. Even so, by dint of specialization in quantum mechanics, chemists like Ingold and his followers were able to rely a good deal still on geometrical reasoning. Wöhler's forest was now revealed as an ordered plantation. Such a revolution of perception was not without its effects on inorganic chemistry, as we shall see in the following chapter.

The Renaissance of Inorganic Chemistry

> Those of us who were familiar with the state of inorganic chemistry in universities twenty to thirty years ago will recall that at that time it was widely regarded as a dull and uninteresting part of the undergraduate course . . . . This state is now past and for the purposes of our discussion we shall define inorganic chemistry today as the integrated study of the formation, composition, structure, and reactions of the chemical elements and their compounds, excepting most of those of carbon.
>
> (R. NYHOLM, *The Renaissance of Inorganic Chemistry*, 1956)

Eclipsed by the systematization of analytical and synthetic organic chemistry, and by the rigour and logic of physical chemistry, which Ostwald had promoted as the under-pinning of the whole of chemistry, until the 1950s inorganic chemistry remained the poor relation of chemistry. To be sure it was the entrée to chemistry at the high-school level where, since the 1880s, the periodic table had offered some sort of systematization and coherence, and it had its own special German-language journal; but once atomic weights had been determined to a few more decimal places, atomic numbers had been found to offer a better rationale for periodicity and for the differentiation of the rare-earth elements, and a few 'missing' elements characterized, there seemed to be few interesting inorganic research problems worth pursuing.

The exception was a group of compounds known as 'complex compounds' or 'complex salts', which, at the beginning of the twentieth century, appeared to offer opportunities for skilled preparative chemistry, adventures in stereochemistry and opportunities for controversy and debate over their states of valency and structure. Yet, by 1914, most chemists agreed that Alfred Werner's explanation of these compounds in terms of his theory of co-ordination, rather than Scandinavian chemists' appeal to analogies with organic compounds, had solved the puzzles. In publishing his *New Views of Inorganic Chemistry* in 1905, it appeared to many that Werner had left few stones unturned in the field of co-ordination chemistry. All that remained to do was to summarize and entomb what was known about chemical elements – as was done in the bravado compilations of John Newton Friend (1881–1966), *Textbook of Inorganic Chemistry* (22 vols, 1914–37), and by Joseph William Mellor in his *Comprehensive Treatise on Theoretical and Inorganic Chemistry* (16 vols, 1922–37). Both surveys retain their value for accurate historical documentation.

Like organic chemistry, inorganic chemistry was to be invigorated by quantum mechanics and the advent of new forms of instrumentation that allowed the investigation and interpretation of physical structure. Werner's co-ordination theory was then found to offer rich opportunities for theoretical speculation, model-building, the preparation of compounds in unusual valency states and the chance to break down the distinction between inorganic and organic chemistry through the 'intermarriage' of organic groups with metal atoms in co-ordination complexes. The books of Sidgwick and Pauling, together with *Modern Aspects of Inorganic Chemistry* (1939) by H. J. Eméleus and J. S. Anderson, did much to stimulate a new generation. The Second World War's atom bomb project led to the discovery of a whole new group of 'artificial' elements and, partly through its secrecy, stimulated chemists' imaginations, as well as stimulating further preparative work in co-ordination chemistry in order to achieve separations of isotopes or minute quantities of new elements and their compounds. The petroleum industry's post-war awareness that nickel complexes catalysed cyclizations and carbonylations of olefins and acetylenes also encouraged research grants for the investigations of transition-metal chemistry. The sensational discovery in 1962 that a generation of chemists had been gulled into believing that the rare gases could not form compounds completed the renaissance of inorganic chemistry. In the same year, the opening editorial of *Inorganic Chemistry* could declare:

> The limits of inorganic chemistry are difficult to define. Its subject matter may range from the limits of physical and organic chemistry to the edges of theoretical physics.

Despite the launch of the series *Inorganic Syntheses* in 1939 and the important contributions to co-ordination chemistry made by Americans such as John C. Bailar Jr (*b*. 1904), Melvin Calvin (*b*. 1911) and Fred Basolo (*b*. 1920), as well as the Russians, Aleksandrovich Chugaev (1873–1922) and Il'ya Il'ich Chernyaev (1893–1966), this 'renaissance of inorganic chemistry', as Ronald Nyholm termed it in 1956, was very much a distinctive contribution of Australian chemists. Since this was the first time that the Australasian continent entered onto the world's chemical stage, part of this chapter will be concerned to identify how Australia built up a research tradition in this area. Comparisons with the Japanese will be appropriate, since both nations began to institutionalize science seriously in the 1870s. However, as Nyholm and other co-ordination chemists of the 1950s were the first to admit, the reawakening of inorganic chemistry would never have been possible without the secure foundations that were laid by Werner at the end of the nineteenth century and by Sidgwick in the 1920s. It is, therefore, to Werner that we first turn.

WERNER'S NEW IDEAS

The principal historian of co-ordination chemistry, George B. Kauffman, makes the undeniable point that Alfred Werner (1866–1919) was, and is, synonymous with co-ordination chemistry, the field in which he played 'a central and monopolistic role'. Werner, a French- and German-speaking Alsatian from the industrial town of Mulhouse, studied chemistry with the fiery stereochemist, Arthur Hantzsch (1857–1935) at the well equipped Eidgenössisches Polytechnikum in Zürich. In his doctoral dissertation in 1890, Werner succeeded in demonstrating that the stereo-isomerism associated with tetrahedral carbon was also found in trivalent nitrogen. During the 1880s, Victor Meyer and others had prepared the dioximes of benzil in three different forms. Werner's explanation, which he published with Hantzsch in 1890, was that the dioximes were an example of van't Hoff's geometric *cis–trans* isomerism:

Werner's doctoral work was a great stimulus to stereochemical studies, and by the end of the decade Armstrong's pupil, William Jackson Pope (1870–1939), had succeeded in resolving a quaternary ammonium compound by using camphor acids and other optically active substances.

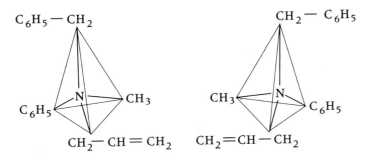

allylbenzylmethylphenylammonium ion
enantiomorphs resolved by Pope and Peachey (1899)

Thus encouraged, Pope and others went on to resolve the racemates of large numbers of substances in which nitrogen, sulphur, selenium and tin, and not carbon, were the centres of asymmetry. As John Read has hilariously described, work on selenium compounds at Cambridge, where Pope became Professor in 1908, was particularly difficult because of the sensational odours that clung to the chemists' bodies for months, rendering social intercourse impossible. This classical form of stereochemistry continued until the 1930s when the advent of X-ray analysis, dipole measurement and infrared spectroscopy expanded stereochemistry to embrace all chemical substances whether optically active or not. Here Werner's co-ordination theory was to come into its own.

In completing his *Habilitationsthesis*, necessary for an academic position in a German-speaking university, Werner had turned his attention to the nature of chemical affinity and valency. On the strength of this preliminary version of his co-ordination theory he became a Privatdocent at the Zürich Polytechnic before, in 1893, taking the Chair of Chemistry at the University of Zürich, where he built up a very successful research school.

Although Frankland's and Kekulé's theory of valency had provided an exceedingly satisfactory explanation for the structures of carbon compounds and the simpler compounds of inorganic chemistry, as we saw, there was debate whether elements had fixed or variable valencies. Some of this debate hinged on the puzzling structures of minerals and recalcitrant substances such as organo-metallic compounds and metal complexes such as metal hydrates and ammines (metals combined with ammonia). There were dozens of bizarre theories of mineral structure, none of which proved satisfactory until X-ray analysis and the crystallographic work of the Braggs and Linus Pauling in the 1920s revealed that chemists had been making false assumptions all along. Organo-metallic compounds seemed a simpler problem because, by the association of ideas, they could be imagined to follow the structural rules of organic chemistry. From there it was but a small step to conceive that the so-called 'molecular compounds' such as ammines were linked together in chains like carbon atoms.

The 'chain theory' was first developed by the Swede, Christian W. Blomstrand (1826–97), as a simple extension of Kekulé's supposition that diazo compounds had their radicals linked together through nitrogen:

$$C_6H_5—N\!\!=\!\!N—C_6H_5$$
azobenzene

Where metals formed hydrates, or ammines (the term was not coined by Werner until 1897), Blomstrand suggested in his tremendously influential *Die Chemie der Jetztzeit* (The Chemistry of Today) that one way of avoiding the increase of a metal's normal valency would be to assume the formation of a polymeric chain. Thus, a potassium tetravalent platinum hexachlorine complex could be written

Blomstrand's experience with ammines suggested to him that their nitrogen should be regarded as quinquevalent, rather than trivalent. Consequently, in contradistinction to Kekulé, he preferred to write azo compounds with a triple bond:

$$C_6H_5 \text{ ----- } N \text{ ----- } C_6H_5$$
$$\text{|||}$$
$$N$$

When Emil Fischer derived phenylhydrazine from diazo compounds in 1875, Kekulé's formulation seemed preferable. But this was not the end of the matter since, in many reactions, diazobenzene, $C_6H_5.N:N.OH$, seemed to react in an isomeric form of phenylnitrosamine, $C_6H_5.NH.NO$. The confirmation of this isomerism by Eugen Bamberger (1857–1932) in 1894, soon after he had been appointed to the Zürich Polytechnic, led to a violent controversy with Hantzsch, who by that time had succeeded Fischer at Wurzburg. We need not follow this polemical exchange, which lasted until 1902, except to observe that Hantzsch perceived that geometrical stereochemical effects were in operation,

$$C_6H_5.N \qquad\qquad C_6H_5.N$$
$$\text{||} \qquad\qquad\qquad \text{||}$$
$$KSO_3.N \qquad\qquad N.SO_3K$$
$$\text{syn} \qquad\qquad\qquad \text{anti}$$

and he urged organic chemists to pay more attention to the ideas of co-ordination and stereochemistry that his pupil Werner had announced. Ironically, Blomstrand himself did not believe in fixed valencies, and it was this that allowed Werner to conceive such compounds very differently.

As an admirer of Berzelius' electrochemical theory, Blomstrand was convinced that, because combination depended upon the neutralization of charges, and these varied with the nature of the reagent or attacking group, the saturation capacities, or valencies, were bound to be variable. Werner, while disagreeing with Blomstrand's structures, was to exploit this notion of the expansibility of valency to the full.

Like Kekulé, Werner claimed that his theory flashed through his mind while he was sleeping fitfully; by tea-time of the following day he had written one of the most intellectually exciting and cogent papers in the whole history of chemistry, 'Beitrag zur Konstitution anorganische Verbindungen', which was published in the new *Zeitschrift für anorganischen Chemie* in 1893.

In this revolutionary paper, Werner began with the observation that the known ammine and hydrate salts of cobalt and copper were divisible into two groups – those in which the maximum ratio of ammonia or water to metal was 6 : 1 or 4 : 1, e.g.

$$Co(NH_3)_6Cl_3 \qquad \text{and} \qquad Cu(NH_3)_4(NO_3)_2$$

Although not all members had been isolated, each group formed a series of complex compounds in which the amount of ammonia or water was gradually reduced to zero, viz.

$$M(NH_3)_6X_3 \qquad M(NH_3)_5X_3 \qquad M(NH_3)_4X_3$$
$$M(NH_3)_3X_3 \qquad \dots \qquad MX_3$$

Werner paid most attention to cobalt salts as models for his argument because they had received a great deal of attention from Edmond Frémy (1814–94) in France and Sophus Jørgensen (1837–1914) in Denmark. Both men had been attracted by the dazzling beauty of the different colours of the various cobalt salts; and Frémy in 1852 had devised a complicated, and not always consistent, colour nomenclature to differentiate them. For example, all complexes containing six NH_3 or HO groups became 'luteo' compounds whether or not they were yellow in colour (see table 15.1):

TABLE 15.1 *Colour names given by Frémy.*

Name	Colour	Example
Flavo	Brown	*cis*-$[Co(NH_3)_4(NO_2)_2]^+$
Croceo	Yellow	*trans*-$[Co(NH_3)_4(NO_2)_2]^+$
Luteo	Yellow	$[Co(NH_3)_6]_3^+$
Praseo	Green	*trans*-$[Co(NH_3)_4H_2O]^+$
Roseo	Rose-red	$[Co(NH_3)_5H_2O]^{3+}$
Purpureo	Purple	$[Co(NH_3)_5Cl]^{2+}$
Violeo	Violet	*cis*-$[Co(NH_3)_4Cl_2]^+$

From E. Frémy, *Annales de Chimie Physique*, **35** (1852): 22.

$$Co(NH_3)_6X_3 \qquad Co(NH_3)_5X_3$$
luteo   purpureo

$$Co(NH_3)_4X_3 \qquad Co(NH_3)_3X_3$$
praseo   hexamino

The 'hexamine' notation sprung from the fact that until 1890 cobalt chloride was assumed to be Co_2Cl_6, cobalt hexachloride.

Werner next pointed out (like Laurent in his nucleus theory) that, over a range of metals such as cobalt, nickel, copper, rhenium and platinum, their ammonium salts, $M(NH_3)_6X_3$, formed three subclasses according to whether the metal was tetra-, tri- or divalent,

$$M^{IV}(NH_3)_6X_4 \qquad M^{III}(NH_3)_6X_3 \qquad M^{II}(NH_3)_6X_2$$

each of which could lose ammonia to form a new 'purpureo' salt, e.g.

$$Cr(NH_3)_6Cl_3 \rightarrow NH_3 + Cr(NH_3)_5Cl_3$$

However, whenever this reaction was carried out, Werner pointed out, one of the acid residues ceased to be ionic, as was shown by the different reactions with potassium hexachloroplatinate of the parent and daughter salts. Whereas the mother compound precipitated a platinum–cobalt complex salt, the penta-ammonium salt did not:

$$2Co(NH_3)_6Cl_3 + 3K_2PtCl_6 = 6KCl + [Co(NH_3)_6]_2(PtCl_6)_3$$
$$Co(NH_3)_5Cl_3 + K_2PtCl_6 = 2KCl + Co(NH_3)_5.Cl.PtCl_6$$

It was this 'contradictory' observation that led Werner to overthrow 'contemporary views of the constitution of salts' and to represent the cobalt salts ionically with ammonia bound directly to the metal,

rather than by Blomstrand's and Jørgensen's

If Werner was right, a further ionic praseo salt was possible,

$$\begin{pmatrix} & (NH_3)_4 & \\ Co & & \\ & X_2 & \end{pmatrix} X$$

however, in 1893, this was hardly evidence against Jørgensen's chain formula

$$M \underset{\diagdown}{\overset{\diagup X}{\longrightarrow}} X$$
$$NH_3-NH_3-NH_3-NH_3-X$$

since the final X in his chain was also ionic. A stronger case against Jørgensen was that removal of one more ammonia produced a non-ionic compound that had no basic properties at all. Whereas Werner's formulation

$$\left(M \begin{array}{c} (NH_3)_3 \\ \\ X_3 \end{array} \right)$$

made this obvious, Jørgensen's

$$Co \underset{\diagdown}{\overset{\diagup X}{\longrightarrow}} X$$
$$NH_3-NH_3-NH_3-X$$

still implied ionic behaviour. But no precipitation with K_2PtCl_6 occurred. Moreover, Jørgensen's formula suggested that it ought to be possible to remove further ammonia. When this was attempted, however, instead of

$$\left(M \begin{array}{c} (NH_3)_2 \\ \\ X_3 \end{array} \right)$$

which simply did not exist, chemists always found the ammonia replaced by another acid radical to form a new complex of the form

$$\left(\text{M} \quad \genfrac{}{}{0pt}{}{(NH_3)_2}{X_4} \right)$$

These 'tetraminemetal salts', renamed 'diammine compounds' by Werner, were already well known, having been prepared by Otto Erdmann (1804–69) at the University of Leipzig in the 1840s. The complete argument gave Werner a series of valency transitions from a positive metal ammine to a negative ammine ion:

$$[Co(NH_3)_6]^{III}(NO_2)_3 = NH_3 + \begin{bmatrix} CO(NH_3)_5 \\ NO_2 \end{bmatrix}^{II}(NO_2)_2$$
$$\text{xantho}$$

$$\begin{bmatrix} Co(NH_3)_5 \\ NO_2 \end{bmatrix}^{II}(NO_2)_2 = NH_3 + \begin{bmatrix} Co(NH_3)_4 \\ (NO_2)_2 \end{bmatrix}^{I}NO_2$$
$$\text{croceo}$$

$$\begin{bmatrix} Co(NH_3)_4 \\ (NO_2)_2 \end{bmatrix}^{I}NO_2 = NH_3 + \begin{bmatrix} Co(NH_3)^3 \\ (NO_2)_3 \end{bmatrix}^{0}$$
$$\text{hexammine cobalt}$$

$$\begin{bmatrix} Co(NH_3)_3 \\ (NO_2)_3 \end{bmatrix}^{0} + NO_2^- = \begin{bmatrix} Co(NH_3)_2 \\ (NO_2)_4 \end{bmatrix}^{-1} + NH_3$$
$$\text{tetramminecobalt}$$

$$\left[\begin{array}{c} Co(NH_3)_2 \\ (NO_2)_4 \end{array}\right]^{-I} +K \quad = \quad \left[\begin{array}{c} Co(NH_3)_2 \\ (NO_2)_4 \end{array}\right]K$$

potassium diamminecobalt nitrate

We need not follow Werner further in his examination of how platinum ammine complexes, or the hydrates of both cobalt and platinum, could be brought to order in a similar fashion. Three general comments are, however, in order. .

First Werner's co-ordination of water directly to the metal not only solved the problem of water of crystallization, but formed a bridge between the hydrate theories of Mendeleev and others and the new dissociation theory of Arrhenius. Conductivity and dissociation were dependent on the nature of solvents because only those solvents which can combine with metal salts to form co-ordination radicals are able to allow electrolytic conduction. The dissociation of copper sulphate was *not*

$$CuSO_4 \rightarrow Cu^{2+} + SO_4^{2-}$$

but

$$[Cu(H_2O)_6]SO_4 \rightarrow Cu(H_2O)_6^{2+} + SO_4^{2-}$$

In fact, later studies have shown that not all water of crystallization necessarily forms part of a hydrated cation.

Secondly, stimulated by van't Hoff's vision of molecules in space, Werner asked how such radical complexes as MR_6 and MR_4 were to be represented spatially and with what consequences for their chemical properties? Werner's new viewpoint would force inorganic chemists to think stereochemically. There could be little argument that the simplest way to arrange six groups around a metal in MR_6 was octahedrally. The consequence of this structure would be the existence of two enantiomorphs according to whether the second acid radical was in the plane or at the apex:

Ironically, Jørgensen's 'beautiful experimental work', as Werner acknowledged it, had already shown that the praseo salts of cobalt formed two series of ethylenediamine (en) salts, green (praseo) and violet (violeo), which were identical in composition. Werner took these to be examples of geometrical isomerism even though Jørgensen had explained them by conventional structure theory by supposing that the valencies of cobalt in its three bonds were non-equivalent, or that en itself could assume alternative structures. A similar collision of viewpoints occurred over Werner's claim that the MX_4 radical would be square planar, so that the platinum compound $Pt(NH_3)_2Cl_2$ would then have two geometric isomers (it could not be tetrahedral since that would have produced optical activity, which was not observed):

$$
\begin{array}{ccc}
NH_3 & & NH_3 \\
| & & | \\
Cl - Pt - Cl & & NH_3 - Pt - Cl \\
| & & | \\
NH_3 & & Cl \\
\textit{trans} & & \textit{cis}
\end{array}
$$

Such 'platinosemidiammine' complexes had been prepared by both Blomstrand and Arrhenius' teacher, Per Cleve, who both portrayed them, chain fashion, as

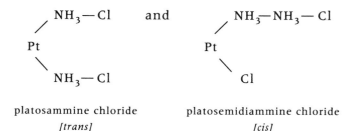

platosammine chloride   platosemidiammine chloride
       [trans]   *[cis]*

But Werner's ionic arguments cast doubt upon such formulations.

The third point about Werner's modestly titled 'contribution' to the constitution of inorganic compounds was the revolution in valency theory he was demanding. How could a divalent copper atom bond six ammonia radicals to itself? In one sense Werner's agnostic answer was that he had no idea and that he was proceeding solely experimentally and pragmatically from the fact that copper and many other metals did behave in this manner. On the other hand, because his entire interpretation stood 'in opposition to our present views on the constitution of the compounds as they have evolved from a study of carbon compounds',[1] he felt bound to speculate about the nature of valency. His views were undoubtedly derived from the theory of residual affinity that Armstrong had developed between 1885 and 1886. According to this[2]:

> Whatever be the nature of chemical affinity, it is difficult to avoid the conclusion that the 'charge' of a negative radical especially is rarely if ever given up at once: that its affinity is at once exhausted. It would also appear that the amount of residual charge – of surplus affinity – possessed by a radical after combination with others depends both on its own nature and that of the radical or radicals with which it becomes associated.

In Werner's model, although the valency force was equally distributed in space, it could be imagined to work within an inner and outer sphere of influence. Radicals bound directly to a metal formed a complex radical within the metal's inner valency shell, which he marked off with square brackets. In 1902 he called the valency that the complex exerted the *Hauptvalenz* or primary valency; its value was equal 'to the [algebraic] difference of the valency of the metal atom and the valency of the monovalent groups of the first sphere completely independent of the molecules present in the first sphere such as H_2O, NH_3, and so on'.

$$Co^{III} \ (NH_3)_6 \qquad 3 \ - \ 0 \ = 3 \qquad Co \ (NH_3)_6 X_3$$

$$\begin{pmatrix} Co^{III} \ (NH_3)_3 \\ \\ (NO_2)_3 \end{pmatrix} \qquad 3 \ - \ 3 = 0 \qquad \begin{pmatrix} (NH_3)_3 \\ \\ Co \\ \\ (NO_2)_3 \end{pmatrix}^0$$

$$\begin{pmatrix} Co^{III} \ (NH_3)_2 \\ \\ (NO_2)_4 \end{pmatrix} \qquad 4 \ - \ 3 = 1 \qquad \begin{pmatrix} (NH_3)_2 \\ \\ Co \\ \\ (NO_2)_4 \end{pmatrix} K$$

$$Fe^{II}Cy_6 \qquad 6 \ - \ 2 = 4 \qquad (FeCy_6)^{II}K_2$$

$$Pt^{IV}Cl_6 \qquad 6 \ - \ 4 = 2 \qquad (PtCl_6)^{II}K_2$$

As recorded in Kauffman[3]:

> The manner of functioning of molecules like NH_3, H_2O and so on is specifically a quite peculiar one; it can

perhaps be defined as follows: These molecules have
the property of shifting the places of functioning of the
force of affinity of the metal from the first sphere, in
which it generally achieves activity, to a sphere further
removed from the metal atom.

It was, he suggested, as if the metal were a positive sphere
surrounded by a neutral shell of water or ammonia whose
inner surface was rendered negative and, consequently,
its outer surface positive. As we have seen, this imagery,
though not the details, was to influence G. N. Lewis'
first thoughts on chemical bonding in 1902, as well
as stimulating Flürscheim's earliest views on alternating
affinity in carbon chains. At first Werner used dotted lines
for the secondary (*Nebenvalenz*) valency bonds co-ordinating
groups with the metal atom, but he soon abandoned it for
typographical conformity.

Werner called the number of groups combining with
a metal to form a complex radical the 'co-ordination
number' and he noted that, except in the case of carbon,
which had hitherto prevented the differentiation, this
value differed from the valency, which only 'indicates
the maximum number of monovalent atoms which can
be bound directly to the atom in question'. (For example,
cobalt(III) has a valency of three, but may have a co-
ordination number of six.) The term 'ligand' was first
coined to describe the atoms or groups co-ordinated to
a metal by Alfred Stock (1876–1946) in 1916 when
he suggested an improved systematic nomenclature for
inorganic compounds. However, the term did not come
into general use until the 1950s. It was Werner who
abolished the confused nomenclature of complexes based
on the colours of salts and who employed names based on
the ligands surrounding the metal.

Although German chemists were quite receptive towards
Werner's views, British chemists were unresponsive or
hostile. An unhelpful abstract in the *Journal of the Chemical*

Society — 'a theoretical paper devoted to a discussion of the so-called ammonia-metallic compounds' — was hardly conducive to the perusal of Werner's work, while a very large number of misprints in the 1893 paper must have been confusing. Of course, the translation of Werner's *New Views* in 1911 finally ensured the wider dissemination of the theory, though the mint condition of Edgar Fahs Smith's Philadelphia copy suggests that he did not use it for lectures. Before then, however, chemists had become aware of the strengths of Werner's position because of the ingenuity with which he defended them against the equally ingenious criticism of Jørgensen. If we follow Karl Popper's view that the hallmark of a scientific, as opposed to a non-scientific, doctrine is its falsifiability, then Werner's theory is a bold example of fallibilism. One example, which links Werner's work with the new approach of the new physical chemistry, must suffice.

As we saw in chapter 10, Hittorf's and Kohlrausch's investigations of the independent migrations of ions in electrolysis had shown that the equivalent (molecular) conductivity of an electrolyte equalled the sum of the conductivities of the anion and cation. Their experimental techniques had shown the way to determine the number of ions in an electrolyte, which had proved significant in Arrhenius' interpretation of the van't Hoff factor, i. Since Werner's interpretation of complex ions as forming a substituted series could be falsified on the grounds of ionization behaviour, Werner was keen to show that their electrolytic properties followed his interpretation, while at the same time falsifying that of Jørgensen. Together with another former student of Hantzsch, the Italian Arturo Miolati (1869–1950), Werner showed how the molecular conductivities of co-ordination compounds decreased to zero as successive molecules of ammonia were replaced in $[Co(NH_3)_6](NO_2)_3$ to $[Co(NH_3)_3](NO_2)_3$ and then, beautifully, arose again as the cation became the anion in $K[Co(NH_3)_2(NO_2)_4]$ (see figure 15.1). He wrote[4]:

FIGURE 15.1   Molecular conductances of cobalt(III) series.

According to this thoroughly good agreement between the results obtained and the ones theoretically expected, we can consider as well founded the constitutional theory of the more complex inorganic compounds (hydrates, metal–ammonia salts, and double salts) which is derived from the hypothesis of the coordination number.

Ironically, although Werner and Miolati's experiments seem so convincing today, Jørgensen initially welcomed them as confirming his own views. Indeed, his chain formulae, as we have seen, could be adjusted to allow a variable number of ions, except for the case of triamminecobalt nitrate, which he claimed unable to prepare. According to Jørgensen, the specimen Werner was using was a different compound altogether. Werner's answer to this was to prepare dichlorocobalt chloride, $Co(NH_3)_3.(H_2O)Cl_3$. On the supposition that this was

$$\begin{pmatrix} (NH_3)_3 \\ Co \quad H_2O \\ Cl_2 \end{pmatrix} Cl$$

he predicted that it would have only one unit of conductivity, whereas Jørgensen's structure

$$Co \diagup Cl$$
$$Co \text{---} Cl$$
$$\diagdown NH_3\text{--}NH_3\text{--}NH_3\text{--}H_2O\text{--}Cl$$

would allow three ions. Although the measurements had to be made at low temperatures, Werner's prediction proved correct.

Not unexpectedly, Jørgensen was not convinced, since he could again reshuffle his formulae to argue that two of the chlorines were more strongly held when associated with an ammonia chain. In the end, what did convince Jørgensen were Werner's stereochemical arguments. In 1889 Jørgensen had begun to use a bidentate ligand, ethylenediamine (en), $C_2H_4(NH_2)_4$. He explained the isomerism of cobalt–en complexes as due, not to stereoisomerism, but to two possible linkages of the en molecule:

He challenged Werner in 1895 to produce two geometric enantiomorphs of cobalt tetrammine. As we have seen, Werner had already supposed that these would have an octahedral structure. The praseo salts of $[Co(NH_4)_4Cl_2]X$ were already known, but the unstable isomeric violeo salts proved very difficult to isolate. It was not until November 1907 that Werner was successful. Before reporting the matter in *Berichte*, he sent samples to Jørgensen in Denmark:

> I am taking the liberty of sending you . . . a sample of the long-sought ammonia-violeo series $[Cl_2Co(NH_3)_4]Cl$ and hope that you will take pleasure in it.

Jørgensen, a perfect Danish gentleman, did so and finally admitted that Werner's co-ordination theory, with its superior stereochemical perspective, was a better explanation of complexes than the chain theory he and Blomstrand had espoused for so long.

Werner's triumph was completed in 1911 when he found a way of resolving *cis* stereoisomers into their theoretical enantiomorphs, including ones containing ethylenediamine:

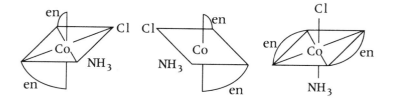

(Note that two *cis* forms are themselves optically active.)

His social triumph was completed in 1913 when he was awarded a Nobel prize. The few critics who had objected that carbon could in some way be responsible for the isomerism of his enantiomorphs because he had used asymmetric carbon systems to resolve the cobalt and platinum stereoisomers were quietened in 1914. In his final triumph before his career was cut by five years of mentally debilitating illness, he resolved the non-carbon system tris[tetrammine-μ-dihydroxo-cobalt(III)cobalt(III)],

$$\left[Co \left(\begin{array}{c} OH \\ \\ OH \end{array} \quad Co \quad (NH_3)_4 \right)_3 \right] Br_6$$

thus showing once and for all that there is 'no difference between carbon compounds and purely inorganic ones'.

It is a curious fact that, despite Werner's success in establishing a large international research school of co-ordination chemistry at the University of Zürich, few of his pupils and associates maintained their interest in the field or made their own independent reputations in it. This is partly explained by the already mentioned feeling that Werner had answered almost everything that was worth investigating in co-ordination chemistry. Kauffman, however, has drawn attention to the fact that, with the kindest of motives, Werner made a habit of always getting an assistant to investigate a research problem in miniature to test its feasibility before handing it to a doctoral candidate. While this must have given a tyro confidence, it meant that Werner's doctorate theses were pretty routine and unimaginative. By lacking an opportunity to make mistakes and to think for themselves, very few of Werner's pupils made significant contributions to chemistry. Only one, Paul Karrer (1889–1971), who turned to vitamin synthesis, won a Nobel prize.

SIDGWICK'S ELECTRONIC INTERPRETATION OF CO-ORDINATION CHEMISTRY

In 1927 Nevil Vincent Sidgwick (1873–1952), a nephew of Benjamin Brodie, who was Reader in Chemistry at the

University of Oxford, published an influential reworking of Werner's theory in terms of Bohr's theory of spectra and atomic constitution and Lewis' views on valency and chemical combination. Sidgwick had received a solely classical education at Rugby School and did not begin science seriously until he was sixteen. In 1895, after obtaining first class honours in Natural Sciences at Oxford, he decided to resume the classics, and in 1897 obtained another first class degree. This double degree in the arts and sciences was important to Sidgwick's success at Oxford, where as late as 1900 men of science were still regarded as an inferior breed of gentlemen. In fact, despite his early intellectual promise, his research career as a chemist was disappointing. Postgraduate studies at Leipzig and Tübingen identified him as a physical organic chemist, but by the time he was forty and a Fellow of Lincoln College, Oxford (where he spent his entire career), Sidgwick had published scarcely a dozen papers and none of any significance.

Like J. B. Cohen earlier, Sidgwick was to find his true métier collecting and systematizing information as a writer. In 1910 he published a useful book on *The Organic Chemistry of Nitrogen*, which applied physical chemical ideas to problems of structure, reaction and stereochemistry. A long meeting with Ernest Rutherford while voyaging to Australia in 1914 for an overseas meeting of the British Association for the Advancement of Science brought about his interest in atomic structure, and from then on he began eagerly to follow the work of Bohr, Lewis and Langmuir. He was present at Lowry's important Cambridge Faraday Society discussion in 1923, from which emerged *The Electronic Theory of Valency* in 1927. As his devoted pupil and friend, Leslie Sutton, has remarked of this text[5]:

> It is curious to realise that the physical basis on which he built was already out of date, for the system of quantum numbers which he used had been abandoned by spectroscopists, and by 1927

quantum mechanics had been developed. For the relatively simple needs of the time, this did not much matter. His grasp of theory was enough to be useful, and he saw how it could be applied to chemical problems . . . . This was much more than a textbook. The new correlations in it gave a fresh unity to the whole of chemistry: the division between inorganic and organic chemistry was finally broken down. By its comprehensiveness it convinced; by its lucidity it delighted. It became a classic.

Like Pauling's *Nature of the Chemical Bond*, which ultimately replaced it, Sidgwick's *Electronic Theory* helped to reawaken the dormant interest in inorganic chemistry in English-speaking countries. Sidgwick recognized three different linkages between elements: the polar or ionizable bonds between oppositely charged ions; the non-polar, covalent, shared electron pair of Lewis and Langmuir; and the co-ordinate linkages of Werner, which he also recognized as covalent. Insofar as the shared pair was drawn from one and the same atom, Sidgwick preferred the term 'covalent link' for the case of ligands donating their shared pairs to a metal acceptor atom. This abolished the need for Werner's secondary valency. A co-ordination number was then simply the number of shared pairs donated. Sidgwick also proved a useful conduit for quantum-mechanical interpretations and the notions of Linus Pauling, with whom he became friendly when giving the eleventh in the important series of George Fisher Baker Lectures at Cornell in 1931. Published as *The Covalent Link in Chemistry* (1932), the work was influential in Australia, as we shall see. Sidgwick's authoritative support for the idea of resonance (which he may not have fully understood), as well as Werner's co-ordination theory, ensured that British, American and Australian chemists were fully alive to ways of explaining the stability of inorganic molecules. For example, on the assumption that, electronically, the maximum covalency possible in the second period of the periodic table (Li, Be, B, C, N, O, F) is four, and of the third period (Na, Mg, Al, Si, P, S, Cl) is six, nitric and sulphuric acids could be formulated as

i   ii

where an arrow indicated a co-ordinate link. But sulphur could also be formulated with a valency of six using double bonds

iii

which, though analogous to I, suggested that nitrogen and sulphur bonds were probably all alike. Pauling's suggestion, which Sidgwick readily accepted and publicized, was that nitric and sulphuric acids, like most co-ordination compounds, were resonance hybrids. In this way Sidgwick reconciled Werner's co-ordination theory with traditional structural theory. As Werner himself had noted, carbon was unique in possessing a valency identical with its maximum co-ordination number, and this had tended to make chemists believe organic and inorganic chemistry were built on different structural principles. Sidgwick's view was that[6]:

The conflict could only be temporary: it must ultimately be resolved by the discovery of a more complete theory of valency, of which the structural theory and the coordination theory would prove to be partial aspects. The solution was provided by the electronic theory, with the recognition of the third type of linkage, a covalency in which both electrons are supplied by the same atom.

Sidgwick's recognition that the co-ordinate link was more easily broken than Lewis' ordinary covalency, because little energy was required to return loaned electrons to their ordinarily stable ligands, led him to suggest that the linkage was fundamentally electrostatic in character. This argument was a great incentive to chemical physicists such as John van Vleck (1899–1980). Pfeiffer's application of co-ordination theory to crystallography after he left Werner's service in 1916, together with the vindication of co-ordination by X-ray crystallography in the 1920s, suggested to the mathematically minded physicist that there were close analogies between mononuclear co-ordination compounds and the infinite electrostatic arrays of a crystal lattice. Walther Kossel, Kasimir Fajans and others pursued non-quantum-mechanical electrostatic models of co-ordination in the 1920s. Although these generated linear, tetrahedral and octahedral shapes (since these shapes minimized the electrostatic repulsions of ligands from one another), they failed to produce the square planar shape characteristic of Werner's platinum compounds with co-ordination number four.

A more mathematically sophisticated analysis by Hans Bethe (1906–?), R. Schlipp, W. C. Penney (*b.* 1909) and van Vleck in the 1930s in terms of the d orbitals and paramagnetic susceptibility of transition metals solved this problem. In the gaseous metal ion it was supposed that the d orbitals were equal in energy; but in the presence of ligands, those orbitals lying in the direction of the incoming ligands were raised in energy over those lying away. Unlike previous electrostatic models, the charge distribution was no longer symmetrical around the central metal atom. The gain in bonding energy achieved by filling d orbitals preferentially was termed the 'crystal-field stabilization energy' because the first use of the analysis had been in crystalline solids. As we have seen, in the hands of Pauling and Slater, resonance methods also led to deductions about directional bonding. A square planar nickel complex, for example, was produced by the hybridization of sp²d orbitals. Following the gain in power of molecular orbital treatments of organic compounds in the 1950s, it became possible to amalgamate the crystal and molecular orbital theories. The resulting 'ligand-field theory' developed by Leslie Orgel (*b*. 1927) at Oxford made a dramatic contribution to the renaissance of inorganic chemistry.

One of the most significant aspects of Sidgwick's synthesis was a chapter on atomic and molecular magnetism based upon his reading of *Magnetism and Atomic Structure* by the physicist, E. C. Stoner. Although Faraday had shown in 1845 that all chemical substances are either paramagnetic (like iron), setting themselves parallel to a magnetic field, or diamagnetic, setting themselves transversely to a field, such properties had not been exploited by physical chemists. At the start of the twentieth century, Pierre Curie had shown that, whereas diamagnetic susceptibility was independent of the absolute temperature, paramagnetism was inversely proportional and that these relations were affected by chemical combination. The Curies' colleague, Paul Langevin, had then developed a mathematical model of magnetism in terms of revolving electrons, which was easily modified by quantum mechanics in the 1920s. By the time Sidgwick was writing in 1927, it was clear that the determination of magnetic moments could be used as 'a new and independent means of attack on the problem of molecular structure'. Pauling was to agree, and in *The Nature of the Chemical Bond* he discussed the significance of paramagnetism as an indicator of the presence of unpaired electrons. Yet, although Sidgwick predicted that[7]:

> [there] is scarcely any branch of the inquiry which seems more likely than the magnetic to lead to important developments during the next few years . . .

generally speaking, it was not until the 1940s that the techniques were exploited by inorganic chemists. Then it was to be a particular contribution of the Australian school of co-ordination chemists.

AUSTRALIAN CHEMISTRY

Although the European settlement of Australia coincided with the 'chemical revolution' in 1788, it was not until 1888, when the Australian Association for the Advancement of Science (AAAS) was founded, that the small university-based community of Australian chemists began to organize on European lines. Until then, colonial chemistry was culture-dependent. It mainly served utilitarian ends: the training of doctors and pharmacists and miners. Even in the twentieth century, as we have seen from the Robinsons' brief sojourn in Sydney in 1912, academic chemistry was mainly concerned with the identification and extraction of natural products from the island's strange flora. Eucalyptus oil, for example, became a staple pharmaceutical preparation and made the fortune of the Melbourne pharmacist, Joseph Bosisto (1824–98).

Although little chemical knowledge was required, the discovery of alluvial gold in 1850 stimulated the teaching of chemistry as well as geology and mining technology. The first chemical instructors at the newly founded universities of Sydney (1851) and Melbourne (1853) were imported from Britain and were teachers, not researchers. On the industrial front, as in Germany, Britain and America, it was the pharmacists who were the entrepreneurs and innovators. In 1865, for example, the three Elliott brothers, all druggists, began a sulphuric acid plant and super-phosphate production at a factory outside Sydney. A son, James Elliott (1858–1928), was educated in Berlin with Hofmann before returning to the family business, and this European training set a model for the second generation of Australian industrial chemists. Similar industrial enterprises began in Melbourne and Adelaide (which had strong German connections).

A healthy mechanics' institute movement imported from Britain also encouraged the creation of Technical Colleges. The first of these, the Ballarat School of Mines and Industries, was established in 1870, to be followed by Sydney Technical College in 1878 and the Working Men's College (later Royal Melbourne Institute of Technology) at Melbourne in 1887. Each of these developed large and strong departments of applied chemistry. The training was good, and if anything better than could be obtained in Britain – witness the fact that, in 1915, some seventy-five Australian analytical chemists were sent to Britain to work in specially commissioned munitions factories as part of the Allied war efforts.

The practical emphasis of Australian chemistry was noted resignedly by one speaker at the AAAS in 1892[8]:

> The record of the year with regard to original research work, were it given in its entirety, would read very much like Falstaff's hotel bill, showing but a halfpennyworth of research to an intolerable deal of drudgery. This must be the case with most of us in a new society, who if not engaged in teaching or organisation are compelled to spend our time in assaying minerals or else in the pursuit of the agricultural, sanitary or criminal investigations.

The small amount of pure research at Sydney and Melbourne, where science degrees were established in the 1880s, tended inevitably to be in organic chemistry. Archibald Liversidge (1846–1927), a Londoner who had studied with

Hofmann at the Royal College of Chemistry before taking the Natural Science Tripos at Cambridge, designed and built new chemical laboratories at Sydney before he returned to a career in England in 1907. At Melbourne, his contemporary, David Orme Masson (1858–1937), an Edinburgh chemist appointed in 1886, started work on Arrhenius' electrolytic theory, while his physics colleague, William Sutherland (1859–1911), worked more obscurely on interesting theories of intermolecular forces. Frustrated by his lack of impact, Sutherland abandoned science for journalism; but Masson, a born organizer, formed the Australian Chemical Institute on the model of the British institute in 1918. Starting with a membership of only 372, there were some 800 members by 1930. Because of the huge distances involved in travelling, the Institute only really functioned in its branches and divisions within individual states. By the 1930s, its annual meetings had replaced those of AAAS as the meeting ground for professional chemists.

There were few opportunities for postgraduate research in Australia. Instead, using the facilities of Rhodes Scholarships and 1851 Exhibitions, Australian graduates routinely travelled to Britain for their doctorates. Although the 1851 Exhibitions had been intended to encourage industrial training, most Australians awarded the grant went into academic positions. Even after the introduction of the Ph.D. in Australia (1946) and New Zealand (1948), spurred by free travel by boat and the continuing availability of these scholarships, Europe continued to be a magnet. It must not be thought from this that Australian chemistry remained backward. Apart from the obvious difficulty that chemical journals could arrive six months after having been read by European and American colleagues (this is still a problem, despite airmail), their discussions showed a lively contemporaneity. In 1924, for example, within a year of Lowry's Faraday Discussion, the Adelaide AAAS meeting discussed valency and theories of atomic and molecular structure. However, senior posts, especially at Sydney, went to British chemists – to Liversidge,

Robinson, John Read and James Kenner. Only in 1928 was a native-born Australian, John Earl, awarded a Chair at Sydney. Thirty years later, Australians were holding Chairs overseas, and in 1975 the first Australian chemist, John Cornforth (*b.* 1917), won the Nobel prize for his work on the stereochemistry of enzyme-catalysed reactions.

AUSTRALIAN AND JAPANESE CHEMISTRY

Despite the obvious cultural differences between Australia and Japan – one a sparsely populated European colony, the other a crowded independent nation opting for westernization – the disciplines of physics and chemistry were institutionalized in both countries in the 1870s. When the modernization of Japan began during the Meiji era, the Japanese, like the Australians, saw chemistry in a purely utilitarian light. Even so, chemistry did not have quite the same status and priority as engineering and medicine, so that between 1888 (when doctoral degrees were first awarded) and 1920, only 177 chemical doctorates were awarded compared to 656 in medicine and 366 in engineering. Of these 177 degrees, the majority were in chemical engineering, pharmacy and agricultural chemistry; only twenty-five (14%) were in basic chemistry. Of course, the Japanese faced unusual language difficulties. Once 'Japanization' had occurred and European (mainly British) chemists had been dismissed, Japanese chemistry lecturers taught in whatever European language, French, English or German, their postgraduate lecture notes were in. The absence of a Japanese chemical vocabulary made lecturing in Japanese impracticable until the publication of the *Compilation of Chemical Terms* in 1891. A Tokyo (from 1921, Japan) Chemical Society (Kagaku Kai) was founded by foreign teachers as early as 1878, and its journal, *Kagakukai-shi*, founded in 1880, became the principal organ for encouraging European-style research in pure chemistry.

Not until 1972 did the Japanese start an English-language journal, *Chemical Letters.*

The political and cultural differences between Australia and Japan were such that, although both countries sent graduates to Europe for further training, Japanese chemists who showed academic promise often had this promise stopped by bureaucracy; alternatively, they became bemused by a tacit code that a university teacher's task was solely to introduce up-to-date knowledge and practice from America or Europe and not to encourage native innovation. A cultural hierarchical fear of challenging an older peer or teacher also inhibited criticism and novelty and discouraged co-operative research.

Shibata Yūji, who found work on stereochemistry with Hantzsch and Werner uncongenial, was excited by research on rare-earth chemistry when studying with Georges Urbain (1872–1938) in Paris. However, he had no opportunity to pursue such interests after his return to Japan. Nagai Nagayoshi (1845–1921) was able to spend fourteen years studying chemistry in Berlin with Hofmann, whose personal assistant he became. He assumed Germanic, liberal and cosmopolitan mannerisms, converted to Catholicism and added 'Wilhelm' to his name in Hofmann's honour. However, when he returned to a Chair of Pharmacological Chemistry in Tokyo in 1884, he immediately came into conflict with Sakurai Joji. The latter had studied with Alexander Williamson in London, where he had published a series of very competent papers on organo-mercury compounds and on the molecular weights of solutions. Socially, he seems to have adopted the English disease of class distinction. Called back to the Chair of Theoretical Chemistry in Tokyo in 1881, he published little further work and soon became absorbed in university administration. Sakurai, who clearly saw himself as the intellectual leader of Japanese chemistry, had Nagayoshi dismissed from the university on the grounds that pharmacological chemistry was not a worthy subject in an academic university!

Subsequently, Nagayoshi worked for the Ministry of Education until he obtained his Chair back in 1893.

Others, like Haga Tamemasa, a pupil of Edward Divers (1837–1912), an English chemist who taught in Japan between 1873 and 1899, proved incompetent teachers. But if Japan lacked a chemical leader of the quality of Masson at Melbourne, it had a model in Ikeda Kibunae (1864–1936) for the commercial, financial and industrial possibilities of chemistry. Following training in Berlin, where he learned physical chemistry, Ikeda joined Sakurai's department in 1896. Always intrigued by the chemistry of taste, in 1908 he discovered and patented a method for making monosodium glutamate from hydrolysed kelp protein. The production of this flavour-enhancing agent, although more associated in the European mind with Chinese restaurants, became Japan's first major chemical industry and was an early sign of its future economic miracle.

Like Britain, Australia and America, Japan found itself starved of industrial chemicals, pharmaceuticals and scientific instruments during the First World War. This led to a demand for trained engineers and managers and skilled factory workers, and a consequent expansion of the university system during the 1920s. One beneficiary was Kenichi Fukui (*b*. 1918), who trained as a chemical engineer at the University of Kyoto, where he spent his entire career. An interest in the chemistry of fuels during the Second World War narrowed into work on the quantum mechanics of unsaturated hydrocarbons. The theoretical papers of Coulson and Longuet-Higgins on molecular orbitals inspired Fukui to develop what he called 'the frontier orbital theory of reactions' in 1950. In 1981, together with Roald Hoffmann (*b*. 1937), he became the first Japanese chemist to be awarded the Nobel prize – for his demonstration that the progress of reactions depends upon the geometry and relative energies of the highest recipient molecular orbital of one reactant and the lowest molecular orbital of the other. This insight has, nevertheless, tended to be completely overshadowed by the so-called 'Woodward–Hoffmann rules' generated by Woodward and Hoffmann during the synthesis of vitamin B12 in the 1960s (see chapter 16).

CO-ORDINATION CHEMISTRY IN AUSTRALIA

D. O. Masson, together with B. D. Steele, had investigated the blue copper tartrate complex of Fehling's solution in 1899. They showed their familiarity with Werner's work by demonstrating electrolytically that the anion complex was $[Cu_4C_{12}H_9O_{19}]^{3-}$. However, this early adventure in co-ordination chemistry was not extended until 1919, when Eustace Turner (1893–1966) was appointed to the University of Sydney. Turner's war work had involved him joining Pope's Chemical Warfare Committee at Cambridge, where they had investigated the nature of the complex arsenic compounds, like phenylarsinous dichloride, that the German army was using in trench warfare. When Turner went to Sydney he began serious work on arsines with an Australian colleague, George Burrows (1888–1960). Their first resolution of an arsenic compound in 1921, the phenyl-α-naphthylbenzylmethylarsonium ion, put Australian chemistry firmly on the world map of chemistry. More amusingly, a successful preparation of the arsenic analogue of indole – logically 'arsole' – did not get past the censorious eye of an editor and had to be renamed arsindole!

Turner returned to England in 1921, where he had a distinguished career as an organic chemist at Queen Mary, and Bedford Colleges and a warm friendship with Ingold. Despite only staying in Sydney for two years, he had been the catalyst for Australia's future reputation in co-ordination chemistry. If we simplify matters by staying with the metal–arsine complexes, these were taken up again by Burrows in 1933 and, in amazingly ingenious preparative chemistry, his students acquired the techniques to prepare arsenic complexes of zinc, cadmium, mercury and platinum. It was Burrows' lectures on these compounds in 1936–7 that awakened Nyholm's interest.

Meanwhile, the Tasmanian, David Mellor (1903–80), had joined Burrows at the University of Sydney in 1929. Together with a brilliant student, Frank Dwyer (1910–62), Mellor began to use X-ray crystallography in structural studies of co-ordination compounds and to explore the co-ordination chemistry of palladium. His lectures were firmly based on Sidgwick's book on the *Electronic Theory and the Covalent Bond*. While Dwyer continued his career at Sydney Technical College, Mellor consolidated a physical approach to co-ordination chemistry by studying with Pauling at CalTech in 1939. On his return to Sydney he ensured that Pauling's *Nature of the Chemical Bond* became an undergraduate text – to the benefit of his student David Craig (*b*. 1919), whom he also introduced to magnetic studies. It was Mellor who showed how the magnetic properties of the transition metals could be used to clarify their complicated stereochemistry. This small Sydney school of co-ordination chemistry at its university and technical college was to produce four Fellows of the Royal Society and one Nobel prizewinner.

NYHOLM'S RENAISSANCE

Over a million and a half years ago a black-stained coathanger of sedimentary rocks, bearing loads of lead, silver and zinc minerals, was deposited in the Barrier Ranges of New South Wales. Following their identification by a German immigrant prospector in the 1880s, the mining operations that were established at the township of Broken Hill transformed the Australian economy. Hitherto dependent upon wool and cattle and a little gold, the mines of Broken Hill made Australia into an industrialized nation and one, therefore, that needed chemists.

Anyone born in the acrid atmosphere of Broken Hill

is destined to either love chemistry or to hate it. A sultry, battered mining town, its streets are a veritable periodic table: Chloride Street connects with Sulphide, Oxide and Silica Streets, while 'Cobalt Sulphide' can be used as a map reference for a lover's tryst. In such an environment, and under the stimulus of a first-rate high-school teacher, Ronald Nyholm (1917–71) fell under the spell of chemistry. Like most Australians, Nyholm's ancestry had European roots – his paternal grandfather had been a coppersmith in Finland before emigrating to Adelaide in the 1870s. Nyholm's academic success at school, and his prowess at analytical chemistry, won him a scholarship in 1934 to the University of Sydney, where he studied physical chemistry under Ostwald's pupil, Charles Fawsitt (1878–1960), thermodynamics with Thomas Iredale (1898–1971) and was introduced to co-ordination chemistry by George Burrows.

From Burrows, Nyholm developed a love of arsines; from Mellor a commitment to physical and instrumental studies of co-ordination compounds; and from Dwyer, whom he joined as a lecturer at Sydney Technical College in 1940, his love of, and skill in, preparative chemistry. Together, Dwyer and Nyholm published some ten papers on the complexes of rhodium in the *Journal of the Royal Society of New South Wales*. Given the wartime conditions, it is doubtful whether these papers had much impact on European and American chemists. Even so, with an impressive list of publications to his credit, Nyholm easily obtained an Imperial Chemical Industries (ICI) Fellowship to study with Ingold in London in 1947. This was the same year that Dwyer accomplished the feat of preparing a sexadentate ligand (i.e. one huge molecule co-ordinated octahedrally with a metal) as the highlight of his career. Such feats were to play important roles in post-war syntheses of natural products.

Why should a co-ordination chemist want to study with Ingold? The answer lies in the reputation that Ingold's school had acquired among Australian chemists

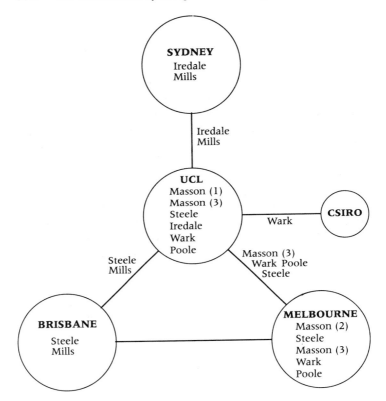

FIGURE 15.2   The origins of inorganic chemistry in Australia.
(From A. Maccoll, *Ambix*, **36** (1989): 87.)

and the pre-war connections that had been made. As
early as 1911, David Masson's son, James Irvine Masson
(1887–1962), had worked at University College, London
(UCL), as Ramsay's personal assistant, his father having
once worked with Ramsay in Bristol. Masson stayed
on as a lecturer until taking a Chemistry Chair at the
University of Durham in 1938. Ramsay had also taught
the Melbourne chemist Bertram Steele (1870–1934), who
was the founder of a chemistry department at the University

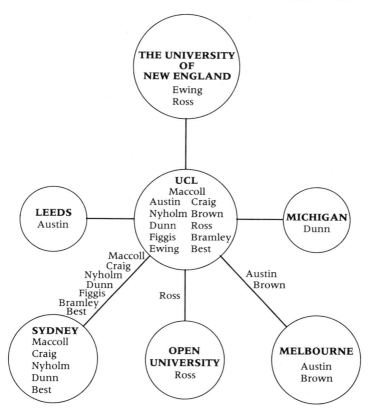

FIGURE 15.3   Inorganic chemistry in the post-war period, in Australia and elsewhere. (From A. Maccoll, *Ambix*, **36** (1989): 89.)

of Queensland (Brisbane) in 1910. During the 1920s, other Melbourne Exhibitioners at UCL included Ian Wark (*b.* 1899) and Nyholm's Sydney teacher, Thomas Iredale. More importantly for the post-war invasion of Australians, H. G. Poole from Melbourne had joined Ingold's staff during the 1930s and collaborated with him on benzene spectroscopy. It was Poole who persuaded the future gas kineticist, Alan Maccoll (*b.* 1914), to use his ICI Fellowship at UCL in 1945. Maccoll, in turn, encouraged his Sydney colleagues, David Craig and Nyholm, to join him in 1946 and 1947 respectively. Ingold personally supervised Maccoll, Craig and Nyholm for their Ph.Ds. Craig, who was to make his name in the field of quantum chemistry, went back to the University of Sydney until 1950, but returned to a Chair at UCL in 1955. Nyholm followed the same pattern. He returned to Sydney Technical College (soon to be the University of New South Wales) in 1951, but rejoined Ingold as Professor of Inorganic Chemistry in 1955, devoting his inaugural lecture to the subject of inorganic chemistry's renaissance. Maccoll never returned to Australia and remained permanently on the UCL staff. By the mid 1950s UCL had also taken on Iredale's student, Tom Dunn (*b.* 1929). He did further work on the spectroscopy of benzene before joining Nyholm's co-ordination chemistry investigations.

Both Ingold and Hughes clearly welcomed this Australian invasion of good-humoured, large-hearted, unstuffy men with their leftish political views. UCL benefited considerably from the new techniques such as gas kinetics, spectrophotometry, co-ordination chemistry and quantum mechanics, which they brought with them or enthusiastically developed while there. In their turn, the Australian and New Zealand universities were to benefit from the skills and ideas of those who returned home. Of course, not all Australians went to UCL. The reputation of Robinson at Oxford for natural products chemistry attracted men like Arthur Birch (*b.* 1915) and J. W. Cornforth, both of whom became outstanding exponents of synthesis.

At UCL for his doctorate in 1950, Nyholm exploited a bidentate ligand, *o*-phenylene-bis-dimethyl arsine (affectionately known as diars), which Joseph Chatt (*b.* 1914) had prepared at Cambridge in 1939 while a postgraduate student of F. G. Mann (1897–1965). Another colleague of Pope, like Turner, Mann had investigated arsenic complexes in the 1920s and 1930s. This ligand proved remarkably useful in stabilizing unusual oxidation states in transition metals, particularly the previously unknown complexes of nickel(III) and nickel(IV). In fact, Nyholm's work showed that the term 'unusual valency state' was of historical significance only. Although single ligands such as NH_3, Cl and H_2O did not provide the right environments for the manifestation of certain oxidation states, with the greater variety of more complicated ligands, such as diars, readily available, 'unusual valency states', identified from measurements of magnetic moments, had become quite normal. For example,

is a Ni(III) diarsine salt prepared by Nyholm in 1950. Its further oxidation gave a Ni(IV) complex, $[NiA_2Cl_2][ClO_4]_2$, where A = diarsine.

Nyholm also had fun using unusual ligands to produce higher co-ordination numbers in transition elements than were usually displayed, for example a seven co-ordinate molybdenum and an eight co-ordinate titanium. The occurrence of such structures immediately raised questions concerning their stereochemistry, a subject Nyholm reviewed with his colleague Ronald Gillespie (*b*. 1924) at length in 1957.

In 1940 Sidgwick and H. M. Powell had argued that the sizes of the valency shells of electrons governed the spatial geometry of the covalencies of multicovalent atoms like the transition elements. According to the 'Sidgwick–Powell rules', the paired electrons in a valency shell were usually arranged in the same way whether or not they were shared (bonded) or unshared (non-bonded). All that mattered was the number of electron pairs: two pairs had to assume a linear form, three a plane trigonal form, four a tetrahedron, and so on. Nyholm and Gillespie refined this electrostatic model by allowing for the fact that electrons of the same spin are repelled more than those with different spins, and that adjacent bonding pairs would repel each other less than bonding pairs repelled lone pairs of electrons. In this way they explained small irregularities in the bonding angles of the regular shapes otherwise predicted (see table 15.2). Their model could not, of course, predict whether a structure would have a particular co-ordination number, since this depended upon the relative sizes and charges of the metal and the incoming ligands, but it brought order to transition-metal chemistry. The model, or variations of it, was widely adopted in teaching, notably in the Nuffield O-level chemistry curriculum in England and Wales with which Nyholm became intimately connected, and the Chemical Bond high school course in America (chapter 11).

Nyholm's powers of rationalization revealed in his lucid undergraduate lectures were most notably displayed in the Tilden Lecture to the (Royal) Chemical Society in 1961. By comparing, contrasting and correlating the properties of transition-metal complexes horizontally and vertically within their periodic table positions, he was able, like Mendeelev, to draw 'attention to gaps and anomalies'. For example, metals like copper, silver and gold, with the electronic configuration $d^{10}s^1$, tend to form metal–metal bonds. Hence complexes in which this configuration occurred might also be expected to display metal–metal bonding, as was indeed the case with Ni, Pd, Pt, Cd, Hg, etc. This then led to the prediction that it ought to be possible

TABLE 15.2 *Stereochemical predictions from ligand-field theory.*

Number of non-bonding d electrons	Unpaired electrons	Four co-ordinate	Six co-ordinate
		⌈ *High spin* ⌉	
0, 10 or 5	0 or 5	Regular tetrahedron	Regular octahedron
9 or 4	1	Square planar	Tetragonal
8 or 4	2	Irregular tetrahedron	Regular octahedron
7 or 2	3	Regular tetrahedron	Slightly distorted octahedron
6 or 1	4	Almost regular tetrahedron	Almost regular octahedron
		⌈ *Low spin* ⌉	
1 or 2	–	–	–
3	1	Almost regular tetrahedron	–
4	0	Regular tetrahedron	Almost regular octahedron
5	1	Distorted tetrahedron	Almost regular octahedron
6	0	Distorted	Regular octahedron
7	1	Square planar	Tetragonal
8	0	Square planar	Tetragonal

From R. Nyholm, *Proceedings of the Chemical Society* (1961): 273.

to synthesize compounds with thallium–thallium, zinc–zinc and cadmium–cadmium bonds. Nyholm's Australian friend, David Craig, has commented[9]:

> Such efforts at systematization and generalization in the broad field of inorganic chemistry, at an unsophisticated theoretical level, were novel and arresting and pointed the way to new areas of attempted synthesis and structural investigation.

In 1950, Chatt, who was working for Imperial Chemical Industries as a research chemist, organized the first biannual conference of co-ordination chemists, which Nyholm attended. It was at this meeting that the term 'ligand' began to be used freely for the first time and that Leslie Orgel revealed the power of the ligand-field theory to decipher the complicated stereochemistry of transition-metal complexes. Chatt invited every British chemist who had published anything on co-ordination chemistry since 1930 to the conference, together with G. Schwarzenbach from Switzerland and K. A. Jensen from Denmark. No Americans were apparently invited. They made barely thirty people! It is a remarkable measure of the strength of co-ordination chemistry in Australia that when Nyholm, Dwyer and Mellor organized a similar conference at Sydney in 1953, over a hundred Australians attended.

Ingold was keen to build up an inorganic research group at UCL to complement his and Hughes' efforts in organic and physical chemistry. He saw, too, that the techniques of reaction mechanisms might be fruitfully applied to inorganic reactions. As early as 1926, Chernyaev had found that, like aromatic compounds, substitutions in co-ordination compounds were never random, but that a negative group such as NO_2 co-ordinated to a metal always 'loosened' the bond of a group situated *trans* to it. In the 1950s, as a form of relaxation, Ingold investigated nucleophilic octahedral substitution in cobalt(III) complexes. By correlating the kinetic characteristics of the substitutions and by studying the involved stereochemistry of the products, he showed the analogues and differences with organic chemistry. Inevitably he used the notation of S_N1 and S_N2.

Although studies of inorganic reaction mechanisms were actively pursued in America by Fred Basolo and Ralph Pearson, they were found to be far more difficult to determine, since, unlike carbon compounds, reactions occurred at more than one centre and were usually much more rapid. Because multisecond rates were so common, kinetic studies had to await the development of the flash photolysis techniques of Norrish and Porter, and the relaxation spectroscopy devised by the German, Manfred Eigen (*b*. 1927) in 1960. It was then found that inorganic substitutions did not exactly follow pure S_N1 or S_N2 kinetics. Subsequently, in 1965, the Americans, Cooper Langford (*b*. 1934) and Harry Gray (*b*. 1935), introduced in their book, *Ligand Substitution Processes*, a classificatory scheme based upon an operational model of the transition state. This had proved necessary because, although many reactions were stoichiometrically bimolecular, the actual mechanism was unimolecular. By distinguishing between a *dissociative* (D) pathway, in which a leaving ligand left an intermediate of lower co-ordination number, and an *associative* (A) step, in which an entering ligand increased the co-ordination number, and calling the combined operation an *interchange* (I), they codified the evidence that A was S_N2, D was S_N1, while I was S_N2. In practice, because the distinction between electrophilic and nucleophilic attack was never clear-cut in co-ordination chemistry, Ingold's notation was not recommended; nevertheless it has continued in use.

Like Ingold for organic chemistry, Nyholm perceived that inorganic chemistry would benefit from the use of large-scale instrumentation for mass spectrometry and spectrophotometry. Indeed, it was Nyholm's contention that[10]:

the impact of quantum mechanics and of modern physical methods of attack are the main reasons for the renaissance of inorganic chemistry, leading to the present period of rapid growth.

Nyholm's membership of the Science Research Council from 1965 helped to ensure the even-handed distribution of funds for such instrumentation between British universities, while his devotion to the cause of chemical education (probably acquired from David Mellor) aided the equally important modernization of the high-school curriculum in

TABLE 15.3 *Nyholm's genealogy of inorganic research.*

PREPARATION————COMPOSITION (analysis)				
Structure		Reactions		
Nature of bond	Stereo-chemistry	Products	Thermo-dynamics	Mechanism of reactions
valency; bond types; quantum interpre-tations (ligand-field theory)	elucidation and correlation with nature of ligand-field interpretation	nature, and steric course of reactions	energetics of reactions	

the 1960s. Nyholm, while lacking Ingold's amazing breadth of chemical knowledge, shared his view of the essential unity of chemistry. Since 1930, UCL had always been an 'integrated department' in which the methods and techniques of the school's divisions of physical, general inorganic, organic and crystallography were applied to whatever problem was at hand. This is illustrated in Nyholm's genealogy of inorganic research (see Table 15.3). Preparations involved the attachment of *organic* ligands and the use of *organic* reagents; structure determinations and the investigations of reactions involved the whole of classical *inorganic* chemistry, the use of *physical* instruments and the whole panoply of kinetic theory, thermodynamics and quantum mechanics. The branches of chemistry had become fused – a fact that Nyholm saw as having profound implications for the way chemistry was taught and the order in which it was delivered.

For example, the old-fashioned and boring qualitative analysis (see chapter 5), appropriate for the days when chemistry lacked instruments and which had been necessary for training metallurgists and food inspectors, was no longer appropriate. Borrowing from industry and from chemical engineering, substances for analysis had to be 'chosen for the *technique* which they teach, rather than as illustrations of *types* of compounds'[11]:

> I believe that we should find more time to enable students to acquire these techniques of inorganic chemistry, as for instance, the handling of substances in the absence of air or moisture, the manipulation of gaseous substances, and reactions involving low or high temperatures. Finally, I am convinced that, in keeping with the new sense of purpose in inorganic chemistry, the maximum opportunity should be provided for the undergraduate to prepare a compound, to establish its purity by analysis, and to investigate as many of its properties by chemical and physical techniques as he [sic] is able to do. This means that we effectively illustrate the wholeness of modern chemistry, and I believe that we thereby develop a genuine enthusiasm for this subject at undergraduate level.

As Ingold's and Hughes' successor to the headship of the department in 1963, Nyholm encouraged this process still further. He recognized that chemistry's boundaries were dissolving and overlapping with interesting areas of physics, biology, geology and mathematics. (Back in Sydney, Dwyer had already moved into enzyme chemistry.) More pragmatically, Nyholm understood that the cost of 'high-tech' instrumentation had become so great – by the 1960s a spectrophotometer was £10 000, a 'cheap' NMR spectrometer £15 000 and a mass spectrometer £30 000 – that the sharing of facilities had become essential; but that undergraduates should be allowed to use them too. Nyholm's untimely death in a car accident in 1971, when he was at the height of his powers, was an enormous loss to British chemistry. But his vision of a revitalized inorganic chemistry as part of a unified chemistry has proved to be correct. In a funeral oration Lord Annan said of Nyholm[12]:

> There are great scientists, and I do not think the worse of them, who are silent, retiring, cool and judicious. Nyholm was not one of them. Wherever he was he raised the temperature. But he raised it, not with pugnacious self-assertiveness, but with bonhomie, good sense and enthusiasm.

CONCLUSION

Werner's co-ordination theory was clearly guided by a belief, drawn from organic chemistry, in the spatial arrangement of atoms. Because the valency of such compounds was a serious issue in the 1890s, Werner was forced to consider this problem over and above the classification of co-ordination compounds. He was thereby compelled to distinguish between non-ionizable anionic groups bound within the first sphere of valency of the metal atom, and ionizable acid anions in a second sphere. This followed from the ionic behaviour of complexes when, for example, ammonia groups were withdrawn from the metal. In other words, groups had to be bound directly to the metal, rather like groups bound to a carbon atom in organic chemistry – a similarity that extended to the isomeric behaviour of the central atom core. The complete central atom complex, together with its attached groups, itself behaved ionically. Werner's problem was to explain this difference in bonding. Why, to take the simplest case, should ammonium chloride be $(NH_4)Cl$? All four hydrogen atoms bonded to the nitrogen were clearly equivalent. Yet, if nitrogen was trivalent, an extra bond had been found from a store of residual valency. Why was this residual valency not different from the other three valencies? In other words, although *a priori* there was a difference between ordinary valency and residual valency, in practice they became equivalent − indeed, identical. Moreover, six subsidiary valencies in $[Co(NH_3)_6]^{3+}$ mysteriously reduce to five in $[Co(NH_3)_5Cl]^{2+}$ and to four in $[Co(NH_3)_4Cl_2]^+$.

Werner was well aware of these puzzles, which undoubtedly deterred some chemists from his theory. These puzzles could not be resolved until the advent of the electronic theory of valency. Here the clarification offered by Lewis and Sidgwick that co-ordination was achieved through the donation of electron pairs by ligand groups, and that a simple application of electrostatic principles explained their stereochemistry, restimulated interest in co-ordination chemistry. This interest became particularly strong in Australia where, after slow beginnings in the 1870s, chemical research took off in the 1920s. Colonial contacts with Great Britain remained important until the 1950s, as is shown by the career of Sir Ronald Nyholm, which spanned positions in Sydney and London.

Whereas Ingold integrated his subject by relating all of his undergraduate teaching to current research and the historical development of organic chemistry, Nyholm, like Mendeleev, looked for common threads among the elements. Twentieth-century experience of co-ordination chemistry has proved very significant. Dwyer, Cornforth and others used it to move into enzyme chemistry, where metals such as cobalt and magnesium play central roles in metabolism. Melvin Calvin's early research on co-ordination compounds proved a stimulus for his study of chlorophyll and for his investigations of the catalytic effects of such materials. Pauling moved into medical chemistry as a result of interest in the co-ordination structure of haemoglobin, with its iron metal base.

The central place of inorganic chemistry is now unquestionable. The synthesis of extraordinary structures and insights into unexpected mechanisms continues. Organometallic chemistry was, for example, transformed with the synthesis of the first sandwich compound, ferrocene, in

1957. The power of transition complexes, especially those of platinum, to catalyse important polymerization reactions has similarly transformed industrial chemistry since 1950. Far from being outplayed, inorganic chemistry in the second half of the twentieth century has proved an essential component of the understanding of biochemistry, analytical chemistry, catalysis, electrochemistry, mineralogy, crystallography, radiochemistry and in all industrial processes involving high temperatures, catalysis and semiconductors.

At the Sign of the Hexagon

Having completed his analytical work, the chemist proposes to re-compose what he has destroyed; he takes as his point of departure the ultimate degree of analysis, i.e. simple bodies, and he compels them to unite with each other and by their combination to re-form the same natural principles which constitute all material beings. Such is the object of chemical synthesis.

(M. BERTHELOT, *Chimie organique fondée sur la synthèse*, 1860)

In September 1931, during the celebrations of the 150th anniversary of the birth of Michael Faraday, a combined electrical and chemical exhibition was held at the Albert Hall in London. The chemical section, arranged by Henry Armstrong, aimed to illustrate how Faraday's discovery of benzene in 1825 had, through the development of chemical industry, brightened people's lives with colourful fabrics and perfumes, produced new synthetic materials such as bakelite, casein plastics and viscose artificial silks, promoted the introduction of colour photography, aided an understanding of the chemistry of the human body, especially that of internal secretions (hormones), and revolutionized health through the drugs industry. Dominating the exhibits close by the great organ was a fourteen-foot high banner bearing benzene's signature, the sign of the hexagon, surrounding which was a frieze carrying a rainbow spectrum built up from the extensive range of subtle dyestuffs available three-quarters of a century after Perkin's discovery of mauve.

Fifty years later, although no comparable exhibition was mounted in honour of Faraday's bicentennial, the magnitude of chemists' contributions to the benefit of society goes beyond anything that Armstrong could have imagined – despite his lyrical enthusiasm for the exploits of industry. Underlying what the American chemical firm of Du Pont called 'better living with chemistry' has been the chemists' ability to synthesize new products and the chemical engineers' ingenuity in industrializing invention. However, with the increasing penetration of chemistry into the weft and warp of rural and urban civilization have come problems of pollution and safety that have damaged the science's reputation and produced a chemophobia among some sections of the public.

SYNTHESIS

By the 1930s, besides being used to establish chemical structures, especially those of natural products, synthesis had long been routinely used to study humanly produced substances (as in Körner's classical investigation of the orientations of aromatic substitutions in 1874), or to test general theories (as in W. H. Perkin Jr's equally classical demonstration in 1883 that small (three, four or five) carbocyclic rings might exist in defiance of Baeyer's strain theory). As we have seen, it was an interpretation of the consequences of Berzelius' radical theory that had led Frankland towards the valency theory of structure and to the organo-metallic compounds that proved extremely significant in laying the foundations of synthetic organic chemistry. At the same time, his friend Kolbe 'confirmed' the validity of the radical theory interpretation by building up carboxylic acids from first principles. For example, Kolbe's synthesis of acetic acid (1843–4):

$$FeS_2 + C \rightarrow CS_2 + Fe \quad \text{Lampadius, 1796}$$
$$CS_2 + 2Cl_2 \rightarrow CCl_4 + 2S \quad \text{Kolbe, 1843}$$
$$2CCl_4 \rightarrow C_2Cl_4 + 2Cl_2 \quad \text{Kolbe, 1844}$$
$$C_2Cl_4 + 2H_2O + Cl_2 \rightarrow CCl_3CO_2H + 3HCl$$
$$\text{Kolbe, 1844}$$
$$CCl_3CO_2H + 3H_2 \rightarrow CH_3CO_2H + 3HCl$$
$$\text{Melsens, 1842}$$

To Marcellin Berthelot, a total synthesis of a compound from its elements demonstrated[1]:

the identity of the forces which act in mineral chemistry with those that act in organic chemistry, by showing that the former sufficed for producing all the effects and all the compounds from which the latter are born.

However, such textbook demonstrations of 'circles of metamorphosis' and of the unity of chemistry, with their frequently low yields of products, were a far cry from the more technical syntheses upon which industrial chemistry was to depend.

The German *Organikern* represented by Adolf von Baeyer and Emil Fischer at the turn of the twentieth century had made the art of structure determination and synthesis at one and the same time the most glamorous and prestigious, as well as tedious and plodding, areas of chemical research. The glamour and prestige were reflected year after year as Nobel prizes were awarded for what seemed incredible feats of synthesis and structure determination. The tedium and mechanically routine nature of much of this structural organic chemistry was reflected in the way generations of schoolchildren and university students were forced to learn ways of adding or subtracting carbon in homologous series, inserting $C=O$ groups or coupling nitrogen atoms to form azo dyestuffs.

In 1861, the Frenchman, Charles Friedel (1832–99), a pupil of Wurtz, struck up an unusual research partnership with an American mining engineer, James Mason Crafts (1839–1917), who was also studying with Wurtz. Crafts returned to the Massachusetts Institute of Technology (MIT) in Boston as a Professor of Analytical Chemistry, but abandoned his position on the grounds of ill health in 1874. He returned to Paris where he re-established a partnership with Friedel. In 1877 they discovered the so-called Friedel–Crafts reaction, whereby an aluminium chloride catalyst transformed organic chlorides into hydrocarbons or acid halides into ketones:

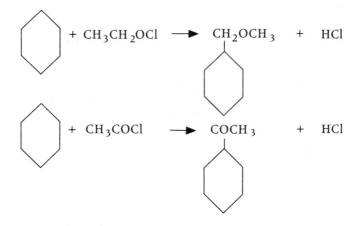

The reaction was particularly useful in preparing homologues of benzene and assumed major industrial significance with the rise of the petrochemicals industry in the 1950s. Aware of the synthetic importance of the reaction they had discovered, particularly its potentiality in petroleum cracking, Friedel and Crafts patented their findings in France and Britain. After Friedel's death, Crafts, in excellent health, returned to Boston to become President of MIT. This was but one of many dozens of 'useful' reactions that became part of the instruction in organic chemistry courses from the 1870s on.

The rewards in the market place and even political corridors for successful structure determinations and syntheses were great. Although Robert Robinson, as we have seen, made highly original theoretical contributions to organic chemistry, and although Christopher Ingold had begun his career as a traditional *Organiker*, Robinson towered over Ingold in fame and prestige for his elucidation of the structure of natural products – the alkaloids, strychnine and brucine, and the colouring matters of flowers, such as the anthocyanins and anthoxanthins.

Other contemporaries of Robinson, such as John Simonsen (1884–1957) and Walter Haworth (1883–1950), devoted themselves almost exclusively to the study of terpenes and sugars, where they were faced with major stereochemical problems and challenges. Yet others, particularly on the Continent, were more concerned with biochemically interesting molecules and the synthesis of vitamins and hormones. Baeyer's pupil, Richard Willstätter (1873–1942), unravelled the structure of chlorophyll and certain enzymes; Thiele's student, Heinrich Wieland (1877–1957), who succeeded Willstätter at the University of Munich in 1925, explored the world of enzymes, alkaloids, pterins and bile acids; while Richard Kuhn (1900–67) astonished the world in 1938 with the synthesis of vitamin A, followed (after a Nobel prize in the interim) by the synthesis of vitamin B6 in 1939. Two other German Nobel laureates, Otto Diels (1876–1954) and Kurt Alder (1902–58), developed in 1928 the addition reaction whereby double-bonded dienes were transformed into cyclic compounds. This Diels–Alder reaction proved to be of tremendous versatility in the synthesis of natural products.

Nor was this structural and synthetic tradition neglected in France, where, for example, Baeyer's pupil, Ernest Fourneau (1872–1949), established a laboratory at the

Pasteur Institute that worked closely with the French pharmaceutical industry in the creation of synthetic anaesthetics such as stovaine, and chemotherapeutic agents such as the first sulphanilamide agent, Prontosil Album, in 1935. During the 1920s, and under the visionary leadership of Heinrich Hörlein, I. G. Farben employed Gerhard Domagk (1895–1964) to test systematically for useful clinical effects the thousands of dyestuffs and their derivatives that their works chemists were synthesizing. On Christmas Day 1932, two of Domagk's workers patented sulphamido chrysoidine ('Prontosil'), the specification noting that this red dye destroyed streptococcal and staphylococcal infections in experimental animals, though not in *in vitro* cultures.

Rapidly confirming Domagk's claims, the Pasteur Institute team of Fourneau, Tréfoül, Nitti and Bovet, in three months of intensive work, had synthesized and tested eighteen other derivatives (most of which shared Prontosil's antibacterial properties) and had drawn the important conclusion that these, as well as Prontosil itself, were decomposed in living organisms into *para*-aminobenzene sulphanilamide, or plain sulphanilamide as it became known after 1937. This was the true bactericide. Since sulphanilamide had been synthesized by Paul Gelmo in 1908, it was not protected by I. G. Farben's patent. Moreover, it was easier and cheaper to prepare, and did not dye patients red! Consequently, the French pharmaceutical firm, the Société Rhône-Poulenc, was free to exploit the work of the Pasteur Institute pharmacologists and to market a 'Prontosil Album'. Similar confirmation of Domagk's findings came from British workers. Sponsored by the Medical Research Council, M. Colebrook and G. Buttle found that Prontosil cured post-natal cases of puerperal fever, while D. Woods and P. Fildes showed in 1940 that sulphanilamides worked by competing for an enzyme associated with an essential metabolite in a bacterium's life cycle.

The 'Robert Robinson of America' between the wars

was Roger Adams (1889–1971). A Harvard graduate, he had trained in Berlin with Willstätter and Diels, before spending his entire career at the University of Illinois. Here he ran one of the largest chemistry graduate schools in the world. In 1914, in order to save on laboratory costs, Adams' predecessor at Illinois, C. G. Derrick, had paid graduate students (including Carl Marvel) during the summer vacation to prepare chemicals that were to be used in undergraduate teaching and research during the following session. This system, which Adams took over, became an invaluable exercise during the First World War when America was unable to purchase pure chemicals from Germany or from American supply companies that, in practice, had bought most of their stocks in Europe. This 'preparations laboratory' scheme appealed to Adams very strongly[2]:

> It was work of national importance, it was good chemical training for the students, and it could be made a strong asset to the research program and the national reputation of the Illinois department; in addition, the very strong practical side of Adams's nature found it satisfactory.

The scheme was so successful financially, because Adams encouraged students to find the cheapest synthetic routes, that after the war the operations were transferred to a commercial company. The scheme was the origin of the annual series of volumes, *Organic Syntheses*, which Adams launched, very profitably, in 1921. Since each synthesis submitted by chemists had to be independently checked and verified in a different laboratory, publication was necessarily slow; but 'Adams's Annual', as Conant described it, soon became renowned for its accuracy and clarity. A measure of its usefulness was that it spawned other series such as *Inorganic Syntheses* (1939), *Organic Reactions* (1942) and *Biochemical Preparations* (1949).

In 1967, Louis and Mary Fieser began the annual *Reagents*

for Organic Chemists. Unlike Gertrude Robinson and Hilda Ingold, who remained in their husbands' shadows and who abandoned chemistry in the 1930s, Mary Fieser (*b.* 1909) became a role model for American women chemists. The Fiesers' *Organic Chemistry* (1944) was a popular book, despite its lack of theoretical commitment, because of its comprehensiveness and attention to natural products, its clever use of graphics, and its readability, which owed much to Mary Fieser's concern for literary style.

In 1922, as a result of fortuitous breakage of apparatus, Adams discovered the catalytic power of 'brown' platinum oxide in hydrogenation reactions. The subsequent use of this catalyst in all sorts of syntheses and preparations brought Adams fame, industrial consultancy positions, and appointments as a government adviser. During the 1930s and 1940s, as narcotics became an increasing social problem in America, Adams was asked to investigate the chemical nature of marijuana, from which he isolated the active constituent, cannabidiol.

Adams, although he hired a physical organic chemist, Charles C. Price (*b.* 1913), to work at Illinois, and although he happily used the new instrumental techniques such as UV and NMR spectroscopy as they became available in the 1950s, never really came to grips with the work of Ingold and Winstein. Consequently, his later work came to seem very old-fashioned and laboratory-oriented – a position that he defended vigorously on the grounds that what industry needed were good laboratory chemists, like his most brilliant student, Wallace H. Carothers.

In this respect, Adams differed from the next generation of American structural chemists, Robert Woodward, Carl Djerassi and Donald J. Cram, who may be taken as representative of the way structural and mechanistic studies invigorated the traditional 'hands on', tacit knowledge, approach of organic chemists after the 1950s, and the way that such 'pure' research came increasingly to respond to external biochemical, biomedical and social interests.

In the 1930s, following the entry of physiologists and biochemists into research on hormones, chemists began to take an interest in the synthesis of steroids because, being in very short supply from natural sources, their clinical use in hormone deficiency diseases was proving prohibitively expensive. It occurred to Russell Marcker, who was then working at Pennsylvania State University, that human steroidal hormones should be preparable by the chemical manipulation of similar steroids that occurred naturally and had been isolated from the sapogenin group of plants. The most desirable plant steroid to work with was diosgenin, which, however, proved to be contained in American plants in too small a quantity to make their commercial exploitation worth while. But one Mexican plant provided large quantities of the female hormone, progesterone, after fairly routine chemical treatment of its extract.

Unable to interest American chemical companies, Marcker, together with a Mexican businessman, set up the Syntex Company in Mexico in 1943 (Syntex = *Synt*hesis + *Mex*ico). Swindled of his share of the profits, Marcker established a rival company of his own, only to find himself the subject of physical and legal harassment. Not surprisingly, Marcker, a talented practical steroid chemist, abandoned industrial chemistry in disgust in 1949, and became a dealer in Mexican antiques. He had, however, succeeded in reducing the price of progesterone by half and laying the foundations of Mexico's present large steroid manufacturing industry. He also seeded the contraceptives revolution.

It was the Vienna-born American, Carl Djerassi (*b.* 1923), who followed Marcker's lead in a more sophisticatedly physical way. A refugee from the Nazi invasion of Austria in 1938, Djerassi joined the CIBA pharmaceutical company's laboratory in New Jersey after graduating in chemistry from a small midwestern university. At the age of only twenty he prepared one of the first antihistamine drugs, pyribenzamine, and seemed set upon a successful career in the pharmaceutical industry. However, excited by the possibilities of steroid research revealed in Louis Fieser's *Natural Products Related to Phenanthrene* (1936), which a CIBA colleague had encouraged him to read, in 1944 Djerassi began postgraduate studies at the University of Wisconsin, where research on the structures and syntheses of steroids was in progress. When he eventually returned to his post at CIBA he discovered that the American company's protocol would not allow him to attempt the synthesis of cortisone because this task had been assigned to the parent company in Switzerland. Frustrated, Djerassi resigned and became research director of Marcker's former, and now respectably run, Syntex Company in Mexico.

In 1951 Djerassi succeeded in devising a simple synthesis of cortisone from starting materials extracted from Mexican yams and sisal. In a later interview he commented[3]:

> When you consider the competitive nature of the problems, particularly the cortisone one, it was extraordinary. Our competitors were Woodward at Harvard, Fieser at Harvard, E. R. H. Jones and his group at Manchester, the entire ETH group at Zürich, and all the pharmaceutical companies, including Merck and CIBA. No one had ever heard of Mexico Syntex, and there we would just come out with one paper after another and beat the entire competition. This was done with people who were extraordinarily excited. We trained the Mexicans ourselves. It was the only time in my life where I did research on a shift basis. We did it in two shifts – we'd work from eight to five and a[nother] group would work from four to midnight.

This cortisone process was, however, doomed commercially when, at about the same time, a rival company found a way of synthesizing it much more cheaply using microorganisms. The tension between fermentation procedures (biotechnology) and laboratory degradation procedures that unravelled structures of natural products, which, in turn, suggested potentially viable synthetic pathways, had begun with the work of Pasteur. It was to be characteristic of the commercial exploitation of organic chemistry in the twentieth century, as the case of penicillin makes clear.

Penicillin, whose antibiotic properties were first revealed by the bacteriologist, Alexander Fleming, in 1928, and more fully realized by Howard Florey and Ernest Chain in 1939, became a crucial drug to manufacture during the Second World War as a magic bullet to fight venereal disease and tropical diseases. Despite being a comparatively small molecule of molecular weight only 350, it contained, in Woodward's words, 'a diabolical concatenation of reactive groups' that seemed impossible to put together. Some thousand chemists grouped at Oxford under Robinson and Florey, and under Adams at Illinois, together with five other universities and seven pharmaceutical companies, were confident that a synthesis of this labile molecule was nevertheless possible. But soon there were serious disagreements and conflicts over the possible structure and therefore the appropriate synthetic strategy, and synthesis during the war proved impossible.

Instead, in a crash industrial programme, Florey persuaded American pharmaceutical companies to co-operate on a fermentation process for growing *Penicillium notatum*. By 1944 adequate quantities of the drug were being produced by this method. It was only in 1957, after most chemists had given up penicillin synthesis as hopeless, that John Sheenan (1915–92), who worked on the American synthesis programme during the war, doggedly synthesized the molecule. Unfortunately, his triumph was marred for the rest of his career by long-winded patent litigation.

From hindsight, it is clear that part of the difficulty over penicillin synthesis was caused by the weight of Robinson's authority. On good chemical grounds, based on his long experience, he assumed that one of the key molecular ingredients was an oxazolone-thiazolidine group (the presence of sulphur had actually been missed by the British team until it was put right by Adams in 1943). Although opposed on equally valid chemical grounds by E. P. Abraham and E. Chain, who supported an alternative β-lactam group, Robinson continued to oppose this possibility even after 1945 when X-ray studies by Dorothy Hodgkin clearly showed Abraham and Chain to be correct.

The advent of high-resolution mass spectrometers and NMR spectroscopy in the 1960s made such disputes virtually impossible. Given such tools whereby the four hydrogens in a functional group $CH_3CH_2CH(OH)$ could be distinguished at a glance from an NMR spectrum trace, the structure of penicillin, which took years to unravel in the 1940s, would have been settled in days twenty years later. The determination of structure by chemical means had become history. The post-war organic chemist no longer relied exclusively on 'reverse synthesis' – the identification of degradation products that were reassembled after their own separate synthesis – but on instruments that directly identified organic functional groups (as in low- and high-resolution mass spectrometry and infrared and ultraviolet spectrophotometry), the presence of key atoms such as hydrogen and phosphorus, as well as kinetic-mechanistic information (as in NMR spectroscopy) and optical rotatory dispersion with the spectropolarimeter for the determination of conformation and configuration of molecules.

The use of these analytical instrumental techniques was quickly reflected in American undergraduate texts such as John D. Roberts and Marjorie Caserio, *Basic Principles of Organic Chemistry* (1964), which challenged the reader with a chapter on the spectroscopy of organic compounds before even introducing the alkanes. British and Continental authors and publishers seemed unable to compete with such textbooks. With rare exceptions, such as I. L. Finar, *Organic Chemistry* (1951), American textbooks monopolized the world's teaching market from the 1960s.

Although photography had stimulated interest in photochemistry since the 1840s and photochemical reactions in the gas phase had formed the main part of kinetic theory, organic chemists largely ignored the possibilities of photochemistry until the 1930s. At Cambridge in the 1920s, Ronald Norrish (1897–1978), while working in the physical chemistry laboratory established by Lowry, investigated photolysis using a single arc lamp. Despite rudimentary equipment, Norrish established a large school of photochemical research, which, by the 1930s, had begun to investigate the photolysis of aldehydes and ketones, and the chemistry of free radicals. In 1947, Norrish was joined by George Porter (*b*. 1920), a Leeds graduate who had spent the war years working on radar. It occurred to Porter to apply the pulse techniques of radar – microsecond pulses of electromagnetic radiation – to the investigation of photochemical reactions. In 1949, using a flash lamp, Norrish and Porter showed that free radicals were instantaneously produced. Weaker flashes, activated in short bursts after the first one, enabled spectroscopic photographs to be taken for the identification of reaction intermediates. Once laser beams became available after 1960, flash photolysis proved fruitful in mechanistic studies and the theory of excited states; but it also showed the organic chemist that many of the ring closures demanded in synthesis could be achieved by photochemical, as opposed to thermal, treatment. Both Norrish and Porter received Nobel prizes for their work.

One major effect of the deglamorization of structure determinations by instrumentation in the 1960s was to push organic chemists towards asking questions about function. Todd has explained[4]:

> . . . if you simplify structural work in the way chemists are now doing, structure becomes less of an end to me, and I become more and more interested in function. And this takes me into areas where there are many

things to be considered that organic chemists have never much thought about before.

Just as we saw with Pauling in theoretical chemistry, the post-war tendency has been to push organic chemists closer to biochemistry and towards the structure and function of living systems. Here there were challenging problems of synthesis.

Syntex had waxed profitably from the production of progesterone from Mexican yams. By adding a methyl group to progesterone to form norethindrone, Djerassi succeeded in making a more powerful contraceptive – as shown by the clinical trials of Pincus. As Djerassi's book, *The Politics of Contraception* (1981), revealed, there was intense rivalry between pharmaceutical companies in the 1950s to market a safe female contraceptive pill. Djerassi, who retained strong commercial links after becoming Professor of Chemistry at Stanford University in 1960, also solved many problems in the complex stereochemistry of steroids by developing optical methods of rotatory dispersion and circular dichroism that gave details of structure that could not possibly have been discerned by the nineteenth-century polarimeter. Following his 'retirement' in 1980, unlike many American chemists, who became consultants, he turned to the arts, writing poetry and an interesting science novel, *Cantor's Dilemma* (1989), and supporting a dance company financially.

The amazing ability of twentieth-century chemists to overcome synthetic problems was well illustrated by Donald Cram and George Hammond's *Organic Chemistry* (1959), which, arranged by the mechanisms of reactions rather than by the structures of reactants and products, became a standard college text in the 1960s. In the second edition of 1964, the front end-papers depicted ten compounds that had been synthesized since the first edition had appeared; the back end-papers showed another ten that still eluded synthesis. Cram (*b.* 1919) worked on the penicillin project before training with Fieser at Harvard. The microbiological chemical world of *Penicillium* moulds revealed to him many unique ring and asymmetric carbon systems, while organic chemistry itself seemed like some[5]:

> vast playground on which many new games could be invented, games whose players might engage in civil and international competition to discover the appropriate rules.

In Cram's hands at the University of California at Los Angeles (UCLA), organic chemistry did, indeed, become a game to invent, or design, molecules on paper and then to think of ways of making them in the laboratory. As he has acknowledged, Dewar's views on π complexes were an inspiration to design and synthesis. Amid the games, however, a chemistry of 'host–guest complexation' emerged that held important implications for the pharmaceutical industry and the understanding of how enzymes function. Cram's ability to show how chemists could design synthetic hosts that were the counterparts of the receptor sites of biological chemistry earned him a Nobel prize in 1987.

Like Woodward, Cram emphasizes the intensely visual nature of organic chemistry and the need to be an artist as well as a scientist. In his Indian lecture, 'Art and Science in the Synthesis of Organic Compounds' (1963), Robert Woodward (1917–79), the most extraordinary of all modern synthesizers, said[6]:

> The structure known, but not yet accessible by synthesis, is to the chemist what the unclimbed mountain, the uncharted sea, the untilled field, the unreached planet, are to other men. . . . The unique challenge which chemical synthesis provides for the creative imagination and the skilled hands ensures that it will endure as long as men write books, paint pictures, and fashion things which are beautiful, or practical, or both.

Woodward was brought up in Boston by his widowed mother, who encouraged his boyhood love of playing with chemicals. By the age of twelve, in a home-based laboratory, he had already worked his way through the English translation of Ludwig Gatterman's 'Kochbuch', the *Practical Methods of Organic Chemistry* (1894). Gatterman (1860–1920), a chemist at Freiburg, had done dangerous experiments with the explosive nitrogen trichloride, as well as noticing that the presence of hydrogen cyanide in a laboratory renders a peculiar taste to a cigar! Fortunately, Woodward did not repeat such experiments. Instead, at the age of sixteen, recognized as a genius, he was allowed to matriculate at MIT; by the age of twenty he had completed a doctorate on a partial synthesis of the female hormone, oestrone. This brought him an appointment at Harvard, where he spent the remainder of his extraordinary life in unremitting synthetic labours.

Central to Woodward's approach and success was his use of the latest instrumentation together with the exploitation of the molecular orbital method of understanding structure and mechanism. During the Second World War, Woodward was hired by the Polaroid Company to find a way of producing light polarizers to replace those made from iodoquinine. Because of the Japanese occupation of the Dutch East Indies, natural supplies of quinine from the bark of the cinchona trees that grew in the Indies were unavailable. And since quinine was a valuable anti-malarial drug vital to the waging of a tropical war, Woodward was able to persuade Polaroid to fund his research on its synthesis. Polaroid, having found substitutes for light polarizers, agreed in 1942 to support Woodward and his postdoctoral student, William Doering (*b.* 1922).

Quinine's molecular structure (*pace* Perkin, chapter 5) had been determined by Paul Rabe (1869–1952) at the University of Jena as early as 1908. He had found that one of the primary constituents was quinotoxin, from which quinine could be synthesized. Woodward and Doering's problem, therefore, was the synthesis of quinotoxin, which they achieved in April 1944, only fourteen months after starting with benzaldehyde. Although the synthesis was of no commercial value, since it involved at least fifteen steps just to reach quinotoxin, it made Woodward a famous man. Together with penicillin, chemists were winning the war. Not surprisingly, therefore, with this triumph, Woodward was pressed into the penicillin problem. However, apart from exploiting infrared spectroscopic evidence for a constituent lactam molecule, he was unable to solve the conundrum.

Instead he turned to strychnine, whose structure he elucidated in 1948 and synthesized in 1954. This was followed by adventures with chlorophyll, cholesterol, lysergic acid, reserpine and the antibiotic, cephalosporin, which gained him the Nobel prize in 1965. If these molecules, and many others, involved interesting chemical problems, particularly in view of the large numbers of asymmetric carbon atoms involved (chiral centres), the choice of subjects by Woodward and his competitors in the 1950s and 1960s was largely dictated by the pharmaceutical companies that provided research grants. Cortisone, whose structure Woodward, like Djerassi, unravelled in 1951, involved thirteen steps in the synthesis and six or more chiral centres. Since the combination of six opportunities for two enantiomers leads to the possibility of $2^6 = 64$ stereoisomers, it became imperative for organic chemists to find and choose stereospecific pathways in synthesis.

It became Woodward's goal to avoid the production of racemates at any stage of a synthesis. Mixtures of stereoisomers were an 'inelegance, not to say impracticality'. Here the groundwork laid by the mechanistic studies of Ingold and others earlier this century paid dividends. By thinking through a synthesis mechanistically, in terms of the bonds to be made and broken in three dimensions, Woodward was usually able to predict confidently the feasibility of any particular reaction. On the other hand, it is clear from the prolific work of the Japanese organic chemist, Teruaki Mikaiyama (b. 1927), who, on Woodward's advice, coined the term 'synthetic control' in 1974, that over-zealous use of mechanistic analysis could stifle the creativity of synthesizers. Like Claude Bernard in physiology a century before, Mikaiyama has stressed the continuing importance of purely exploratory experimentation and of the pursuit of the unexpected. It was while trying to prepare samples of α-nitropropionanilide in order to elucidate the mechanism of the thermal dissociation of amides in 1950 that Mikaiyama stumbled upon an unexpected reaction. Close analysis of this led to the discovery that organic molecules, such as nitroalkanes, could be readily dehydrated by isocyanate molecules. Abandoning mechanistic studies, Mikaiyama was led into a long and fruitful programme of research in Tokyo on dehydrating agents, which formed the basis for new synthetic pathways.

In addition to using all the latest instrumental support possible for the rapid identification of intermediate structures, Woodward also exploited the new principle of 'conformational analysis', which Derek Barton (b. 1918) and Odd Hassel (1897–1981) independently developed during the 1950s, and for which they were jointly awarded a Nobel prize in 1969.

Through his charisma and dedication, Woodward instilled a loyalty in his students comparable to those of Liebig a century before. Research students might have little or no chance of publishing a solo paper; nevertheless, his or her participation in the synthesis of a 'Woodward molecule' was a badge of entry into an academic position or into industry (or even, in one case, into history of science). Despite gruelling hours of work expected of them, the sense that organic chemistry was a delightful, logical game, and the sense that their Harvard group was in competition with Robinson at Oxford, or Albert Eschenmoser at the

Eidgenössische Technische Hochschule (ETH) at Zürich, were factors that inspired team research. Organic chemistry was now 'big science' like particle physics.

Interestingly, although they were in direct competition, Woodward was never secretive about his plans and current achievements prior to publication. In 1958, when he and Eschenmoser were competing to synthesize colchicine, a medicinal used in the treatment of gout, Eschenmoser asked Woodward if he knew of a degradation procedure whereby the natural colchicine of the crocus could be made to give a compound they had synthesized in Zürich. Woodward gave the necessary information, knowing full well that it meant that the Swiss had beaten his team to the synthesis.

It was this mutual trust that enabled Woodward and Eschenmoser to collaborate internationally on the biggest remaining problem in natural product synthesis: vitamin B12. Dorothy Hodgkin, after laborious X-ray analyses, had determined the vitamin's structure in 1956. Even so, the synthesis was to take twelve years of combined research, despite the simplification that the vitamin had already been synthesized from cobyric acid. The problem was reduced, therefore, to the synthesis of this naturally occurring cobalt complex. Cobyric acid has four pyrrole rings surrounding cobalt. The problem was not only how to make these rings with the appropriate attached groups, but how to bring the rings together. Because the molecule was asymmetric, the Woodward team studied its left half, the Swiss team the right-hand side. As a result of this division of labour, Woodward made a powerful new theoretical discovery.

In 1958, E. Vogel reported in *Liebig's Annalen* that *cis*-3,4-dicarboxymethoxycyclobutane was easily cleaved to form a stereospecific isomer, *cis,trans*-butadiene. It followed from this example of 'valence isomerism' that, by the 'principle of microscopic reversibility', the reaction ought to be stereospecific in the reverse direction.

cis-3,4-dicarboxymethoxy cyclobutane   *cis-, trans*-butadiene

A few years later, in work on the synthesis of vitamin B, the Dutch chemist, E. Havinga, found that portions of the molecule cleaved photochemically and thermally with different stereochemical results. Such an event could not be explained as a more complex example of a Walden inversion. In 1961, Havinga speculated in *Tetrahedron* that the difference of behaviour might be caused by the different symmetry characteristics of the highest π electron orbitals of conjugated hexatrienes. This point was picked up by Woodward when he was faced by a similar photochemical and thermal contradiction when attempting the synthesis of his half of the vitamin B12 molecule.

In thinking over the stereospecific differences he and Havinga had found, it occurred to Woodward, who was fond of late-night brain-storming sessions with colleagues and students, that, for atoms to bond, two orbitals (whether σ, π or even δ was immaterial) had to be in phase. A given stereochemistry arose precisely because molecules were able to twist around until their appropriate bonding orbitals were in the correct phase. Whereas heat merely agitated molecules, light photons would enable electrons to be promoted to orbitals of a higher energy and a potentially different phase. This might then make it easier for a molecule to twist and so place its orbitals in position for overlap and bonding. Here was a qualitative explanation for the difference between thermal and photochemical reactions. In order to make the explanation quantitative, Woodward consulted with a young Polish-born American theorist, Roald Hoffmann (*b.* 1937), who was then working at Harvard. The resulting 'Woodward–Hoffmann rules', or 'principle of orbital symmetry' that the two men developed between 1965 and 1969 were to earn Hoffmann (together with the Japanese chemist, Kenichi Fukui; see chapter 15) the 1981 Nobel prize. This was two years after Woodward's death.

Meanwhile, application of these rules to both sides of the cobyric acid molecule, together with applications of knowledge derived from the newer inorganic co-ordination chemistry, led to their completion. In the knotty problem of integrating the two halves of the molecule, both the Swiss and the American teams used photochemical reactions extensively, but found different routes to the final product. The two syntheses were published in 1972.

Thereafter, with the main challenges of natural products conquered, chemists turned increasingly towards the challenge of 'invented' molecules, preferably ones with freakish and amusing shapes. The most recent, and sensational, examples are the carbon (C_{60}) 'fullerenes' named after Buckminster Fuller, the architect who designed geodesic domes. With modern computer programs, today's chemists are able not only to print out perfect structural formulae, but to design molecules on their screens before trying to prepare them in the laboratory.

Woodward was no ivory-tower chemist. He held consultancies with Polaroid for nearly forty years, and with Merck and Pfizer for thirty years, while with Ciba-Geigy he established the Woodward Research Institute in Basel in 1963 in order to help stimulate research in an industrial setting. His synthesis of the natural cephalosporin was sponsored by Ciba-Geigy, who reaped the benefit by making molecular variants that combined the desirable attributes of both penicillin and cephalosporin.

INDUSTRIAL CHEMISTRY

For all the rhetoric of nineteenth-century academic chemists in Britain urging the priority of the study of pure chemistry over applied, their students who became works chemists were little more than qualitative and quantitative analysts. Before the 1880s this was equally true of German chemical firms, who remained content to retain academic consultants (for example, A. W. Hofmann by AGFA) who pursued research within the university and who would occasionally provide the material for manufacturing innovation. By the 1880s, however, industrialists were beginning to recognize that the scaling up of consultants' laboratory preparations and syntheses was a distinctly different activity from laboratory investigation. They began to refer to this scaling problem and its solution as 'chemical engineering' – possibly because the mechanical engineers who had already been introduced into works to maintain the steam engines and pumps in an industry of growing complexity were the very men who seemed best able to understand the processes involved. The academic dichotomy of head and hand died slowly.

In Britain, when in 1881 there was an attempt to name the new Society of Chemical Industry as the 'Society of Chemical Engineers', the suggestion was turned down. On the other hand, as a result of growing pressure from the industrial sector, the curricula of technical institutions began to reflect, at last, the need for chemical engineers rather than competent analysts. No longer was mere description of existing industrial processes to suffice. Instead, the expectation was that the processes generic to various specific industries would be analysed, thus making room for the introduction of thermodynamic perspectives, as well as those being opened up by the new physical chemistry of kinetics, solutions and phases.

A key figure in this transformation was the chemical consultant, George Davis (1850–1907), the first Secretary of the Society of Chemical Industry. In 1887 Davis, then a lecturer at the Manchester Technical School (later UMIST), gave a series of lectures on chemical engineering, which he defined as the study of 'the application of machinery and plant to the utilization of chemical action on the large scale'. The course, which revolved around the type of plant involved in large-scale industrial operations such as drying, crushing, distillation, fermentation, evaporation and crystallization, slowly became recognized as a model for courses elsewhere, not only in Britain, but overseas. The first fully fledged course in chemical engineering in Britain was not introduced until 1909 at Battersea Polytechnic in south London; though in America, Lewis Norton (1855–93) of MIT pioneered a Davis-type course as early as 1888.

In 1915, Arthur D. Little, in a report on MIT's programme, referred to it as the study of 'unit operations' and this neatly encapsulated the distinctive feature of chemical engineering in the twentieth century. The reasons for the success of the Davis movement are clear: it avoided revealing the secrets of specific chemical processes protected by patents or by an owner's reticence – factors that had always seriously inhibited manufacturers from supporting academic programmes of training in the past. Davis overcame this difficulty by converting chemical industries 'into a series of separate phenomena which could be studied independently' and, indeed, experimented with in pilot plants within a university or technical college workshop. In effect he applied the ethics of industrial consultancy, by which experience was transmitted[7] 'from plant to plant and from process to process in such a way which did not compromise the private or specific knowledge which contributed to a given plant's profitability'.

At the same time, led by German firms, invention and discovery became industrialized through the establishment of company research laboratories. The model here was the Bayer Company at Barmen (later Elberfeld). When Friedrich Bayer founded his dyestuffs firm in 1861, it was small, poorly equipped and, as in the British alkali industry, its few chemically qualified employees were solely engaged in quality control analyses. Only in the 1880s, following the breakthroughs in the synthesis of alizarin and indigo, and the realization that hundreds of dyestuffs intermediates had potentials as starting points in the manufacture of pharmaceuticals such as Bayer's 'aspirin' (1897), did Bayer begin to invest heavily in research and development at new works at Leverkusen. Here the successes of the structural theory of organic chemistry in the academic university came into their own industrially.

In 1884 Bayer was joined by one of Adolf Baeyer's pupils, Carl Duisberg (1861–1935), whose work on azo dyes proved of considerable commercial benefit to the firm. Given a free hand to rationalize the Bayer laboratories, in 1891 Duisberg opened a new laboratory with space

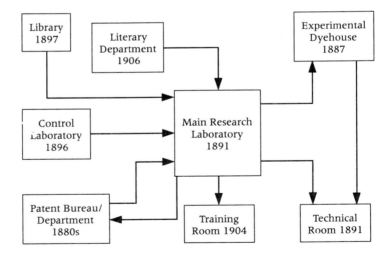

FIGURE 16.1 The infrastructure of the Bayer company at the turn of the century. (Adapted from G. Meyer-Thurow, *Isis*, **73** (1982): 363–83.)

for a dozen research chemists. Around this laboratory Duisberg slowly constructed an infrastructure of support and development facilities. A well stocked library (which by 1910 was subscribing to some 500 periodicals), and a patent bureau, were needed to keep the research chemists up to date with chemical advances and with the innovations of rival firms throughout the world. In 1906 a literary, or abstracts, department had to be added in recognition that it was no longer possible for an individual to keep abreast of the literature. A team of library specialists instead drew up lists and abstracts of reading matter of potential interest to the different lines of research being pursued. An experimental dye house assessed any promising innovations developed in the main laboratory, while a technical room staffed with chemical engineers scaled up the best procedures for manufacture. Successful processes had to be patented, so that the patent library also became a patent filing bureau. In addition, Duisberg found it necessary to open a control laboratory of analysts who routinely investigated the products of rival companies, and a further laboratory to train works chemists.

It was this pattern of industrialized invention, with its potential for expanding the scientific workforce, that became the international model for twentieth-century industry. Research was now a co-operative enterprise within a bureaucratic structure and in which a company, rather than a particular chemist, became the collective inventor.

In his *Essay on Population* (1798), Malthus argued that, since food supplies could never keep pace with population growth, poverty, famine, death and misery were ineluctable consequences of life. Although famous for its use by Darwin to evoke the mechanism of natural selection for evolution, the Malthusian spectre haunted the nineteenth century. Indeed, had yields per acre not been increased in the 1840s by nitrogen and phosphorus fertilizers, or American wheat been introduced to Europe in the 1870s, there might well have been famine in England, Wales and Scotland, as there was in Ireland in the 1840s.

Even so, at the end of the century, the chemist, William Crookes, could argue in a Presidential Address to the British Association that supplies of nitrogen fertilizer were finite and that, if food supplies were to be further increased to ward off the Malthusian threat, some means would have to be found to tap the vast reservoir of nitrogen in the air[8].

> It is the chemist who must come to the rescue of the threatened communities. It is through the laboratory that starvation may ultimately be turned to plenty.

Following the eighteenth-century nomenclature of Stephen Hales, chemists referred to this as the problem of fixation of nitrogen. The rise of the Nobel explosives industry based upon nitroglycerine and dynamite was also to increase demand for nitric acid and therefore of a convenient method of synthesis from nitrogen.

One obvious way of fixing nitrogen was to use the method long ago discovered by Cavendish whereby nitrogen and oxygen were sparked together to form oxides of nitrogen from which nitric acid could be prepared. The snag was that, industrially, such a process demanded extremely high temperatures (2000–3000°C) and therefore uneconomic amounts of electricity. Since such a process was only viable with cheap hydroelectricity, it was only worked for some years in Norway after 1903 when a process was perfected by Olaf Birkeland (a physicist) and Sam Eyde (an engineer). Despite its limitations, the Birkeland–Eyde process attracted the attention of academic chemists such as Fritz Haber (1868–1934) and Walther Nernst (1864–1941), who were interested in the thermodynamics of reactions. In 1903 Haber showed that ammonia could be synthesized at the not unreasonable temperature of 1000°C if an iron catalyst was used:

$$3H_2 + N_2 \rightarrow 2NH_3$$

However, the yield was infinitesimal and of no commercial significance.

To Haber's embarrassment, this was publicly challenged by Nernst, who pointed out that Haber had paid insufficient attention to pressure as a factor in driving the equilibrium to the right. Haber therefore reinvestigated the matter thoroughly from first principles and derived optimum thermodynamic conditions for the reactions. Using an osmium, uranium carbide or iron catalyst, a pressure of 200 atmospheres (402 kPa) and a temperature of 500°C, Haber persuaded the firm of BASF that the synthesis did have commercial possibilities. That was in 1909. It took the engineer, Carl Bosch (1874–1940), and the firm's chief chemist, Alwin Mittasch (1869–1953), a further five years to scale up the process. One of the chief problems was the design of a pressure converter of some 65 tons, which involved Krupps in the development of new steel forging techniques. Bosch also had to develop a cheaper method for preparing hydrogen, since electrolysis of water was far too expensive. (Nitrogen was available from industrial plants via liquefaction of air by this date.) Bosch achieved this by passing steam over coke. The process also provided abundant cheap supplies of hydrogen for Zeppelin's airships and for manufacturers of margarine.

The first pilot plant for ammonia synthesis was built by BASF at Ludwigshafen in 1913. With the outbreak of war this pilot plant was quickly enlarged to a production capacity of 60 000 tons (61×10^6 kg) of ammonia per annum, thus making Germany potentially, if not actually, self-sufficient in nitric acid for explosives production. Although the conquest of ammonia synthesis was widely publicized (Haber was to be awarded the Nobel prize for chemistry in 1919 even though he had directed research on gases for chemical warfare; and Bosch received the Nobel prize in 1931), BASF revealed nothing concerning the economics of production. When war broke out in 1914, and British supplies of nitrate for fertilizer and explosives were blockaded by U-boats, Britain and her allies were forced to look closely at the economics of the synthesis. Drawing the erroneous conclusion that the process was prohibitively expensive, the British government developed instead the cyanamide process, which German chemists had used as a route to cheap fertilizers since the 1890s. In this, calcium carbide absorbed nitrogen directly to form the fertilizer, calcium cyanamide. The cyanamide could also be decomposed with steam to form ammonia, which, complemented by ammonia recovered from gasworks, could be converted to nitric acid for the explosives industry.

The British invested heavily in cyanamide factories only to discover in 1919, when BASF's books were inspected, that estimates of the costs of ammonia synthesis had been way out. Consequently, in the 1920s, and very rapidly, the Haber–Bosch process was introduced in Britain and America and soon superseded all rivals. Moreover, its introduction acted as a stimulus and model for all subsequent twentieth-century industry, almost all of which began to involve high-pressure synthesis. As Haber's son has put it[9]:

> The construction of huge plants, designed to handle continuously large volumes of high temperatures and pressures, imposed novel operating practices on works engineers, and contributed to the rapid development of chemical engineering, and also to improved types of steel, and new designs of valves and gas compressing machinery.

He adds that 'the impact of the ammonia synthesis may be compared in significance with the adoption of petroleum and natural gas for chemical manufacture in Europe in the 1950s and 1960s'.

The Haber–Bosch process was of considerable social, economic and scientific importance. Scientifically it was an elegant study of the thermodynamics of gaseous reactions and a demonstration of its commercial significance; socially and economically, it resolved the spectre of Malthus and of starving millions; environmentally, with its absence of waste products and polluting odours, it was a model for a cleaner and more socially responsible industry.

Apart from cleaner and more efficient processes suggested by electrochemical processes in the alkali industry and by ammonia synthesis, twentieth-century industry has also been concerned with the economics of scale and scope, including the transfer from wasteful and inefficient batch manufacture to continuous flow. This has been made possible by the exploitation of the remarkable powers of catalysts and through process control by instrumental monitoring. The key factor has been the development of the petrochemicals industry since the 1920s, when chemical engineers at MIT first devised quantitative tools for analysing fractional distillations, and when John Griebe was hired by the Dow Company to develop automatic control technology. Later, in the 1940s, industrial analysis was further refined by the development of infrared spectroscopy – to the enhancement of post-war research in organic chemistry.

But it has been the chemical industry's ability to substitute a cheaper synthetic product for a natural one, followed by the exploitation of such materials in novel applications, that has been the real hallmark of twentieth-century industry in the public mind. The process may be said to have begun in 1861 when a Birmingham electrochemist, Alexander Parkes (1813–90), prepared a malleable solid by mixing nitrocellulose with wood naphtha (a mixture of methyl alcohol, acetone, acetic acid and methyl acetate formed during the distillation of wood). Patented as 'Parkesine' and advertised as a high-quality sculpting material, it had little commercial success until a former partner, Daniel Spill (1832–93), prepared a better material, Xylonite, from the unpromising brew of nitrocellulose, alcohol, camphor and castor oil. Parkes' and Spill's Xylonite Company then moulded what was in effect cellulose nitrate under pressure to form such objects as combs and shirt collars. These found a ready sale among the lower-middle-class market of insurance agents and commercial travellers. From 1884 Xylonite was adopted by the Sheffield cutlery trade as a cheaper material than bone for knife handles.

These developments were purely empirical. The explosive, nitrocellulose, had been discovered in 1846 by the Swiss chemist, Christian Schönbein (1799–1869), the discoverer of ozone, when he nitrated cotton fibres. Although its exploitation as a safe explosive only began in the 1880s, Schönbein found that a solution of nitrocellulose in an ether/alcohol mixture produced a hard transparent film that he called 'Collodion'. This substance found a use as a waterproof dressing for protecting minor wounds and as a basis for photographic film. Spill's development of Xylonite, therefore, was little more than that of finding a plasticizer (camphor) to render Schönbein's Collodion pliable.

Parkes' material, which had the unfortunate property of easy deformation and flammability, was improved in 1870 by the American inventor, John Wesley Hyatt (1837–1920). Hyatt was specifically searching for a substitute for costly ivory that was imported to make billiard balls, and for the expensive tortoise-shell used as the backing for mirrors, hair and tooth brushes. His new product, 'Celluloid', proved a commercial success, despite its flammability in proximity to cigars and cigarettes, mainly because Hyatt realized that nobody would use an unfamiliar material unless it was demonstrated palpably to resemble and to be equally as good as a familiar material. Hyatt was also undoubtedly fortunate that Celluloid became the basis of the roll film developed by George Eastman in 1889, thus ensuring constant sales through two popular leisure and entertainment pursuits, those of snapshots and movie-going.

The market success of these 'plastics' – the word was not used in a generic sense until the 1920s, the 'plastic age' – and the pressure of patents soon stimulated experiments with other natural products such as urea and milk. Since milk was an end-product of the cellulose digestion of a cow, this abundantly available food was a logical choice for investigation. In 1897 a German firm was commissioned to produce white writing slates for the use of elementary schoolchildren. By adding formaldehyde to milk the Bavarian chemist, Adolf Spitteler, prepared a hard ivory-like substance that was marketed as 'Galalith' and used in button-making. This was, in fact, the casein first identified by Berzelius in 1814 and pronounced a protein by Mulder in 1838. Galalith, which was licensed for manufacture throughout Europe under such names as 'Erinoid' and 'Lactoid', gave the Belgian photographic chemist, Leo H. Baekeland (1863–1944), who emigrated to New York in 1889, the idea of experimenting with formaldehyde as a plasticizer.

Synthetic organic chemists had repeatedly reported coming across reactions in which dark-coloured, tarry and resinous-smelling materials, which resisted all attempts at crystallization and molecular weight determination, had been thrown down the sink. By the careful examination of the conditions of one such reaction, between phenol and formaldehyde, Baekeland was able to develop a thermosetting plastic he called 'Bakelite' and which he planned initially to market as a substitute for lac and shellac. When production began in 1910, however, Bakelite found a ready use as an electrical insulator, while its malleability, sturdiness and artistic 'blackness' made it aesthetically appealing for the manufacture of telephones and other household appliances. Colour came during the 1920s with the manufacture of urea-based resins, which could be mixed successfully with pigments.

The plastics age was born in trial and error and the dogged exploitation of well tried chemical reactions on pre-existing natural polymers such as cellulose. The academic study of the chemical structure of these plastic resins, as well as of natural products such as rubber, scarcely began before the 1920s. It was crucially dependent upon the advent of X-ray analysis by the Braggs and of the ultracentrifuge by Svedberg after 1924.

Initially, following the enormous success of Emil Fischer in working out the three-dimensional structures of sugars and proteins, it was supposed that such molecules consisted of long chains of repeated glucose and peptide units aggregated together and bonded by weak intermolecular forces. Although the repetition of a simple unit was a recognition of the polymeric nature of such molecules, including rubber, there was little inkling of their 'macromolecular' nature until the classically trained German organic chemist, Hermann Staudinger (1881–1965), urged this view as a proper deduction from conventional valency theory. Such was the weight of biochemical theoretical presumption of the basic molecular simplicity of these molecules, or 'micelles', however, that Staudinger did not carry the day much before 1930. His supporters, like Herman Mark (*b.* 1895), while disagreeing with him in detail, exploited the growing physical evidence for giant molecules and introduced new ideas, such as those of flexible chains. Mark, who emigrated to America in 1938, went on to create a large and innovative polymer research school at Brooklyn Polytechnic Institute in New York. During the 1930s, American research on free-radical reactions revealed some of the mechanisms of polymer formation, while the brilliant preparative chemist, Carl Marvel (1894–1988), a former associate of Adams at Illinois, became deeply involved in America's synthetic rubber programme and with Du Pont's polymer projects.

American organic chemists proved more receptive than their European competitors to the idea of macromolecules, and so did their industrial companies. Inspired by the obvious success of German industrialization of research, firms such as Du Pont moved away from their founders' interests (in the case of Du Pont, this had been gunpowder manufacture), and found profit and strength in diversi-

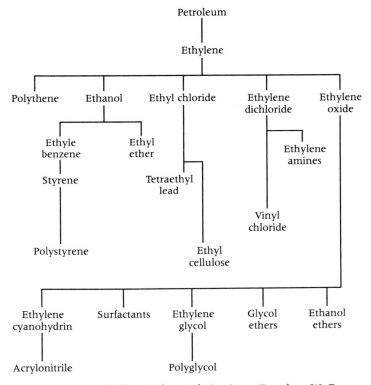

FIGURE 16.2   Ethylene (ethene) derivatives. (Based on W. F. Furter, *History of Chemical Engineering* (Washington, DC: American Chemical Society, 1981), p. 308.)

fication. But this choice made a strong research and development base imperative. In 1928 Du Pont hired one of Roger Adams' associates from the University of Illinois, Wallace H. Carothers (1896–1937). At the company's headquarters in Wilmington, Delaware, Carothers chose polymerization for research. Using exacting standards of purification, Carothers brought fundamental order to the production of polymers by showing that the principal methods of generation were by means of addition and condensation reactions. It was from this fundamental research, in which Paul Flory (1910–85) assisted with physical chemical investigations, that Carothers developed the new polyamide fibre that Du Pont marketed as 'Nylon' in 1938. Although the first industrial scientist ever to be honoured by election to the National Academy of Science, Carothers was prone to depression. Convinced that he was a failure as a scientist, he committed suicide in 1937, two years after formulating nylon:

Nylon was Du Pont's greatest money-spinner; but the industrial process of manufacture from adipic acid and hexamethylenediamine vented enormous volumes of carbon dioxide into the atmosphere. At about the same time, and motivated by the same research imperatives, R. O. Gibson and E. W. Fawcett, working for ICI in England, made the serendipitous discovery of 'Polythene' (polyethylene) while investigating the effects of high pressures on organic materials. Nylon and polythene proved the value of industrial research. After the war, in which both materials played important roles as materials for parachutes and radar insulators respectively, Karl Ziegler (1898–1973) and Giulio Natta (1903–79) developed catalytic methods using transition-metal complexes for making polythene and other similar polymers at atmospheric pressure. The application of these organo-metallic catalysts by the petroleum industry was a key factor in the renaissance of inorganic chemistry in the 1950s (chapter 15).

Since Henry Ford pioneered assembly-line production of petrol-driven motor cars in 1909, America has been a country on wheels. But these wheels were dependent upon expanding supplies of the motor fuel, gasoline (petrol). Following the discovery of petroleum supplies in Pennsylvania and Russia in the 1860s, its chief use had been the distillation fraction that was used as an illuminating oil, paraffin oil or kerosene. Apart from other uses as solvents and lubricating oils, the remaining petroleum light fractions (i.e. those dangerously flammable parts that boiled off below 80°C) were allowed to go to waste. However, with the rise of public electricity supplies in urban areas, sales of kerosene plummeted while there was an increasing demand for the lighter gasolene. Petroleum companies were therefore forced either to search for new sources of oil, or to find ways of increasing the yields of gasolene fractions. The latter path was a stimulus for the development of continuous methods of distillation (as opposed to the time-consuming, messy and wasteful batch method), and the introduction of vacuum distillation technology from the sugar refining industry. The most important consequence, cracking, was of the greatest long-term significance for the diversification of the industry.

Nineteenth-century chemists had found that petroleum was a complicated mixture of paraffins and olefins. The fact that high molecular weight paraffins could be decomposed under heat and pressure ('cracking') to form the lower molecular weight olefins that chiefly gave petrol its desirable properties was first exploited by the Standard Oil Company of Indiana in 1913. Thermal cracking, succeeded by catalytic cracking in the 1940s, enabled the petroleum industry to more than double its output of petrol in the inter-war period. It also led to a greater understanding of petroleum chemistry and to the realization that, as a rich source of reactive olefins, petroleum, like coal, was a potential starting point for the synthesis of other chemicals.

During the 1930s some American chemical firms began to exploit petrochemicals; for example, to prepare ketones as solvents, to produce the automobile engine antifreeze, ethylene glycol, and to make styrene (ethylbenzene) for artificial rubber. European chemical industry remained steadfastly coal-based; indeed, because it was cut off from petroleum supplies, Germany continued to use coal for its chemical industries throughout the Second World War, at which time both Britain and America turned to oil as an additional source of chemicals. This was especially the case for toluene for explosives and styrene for artificial rubber, America's East Asian supplies of natural rubber having been suspended by the Japanese. Synthetic polymer products also found wartime uses that were adaptable to peacetime domestic markets. Even the old alkali trade was affected as traditional soaps gave way to new synthetic detergents. By the 1950s the age of coal had passed (permitting governments the gesture of Clean Air Acts) and the chemical industry had become based upon petroleum and natural gas. Chemistry became a key factor in world politics as the Middle East became identified as the richest source of petroleum. In the US alone, the total production of petrochemicals rose from 500 000 metric tonnes in the 1940s to 200 million tonnes in the 1980s.

As the engineering of the internal combustion engine increased in efficiency, and as air travel became important, so there came a need to purify gasolene by increasing its octane number (an arbitrary scale introduced in 1926 that correlated a fuel's burning efficiency with the amount of iso-octane, $(CH_3)_2CH-CH_2-C(CH_3)_3$, in the sample). Cracking procedures helped in the production of branched-chain paraffins like octane; but it was also found necessary to search for an inhibitor to prevent the formation of straight-chain paraffins like heptane, $CH_3(CH_2)_4CH_3$, which produced severe knocking in engines. After several years of hit-and-miss testing, followed by guidance from the periodic table, the General Motors engineer, Thomas Midgley (1889–1944), found that lead tetraethyl prevented knocking. In order to prevent the lead oxide that was formed in the engine from fouling sparking plugs and valves, ethylene bromide was also added – causing the Dow Chemical Company to expand its production of bromine from salt wells. Marketed initially as 'ethyl gas', the potentially damaging effects of venting volatile lead bromide into the atmosphere were minimized before the 1950s despite several fatalities in the manufacture of lead tetraethyl during the 1920s until adequate safety precautions were taken.

Midgley was also responsible for identifying dichlorodifluoromethane (CCl_2F_2) as a refrigerant that was neither toxic nor flammable (like ammonia and methyl chloride). Fluorine compounds were identified as the most likely candidates for testing as refrigerants not from:

> plottings of boiling points, hunting for data, correlations, slide rules, log paper, eraser dirt, pensil shavings and all the rest of the paraphernalia that takes the place of tea leaves and crystal spheres in the life of the scientific clairvoyant,

as Midgley jokingly pretended, but by once more carefully considering the sequence of physical and chemical properties encapsulated in the periodic table. The chloro-fluorocarbons (CFCs), or 'Freons' (as Du Pont called them), revolutionized refrigeration. They also found application in America's huge air-conditioning industry, as well as in aerosols.

Some thirty years after Midgley's death, in the 1970s, there were reports that lead emitted from combusted petrol was interfering with human health and possibly damaging the development of children's brains; at the same time, CFCs were implicated in the destruction of the earth's ozone layer, causing more ultraviolet light to reach the earth's surface and inducing skin cancers. As Lady Bracknell might have said: 'to invent one environmental hazard may be regarded as a misfortune, to have invented two looks like carelessness'. Yet, of course, at the time, Midgley was showing how chemistry could be exploited to solve particular industrial problems.

CHEMISTRY AND THE ENVIRONMENT

Following the 'success' of the chemical industry during the First World War, which was widely interpreted as 'the chemists' war', the 1920s saw a strong movement to sell chemistry to the public and to the American government. As Du Pont's famous 1935 slogan, 'Better Things for Better Living Through Chemistry', and a huge educational and publishing programme aimed to demonstrate, a new chemical age was dawning. A trade tariff was passed by Congress in 1922 to protect American chemical industry against Germany 'not only as a punishment for their hideous crimes, but as a mark of respect and honor to the men who have given up their lives to the cause of freedom'. In practice this allowed the Chemical Foundation, which under Francis Garvan had become the national repository of the German patents seized by the federal government as war booty, to further the interests of the larger chemical companies and to urge the support of scientific research and development to a greater extent. This did not materialize, of course, as the depression and the high costs of Roosevelt's New Deal carried the day.

Besides launching a number of educational initiatives, like the sponsorship of a *Journal of Chemical Education*, one of the Chemical Foundation's more interesting experiments was its backing for a Chemurgic Farm Council that had been set up by a Dow Company chemist, William J. Hale, in 1934. Hale had coined the term 'chemurgy', meaning chemistry at work, in the same year, though the ideas went back to the 1920s. Chemurgy's purpose was to use surplus farm produce to furnish raw materials for chemical industry, namely to exploit what Hale called Nature's three musketeers, cellulose, vegetable oil and alcohol ('Agrol'). According to Hale, the replacement of the horse by the internal combustion engine, which did not use cellulose and which produced no useful fertilizer, had wrecked the agricultural cycle. Hence the agricultural depression. If America were to exploit the potential of chemurgy, it would return to a natural recycling pattern and solve the depressed state of American farming, render America self-sufficient and, in by-passing the need for any foreign trade [*sic*], it need never again be involved in European wars.

Although some of the ideas of the chemurgists were investigated by the Board of Agriculture and are reflected in the continuing importance of fermentation processes, the power of the automobile lobby, the refusal of the Republicans to adopt the Farm Council's policies, the death of Garvan in 1937, and the demise of the Foundation's monopoly of patents in the late 1930s, all told against it. By 1938 the chemurgic movement had all but disappeared – to reappear, in a different context, as the Green movement in the 1960s. In any case, the advent of the Second World War eliminated the problems of farm surpluses and unemployment as far as America was concerned. Arguably, however, as the physicists emerged from the war covered in glory, the chemical community has never regained the bright and attractive image it had during the 1920s and 1930s.

For with the petroleum chemists' synthetic success and prowess in providing housewares, processing foods, devising new medicines, beautifying gardens and decors and increasing agricultural yields, came the side effects of pollution and danger and the whole question of cost–benefit. In 1962 the natural history writer, Rachel Carson (1907–64), drew attention to the long-term effects of the introduction into the ecosphere of synthetic chemicals like pesticides[10]:

TABLE 16.1   *Chemists and the environment.*

1947 Aluminium nitrate fire in ship moored in Texas City harbour causes explosions at adjacent Monsanto styrene polymer plant. Many deaths

1950 US House of Representatives investigates 850 chemicals used in food processing. Substances found carcinogenic in animals to be banned

1961 Thalidomide found to cause birth deformities

1962 Rachel Carson publishes *Silent Spring*

1965 ACS issues 'The Chemist's Creed'; use of 'Agent Orange' in Vietnam War 1965–75

1968 Lake Erie pronounced dead from pollution

1970 On 22 April, 20 million people observe first 'Earth Day'

1971 Establishment of Environmental Protection Agency (EPA) in USA; 'Dow shall not kill' protests on US university campuses against Dow's manufacture of napalm

1972 EPA bans DDT; acid rain identified

1974 Reports that CFCs destroy ozone layer; ICI's caprolactam (nylon) works explodes at Flixborough

1976 US Toxic Substances Act: all chemicals in commercial use to be tested; Givaudan-La Roche pesticides plant at Seveso, Italy, releases dioxins

1978 Toxic leak from chemical dump owned by Occident Chemical Company at Niagara; EPA long-term ban on aerosols

1979 Radiation leak at Three Mile Island, Harrisburg, Pennsylvania

1980 Several reports on effects of lead in the environment

1983 Times Beach, Missouri, evacuated after dioxin leak

1984 Union Carbide plant at Bhopal, India, releases 30 tonnes of methyl isocyanate and kills 2500 people; hole in ozone shield announced

1986 Acid rain from coal burning causes concern in Europe and Canada; Chernobyl nuclear power plant explosion

1987 Some 24 countries agree to freeze production of CFCs (Montreal Protocol)

1988 US Federal law to test all pesticides for toxicity; UK signs directive agreeing on 60 per cent reduction of SO_2 emissions by 2003

1990 UK Food and Environment Protection Act

1992 Earth Summit at Rio de Janeiro

By their very nature chemical controls [of pests] are self-defeating, for they have been devised and applied without taking into account the complex biological systems against which they have been blindly hurled. . . . The balance of nature is not the same today as in Pleistocene times, but it is still there: a complex, precise, and highly integrated system of relationships between living things which cannot be ignored any more than the law of gravity can be defeated with impunity by a man perched on the edge of a cliff. The balance of nature is not a *status quo*; it is fluid, ever shifting, in a constant state of adjustment. Man, too, is part of this balance. Sometimes the balance is in his favor; sometimes – and all too often through his own activities – it is shifted to his disadvantage.

The reaction to *Silent Spring* was immediate and world-wide. An Environmental Protection Agency (EPA) was established in the USA to monitor the effects of a number of laws passed to protect air, water, soil plants and animals endangered by the presence of the chemicals that were being produced by humankind. Twenty-five years later, in 1987, in a symposium 'Silent Spring Revisited', it was clear that Carson's influence had led to technologies being assessed in terms of benefits weighed against risks, rather than for benefits alone, and that governments worldwide were concerned with legislation to ensure (though not to guarantee) human safety.

As the historian of technology, Melvin Kranzberg, has explained, 'technology is neither good nor bad' in itself. This does not mean that it is neutral[11]:

> Many of our technology-related problems arise because of unforeseen consequences when apparently benign techniques are employed on a massive scale. Hence many technical applications that seemed a boon to mankind when first introduced become threats when their use becomes widespread.

The most spectacularly awful consequence of long-term ignorance in the 1950s was the administration of thalidomide ($C_{13}H_{10}N_{10}O_4$) as a sedative to prevent nausea during pregnancy. Although the *dextro* form of the drug is safe and effective, the *laevo* form present in the unresolved drug turned out to be a mutagen, and had to be banned in 1961.

Sequestrants, emulsifiers, stabilizers, buffers, surfactants, preservatives, E-numbers and flavouring agents have for many people 'become the best appetite suppressants since cod-liver oil and potassium permanganate'. Half the problem is one of language, and therefore of education. A spicy dish of peppers, courgettes, onion and tomatoes, bound with eggs and cheese, flavoured with cumin, cinnamon and cayenne, and served with a cucumber and yoghurt salad, sounds a delicious summer recipe. The chemists' version of denatured proteins, polypeptides, amino acids, mono-, di- and polysaccharides, cellulose, cholesterol (the bugbear of the 'Uesanians'), linoleic, linolenic, arachidonic (good heavens, spiders!), lactic, propionic and butyric acids, oleic and palmitic triglycerides, lecithin, retinol, calciferol, phytomenadione, cobalamin, ascorbic acid, *para*-isopropylbenzaldehyde, capsaicin and cinnamaldehyde, besides being very long-winded, also sounds a lethal cocktail.

Given that financial support for 'pure science' is now closely geared to the needs and priorities of governments and commercial industries, sociologists of science agree that science can no longer claim neutrality. As far as moral accountability is concerned, neither academic nor industrial chemists can separate basic research from its applications and consequences. Faced by poor ratings in the public estimation, by diminishing recruitment of students to read chemistry at university, and by the continuing vociferous concerns with the effects of chemistry on safety, health and the environment, American chemical firms have recently launched a 'Responsibility Care Program'. In future, only manufacturers who agree,

> constantly and continuously to improve performance
> – *no matter what base they start from* – through the
> implementation of a series of codes of performance
> objectives addressing community awareness and
> emergency response, pollution prevention, process
> safety, employee health and safety, distribution and
> product stewardship

will be allowed membership of the American Chemical Manufacturers' Association. In the wake of forthcoming legislation by the European Community involving the civil liability of the chemical industry, it also appears that European chemical manufacturers will overhaul their operations and improve the environmental impact of their businesses.

While the repair of the chemical industry's image, and of chemistry itself, is a performance challenge for the 1990s, it is clearly also one of historical awareness. As an editorial in the *Beckman Center News* put it recently[12]:

> Our chemical heritage – the record of our achievements and our shortcomings – has a vital role to play in developing a more adequate public understanding of science. The past must be preserved, deployed, and made known. We all – whether Chief Executive officers, chemical scientists, school teachers, or representatives of the media – need a better understanding of the human dimensions of the chemical sciences. Chemical history, our chemical heritage, can help inform our decision making. A positive view of the past chemical achievements will lend a modest but firm realism to our plans for the future.

The 'sign of the hexagon' points forwards and backwards. 'In my beginning is my end; in my end is my beginning.'

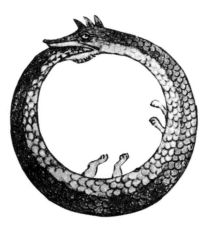

Epilogue

Organic chemistry before Kekulé spread his wings was like a merrily splashing torrent; there were so many stones in the water that one could still cross it without getting wet. Today, the torrent has become a deep and massive stream; the eye can hardly see the opposite bank, and proud, richly loaded fleets rock gently on its broad surface.

With the concept of the benzene ring the number of organic compounds all at once seems, one might almost say, to have increased to infinity. In the benzene nucleus we have been given a soil out of which we can see with surprise the already-known realm of organic chemistry multiply, not once or twice but three, four or six times just like an equivalent number of trees. What an amount of work had suddenly become necessary, and how quickly were busy hands found to carry it out! First the eye moves up the six stems opening out from the tremendous benzene trunk. But already the branches of neighbouring stems have become intertwined, and a canopy of leaves has developed which becomes more spacious as the giant soars upwards into the air. The top of the tree rises into the clouds where the eye cannot yet follow it. And to what an extent is this wonderful benzene tree thronged with blossoms! Everywhere in the sea of leaves one can spy the slender hydroxyl bud; hardly rarer is the forked blossom which we call the amine group, the most frequent is the beautiful crossed-shaped blossom we call the methyl group. And inside this embellishment of blossoms, what a richness of fruit, some of them shining in a wonderful blaze of colour, others giving off an almost overwhelming fragrance! Understandably, there is also no dearth of industrious workers busily striving to collect the harvest. Keen climbers have already clambered up to the third or fourth branch; some of them we can see working at a dizzy height. Most of them, however, are in the bottom branches of the benzene tree. Some have collected enough and are about to get down, others still cannot separate themselves from the rich harvest, and yet others are quarreling with their neighbours about the harvest . . .

(A. W. HOFMANN, speech at the Kekulé 'Benzolfest', 1890)

APPENDIX

History of Chemistry Museums and Collections

This partial listing draws upon and updates John H. Wotiz, 'Chemistry museums of Europe', *ChemTech* (April 1982): 221–8 and J. W. van Spronsen, *A Guide of* [sic] *European Museums and Expositions on Chemistry and History of Chemistry* (Budapest, 1981).

AUSTRALIA
Sydney

Powerhouse, Museum of Applied Arts and Sciences: Australian phytochemistry

AUSTRIA
Vienna

Technisches Museum (Mariahilferstrasse 212), Welsbach and rare earths chemistry

BELGIUM
Ghent

Museum for Science and Technology (Korte Meer 9): Kekulé's laboratory equipment

CZECHOSLOVAKIA
Prague

The Little Gold Street, Hradčany Castle: alchemy

DENMARK
Copenhagen

Carlsberg Brewery Laboratory (Gamle Carlsbergvej 10): work of Kjeldahl, Sørensen, etc.

FRANCE
Dole Maison Natale de Pasteur (Rue de Couveil): Pasteur

Paris Conservatoire Naturelle des Arts et Métiers (292 rue Saint Martin): Lavoisier's apparatus
Pierre et Marie Curie Museum (11 rue Pierre et Marie Curie): radioactivity
Pasteur Museum, Institut Pasteur (25 rue du Docteur Roux): Pasteur mausoleum and apparatus
La Villette (211 Avenue Jean Javres): chemistry galleries of National Museum of Science and Industry

GERMANY
Berlin Humboldt University, Nernst Museum of Physical Chemistry

Darmstadt Technische Hochschule, Kekulé Sammlung (Peterstrasse 22): Kekulé exhibit and archive

Giessen Liebig Museum (Liebigstrasse 12): Liebig's laboratories

Göttingen Museum der Göttingen Chemie, Institute of Inorganic Chemistry, Göttingen University: Wöhler and other Göttingen chemists

Grossbothen Haus Energie, Wilhelm Ostwald Museum

Heidelberg Deutsches Apotheken Museum, Heidelberg Castle: German pharmacy

Höchst Höchst Company Museum (Schlossplatz): dyestuffs history

Munich Deutsches Museum (Museum Insel): chemical galleries

GREAT BRITAIN
Edinburgh Royal Scottish Museum (Chambers Street): apparatus of Black, Playfair and others

London	Royal Institution (21 Albemarle Street): Faraday, Frankland apparatus Science Museum (Exhibition Road): chemistry and industrial galleries University College London, Chemistry Department (20 Gordon Street): Ramsay, etc.
Manchester	Greater Manchester Museum of Science and Industry (Liverpool Road Station): Dalton, Frankland, Roscoe
Oxford	Museum of History of Science (Broad Street): Moseley, glyptic formulae, etc.
St Andrews	Chemistry Department, John Read Collection: alchemy, balances, sugar derivatives
Widnes	Catalyst, Museum of Chemical Industry: alkali industry

ITALY
Como	Volta Museum (Viale Marconi): Volta and electrolysis

RUSSIA
St Petersburg	Mendeleev Museum (Universitetskaya nab. 3): periodic law

SWEDEN
Stockholm	Berzelius Museum (Lilla Frescativ 4): Berzelius' apparatus

SWITZERLAND
Basel	Swiss Museum of History of Pharmacy (Totengaesslein): Paracelsus and pharmacy
Zürich	Zürich University, Inorganic Chemistry Institute (Winterthurerstrasse): Werner

USA

Cincinnati, Ohio	University of Cincinnati, Chemistry Department, Oesper Laboratory: books, instruments, laboratory displays
Leominster, Mass.	National Plastics Museum: polymer history
Lexington, Ky.	Transylvania University: early chemical apparatus
Midland, Mich.	Dow Museum: career of Herbert Dow, and company history
Northumberland, Pa.	Joseph Priestley House: laboratory and home
Philadelphia, Pa.	Beckman Center for History of Chemistry (Divinity School, Walnut Street): library, instruments, archives, oral histories
Washington, DC	Smithsonian Institution, National Museum of American History: electrical gallery
Wilmington, Del.	Du Pont Museum: history of the company

NOTES

INTRODUCTION
1 Hermann Kopp, *Die Entwicklung der Chemie in der neueren Zeit* (Munich, 1873), p. ix.

CHAPTER 1
1 Justus von Liebig, *Familiar Letters* (1859), p. 53.
2 W. Ganzenmuller in Jost Weyer, 'The Image of Alchemy in 19th and 20th century Histories of Chemistry', *Ambix*, **23** (1976): 75.
3 E. J. Sheppard, *Ambix*, **17** (1970): 69–84; and in C. Meinel (ed.), *Die Alchemie in der europaischen Kultur- und Wissenschaftsgeschichte* (Wiesbaden: Harrassowitz, 1986).
4 William Newman, *The Summa Perfectionis of Pseudo-Geber* (Leiden: E. J. Brill, 1991), p. 40.
5 A. R. Butler and J. Needham, *Ambix*, **27** (1980): 69–76.
6 Vannoccio Biringuccio, *Pirotechnia* (1540); transl. in C. S. Smith and M. T. Gnudi, *The Pirotechnia* (New York: Basic Books, 1942), p. 40.

7 J. R. Partington, *A History of Chemistry* (London: Macmillan, 1962–70), vol. 2, p. 428.
8 B. J. T. Dobbs, *The Foundations of Newton's Alchemy* (Cambridge: Cambridge University Press, 1975), p. 3.
9 Frederick Soddy (1917); see G. B. Kauffman, 'The Role of Gold in Alchemy', *Gold Bulletin*, **18** (1985): 118.

CHAPTER 2
1 Marie Boas, 'An Early Version of the *Sceptical Chymist*', *Isis*, **45** (1954): 153–68.
2 Yung Sik Kim, 'Another Look at Robert Boyle's Acceptance of the Mechanical Philosophy', *Ambix*, **38** (1991): 8.
3 See A. G. Debus, *Annals of Science*, **23** (1967): 144.
4 See J. R. Partington, *A History of Chemistry* (London: Macmillan, 1962–70), vol. 2, p. 639.

CHAPTER 3
1 A. L. Lavoisier (1772); see M. Fichman, 'French Stahlism and Chemical

Studies of Air', *Ambix*, **18** (1971): 121.
2 A. L. Lavoisier (1773); see J. B. Gough, in H. Woolf (ed.), *The Analytic Spirit* (Ithaca, NY: Cornell University Press, 1981).
3 See M. Fichman, *Ambix*, **18** (1971): 118.
4 See H. Guerlac, *Lavoisier, the Crucial Year* (Ithaca, NY: Cornell University Press, 1961), p. 227.
5 See R. Siegfried, *Isis*, **63** (1972): 74.
6 A. L. Lavoisier (1779); see M. P. Crosland, *Isis*, **64** (1973): 307.
7 E. B. Condillac (1781); A. L. Lavoisier (1790), p. xiii.

CHAPTER 4
1 A. L. Lavoisier (1790), p. xxiv.
2 J. Dalton, *A New System of Chemical Philosophy* (Manchester, 1808), p. 216.
3 J. Dalton (1803); see F. Greenaway, *John Dalton and the Atom* (London: Heinemann, 1966), p. 130.
4 J. Dalton (1811); see A. Thackray, *Isis*, **57** (1966): 42.
5 H. Davy (1808); see C. A. Russell, *Annals of Science*, **15** (1959): 16.
6 See J. R. Partington, *A History of Chemistry* (London: Macmillan, 1962–70), vol. 4, p. 42.
7 See D. S. L. Cardwell (ed.), *John Dalton and the Progress of Science* (Manchester:

Manchester University Press, 1968), p. 261.
8 See W. H. Brock, *From Protyle to Proton* (Bristol: Adam Hilger, 1985), p. 105.
9 See D. S. L. Cardwell, *op.cit.*, p. 268.

CHAPTER 5
1 F. Szabadváry, *History of Analytical Chemistry* (Oxford: Pergamon, 1966), p. 5.
2 See J. S. Fruton, *Contrasts in Scientific Style* (Philadelphia: American Philosophical Society, 1990), p. 68.
3 See F. Szabadváry, *op.cit.*, p. 176.

CHAPTER 6
1 A. Laurent, *Méthode de chimie* (Paris, 1854), preface.
2 A. Laurent, Thesis (1837); see N. W. Fisher, *Ambix*, **20** (1973): 118.

CHAPTER 7
1 F. A. Kekulé (1859); see N. W. Fisher, *Ambix*, **21** (1974): 37.
2 F. A. Kekulé (1857).
3 F. A. Kekulé (1858); see J. R. Partington, *A History of Chemistry* (London: Macmillan, 1962–70), vol. 4, p. 536.

CHAPTER 8
1 J. Black, *Lectures on the Elements of Chemistry* (Edinburgh, 1803), vol. i, p. 547.
2 W. Cullen (*c.* 1766); see A. L. Donovan, *Philosophical*

Chemistry in the Scottish Enlightenment (Edinburgh: Edinburgh University Press, 1975), p. 98.

3 W. Cullen (*c.* 1766); see A. L. Donovan, *ibid.*, p. 107.

4 C. C. Gillispie, *Isis*, **48** (1957): 153.

5 J. R. Partington, *The Alkali Industry* (London, 1919), p. 2.

6 R. Blatchford, *Dismal England* (1899), p. 15.

CHAPTER 9

1 D. Mendeleev, *Principles of Chemistry* (1902 [1905]), vol. i, p. xvii.

2 F. Paneth, *Angewandte Chemie*, **37** (1924): 421.

3 W. Ramsay, *Gases of the Atmosphere* (1896), p. 193.

4 H. Moseley, *Philosophical Magazine*, **26** (1913): 1024.

5 H. Roscoe, *Reports of the British Association for the Advancement of Science* (1887): 10.

6 See B. Bensaude-Vincent, *British Journal for the History of Science*, **19** (1986): 7.

7 See H. M. Leicester, *Journal of Chemical Education*, **34** (1957): 333.

8 See H. M. Leicester, *Chymia*, **1** (1948): 70.

CHAPTER 10

1 M. J. Nye, *Science in the Provinces* (Berkeley: University of California Press, 1986), p. 82.

2 See M. J. Nye, *ibid.*, p. 109.

3 See H. C. Jones, *The Theory*

of Electrolytic Dissociation (London and New York, 1900), p. 78.

4 See R. G. A. Dolby, *Historical Studies in the Physical Sciences*, **7** (1976): 389.

5 See A. J. Ihde, *Chemistry as Viewed from Bascom's Hill* (Madison, Wis.: Department of Chemistry, University of Wisconsin, 1990), p. 322.

CHAPTER 11

1 E. Frankland, *Lecture Notes for Chemical Students* (1866), preface.

2 See B. Gee and W. H. Brock, *Ambix*, **38** (1991): 29–62.

3 See J. C. Slater, *Introduction to Chemical Physics* (New York, 1939), p. viii.

4 See H. S. Van Klooster, *Chymia*, **2** (1949): 9.

CHAPTER 12

1 J. Liebig (1834); see Jakob Volhard, *Justus von Liebig* (Leipzig, 1909), vol. i, p. 326.

2 See *Chemical News*, **3** (1861): 1–2.

3 See *Nature*, **130** (1932): 603.

CHAPTER 13

1 L. Pauling, *The Nature of the Chemical Bond* (Ithaca, NY: Cornell University Press, 1939), p. vii.

2 See J. W. Servos, *Physical Chemistry in America from Ostwald to Pauling* (Princeton, NJ: Princeton University Press, 1990), p. 310.

3 E. Frankland, *Journal of the Chemical Society*, **19** (1866): 377.

4 See J. W. Servos, *op.cit.*, p. 119.

5 See J. W. Servos, *Journal of Chemical Education*, **61** (1984): 6.

6 J. H. Hildebrand, 'G. N. Lewis', *Biographical Memoirs of the National Academy of Sciences*, **31** (1958): 212.

7 G. N. Lewis, *Journal of the American Chemical Society*, **35** (1913): 1448–55.

8 G. N. Lewis, *Valence and the Structure of Atoms and Molecules* (New York, 1923), p. 30.

9 See W. B. Jensen, 'Abegg, Lewis, Langmuir and the Octet Rule', *Journal of Chemical Education*, **61** (1984): 196.

10 G. N. Lewis, *op.cit.* (1923), p. 53.

11 G. N. Lewis, *op.cit.* (1923), p. 79.

12 L. Pauling, *Daedelus*, **99** (1970): 988.

13 L. Pauling, *ibid.* (1970): 1005.

14 R. S. Mulliken (1964); see D. A. Ramsay and J. Hinze (eds), *Selected Papers of Robert S. Mulliken* (Chicago: University of Chicago Press, 1975), p. 9.

15 R. Paradowski, *The Structural Chemistry of Linus Pauling*, Ph.D. Thesis, University of Wisconsin, 1972, p. 549.

CHAPTER 14

1 J. H. S. Green in J. H. Ridd, *Studies on Chemical Structure and Reactivity* (London: Methuen, 1966), p. 269.

2 A. Lapworth, *Journal of the Chemical Society* (1898): 445.

3 See M. D. Saltzman, *Natural Products Chemistry*, **4** (1987): 54.

4 R. and G. Robinson, *Journal of the Chemical Society* (1917): 962.

5 A. Lapworth, *Journal of the Chemical Society* (1922): 423.

6 W. O. Kermack and R. Robinson, *Journal of the Chemical Society* (1922): 121.

7 See M. D. Saltzman, *Journal of Chemical Education*, **57** (1980): 487.

8 See T. I. Williams, *Robert Robinson. Chemist Extraordinary* (Oxford: Clarendon, 1990), p. 80.

9 See M. D. Saltzman, *op.cit.* (1980): 488.

10 H. E. Armstrong, *Journal of the Society of the Chemical Industry* (22 February 1929): 196.

11 C. K. Ingold, *Biographical Memoirs of the Royal Society*, **10** (1964): 154.

12 L. P. Hammett, *Journal of Chemical Education*, **43** (1966): 467.

13 M. D. Saltzman, *Journal of Chemical Education*, **63** (1986): 593.

14 C. K. Ingold, *Structure and Mechanism in Organic Chemistry* (Ithaca, NY: Cornell University Press, 1953), p. 167.

15 M. J. S. Dewar, *The*

Electronic Theory of Organic Chemistry (1949), p. 161.

16 J. D. Roberts, *The Right Place at the Right Time* (Washington, DC: American Chemical Society, 1990), p. 89.

CHAPTER 15

1 G. B. Kauffman, *Classics in Coordination Chemistry* (New York: Dover, 1968), p. 80.

2 See C. A. Russell, *The History of Valency* (Leicester: Leicester University Press, 1971), p. 207.

3 G. B. Kauffman, *op.cit.*, p. 82.

4 G. B. Kauffman, *op.cit.*, p. 115.

5 L. E. Sutton, *Proceedings of the Chemical Society* (1958): 314.

6 N. V. Sidgwick, *The Electronic Theory of Valency* (Oxford, 1927), p. 112.

7 N. V. Sidgwick, *ibid.*, p. 218.

8 See I. D. Rae in R. M. MacLeod (ed.), *The Commonwealth of Science* (Oxford: Oxford University Press, 1988), p. 171.

9 D. Craig, *Biographical Memoirs of the Royal Society*, **18** (1972): 457.

10 R. Nyholm, *The Renaissance of Inorganic Chemistry* (London, 1956).

11 R. Nyholm, *ibid.*

12 See D. Craig, *op.cit.*, p. 450.

CHAPTER 16

1 M. Berthelot, *Chimie organique fondée sur la synthèse* (Paris, 1860), p. xxv; see C. A. Russell,

Ambix, **34** (1987): 177.

2 D. S. Tarbell and A. T. Tarbell, *Roger Adams, Scientist and Statesman* (Washington, DC: American Chemical Society, 1981), p. 54.

3 C. Djerassi, Interview (1985); typescript in Beckman Center for the History of Chemistry, Philadelphia.

4 See 'An interview with Lord Todd', *Chemistry in Britain*, **10** (1974): 211.

5 D. J. Cram, *From Design to Discovery* (Washington, DC: American Chemical Society, 1990), p. 7.

6 R. B. Woodward, in *Pointers and Pathways in Research* (Bombay: CIBA of India, 1963), p. 21.

7 See J. Donnelly, *Annals of Science*, **45** (1988): 562.

8 W. Crookes, *Reports of the British Association for the Advancement of Science* (1898): 4.

9 L. F. Haber, *The Chemical Industry, 1900–1930* (Oxford: Clarendon, 1971), p. 91.

10 R. Carson, *Silent Spring* (London: Hamish Hamilton, 1963), p. 246.

11 M. Kranzberg, in S. H. Cutliffe and R. C. Post, *In Context. History and the History of Technology* (Bethlehem, PA: Lehigh University Press, 1989), p. 245.

12 Editorial, *Beckman Center for the History of Science News*, **9** (1992), spring.

BIBLIOGRAPHICAL ESSAY

Places of publication are London unless cited otherwise. Publishers' names are given only for books published after 1960, unless they are of historical interest.

Of continuing value are the untranslated works of Hermann Kopp, *Geschichte der Chemie*, 4 vols (Braunschweig, 1843–7) and *Die Entwicklung der Chemie in der neueren Zeit* (Munich, 1873); but for most purposes English readers will use James Riddick Partington, *A History of Chemistry*, 4 vols (Macmillan, 1962–70). The second part of vol. 1, on Arabic and medieval chemistry, was not published. Partington's survey, which curiously ignores Kopp, effectively stops at about 1920, but can be complemented by the readable and accurate *The Development of Modern Chemistry* (New York: Harper and Row, 1964) by Aaron J. Ihde, which also contains a comprehensive bibliography. Note also Dean Stanley Tarbell and Tracy Tarbell, *The History of Organic Chemistry in the United States, 1875–1955* (Nashville, Tenn.: Folio Publishers, 1986) and C. A. Russell, *The Structure of Chemistry, Units 1–3* (Milton Keynes: Open University Press, 1976).

An excellent guide to secondary literature and to reprints of historically important original papers and books is C. A. Russell (ed.), *Recent Developments in the History of Chemistry* (Royal Society of Chemistry, 1985). For the archives of the chemical industry, see C. A. Russell and P. J. T. Morris, *Archives of the British Chemical Industry, 1750–1914. A Handlist* (British Society for the History of Science, 1988) and George D. Tselos and Colleen Wickey, *A Guide to Archives and Manuscript Collections in the History of Chemistry and Chemical Technology* [in the USA] (Philadelphia: Beckman Center, 1987). Note also Robert P. Multhauf, *The History of Chemical Technology. An Annotated Bibliography* (New York: Garland, 1984).

Although articles on the history of chemistry appear regularly in history of science journals such as *Annals of Science*, the *British Journal for the History of Science* and *Isis*, the subject has its own periodicals in *Ambix* (the journal of the Society for the History of Alchemy and Chemistry, which has appeared since 1937), the *Bulletin of the History of Chemistry* (American Chemical Society, from 1988), the *Beckman Newsletter for the History of Chemistry* (National Foundation for the History of Chemistry, Philadelphia, from 1982; formerly *Center for the History of Chemistry Newsletter*); and *Mitteilungen* (Fachgruppe Geschichte der Chemie der Gesellschaft Deutscher Chemiker, Frankfurt, from 1988). Note especially the annual bibliography published in the *Bulletin*. Since its foundation in 1923, the *Journal of Chemical Education* has been a leading repository of historical articles by chemists and high-school teachers. Pre-war issues in particular contain valuable photographs of European chemical buildings and statues that were subsequently destroyed.

Recent histories of chemistry include Helene Metzger, *Chemistry* (West Cornwall, Conn.: Locust Hill Press, 1991; transl. from French edn. of 1930); Roman Mierzecki, *The Historical Development of Chemical Concepts* (Dordrecht: Reidel, 1991; transl. from Polish edn. of 1985); Hugh W. Salzberg, *From Caveman to Chemist* (Washington, DC: American Chemical Society, 1991); Fred Aftalion, *A History of the International Chemical Industry* (Philadelphia: University of Pennsylvania Press, 1991); David M. Knight, *Ideas in Chemistry. A History of the Science* (Athlone Press, 1992); and John Hudson, *The History of Chemistry* (Basingstoke: Macmillan, 1992).

CHAPTER 1

The integration of the activities of early artisans and technologists, natural philosophers and alchemists is the subject of an exemplary study by Robert P. Multhauf, *The Origins of Chemistry* (Oldbourne, 1966). The origins and development of applied chemistry are surveyed comprehensively from literary sources in J. R. Partington, *Origins and Development of Applied Chemistry* (1935). Archaeological insights first opened up by M.

676 · *Bibliographical Essay*

Berthelot, *Archéologie et histoire des sciences* (Paris, 1906) have been continued in the multi-volumed *Studies in Ancient Technology* (Leyden, 1955) by J. R. Forbes; Martin Levey, *Chemistry and Chemical Technology of Ancient Mesopotamia* (Amsterdam, 1959); F. Tylecote, *A History of Metallurgy* (Institute of Metals, 1976; 2nd edn. 1990); and R. Halleux, *Le probleme des metaux dans la science antique* (Paris: Société d'Édition 'Les Belles Lettres', 1974). Because of its later importance, much attention has been paid to the surviving archaeological and manuscript evidence for distillation. See Forbes (1955); F. S. Taylor, 'The Evolution of the Still', *Annals of Science*, **5** (1945): 183–202; L. Gwei-Djen, J. Needham and D. Needham, 'The Coming of Ardent Water', *Ambix*, **19** (1972): 69–112; and A. R. Butler and J. Needham, 'An Experimental Comparison of the East Asian, Hellenistic and Indian (Gandharan) Stills in Relation to the Distillation of Ethanol and Acetic Acid', *Ambix*, **27** (1980): 69–76.

Multhauf (1966) provides a good overview of the matter theories of the Artistotelians and atomists, while more specialized treatments are available by S. Sambursky, *The Physical World of the Greeks* (1956); E. J. Dijksterhuis, *The Mechanization of the World Picture* (Oxford: Clarendon, 1961); and J. E. Bolzan, 'Chemical Combination According to Aristotle', *Ambix*, **23** (1976): 133–44. There are very readable studies by G. E. R. Lloyd, *Early Greek Science. Thales to Aristotle* (Chatto and Windus, 1970); *Greek Science after Aristotle* (Chatto and Windus, 1973); and *Aristotle: The Growth and Structure of his Thought* (Cambridge: Cambridge University Press, 1968). The continuity of Aristotle's thought in chemistry from the Greeks to nineteenth-century crystallography is wonderfully conveyed in Norma E. Emerton, *The Scientific Reinterpretation of Form* (Ithaca, NY: Cornell University Press, 1984). For a readable English version of Lucretius, *De rerum natura*, see *The Nature of the Universe*, trans. by R. E. Latham (Penguin Classics, 1951, etc.).

The first volume of J. R. Partington's *History of Chemistry* (Macmillan, 1970), which was published posthumously, is unhelpful, but its place is handsomely filled by the fifth 'volume' (in ten parts), *Chemistry and Chemical Technology*, of Joseph

Needham's ambitious survey of *Science and Civilisation in China:* Part 1, *Paper and Printing* (Cambridge: Cambridge University Press, 1985); Part 2, *Spagyrical Discovery and Invention. Magisteries of Gold and Immortality* (Cambridge: Cambridge University Press, 1974) deals with alchemy and includes a magnificent eighty-three-page bibliography of books and articles in western languages; Part 3, *Spagyrical Discovery and Invention. Historical Survey from Cinnabar to Elixirs to Synthetic Insulin* (Cambridge: Cambridge University Press, 1976) is a general survey of Chinese chemistry from antiquity to the twentieth century; Part 4, *Spagyrical Discovery and Invention. Apparatus, Theories and Gifts* (Cambridge: Cambridge University Press, 1980) deals particularly with chemical apparatus; Part 5, *Spagyrical Discovery and Invention. Physiological Alchemy,* is concerned with physiological chemistry; Part 6, unpublished, will deal with the art of war; Part 7, *Military Technology. The Gunpowder Epic*; Part 8, unpublished, will be about weaponry; Part 9, *Textile Technology. Spinning and Reeling*; and Part 10, unpublished, will complete the survey of textile chemistry. Because of its readability, bibliographical strength and extensive digressions into, and discussions of, western alchemy, Needham and his collaborators have provided by far the most interesting, comprehensive and exciting account of pre-seventeenth-century chemistry available.·

Thomas Norton's *Ordinall* (c. 1477) was first printed in English by Elias Ashmole in his *Theatrum Chemicum Britannicum* (1652) and was re-edited by E. J. Holmyard as *The Ordinall of Alchemy* (1928), and by John Reidy for the Early English Text Society (Oxford University Press, 1975). It had first appeared in a Latin translation, *Crede mihi seu*, in 1618 and was reprinted in Latin in the famous compilation of alchemical texts, *Musaeum Hermeticum* (Frankfurt, 1625). The latter was translated into English by the occultist, A. E. Waite, as *The Hermetic Museum Restored and Enlarged* (2 vols, 1893), but only 250 copies were printed. For the translation of Biringuccio, see C. S. Smith and M. T. Gnudi, *The Pirotechnia* (New York: Basic Books, 1942; reprint 1959).

The literature on alchemy is enormous. Especially recommended are Needham (1974 and 1976); A. Coudert, *Alchemy.*

The Philosopher's Stone (Wildwood House, 1980); R. Halleux, *Les textes alchimiques* (Turnhout, Belgium: Brepols, 1979), which provides a balance sheet of current scholarship and a list of unresolved historical problems; and A. Pritchard, *Alchemy. A Bibliography of English-Language Writings* (London: Routledge and Kegan Paul, 1980). E. J. Sheppard's universalist definition of alchemy is found in his 'Alchemy. Origin or Origins', *Ambix*, **17** (1970): 69–84, and finalized in an essay in C. Meinel (ed.), *Die Alchemie in der europaischen Kultur- und Wissenschaftsgeschichte* (Wiesbaden: Harrassowitz, 1986). Note also Marcel Eliarde, *The Forge and the Crucible* (New York: Rider, 1962; reprint, Chicago: Chicago University Press, 1978). The traditionalist view of alchemy as a religious and spiritual quest is examined in Carl Jung, *Psychology and Alchemy* (Routledge and Kegan Paul, 1953) and sumptuously illustrated in J. Fabricius, *Alchemy. The Medieval Alchemists and their Royal Art* (Copenhagen: Rosenkilde and Bagger, 1976). Note also L. H. Martin, 'A History of the Psychological Interpretation of Alchemy', *Ambix*, **22** (1975): 10–20. G. B. Kauffman, 'The Role of Gold in Alchemy', *Gold Bulletin*, **18** (1985): 31–44, 69–78, 109–19, contains a wealth of references and useful information on post-1850 developments. New insights are provided in Z. von Martels (ed.), *Alchemy Revisited* (Leiden: E. J. Brill, 1990). For the origins of the word 'chemistry', see A. J. Rocke, 'Agricola, Paracelsus and Chymia', *Ambix*, **32** (1985): 37–43.

Greco-Roman-Egyptian alchemy is examined in F. S. Taylor, *The Alchemists* (New York: Schuman, 1949; London: Heinemann, 1952; reprint, New York: Arno, 1974) and in the stimulating study, A. J. Hopkins, *Alchemy, Child of Greek Philosophy* (New York, 1934; reprint, New York: AMS, 1967). A scholarly edition of Greek texts, *Les alchimistes grecs*, edited and translated into French, was begun in 1981. Islamic alchemy is best approached through the writings of Eric J. Holmyard, for which see his *Alchemy* (Hardmondsworth: Penguin, 1957; reprint 1968); and William Newman, *The Summa Perfectionis of Pseudo-Geber* (Leiden: E. J. Brill, 1991). For Chinese alchemy, see the aforementioned studies by Needham, and Nathan Sivin, *Chinese Alchemy. Preliminary Studies* (Cambridge, Mass.:

MIT Press, 1968). The warning against misinterpreting artists' representations of alchemical laboratories is found in C. R. Hill, 'The Iconography of the Laboratory', *Ambix*, **22** (1975): 102–10.

Finally, for Newton's alchemical activities, see Betty Jo Teeter Dobbs, *The Foundations of Newton's Alchemy, or, 'The Hunting of the Greene Lyone'* (Cambridge: Cambridge University Press, 1975); *Alchemical Death and Resurrection. The Significance of Alchemy in the Age of Newton* (Washington, DC: Smithsonian Institution, 1990); and her *The Janus Faces of Genius: The Role of Alchemy in Newton's Thought* (Cambridge: Cambridge University Press, 1992).

CHAPTER 2

Robert Boyle's *Sceptical Chymist*, first published in 1661 (2nd edn. 1668), was one of the few scientific books represented in J. M. Dent's Everyman's Library in 1911 when it was republished with an introduction by the chemist, M. M. Patterson Muir. It was reissued as an Everyman in 1964 with a new introduction by E. A. Moelwyn-Hughes. The second edition of *Boyle's Works* (1st edn, 5 vols, folio, 1744), edited by Thomas Birch in 6 vols, quarto, in 1772, was reprinted by George Olms with an introduction by Douglas McKie (Hildersheim, 1965). A facsimile of the 1st edn of *The Sceptical Chymist* was also issued by William Dawson in 1965. For the more readable preliminary version of *Sceptical Chymist*, see Marie Boas, 'An Early Version of the *Sceptical Chymist'*, *Isis*, **45** (1954): 153–68. Note also A. G. Debus, 'Fire Analysis and the Elements in Sixteenth- and Seventeenth-Century Chemistry', *Annals of Science*, **23** (1967): 127–47; H. M. Howe, 'A Root of Van Helmont's Tree', *Isis*, **56** (1965): 408–19; Charles Webster, 'Water as the Ultimate Principle of Nature. The Background to Boyle's *Sceptical Chymist'*, *Ambix*, **13** (1966): 96–107; and Michael T. Walton, 'Boyle and Newton on the Transmutation of Water and Air. From the Root of Helmont's Tree', *Ambix*, **27** (1980): 11–18.

The standard, albeit rather antiquarian, life of Boyle is R. E. W. Maddison, *The Life of the Honourable Robert Boyle,*

F.R.S. (Taylor and Francis, 1969). For Boyle's contributions to chemistry, besides Partington, vol. 2, chap. 14, see the fine study by Marie Boas, *Robert Boyle and Seventeenth-Century Chemistry* (Cambridge: Cambridge University Press, 1958; reprinted, Millward, NY, 1976). For the most recent account of Boyle and alchemy, see Michael Hunter, 'Alchemy, Magic and Moralism in the Thought of Robert Boyle', *British Journal for the History of Science*, **23** (1990): 387–410.

For the iatrochemists, see Allen G. Debus, *The English Paracelsians* (Oldbourne, 1965) and his *The Chemical Philosophy. Paracelsian Science and Medicine in the Sixteenth and Seventeenth Centuries*, 2 vols (New York: Science History Publications, 1977); R. P. Multhauf, *The Origins of Chemistry* (Oldbourne, 1966); and P. M. Rattansi, 'Recovering the Paracelsian Milieu' in William R. Shea (ed.), *Revolutions in Science* (Canton, Mass.: Science History Publications, 1988), pp. 1–25. Paracelsus and van Helmont receive careful treatment in Walter Pagel, *Paracelsus. An Introduction to Philosophical Medicine in the Era of the Renaissance* (Basel: Karger, 1958) and *Joan Baptista van Helmont, Reformer of Science and Medicine* (Cambridge: Cambridge University Press, 1982). The Sylvian acid-alkali theory is discussed in Marie Boas, 'Acid and Alkali in Seventeenth-Century Chemistry', *Archives Internationale de Histoire des Sciences*, **9** (1956): 13–28.

On the corpuscular philosophy, see Marie Boas, 'The Establishment of the Mechanical Philosophy', *Osiris*, **10** (1952): 412–541; Robert H. Kargon, *Atomism in England from Hariot to Newton* (Oxford: Clarendon, 1966); Marie Boas Hall, 'Boyle's Method of Work. Promoting Corpuscular Philosophy', *Notes and Records of the Royal Society*, **41** (1987) 111–43; Christoph Meinel, 'Early Seventeenth-Century Atomism. Theory, Epistemology and the Insufficiency of Experiment', *Isis*, **79** (1988): 68–103; and the revisionist essay by A. Clericuzio, 'A Redefinition of Boyle's Chemistry and Corpuscular Philosophy', *Annals of Science*, **47** (1990): 561–89.

On Newton's particle theory and the development of eighteenth-century chemistry, see Arnold Thackray, *Atoms and Powers. An Essay on Newtonian Matter Theory and the Development of Chemistry* (London: Oxford University Press, 1970); Robert E.

Schofield, *Mechanism and Materialism. British Natural Philosophy in the Age of Reason* (Princeton, NJ: Princeton University Press, 1970); A. L. Donovan, *Philosophical Chemistry in the Scottish Enlightenment. The Doctrines and Discoveries of William Cullen and Joseph Black* (Edinburgh: Edinburgh University Press, 1975); and J. R. R. Christie and M. J. S. Hodge (eds.), *Conceptions of Ether: Studies in the History of Ether Theories* (Cambridge: Cambridge University Press, 1984), especially Christie's 'Ether and the Science of Chemistry, 1740–1790', pp. 85–110. Maurice Crosland's 'The Development of Chemistry in the Eighteenth Century', *Studies on Voltaire* (1963): 369–441, remains an invaluable guide.

The post-Boyle development of ideas about air, combustion and respiration is analysed by Robert G. Frank Jr, *Harvey and the Oxford Physiologists. A Study of Scientific Ideas* (Berkeley: University of California Press, 1980); and Audrey B. Davis, *Circulation Physiology and Medical Chemistry in England, 1650–1680* (Lawrence, Kans.: Coronado, 1973). Apart from Partington (vol. 3, chaps 17 and 18), the best account of Stahl's phlogiston theory remains John H. White, *The Phlogiston Theory* (1932), and Hélène Metzger, *Newton, Stahl, Boerhaave et la doctrine chimique* (Paris, 1930). Note also D. R. Oldroyd, 'An Examination of G. E. Stahl's Philosophical Principles of Universal Chemistry', *Ambix*, **20** (1973): 36–52; M. Teich, 'Circulation, Transformation, Conservation of Matter and the Balancing of the Biological World in the Eighteenth Century', *Ambix*, **29** (1982): 17–28; and M. Teich, 'Interdisciplinarity in J. J. Becher's Thought', *History of European Ideas*, **9** (1988): 145–60. On cameralism, see Bruce T. Moran (ed.), *Patronage and Institutions. Science, Technology and Medicine at the European Court, 1500–1750* (Woodbridge, Suffolk: Boydell, 1991).

Finally, on chemistry and communication during the period, see Owen Hannaway, *The Chemist and the Word* (Baltimore: Johns Hopkins University Press, 1975); and Jan V. Golinski, 'Chemistry in the Scientific Revolution: Problems of Language and Communication', in D. C. Lindberg and R. S. Westman (eds.), *Reappraisals of the Scientific Revolution* (Cambridge: Cambridge University Press, 1990), pp. 367–96.

CHAPTER 3

Lavoisier's *Traité élémentaire de chimie présenté dans un ordre nouveau et d'apres les découvertes modernes* appeared in two volumes in 1789. The single-volume English translation by Robert Kerr, which was published at Edinburgh in 1790, has been republished as a paperback, *Elements of Chemistry* (New York: Dover, 1965; and reprints). The literature on Lavoisier is vast and only a small selection of material that has appeared since the bibliographical review by W. A. Smeaton in *History of Science*, **2** (1963): 51–69 will be noted here. All Lavoisier students owe debts to Douglas Mackie, *Antoine Lavoisier* (1935; revised 1952) and Henry Guerlac, *Lavoisier, the Crucial Year* (Ithaca, NY: Cornell University Press, 1961) and the latter's 'Lavoisier' entry in the *Dictionary of Scientific Biography*, which was also published separately as *Antoine Laurent Lavoisier* (New York: Scribner, 1975). An excellent overview is given by M. P. Crosland, 'Chemistry and the chemical revolution;', in G. S. Rousseau and R. Porter (eds.), *The Ferment of Knowledge* (Cambridge: Cambridge University Press, 1980), pp. 389–416. This has a good bibliography. Lavoisier's laboratory notebooks have received careful scrutiny by F. L. Holmes, *Lavoisier and the Chemistry of Life* (Madison, Wis.: University of Wisconsin Press, 1985). This also provides a splendid survey of the Lavoisier literature. Phlogiston as a modification of the universal ether is discussed in G. N. Cantor and M. J. S. Hodge (eds.), *Conceptions of the Ether* (Cambridge: Cambridge University Press, 1981). Special bicentennial issues of *Bulletin of the History of Chemistry*, **5** (1989), *Osiris,* **4** (1988) and *Ambix,* **36** (March 1989) cover a range of issues and controversies.

Rouelle's influence on Lavoisier and the introduction of the phlogiston theory to France is examined by Martin Fichman, 'French Stahlism and Chemical Studies of Air, 1750–1770', *Ambix,* **18** (1971): 94–122. Lavoisier's early unpublished essays on air have been analysed by J. B. Gough, 'Lavoisier's Early Career in Science: An Examination of Some New Evidence', *British Journal for the History of Science,* **4** (1968): 52–7; R. Siegfried, 'Lavoisier's View of the Gaseous State and its Early Application to Pneumatic Chemistry', *Isis,* **63** (1972): 59–78, which prints extracts; R. E. Kohler, 'Lavoisier's Rediscovery of the Air from Mercury Calx: A Reinterpretation', *Ambix,* **22** (1975): 52–7; and J. B. Gough, 'The Origins of Lavoisier's Theory of the Gaseous State', in H. Woolf (ed.), *The Analytic Spirit* (Ithaca, NY: Cornell University Press, 1981). An important perspective on Lavoisier's elements is given in R. Siegfried and B. J. T. Dobbs, 'Composition, a Neglected Aspect of the Chemical Revolution', *Annals of Science,* **24** (1968): 275–93. See also A. M. Duncan, 'The Functions of Affinity Tables and Lavoisier's List of Elements', *Ambix,* **17** (1970): 28–42; Perrin's (1973) *Ambix* essay below; Theodore M. Porter, 'The Promotion of Mining and the Advancement of Science: The Chemical Revolution of Mineralogy', *Annals of Science,* **38** (1981): 543–70, whose title disguises the light the article throws on the concept of the element; and R. Siegfried, 'Lavoisier's Table of Simple Elements; Its Origins and Interpretation', *Ambix,* **29** (1982): 29–48. The series of essays by the late Carl E. Perrin are worth reading in continuity: 'Prelude to Lavoisier's Theory of Calcination. Some Observations on *mercurius calcinatus per se*', *Ambix,* **16** (1969): 140–51; 'Early Opposition to the Phlogiston Theory – Two Anonymous Attacks', *British Journal for the History of Science,* **5** (1973): 128; 'Lavoisier, Monge and the Synthesis of Water – Pure Coincidence?, *British Journal for the History of Science,* **6** (1973): 424–8; 'Lavoisier's Table of the Elements: A Reappraisal', *Ambix,* **20** (1973): 95–105; and 'The Triumph of the Antiphlogistians', in Woolf, *Analytic Spirit* (1981).

On apparatus, see T. H. Levere, 'The Interaction of Ideas and Instruments in Van Marum's Work on Chemistry and Electricity', in G. L'E. Turner and T. H. Levere (eds.), *Martinus van Marum. Life and Work* (Leyden: Noordhoff, 1973), chap. 3.

For theories of acidity, see H. E. Le Grand, 'A Note on Fixed Air: The Universal Acid', *Ambix,* **20** (1973): 88–94; M. P. Crosland, 'Lavoisier's Theory of Acidity', *Isis,* **64** (1973): 306–25; and H. E. Le Grand, 'Lavoisier's Oxygen Theory of Acidity', *Annals of Science,* **29** (1972): 1–18.

The 'mythology' of Lavoisier as *the* founder of modern chemistry, as well as his own view of history, are discussed by Bernadette Bensaude-Vincent, 'A Founder Myth in the History of Science? The Lavoisier Case', in L. Graham, W.

Lepenies and P. Weingart (eds.), *Functions and Uses of Disciplinary Histories* (Dordrecht: Reidel, 1983), pp. 53–78. For the view that Lavoisier's achievement was physical rather than chemical, see Evan M. Melhardo, 'Chemistry, Physics and the Chemical Revolution', *Isis*, **76** (1985): 195–211; and the special issue of *Osirus* (above).

On Black, see H. Guerlac's essay in the *Dictionary of Scientific Biography*, vol. 2 (1970), pp. 173–83; and C. E. Perrin, 'A Reluctant Catalyst: Joseph Black and the Edinburgh Reception of Lavoisier's Chemistry', *Ambix*, **29** (1982): 141–76. For Scheele, see W. A. Smeaton, 'Carl Wilhelm Scheele (1742–1786)', *Endeavour*, **10** (1986): 28–30. For Priestley, see F. W. Gibbs, *Joseph Priestley: Adventures in Science and Champion of Truth* (Nelson, 1968); and J. G. McEvoy, 'Joseph Priestley, "Aerial Philosopher": Metaphysics and Methodology in Priestley's Chemical Thought from 1772 to 1781', *Ambix*, **25** (1978): 1–55, 93–116, 153–75 and **26** (1979): 16–38. For Berthollet's conversion to Lavoisier's chemistry, see H. E. Le Grand in *Ambix*, **22** (1975): 58–70. Finally, for Fourcroy and Guyton, see W. A. Smeaton, *Fourcroy. Chemist and Revolutionary 1755–1809* (Cambridge: Heffer, 1962) and his 'Guyton' in the *Dictionary of Scientific Biography*, vol. 5.

CHAPTER 4

Dalton's *A New System of Chemical Philosophy*, vol. 1, part 1, was published in Manchester and London in 1808. Part 2 appeared in 1810 and the first part of a second volume in 1827. There was no second part of vol. 2. The two volumes were reproduced in facsimilé by William Dawson (London, 1953). The best studies of Dalton's career are Frank Greenaway, *John Dalton and the Atom* (Heinemann, 1966) and Elizabeth Patterson, *John Dalton and the Atomic Theory* (New York: Doubleday, 1970). There is also a wealth of detail in D. S. L. Cardwell (ed.), *John Dalton and the Progress of Science* (Manchester: Manchester University Press, 1968). For a complete list of Dalton's work, see A. L. Smyth, *John Dalton, 1766–1844. A Bibliography of Works by and about him* (Manchester: Manchester University Press, 1966). Derek Gjertsen includes a chapter on Dalton's *New System* in his *The Classics of Science* (New York: Lilian Barber, 1984).

The eighteenth-century background to Dalton is brilliantly portrayed in Arnold Thackray, *Atoms and Powers. An Essay on Newtonian Matter Theory* (Oxford: Oxford University Press; Cambridge, Mass.: Harvard University Press, 1970). This study had been preceded by a series of essays that explored the origins of Dalton's theory, notably 'The Emergence of Dalton's Chemical Atomic Theory: 1801–08' *British Journal for the History of Science,* **3** (1966): 1–23. This and other essays are reprinted in A. Thackray, *John Dalton: Critical Assessments of his Life and Science* (Cambridge, Mass.: Harvard University Press, 1972). Still pertinent is H. E. Roscoe and A. Harden, *A New View of the Origin of Dalton's Atomic Theory* (1896). Partington, vol. 3, provides a deep and detailed analysis of the work of Dalton and his contemporaries. Other significant Dalton essays include: S. H. Mauskopf, 'Thomson Before Dalton: Thomas Thomson's Considerations of the Issue of Combining Weight Proportions Prior to his Acceptance of Dalton's Chemical Atomic Theory', *Annals of Science,* **25** (1969): 229–42; and 'Hauy's Model of Chemical Equivalents: Daltonian Doubts Exhumed', *Ambix,* **17** (1970): 182–91; and W. V. Farrar *et al.*, 'William Henry and John Dalton', *Ambix,* **21** (1974): 208–28. See also A. J. Rocke, *Chemical Atomism in the Nineteenth Century* (Columbus, Ohio: Ohio State University Press, 1984) for the fundamental distinction between chemical and physical atomism.

For a general overview of nineteenth-century matter theory, besides Rocke, see D. M. Knight, *Atoms and Elements* (Hutchinson, 1967), and W. H. Brock (ed.), *The Atomic Debates. Brodie and the Reception of the Atomic Theory* (Leicester: Leicester University Press, 1967). The latter deals with scepticism towards atomism. For Prout's hypotheses see W. H. Brock, *From Protyle to Proton. William Prout and the Nature of Matter 1785–1985* (Bristol: Adam Hilger, 1985).

There is no history of the chemical equation apart from L. G. Oltra, *Aproximación a la evolución histórica de los mêtodos de ajuste de las ecuaciones químicas* (Alicante, Spain: Instituto de Cultura Juan Gil-Albert, 1990); but for some English suggestions, see

R. M. Caven and J. A. Cranston, *Symbols and Formulae in Chemistry* (1928) and M. P. Crosland, *Historical Studies in the Language of Chemistry* (1962; reprint, New York: Dover, 1978). On Berzelius, see J. Erik Jorpes, *Jac. Berzelius: His Life and Works* (Stockholm: Almquist and Wiksell, 1966; revised, Berkeley, 1970) and the difficult analysis provided by Evan M. Melhardo, *Jacob Berzelius. The Emergence of his Chemical System* (Stockholm: Almquist and Wiksell; Madison, Wis.: University of Wisconsin Press, 1981). C. A. Russell has published two clear essays on 'The Electrochemical Theory of Berzelius' in *Annals of Science*, **19** (1963): 117–26 and 127–45; and also an edition of Berzelius' *Essai sur la théorie des proportions chimiques* (New York: Johnson Reprint, 1972). For Russell's essays on Davy's electrochemical system see *Annals of Science*, **15** (1959): 1–13, 15–25, and **19** (1963): 255–71. There is a sound life of Davy by Sir Harold Hartley, *Sir Humphry Davy* (Nelson, 1966; reprint, EP Publishing, 1973). Note also Sophie Forgan (ed.), *Science and the Sons of Genius. Studies on Humphry Davy* (Science Reviews, 1980).

Although I have deliberately played down Avogadro in this chapter, readers may like to consult Mario Morselli, *Amedeo Avogadro* (Dordrecht: Reidel, 1984); N. G. Coley, 'The Physico-Chemical Studies of Amedeo Avogadro', *Annals of Science*, **20** (1964): 195–210; S. H. Mauskopf, 'The Atomic Structural Theories of Ampère and Gaudin: Molecular Speculation and Avogadro's Hypothesis', *Isis*, **60** (1969): 61–74; N. Fisher, 'Avogadro, the Chemists, and Historians of Chemistry', *History of Science*, **20** (1982): 77–102 and 212–31; and J. H. Brooke, 'Avogadro's Hypothesis and its Fate', *History of Science*, **19** (1981): 235–73. Finally, on Berthollet and mass action, see F. L. Holmes, 'From Elective Affinities to Chemical Equilibria: Berthollet's Law of Mass Action', *Chymia*, **8** (1962): 105–45; and Satish Kapoor, 'Berthollet, Proust and Definite Proportions', *Chymia*, **10** (1965): 53–110.

CHAPTER 5

William Gregory's English translation of J. J. Liebig, *Anleitung zur Analyse organischer Körper* was published as *Instructions for the*

Analysis of Organic Bodies (Glasgow and London, Richard Griffin and Thomas Tegg, 1839). This fifty-nine-page monograph was enlarged by Liebig in a second edition (1853), and retranslated by his pupil, A. W. Hofmann, as *Handbook of Organic Analysis* (London, 1853). This contains an account of Hofmann's pioneering use of coal gas as a heating agent. A preliminary version of Liebig's analytical apparatus was reported by him in *Annalen der Physik*, **21** (1831): 1–43. The other important German analytical texts are Heinrich Rose, *Handbuch der analytischen Chemie* (1829); C. R. Fresenius, *Anleitung zur qualitativen chemischen Analyse* (Bonn, 1841) and *Anleitung der quantitativen chemischen Analyse* (Braunschweig, 1846), English editions of which by J. L. Bullock appeared in the same years; and Heinrich Will, *Anleitung zur qualitativen chemischen Analyse* (Heidelberg, 1846), which Hofmann simultaneously translated into English in the same year for use at the RCC.

The most detailed account of the history of analysis is Ferenc Szabadváry, *History of Analytical Chemistry* (Oxford: Pergamon, 1966), which first appeared in Hungarian in 1960. Other useful sources are E. von Meyer, *History of Chemistry* (2nd edn, 1898), pp. 141–5, 384–99; M. Dennstedt, 'Die Entwicklung der organischen Elementaranalyse', *[Ahrens] Chemischer und chemischtechnischer Vorträge*, **4** (1899): 1–114; A. J. Berry, *From Classical to Modern Chemistry* (Cambridge, 1954), chap. 6; W. A. Campbell and C. E. Mallen, 'The Development of Qualitative Analysis from 1750 to 1850', Part I, *Proceedings of the University of Durham Philosophical Society*, **13A** (1959): 108–18; Part II, *ibid.*, (1960): 168–73; Part III, *Proceedings of the University of Newcastle-upon-Tyne Philosophical Society*, **2** (1971–2): 17–24; and Part IV, *ibid.*, **2** (1976): 69–76; E. Rancke-Madsen, *The Development of Titrimetric Analysis till 1806* (Copenhagen, 1958); F. Greenaway, 'The Early Development of Analytical Chemistry', *Endeavour*, **21** (1962): 91–7; A. J. Ihde, *The Development of Modern Chemistry* (Harper and Row, 1964), chaps 11 and 21 (good bibliographies); W. V. Farrar, 'The Origin of Normality', *Education in Chemistry*, **4** (1967): 277–9; and W. H. Brock, *From Protyle to Proton* (Bristol: Adam Hilger, 1985), chap. 2. For Arthur Vogel's textbooks, see his obituary, *Chemistry in Britain* (1966): 548.

On purity, see E. F. Caldin, *The Structure of Chemistry* (London: Sheed and Ward, 1961); N. W. Pirie, 'Concepts Out of Context', *British Journal of the Philosophy of Science*, **2** (1951–2): 273–7; and L. Principe, 'Chemical Translation and the Role of Impurities in Alchemy', *Ambix*, **34** (1987): 21–30. The key 'texts' are M. E. Chevreul, *Considérations générales sur l'analyse organique et sur ses applications* (Paris, 1824); and S. P. Mulliken, *Method for the Identification of Pure Organic Compounds* (Boston, 1899–1904). The commercial production of 'pure' chemicals may be followed in the successive editions of Henry Schenck, *Chemical Reagents. Their Purity and Tests* (New York: Merck & Co., 1914); *'AnalaR' Standards for Laboratory Chemicals* (Chadwell Heath, Essex, 1934); and *Reagent Chemicals* (Washington, DC: American Chemical Society, 1951).

On the supply of laboratory apparatus, see Michael Faraday, *Chemical Manipulation* (1827) and J. J. Griffin, *Chemical Recreations* (Glasgow, 1834, and later editions); B. Gee and W. H. Brock, 'The Case of John Joseph Griffin. From Artisan-Chemist and Author-Instructor to Business-Leader', *Ambix*, **38** (1991): 29–62; and F. Kraissl, 'A History of the Chemical Apparatus Industry' [in USA], *Journal of Chemical Education*, **10** (1933): 519–23. Note also *Das Laboratorium. Eine Sammlung von Abbildungen und Beschreibungen der besten und neuesten Apparate zum Behuf der practischen und physicalischen Chemie* (Weimar, 1825–41).

The significance of distillation in Renaissance medical chemistry is dealt with by R. P. Multhauf, *The Origins of Chemistry* (Oldbourne, 1966) and A. C. Debus, 'Solution Analysis Prior to Boyle', *Chymia*, **8** (1962): 41–60. See also W. Eamon, 'Robert Boyle and the Discovery of Chemical Indicators', *Ambix*, **27** (1980): 204–9, which argues for the artistic origin of indicators; and Marco Beretta, 'T. O. Bergman and the Definition of Chemistry', *Lychnos* (1988): 37–67. The destructive distillation story is told by M. Nierenstein, 'A Missing Chapter in the History of Organic Chemistry: The Link Between Elementary Chemical Analysis by Dry-Distillation and Combustion', *Isis*, **21** (1934): 123–30; E. N. Hiebert, 'The Problem of Organic Analysis', in I. B. Cohen and R. Taton (eds.), *L'Aventure de la Science. Mélanges Alexandre Koyre* (Paris: Herman, 1964), vol. 1, pp. 303–25; and F. L. Holmes, 'Elementary Analysis and the Origins of Physiological Chemistry', *Isis*, **54** (1963): 50–81, and his monograph, *Eighteenth-Century Chemistry as an Investigative Enterprise* (Berkeley: Office for History of Science and Technology, University of California, 1989).

My comments on research schools are based on J. B. Morrell, 'The Chemist Breeders: The Research Schools of Liebig and Thomas Thomson', *Ambix*, **19** (1972): 1–46; G. L. Geison, 'Scientific Change, Emerging Specialities and Research Schools', *History of Science*, **19** (1981): 20–40; and Joseph S. Fruton, *Contrasts in Scientific Style. Research Groups in the Chemical and Biochemical Sciences* (Philadelphia: American Philosophical Society, 1990). See also W. H. Brock, 'Liebig's Laboratory Accounts', *Ambix*, **19** (1972): 47–58. Finally, for Liebig, the best current guides are F. L. Holmes' entry in the *Dictionary of Scientific Biography*, and Carlo Paoloni, *Justus von Liebig. Eine Bibliographie sämtlicher Veröffentlichungen* (Heidelberg: Carl Winter Universitäts Verlag, 1968). A revised edition of this has been promised. Two very important unpublished doctoral theses on Liebig are: Bernard Gustin, *The Emergence of the German Chemical Profession 1790–1867* (University of Chicago, 1975), which emphasizes the pharmaceutical roots of Liebig's success; and E. Patrick Munday, *Justus von Liebig and the Chemistry of Agriculture* (Cornell University, 1990), which examines the role of patronage during Liebig's early career, besides discussing Liebig's decision to turn to agricultural chemistry. Note finally, Munday's 'Social Climbing Through Chemistry: Justus Liebig's Rise from the nieder Mittelstand to the Bildungsbürgertum', *Ambix*, **37** (1990): 1–19; and Ulrika Thomas, 'Philipp Lorenz Geiger and Liebig', *Ambix*, **35** (1988): 77–90.

CHAPTERS 6 AND 7

Laurent's posthumous *Méthode de chimie* was published in Paris in 1854. The English translation, with rectifications and clarifications by William Odling, appeared as *Chemical Method, Notation, Classification, and Nomenclature*, and was published by the Cavendish Society in 1855. On Laurent, see Partington, vol. 4, chap. 12; Clara deMilt, 'August Laurent, Founder of Modern Organic Chemistry', *Chymia*, **4** (1953): 85–114; Satish C. Kapoor, 'The Origins of Laurent's Organic Classification', *Isis*, **60** (1969): 477–527 and the same author's entry on Laurent in the *Dictionary of Scientific Biography*; J. H. Brooke, 'Chlorine Substitution and the Future of Organic Chemistry. Methodological Issues in the Laurent-Berzelius Correspondence (1843–1844)', *Studies in the History and Philosophy of Science*, **4** (1973): 47–94; and J. H. Brooke, 'Laurent, Gerhardt, and the Philosophy of Chemistry', *Historical Studies in the Physical Sciences*, **6** (1975): 405–29.

For the general problem of classification in early organic chemistry, and explanations of the radical and unitary theories, see Leopold Gmelin, *Hand-Book of Chemistry*, vol. 7 (= *Organic Chemistry*, vol. 1), transl. by Henry Watts for the Cavendish Society (1852). Watts was plagued throughout the translation by Gmelin's decision to use the standard O = 8, or water = HO. See also Satish C. Kapoor, 'Dumas and Organic Classification', *Ambix*, **16** (1969): 1–65; and the three important articles by N. W. Fisher, 'Organic Chemistry Before Kekulé, *Ambix*, **20** (1973): 106–31, 209–22; and 'Kekulé and Organic Classification', *Ambix*, **21** (1974): 29–52. The pre-Cannizzaro revolution in atomic weights is analysed in A. J. Rocke, 'The Quiet Revolution of the 1850s: Scientific Theory as Social Production and Empirical Practice', in S. Mauskopf (ed.), *The Chemical Sciences in the Modern World* (Philadelphia: University of Pennsylvania Press, 1992). The modern perspective offered by W. Hückel, *Theoretical Principles of Organic Chemistry* (1955), vol. 1, chap. 1, is also useful.

Among the best accounts of the development of structural organic chemistry in English are: M. M. Patterson Muir, *A History of Chemical Theories and Laws* (1907; reprint, New York, 1975), chap. 9; O. Theodor Benfey, *From Vital Force to Structural Formulas* (Boston: Houghton Mifflin, 1964), which is best read in conjunction with the same author's translations and reprints, *Classics in the Theory of Chemical Combination* (New York: Dover, 1963); C. A. Russell, *The Structure of Chemistry, Units 1 and 2 of The Nature of Chemistry*, a third-level science course (Milton Keynes: The Open University, 1976); and Alan

J. Rocke, *Chemical Atomism in the Nineteenth Century* (Columbus, Ohio: Ohio State University Press, 1984).

Kekulé's metaphor of the two streams of organic chemistry comes from his Benzolfest speech of 1890. See the translation by O. T. Benfey in *Journal of Chemical Education*, **35** (1958): 21–3. On Kekulé, besides Fisher (above), see the *Dictionary of Scientific Biography;* Partington, vol. 4, chap. 17; Richard Anschütz, *August Kekulé*, 2 vols (Berlin, 1929) – the second volume consists of reprints of Kekulé's papers; O. T. Benfey (ed.), *Kekulé Centennial* (Washington, DC: American Chemical Society, 1966), which contains many interesting essays; E. N. Hiebert, 'The Experimental Basis of Kekulé's Valence Theory', *Journal of Chemical Education*, **36** (1959): 320–7; A. J. Rocke, 'Hypothesis and Experiment in the Early Development of Kekulé's Benzene Theory', *Annals of Science*, **42** (1985): 355–81; and A. J. Rocke, 'Kekulé's Benzene Ring and the Appraisal of Scientific Theories', in A. Donovan, L. Laudan and R. Laudan (eds.), *Scrutinizing Science* (Dordrecht: Reidel, 1988), pp. 145–61. J. Wotiz, *The Kekulé Riddle* (New York: Springer, 1992) contains essays concerning Kekulé's dreams.

For Couper, see the *Dictionary of Scientific Biography* and Anschütz's biography, *Proceedings of the Royal Society of Edinburgh*, **29** (1909): 193–273. Butlerov receives a fair appraisal in Henry M. Leicester, 'Contributions of Butlerov to the Development of Structural Theory', *Journal of Chemical Education*, **36** (1959): 328–9; G. V. Bykov, 'The Origin of the Theory of Chemical Structure', *Journal of Chemical Education*, **39** (1963): 220–4; and C. A. Russell, *The History of Valency* (Leicester: Leicester University Press, 1971), chap. 8, which also provides a thorough appraisal of Kekulé and Frankland.

The advent and development of stereochemistry is described in O. B. Ramsay (ed.), *The van't Hoff–le Bel Centennial* (Washington, DC: American Chemical Society, 1975); O. B. Ramsay, *Stereochemistry*, Nobel Prize Topics in Chemistry (London: Heyden, 1981); and H. A. M. Snelders, 'The Reception of J. H. van't Hoff's Theory of the Asymmetric Carbon Atom', *Journal of Chemical Education*, **57** (1974): 2–7. Note also Stephen Mason, *Chemical Evolution. Origin of the Elements, Molecules and Living Systems* (Oxford: Clarendon, 1991).

Finally, the roots of Kolbe's opposition are discussed in Snelders (1974) and brilliantly by A. J. Rocke, 'Kolbe Versus the Transcendental Chemists: The Emergence of Classical Organic Chemistry', *Ambix*, **34** (1987): 156–68.

CHAPTER 8

James Sheridan Muspratt, *Chemistry Theoretical, Practical and Analytical as applied and relating to the Arts and Manufactures*, was issued in monthly parts by the Glasgow publisher, William McKenzie, between 1854 and 1860. Library copies are usually found bound in two volumes with indexes. McKenzie also issued a revised edition with the same title between 1875 and 1880 in eight volumes with technical plates, and without Muspratt's name. On the Muspratts, see E. K. Muspratt, *My Life and Work* (1918); D. F. W. Hardie, 'The Muspratts and Chemical Industry in Britain', *Endeavour*, **14** (1955): 29–33; and M. D. Stephens and G. W. Roderick, 'The Muspratts of Liverpool', *Annals of Science*, **29** (1972): 287–311. For the tradition of scientific encyclopedias, see Arthur Hughes, 'Science in English Encyclopaedias 1704–1874', *Annals of Science*, **7** (1951): 340–70; **8** (1952): 323–67; and **9** (1953): 233–64.

On the alkali industry, see C. C. Gillispie, 'The Discovery of the Leblanc Process', *Isis*, **48** (1957): 152–70; M. H. Mathews, 'The Development of the Synthetic Alkali Industry in Great Britain by 1823', *Annals of Science*, **33** (1976): 371–82; and A. E. Dingle, 'The Monster Alliance. Landowners, Alkali Manufacturers and Air Pollution 1828–64', *Economic History Review*, **35** (1982): 529–48. The standard histories of chemical technology, for which see R. P. Multhauf, *The History of Chemical Technology. A Bibliography* (New York: Garland, 1984), all deal with alkali. Among the best are: J. Fenwick Allen, *Some Founders of the Chemical Industry* (London and Manchester, 1906); J. R. Partington, *The Alkali Industry* (1919); Stephen Miall, *A History of the British Chemical Industry* (1931); Archie and Nan Clow, *The Chemical Revolution* (1952); T. C. Barker and J. R. Harris, *A Merseyside Town in the Industrial Revolution. St Helens* (Liverpool, 1954); L. Haber, *The Chemical Industry in the Nineteenth Century*

(Oxford, 1958), which includes European developments; D. F. W. Hardie and J. D. Pratt, *A History of the Modern British Chemical Industry* (Oxford: Pergamon, 1966); W. A. Campbell, *The Chemical Industry* (Longman, 1971); and the excellent study by Kenneth Warren, *Chemical Foundations. The Alkali Industry in Britain to 1926* (Oxford: Clarendon, 1980). See also Smith below.

For the relationship between philosophical chemistry and eighteenth-century chemical improvements, see Arthur L. Donovan, *Philosophical Chemistry in the Scottish Enlightenment* (Edinburgh: Edinburgh University Press, 1975). In a confirmation of the Clows' thesis, A. E. Musson and E. Robinson, *Science and Technology in the Industrial Revolution* (Manchester: Manchester University Press, 1969), provides case histories to demonstrate the science-based nature of the industrial revolution. Note also A. Thackray, 'Science and Technology in the Industrial Revolution', *History of Science*, **9** (1970): 76–89.

On the dye industry, in addition to the general works already cited, see John Beer, *The Emergence of the German Dye Industry* (Urbana, 1959); *Perkin Centenary London, 100 Years of Synthetic Dyestuffs*, Supplement No. 1 of *Tetrahedron* (New York: Pergamon, 1958); E. Homburg, 'The Influence of Demand on the Emergence of the Dye Industry', *Journal of the Society of Dyers and Colourists*, **99** (1983): 325–33; M. R. Fox, *Dye-Makers of Great Britain 1856–1976* (Manchester: ICI, 1987); D. H. Leaback, 'Perkin's Pioneering Enterprise', *Chemistry in Britain*, **24** (1988): 787–90; and A. S. Travis, 'Perkin's Mauve: Ancestor of the Organic Chemistry Industry', *Technology and Culture*, **31** (1990); 51–82, and his *The Rainbow Makers* (Bethlehem, PA: Lehigh University Press, 1992).

On French developments, see Henry Guerlac, 'Some French Antecedents of the Chemical Revolution', *Chymia*, **5** (1959): 73–112; and the authoritative study by J. G. Smith, *The Origins and Early Development of the Heavy Chemical Industry in France* (Oxford: Clarendon 1979).

Academic relations between chemistry and industry are analysed in Robert Bud and Gerrylyn K. Roberts, *Science versus Practice: Chemistry in Victorian Britain* (Manchester: Manchester University Press, 1984).

CHAPTER 9

There were eight editions of Mendeleev's *Principles of Chemistry* during his lifetime and posthumous Russian editions continued until the 13th edn, 1932–47. The 5th, 6th and 7th edns were translated into English in 1891, 1897 and 1905 (reprinted New York, 1969). The historian of chemistry is well served for access to original sources on the classification of the elements in D. M. Knight (ed.), *Classical Scientific Papers. Chemistry II* (Mills and Boon, 1970). The definitive account of the periodic law is J. W. van Spronsen, *The Periodic System of Chemical Elements. A History of the First Hundred Years* (Amsterdam: Elsevier, 1969). The standard Russian biography of Mendeleev by N. A. Figurovsky, *Dmitry Ivanovich Mendeleev* (Moscow: CCCP, 1961), has never been translated into English. The older English 'lives' cited by Partington, vol. 4, p. 893, are probably no longer reliable. The interested reader should begin with B. N. Kedrov's excellent Mendeleev entry in the *Dictionary of Scientific Biography*. English sources that exploit Russian archives or Russian language sources include Henry M. Leicester, 'Factors Which Led Mendeleev to the Periodic Law', *Chymia*, 1 (1948): 67–74; Don C. Rawson, 'The Process of Discovery: Mendeleev and the Periodic Law', *Annals of Science*, 31 (1974): 181–204, which uses archival material; and Bernadette Bensaude-Vincent, 'Mendeleev's Periodic System of Chemical Elements', *British Journal for the History of Science*, 19 (1986): 3–17. Excerpts from Mendeleev's *The Oil Industry of Pennsylvania* (1876) have been translated by H. M. Leicester in *Journal of Chemical Education*, 34 (1957): 333–43. There is a good review of Mendeleev's work in physical chemistry by T. E. Thorpe, 'Scientific Worthies, XXVI. Dmitri Ivanowitsh Mendeleeff', *Nature*, 40 (1889): 193, reprinted in Thorpe's *Essays in Historical Chemistry* (1894), pp. 350–65. For Roscoe's genealogical simile, see his Presidential Address, *Reports of the British Association for the Advancement of Science* (1887): 3–28.

For Moseley's clarification of the periodic law, see his 'The High-Frequency Spectra of the Elements', *Philosophical Magazine*, 26 (1913): 1024–34 and 27 (1914): 703–13. See also, John L. Heilbron, *H. G. J. Moseley. The Life and Letters of an English Physicist, 1887–1915* (Berkeley: University of California

Press, 1974); W. A. Smeaton, 'Moseley and the Numbering of the Elements', *Chemistry in Britain*, **1** (1965): 353–5; P. M. Heimann, 'Moseley and Celtium: The Search for a Missing Element', *Annals of Science*, **23** (1967): 249–60; and P. M. Heimann, 'Moseley's Interpretation of X-Rays', *Centaurus*, **12** (1968): 261–74.

The story of the discovery of the rare gases is told in W. Ramsay's *Gases of the Atmosphere* (1896); M. W. Travers, *Discovery of the Rare Gases* (1928); M. W. Travers, *A Life of Sir William Ramsay* (1956); J. R. Strutt, *John William Strutt, Third Baron Rayleigh* (1924), reissued as *Life of Lord Rayleigh* (Madison, Wis.: University of Wisconsin Press, 1968); Erwin N. Hiebert, 'Historical Remarks on the Discovery of Argon, the First Noble Gas', in Herbert H. Hyman (ed.), *Noble Gas Compounds* (Chicago: University of Chicago Press, 1963), pp. 3–20; and R. F. Hirsh, 'A Conflict of Principles: The Discovery of Argon and the Debate over its Existence', *Ambix*, **28** (1981): 121–30. On M. W. Travers, see D. McKie, *Proceedings of the Chemical Society* (1964): 377–8; and C. E. H. Bawn, *Biographical Memoirs of the Royal Society*, **9** (1963): 301–13. For the breakdown of the 'inertness' dogma, see Hilda and George E. Hein, 'The Chemistry of Noble Gases – A Modern Case History in Experimental Science', *Journal of the History of Ideas*, **27** (1966): 417–28; Hannah Gay, 'Noble Gas Compounds: A Case Study in Scientific Conservatism and Opportunism', *Studies in the History and Philosophy of Science*, **8** (1977): 61–70; G. B. Kauffman, 'The Discovery of Noble Gas Compounds', *Journal of College Science Teachers*, **17** (1988): 264–8, which includes Bartlett's own account; Hyman (1963); and John H. Holloway, *Noble Gas Chemistry* (Methuen, 1968). Neil Bartlett's paper, 'Xenon Hexafluoroplatinate(V), $Xe^+[PtF_6]^-$', was published in *Proceedings of the Chemical Society* (June 1962): 218. Pierre Laszlo and G. J. Schobilgen, 'The Discovery of Noble Gas Compounds', *Angewandte Chemie*, **100** (1988): 495–506, emphasizes German work following Bartlett's announcement.

The best general account of the elements is the handsomely illustrated *Discovery of the Elements*, 7th edn (Easton, Pa: Journal of Chemical Education, 1968) by Mary Elvira Weeks and Henry M. Leicester. For 'masurium' and rhenium, see P. H.

M. van Assche, 'The Ignored Discovery of the Element Z = 43', *Nuclear Physics*, **A480** (1988): 205–14. On francium, see J. A. Cranston, 'A Contribution to the History of Francium', *Chemistry in Britain*, **4** (1968): 66; and G. B. Kauffman and J. P. Adloff, 'Marguerite Perey and the Discovery of Francium', *Education in Chemistry*, **26** (1989) 135–7. On the puzzle of the rare earths, in addition to Spronsen (1969), and Weeks and Leicester (1968), see Robert DeKosky, 'Spectroscopy and the Elements in the Late Nineteenth Century: The Work of Sir William Crookes', *British Journal for the History of Science*, **6** (1973): 400–23. The story of the actinides can be followed in Glenn T. Seaborg, 'Some Recollections of Early Nuclear Chemistry', *Journal of Chemical Education*, **45** (1968): 278–89; and A. G. Maddock, 'Concepts and Techniques in the Discovery of the Actinide Elements', *Inorganic Acta*, **139** (1987): 7–12. For O. T. Benfey's spiral ('snail') periodic table, see *Chemistry*, **43** (1970): 27.

CHAPTER 10

The most recent authoritative and definitive treatment of physical chemistry is John Servos, *Physical Chemistry from Ostwald to Pauling. The Making of a Science in America* (Princeton, NJ: Princeton University Press, 1990). My interpretation has also been greatly guided by R. G. A. Dolby, 'Debates Over the Theory of Solutions: A Study of Dissent in Physical Chemistry in the English-Speaking World in the Late Nineteenth and Early Twentieth Centuries', *Historical Studies in the Physical Sciences*, **7** (1976): 297–404; Erwin N. Hiebert, 'Developments in Physical Chemistry at the Turn of the Century', in C. G. Berhard, E. Crawford and D. Sörbom (eds), *Science, Technology and Society at the Time of Alfred Nobel* (Oxford: Pergamon, 1982), pp. 97–114; and three excellent reviews by Keith J. Laidler, 'Chemical Kinetics and the Origins of Physical Chemistry', *Archives for the History of the Exact Sciences*, **32** (1985): 43–75; 'Development of the Theory of Catalysis', *ibid.*, **35** (1986): 345–74; and 'Chemical Kinetics and the Oxford College Laboratories', *ibid.*, **38** (1988): 197–283. There are good accounts of the 'three musketeers' of physical chemistry, Arrhenius, Ostwald and van't Hoff, in the *Dictionary of Scientific Biography*; but also note H. A. M. Snelders, 'J. H. van't Hoff's Research School in Amsterdam (1877–1895)', *Janus*, **71** (1984): 1–30. Among original writings, I have used (with caution), Harry C. Jones, *The Theory of Electrolytic Dissociation* (London and New York, 1900; 2nd edn, 1904) and his posthumous *Nature of Solutions* (New York, 1917). On Jones, see William B. Jensen, 'Harry Jones Meets the Famous', *Bulletin of the History of Chemistry*, **7** (1990): 26–32, as well as Servos. The writings of Arrhenius, van't Hoff and Ostwald on solution theory are available in English as Alembic Club reprints and in German in Ostwald's Klassiker series; but I have used Jones' translations in the Harper Scientific Memoirs series, vol. 4, *The Modern Theory of Solution* (New York and London, 1890). Full bibliographies of their writings are found in Partington, vol. 4, whose section on 'Physical Chemistry', pp. 569–746, is an indispensable guide. Another source of value in gauging the contemporary mood is M. M. Pattison Muir, *A History of Chemical Theories and Laws* (Cambridge, 1907; reprinted, New York: Arno, 1975). Muir was the first English convert to the ionic theory. Van't Hoff's historical account of his researches is in *Berichte deutschen chemischen Gesellschaft*, **27** (1894): 6–20. Like much of his writing, it reads like disconnected lecture notes and is difficult to follow.

For Kahlenberg's opposition to the ionists, besides Servos and Dolby, see the history of the University of Wisconsin's Chemistry Department by A. J. Ihde, *Chemistry as Viewed from Bascom's Hill* (Madison, Wis.: Department of Chemistry, University of Wisconsin, 1990). His long section on Kahlenberg complements his essay on the same subject in G. Dubpernell and J. H. Westbrook (eds.), *Select Topics in the History of Electrochemistry* (Washington, DC: Electrochemical Society, 1978). This book also contains a valuable revaluation concerning the dating of Arrhenius' dissociation hypothesis by R. S. Root-Bernstein, pp. 201–12. The later fortunes of the ionic theory can be followed in John Wolfenden's entertaining 'The Anomaly of Strong Electrolytes', *Ambix*, **19** (1972): 175–96; Gordon R. Freeman, 'The Naming of Evolving Theories' [on Milner], *Journal of Chemical Education*, **62** (1985): 57–8; and A. J. Berry,

Modern Chemistry (Cambridge, 1946), chaps 2 and 7. On hydrogen ion concentration studies, see F. Szabadváry, 'The Concept of pH', *Journal of Chemical Education*, **41** (1964): 105–7; and his *A History of Analytical Chemistry* (Oxford: Pergamon, 1966). For Guldberg and Waage and the law of mass action, see Laidler, the *Dictionary of Scientific Biography* and F. L. Holmes, 'From Elective Affinities to Chemical Equilibria: Berthollet's Law of Mass Action', *Chymia*, **8** (1962): 105–45. For Kopp, who is surprisingly ignored by fellow historian Partington, see Max Speter, 'Vater Kopp', *Osirus*, **5** (1938): 392–460. Finally, Raoult's isolated genius is sympathetically portrayed in Mary Jo Nye, *Science in the Provinces* (Berkeley: University of California Press, 1986).

CHAPTER 11

Cannizzaro's programme is described in his *Sketch of a Course of Chemical Philosophy* (Edinburgh: Alembic Club, 1910; reprinted 1969), a translation from *Il Nuovo Cimento*, **7** (1858): 321–66. George Challoner's edition of Edward Frankland's lectures to teachers was published as *How to Teach Chemistry* (London, 1872; Philadelphia, 1875). Earlier, Frankland published *Lecture Notes for Chemical Students* (1866; 2nd edn, 2 vols, 1870–2; 3rd edn of vol. 2 only (organic), 1881). On Frankland's chemical training, see Colin A. Russell, *Lancastrian Chemist: The Early Years of Sir Edward Frankland* (Milton Keynes: Open University Press, 1986); a sequel covering Frankland's mature years is expected. On Frankland's contributions to water analysis, see Christopher Hamlin, *A Science of Impurity. Water Analysis in the Nineteenth Century* (Bristol: Adam Hilger, 1990). Frankland was much influenced by A. W. Hofmann, *Introduction to Modern Chemistry, Experimental and Theoretic, Embodying Twelve Lectures delivered in the Royal College of Chemistry* (1865; German edns Brunswick, 1866 and later). Armstrong's many writings on chemical education are found in his *The Teaching of Scientific Method* (1903; 2nd edn, 1910; 3d edn, 1925). The most important of these are reprinted with an introductory essay in W. H. Brock, *H. E. Armstrong and the Teaching of Science*

1880–1930 (Cambridge: Cambridge University Press, 1973). For Ida Freund's use of illustrative experiments at Cambridge, see her posthumous and incomplete *The Experimental Basis of Chemistry. Suggestions for a Series of Experiments Illustrative of the Fundamental Principles of Chemistry* (Cambridge, 1920).

The history of science teaching in Britain is the subject of David Layton, *Science for the People* (Allen and Unwin, 1973) and his *Interpreters of Science. A History of the Association for Science Education* (ASE/John Murray, 1984). See also G. K. Roberts, 'The Liberally-Minded Chemist. Chemistry in the Cambridge Natural Science Tripos', *Historical Studies in the Physical Sciences,* **11** (1980): 157–83; and E. Jenkins, *From Armstrong to Nuffield. Studies in Twentieth-Century Science Education in England and Wales* (John Murray, 1979), which is very informative. On the Nuffield chemistry project, see Marjorie Waring, *Social Pressures and Curriculum Innovation. A Study of the Nuffield Foundation Science Teaching Project* (Methuen, 1979). The CHEM Study project is immortalized in Richard J. Merrill and David W. Ridgway, *The CHEM Study Story. A Successful Curriculum Improvement Project* (San Francisco: W. H. Freeman, 1969). It is unfortunate that nothing comparable has been written on the Chemical Bond project. My own remarks are based on Laurence Strong (ed.), *Chemical Systems* (St Louis: McGraw-Hill, 1964) and conversations with Drs. L. Strong and O. T. Benfey. Note, however, J. S. Pode, 'CBA and CHEM Study: An Appreciation', *Journal of Chemical Education,* **43** (1966): 98–103. On the international front, O. T. Benfey and S. L. Geffner (eds.), *International Chemical Education. The High School Years* (Washington, DC: American Chemical Society, 1968) is very helpful. For a polemical view of the chemical curriculum, see Jonathan Stark, 'Class Struggle Among the Molecules', in Trevor Pateman (ed.), *Counter Course* (Harmondsworth: Penguin, 1972), pp. 202–17.

The Griffin story is the subject of Brian Gee and W. H. Brock, 'The Case of John Joseph Griffin. From Artisan-Chemist and Author-Instructor to Business-Leader', *Ambix,* **38** (1991):29–62. Helpful on the development of the American system of chemical education are F. W. Clarke, *A Report on the Teaching of Chemistry and Physics in the United States*

(Washington, DC, 1881); Bruce V. Lewenstein, 'To Improve Our Knowledge in Nature and Arts: A History of Chemical Education in the United States', *Journal of Chemical Education*, **66** (1989): 37–44; Larry Owens, 'Pure and Sound Government: Laboratories, Playing Fields and Gymnasia in the Late-Nineteenth-Century Search for Order', *Isis*, **76** (1985): 182–94; and Owen Hannaway, 'The German Model of Chemical Education in America: Ira Remsen and Johns Hopkins', *Ambix*, **23** (1976): 145–64. On mathematics and chemical education, see Fathi Habashi, 'Joseph William Mellor (1869–1938)', *Bulletin of the History of Chemistry*, **7** (1990): 13–16; and John W. Servos, 'Mathematics and the Physical Sciences in America, 1880–1930', *Isis*, **77** (1986): 611–29, which fails, however, to note the importance of Daniels.

On laboratories, see E. R. Robins, *Technical School and College Buildings* (1887); J. R. Partington, 'The Evolution of the Chemical Laboratory', *Endeavour*, **1** (1942): 145–50; and B. Gee, 'Amusement Chests and Portable Laboratories: Practical Alternatives to the Regular Laboratory', in F. A. J. L. James (ed.), *The Development of the Laboratory. Essays on the Place of Experiment in Industrial Civilisation* (Basingstoke: Macmillan, 1989), pp. 37–59. The latter also contains an essay on Robins and Armstrong by W. H. Brock, 'Building England's First Technical College: The Laboratories of Finsbury Technical College 1878–1926', pp. 155–70. Note also Jenkins (1979), chap. 7; D. Chilton and N. G. Coley, 'The Laboratories of the Royal Institution in the Nineteenth Century', *Ambix*, **27** (1980): 173–203; and K. J. Laidler, 'Chemical Kinetics and the Oxford College Laboratories', *Archives for the History of the Exact Sciences*, **38** (1988): 197–282. On American developments, see Owens (1985) and Lewenstein (1989) and H. S. Van Klooster, 'The Beginnings of Laboratory Instruction in Chemistry in the USA', *Chymia*, **2** (1949): 1–15.

CHAPTER 12

For the history of chemical societies in the United Kingdom and America, see T. S. Moore and J. C. Philip, *The Chemical*

Society 1841–1941. An Historical Review (1947); R. Bud, *The Development and Early Years of the Chemical Society* (unpublished Ph.D. thesis, University of Pennsylvania, 1980); R. Bud and G. K. Roberts, *Science versus Practice: Chemistry in Victorian Britain* (Manchester: Manchester University Press, 1984); David H. Whiffen and Donald H. Hey, *The Royal Society of Chemistry: The First 150 Years* (Royal Society of Chemistry, 1991); C. A. Russell, N. G. Coley and G. K. Roberts, *Chemistry as a Profession. The Origins and Rise of the Royal Institute of Chemistry* (Milton Keynes: Open University Press, 1977); R. C. Chirnside and J. H. Hamence, *The 'Practising Chemists': A History of the Society of Analytical Chemistry 1874–1974* (Society of Analytical Chemistry, 1974); C. A. Browne and M. E. Weeks, *A History of the American Chemical Society* (Washington, DC, 1952); Herman Skolnik and Kenneth M. Reese, *A Century of Chemistry* (Washington, DC: American Chemical Society, 1976); A. Thackray, J. L. Sturchio, P. T. Carroll and R. Bud, *Chemistry in America 1876–1976* (Dordrecht, Reidel, 1985); and J. Bohning, 'The Continental Chemical Society', *Bulletin of the History of Chemistry*, **6** (1990): 15–21.

For early ephemeral groups, see: J. Kendall, 'Some Eighteenth-Century Chemical Societies', *Endeavour*, **1** (1942): 106–9; W. D. Miles, 'Early American Chemical Societies', *Chymia*, **3** (1950): 95–113; W. H. Brock, 'The London Chemical Society 1824', *Ambix*, **14** (1967): 99–128; and Gwen Averly, 'Social Chemists. Early English Chemical Societies', *Ambix*, **33** (1986): 99–128. Robert Warington, the founder of the Chemical Society of London, is profiled by J. H. S. Green in *Proceedings of the Chemical Society* (Sept. 1967): 241–6. There are few satisfactory histories of Continental societies except Walter Ruske, *100 Jahre Deutsche Chemische Gesellschaft* (Weinheim: Chemie Verlag, 1967) and B. Rassow, *Geschichte des Vereins Deutscher Chemiker* (Leipzig, 1912).

Scientific periodicals in general are the subject of W. H. Brock and A. J. Meadows, *The Lamp of Learning* (Taylor and Francis, 1984) and W. H. Brock, 'Scientific Periodicals', in Rosemary T. Van Arsdel and J. Don Vann (eds.), *Guide to Victorian Periodicals*, vol. 3 (Toronto: University of Toronto Press, 1992). On chemical periodicals, I have drawn on an unpublished paper by Christoph Meinel, 'Communication and Integration. Chemical Journals and the International Transmission of Knowledge in Nineteenth-Century Europe', which he gave at the International Congress on History of Science, Berkeley, Ca, in 1985. See also his 'Nationalismus und Internationalismus in der Chemie des 19. Jahrhunderts', in *Perspektiven der Pharmaziegeschichte* (Graz: Akademische Druck- und Verlagsanstalt, 1983), pp. 225–42, which gives the example quoted of Döbereiner's catalysis. Other treatments include Hörst Harff, *Die Entwicklung der deutschen chemischen Fachzeitschrift* (Berlin, 1941) and, for Crell's journals, Karl Hufbauer, *The Formation of the German Chemical Community 1720–1795* (Berkeley: University of California Press, 1982). American periodicals are the focus of William A. Noyes, 'Chemical Publications', *Journal of the American Chemical Society*, **42** (1920): 2099–115; and Browne and Weeks (1952); while Bancroft's *Journal of Physical Chemistry* is the subject of a chapter in John W. Servos, *Physical Chemistry from Ostwald to Pauling. The Making of Physical Chemistry in America* (Princeton, NJ: Princeton University Press, 1990). On Berzelius' *Jahres-Bericht*, see William Odelberg, 'Berzelius as Permanent Secretary', in T. Frängsmyr (ed.), *Science in Sweden. The Royal Swedish Academy of Science 1739–1989* (Canton, Mass.: Science History Publications, 1989), pp. 124–47. For a unique biography of a journal, see Thomas Hapke, *Die Zeitschrift für physikalische Chemie* (Herzberg: Verlag Traugott Bautz, 1990). On line notations, see W. J. Wiswesser, *A Line-Formula Chemical Notation* (New York: Crowell, 1954).

On Crookes, see my essay in *Dictionary of Scientific Biography* and Fournier D'Albe, *The Life of Sir William Crookes* (London and New York, 1924). There are generous reproductions from *Chemical News* in D. M. Knight (ed.), *Classical Scientific Papers. Chemistry* (Mills and Boon, 1968) and *Classical Scientific Papers. Chemistry, Second Series* (Mills and Boon, 1970).

CHAPTER 13

Copies of Linus Pauling, *The Nature of the Chemical Bond and the Structure of Molecules and Crystals. An Introduction to Modern Struc-*

tural Chemistry (Ithaca, NY: Cornell University Press, 1939; 2nd edn 1940; 3rd edn 1960) can be found in most libraries, though the first edition less easily. Pauling supplies references to the six papers upon which the book was based. Pauling's other books include *College Chemistry* (San Francisco: W. H. Freeman, 1950; 2nd edn 1955; 3rd edn 1964) and *The Chemical Bond* (Ithaca, NY: Cornell University Press, 1967). The other primary sources used in this chapter were J. J. Thomson, *Electricity and Matter* (Cambridge, 1904); J. J. Thomson, *The Corpuscular Theory of Matter* (Cambridge, 1907); W. Ramsay, 'The Electron as Element', *Journal of the Chemical Society,* **93** (1908): 774–88; K. G. Falk and J. M. Nelson, 'The Electron Conception of Valence', *Journal of the American Chemical Society,* **32** (1910): 1637–54; W. C. Bray and G. E. K. Branch, 'Valence and Tautomerism', *ibid.,* **35** (1913): 1440–8; G. N. Lewis, 'Valence and Tautomerism', *ibid.,* **35** (1913): 1448–55; J. J. Thomson, 'The Forces Between Atoms and Chemical Affinity', *Philosophical Magazine,* **27** (1914): 757–89; G. N. Lewis, 'The Atom and the Molecule', *Journal of the American Chemical Society,* **38** (1916): 762–88; I. Langmuir, 'The Arrangement of Electrons in Atoms and Molecules', *ibid.,* **41** (1919): 868–934; 'The Electronic Theory of Valency. A General Discussion', *Transactions of the Faraday Society,* **19** (1923): 450–537; J. J. Thomson, *The Electron in Chemistry* (Philadelphia: Franklin Institute, 1923); and G. N. Lewis, *Valence and the Structure of Atoms and Molecules* (New York, 1923; reprint, New York, 1967).

Despite its title, John W. Servos, *Physical Chemistry in America from Ostwald to Pauling* (Princeton, NJ: Princeton University Press, 1990) only deals briefly with Pauling's contributions in its sixth chapter. It is, however, excellent for understanding the background to the rise of CalTech. Pauling has written a number of autobiographical pieces, including 'Fifty Years of Physical Chemistry in the California Institute of Technology', *Annual Reviews of Physical Chemistry,* **16** (1965): 1–14; and 'Fifty Years Progress in Structural Chemistry and Molecular Biology', *Daedelus,* **99** (1970): 988–1014. There is an excellent Ph.D. thesis by Robert Paradowski, 'The Structural Chemistry of Linus Pauling' (University of Wisconsin, 1972); it is understood that Professor Paradowski is revising this for publication. More journalistic, and annoyingly repetitious, is Anthony Serafini, *Linus Pauling. A Man and His Science* (New York: Paragon House, 1989). For Pauling's role in the 'race' for the double helix, see Robert Olby, *The Path to the Double Helix* (Macmillan, 1974), pp. 272–89.

Any study of the chemical bond must be indebted to four superb studies by Robert E. Kohler Jr, 'The Origins of G. N. Lewis's theory of the Shared Pair Bond', *Historical Studies in the Physical Sciences*, **3** (1971): 342–76; 'Irving Langmuir and the "Octet" Theory of Valence', *ibid.*, **4** (1972): 39–87, which prints a number of letters between Lewis and Langmuir; 'The Lewis-Langmuir Theory of Valence and the Chemical Community, 1920–1928', *ibid.*, **6** (1975): 431–68; and 'G. N. Lewis's views on Bond Theory, 1900–1916', *British Journal for the History of Science*, **8** (1975): 233–9. The last paper explores a connection between Werner and Lewis. A stimulating symposium on Lewis was published as a series of papers in *Journal of Chemical Eduction*, **61** (1984): 5–21, 93–115 and 185–202. All of Langmuir's papers have been republished in a collected edition, the first volume of which contains biographical essays by Albert Rosenfield, J. H. Hildebrand and E. K. Rideal, *Langmuir, the Man and the Scientist* (Oxford: Pergamon, 1962).

Other useful studies that deal with bonding include: E. Campaigne, 'The Contributions of Fritz Arndt to Resonance Theory', *Journal of Chemical Education*, **36** (1959): 336–9; G. V. Bykov, 'Historical Sketch of the Electron Theories of Organic Chemistry', *Chymia*, **10** (1965): 199–253, which provides a Russian perspective; C. A. Russell, *A History of Valency* (Leicester: Leicester University Press, 1971); M. Saltzman, 'J. J. Thomson and the Modern Revival of Dualism', *Journal of Chemical Education*, **50** (1973): 44–59; Anthony N. Stranges, *Electrons and Valence. Development of the Theory 1900–1925* (College Station, Texas, 1982); E. Mackinnon, 'The Discovery of New Quantum Theory', in T. Nickles (ed.), *Scientific Discovery. Case Studies* (Dordrecht: Reidel, 1983), pp. 261–72; D. A. Bantz, 'The Structure of Discovery: Evolution of Structural Accounts of Chemical Bonding', *ibid.*, pp. 291–329; W. B. Jensen, 'Abegg, Lewis, Langmuir and the Octet Rule', *Journal of Chemical Education*, **61** (1984): 191–200; Denis Quane, 'The

Reception of Hydrogen Bonding by the Chemical Community, 1920–1937', *Bulletin of the History of Chemistry*, **7** (1990): 3–13; Jozef Hurwic, 'Reception of Kasimir Fajan's Quanticule Theory of the Chemical Bond', *Journal of Chemical Education*, **64** (1987): 122–3; and Reynold Holmen, 'Kasimir Fajans', *Bulletin of the History of Chemistry*, **4** (1989): 15–23 and **6** (1990): 7–15. For orientation on French and German physical chemistry, besides Bykov and Kohler, see Jules Guran and Michael Magat, 'A History of Physical Chemistry in France', *Annual Review of Physical Chemistry*, **22** (1971): 1–23; and W. Jost, 'The First 45 Years of Physical Chemistry in Germany', *ibid.*, **17** (1966): 1–14. Analogous essays on the situation in other countries form the lead article in other years of this review.

The relevant developments in spectroscopy and molecular orbital theory can be gleaned from Robert S. Mulliken, 'Molecular Scientists and Molecular Science; Some Reminiscences', *Journal of Chemical Physics*, **43** (1965), Suppl. 2–11, which is reprinted in D. A. Ramsay and J. Hinze (eds.), *Selected Papers of Robert S. Mulliken* (Chicago: University of Chicago Press, 1975), which also prints the 1964 interview with T. S. Kuhn. See also Gerhard Herzberg, 'Molecular Spectroscopy: A Personal History', *Annual Review of Physical Chemistry*, **36** (1985): 1–30; Charles Coulson, *Valency* (Oxford: Oxford University Press, 1952; 2nd edn 1961); R. Daudel, R. Lefebvre and C. Moser, *Quantum Chemistry Methods and Applications* (New York: Interscience, 1959); G. V. Bykov, *Electronic Charges of Bonds in Organic Compounds* (New York: Pergamon/Macmillan, 1964); and M. J. S. Dewar, *The Molecular Orbital Theory of Organic Compounds* (New York: McGraw-Hill, 1969). The Royal Society's obituaries of Coulson, Hückel and Mulliken are enlightening: *Biographical Memoirs of the Royal Society*, **20** (1974): 75–134; **28** (1982): 153–62; and **35** (1990): 329–54. The *Dictionary of Scientific Biography* entries for Bohr, Fritz London and Schrödinger are also helpful.

CHAPTER 14

The primary text is C. K. Ingold, *Structure and Mechanism in Organic Chemistry* (Ithaca, NY: Cornell University Press, 1953),

828 pp. A second, much larger, edition, published in the same place in 1969, ran to 1266 pp. The core of the book is based on Ingold's 'Principles of an Electronic Theory of Organic Reactions', *Chemical Reviews*, **15** (1934): 225–74. On Ingold's life, see J. H. Ridd (ed.), *Studies on Chemical Structure and Reactivity* (London: Methuen, 1966), especially the essay by J. H. S. Green; and C. W. Shoppee, 'Christopher Kelk Ingold 1893–1970', *Biographical Memoirs of the Royal Society*, **18** (1972): 349–71. The latter provides a complete list of papers, but is a pretty unreadable text. For Ingold's teacher, D. R. Boyd, see the obituary by N. K. Adam, *Journal of the Chemical Society* (1956): 2568–9. Critical light is thrown on Ingold, as well as Robinson, in a symposium on Sir Robert Robinson published as a special issue of *Natural Products Chemistry*, **4** (1987): 3–72. In this, note particularly M. D. Saltzman, 'The Development of Sir Robert Robinson's Contributions to Theoretical Chemistry', pp. 53–60, and J. Shorter, 'Electronic Theories of Organic Chemistry: Robinson and Ingold', pp. 61–6. To these must be added M. D. Saltzman, 'The Robinson-Ingold Controversy. Precedence in the Electronic Theory of Organic Reactions', *Journal of Chemical Education*, **57** (1980): 484–8. Robinson is the subject of a hagiographical obituary by Lord Todd and J. W. Cornforth, *Biographical Memoirs of the Royal Society*, **22** (1976): 415–527. Robinson's own autobiography, *Memoirs of a Minor Prophet* (Amsterdam: Elsevier, 1976), is embarrassingly unsatisfactory. T. E. Williams, *Robert Robinson. Chemist Extraordinary* (Oxford: Clarendon, 1990) portrays the man, but ignores most chemical detail. Note also M. D. Saltzman, 'Sir Robert Robinson. A Centennial Tribute', *Chemistry in Britain* (1986): 543–8.

Ingold's collaborator, E. D. Hughes, is the subject of a sympathetic and readable essay by Ingold in *Biographical Memoirs of the Royal Society*, **10** (1964): 147–82; and Peter B. De La Mare, 'E. D. Hughes', *Proceedings of the Chemical Society* (1964): 97–100. The polemical skills of Ingold and Hughes are the subject of a light-hearted, but informative, essay by Derek Davenport, 'On the Comparative Unimportance of the Invective Effect', *Chemtech* (Sept. 1987): 526–31. The amazing career of Robinson's one-time collaborator, W. O. Kermack, is movingly conveyed in *Biographical Memoirs of the Royal Society*, **17** (1971) 415–527.

General, as well as specific, treatments of the development of physical organic chemistry include C. A. Russell, *The History of Valency* (Leicester: Leicester University Press, 1971), chap. 16; G. V. Bykov, 'Historical Sketch of the Electron Theory of Organic Chemistry', *Chymia*, **10** (1965): 199–253; Louis P. Hammett, 'Physical Organic Chemistry in Retrospect', *Journal of Chemical Education*, **43** (1966): 464–9; Leon Gortler, 'The Physical Organic Community in the United States, 1925–50', *Journal of Chemical Education*, **62** (1985): 753–7; M. D. Saltzman, 'The Development of Physical Organic Chemistry in the United States and the United Kingdom: 1919–1939, Parallels and Contrasts', *Journal of Chemical Education*, **63** (1986): 588–93; M. D. Saltzman, 'Arthur Lapworth. The Genesis of Reaction Mechanism', *Journal of Chemical Education*, **49** (1972): 750–2; and John Shorter, 'Hammett Memorial Lecture', *Progress in Physical Organic Chemistry*, **17** (1990): 1–29.

On the development of kinetics, see the two papers by K. J. Laidler, 'Chemical Kinetics and the Origins of Physical Chemistry', *Archives for the History of the Exact Sciences*, **32** (1985) 43–75; and 'Chemical Kinetics and the Oxford College Laboratories', *ibid.*, **28** (1988): 197–283; K. J. Laidler and M. Christine King, 'The Development of Transition State Theory', *Journal of Physical Chemistry*, **87** (1983): 2657–64; and M. Christine King, 'Experiments with Time', *Ambix*, **28** (1981): 70–82; **29** (1982): 49–61; and **31** (1984): 16–31. The significance of the Welsh school is scarcely apparent in the obituary of K. J. P. Orton, *Journal of the Chemical Society* (1931): 1042–8.

For post-Ingold mechanistic and theoretical developments, see Dean Stanley Tarbell and Tracy Tarbell, *Essays on the History of Organic Chemistry in the United States 1875–1955* (Nashville, Tenn.: Folio Publishers, 1986); and Paul D. Bartlett, 'The Scientific Work of Saul Winstein', *Journal of the American Chemical Society*, **94** (1972): 2161–8. Other essays on Winstein are to be located in *Progress in Physical Organic Chemistry*, **9** (1972) and *Biographical Memoirs of the National Academy of Science*, **43** (1973): 321–53. For the non-classical ion debate, see Paul D. Bartlett (ed.), *Non-Classicial Ions. Reprints and Com-*

mentary (New York: W. A. Benjamin, 1965); Herbert C. Brown, *Boranes in Organic Chemistry* (Ithaca, NY: Cornell University Press, 1972); Herbert C. Brown, *The Non-Classical Ion Problem* (New York: Plenum, 1977); John D. Roberts, *The Right Place at the Right Time* (Washington, DC: American Chemical Society, 1990), which is bitterly frank; and Editorial, 'Resolution of the Norbornyl Cation Debate Remains Elusive', *Chemistry and Engineering News* (4 April 1983): 21–3. The best, sophisticated review is Edward M. Arnett, Thomas C. Hofelick and George W. Schriver, 'Carbocations', in Maitland Jones Jr and Robert A. Moss (eds.), *Reactive Intermediates*, **3** (1985): 189–226.

Other useful sources are the successive editions of Alfred W. Steward, *Recent Advances in Organic Chemistry* (1908, 1911, 1918, etc.); W. A. Waters, *Physical Aspects of Organic Chemistry* (1935, 1937, 1942 and 1950); H. B. Watson, *Modern Theories of Organic Chemistry* (Oxford, 1937, 1941); and A. E. Remick, *Electronic Theories of Organic Chemistry* (New York, 1943). The early history of tautomerism is the subject of the monograph by Ingold's Leeds colleague, John W. Baker, *Tautomerism* (1934). Finally, indispensable for the historian, as well as the critical chemist, is Walter Hückel, *Theoretical Principles of Organic Chemistry*, 2 vols (Amsterdam and London, 1955–8).

CHAPTER 15

Ronald Nyholm's inaugural lecture at University College on 1 March 1956 was published as *The Renaissance of Inorganic Chemistry* (University College, H. K. Lewis, London, 1956). Since this is already difficult to locate, readers should consult the abbreviated version that Nyholm published in *Journal of Chemical Education*, **34** (1957): 166–9. Internal evidence also shows that the lecture was based upon his Presidential Lecture to the Royal Society of New South Wales given the year before: 'Magnetism and Stereochemistry', *Journal and Proceedings of the Royal Society of New South Wales*, **89** (1955): 8–29. On Nyholm's career, see the obituaries by David Craig, *Biographical Memoirs of the Royal Society*. **18** (1972): 445–62, which lists Nyholm's papers; Alan Maccoll, *Chemistry in Britain* (1972): 341; and John Chatt's moving 'A Tribute to Sir Ronald Nyholm', *Journal* *of Chemical Education,* **51** (1974): 146–9. For Nyholm's views of unified chemistry, see his 'Future of the [UCL] Department' in J. H. Ridd (ed.), *Studies on Chemical Structure and Reactivity* (London: Methuen, 1966), pp. 275–82. For mining and the street names of Broken Hill, see R. H. B. Kearns, *Broken Hill 1883–1893. Discovery and Development* (Broken Hill, NSW: Broken Hill Historical Society, 1973; 3rd edn 1987), and the sequel, *Broken Hill, 1894–1914. The Uncertain Years* (1974; 3rd edn 1987); and Geoffrey Blainey, *The Rise of Broken Hill* (Melbourne: University of Melbourne Press, 1968).

The Australian bicentennial in 1988 brought forward a number of useful articles on the history of Australian chemistry. David Philip Miller, 'Writing the History of Australian Chemistry. What Are the Questions?', *Chemistry in Australia,* **55** (1988): 239–42; Ian D. Rae, 'Chemists at ANZAAS – Cabbages or Kings?' in R. M. Macleod (ed.), *The Commonwealth of Science* (Oxford: Oxford University Press, 1988), pp. 166–95; I. D. Rae, 'A History of Chemistry in Australia', *Chemistry in Australia,* **56** (1989): 432–9, which has a bibliography that includes university departmental histories; and Alan Maccoll, 'Australians at University College, London, 1899–1988', *Ambix,* **36** (1989): 82–90. Note also Anthony T. Baker and Stanley E. Livingstone, 'The Early History of Coordination Chemistry in Australia', *Polyhedron,* **4** (1985): 1337–51. New Zealand chemistry awaits its historian and the only source is the uninspiring official *Chemistry in a Young Country* (Christchurch: New Zealand Institute of Chemistry, 1981), edited by P. P. Williams, and the more helpful perspective in Rae (1988).

It is also difficult to gain a perspective on Japanese chemistry. Incidental remarks in J. R. Bartholomew, *The Formation of Science in Japan* (New Haven: Conn.: Yale University Press, 1989) are useful, as are R. D. Home and M. Watanabe, 'Physics in Australia and Japan: A Comparison', *Annals of Science,* **44** (1987): 215–35 and 'Forming New Physics Communities: Australia and Japan, 1914–1950', *ibid.,* **47** (1990): 317–45. Note also J. Harris and W. H. Brock, 'From Giessen to Gower Street. Towards a Biography of Alexander William Williamson, 1824–1904', *Annals of Science,* **32** (1974): 95–130, which discusses the education of Japanese chemists in London.

The basic text of co-ordination chemistry is Alfred Werner, *Neuere Anschauungen auf dem Gebiete der anorganischen Chemie* (Braunschweig, 1905; 2nd edn 1909; 3rd edn 1913; later posthumous edns were produced by pupils). The second edition was translated into English by E. P. Hedley as *New Ideas on Inorganic Chemistry* (London, 1911). G. B. Kauffman has published hundreds of monographs and papers on Werner and the history of co-ordination chemistry. Among the most useful are: 'Sophius Mads Jørgensen and the Werner–Jørgensen Controversy', *Chymia*, **6** (1960): 180–204; *Alfred Werner – Founder of Coordination Chemistry* (New York: Springer, 1966); *Classics in Coordination Chemistry*, 3 vols (New York: Dover, 1968 and 1976); and 'General historical survey [of co-ordination chemistry] to 1930', in Sir Geoffrey Wilkinson (ed.), *Comprehensive Coordination Chemistry* (Oxford: Pergamon, 1987), pp. 1–20. Also useful are D. P. Mellor, 'Historical Background and Fundamental Concepts', in F. P. Dwyer and D. P. Mellor (eds.), *Chelating Agents and Metal Chelates* (New York: Academic Press, 1964), pp. 1–50; and W. H. Brock, K. A. Jensen, C. K. Jørgensen and G. B. Kauffman, 'The Origin and Dissemination of the Term Ligand in Chemistry', *Ambix*, **28** (1981): 171–83, which is reprinted in *Polyhedron*, **2** (1983): 1–7. See also C. H. Langford and H. B. Gray, *Ligand Substitution Processes* (New York: W. A. Benjamin, 1966).

For Sidgwick's reinterpretation of Werner, see N. V. Sidgwick, *The Electronic Theory of Valency* (Oxford, 1927). For a stimulating portrait, see Leslie E. Sutton, 'Nevil Vincent Sidgwick', *Proceedings of the Chemical Society* (1958): 310–19. For a highly technical historical treatment of ligand-field theory, see the papers by Carl J. Ballhausen, 'Quantum Mechanics and Chemical Bonding in Inorganic Complexes', *Journal of Chemical Education*, **56** (1979): 215–18; 'Valency and Inorganic Metal Complexes', *ibid.*, 357–61; and 'The Spread of the Ideas', *ibid.*, 294–7. Less demanding is Andrew D. Liehr, 'Molecular Orbital, Valence Bond and Ligand Field Theory. A Comparison of Theories', *Journal of Chemical Education*, **39** (1962): 135–9.

For other miscellaneous topics referred to, see: W. C. Fernelius, 'History of Inorganic Synthesis', *Journal of Chemical Education*, **63** (1986): 500–1; for a hilarious account of Pope and

Read's work on the stereochemistry of selenium compounds, see John Read, *Humour and Humanism in Chemistry* (1947), pp. 288–92. Note also W. J. Pope's 'Forty Years of Stereochemistry', *Chemistry and Industry*, **51** (1932): 229–32. Blomstrand's work and influence are treated in C. A. Russell, *The History of Valency* (Leicester: Leicester University Press, 1971), and the Hantsch-Bamberger controversy receives generous treatment in Partington, vol. 4, pp. 842–7. As with his treatment of organic chemistry, the most stimulating and philosophical treatment of inorganic chemistry up to 1950 is W. Hückel, *Structural Chemistry of Inorganic Compounds*, 2 vols (London and New York, 1950–1), translated from *Anorganische Struktur Chemie* (Tubingen, 1949) by L. H. Long.

CHAPTER 16

The title is taken from H. E. Armstrong's report on the 150th anniversary celebration of Faraday's birth, an exhibition at the Albert Hall, *Chemistry and Industry*, **50** (1931): 774–6, 793–4. On the development of organic synthesis, see M. Berthelot, *Chimie organique fondée sur la synthèse* (Paris, 1860), on which see the critique by C. A. Russell, 'The Changing Role of Synthesis in Organic Chemistry', *Ambix*, **34** (1987): 169–80. I have benefited from Mary Ellen Bowden's *R. B. Woodward and the Art of Chemical Synthesis* (Philadelphia: Beckman Center, 1992) and the travelling exhibition it accompanied. See also D. Stanley Tarbell and Ann Tracy Tarbell, *Roger Adams, Scientist and Statesman* (Washington, DC: American Chemical Society, 1981); Carl Djerassi, *Steroids Made it Possible* (Washington, DC: American Chemical Society, 1990); Donald J. Cram, *From Design to Discovery* (Washington, DC: American Chemical Society, 1990); Derek H. R. Barton, 'Some Reflections on the Present Status of Organic Chemistry', in *Science and Human Progress* (Pittsburgh: Mellon Institute, 1964), pp. 85–100, which is excellent on the instrumental revolution; John C. Sheehan, *The Enchanted Ring. The Untold Story of Penicillin* (Cambridge, Mass.: MIT Press, 1982); John D. Roberts, *The Right Place at the Right Time* (Washington, DC: American Chemical Society,

1990); R. B. Woodward, 'Art and Science in the Synthesis of Organic Compounds: Retrospect and Prospect', in *Pointers and Pathways in Research* (Bombay: CIBA of India, 1963), pp. 1–21; Russell E. Marker, 'The Early Production of Steroidal Hormones', *CHOC News* (Philadelphia), **4**(2) (1987): 3–6; C. Djerassi, *The Politics of Contraception* (San Francisco, W. H. Freeman, 1981), postscript; and George A. Olah (ed.), *Friedel–Crafts and Related Reactions* (New York: Interscience, 1963), vol. 1, chap. 1, which is historical. The Japanese method of discovering and inventing new reactions is discussed in Teruaki Mukaiyama, *Challenges in Synthetic Organic Chemistry* (Oxford: Clarendon, 1990).

Trevor I. Williams, *Robert Robinson Chemist Extraordinary* (Oxford: Clarendon, 1990) gives the context of Robinson's natural products investigation. See also Lord Todd, *Time to Remember. The Autobiography of a Chemist* (Cambridge: Cambridge University Press, 1983), which is extremely readable; also 'Chemistry of Life. An Interview with Lord Todd', *Chemistry in Britain*, **10** (1974): 211–13. On flash photolysis and the rise of organic photochemistry, see 'Ronald Norish 1897–1978', *Biographical Memoirs of the Royal Society*, **27** (1981): 379–424; and 'Quick as a Flash. An Interview with Sir George Porter', *Chemistry in Britain*, **11** (1975): 398–401. Mary Fieser is profiled by Stacey Pramer in *Journal of Chemical Education*, **62** (1985): 186–91. On women chemists generally, see G. Kass-Simon and Patricia Farnes (eds.), *Women in Science. Righting the Record* (Bloomington, Ind.: Indiana University Press, 1990). For radical chemistry and its industrial exploration, see W. A. Waters and F. R. Mayo, 'The Significance of the Work of M. S. Kharasch in the Development of Free Radical Chemistry', in W. A. Waters (ed.), *Vistas in Free Radical Chemistry*, *Tetrahedron* Suppl. No. 3 (Oxford, 1959).

The unpublished 'Arthur Clay Cope Award and Address' given by R. B. Woodward to the ACS on 28 August 1973 (copy at Beckman Center) reveals how he came upon orbital symmetry. For a very readable account of the synthesis of invented molecules, see Alex Nickon and Ernest F. Silversmith, *Organic Chemistry: The Name Game. Modern Coined Terms and Their Origin* (New York: Pergamon, 1987).

On twentieth-century chemical industry and engineering, see George Davis, *Handbook of Chemical Engineering* (1901); *Jubilee of the Society of Chemical Industry* (1931); L. F. Haber, *The Chemical Industry, 1900–1930. International Growth and Technological Change* (Oxford: Clarendon, 1971); William F. Furter (ed.), *History of Chemical Engineering* (Washington, 1980); William F. Haynes, *American Chemical Industry*, 6 vols (New York, 1945–54) – the sixth volume contains over 200 company histories; Terry S. Reynolds, *75 Years of Progress. A History of the American Institute of Chemical Engineers, 1908–1983* (New York: AICE, 1983); A. Thackray, J. L. Sturchio, P. T. Carroll and R. Bud, *Chemistry in America, 1876–1976. Historical Indicators* (Dordrecht: Reidel, 1985); and three essays by James Donnelly, 'Misrepresentations of Applied Science. Academics and Chemical Industry in Late Nineteenth-Century England', *Social Studies Science*, **16** (1986): 195–234; 'Chemical Engineering in England 1880–1922', *Annals of Science*, **45** (1988): 555–90; and 'Origins of the Technical Curriculum in England During the Late Nineteenth and Early Twentieth Centuries', *Studies in Science Education*, **16** (1989): 123–61. Note also Georg Meyer-Thurow, 'The Industrialisation of Invention', *Isis*, **73** (1982): 363–83; and John K. Smith, 'The Evolution of the Chemical Industry. A Technological Perspective', in Seymour H. Mauskopf (ed.), *Chemical Sciences in the Modern World* (Philadelphia: University of Pennsylvania Press, 1992).

For an excellent annotated bibliography of chemical firms, see Jeffrey L. Sturchio (ed.), *Corporate History and the Chemical Industries* (Philadelphia: Beckman Center, 1985), to which add the important study by David A. Hounshell and John K. Smith, *Science and Corporate Strategy: Du Pont R&D, 1902–1988* (New York: Cambridge University Press, 1988). For specific processes mentioned in the text, see Sir William A. Tilden, *Chemical Discoveries in the Twentieth Century* (1917; esp. 6th edn, 1936); Earl Lishey, *The Housewares Story* (Chicago: National Housewares Manufacturers Association, 1973); Robert Friedel, *Pioneer Plastic: The Making and Selling of Celluloid* (Madison, Wis.: University of Wisconsin Press, 1983); Peter J. T. Morris, *Polymer Pioneers* (Philadelphia: Beckman Center, 1986); Peter H. Spitz, *Petrochemicals. The Rise of an Industry* (New York:

Wiley, 1988); Peter J. T. Morris, *The American Synthetic Rubber Research Program* (Philadelphia: University of Pennsylvania Press, 1989); A. Benninga, *A History of Lactic Acid Making* (Dordrecht: Reidel, 1990); and G. B. Kauffman, 'Midgley: Saint or Serpent?', *ChemTech* (December 1989): 717–25.

On the movement to promote chemistry in the 1920s and 1930s, see Thackray, *et al.* (1985); William J. Hale, *The Farm Chemurgic. Farmward the Star of Destiny Lights Our Way* (Boston, 1934); Wheeler McMillen, *New Riches from the Soil* (New York, 1946); and Carroll W. Pursell Jr, 'The Farm Chemurgic Council', *Isis*, **60** (1969): 307–17. For the reaction against 'chemicals', see Rachel Carson, *Silent Spring* (Hamish Hamilton, 1963); Hugh D. Crone, *Chemicals and Society. A Guide to the New Chemical Age* (Cambridge: Cambridge University Press, 1986); and M. Kranzberg, 'One Last Word – Technology and History', in Stephen H. Cutcliffe and Robert C. Post (eds.), *In Context. History and the History of Technology* (Bethlehem, PA, Lehigh University Press, 1989), pp. 244–58.

For Hofmann's epilogue, see W. H. Brock, O. T. Benfey and S. Stark, 'Hofmann's Benzene Tree at the Kekulé Festivities', *Journal of Chemical Education*, **68** (1991): 887–8.

INDEX

methane 249, 250, 366, 554
methyl iodide 516–7, 523
methyl isocyanate 659
methyl orange 184
Meusnier, J. 110
Meyer, L. 162, 321–2, 329, 350
Meyer, V. 260, 573
Michael, A. 517–21, 533
Michaelis, L. 385
microgravimetry 182–3
Midgley, T. 655–6
Mikaiyama, T. 636
milk 193, 196, 649
  of magnesia 142
Miller, W.A. 357, 373
Millikan, R.A. 492
Milner, S.R. 393–4
mineral water 90, 99, 179
mineralogy, early 80, 90–91, 119,
  181, 187, 317
minima naturalis 18, 21, 55, 65,
  130
mining
  Australian 604–5
  early 18, 27–8, 79–80, 90
  education 420, 430
Miolati, A. 587–8
Mirsky, A.E. 499
Mitscherlich, A. 151, 158, 223,
  367, 368
Mittasch, A. 645
mixts 81–2
models 146–7, 224, 258–9, 463,
  500; *see also* cubic atoms
  plum-pudding atomic model
Mohr, C. 183–4
Moigno, L'abbé 456
Moissan, H. 337, 340
mole 422
molecular
  compounds 252, 575
  conductivity 376–8, 383–4,
    390–91, 392, 393, 587–8
  depressions 363–5
  groupings 227
  orbital (MO) theory 394, 487,
    500–5, 531, 552, 558–69,
    602, 634

symmetry 533
  volumes 357, 360
  weights 228–30, 353, 358, 362,
    377, 463, 601
molecules 222–3, 224
molybdenite 493–4
molybdenum 343, 609
Mond, L. 289–91, 293
Monge, G. 112
monosodium glutamate 602
mordants 276, 300
Morley, E.W. 183
morphine 296
Morrill Land Act 431
Morveau, Guyton de *see* Guyton
  de Morveau
Mosander, C.G. 327
Moseley, H.G. 192, 330, 340–42,
  353, 410, 475, 488
Mulder, G.J. 649
Mulliken, R.S. 500–502
Mulliken, S.P. 175, 420, 500
multiple proportions 144, 152
multiplicity, maximum 496
Munby, A.E. 428
murexide 299
muriatic acid 116, 120, 149, 276
murium 116
Murray, J. 186
Muspratt, J. 276, 277, 281–2, 289,
  293
Muspratt, J.S. 270, 274–6, 293–5,
  297
Muspratt, M. 291
mysticism and alchemy 16
Nagayoshi, N. 601–2
napalm 658
naphthalene 223–4, 225, 312,
  555, 557
Napoleonic wars 280
Naquet, A. 268
narcotics 626
National Curriculum 410
National Science Foundation 424
Natta, G. 653
natural gas 646, 654
Nature 305, 332, 387, 437, 454
Nef, J. 552